P9-CEA-402
DELAFIELD PUBLIC LIBRARY

EQUATION FOR EVIL

Also by Philip Caputo

Means of Escape

A Rumor of War

Horn of Africa

DelCorso's Gallery

Indian Country

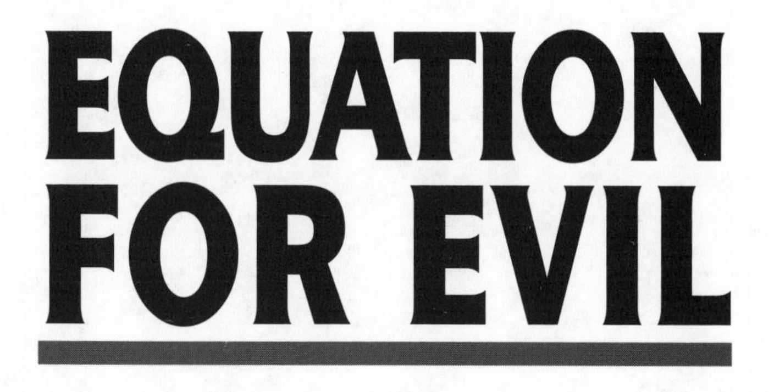

EQUATION FOR EVIL

A NOVEL

Philip Caputo

HarperCollinsPublishers

DELAFIELD PUBLIC LIBRARY

EQUATION FOR EVIL. Copyright © 1996 by Philip Caputo. All rights reserved. Printed in the United States of America. No part of this book may be used or reproduced in any manner whatsoever without written permission except in the case of brief quotations embodied in critical articles and reviews. For information, address HarperCollins Publishers, Inc., 10 East 53rd Street, New York, NY 10022.

HarperCollins books may be purchased for educational, business, or sales promotional use. For information please write: Special Markets Department, HarperCollins Publishers, Inc., 10 East 53rd Street, New York, NY 10022.

FIRST EDITION

Designed by Alma Hochhauser Orenstein

Library of Congress Cataloging-in-Publication Data

Caputo, Philip.
Equation for evil : a novel / by Philip Caputo. — 1st ed.
p. cm.
ISBN 0-06-018360-8
1. Asian American children—Crimes against—California—Fiction. 2. White supremacy movements—California—Fiction. 3. Police psychiatrists—California—Fiction. I. Title.
PS3553.A625E68 1996
813'.54—dc20 95-46706

---

96 97 98 99 00 ❖/HC 10 9 8 7 6 5 4 3 2 1

This book is for the lady, Leslie Blanchard Ware

Acknowledgments

WITH GRATITUDE TO MY EDITORS, HARPERCOLLINS Vice President and Associate Publisher Gladys Carr and Frances Miller, for their patience and suggestions. My thanks also to Phil Yee and Allan Benitez, special agents, California Department of Justice, and Faye Springer, senior criminalist, California Bureau of Forensic Services, for sharing their professional secrets with me, and to Dr. Bruce Shimmelman, for his insights into forensic psychiatry.

Prelude

A Native Son of the Golden West

DUANE BOGGS, WAKING EARLY ON WHAT HE HOPED would be the last day of his life, looked out the window and saw no light in the sky. There would have been none in his room, room 102 of the Camino Real Motel, if not for the faint glow slithering through the filmy curtains from the floodlights of the convenience store half a block away on the frontage road. For ten or fifteen seconds, he lay without moving and listened to the tinny ring of his alarm clock wind down into silence. From outside came the sound of cars and trucks climbing the overpass on Highway 99. Boggs sat up slowly, yawned, and rubbed his eyes clear of sleep. The clock's luminous hands drew a pale vertical stripe in the darkness. Six A.M. The only thing that had ever given him a reason to get out of bed at this time, or at any time before noon, had been school or work, and he'd quit school at fourteen and hadn't held a job for longer than three months in his life. He hated the morning, and the earlier it was the more he hated it. The mere sight of dawn made him feel like a ruptured blow-up toy, absent the muscle, bone, and will to rise and face the new day. Often, before going to sleep, he would walk the streets till well past midnight or drink himself into a stupor just to make sure he didn't see even a minute of the hour when the sun extended its bright arms over the world and held out its phony promise of a fresh beginning. He preferred to sleep well into the afternoon, or, better yet, until dusk—dusk, the dawn of night.

Today was different. His feelings on this, his life's last morning, were those of a convict on the day of his release. He wanted to see as much of the day as he could, to savor each moment, knowing that each was bringing him closer to the final one. If everything went according to plan he'd be free and gone before the evening news, and the whole world would know it because he was going to be *on* the evening news. The lead story, no doubt about it.

He stretched and swung his feet onto the cheap, wine-red carpet that rubbed his soles like a scouring pad. He switched on the nightstand lamp. Its light, mottled by the mildewed shade, flooded over an army of toy soldiers deployed throughout the room: blue infantrymen with arms crooked to throw grenades, red ones charging with bayonets fixed, green ones hunched behind tiny plastic machine guns. The sight made his heart beat faster. He was a soldier now, a sacrificial warrior with a purpose, a direction, a mission. Hezbollah.

No . . . Hezbollah meant "party of God." Fedayeen meant sacrificial warriors. Or was it mujahadeen? Sand niggers couldn't make up their minds what they meant with all their oogabooga talk. Boggs looked into the minifridge and took out the last beer in the six-pack he'd bought last night at the convenience store. He downed half of the can before going into the bathroom to shave.

They darted for the cracks and crannies as soon as the light went on. They were so fast—here then not here—he would have thought them fleeting hallucinations if he didn't see the dead ones lying beneath the sink. Boggs hated cockroaches. He'd waged war against them all his life with powders and sprays and homemade poisons in the dumps he'd lived in with his mother, the dumps he lived in on the road: trailer parks like that one down in Florida, where on nights thick with the stench of sewage and low tide, lean, dark Marielitos shot each other in duels over crack and women; in rooming houses in the kinds of neighborhoods where the rent came due on the same day the welfare checks were issued, and in motels like this one, LOW RATES DAY WK MO—XXX MOVIES. In all the places he'd been, coast to coast and border to border, *la cucaracha* appeared to remind him that he had to live with the lowest of the low. He, a native-born son of the San Joaquin Valley, had to live in dumps and scrape by on dead-end jobs while wetbacks and beaners and boat people got everything handed to them. That was *la cucaracha*'s message and so he killed them whenever he could.

Kneeling under the sink, he picked up the dead roaches with a piece of toilet paper and dropped them into the toilet bowl. A watery grave for *la cucaracha.* These had been killed by one of his own concoctions: Doritos soaked in Black Leaf, a nicotine concentrate. The roaches had died of a nicotine overdose.

"Proves that roaches shouldn't smoke," he said, addressing the film-dulled, blue-green tile walls. He urinated on the insects, flushed them down, and then lathered his face with shaving cream.

It was a face that some women, and some men as well, had called handsome. His cheekbones were high like an Indian's and his eyebrows, hair, and mustache were Indian black—Grandpa Clovis said there was Choctaw blood in the family—but his skin was white and his eyes pale green, the color of shallow seawater over white sand yet lacking seawater's clarity and softness. He shaved carefully around his mustache, trimming it with light strokes of the razor. He wanted to look good for his appearance on the evening news.

By the time he finished dressing in his combat boots and camouflage pants, the sky had gone from black to oyster. Standing by the window and smoking a cigarette, Boggs watched the convenience store's floodlights go off. Its sign, atop a high pole so it could be seen from the overpass, continued to flash GAS 4 LESS—FOOD MART. A trucker pushed his eighteen-wheeler up the overpass. The rig whined, seemed to give a cough of relief when it reached the top, then rumbled down the other side toward Fresno, or L.A., or San Diego. Boggs pictured some red-eyed redneck long-hauler listening to a country station to stay awake. Farm report. News. Weather. Music. Good morning to you, truckdrivin' man!

He turned away from the window, shook another cigarette from the crumpled pack on the dresser, and flicked on the TV. A local early-morning news show. The interviewer, one of those TV bitches, was talking to a fat guy with curly, reddish hair. A politician or a cop. Boggs reached into the black AWOL bag beside the bed, drew out his stainless-steel Taurus, cocked it and held it with both hands, aiming at the red-haired guy's head. He was talking about a gang problem in San Joaquin, Asians versus Latinos. "Let 'em have at it," Boggs said to the two figures on the screen. His finger took up trigger slack and the hammer fell with a click. "BAM! Kill each other off, save us the trouble."

The pretty interviewer, done with the gang problem, turned things over to a weatherman who stood in front of satellite photographs of clouds and storm fronts swirling. The weather in the Valley was going to be clear and unseasonably warm, with visibility of such and such. . . .

I ain't gonna need a lot of visibility, he thought, and kneeled down and pulled Calvin out from under the bed. It was wrapped in a canvas tarp on which he had drawn, in black Magic Marker, Calvin of *Calvin and Hobbes,* his favorite cartoon strip. He paused a moment to admire his artwork. It was pretty good: the scowling face, the hairdo that looked like spikes growing out of Calvin's skull. Boggs had made the drawing last night while he drank a few beers to help him get to sleep early. Drawing always relaxed him, made him feel more in control of things. He didn't know why. He was not bad at it. Art was one of the few subjects he'd passed in school, and in those days, when he still believed in the illusion of a future, he'd dreamed of becoming a famous cartoonist or an illustrator for the comic books.

He unrolled the tarp, the face of Calvin the cartoon character peeling away from Calvin the Street Sweeper. A mean gun for a mean world: a semiautomatic twelve-gauge with folding paratrooper stock, a twelve-round detachable drum magazine, and a ported barrel to dampen the recoil. It would sweep the streets clean of scum, all right. He'd bought the weapon in Florida from a cracker named Willy Owens, and Willy had told him it could fire twelve rounds in three seconds flat. Pop the magazine, load the spare, and you could put out more double-ought buckshot than a claymore. "A real crowd pleaser," Willy had said. "You can take out a mob with this all by your lonesome. Have 'em stacked up like trashbags back of a busy restaurant on Friday night, yes, sir."

He uncased the shotgun, disassembled it, and laid the parts on the tarp. Willy had told him to keep the gun spotless because a Retaliator's major flaw was a tendency to jam. And this one had jammed just a few days ago, when Boggs was practicing with it up in the mountains. He got out his cleaning rod, bore brush, patches, and bottle of nitro solvent and swabbed the barrel, scrubbed the trigger mechanism and receiver, and then put the whole thing back together, loving the sound and the feel of the pieces fitting into one another, the smell of oil on unforgiving steel.

When the weapon was reassembled, he loaded both magazines, locked one into the shotgun, put the spare into a belly-pack, and belted the pack to his waist. The weight of the magazine pulled it low over his hips. He held Calvin at high port and posed in front of the tarnished dressing mirror bolted to the back of the door. The mirror threw back an image of a young man whose knobby shoulders, prominent collarbone, and nearly meatless ribs showed through his tight-fitting army T-shirt. Boggs set the gun down momentarily and pulled a flak jacket out from under the bed. He put it on and looked in the mirror again. Okay, he looked okay now, bigger and bulkier.

He snapped the gun to his hip and remembered the first time he fired it, in a patch of Everglades not far from Willy's house. Even with earplugs on, the gun sounded like the wrath of God. Bambambam. Twelve rounds. Three seconds.

Now, in the Camino Real Motel, on the frontage road off Highway 99 in the city of San Joaquin, Duane Boggs drew in a deep breath to inflate his narrow chest, his imagination expanding it further until, in his eyes, it looked like a weight lifter's. He bent his knees into a combat crouch, aiming Calvin at his reflection, the reflection aiming back at him,

"Bam! Bambambam!"

He swept the gun back and forth.

Bambambam!

Hezbollah.

He holstered the Taurus, threw on a camie shirt and let the tails hang out to hide the gun's bulge, wrapped Calvin in a blanket, and went out to his truck, a gray, clapped-out '73 Dodge. The morning was fine and fresh and smelled of oleander. He started the truck. A puff of blue smoke shot out the exhaust pipe. That makeshift ring job he'd tried at Grandpa Clovis's place hadn't worked out, but what the hell, nothing ever worked out. Grandpa, that retard Okie full of Jesus fevers. Whole damned family a bunch of retards except for Dearest Mom. Dumb she wasn't.

That was Boggs's final thought before he pulled out onto the frontage road, leaving in the room everything he owned: his clothes, his shaving tackle, his soldiers. He wouldn't need any of it anymore.

Friday, April 16th, 1993

TALL, BIG-BONED JOYCE DELUCA, HER RIDE IN THE darkness done, led Ghost to the barn. As she walked, the lead rope sagging behind her, a breeze stirred her long, light hair, fanned out beneath her riding hat, and the horse blew steam in the cool foothills air and shied as if sensing danger though Joyce knew no danger was near. The high-strung mare had been unusually skittish all morning, taut muscles quivering like drawn bow strings, and almost bolted once, Joyce short-reining her, gentling her with soft words. Steady, girl . . . What's got into you . . . ? Steady now. . . .

A difficult, exasperating animal, yet Joyce loved her for her unpredictability and for her color—a bluish gray set off by a black mane. Two summers ago, she had seen the mare for the first time, running with a herd across a New Mexican mesa below the reddish, sage-speckled slopes of the Mogollons. It was late afternoon, and a thunderstorm to the east raised a purple-black wall as solid-looking as the mountains. The sunlight reflecting off the clouds had an eerie cast that made the blue roan look supernatural, like a spirit horse out of some Apache myth. The sight brought a tightness to Joyce's chest and she bought the horse on the spot from the outfitter who'd guided Alex and her on a week-long ride.

Under the barn's eave, she got out her hoof pick and curry brushes and reached to shackle a crosstie to Ghost's bridle. Suddenly, the pale mare spooked, backing hard and tossing her head so the lead rope swung like a whip and cracked Joyce an inch below her eye. Both eyes began to tear and she grabbed the lead high up and jerked it and kicked Ghost hard in the ribs.

"Damn you!"

The horse settled down immediately. It had been one of Ghost's unexplainable fits, over in a second. Instantly, Joyce's temper cooled and guilt overcame her. She wasn't sentimental about disciplining horses when they needed it, but that whack had been gratuitous and misdirected: had been a show of the anger that had been in her when she woke up before dawn and had stayed in her, lodged like a bone, and not even an hour's hard riding enough to get it out.

"Sorry, girl," she said, patting the mare's neck. "Okay? Sorry."

She snapped the crossties, undid the cinch straps, and, enjoying the smells of old oiled leather and horse sweat, pulled the saddle off and laid it over a rail. Alex had given her the saddle for her thirty-fifth birthday, which was getting to be longer ago than she cared to remember.

Twenty minutes later, she had everything done—the mare curried and put in the stall, saddle and bridle stowed in the small tack room. Joyce could think of nothing else to delay her return to the house, and she started toward it with stiff strides that suggested a Civil War soldier marching toward an enemy battery.

She wished she could go to work as she was, in jodhpurs and boots. She wished she did not have to enter the big house of quarried stone where she would have to look at Alex's long, somber face and behave as if nothing were wrong. She did not want to give the sharp-eared, sharp-eyed Theresa the slightest evidence that she and Alex had been quarreling. Theresa had been with the DeLucas for years and had become Alex's surrogate mother since his own had died. If she thought there was trouble in the marriage she would speak to Alex with glances and well-timed silences calculated to inspire remorse and guilt. *This unhappiness is what you get, Alejandro, it's your punishment for breaking the laws of the Church.*

Her thoughts were interrupted by a loud rustling and crashing among the tangled sycamore and cottonwood in the ravine that writhed through the DeLuca vineyards. The noise sounded like a large animal running. She paused and listened. The noise stopped. A deer? Or something else? Maybe Ghost had heard or sniffed some menace human senses could not. As she looked into the ravine, where pools of night lingered in the low spots, an apprehensiveness rippled up her back and down her arms. Last week, the local paper reported that a cow had been killed by a marauding cougar on a high range in the Sierras, but Joyce couldn't imagine what would drive a mountain lion into this winemaking country, unless it had acquired a taste for zinfandel.

She stood still and alert for another few seconds, but heard nothing, saw nothing. Her gaze rising from the gully toward the regimented rows of vines on the hillsides, she blamed the noise on a flock of birds, a trick of the wind. Far off, crows or buzzards gyred like smoke above a hill topped by fir trees. She doubted they were eyeing a predator's kill; yet the possibility that something lethal lurked in this serene landscape seemed to darken its character. Even the vines looked a little sinister, canes twisting like serpents over the trellis wires.

The kitchen smelled of coffee and the batter that Theresa, a bowl locked in the crook of one fleshy arm, was mixing by hand. She was dressed in a green sweat suit and tennis shoes, a costume that did not go with her heavyset figure, her lined face, with its look of reserve, her thick hair pulled into a stern, matronly bun. She would have looked more appropriate draped in the black of a nineteenth-century duenna.

"Well, hello there, Joyce." Thirty years in the United States had taught Theresa gringo informality, which suited Joyce: having help troubled her prairie sense of democracy, and she could not have borne being addressed as Senora DeLuca.

"So, where will you go riding this morning?"

"I've already been," Joyce said, and took her hat off and fluffed her hair.

Theresa, not missing a beat with the wooden spoon, regarded her with narrowed eyes.

"You went riding in the dark?"

"Yep."

"I cannot believe you went riding around these hills in the dark. Alone."

There was a note of disapproval in her husky voice. Another point in Joyce's disfavor, more evidence that she was peculiar, unsuited for Alejandro. Theresa's heart remained loyal to Elaine, Alex's first wife. Elaine would not have done anything so foolishly daring as to ride a horse in the dark. She didn't ride at all. Joyce took a mug from the wall rack beside the stove and filled it from the ancient, enameled pot Theresa insisted on using in place of the electric coffee-maker.

"Someday I'll tell you about the midnight ride of Sybil Luddington, another mad gringa. A revolutionary heroine. The lady Paul Revere."

To this capsule history lesson Theresa responded by raising her black eyebrows—a gesture of impenetrable meaning, or no meaning at all. Then, graceful and light on her feet, as plump women sometimes are, she glided swiftly across the kitchen and put the bowl in the refrigerator.

"What is that?"

"Ricotta and other things. Filling for tonight's lasagna."

"I went riding early because I've got to go in early and pick up my bilingual aide," Joyce said, annoyed that she felt compelled to offer a justification. "We're taking the class to Sutter's Mill. Teach them about the forty-niners and the Gold Rush, although I really don't think a bunch of Cambodian and Vietnamese kids are going to be much interested in that."

"Everyone is interested in finding gold."

"Verdad," Joyce said, and left.

She passed through the hall on her way to the bedroom, but paused under the archway to the living room, where Alex was reading the *Wall Street Journal* with the aid of his glasses, a magnifying glass, and a three-way light turned to its brightest. A breeze guttering down the chimney ruffled the remnants of yesterday's fire in the fireplace and breathed into the room, faintly, a scent of charred wood and ashes. It was a big, dim room with varnished beams and a lot of antique furniture that spoke of missions long gone to dust, of long-buried *haciendados.* What had made Joyce pause was the picture of age Alex presented there, his Ben Franklin glasses pushed down to the tip of his nose, the creases in his lugubrious face deepened by the shadows. Of course he was no kid—fifty-two this year—but she saw in him now a prefiguration of the old man he would become.

Sipping her coffee, she watched him as he moved the magnifying glass up and down the stock tables, pretending to be too absorbed to notice her. He took out a pocket calculator, made computations. Joyce knew what he was up to, besides ignoring her. He, too, was still upset about last night's quarrel and was seeking to calm himself with the cool arithmetic of profit and loss. Before he went into commercial real estate and became one of the more successful land speculators in central California, he'd found refuge from emotional turmoil by taking long walks through the vineyards first planted by his great-grandfather and nurtured by every generation of DeLucas since. But the vineyard was poetry, and Alex had no time for that anymore. Nowadays he preferred the unambiguous facts of the stock market. They told him where he stood, and he liked to know where he stood. He did not like it when life got messy, when the unruly heart, whether his own or someone else's, threatened to subvert the order of his days. His divorce had given him enough mess to last a lifetime.

"How are we doing?" she asked.

Feigning surprise at the sound of her voice, he straightened his shoulders as he half-turned to face her, a question in his deep-set brown eyes. Joyce gestured at the *Wall Street Journal.*

"I meant that."

"Pharmaceuticals down, cyclicals up," he answered in his rich, solemn baritone. A beam of sunlight slicing through one of the casement windows lifted the shadows from his face and erased its appearance of a premature old age. "In a nutshell, we're about eleven percent ahead for the year."

"Thanks for the report. I won't be at breakfast. Have to get in early."

"How was the ride?"

"Okay. Theresa thinks I'm a little loco for riding in the dark."

"Theresa," he said through a thin smile. "Old Mother Hubbard."

"Ghost was a tad jumpy."

Alex squinted and raised a finger to his cheek.

"She give you that?"

"Yeah. Tossed her head. The lead rope . . . "

"Never know what she'll do. Sometimes I think we were had by that Marlboro man."

"We weren't had, okay? I know horseflesh. She's just temperamental."

"Or half a quart low."

"Something might have spooked her. You don't think that cougar . . . "

"Last one in this neck of the woods was shot by my great-granddad. 1887."

"I've got to get ready."

She went upstairs, showered, and put on her makeup and brushed her hair, alert for signs of gray. She had hoped for a signal that Alex was having second thoughts: a word, a gesture.

She took off her robe and backed away from the mirror so she could see her naked self from her hair down to her somewhat oversize feet. Her body had hardly changed since she was twenty-five, but that did not please her this morning. The woman staring back at her had the overexercised look she had seen in obsessively active, middle-age females. *Preserved, pickled* were the words that came to her mind. Breasts never suckled out of shape by a greedy little mouth; flat, hard belly innocent of stretch marks; thighs sinewed from riding and hiking, unblemished by the burst blue veins that tattooed her mother's after she'd given birth to the second of her two huge baby daughters. Joyce had weighed nine pounds at birth, her younger sister, Kristen, nine and a half. "Like shitting a watermelon," Joyce had once overheard her mother tell a friend, and that repulsive image—of her infant self as giant turd—had stayed with her all her life, sparing her any unrealistic notions about the miracle of childbirth.

After Kristen was born, their mother had her tubes tied—no more squalling excreta for her—and didn't try to "get her figure back," as women said in those days. Joyce had felt shock and disgust one hot summer when she saw her mother stripped in the dressing room of a lake resort. I'm never never going to look like that, she'd thought then; now she found something to be admired and envied in her mother's loss of beauty, as a handsome but untested young man might admire and envy a warrior's disfigurements. Was childbirth the fullest expression of womanhood? Was a woman who had never given birth the less for it, condemned to some eternal girlhood? What about all the women who could not get pregnant?

Fill me up, fill me, she'd cried the first time she and Alex made love. She heard herself crying it out again in her imagination, and saw herself, ass bearing down hard on the bed, he plunging into her *fill me up* and he does, sending ten million of the little bastards on a spawning run to batter her ovum's walls and one of them gets through *fill me up, oh, do.*

Then he was at the bedroom door, as if the fantasy had beckoned him. He started to come in and she told him to wait, she wasn't finished dressing.

"What the hell? This the Victorian age? A guy can't see his wife with her clothes off?"

She quickly put on khakis, sneakers, and a pullover, then opened the door.

"I've got the green light?" Alex mimicked a courtier's bow. "It's permitted to enter her ladyship's chambers?"

"I hate it when you try to be comic. You and comedy clash."

"I thought I was being ironic, not comical."

"Look up *ironic* in the dictionary. You'll see that you weren't."

"Teacher. Mizzzz DeLuca . . . "

He moved through a cube of window light into a shadowed corner of the room, where he sat resting both arms royally on the arms of the chair.

"I think we need to talk."

"I really do have to get in early."

"Is this jaunt timed to the minute?"

"It's not a jaunt. It's a field trip." She took a chair in the corner opposite Alex, putting between them the desk where she wrote letters and corrected papers. "I suppose you want to talk about what we've talked about."

"I think the air needs clearing."

"Talked and talked and talked about and now you've settled it, so there really isn't anything to talk about, is there?"

He twisted around in his chair.

"I can't look at you, us sitting like this."

"I don't particularly want you to look at me."

"Oh, for Christ's sake . . . "

He rose, and passing again through the light that gilded the gray in his hair, sat on the edge of the bed, his big, awkward-looking hands clasped between his knees.

"Answer me one question. Do you want to have a baby or not?"

"Talked and talked and talked."

"You can't make up your mind. You've been saying that for months. Maybe yes, maybe no. To me, that means no."

"To me, that means I don't know. There are times when I want one, times I don't. Okay?"

"The times you do—why?"

"I know what you're up to. I'll give you my reasons and you'll show me why they're unsound. Your little railroad track of Jesuitical logic. "

"Franciscans. I was taught by Franciscans."

"Your Franciscan logic, then. Anyway, who cares what my reasons are? You know you don't want one. You don't want to be tossing a football to little junior with a pacemaker in your heart. You don't want to go to a high school graduation and be mistaken for a grandparent."

He let out a breath.

She looked out the window, which squared a picture of vineyards and walnut groves and the barn and the winery below the hill where Alex dry-farmed the century-old vines that made their zinfandel classico. The gravel road she used as a bridle path ran alongside the hill, disappeared, reappeared atop another hill farther on, disappeared again, and then all she could see were foothills, splashed with purple lupine and California poppy as they mounted toward the high Sierra, its white peaks towering over all.

"What's that old saying about lupine?"

"That you'll find gold under where it grows."

"I love this place," she said quietly. "I don't want to leave here. Not ever."

"That's how I've always felt about it."

"But it isn't mine. None of it. Not this house, not those vineyards. None of it belongs to me. It never will."

"What are you talking about?"

She turned to him.

"I'm kind of a visitor here, aren't I?"

"Visitor? You're my wife . . . "

"You said it a couple of minutes ago. I'm living in this house. It isn't mine the way it was Elaine's. Still is, in some ways."

"Hon, what's the . . . Have you forgotten, I transferred title to the house. . . . She doesn't . . . "

He paused and pulled his brows together, in the same way Joyce had seen her students do when stumped by a test. She looked at her watch and stood up.

"I really have to go."

"I wanted to clear the air. Still seems pretty foggy to me."

"Okay. There is no good reason for that operation. I don't want you to go through with it. I insist you don't. If you do, I'll probably hate you for it. How's the fog now?"

He looked at her gravely, then got to his feet and paced the room, the vague odor of ashes trailing after him.

"You're not saying that you'd leave?" he asked, as if that were beyond imagining.

"Theresa would love that. By her lights we're living in sin. Who else would love it? Your kids. They still think you would have gone crawling back to Mama if I hadn't come along. Think of all the people I'd make happy."

It thrilled her to see that she'd wounded him, and then she felt the way she had after she kicked the mare.

"All I want is for us to go on like we have," he said. "That's the whole reason I've been thinking about doing this."

"What are you afraid of? That I'd go off the pill without telling you? If you want, I'll use a diaphragm too, and insist you wear a condom," she said wickedly. "Just in case one of the little sneaks found a way through all that armor, I'd load up on spermicide. Turn myself into a reproductive death-trap . . . "

"Damnit, Joyce, we discussed this . . . "

"*We* did not discuss a damn thing and that's the whole point. You told me what you decided to do. That's your idea of a discussion. Julius goddamned Caesar."

"Who said anything about deciding? I said I was considering it, all right? Con-sid-er-ing."

"You've made up your mind. Don't kid me. I could see it in your face. That look you get. Like this." She stuck out her chin and drew her lips into a tight, upside-down U. "Like those old pictures of J. Edgar Hoover."

He gave her his back and stood silhouetted by the sunlight flowing through the window. "A kid would ruin it, everything we've had together."

"All that operation would tell me is that you don't trust me."

He turned around.

"It's accidents I'm afraid of. It's me I don't trust."

This was new to Joyce.

"That means what exactly?"

"I don't want it ruined, that's all, and it would be."

"It's not like you to be enigmatic."

"The trips to Tuscany, the weekends in San Francisco. All that. I don't want all that ruined."

"What has 'all that,'" she said with rising anger, "got to do with not trusting yourself?"

"You've got to get going and so do I. Zoning board has a ten o'clock hearing. They're going to rule on the variance for that—"

"So that's it?" she interrupted.

He put his hands in his back pockets and shrugged and the brief, jerky movement of his shoulders somehow made her despise him. She went to the closet and put on her suede jacket, another of his birthday presents. Her thirty-sixth. Or was it the thirty-seventh?

"In other words, now that *you've* decided you don't want to talk about it anymore, we're through talking about it."

"You said you were in a hurry."

"Fine. Let's not talk about it ever again." She smiled brightly. "And I promise I won't hate you too terribly long. So you can go ahead with it, and since it's foolproof you want, darling, you might tell the doctor to cut your balls off while he's at it."

He leaned backward, as if she'd slapped him. Before he could retaliate, she left the house and walked quickly down the flagstone path toward the garage, her feet stirring the cherry blossoms that lay along it. The birds far off still circled, dark specks against the bright, untextured sky.

▬ ▬ ▬

On the freeway, she kept a sharp eye out for the highway patrol. She eased up on the gas as she approached an overpass—a nook favored by state troopers out to fill their monthly quota—and went through at a sedate sixty before accelerating to eighty. A vibration in the steering wheel reminded her that the Nissan needed an alignment and forced her to trim five miles off her speed. Seventy-five was an easy cruise down the highway, which ran straight as a plumb line across the San Joaquin Valley. Level and wide, the Valley reminded her of western Minnesota, though it lacked the vast and somehow threatening vacancy of the midwestern plains. The Sierras in the east and the coastal ranges in the west—visible boundaries never more than fifty miles away—promised quick relief from the monotony of a horizontal landscape. Back home—Joyce still thought of Minnesota as home, though she'd left fourteen years ago—you could drive two hundred miles in any direction and the highest thing you'd see would be a grain silo or a windmill, its vanes turning in a wind unchecked by anything more than a barbed wire fence or a farmer's cottonwood windbreak.

She crossed a branch of the Calaveras. Placidly winding toward a walnut grove in full blossom, it did not seem like the same river that had drowned one of her students, Vanna Lim, in a spring flood last year. Now migrant pickers in bright shirts bowed and stooped in a field beside the grove and fallen blossoms blew over them like confetti over a parade. A peat fire was burning in a distant tule marsh. The smoke whirled in a funnel that recalled the dreadful shape of a tornado, then drew out into a long, black reef that lay over the land between her and the city, giving the impression that she was farther from it than she was. She looked at the clock. Almost eight. If traffic wasn't heavy she would be on time to pick up Sokhim. She wished she hadn't made that last remark to Alex. She'd read somewhere that depression was frozen rage. Was the opposite true? Rage as molten depression? It was the idea of foreclosed hope that depressed her. Nature was going to do its own foreclosure in a few years anyway, so why did he feel compelled to hurry things?

A green and white sign appeared. SAN JOAQUIN—NEXT 3 EXITS. She slowed down and, putting Alex and the quarrel out of her mind, slipped into the right lane. The exit ramp made a long curve onto Calaveras Avenue, the street that ran the whole dreary, anarchic breadth of San Joaquin and its suburbs. Joyce had tried to like this city where she had taught for so long, but it never requited her attempts at affection. It was a cowtown without rural virtues, an inland seaport—linked to the distant Pacific by a navigable river—without a grain of salty glamour, a cannery town as hard and sharp-edged as a hex nut. Thirty years ago, Alex had told her, it had been a third its present size, a backwater where ranchers and farmers came to shop, drink, watch a movie, and see to the shipping of their grain and cattle. Now, swollen by tides of Asian refugees and Bay Area exiles who could no longer afford San Francisco or those parts of Oakland where the murder rate wasn't off the charts, San Joaquin had grown big enough to accommodate modern metropolitan horrors, from crack to gangs.

As she followed Calaveras toward downtown, she felt as if she were in the shaft of an archaeological dig that had been turned from the vertical to the horizontal. A century of the city's history passed before her in twenty minutes. On the outskirts were strip malls and the planned communities of today: enclaves surrounded by security walls from which pennants flew gaily to attract home buyers. The walls and pennants made each suburban patch resemble a medieval town decked out to welcome a visiting king—provided he could get past the private guards manning the electronically controlled gates against criminal invaders from the slums. The next layer, consisting of split-levels, each with its proud picture window and emblem of lawn, dated from the Eisenhower era, when walls and guards weren't needed and a home of his own lay within the grasp of every working man with a job. Rows of clapboard cottages recalling Steinbeck's California followed, then a strata of turreted Victorians with wide verandahs upon which cattle kings and mine barons and other ranks of commercial nobility once passed their prosperous evenings. Front yard signs told what had become of their castles. ROOMS FOR RENT . . . LEGAL AID CLINIC . . . SOCIAL SERVICES DEPT. ANNEX . . . ROOMS FOR RENT . . .

At last she came to Sutter Square, a broad green shaded by white oak and palm and with a fountain in its center, flinging spray over beds of poppy and marigold bright as wedding bands. Locking her doors and windows, she turned onto Fremont, a scary street but the shortest route to Sokhim's apartment. Fremont had been queen of San Joaquin's commercial and entertainment life, but the screens of the movie theaters had been blank since the days Doris Day and Rock Hudson held pillow talks, and the department stores were now either vacant lots or the lowest sort of discount houses, steel grates shielding their windows against thieves and vandals.

A red light caught her at the intersection where the Southern Pacific tracks ran past the abandoned passenger station. She was tempted to run the light—even in broad daylight, this wasn't a neighborhood for a woman alone to linger. A crackhead or schizo appeared to be staring at her as he danced a patternless jig under a marquee that advertised the theater's only feature: —LOSED. Next door, fidgeting and scratching their forearms, three winos waited for a liquor store to open and the day's first swallow of Night Train or Mad Dog. Another man sat beside the building, holding a sign: HIV POSITIV & HOMELISS—PLS HELP. My God, what succor did he expect to find on this derelict street of derelict men? Her eyes moved from him toward the train station's bleached rose walls, blackened by gangs' tribal markings, by peculiar nicknames—VERT . . . EROC . . . MERLIN—by bizarre drawings and indecipherable runes. Nonsense sprayed by punks who should have been doing their homework instead of wandering the streets with aerosol cans. The end of language, a devolution to primitive glyphs and pictographs that said law and learning and government would not triumph in the end; entropy would.

VERT . . . EROC . . . MERLIN . . . Sounds like some weird law firm, she thought, and pounced on the gas when the light flashed green. Down the block was evidence that some graffiti writers still believed in conventional communication. She didn't like the messages but at least could understand them.

EAT SHIT AND DIE, WHITEBOY . . . AFTER YOU, JIGABOO . . . GOOKS GO HOME . . . BOAT PEOPLE BACK TO YOUR BOATS . . .

The esperanto of hate.

Traffic was heavy on the drawbridge that took her over the river to the west side of town. She pulled to the curb beside a small, shady park across from the Park Lane Apartments, a tony name for four drab blocks of two-story buildings arranged in a rectangle, with a courtyard in the middle. Old Plymouths, Fords, and Chevys, a few up on blocks, formed a rusty necklace around the compound. At the entrance to the courtyard, three brown Khmer workmen were assembling long-handled paint rollers. Joyce went jauntily up a path worn into a groove, and then noticed that the men had stopped their work and were staring at her. At first, she thought they were only curious, possibly wondering if this tall blonde was a landlord with an eviction notice or a social worker on a checkup. But as she drew closer, she saw hostility on their faces. At their feet were cans of whitewash and paint. In bright blue letters, someone had sprayed a message across half a wall facing the passageway into the courtyard.

CAT EYES EAT DOG MEAT & W.A.R. EATS CATS!!!

Children were everywhere inside the courtyard, which had been trampled long ago into grassless dust hard as pavement. Three boys shot marbles in the dirt; girls played a jumping game with a chain of rubber bands and were watched by teenage boys in satiny jackets and high-top sneakers. Across the way, an old woman in a brilliant sarong cooked over an oven outside her apartment and the smoke rose swirling into the light. Joyce climbed a set of grimy stairs to the second-floor balcony and smelled the old woman's cooking and heard Khmer laments playing on radios and tape recorders. The whole dense texture of foreign life crowded in on her and made her feel as if she had left her country, but the games and toys and dress of the kids, like the American slang on their lips, told her she hadn't. A Brooklyn ghetto might have been like this eighty years ago, she thought. Old people clinging to the ways of an old land, their kids becoming strangers.

"Good morning, Joyce. So happy to see you!" Sokhim said in the somewhat stilted tones learned at her English lessons. She looked stunning, as usual. Dark oval eyes, skin the color of antique ivory, hair piled up like a turban made of raven's wings. Joyce stepped into the cramped apartment, her head missing by only an inch or two the big colored ball that hung from the middle of the ceiling. Sparkling garlands spread from it in all directions and made the room look as if it had been decorated for a party.

"Sit down, please," Sokhim said with barely audible D's and T's as she gestured at an unmade sofabed. "I am sorry for the bed. . . . So sloppy! Mrs. Or again. Early, early this morning, very frightened . . . She asked to stay and slept so late!"

Joyce waved away the apology.

"Some tea?"

"No, thanks. We should be going."

"Yes, of course. One moment."

Sokhim went into the bedroom, where, leaping fluidly between Khmer and English, she passed last-minute instructions to her three children and Pandra.

The toilet flushed. Mrs. Or, frail as thread, came out of the bathroom in an ankle-length silk skirt, a white blouse, and checkered shoulder sash. She stood in the doorway for a moment and, sensing a stranger's presence, looked in Joyce's direction with fearful eyes that could see and yet did not. She called out to Sokhim. The two women spoke briefly: an exchange in which Joyce heard her name uttered by Sokhim with emphasis and some irritation. *Joyce DeLuca, Joyce . . .* Mrs. Or, the fear fading from her eyes, adjusted her sash, smoothed her blouse. Wraithlike, she moved into the living room and greeted Joyce with a slight bow.

"Good morning, Mrs. Or."

The corners of the woman's mouth twitched slightly in what might have been an attempt at a smile. Then, in the uncanny way the blind can find their way through a crowded room, she passed in a whisper of silk around a floor mat on which breakfast bowls awaited washing, and sat on the rumpled sofabed.

She faced the Chuns' family altar, a shrine of an ancient and exotic faith made out of the modern and commonplace: Woolworth's dust ruffles and table linens, Mylar and tinfoil. Joss sticks awaited burning in a Tupperware bowl. A portrait of Buddha torn from a magazine and enclosed in a ready-made frame hung over the altar and the walls around it were covered with photographs of dead relatives. The Khmer Rouge had provided the Chuns—and a million other Cambodians—with a gallery of those.

Mrs. Or, lone survivor of a clan once numbering forty, was exceptionally rich in that regard. Husband, four children, grandparents, aunts, uncles, cousins, brothers—all hacked, shot, beaten, or starved to death in rice paddy and jungle. One day in 1978, the Khmer Rouge tied her up and forced her to watch as her last living child, a four-year-old boy, was picked up by the ankles and bashed headfirst against a tree. Mrs. Or screamed and screamed, felt something drill through her skull like a bullet, and had not seen a thing since.

Carrying a leather shoulder bag, a crimson peony pinned to her hair, Sokhim returned from the bedroom. She squatted in front of Mrs. Or and, holding the blind woman's hands in hers, spoke to her gently, the Khmer words sounding in Joyce's ears like music. Except for a slight frown, Mrs. Or made no response to whatever was being said. Sokhim said a few more words, then rose and went to the door. Mrs. Or turned toward it and spoke sharply, holding up a thin, brittle finger in what appeared to be a rebuke. Sokhim started to respond, had second thoughts, and left.

"Is she angry about something?" Joyce asked as they walked along the balcony toward the stairs.

"Oh, maybe. I tell her every day not to be frightened. Khmer Rouge are not here and no one is going to kill her. Every day the same. I tell her every day to go back to the clinic. The doctors know nothing wrong with her eyes. In her mind. That's what I tell her just now."

"Hysterical blindness."

"What is that word? What kind blindness?"

"Hysterical. A kind of madness that makes a person not see anymore."

With a diligence Joyce wished for in her students, Sokhim withdrew a notebook and ballpoint from her shoulder bag and stood at the top of the stairs, poised to write.

"You will spell it for me, please?"

Joyce did, and they went down, the concrete steps so dusty their feet left prints.

"But what did you say that made her angry?"

"To see doctor! She doesn't want doctors to cure her eyes. Doesn't think it is the right thing to do. She said something strange to me when we leave. Difficult for me in English, one moment." Sokhim paused, her lips moving as she translated the Khmer to herself. "She says, 'I have seen the true things . . . ' No. 'I have seen the truth of things.' Yes, that's right. 'I have seen the truth of things. The world is become . . . ' No. *Has.* 'The world has become too terrible for me to look at. It is too terrible for you to look at, but you can because you do not see the truth of things.'"

They walked past the workmen painting over the graffiti.

"This is what frightens her." With a languorous movement, Sokhim pointed at the letters faintly showing through the thin whitewash. "She hears them, the men who did this. She hears so well! She comes to our apartment. 'Khmer Rouge here, come to kill us,' she says. 'We must run!' Mrs. Or, she thinks everything is Khmer Rouge. She hears children on their bikes and thinks they are Khmer Rouge. I make her calm, but very soon I can hear these men. Know they are not Cambodian because I can hear them speaking English. Then they call out, 'Cat eyes! Cat butts! Go home! You don't belong here!' Then I hear their car go away, very fast. Like this." She mimicked the sound of squealing tires. "What is this W.A.R.? Like war? Like fighting?"

"The White Aryan Resistance. A white supremacist group. Racists."

"White Ah . . . Ar . . . "

"Air-ee-an. Another word for white people."

Pen and notebook came out again as the two women passed by a knot of noisy children waiting for the school bus. Joyce spelled the word, Sokhim wrote it down, the tip of her tongue peeking through a corner of her lips.

"They are making a resistance against what?"

"I guess the future. Maybe the present. Maybe both."

They drove off toward the McKinley Intermediate School. Realizing that her answer had done more to confuse than enlighten, Joyce explained that the Aryan Resistance was bands of angry young white men, down on their luck and filled with frustrations and a conviction that people with dark skin were to blame for their misfortunes and failures.

"They're more like street gangs than anything else. Usually they beat up on blacks, but there aren't enough blacks in this town to count."

"But there are many of us."

Joyce nodded.

"They think we eat dogs." Sokhim let out a high light laugh. "How silly. We are cats who eat dogs. I am thirty-five years in age and never have I eaten a dog. Even in Cambodia, Joyce! When we were starving! Not even there did I eat a dog."

"I have," Joyce declared, and saw, in her peripheral vision,

Sokhim's slender eyebrows arch in surprise. "In a Chinese restaurant in Sacramento."

"Ah, yes! Chinese. Now *they* eat dogs."

"It wasn't on the menu. A couple of days after we ate there—Alex and I—we read in the papers that the health department closed them down. They found dog meat in the beef chow mein. Cats, too. A big scandal."

"Cats?" Sokhim asked with a grimace. "Cats and dogs. No, Joyce. You did not eat a *cat*?"

"Not that I know of. Dog for sure."

"So. You should say to those white gang people, the W.A.R. people, 'I am a white person and I have eaten a dog and I liked it!'" Sokhim's laugh was lovely as a wind chime. "That's what you should say. Then maybe they will stop saying we do."

"Doubt it. They'd find something else. That you dry your meat and vegetables outside. That you cook outside. That you're too short. Too dark. Or maybe not dark enough. That you don't work. Or you work too much. That's where hate has it over love, Sokhim. You can always find something to hate in somebody else."

They were passing through the Eisenhower era of split-levels, picture windows, and lawns. Sokhim folded her hands in her lap and gazed pensively at the houses, lined up behind rows of straight and soldierly royal palms.

"This is so hard, so hard," she said. "Understanding this country. In Cambodia we don't have gangs. We don't have word for gangs. We don't know what a gang is until we come here and now our boys in gangs to protect themselves from white gangs and Spanish gangs. We don't understand. Cat eyes. Cat butt. You know, we don't have racism in Cambodia . . . "

"That's because you're all the same. It's when people are different . . . "

"But we don't have it."

Joyce checked an impulse to say, "With the Khmer Rouge around, racists would be superfluous," and to remind her companion of the venerable enmities that had caused the Vietnamese, Cambodians, and Laotians in the city to segregate themselves into ethnically pure enclaves a Balkan politician would envy. She drove on in silence, musing upon Mrs. Or's parting words. Was it possible to see too clearly? To apprehend the truth of things so completely that, like someone staring without protective glasses into a solar eclipse, you went blind from it? Seared the retinas of your mind?

"I don't understand how she does it," she said, thinking aloud.

"Yes?" said Sokhim.

"Mrs. Or. I don't understand how she does it. Goes on living, I mean. Doesn't go crazy. I couldn't do it."

"Do you remember what I tell you? About karma?"

Joyce nodded and asked what Mrs. Or could have done in a past life to deserve what had happened to her in this one.

"I know. Very hard for you to understand."

"The punishment didn't fit the crime. Mrs. Or would have had to have been Genghis Khan."

"All the same, she believes these terrible things happen to her because her karma is so heavy. Buddha spares her from death so she can lighten her karma. She lives like, you know the word . . . a woman monk?"

"Nun."

"Yes, like nun. She follows the eightfold path. She speaks right. Thinks right. Eats right. And gives her great gift to the people. She is fortune-teller, you know. That is her gift."

Joyce, turning onto a side street, glanced at Sokhim to see if she was serious. She was.

"You remember last year, when the three boys are drowned in the river? During the big rainstorm? You were there when they find the bodies, I think."

"One of the boys was in my class. Vanna? He was one of my better kids. I've got his younger brother this year. God, that was a damned shame. The parents were holding this ceremony . . . "

"Yes! Because Mrs. Or tells them to. These parents go to her, asking her, 'What must we do to find the bodies? Very important for Buddhist to have the body for proper burial, you know. Mrs. Or, she instructs them to go to the river with offerings of food and to pray and to bring a monk to call on the river spirits to release the bodies. If they do this for two days, on the night of the second day the bodies will be found."

Joyce said nothing, goosebumps rising on her arms. Sokhim looked at her coyly.

"So, what do you think? This is coincidence?"

"Well . . . "

"The people don't think so. They think the river gives up the bodies because it was convinced to, and Mrs. Or, she foresees this.

You know, I think that also is why she won't go to the clinic for help. She believes Buddha takes away her eyes for this present world so she can see into the future and in this way lighten her karma."

▬ ▬ ▬

The William McKinley school covered a square city block: a one-story, L-shaped classroom building of buff-colored stucco, a gym, and a playground and ball field enclosed by a cyclone fence. The surrounding neighborhood was one of fathers who went to work and mothers who stayed home with kids, and its antiquated, *Saturday Evening Post* atmosphere made the writing on the school's front wall seem uglier, more jarring and menacing than what she had seen at the Park Lane Apartments.

CAT EYES EAT DOG MEAT & W.A.R. EATS CATS!

Fran Bigelow, the principal, was standing near the front doors with Gillis, the chief custodian. They were looking at the graffiti.

"Nice, isn't it?" Fran said as Joyce and Sokhim came up the front walk, only minutes ahead of the school buses. A short, caramel-colored woman with prematurely gray hair, Fran had been named principal this year.

"They did the same thing over at the Park Lane," Joyce said with a half-turn toward Sokhim. Standing between the two women, she felt pasty and monumental, like a statue molded out of dough. "Must be the same people. Same message. Same blue paint."

Fran's lips drew into a dash. "They must have had a busy night. The principal at Elgin called me a few minutes ago. Same endearing sentiments on his wall. Ditto for the Taylor Homes, where all the Vietnamese live. Not very creative, are they?"

Joyce looked at the writing and felt violated and angry and frightened, like someone whose home had been ransacked by burglars.

"What do you expect from white trash?" she said. "I'll bet some local boys did this. Our very own San Joaquin Valley rednecks. California good old boys. Like to bang around in pickup trucks, listening to their daddy's old Merle Haggard tapes and calling everybody who doesn't look like them gooks and niggers and beaners. Those creeps make it impossible for me to read *The Grapes of Wrath* with any degree of sympathy."

"I know the type," Fran said. "I also know the black version."

The school buses pulled up and formed a yellow and black line that stretched almost to the street corner. Doors opened with wheezes and snaps, and students spilled out and flowed in colorful streams down the sidewalks, across the playground and ball field: sixth-graders still wearing the charm of childhood, eighth-graders awkwardly treading the border between childhood and adolescence. Their shouts and laughter released the neighborhood from the oppressive residential quiet that would return at the first bell. A lot had changed in the years Joyce had taught at McKinley. When she began, most of her students were towheads; now most had straight black hair and spoke among themselves in tongues that sang like birds. But the morning ritual had not changed, nor had it lost its magic. The start of a new day, with a new day's hope—too often disappointed yet fulfilled enough to make the effort worthwhile—that her students would end the day more enlightened than they had been at the beginning. A simple thing, and a joy.

"You're off to Coloma today, aren't you?" Fran asked.

Joyce nodded.

"The flyers went out to the parents? The Asians, I mean."

"Well, I gave them to the kids to take home." She turned to Sokhim. "The parents know their children are going to be late coming home today?"

"Oh, yes. I think so."

"Sokhim translated the flyers into Khmer for us," Joyce said.

"Good. With all this crap going on, I don't want parents calling up, wondering why their kids aren't home at the usual time." She pointed at the wall with her thumb. "I called the police. Asked them to have a patrol car cruise by here at lunch period and when school's out. Just in case."

"In case of what?" Joyce asked, slightly alarmed. "We didn't get any phone threats, did we?"

"Nothing like that. But when it comes to these Nazi creeps, or whatever the hell they call themselves, you never can tell." Fran pivoted on her heels and led the way inside. Behind her, Joyce glanced warily at the graffiti, the way she might at a vicious dog. The words did seem strangely alive, as if, imbued with the hate of the men who had written them, they had the power to lunge from the wall and draw blood.

She spent twenty minutes of the first period quizzing the class on the history of the Gold Rush.

"Who first found gold in California?"

A hand shot up in the back of the room: Billy Pate, red-haired and eager.

"Captain John Sutter."

Joyce shook her head and scanned the rows of white and brown and saffron faces. No one moved or spoke. Her eyes fell on Paul Lim, brother of the drowned Vanna. He was tall for a Cambodian and had crooked teeth and a bowl haircut.

"Paul, can you tell us? Who discovered gold in 1849?"

He glanced uncertainly at Sokhim, who put the question in Khmer.

"James Wilson Marshall," the boy said, his tongue picking its way through the thickets of treacherous consonants.

"That's correct," Joyce said, and wrote the name on the blackboard in her clear, curving hand. Those old-fashioned penmanship classes. "Now who knows where the gold was found?"

Once more she was met by blank and silent faces.

"Oh, come on. This is easy. Where are we going at the end of this period?"

Rose Ortega's arm rose tentatively.

"Coloma?"

"Is that an answer or a question, Rose?"

"An answer."

"Be more specific."

Rose's thick eyebrows knit in thought.

"Sutter's Mill."

"Yes. In the tailrace of Sutter's Mill, which is on what river?"

Waiting for a response, Joyce looked out the window. Dappled light fell through the trees onto the bus that was to take them to Coloma. It was the one the school used for field trips, a boxy vehicle nearly as long as a city bus. A battered pickup truck cruised by, spewing exhaust fumes as thick as sprayed insecticide over the school lawn. A California good old boy, listening to Merle Haggard?

"Well?" she said to the class, keeping her back to them to signal her disapproval of their performance. Suddenly, sadness washed over her and she mentally left the room, picturing herself in the place of the elderly woman who was shuffling down the sidewalk across the street. A vasectomy. She was going to outlive Alex by many years, and saw a long, lonely widowhood stretching before her.

A voice behind her spoke in a near whisper.

"The American River, Mrs. DeLuca."

She faced the class. The voice belonged to Sandra An, a girl with a perpetually downturned mouth and her shyest pupil.

"That's right!" she said, with an enthusiasm she hoped would encourage the girl. Joyce identified with her, for she had been withdrawn and awkward when she was in school.

She went on with the quiz until a restlessness swept through the classroom like a wind. The kids, anxious for their day in the open air, began to look out the windows, to squirm in their seats and fidget with pencils and notebooks. When she announced that it was time to board the bus, she had to shout, "Quietly!" to restrain them from rushing the door in a mass.

They filed down the corridor. Wall lockers, redolence of floor wax, school. Sokhim seemed as impatient as the students; without a car and with three children to take care of, she led a confined life.

Outside, as the kids climbed into the bus, Joyce conferred with the driver about the route and schedule. He was an older man, with a hard, spare face.

"Blecch! It stinks in here," someone said in the bus. Others began to cough.

Joyce stepped up and caught a strong odor of exhaust fumes.

"Is there something wrong with the engine?" she asked the driver. "It smells like a garage in here."

"The engine isn't runnin'," he answered with a sly look. "It was some fella burnin' more oil than gas. Come by twice and near to choked me to death. Thought they had laws against that. Emission control."

The man's speech clung to the twangs and rhythms of the Southwest. Eee-mission control. Probably came out here as a young boy. Out of the Dust Bowl in a jalopy piled high with old furniture, a Dorothea Lange photograph.

"If it's all right with you, I'll let the kids open the windows for a while."

"I don't mind, long as none of 'em sticks their head or arms out. Got rules to abide by."

Later, with her pupils settled down for the long ride, Joyce sat in a rear seat beside Sokhim. On the freeway, the bus lumbered along in the slow lane. Westward lay the part of the San Joaquin Valley known as the Delta for the rivers and canals and sloughs that spread through it like blue arteries. Off to the north, thick black smoke continued to rise into a cloudless sky, but Joyce could not tell if it was the same peat fire she had seen earlier or a new blaze.

"You know, this makes me think of Cambodia," Sokhim said, her face glued to the window. "All the rivers, the farms, the green."

"I've seen pictures of it. It's a beautiful country. Do you miss it much?"

"No!" Sokhim answered sharply; then she turned from the window with a smile, to show that she'd meant no offense by her tone.

"You wouldn't want to go back? If they ever get things settled over there."

"Never settle things over there. Never. If there is one Khmer Rouge still living, things never settled. Anyway, Khmer Rouge are not the only reason I don't want to go back." She leaned toward Joyce and lowered her voice to a conspiratorial undertone. "Women here so free!"

"Uh-oh, we've corrupted you," Joyce said with a laugh. "But we're not as free as you think. Nobody is. We're all trapped by biology."

Sokhim gave her a puzzled frown.

"Yes?"

"Oh, nothing. I say goofy things sometimes."

Joyce leaned back and closed her eyes. She supposed it was the glory and the curse of the American to live by the illusion that all things were possible, that anything you get into can be gotten out of, that the idea of fate or destiny belonged in a stale Old World museum. Yet biology was fate, wasn't it? Women knew that in their marrow, while for men it was an abstraction understood only as an equation or a law of physics is understood.

A fire truck wailed past. The kids on the left side of the aisle pointed out the windows, shouting, "A fire! A fire!" An entire wheat field was ablaze. Pillars of flame rose flashing out of the wheat, then vanished in an instant, consuming the subterranean gases that had given them their moment of life. A fireboat, streams shot from its water cannons making vague rainbows, chugged up and down a slough bordering the field. The smoke nearest the ground looked as solid as tar. As it rose, it thinned gradually into a gauzy curtain that drew itself across the arch of the sky and over the freeway and the fields beyond before it dissipated into a haze. The bus passed beneath the pall and a stench of sulphur blew in through the windows. The sunlight changed tone, taking on the ominous yellow cast that sometimes prophesies a thunderstorm.

Billy Pate, his eyes fastened on the blaze, asked what had caused it, and Joyce explained that beneath the Delta's topsoil lay beds of rotting tule reeds—the remnants of primeval marshes. As the reeds decomposed they formed an organic substance called peat, which had the same chemical composition as coal.

"As a matter of fact, Billy, under pressure and over many thousands of years, peat becomes coal. Sometimes it spontaneously combusts and smolders like an underground furnace. If a peat fire bursts to the surface and gets out of hand, like this one, it can destroy whole orchards, acres of crops."

Billy looked appropriately impressed. The very earth beneath your feet suddenly exploding into flame. Joyce looked back a last time and, like a child who invents dragons out of clouds and monsters out of shadows, she imagined that the flames leaping briefly into life were the vengeful ghosts of Indians, summoned to haunt the living souls who now walked and plowed upon their graves in the secret marshes.

What a perfectly strange idea. The argument with Alex, the vandalism at the school . . . She must be a little overwrought, and yet she shivered as she watched the flames licking out of the ground, the smoke spreading in long tendrils across the land.

The bus passed through Sacramento suburbs. The driver left the freeway and got onto Highway 50, which bore them eastward into rolling ranch country where grazing Herefords daubed the hillsides and lone bulls lazed in the shade of the trees. The landscape evoked sentimental images of Old California: vast rancheros granted by Spanish kings, vaqueros wearing leather breeches. Road signs sang to passing motorists.

FIND YOUR DREAM AT RANCHO DEL LAGO . . . RANCHO BUENAVISTA—CALIFORNIA LIVING—SINGLE-FAMILY HOMES STARTING AT ONLY . . .

The new subdivisions lay well off the highway, at the ends of new access roads. Obscured by distance and the dust and spring pollen in the air, they looked as vague and intangible as the dreams that lured people to them.

Alex was partly responsible for a couple of those developments. He had sold the land to the men who had built them. Joyce's future widowhood might be long and lonely but not poor, thanks to his keen eye for the right deal at the right price.

He trusted himself with all that money hanging in the balance, but not in this other business. What the hell did he mean by that? *It's me I don't trust.* That he'd cheat on her if she got pregnant? Whatever he meant made no difference. Joyce blamed herself. Years ago, she should have foreseen that this longing would rise in her as she approached forty. Biology is fate.

The bus entered Placerville, then turned north onto Highway 49. Tight and twisting, it climbed into the foothills of the Motherlode Country. Motherlode—Eve of all riches, the great, inexhaustible reef of gold the fever-eyed forty-niners sought but never found, a myth, one of California's earliest intangible dreams. The driver slowed to negotiate the sharp bends. The country grew wilder and steeper, creased by ravines through which dark streams flowed.

The smell of exhaust again filled the inside of the bus. Sokhim started to rub her eyes.

At first, Joyce thought the fumes had irritated them; then she saw that Sokhim was crying.

"What's wrong?"

Sokhim's hand reached above her ear to press the crimson flower, then dipped into her bag for a tissue.

"Nothing. Please forgive."

"Are you sure?"

"Something you say."

"That *I* said?"

"Pandra. I am thinking about him, maybe too much I think. He has not even try to find work. Not even try to come with me to English lessons. All day, all night in the apartment except in the evening. Then he and the other men listen to news from Cambodia. It is—has—it has been like this for years now."

Joyce, wondering what she could have said to have brought this on, heard in her companion's voice the sadness, anger, and contempt of a strong woman married to a man who had lost his strength. She knew the story of how, armed only with a machete and a shotgun, Pandra had led Sokhim and their then only child out of Cambodia toward the Thai border, traveling at night past annihilated villages where the wind piped through human rib cages and the eye sockets of mounded skulls. Pandra walked always ahead and told Sokhim that if they ran into any Khmer Rouge, he would shoot the first with the shotgun and charge the others with the machete so she and the child could get away.

That was the kind of man he had been, but in America, torn from his farm and his ancestors' graves, he had grown aimless and indifferent, content to live off welfare. For a while, he'd worked in a downtown diner as a dishwasher, the only work he knew besides farming; the Khmer Rouge had made him a dishwasher after they took over his village. One night in the diner, Pandra fell far behind. The owner yelled at him. Certain the man was going to kill him, as the Khmer Rouge would have done, he ran out and fled back to the apartment and had hardly left it since.

"So many men like him," Sokhim was saying, "they don't try to learn English, don't try to find job. Only listen to the radio and talk about when they can go back to Cambodia."

"So that's what I said . . . "

"'Ah!' say these men. 'There is peace treaty. Soon we go back home. Ah! Prince Sihanouk soon to return to power. Soon we go back home. Ah! United Nations has sent peace force. Soon there will be peace and we go back home.'"

"And you can't do that," said Joyce, pressing a sisterly hand on Sokhim's knee. "Or won't."

"I am good Buddhist wife, so if Pandra . . . "

They were pitched forward violently. Joyce's forehead struck the chrome bar atop the seat in front of her. Brakes squealed, the bus shuddered and swerved to a stop. Several children cried out. There were smells of smoke and scorched rubber. Toward the front, Rose Ortega stood in the aisle, a hand cupped to her bleeding nose. A few other kids were half out of their seats, pointing through the windshield. The driver, turning the wheel hard with one hand, the other working the gearshift, called for everyone to sit down. Shaking her head to clear it, Joyce touched her forehead lightly. A lump was rising above the bridge of her nose. Looking out, she saw that the rear of the bus was almost on the shoulder. Below, a hill sheared so steeply it was brother to a cliff. A bluff walled the other side of the road.

The driver eased the bus forward a couple of yards, stopped, turned the wheel, backed up ever so slowly, stopped again, and turned the wheel in the opposite direction. Joyce rose unsteadily and started up the aisle, telling the children to keep their seats and be calm.

"You too, lady," the driver ordered. "I got to get this vehicle straightened out and backed up. Helluva accident just ahead! Pickup blockin' the road! On fire!"

She rushed to the front and saw it through the flame-stitched

DELAFIELD PUBLIC LIBRARY

smoke roiling out of the driver's side window: a gray truck astride a curve fifty or sixty feet away. In a moment, the cab was ablaze.

"Musta happened ten seconds before we got . . . Didn't even see him till we come 'round that bend back of us. . . . I'll be damned if it ain't the same one."

"Same?"

"Lady, siddown. Got to get us around that curve back behind us before his tank blows." The driver pulled a knob and the front door flapped open. "Just in case. You and that other lady stand by the emergency door."

As the bus crawled in reverse, she moved to the rear and stood with her hand on the emergency door handle, her heart beating against her ribs.

Sokhim looked up with a calm that made Joyce ashamed of her fear.

"What is happening?"

"An accident. We're all right. . . ."

A loud, hollow boom, as of a huge kettle drum struck once, was followed by a sharp crack and the crystalline sound of shattering safety glass. The bus jerked to a stop again, throwing Joyce forward so that she lost her grip on the emergency handle. The horn was blaring, and over its harsh monotone children screamed in a way she had never heard anyone scream before. The windshield had been blown to pieces, kids were bleeding from shards of glass, and the horn was stuck because the driver was slumped over the steering wheel.

For a fraction of an instant, she thought he'd had a heart attack, but an astonishing quantity of blood lay puddled at his feet. The truck must have exploded and a piece of it shot through the window and struck him. Children leapt from the seats and charged all at once for the front door, some slipping in the blood and the rest jamming themselves in the stairwell. Smoke bearing the stink of burning gasoline rolled through the broken windshield. Then a dozen children, coughing and shrieking, flew down the aisle and flung themselves in a mass against Joyce and Sokhim, pinning them to the emergency door. Joyce groped behind her back for the handle. She couldn't find it. In the same moment, a series of roars, following one another so rapidly they were as one thunderous noise, came from outside, toward the front of the bus. There was another roar, and through a rent in the smoke she saw Billy Pate, with an arm blown off at the shoulder, thrown backward up the stairwell and against the dead driver.

The man suddenly appeared, as if he had risen out of the smoke or as if the smoke, like the stuff that whirls out of a fairy tale genie's bottle, had composed itself into the figure of a man. He was standing beside the driver's seat, straddling the body of Billy Pate. The man was tall and thin . . . black hair . . . headset over his ears, like the kind skeet shooters wore . . . a military uniform . . . flak jacket . . . words, symbols drawn on it in yellow . . . a black, short-barreled gun at his hip . . . a pasty face . . . no expression. . . . Seeing everything in slow-motion, Joyce watched him make a half-turn to the right and fire the gun into a seat, and she knew a child had been hiding there because blood spattered against the window in a way that reminded her of mosquito blood on a windshield, only there was so much more of it. The gunshot had been so loud in the enclosed space it pierced her eardrums so that she could hardly hear the horn anymore, or the children's screams, or Sokhim's, or her own. Quickly and calmly, the gunman detached the round magazine under his weapon, dropped it, and reached into a belly-pack.

"Oh, please, please! No!"

He fixed her for a moment with pale eyes flat and lifeless, eyes that looked like tinted green contact lenses, then drew another magazine out of the belly-pack and began to fit it into the gun.

"God, no!"

Sokhim yelled something. Joyce fell outside, on her back on the road. Sokhim had wrenched open the emergency door and everyone had tumbled out like fish from a net.

They got to their feet and ran for the bend in the road. With the steep hill on one side and the bluff on the other, there was nowhere else to go; if they could get around the bend, maybe they would find level ground and woods to hide in. From inside the bus, the gunman fired a single shot.

Joyce outstripped the others in no time. She rounded the curve, and yes . . . flat ground . . . woods. . . . But Sokhim, the kids . . . She spun around to run back as they came toward her, scattered and strung out along the road. The pale killer was running after them. He stopped, raised the gun to his shoulder, and aimed at the last child in the pack. Rose Ortega. Sometimes the unimaginably horrible has the same arresting power as the ineffably beautiful. Joyce could not move. The gun crashed, the noise pealing over the hills, and Rose somersaulted and flopped on her back and lay still.

The gunman swung the weapon on Paul Lim.

Joyce sprang across the road, scooped Paul up as if he weighed nothing, and ran with him in her arms, ran as if she herself were weightless. She could not feel the pavement beneath her feet. She heard another roar, tripped, and went down belly first atop Paul, who cried out. Somehow she had the presence of mind to grab his wrist and pull him with her as she rolled into a brushy culvert. She tried to rise and flee into the sheltering woods, but one leg crumpled and she fell against the slope of the culvert. The leg felt warm and wet. She looked down. Blood was spreading across her trousers, an inch or two above her knee. A hot, bilious lump rose in her throat. She forced it back down, forced herself not to make a sound, and clamped a hand tightly over Paul's mouth.

"Shhhhhh . . . "

Paul gazed up at her, stunned.

"Shhhhhh . . . "

The gunman stood in the middle of the road, close enough for Joyce to see his eyes again. He was very young, not much more than a kid himself. Nineteen, twenty maybe. He was bent over, frantically pulling a rod or lever on the side of the barrel.

"Goddamn you!" he yelled. If he hadn't yelled, she would not have heard him for the blaring of the bus horn and the ringing in her ears.

"Goddamn you! Fucked up! It's all fucked up!"

It was an anguished cry—the only emotion Joyce had seen him display. He sounded so hurt and frustrated that, for one bizarre split second, she felt sorry for him. In the next split second, watching him toss the weapon aside, a white rage rose in her. She would have strangled him with her bare hands if she'd been able. A fortunate thing she wasn't, because he reached under his flak jacket and drew a pistol from his back pocket. It flashed like a mirror in the sunlight as he waved it this way and that, his white-green eyes flicking in synchronization with the movements of the gun. Then, gripping the pistol in both hands, he fired down the road, in the direction Sokhim had fled with the others. Joyce saw a red circle on the pavement, thought it was blood. . . . No . . . Sokhim's flower. The man fired another shot and shouted something Joyce could not quite make out. . . .

Race! . . . Victory! . . . Something like that.

Then he pivoted and looked straight at her and Paul.

I see my death, here is my death. . . .

He took a step toward them and stopped.

Here is death.

The bright pistol at his side.

She waited for him to raise it, waited for her death. Light reflected off the pistol and reached out like an arm. It swept across her face, she squinted against the silver glare, and feeling weak and drowsy, she rose into the air, light as ash. Some part of herself—soul, spirit, or mind—levitated over her bleeding body and understood that all that had seemed important only minutes ago was unimportant. She did not see her life pass before her in a flash of images; she saw it in a single static picture, from its beginning to this moment. Really, it was not a picture so much as a swift comprehension, as when the solution to a difficult mathematical problem suddenly becomes clear. "I understand now, yes" were the words that went through her mind, though she did not know precisely what it was she understood.

A siren. She heard one in the distance. Or was it close and only sounded distant to her? The far-off wailing restored her buoyant spirit to her body, returned her to the reality of terror and pain and blood and slaughtered children. Children massacred, her children. Rose Ortega, lying out there on the road, almost torn in half, and Billy Pate . . . Her hand still covered Paul Lim's mouth; she had never let him go. The siren was louder, but still far off. A siren, yes. But who out here could have called the police so soon? Out on the road, the gunman turned toward the sound. He looked around with quick, nervous jerks of his head, as if he were confused or frightened. He stuck the gun behind his ear, stood there for a second or two poised to shoot himself, and then sprinted into the woods, yelling again. The same words as before. Victory! . . . Race! Race? *Race*. Racial victory? Oh, God. W.A.R. He was one of them. *W.A.R. eats cats.* She should have known, Fran should have known. The same . . . *the same truck* . . . the one she'd seen out the classroom window . . . Came by twice, he'd said. . . . Must have circled the block, waiting for the bus to leave. . . .

She heard a gunshot in the woods, not very far off. Just the one and no more. Her mouth tasted of wool and salt and was so dry her tongue stuck to the roof. She turned her head aside and vomited. Her hand relaxed its grip on Paul and fell on the side of her right thigh. Through the blood on her trousers, she felt the buckshot's ragged punctures in her flesh, and drew in deep breaths to quiet her heartbeat. There wasn't any pain. Reading news stories about murders and shootings, she had imagined that getting shot would hurt terribly. The same truck. W.A.R. eats cats. Maybe the pain would come later. No matter how bad it was, she would be grateful that she was alive to feel it. I hurt, therefore I am. She lay back and looked up at the mild, unblemished sky.

Interlude

The People of the Neighborhood

HUMMING AND WHINING LIKE GIANT APPLIANCES, remote vans and satellite trucks lined both sides of the street in front of the William McKinley Intermediate School. Cables writhed across the sidewalk and the school lawn, bearing signals that steel dishes on the truck roofs shot toward tiny steel balls spinning far above the planet, toward repeater stations atop distant mountains. The people of the neighborhood stood on their front porches or in their front yards, watching the spectacle of mass communication that had disrupted their routine mornings. Some of them could not get to work or to doctor's appointments or to the grocery store because the vehicles blocked their driveways, but no one complained or asked the drivers to move the equipment humming with powerful electronic mysteries.

There were several reasons for this reluctance. The thrill of seeing the familiar faces of reporters and local news anchors in the flesh was one, but the main reason was this: the people of the neighborhood knew that the spectacle unfolding before them was a necessary, almost a sacred, ritual that must not be interfered with in any way. This ritual was called *coverage*. Television was a way of life for the people of the neighborhood; they took miniature TV sets to sporting events, took them on vacations to the seashore, to national parks, even to campsites deep within what remains of the North American wilderness. That intimacy with the medium was the reason they understood that the *coverage* of an event was more important than the event. The reporters and cameramen and the technicians in the vehicles beaming signals into outer space and onto distant mountain peaks were here in the name of structure and order. They were here to provide narrative: beginning, middle, end. Priests and priestesses of *coverage*, they were here to make, through their magic, the incomprehensible comprehensible.

They had been doing exactly that since Friday, which had been Act One of the horror that almost everyone, on TV and off, called "The Tragedy" because they didn't know what else to call it.

Because the McKinley School was across the street, around the corner, down the block, the people of the neighborhood were more stunned by "The Tragedy" than people elsewhere. They had a hard time fitting the event into their understanding of the world. It expanded their conception of the possible beyond the limits of the acceptable. They would have found it easier to believe that the school bus, on that balmy cloudless morning, had been destroyed by a meteor. If they had not been Americans of the late twentieth century, but, say, Native Americans of the fifteenth, they would have turned to tribal shamans for answers and guidance. If they had been Americans of their grandparents' generation, they would have sought out priests and ministers.

The people of the neighborhood turned on their televisions.

Their televisions helped them fit the event into their understanding of the world by reducing it to images that fit within a screen. Their televisions made the alien familiar through the familiar ceremonies of *coverage*.

Thus, Act One, "The Crime," the Friday nightly news . . .

A WIDE, ESTABLISHING SHOT of the road where the bus was ambushed, the surrounding foothills, the reporter voicing over . . . "This is California's Motherlode Country" . . . The people of the neighborhood, gathered around their flickering shrines, finished the sentence in their minds . . . *but this picturesque part of the Golden State became a scene of horror Friday morning when . . .*

The ambush was then described in precise order, so that it sounded as structured as a movie. . . . "Bob, it looked like a war zone out here . . ."

TIGHT FULL, a photograph of the killer, and he became in a twinkling not an arbitrary impersonal force but someone with a face and name . . . CUT TO LIVE SHOT, reporter at the scene, mike in his hand . . . "The question everyone is asking is 'Why?' . . . But the only man who could answer that is . . . " Again the people of the neighborhood knew what the reporter was going to say, they wanted him to say it, it was part of the ritual, and they uttered the words to themselves before the reporter spoke them . . . *is dead by his own hand* . . .

Thus Act Two, "The Aftermath," the weekend news . . .

A poignant SYMBOL SHOT . . . a child's coffin being lowered into a grave, WIDE on Buddhist monks, chanting . . . Reporter voices over . . . "They began to bury their dead in San Joaquin today . . . " TIGHT ON grieving mother, SOUND UP FULL as she wails . . . CUT TO LIVE SHOT, reporter in cemetery . . . "Shock and disbelief have spread throughout the Asian community in this Central Valley city . . . Vietnamese, Cambodians, and Laotians, who fled the killing fields of Southeast Asia . . . *only to have their dreams of a better life in America shattered by violence* . . ."

The hearts of the people cried out for a life-affirming story, and their televisions gave it to them in the tale of the two heroines, Sokhim Chun and Joyce DeLuca . . . Interview with Sokhim Chun in her apartment . . . CUT TO reporter in front of a Sacramento hospital . . . "On the sixth floor of this hospital, seventh-grade teacher Joyce DeLuca is recovering from an operation . . . her condition is described as good . . . "

The massacre also cried out for explanations, and the television crews provided those as well. EXTERIOR WIDE, a cannery, reporter voice-over . . . "Mass child-murderer Duane Boggs worked on the loading dock of this United Foods cannery last summer . . . TIGHT FULL on Joshua Somers, a foreman . . . "He kind of stuck to himself most of the time . . . Most of the guys thought he was hard to work with . . . He seemed angry about everything . . . a bomb waiting to go off . . . " CUT TO LIVE SHOT, reporter, "Meanwhile, detectives and psychologists are struggling to identify the demons that raged through . . . " And then came the interviews with the experts . . . TIGHT ON Dr. Thomas Renfro, professor of criminology . . . bookshelves in background, cluttered desk . . . "The ultimate act of terrorism against society is to harm or kill children . . . And the ultimate revenge is to then kill yourself, thus denying society justice . . . "

Of course! That's why he did it. Terrorism . . . revenge . . . hate . . . angry loner . . . bomb waiting to go off . . . Now we can name the demons that raged through Duane Leonard Boggs . . .

Thus Act Three, "Life Goes On . . . "

That was this morning's drama. The president of the San Joaquin Consolidated School District, in a televised press conference, announced that the William McKinley Intermediate School would open its doors on Monday, as usual. Classes would go on, it would be best for the children to continue as before, to *begin picking up the pieces of their lives* . . .

Now everyone was waiting for the school buses to arrive. Everyone was waiting to see if the parents and children shared in the brave determination of the school district president to carry on. Would they play their roles in Act Three? Would the buses arrive full or empty?

Monday, April 19th

FOR HIS SINS, GABRIEL CHIN HAD TO SHUTTLE FROM one training and refresher course to another, a wandering scholar of advanced police science. It was the Bureau's way of keeping him busy during his suspension from regular duties. He was to spend this week in blood—blood splattered and splashed and misted as fine as aerosol spray, the blood of calves sacrificed to further the progress of modern crime detection. Blood was a substance he knew something about, having seen a lot of it, and so he hoped this week would be less torturous than last, when he'd attended tutorials on flame spectroscopy. A whole week, squinting at calibration graphs showing the amounts of cocaine extracted from addicts' hair follicles with a device called an ITS-40 ion trap mass spectrometer interfaced to a Varian 3400 gas chromograph.

The classroom confinement often made him feel like tearing down walls out of sheer boredom. He craved action and suffered fits of restlessness and irritability when his craving wasn't satisfied. Krimsky, his supervisor in the Sacramento field office, had counseled him to keep cool, keep calm. He should consider himself lucky—he was being introduced to the cutting edge, the game of cops and robbers as it was going to be played in the twenty-first century. For that matter, he should consider himself lucky to still be employed by the California Department of Justice.

Adrienne and the kids were happy with his normal hours. For the duration of his suspension, he would be a husband and dad like other husbands and dads, home for dinner, in bed by ten, and no three A.M. summons to some desolate highway where a perforated body had been found in a trunk. But he missed those calls and the stark theatrics of patrol car and ambulance lights flashing in the darkness, the anticipation that tingled in him as he began to gather clues to a new mystery, the excitement of plaiting those clues into a seamless net of evidence and then dropping it on a suspect. Without the spice of the unexpected, life tasted like oatmeal, a diet that made him miserable. Adrienne, Leland, and Eleanor paid for his home-for-dinner, in-bed-by-ten regularity by enduring his spells of irascibility and watching him pace the backyard like a high-strung hunting dog with no room to run and no game to chase.

This state of affairs had forced Gabriel, not a reflective man, to confront a truth about his nature that he'd been aware of but never had the inclination to look in the face: he couldn't stand normality. Not only his livelihood, but his happiness depended on the abnormal, on the existence of murderers and rapists and gangbangers and other violators of the laws of God and man. That strange symbiosis between cop and criminal. Well, he was going to have to learn to cope with everyday life one of these days. He was only forty-four, but retirement came early in his profession. In less than seven years, he would have his twenty-five in with the Bureau, and probably would have to choose between retirement and a desk job like Krimsky's. Unlike a lot of cops, with their fantasies of buying a small ranch or taking to the road in Winnebagos, he dreaded retirement. Those idle years yawned out there in his future with a bleak and terrifying emptiness, like the Mojave at night.

Until his recent fall from grace his disciplinary record had been impeccable, but he had fallen hard, and now, nearly a month into his suspension, he had to spend a week learning blood-spatter analysis. With twenty other students—crime lab technicians, plainclothesmen, small town and county cops in the varied uniforms of their departments—he sat at a long table in a windowless room on the bottom floor of the State Department of Law Enforcement's headquarters in Sacramento. This gargantuan structure, the largest law enforcement building in the country after the FBI's in Washington, seemed to enfold Gabriel in a motherly embrace. Though he could not hear them, he was aware of the square gray mainframes whirring in climate-controlled rooms as they processed countless bytes of information on every felon in California from the pettiest purse snatcher to the most cunning serial killer; though he could not see them, he could picture the video terminals on the floors above, each terminal capable of displaying any one of seven million fingerprints at the touch of a few keys; and though he could not touch them, he sensed the weight of the ten million criminal case files that crowded the stacks floor to ceiling in the records rooms. The nearness of all this reminded him, as he fought back a yawn, of Krimsky's advice to consider himself lucky. Down in L.A., Lockheed engineers were serving Big Macs or standing in unemployment lines with high school dropouts, but Gabriel Chin was assured of a job if he behaved himself. He was employed by California's only remaining growth industry.

Roger Willow, the lecturer, entered the room. As slender as his name, he was wearing a white smock, paper hat, and plastic faceshield with the visor turned up. He looked like a cross between a surgeon and a riot policeman.

"Blood on a wall—something most of you have seen," he began in his dry, flat voice. "It's a mess, and yet . . . and yet it's not a mess. It means something. It's like animal tracks in the woods. If you're a good woodsman, you can read the tracks. That's what blood-spatter interpretation is all about. By the end of this week, you'll be able to study blood spatters and know what kind of instrument made the blows, how many blows were struck, and the positions of the victim and the assailant. . . ."

Gabriel, sitting between a Sacramento detective and a Stockton patrolwoman, wrestled back another yawn. He knew Willow, who had done the lab work on two of his murder cases. Chemist and mathematician, he was a minor genius in the far-out realms of criminalistics and also a man who could make the Second Coming sound as interesting as an assembly manual.

"We will be using basic trigonometry to figure these things out," he droned. "We will create blood spatters and study them to see if what happens corresponds to the theory of what should happen. . . ."

This is going to be agony, Gabriel thought. He fiddled with his protractor and rule, the instruments with which he was to plot the trigonometry of death inflicted by bludgeon and bullet, knife, hatchet, and saw.

Willow turned his back and wrote on the blackboard: *Chaos Theory.* "Now what is that? you ask." Willow gazed at the class, his lips as thin and straight as an equal sign. "A type of mathematics that describes the indescribable—phenomena that cannot be handled by classical mathematics. And what phenomena? you ask. The motion of fluids through a medium among others. In our case, blood. You see, in the sheer force of liquids, you get turbulence effects, you get viscosity effects . . . "

Viscosity? Turbulence effects? What did any of this have to do with catching crooks and killers? The Stockton patrolwoman, her head bowed as if in prayer, took notes. Everyone was taking notes. On what? Maybe he should as well, so he wouldn't look lazy or stupid in front of all these ordinary cops. He couldn't hide that he belonged to the state's elite law enforcement agency; he was wearing his field uniform, a midnight blue jumpsuit with a golden sleeve patch and badge proclaiming: SPECIAL AGENT . . . CALIFORNIA DEPT. OF JUSTICE.

Gabriel usually worked in plainclothes. The uniform was for a photographer's shoot late this afternoon. Despite his disgrace, he was going to pose for a recruiting poster designed to show that the Bureau was an equal opportunity employer. In a group that included two female agents, two white men, one Hispanic, and one black, he was to be the token Asian. Though he was a fourth-generation Californian who spoke only one word of Chinese and preferred poker to mah-jongg, his appearance filled the bill. He hadn't inherited his mother's soft Cantonese features, but those of his father's ancestors: people of the Manchurian plains, with sharp angles carved into their faces by the iron winds of high Asia. His nose, broken in a tae kwon do tournament ten years ago, added a menacing touch appropriate to a lawman. "You're perfect, Gabe," said Krimsky, who had volunteered him as a model. "You look like you were a drill sergeant in the Golden Horde."

". . . so to give you an overview of the theory—you won't need to know this, but it's good to know it"—Willow's voice hummed like an air conditioner—"chaos math is based on imaginary numbers and functions of complex variables . . . "

Functions? Complex variables? He looked up and down the table. Heads remained bowed over notebooks, pens moved, and he could not see a glazed or confused eye in the bunch. Did they understand Willow's Swahili? He should not set a bad example. He pushed back in his chair and, holding his notebook on his crossed leg so no one could see what he was doing, began to make scramblers.

CHAOS
AOSCH
HACOS

Hacos. A burrito and two chicken hacos, por favor.

". . . so with computers we can run the functions out to infinity. We discover that they are fairly smooth and normal at first, but eventually they get into a chaotic shape. Things break down, so to speak, become disorganized and unpredictable . . . "

HASCO
COSHA
CSHAO

Could be a Chinese name. How do you do, Mr. Cshao? No, too many consonants. Maybe a Czech name.

". . . thus, chaos math describes things going from a stable to an unstable state, like storm systems or something as simple as cigarette smoke. It rises in a tidy column, then spreads and swirls, but no two cigarettes, even identical ones, disperse smoke in the same way. Yet some things can be predicted. In a manner of speaking, this math is the language of chaos. But what does that say? Chaos isn't truly chaos. It's order disguised as disorder, a sheep in wolf's clothing, you might say . . . "

SCHOA
OCSHA
SOCHA

Socha. So cha cha cha. I've got to get out of this! A week is going to drive me, cha cha cha, into the nuthatch.

"But I think things will be much clearer if you can see how the theory is applied to the effects of impacts upon human flesh. If you would, please gather around me at the other end of the lab."

Chair legs scraped on tile as the students rose and followed Willow to where several cardboard crates, each over six feet high, open on one end, and wrapped in butcher's paper, stood like washing machines in a Laundromat. A store-window mannequin was in the opening of each crate. One was standing, another sitting, another knelt on its plastic knees. Weapons were arrayed on a table—a lead pipe, a length of rebar, a car's radio antenna.

"The heads of these dummies," Willow said, picking up the lead pipe, "simulate the human skull. Styrofoam affixed with sponge soaked in calf's blood, covered with plastic and painted with latex. Please stand aside and I'll demonstrate."

He pulled the visor over his face, and the Stockton patrolwoman and the Sacramento detective and the small town cops in their uniforms of blue, brown, and tan swung like a gate to get out of his way. Willow stood behind the mannequin, and raising the pipe over its head, projected on the wall a shadow that was an image out of a cheap thriller. He swung the pipe once and again, cracking the plastic with the first blow, crushing it with the second. Blood exploded into the box, splattering the butcher's paper with gobs and streaks that resembled paint flung from a brush.

Willow flipped up the smeared visor. His smock now looked as messy as a meatpacker's coveralls at the end of a shift.

"Please take a close look and imagine that you have come upon a crime scene that looks like this. You will note the main patterning, and here at the edges, outlying slashes."

Then a voice squawked through a speaker in the ceiling: "Special Agent Chin, a call for you at station eighteen. Special Agent Gabriel Chin, station one-eight."

Gabriel looked up, the hope of deliverance shining in his black eyes.

"Special Agent Chin," crackled the disembodied voice again, "an urgent call at station one-eight."

"You'd better get that," Willow said, annoyed by the interruption. "One-eight is my office. It's way down at the other end of the hall."

Please please please, Gabriel thought, walking quickly down a corridor lit by recessed lights in square, frosted panes.

He passed laboratories, airless cubicles innocent of sunlight. Few cops inhabited this subterranean world. CCI it was called, for California Criminalistics Institute, a kind of research center where Ph.D.'s like Willow devised improved methods of gathering evidence. Gabriel went by one hidey-hole occupied by a balding little man whose sole function was to test gimmicks marketed by mail order scam artists and find out if they had any use, either in committing crimes or in solving them. Last week, he'd called Gabriel into his lair to show him a device its inventor claimed could boost brain power. You patched a few wires to your temples, flipped a switch, and became an instant genius. He'd declined the little man's invitation to try it out, although now he wished he had. Maybe it would have helped him understand what a complex variable was.

Funny, when you thought about it—all these resources dedicated to getting the goods on some murderer or arsonist who probably hadn't finished high school. And the criminal population was flourishing despite all the fancy technology and techniques that were supposed to keep it under control. Not that criminals had grown more crafty and sophisticated. The ones Gabriel had put behind bars in the last few years were far more careless than those he'd collared early in his career. Their amateurishness often disappointed him; it took the challenge out of the pursuit. It also scared him, filling him with a kind of spiritual fear, because it wasn't an amateurism born of stupidity: the new breed of criminals didn't care if they got caught. Like insects or viruses that had mutated to resist a pesticide or vaccine, they'd become immune to fear of punishment. They expected to be sent to prison, even wanted to be. Do the crime, do the time, hey, three to five in Soledad or San Quentin was no big deal, it was a badge of honor, a rite of passage, a thug's bar mitzvah. The ones who chilled him most were street gangsters like Pham Van Trinh, the Moonlight Dragon who was the cause behind his suspension. They represented something too strange and enormous for Gabriel's comprehension, an evil so alien that it seemed to have come to earth on a meteor. Stone-eyed, stone-cold killers immune even to fear of execution, immune to all human feeling, Trinh and his kind were mutants. They walked and talked and looked like human beings, but the things they did testified that they had to be something very different inside.

He entered Willow's office and picked up the phone. It was Krimsky, calling from the field office in Rancho Cordova.

"Thanks for your prompt response," Krimsky said in the mellow, rich tones of a two-pack-a-day smoker. "You must have been having a good time."

"I witnessed a horrible crime. A window dummy bludgeoned to death by a chemist, the most boring man in California."

"Your school days are over, Gabe. The A.G. wants to see you at one. Her office. One sharp."

Gabriel paused and looked at the deadly texts in Willow's bookcase. Differential Equations. Organic Chemistry.

"Who?" he asked.

"The A.G. Your boss, my boss, the Director's boss? One o'clock"—there was a clicking on the line—"ah, shit, another call coming in. Got to put you on hold for a second."

His stomach tumbled as he waited. On the wall in front of him were two striking but weird paintings, one of something that looked like a golden bat flying at night, another of a huge greenish eye set in a Persian carpet. The A.G. In eighteen years with the Bureau, he had never seen the inside of the attorney general's office. There could be only one reason for a summons to so high an audience: someone had leaked the story of how he'd gone much too far while interrogating Pham Van Trinh. Now the A.G. was going to cover her ass by making an example of him. A temporary suspension would not be seen by the media and the ACLU as punishment severe enough for a special agent who'd done what he had.

"Still there?" Krimsky asked, coming back on the line.

Gabriel pictured the square face, the fifties-style crew cut, the burning Camel between his thick fingers.

"Yeah. I hate suspense, Bob. Am I getting the ax?"

Krimsky barked out a laugh.

"If you were, do you think Ruggerio would do it in person? Uh-uh. I'd be the one to swing it. I've got a message on my desk from the Director himself. You're being assigned to the school bus massacre case. Ruggerio's task force. You're familiar with it?"

"Just what I read in the papers."

"I won't mince words. All you're going to be is a legman for the headshrinker she's hired to figure out why that Boggs guy did what he did. Heartland . . . no, Heartwood. You'll be helping him interview people who knew Boggs, his family, guys he worked with. It's called a psychological autopsy. Do a good job on this, you'll be off suspension when it's done. I'm told it should take a month, six weeks at most. Questions?"

He took a few moments to absorb this information and decide what he thought about it. He thought a month of legging for a shrink was better than a week of Willow. At least he would be back on the street, his natural habitat.

"Sure I've got questions. One, what the hell is a *psychological* autopsy?"

"I'm not real sure myself. It's something these forensic shrinks do to figure out why somebody did something after that somebody's too damned dead to say why himself."

"I don't get it. The case is closed. We've got the victims, we've got the weapon, we've got the perp and he's dead. Killed himself. Who gives a shit why he did it?"

"Christ, a psychopath ambushes a school bus with a semiauto shotgun. Fourteen out of twenty-six kids die. Four more and a teacher wounded. Just about the whole country wants to know why . . . don't you?"

"Usually I want to find out the motive when it helps me collar the bad guy. How did I get tapped for this? It sounds like the kind of thing Watts would eat up. Right down his weirdo alley. He likes this shrink stuff."

Frank Watts was the Bureau's criminal profiler, an alleged expert in kinky killers and rapists.

"Only you could look this gift horse in the mouth," Krimsky said sternly. "You've been picked for the same reason you got the modeling job for the poster. Watts is whitebread. Some big Asian civil rights group from the Bay Area has been putting the screws on the governor because most of the victims were Vietnamese or Cambodian. They're at least half-convinced that the massacre was a neo-Nazi operation. Keep in mind that Ruggerio's planning to run for the U.S. Senate. So if it turns out that hate groups *didn't* have anything to do with this, she's going to want at least one Asian face right beside her to give her credibility when the report's done and she holds the standard press conference. And you're that face."

"I'm used to going after live bad guys, not looking for the motives of a dead one."

"Yeah. A manhunt for a motive. It's funny, all right, but you never know what'll turn up."

He heard the change in Krimsky's voice.

"Is there something I'm missing?" he asked, his interest piqued.

"No. I don't know any more about this case than you do, but you know my rule of thumb . . . "

"If Mother Teresa tells you what time it is, check your watch," Gabriel said. "One other question. How much does Ruggerio know about . . . "

"Put it this way, if she knew even half of it, you'd now be a Kmart security guard. The boss kept his promise. It never left the field office and that's where it'll stay."

- - -

On the wings of her last Demerol shot, Joyce DeLuca ascended to the ceiling and gazed down on herself, lying between the raised sides of her hospital bed like an infant in a crib. Her left leg, its cast blackened by the signatures of her visitors, was held in a suspended kick by a cable and a polished stainless steel pulley. A monitor connected to her right middle finger by a wire and clip flashed her pulse in red numerals on a monitor: . . . 72 . . . 73 . . . 74 . . . 74 . . . 72 . . .

Death, the bright gun at his side.

Hovering, she felt superior to her bodily half, morally and physically above its pain, its frailties and tiresome needs. How pleasant to be up here, free of entrails, of nerves that scalded when the Demerol wore off.

She flapped her arms and flew past the TV set and over the bed separated from hers by a plastic curtain. The bed was empty. Owing to her condition as a gunshot victim, a condition not as common in Sacramento as in L.A. and Oakland, she had been given the room all to herself. It was on the cardiology floor and was filled with devices that possessed the austere, functional beauty of high technology and made her feel, as she levitated, like an astronaut weightless in a space-shuttle cockpit. She wanted to send a message back to earth, but what would she say, what intelligence did she have to bring back from the realm she had been shot into shortly before noon on Friday?

She turned and sailed to the other side of the room, which faced the street, and hung suspended above the get-well bouquets whose scent reminded her of her father's funeral, so long ago. Looking down, she could see the bald spot atop Alex's head as he stood by the window. Odd, she'd almost forgotten that he was here, visiting again. His fifth or sixth visit since Friday. Now he was standing by the window, making the idle small talk people do in the presence of someone who has had a brush with death, who has felt and survived the touch of the Great Mystery.

All her visitors—Fran Bigelow and her fellow teachers, her mother and her sister, who arrived from Minneapolis Saturday afternoon—began to babble about the most mundane topics after they told her how appalled they were by what had happened but how joyful that she hadn't been too seriously hurt. It was as if, sensing and fearing some irreversible change in her, they engaged her in petty chatter and gossip to reassure themselves that she had not been severed from the world of everyday concerns. Kristen had gone on at length about her two boys, Eric and Peter, and Mom discoursed on this year's winter and Joyce did not have the heart to tell them she did not give a damn about her nephews and the weather in Minnesota.

Now Alex was buzzing about an argument he'd had with Jack Crenshaw, the oenologist who managed the winery so Alex could concentrate on his commercial real estate deals.

"He's convinced we could decrease our spacing a couple of feet, boost our yield . . . " Alex was saying.

Maybe he was trying to be a dear, trying to take her mind off the pain and all the other things. He knew that she'd become interested in viticulture so she would sound knowledgeable when she and Marge Crenshaw, Tom's wife, served as hostesses at weekend wine-tastings. Would you like to try our zinfandel classico? Our Barbera? Cabernet Franc? The wine proffered in a small plastic chalice. It has a nice finish, doesn't it? A lot of it's in the grape. Have some bread. Have some cheese. Try our Serene, please. A nice blend of syrah, grenache, and carignane.

Alex thought she was still interested, or hoped she was, hoped she was still his Joyce. Of course she wasn't anything of the sort. How could she be?

". . . what I can't seem to get into that college boy's head is that we need eight-foot spacing on that tabletop because the slope is under five degrees, and the mountains block the morning sunlight, so . . ."

Alex was six-two, so it was unusual to be able to look down on the top of his head. Also amusing. His bald spot was the size of a demi-tasse saucer but not as white. From the corridor outside came the shuffle of slippered feet, a gurney's rattle, voices.

". . . were far enough north to justify closer spacing, I told him, but not what he was suggesting . . . "

The Demerol flowing warmly through her made his voice sound far off. The drug did not numb the pain; it divorced her from it by separating her from her body. She liked the feeling, but it was only a poor counterfeit of the ascension she had experienced in the culvert. The rapture wasn't there.

". . . damned grapes would be too sweet, I told him. My great-granddad knew that and he never heard of computer sunlight-to-slope indexes . . . "

Really a dear. He'd slept on the adjoining bed Friday and Saturday nights because she'd been near delirium and unable to understand that the pale gunman was dead and could not harm her or anyone ever again.

Joyce turned lazy circles on the ceiling. She banked right, banked left by dipping one arm and then the other. She flew to each corner of the room, exploring it from different angles. How pretty from any angle were all the floral arrangements. One was lilies. The white blossom of death but also of resurrection. She had died out there on the road and had been reborn. Now, like any newborn, she needed time to figure out who she was.

". . . settle on six or seven feet. We do need to boost our yield. Karla is already well ahead of us . . . "

A dear, but she really truly did not give a damn about Karla's yield per acre or any of it.

"Alex . . . " she said drowsily, turning toward him.

He stopped talking, his somber brown eyes falling on her.

"Alex, I . . . "

"What is it? Do you need something?"

She smiled affectionately.

"I need for you to be quiet."

He looked hurt for an instant, then recovered himself.

"Sorry, Joyce. I guess I was rattling on . . . " He moved toward her and took her hand.

"Anything else? Should I buzz the nurse?"

She smiled again and slowly shook her head. What she needed, besides his silence, was to know why she had lived while all those children had not.

She hated to think this, but she wished Sokhim were here instead of Alex. Sokhim would not blather on about one thing and another to reassure herself that Joyce had not been sprung loose from the ordinary world of ordinary concerns. More than anyone, she understood that that world, which seemed so solid to most people, was really as insubstantial as smoke and could vanish in an instant, in the time it took to pull a trigger. Sokhim knew that the unimaginable was possible, that nothing could be counted on, that every moment of life was precarious and therefore precious beyond measure. Joyce supposed this was what was meant by the tragic view of life. All right, it was the tragic view. It wasn't a popular view in a society that had invented the TV sitcom.

Sokhim had called on her yesterday afternoon, bringing as a gift one of her watercolors—a lush, cheerful landscape drawn from her memories of her homeland before it had become a killing field. The picture showed a temple with a swooping tile roof and purple bougainvillea splashed over its courtyard wall. Beside it was a lotus bed in which a young woman, poling a basketlike boat, was gathering blossoms.

"This temple was near to Battambang, where I was born," Sokhim had said, sitting in the contour chair Alex now stood behind. "But no lotus flowers grow there. I make that up!"

She had looked at the Cambodian woman, and as though seeing

her for the first time, was struck by how small she was. Five feet at the tallest. Wearing a long, traditional skirt in a floral print as brilliant as the pink flowers in the watercolor, she suggested a figurine. One made of steel rather than ceramic. From what well did she draw her inner strength?

She apologized that she could not stay for long, explaining that she had to return for a community meeting among San Joaquin's Vietnamese, Cambodians, and Laotians.

"This has brought us together like no other thing," she'd said. "We want to make a petition to the governor. To do something to stop attacks on us. Maybe it was the W.A.R. people who did this terrible thing. The ones you told me about. This is what the newspapers and the television are saying."

"And your neighbors at Park Lane, what are they saying?"

"They are very confused. Most, I think, are saying that this happened because Americans hate us. They are saying like you told me, Joyce. The Americans hate us because of how we cook, how we live, how we look. They hate us so much that they kill our children. She paused, her lips pursing. "Not you, Joyce. They don't say this about you. Because of what you did, they are very respectful for you."

Joyce turned on her side, careful not to pull the IV tube loose, and gazed directly into Sokhim's face.

"I don't know why. What I did was to run. I ran away."

"We all did. What else could we do?"

"I ran faster. Ran ahead of you and the kids. I . . . "

The IV bottle rattled on its metal stand as she waved her hand to dismiss her supposed heroism. She did not remember running as a volitional act; it was as if she'd been helplessly propelled down the road, like debris in a gale.

"You come back, though," Sokhim said. "You save Paul Lim's life! I have spoken to his mother. She has burned joss for you. She says you will be remembered always at her family altar. To her, you are herowoman. This is how you say? Herowoman?"

"Heroine," Joyce said, smiling a little as she watched Sokhim reach into her purse for her notebook and pen. "And that's spelled, H-E-R-O-I-N-E."

H-E-R-O-I-N-E, she said to herself. Was she really? *He* could have shot Paul and her as they lay in the culvert, but something moved him to run off into the woods and turn the bright gun on himself. Whatever had made him do that, whether an inner impulse or some outer power, was what had saved Paul Lim's life. Thinking about this and her special place at the Lim family altar, she asked Sokhim about Mrs. Or. Had she offered any wisdom about the massacre, she, the blind prophetess who'd told what had to be done to break the river gods' covetous grip on Vanna's body?

"Mrs. Or, she tells everyone that the children are killed because we forget what happened to us in Cambodia," Sokhim reported with an undertone of skepticism. "It happened to make us not forget again."

"I understand her better now. About seeing into the truth of things? Sometimes I envy her. Sometimes I wish I'd gone blind so I didn't see what I did. When Billy Pate . . . " She smothered a cough. "That poor boy . . . "

And then something seemed to draw the air out of her lungs.

Sokhim reached across the tray cluttered with paper pill cups and patted the back of her hand with a palm cool, dry, and soothing.

"You should cry, Joyce. I did. All night Friday, yesterday. You must cry. This is what I've told Mrs. Or many times. You must cry, then maybe you will see again."

Joyce could understand the simple folk wisdom in this advice, but she did not cry and also understood why Mrs. Or could not or would not. There were some horrors that would be trivialized by tears.

Sokhim, with a glance at her watch, said she had to leave, but took a moment to tape the watercolor to the wall opposite the foot of the bed. That way, it would be the first thing Joyce saw when she woke in the morning.

"You know what I told Mrs. Or? That she is wrong. I remember Cambodia. Pandra does. Each time we burn joss and see the pictures of our dead brothers and sisters, we remember, but I told her, 'We do not make ourselves blind from this remembering. We do not make ourselves blind to the beauty that is still in this world.' So I put this picture here for you, Joyce."

A nurse's aide came in, abruptly ending Joyce's reverie. The aide asked how she was feeling, then took her temperature with a digital thermometer that made an electronic warble when it was ready. Ninety-nine-point-five. The aide applied a blood-pressure compress and pumped the bulb while Joyce looked at the watercolor—the gorgeous drapery of bougainvillea, the thick green pads like tiles on the lotus bed. The lotus also a lily. Resurrection. The flower of forgetfulness in some places. How, amid such beauty, could the Khmer Rouge have murdered millions? She sensed that that was not the sort of question Sokhim would want her picture to provoke. One twenty-six over seventy-nine. The aide noted the reading on Joyce's chart, then left, her starched skirt making a papery sound.

Alex quietly drew the chair beside her bed and sat down.

"Your blood pressure sounds good. You're going to be all right, honey."

She did not say anything.

"Maybe this isn't the right time to tell you, but I want you to know that I'm not going to let this rest."

That solemn baritone.

Joyce questioned him with a look.

"This should never have happened," he answered. "No reason it had to."

She felt herself being lowered from the ceiling, toward a reunion with her pain.

"But it did," she said.

"There were reasons, sure, but none of them good."

"Oh? Tell me. Tell me, if you know. I want to know. Good reasons, bad. Any reason would do right now."

"The son of a bitch who did this to you had an arrest record as long as my arm. He'd been in psychiatric treatment. In the county mental health clinic in San Joaquin. Taxpayers' money. Our money. What was he doing loose on the street? How did he get his hands on those guns?"

Alex's jaw tightened. Behind him, the lilies shone in the sunlight flooding through the window.

"He did it to more than me, Alex."

"Yeah, but you're the one I'm married to. I'm going to find out who was responsible. To see you like this . . . "

She felt a rush of affection; the kind a mother would feel for a small son vowing to beat up a man who'd mistreated her. Then the first jolt of pain shot burning from her knee to her hip; another went from her knee to her ankle, and then the two joined to form an endless loop. The doctors said she had been lucky: had she been five yards closer, the shot pattern would have been much tighter and nearly torn her leg in half at the knee. As it was, no ligaments had been severed, no bones broken, though a couple of pellets had penetrated to the bone. Nerve and tissue damage, that was all. Okay, she'd been lucky. She just did not feel lucky right now.

"It's not going to be for the money, you know that," Alex was saying. "We've got more than enough. We'll donate the money to the families of those kids. Maybe set up a scholarship fund."

"That'd be nice." Another jolt struck her and she stiffened. It would get worse and worse until the nurse came and separated her from it once more with a syringe. She looked at the watercolor and tried to think of the beauty that was still in this world. Her glance shifted to the pulse-rate monitor: 72 . . . 72 . . . 73 . . .

"There'll be some problems. Who had authority? But somebody was responsible for that son of a bitch being on the street and they are going to be brought up short. I've already called my lawyer."

She wanted to laugh, but the pain would not let her. He might as well sue a geologist for causing an earthquake, a weatherman for a tornado. Sue the heavens for the bolt of prairie lightning that strikes a barn and burns it.

"Alex," she said through gritted teeth, "this isn't something you can take to court. What are you going to prove?"

"Maybe we can get a few things changed so something like this doesn't happen again."

His long face with its hollow cheeks, the spray of lilies behind him.

"Then something else will," she said.

Functions of complex variables . . .

Like a song stuck in his head, Willow's lecture played in Gabriel's inner ear, distracting him from John Coltrane's interpretation of "Lush Life."

He was in a good mood after Krimsky's call. All he had to do was wear out a little shoe leather for a shrink and he'd be back to being a real cop, a wandering scholar of police science no more. He took an hour to read the clippings on the Motherlode Massacre, as the media called it, and then, with time to kill before the attorney general's meeting, went to his rust-brick ranch in "The Pocket," a suburban peninsula formed by a wide bend in the Sacramento River.

He settled down with his Fender in the family room, his favorite room in the house. Having grown up a postal clerk's son on the lower end of Sacramento, he'd always aspired to a house in the suburbs, with rooms that looked like those in the home improvement magazines.

And that is exactly what his family room looked like: paneled walls, brick fireplace, bookcase of unread books, an entertainment center with a wide-screen TV and a CD player, sliding-glass doors opening onto a patio where a barbecue grill and striped lounge chairs promised placid joys blessed by the incense of charcoal-broiled hamburgers.

There were a few individual touches to his interior decoration, like the trophy case agleam with silver cups and brass statuettes won in tae kwon do matches. Beside the case, a wall photograph showed a younger Gabriel in midair, driving a foot toward an opponent's chest. He still worked out occasionally, but a spinal condition with the tongue-tripping name of unstable spondololysthesis had taken him out of competition seven years ago. Also age. In his final tournament bout, against a twenty-four-year-old, he'd seen a kick coming, but he was too slow in blocking it and so received the broken nose that now made him look like a drill sergeant in the Golden Horde.

He took up jazz guitar, a much safer hobby, after he and Adrienne had been invited to a club by her new boss at the dental clinic, a jazz fan. Their table was close to the band, a local quintet of mediocre abilities, except for the guitarist, whose riffs and voicing brought approving nods from the aficionados in the crowd. Gabriel had no musical background, but listening to the man play touched something deep inside him. He hired a tutor, a kid in his late twenties who worked in a J Street music store and wore an earring and black leather trousers. Gabriel took a year to learn the basics, enrolled in a sight-reading course at the community college, but didn't finish because he was in Homicide then and too busy to keep up with the classwork. He remained a musical illiterate, learning standards by ear. The kid with the earring suggested that if he stayed at it, maybe, *maybe* he'd be good enough one day to play cheap weddings.

He did stay at it, though not because he was ambitious to play weddings, cheap or otherwise. Much as he relished police work, he needed a sanctuary from it. The martial arts had been his way of relaxing; they called for so much concentration they took his mind off the world of gangbangers and murderers. Music became his substitute. It demanded the same discipline and concentration. Without its refuge, he was afraid that he would become like most other veteran cops: cynical, embittered, burned-out.

He'd been practicing "Lush Life" for an hour now, struggling to stay with the changes, but he couldn't stay focused; he had to leave in a few minutes.

When the piece ended, he switched the CD player off, and the house became filled with the deep silence of midday in the suburbs, when a clock's tick can sound like a footfall. It made him uneasy. This stillness, this emptiness, this was how the house would be if ever he lost Adrienne and the kids. Married eighteen years now, an epoch in a profession where most marriages had the lifespan of a gypsy moth.

He propped the Fender beside the bookcase. His family smiled at him from out of an eight-by-ten frame on a lower shelf: Adrienne, girlish-looking in her black bangs, a serious Leland on one side, Eleanor smiling on the other. Earlier photos of the children were on a shelf above. How similar they looked to the kids whose photographs had been in the clippings. Was there now, in some other silent, empty house, a Cambodian or Vietnamese staring at a photo of a dead son or daughter? What was it like to lose a child that way? The thought of it struck him like the air from a morgue freezer. He ached suddenly to draw his family close to him and protect them from the malignancy that seemed to be everywhere now, a toxic cloud of violence.

He went to the bedroom and put on a tie—he'd doffed his uniform, figuring civilian clothes would be more appropriate for the attorney general's office—and buckled his Glock to his waist. The bulky 9-millimeter wasn't as concealable as a snub-nose .38, but in an age when criminals were armed like guerrilla fighters, the firepower in the seventeen-shot semiautomatic was reassuring.

Outside, strands of heat rose from the roof of his black Ford like transparent cobras, but the cold he'd felt in the house clung to him. A dread of loss, almost like a premonition. Where was Leland now? Probably in the high school cafeteria, eating lunch with his wrestling teammates. And Eleanor? At noon recess in her intermediate school. Adrienne would be taking one last patient before going to lunch herself. He saw her perched on a stool, short hair falling on the back of her collar, her hands in latex gloves holding a mirror as she checked for periodontal disease, gingivitis. In a flash, the patient reaches under the apron fastened over his torso, pulls out a gun, shoots Adrienne, and then rampages through the office, firing at everyone. He is the maddened, spurned lover of the receptionist, whom he executes with a shot to the head before killing himself with his last bullet.

Imagining all this as he backed out of his driveway, Gabriel was surprised to find within himself real fear. If seventh-graders could be massacred on a field trip in the country, then anything was possible.

Gangbangers could burst into Leland's cafeteria, spray the place with Uzis, Eleanor could be snatched by a sadistic pedophile. . . .

Functions of complex variables . . . chaos is really order cloaked as disorder, a sheep in wolf's clothing. . . .

Right, Willow, and what about disorder masquerading as order? Twenty-six kids climb on a bus to learn about the Gold Rush and fourteen end up blown out of existence by a nut with a riot gun.

Gabriel shook his head, as if by that motion he could fling the ugly thoughts out of his brain, and turned on the radio. The news was full of the stand-off in Waco. ATF and FBI agents were poised to assault the cultists' fortress at any moment. Religious nuts with the weapons of a marine battalion. He switched the radio off and put a Wes Montgomery tape in the cassette player, and cruised slowly up his street past ranch and mission-style houses whose lawns had the waxy, too-green look of artificial turf. A flush of satisfaction rose in him as the houses paraded by, some with Lexuses and BMWs in the driveways. Though he had a low opinion of lawyers, he was pleased to have lawyers for neighbors, and doctors, and a couple of state assemblymen, though he didn't think much of politicians, either. Mike, his older brother, now a six-figure CPA, Mike, who had gone to USC while Gabriel patrolled the Mekong waterways, Mike, who'd been a rising star at Peat Marwick's San Francisco office while Gabriel pounded a beat in the Mission District, could no longer patronize him.

At the subdivision's entrance, marked by two low, curving brick walls, each bearing the words RIVER TERRACE, he waved to the gray-haired security guard who sat in a booth all day and checked visitors in and out. The guard was a symbolic deterrent, like a keep-off-the-grass sign in a public park. If some robber or child molester wanted to get in, he could do it easily; the malignancy wasn't going to be stopped by a glorified doorman.

The trip downtown was an easy sail down the freeway, which tunneled between wood and concrete safety walls. Homeboys in an old Pontiac, rap music thundering through custom speakers, pulled abreast of Gabriel's Ford. The rap overwhelmed Wes Montgomery as he riffed in rhapsodic octaves on "Snowflake." A kid in the Pontiac's backseat, his baseball cap skewed sideways, was checking Gabriel out. Probably came from the gangbanger turf east of Fremont. Off to a lunch-hour driveby? Maybe a quick carjacking before afternoon classes? Racist thoughts, but not unreasonable. The kid kept looking with that blank stare they adopted in the ghetto these days. No fear, no anger, no menace. Empty eyes in a face blank and hard as a brick wall. *Boom thud thud thud boom.* He turned up the volume on his cassette player, but Montgomery's lone Gibson was helpless against that cannonlike percussion. The Pontiac stayed even with him, the homies trying to decide if his Ford really was what it looked like: an unmarked police car. If the kids had X-ray vision they could look under the hood and see the real giveaway: a V8 out of Detroit's bygone heyday. In this car, Gabriel could outrace a hurricane. *Boom thud thud thud boom.* The rap singer snarled some anthem of nihilistic ghetto rage. That straight-out-of-Compton, *fuck-you* fury of young men who know they're expendable, surplus humanity at the bottom of the heap. Gabriel thought he understood where it came from. Like the 'Nam grunts, in a way. Don't mean nothin', they used to say. My life, your life. Don't mean nothin' don't mean a thing. The homeboys hung with him, the kid in the backseat continuing to inspect him, the rapper's staccato chant getting on his nerves. Maybe the kids thought he was a Korean and were trying to intimidate him. Koreans were the new villains in ghetto mythology. Can't tell us apart, right? Well, eat my emissions, homies. He floored the pedal and shot away from the Pontiac like a sci-fi flying saucer from a prop-driven fighter plane. When the needle touched ninety, about two seconds later, he eased back to sixty-five.

Gliding off the exit ramp, he passed the remnants of Sacramento's Chinatown: a few restaurants, a temple with a curvilinear roof, like a Mandarin palace. The neighborhood was more a tourist attraction than anything else, like the mock frontier "Old Sacramento" near the river. The Chinese in this city weren't like those in San Francisco or New York, penned up in ethnic paddocks. They had scattered and blended into its suburbs, as he and Adrienne had.

Why did blacks act as if they had sole ownership of the bias victim franchise? All right, yeah, they had more claim to it than other minorities. His uncle, Jimmy Chin, used to tell a story about his army days in Georgia. He'd stopped at a gas station with white and colored washrooms and couldn't figure out which one was for him. The redneck attendant told him, "If you ain't nigger, you're white."

Okay, so it was easier to be Chinese, but not all that easier. Gabriel's great-grandfather on his father's side had come to America a virtual slave laborer, one of the coolie legions imported to spike track for the Central Pacific. An immigrant on his mother's side, after a month of squalid detention on Angel Island, was nearly stoned to death by a white mob when he set foot on the mainland.

More than a century removed from those unhappy times, Gabriel had experienced so little prejudice that he felt a little ashamed, as if he had missed out on some terrible yet grand test of his character. ABC, American-Born Chinese, like his father and grandfather. Dad left home at sixteen to cook on a Nevada cattle ranch and then was drafted as a rifleman with a Texas division in World War Two. His English had a cowboy twang. He'd lost the Chinese language and the culture with it. When Gabriel's grandfather died in 1980, his father had to go to the Chin family association for advice on the proper burial rituals and then had to enlist a stranger to conduct the ceremony of chasing devils away from the old man's grave. Gabriel had grown up white, or rather, had not grown up Chinese. He went to Lincoln High with guys named Wong and Lee, but also O'Mara and Fanelli and Sanchez. Hung around drugstores, read comics, listened to Elvis and the Stones, popped hubcaps and acted bad, rumbling into drive-in parking lots in Fanelli's '57 Chevy. The most bigotry he encountered came from his own family, especially from his mother's side. His maternal grandmother, an iron-willed woman who raised five children alone after her husband died, told him she would disown him if he dated a white girl, much less married one. It was she who insisted he go to Chinese school, but that ended with his expulsion for breaking a basketball hoop in a fit of destructive boredom. The only Chinese word he learned was the only one he knew to this day: *hoydoy*—bad boy.

He drove up N Street, skirting Capitol Park, with its cool gardens and tall, transplanted sequoia. ABC. A militant Chinese once called him a "Twinkie," yellow on the outside, white on the inside. What did it mean to be white on the inside? Gabriel thought it meant to be an American. It meant that although your blood ancestors came from Canton or Shanghai, your spiritual ancestors were Thomas Jefferson and Abraham Lincoln. All the ethnic and racial consciousness in fashion since the sixties annoyed him, although he was struck, every now and then, by reminders that he was different. Two years ago, when he was called to assist in a murder investigation in Oroville, as Okie a town as you could find anywhere, the locals stared at him as if he came from another planet. "Don't mind them folks," said the town police chief. "They're just curious, wondering what a chink's doing here."

But most of the time, he was no more aware of his amber skin and Asian eyes than he was of shoe size or sleeve measurement. Which was why, as he turned on Fifteenth Street at the far end of the park, he was startled by a feeling that he had become suddenly conspicuous. It crawled up his arms and back and prickled on his chest like hives. Stopped by a traffic light, he imagined the pedestrians crossing in front of him were muttering "Chink." Gook. Slant-eye. He imagined that the people at the bus stop across the street were staring at him like the townsfolk in Oroville. So powerful was this sensation that he turned to stare back at them, and was embarrassed to see that they had taken no notice of him at all.

He parked in the Justice Department lot and walked to the main entrance with the feeling that he was in someone's gunsights: a sense of dread he had known in the war, his finger on a 50-caliber's trigger while the patrol boat chugged down some brown river cleaving a gallery through jungles where danger waited unseen. The image reminded him of how vulnerable he was now. In Vietnam, he had a weapon powerful enough to cut down small trees, a gun turret to shield his body. All he had now was a 9-millimeter pistol, and without him near, his children had nothing at all. They were fifth generation, they had typical American desires for success, cars, a house bigger than their parents, but none of that could protect them from hate. The same hate that had flung stones at his ancestor over a hundred years ago but flung bullets now.

■ ■ ■

He entered the Justice building, its six drab stories suggesting that the administration of justice was an uninspiring and unglamorous enterprise, like manufacturing drywall. A guard seated behind a wall of bulletproof glass looked at his ID and buzzed him through. He rode the elevator to the top floor, where a dour receptionist punched an electronic combination lock and ushered him into the attorney general's inner office. Everybody's behind locked doors these days. Locked doors and security guards. To keep the malignancy at bay.

He'd previously seen Eileen Ruggerio only on television or in photographs and had expected her to be a woman of Amazonian stature, like her federal counterpart in Washington, Janet Reno. But as she rose from a conference table at the far end of the spacious room and bustled toward him, he noticed, with some disappointment, that even in her low heels she was four or five inches shorter than he, and he was just shy of five-nine.

"Special Agent Chin, good afternoon!" she said heartily, offering her hand. Gray streaked her short brown hair, and her round face would have looked kind and matronly but for the frown lines that creased her forehead. A pair of bifocals hung from her neck by a chain. "Glad to see you're on time. Dr. Heartwood seems to be running late."

"Deliberately, give you five to one on that," grumbled one of the four men seated at the walnut table. Cupping Gabriel's elbow in her hand, Ruggerio led him across the thick green carpet to the table, which bore on its gleaming surface file folders, water glasses, and a silver pitcher. The windows behind framed a cityscape: the capitol dome, church spires, a geometry of tar and shingle and tile roofs.

"Gentlemen," Ruggerio said, "this is Special Agent Chin. He's the one who'll be working with Lee Heartwood on the autopsy, assuming Lee gets here sometime today. Gabriel . . . is that all right?" she asked, turning to him. "Gabriel?"

"Whatever. You're the general." He felt uncharacteristically unsure of himself, like a seaman in the officer's wardroom.

She let out a laugh that sounded like a small dog's yip.

"Then Gabriel it is. Gabriel, this is Gates Landau, my chief deputy."

Tall and sallow, his hairline pointed in a sharp widow's peak, Landau stood and gave the brusque, limp handshake of someone with little patience for even elementary courtesies. The stocky blond man beside him was Fred Silcox, the supervising deputy.

"And these gentlemen are Harry Yuen and Bill Benedetto." Ruggerio extended her arm toward the two men at the far end of the table. Yuen, a young, moonfaced Cantonese, stylishly dressed in a suit with padded shoulders, embarrassed him by giving him a soul brother's handclasp. Benedetto, wearing a shabby sportcoat without a tie, was about the same age as Yuen, but his sour expression made him look older. When he shook hands, Gabriel felt the strong, callused grip that comes from hard physical labor.

"Harry is legal counsel for the Asian-American Defense League in San Francisco, and Mr. Benedetto is with the Tubman Committee . . . "

"The Harriet Tubman Committee," he elaborated, scowling. "I run an auto-body shop by trade, but I do this on the side. Here . . . " He reached into a briefcase of cracked, faded leather and handed

Gabriel a tabloid newspaper. The masthead bore a drawing of a black woman and the slogan "Down with the KKK, Down with a Racist USA!" Beneath that was a headline for the lead story: "Did The Order Give the Order for Motherlode Massacre?"

He handed the paper back to Benedetto.

"The Klan?"

"We monitor and expose the activities of the Klan on the West Coast and in the Pacific Northwest," he explained in a deep, hypnotic voice. "But we also keep tabs on other white supremacist groups. The Aryan Nation, the neo-Nazi skinheads, the National Socialist Vanguard . . . "

Ruggerio, taking her seat at the head of the table, cut Benedetto off with an imperious wave, raised her glasses, and looked at Gabriel closely.

"Mr. Yuen's organization has asked us to look into the massacre. And Mr. Benedetto . . . well, Gates asked him to join us because he, his committee, that is, has a perspective on what happened Friday that might pertain to what we're trying to do here."

The door swung open and the receptionist escorted into the room a balding man a little taller than Gabriel. He had a prominent nose and brown, intense eyes, and the hair at the sides and on the back of his head curled like shavings in a pipe-fitter's shop. His dark suit appeared to be custom-cut, and if those weren't Guccis on his feet, they were a superb imitation. Gabriel had survived over twenty years as a law enforcement officer by his ability to judge people at a glance. And his immediate impression of the man who sauntered across the carpet like a golfer across a fairway was of a man full of himself. The expensive suit and shoes, the perfectly knotted tie, the monogrammed briefcase, the studied, casual walk that showed he wasn't rushed despite being ten minutes late.

"Eileen! God, I'm sorry," he said, and flashed a Rolex, which he looked at with feigned dismay, as if he had only that moment realized he'd kept everyone waiting. "Two calls at the last minute . . . "

"I'm sure they were important, Lee," Ruggerio said coolly.

"Hope you're not going to take me out to the woodshed."

"You're too geriatric for woodsheds. Sit down and let's get started."

Heartwood's smile looked forced, and Gabriel detected a couple of other false notes in his confident air: a hand raised to his tie to make sure it was straight, a tug at his jacket sleeve to make sure the correct amount of shirt cuff showed. The man's self-assurance rested on a shaky foundation of self-doubt. If the psychiatrist were a criminal, Gabriel estimated he could crack a confession out of him in less than an hour. Just find out what the self-doubts were and work on them.

Ruggerio introduced Heartwood around.

"So you're the investigator who's going to give me a hand," he said, sitting next to Gabriel.

"Special agent." He noticed that the psychiatrist carefully undid the inside button of his suit jacket, which led him to conclude that Heartwood prized the suit. Probably the only expensive one he owned. And the Rolex, on closer inspection, turned out to be a knockoff. A guy with a taste for the finer things but not the wallet. Probably divorced with expenses. Tuitions, child support, alimony. "I'm a special agent, not an investigator."

Heartwood said nothing and looked at Ruggerio.

"Special agent Chin comes highly recommended, Lee. I'm sure you two will work well together. Gabriel and Leander. Sounds rather biblical."

"Leander's Greek."

"Pedant. So, *now* shall we get started? Since Gates is going to be in direct charge, I'll let him explain what this investigation is all about."

"Be glad to, Eileen." Landau opened a folder and began to read from prepared notes. "We want to answer three major questions. First and foremost—what led to this horrible crime, which has set a record of sorts—"

"Worst of its kind in California history," Heartwood interrupted. "So says the L.A. *Times*. A clue right there. Stats are important to creeps like Boggs."

Landau expelled a petulant sigh.

"*If* you don't mind, Lee. . . . As I was saying, our first question is, what led Boggs to target schoolchildren, particularly Asian children? Second, was this massacre in any way connected to ongoing incidences of violence and harassment against Southeast Asians, particularly in the San Joaquin area?" He looked up from his notes. "I think we're all aware that these incidents have increased ever since the John Deere plant closed in San Joaquin four years ago. Whether these acts of violence and vandalism have been committed by disgruntled laid-off workers or someone else, we don't know. We do know that Southeast Asians have increasingly become scapegoats. White supremacist groups, the Aryan Resistance in particular, have sent agitators into San Joaquin in an attempt to exploit racial tensions to recruit new members. And we know that on the night before the massacre, the Resistance or someone sympathetic to them painted racist graffiti on the walls of two San Joaquin schools and of apartment blocks where Asians live. So we have to consider if Boggs was acting on the orders of the Aryan Resistance or some other group. If he was acting on his own, did he feel, considering the extent of anti-Asian sentiment in San Joaquin, that he would have, as it were, a community of support for a crime even as awful as this one? Those are the questions we hope the psychiatric autopsy will answer . . . "

"Can I make a comment here?" Heartwood asked.

"Since you're going to anyway, go ahead," said Ruggerio.

"Let's not forget, before we go sailing off on this Asian-bias angle, that the bus driver was white, the wounded teacher was white, and that several of the children, both wounded and dead, were white or Hispanic. Okay, okay? Maybe Boggs just hated kids, regardless of race, creed, color, or national origin. A real democratic killer."

"Nevertheless," Landau said, "the majority of his victims were Southeast Asians. The final question we want answered is, are there lessons to be learned from this tragedy? Is there any way it could have been prevented, any way we can reduce the chances of its happening again? That's the angle Fred Silcox and I will be looking at. Fred, why don't you say a few words about that?"

Silcox cleared his throat and opened a yellow legal pad, filled with dates.

"I'll be brief because we don't know a helluva lot," he said in a slow, western drawl that spoke of a rural upbringing. "About all we can say for sure is that Boggs was one sick white boy. What we've got here is a guy who slipped through cracks in the criminal justice system, cracks in a publicly funded mental health system. He was in a social security program for substance abusers. To be eligible, he had to be enrolled in a rehab program, and he was—for about a week or two. Dropped out, but through somebody's screwup, he kept getting his checks anyway. Finally, cracks in the gun laws. Despite his criminal record, he bought his pistol legally from a San Joaquin gun store. I've asked the Superior Court for an order to release his clinical records. Dr. Heartwood, I reckon you'll be interested in those when we get them."

"You bet. How long?"

"Not as long as usual," Ruggerio said. "I'll make sure the judge expedites things." She leaned forward, clasping her hands. "So I hope everyone is clear about who does what. Lee, I know there's a question on your mind. Why did we assign Gabriel to assist you? Because of the possibility that a criminal conspiracy existed between Boggs and some hate group or other. If you turn up evidence of that in the course of the autopsy, we want a skilled investigator there to follow up. It's part psychiatric work, part police work. Questions?"

Heartwood paused, clicking his tongue. "On Saturday, you told me you didn't buy the theory that this was a political crime. A lone nut with a lot of firepower is what you said. What made you change your mind?"

"My mind isn't changed exactly. Gates, perhaps you . . . "

"Be glad to, Eileen. Mr. Yuen and Mr. Benedetto have offered views on this that make me wonder." Landau turned a friendly gaze on the two men. "Harry, maybe you and Mr. Benedetto could share some of your thinking on this."

"Okay if I stick my two cents in first?" Gabriel asked. He had a thought he knew would sound outlandish.

"Good Lord. I need a referee. Let's hear it," said Ruggerio.

"If Mother Teresa tells you what time it is, check your watch." He grinned nervously and saw that no one else thought the quip funny. "What I mean is, the first thing I learned in the Bureau was to assume nothing except that everything's possible until you narrow the possibilities down. Why is everybody going on the assumption that if Boggs wasn't a lone nut, then he was with a hate group?"

"Because those do seem the most plausible possibilities," Landau said superciliously. Gabriel couldn't make up his mind whom he disliked more, Landau or Heartwood.

"There might be others . . . " He hesitated. "I'd like to run a background check on every kid who was on that bus."

"Yes?" asked Landau, frowning.

"Last year, I worked on a case in Fresno. A Vietnamese gang, the Valley Tigers, paid a white guy to do a hit on another Asian gang so the cops would think it was a bias crime, not a gangland assassination."

He paused and scanned the faces around the table and saw that everyone was a little embarrassed, as if he'd just belched.

"I find what you're suggesting a little hard to believe," Yuen said with a pro forma smile of politeness. Old Bay Area Chinese, Gabriel judged. Stanford Law, probably. Dad probably made a fortune in import-export.

"It's called victimology. You look at the victims and try to find every possible reason why someone would want to kill them."

"But to suggest a street gang, just to make a hit on one kid, would kill everybody and hire Boggs to do it," Yuen said. "I mean, vicious as they are . . . To do something like that to their own kind, well . . . "

Feeling more sure of his ground, Gabriel half-turned to face Yuen directly.

"Last case I was on, a Viet gang did a B-and-E on a Vietnamese couple down in Stockton. Home invasions are their specialty. Refugees keep their money and gold and jewels at home, like they did in the old country. The gangbangers broke in, the couple wouldn't tell them where the stuff was, so they boiled a pot of water on the stove, took the couple's kid, a two-year-old, and dipped him into the pot and held him there, boiling him like a goddamned lobster. They found out what they wanted to know but the kid died. How's that for racial solidarity, Mr.Yuen?"

"We see what you're getting at," Landau said. "If you want to background the victims, go ahead. But keep in mind that we can't afford to spend a lot of time and money on wild-goose chases."

"I understand." Gabriel stifled his resentment at the choice of words. "But we don't know which geese are wild yet. And there's more than one or two in the flock."

"I believe it's *skein*," Heartwood said, slouching and looking distractedly at the ceiling.

Landau rubbed the two bays of bare skin alongside his widow's peak.

"We're losing focus here. Losing a certain . . . *focus*. Have you reviewed the facts of this case, Gabriel?"

"I read the news clips. I didn't get word about this assignment until this morning," he answered, flushing. If Landau knew how he'd whiled away those hours. Listening to Coltrane.

"Then I'll bring you up to date. The ballistic tests, right here"—he tapped the folder with a forefinger—"show that the bullet that killed Boggs came from this pistol, a Taurus nine-millimeter semiautomatic. His gun. Bought it March twenty-third for three hundred and sixty dollars, picked it up fifteen days later . . . "

"Where'd he get that kind of money?" Gabriel asked.

"Could have been a loan from certain people," Landau answered. "Boggs's prints were on the weapon and the coroner's opinion is that the wound and other evidence were consistent with suicide. Please have a look at the deceased perpetrator."

Landau removed an eight-by-ten photograph from the folder and held it facedown over the table and Gabriel saw in the table's polished surface a reflection of the photo and Landau's long, thin hand. He took the photo, its back bearing the stamp of the El Dorado County Sheriff's Department, and turned it over. It showed Boggs lying facedown on a slablike rock, darkened by blood. In his camouflage trousers and flak jacket, with the 9-millimeter a few inches from his half-closed hand, he resembled a soldier fallen in some desperate, close-quarters fight. Gabriel studied the photo for a few moments. There was something wrong, something that puzzled him, but he could not put his finger on what and handed the photo back to Landau.

"Can I get a print of that?"

"You and Dr. Heartwood will be given copies of everything. Photos, ballistics tests, coroner's report." Landau made a diamond with his hands and held the diamond over his mouth, as though calling to someone in the distance. "Now then, would you care to speculate, since you were doing so much unfocused speculation, why would a gangland hitman, presumably hired for money, commit suicide? Was he planning to spend it in hell? Doesn't add up."

"It doesn't add up if he was some neo-Nazi terrorist, either. What did they do? *Tell* him to commit suicide? And if they did, how could they be sure he'd go through with it?"

"If The Order told him to, they wouldn't have to worry about supervision," said a grimacing Benedetto. "When you join The Order you take an oath to commit suicide to avoid capture." He looked at Ruggerio. "Is it all right if I have my say? I'd like to have my say now."

"I think that's why Gates invited you," she answered, her voice implying that she had not fully approved of the invitation.

Benedetto pulled from his briefcase more copies of his society's tabloid and two thick sheafs of Xeroxes, each clamped with a binder clip—photocopies of a book, its title page facing up. *The Turner Diaries.* Benedetto gave them to Gabriel and Heartwood and, threading his knobby fingers, lowered his chin to the backs of his hands.

"I am not a lawyer. I am not a psychiatrist. I knock dents out of cars, but right there in front of you is evidence that The Order may have thought up Boggs's mission and assigned him to carry it out."

He spoke in the clear, theatrical voice of a preacher, and the shimmer in his eyes was the same Gabriel had seen in the eyes of cult followers and Moonies and true-believers with congregations of one.

"Tell them what The Order is," Landau said. "Not everybody's heard of it."

"It's an army. A secret army. It's an underground army in the White Aryan Resistance. It was started back in the early eighties by a guy named Matthews, Robert Matthews, and he got the idea from that book in front of you, from *The Turner Diaries*. It's a futuristic novel, but it's really kind of the neo-Nazi Book of Revelations. It claims to foretell how the white Aryan revolution will come about. To get into The Order you have to commit an act of violence against a minority and take an oath to kill yourself if you're in danger of being captured. That's what Matthews himself did back in '84, when the FBI cornered him. . . . "

"And you're saying that Boggs was a soldier in this, ah, underground army?" asked Heartwood.

"People in our Southern California office have information that Boggs knew some W.A.R. skinheads when he was down there. As you must know, Boggs and his younger half-brother, Jacob Tipton, were arrested in San Bernardino County last summer for firing an assault rifle in the national forest. Maybe they were training. Boggs got away with buying a pistol legally, but he could not have legally bought an assault rifle, not in this state anyway. The W.A.R. skins may have supplied him with it. Then there's the schoolteacher's statements to the cops. She heard him yell 'Victory for the race' or something like that. Well, 'Hail Victory' is a kind of salute in the Aryan Resistance. A salute like the Nazis' 'Sieg Heil.' The teacher also said she heard sirens before Boggs killed himself. It's possible he—"

"Mistook them for police sirens," Heartwood interrupted.

"Right. For police sirens. Right."

"What kind of sirens were they?" Gabriel asked.

Landau answered, "Ambulance. One of those freak things. A man had a heart attack in the state park the kids were going to. An ambulance was on its way from Placerville right after the massacre took place. The paramedics were the first ones to discover it. That must have been something, thinking they're going to treat a heart attack and finding that."

"Boggs of course didn't know it was an ambulance," Benedetto said. "Mistook it for the police and killed himself to fulfill his oath. And then there are the symbols on his flak jacket. The symbols he painted on his flak jacket. In those papers I've given you, you will see a news photo of the El Dorado County sheriff holding up Boggs's flak jacket. You will also find copies of the Aryan Resistance newsletter. Take a look at them."

Gabriel shuffled through the stack and found the newsletter and the photo. Heartwood smothered a yawn.

Benedetto said, "You see? Boggs painted a cross in a circle on both sides of his flak jacket. And if you look at the masthead on the newsletter you will see the official symbol of the Aryan Resistance. A cross in a circle! It's an ancient Norse rune that the Resistance adopted. When I picked up the paper Saturday morning and saw that on Boggs's flak jacket, I got a chill. A chill ran through me. It was like he, like The Order, was sending a nonverbal message."

He waited to let his information sink in. Gabriel thought that this goose was wilder than anything he could have imagined.

"Are we going to hear what this chilling message is?" Heartwood asked.

"Maybe it's started. It's right in there. In that novel. In *The Turner Diaries*." Benedetto's eyes looked fevered now. "Pages one-forty-five and one-fifty. The book says the precondition for the fascist revolution will be chaos and anarchy, a climate of fear, which lead to government repression and then to the white racial revolution. This climate of fear will be created by The Order, who will commit a series of violent acts, but make them look random. This massacre may have been the first shot in the campaign. And Boggs was the perfect candidate. A loner and a loser who was probably looking for some organization or some cause to identify with."

"I don't fix fenders, Mr. Benedetto. So don't you start psychoanalyzing."

"Well, I was only . . . "

"I'm being paid taxpayers' money to look into Mr. Boggs's mind, not you." Heartwood pushed his chair back from the table, linked his hands behind his head and looked at Landau. "Gates, since he's your guest here, maybe you can explain why he's wasting our time with this dizzy bullshit."

"Lee, be civil," Ruggerio said.

"We don't think it's necessarily dizzy bullshit," said Yuen angrily. "We don't endorse Mr. Benedetto's opinions, but we don't dispute them, either. We certainly have to wonder if Boggs was influenced by neo-Nazis even if he wasn't acting under their orders."

Heartwood abruptly stood.

"I'll make a couple of points here. Let's say Boggs thought the sirens were the cops and let's say he was in this secret army and took an oath to avoid capture. Number one, he wasn't in any danger of being captured at that moment. He wasn't cornered. The sirens were way off in the distance, or so I've read. Number two, he was in the boondocks. Plenty of woods and foothills to escape into, hide in. As a matter of fact, he did run into the woods. That's where he shot himself."

"And how do you explain that?" asked Benedetto, glaring like an insulted child.

"Frankly, I don't know. Maybe he liked trees."

"And the teacher. The teacher said . . . the cops, I mean. The cops told the media that the teacher told them she saw Boggs raise the gun to his head like he was going to shoot himself on the road and then he ran into the woods."

"And doesn't that suggest someone not in complete control of himself and the situation? Why would this cold-blooded, cool-headed assassin you're talking about start to kill himself, then think better of it, then run into the woods and do it anyway for no reason? Then let's take a look at what he did before that. That teacher, DeLeo . . ."

"DeLuca," Landau said, twirling a pencil against his cheek. "Joyce DeLuca. Get the names right, Lee."

"DeLuca. Thank you, Gates. She sees him get frustrated when the shotgun jams, then fire blindly down the road with the pistol. He's acting more like the typical mass killer than the steely-eyed terrorist. Out of control. He spots the DeLuca woman and the kid in the ditch. She's wounded, can't escape. Now if this guy is on a mission to wipe out a school bus, what would he do? Kill them both. Okay? Instead he yells some crazy stuff about a victory and blows himself away. Some terrorist."

Heartwood had spoken rapidly but clearly, like a machine gun: the speech of someone accustomed to winning arguments through a kind of verbal-fire superiority. The assault seemed to have overwhelmed Benedetto. He sat in silence for several seconds, chewing on his tongue.

"It's very possible he had orders to kill himself no matter what. If in fact this was planned to look like the random act of a madman. Maybe . . ."

Even Landau was looking pained now. He reached across the table for the pitcher and filled his glass.

"Put yourself in the shoes of your neo-Nazi masterminds," said Heartwood patronizingly. "You order a guy like Boggs to kill himself. Suppose, as Gabriel's suggested, he screws it up or chickens out at the last minute and gets caught? He can identify you. And there goes your diabolical scheme to make the crime look like the random act of a suicidal madman."

Benedetto looked around the table, silently appealing for help. Heartwood swept his briefcase off the table.

"Eileen, Gabriel and I had better get started establishing some facts about Mr. Boggs. I think we've heard enough fairy stories for one day."

Ruggerio, blushing slightly, laid her palms flat and pushed herself to her feet.

"Anything more, Gates?"

"The shotgun."

"Oh, that."

"What about the shotgun?" asked Gabriel. Murder weapons at least were something he understood.

"Stolen, along with other assault weapons, in a sporting goods store robbery in Hialeah, Florida, last year," Landau said. He threw a glance at Benedetto, whose dour face brightened. "The El Dorado sheriff just got that information late this morning from the Feds. It'll be on the news tonight. Some of the guns were never recovered, but three men were arrested, two for the robbery, the third for receiving stolen property. All three belonged to the Florida Klan and the Church of the Creator, a white supremacist sect based in Florida. The first two were convicted, but the third, the alleged fence, got off on a technicality. Name of William Owens. Last heard of in Dade County, working for a roofing contractor. McNeeley and Sons. The same company Boggs worked for when he was in Florida, just before he came back home to California six weeks ago. You might look into that, Gabriel, while Dr. Heartwood looks into Boggs's toilet training."

Ruggerio winced. Looking sidelong at Heartwood, she made a quick movement with her head—a subtle command that he sit down. As he did, she turned with a strained smile to Yuen and Benedetto.

"Thanks for letting us hear your concerns and your views. Would you mind leaving us alone? It looks like we have some differences that need to be ironed out in private."

After the two men left, she frowned at Heartwood and Landau like a teacher at misbehaving schoolboys.

"Dizzy bullshit. Tactful, Lee."

Heartwood shrugged and spread his arms.

"That Benedetto guy sounded like one of the nuts who come out of the woodwork every time something like this happens. I'm surprised we didn't have a delegation who thinks Boggs was a Satanist."

"We've gotten calls and mail from that sector," Ruggerio said. "And from a guy in Oregon who's sure Boggs was a prophet of the Antichrist. But I didn't ask them here, did I? What Gabriel said about assumptions makes sense. Let's not rule out any reasonable theory until we have to. Maybe Benedetto is a little, oh, intense, but the idea of white supremacist involvement isn't completely off the wall."

"Explains Boggs's suicide," Landau interjected. He pinched his eyebrows, ploughing wavy furrows into his high forehead.

Heartwood tensed and said, "The major purpose of a psychiatric autopsy is to determine why someone committed suicide. So what do you need Gabriel and me for, since you've got the answer?"

Landau started to respond, but Ruggerio stopped him, gaveling for silence with a pencil.

"Will you two bury your hatchets?" she said. "The Driggs case was four years ago. What are we dealing with here? Multiple murder without apparent motive. Multiple murder of *children.* Forget for a moment whether this was neo-Nazis and just ask yourself, 'Why children?' That's the focus, the only question that really matters here. I want to know why, the people of this state want to know, why children? Fourteen of them. Fourteen!" Her voice, growing sharper and thinner and more brittle with each sentence, cut the stale office air like a crystal razor. "I don't give a damn about his suicide, either. I'm just happy he did himself in. Saved me a crisis of conscience because I swear to God if he lived, I would have reversed my opposition to the death penalty, walked him down the last mile myself and watched him die, and then would've gone home that night and slept the sleep of the just."

She picked up her legal pad and strode to her desk, her heels leaving prints in the carpet.

"Worst crime of its kind in California history." She snorted and slapped the pad on the desk. "Of its *kind* in *California* history. What in the hell are we coming to when we have to classify these monstrosities by type and locale? What that miserable bastard did should have been the worst crime of any kind anywhere at any time."

She dropped into her chair. Though its tall back, rising several inches above her head, and the expansive desk crowded with stacked file folders dwarfed her, the profundity of her anger made the furniture and the room itself seem too small for her.

The four men, arrested by her outburst, remained in their seats, heads turned toward her.

She opened a folder and, resting her knuckles against her cheeks, began to read. Heartwood, Landau, and Silcox briefly traded uncertain glances, then got up and stood in front of her desk, waiting. Gabriel followed them.

She looked up at the silent men.

"Well, what the hell are you all standing around for? The meeting's over. Get to work."

"My car or yours?" Heartwood asked as they entered the garage. He pointed at an apple-red Porsche snuggled between a concrete pillar and a minivan. It was scrupulously clean, but looked ten years old and had several dents big enough to be seen but too small to justify the expense of fixing them.

"We'll take mine," Gabriel said.

A dispatcher, delivering a coded message, squawked on the police radio concealed inside the glove compartment. Gabriel shut it off and pulled out on Fifteenth Street, passing through the seedy neighborhood that clung to the edge of Capitol Park like a barnacle. A shirtless, shoeless vagrant pushed a shopping cart piled high with filthy clothes and a rolled-up quilt past a cut-rate liquor store. Tonight, he and the rest of the homeless army would bivouac beneath the sequoia in the park, its walkways now filled with assemblymen and bureaucrats and hopeful lobbyists bearing promises and petitions.

"The meeting, what were your impressions, opinions," Heartwood said suddenly and with a note of impatience, as if hearing Gabriel's opinions were an unpleasant duty to be got through as quickly as possible.

"Well, I'd say that Ruggerio is no wallflower."

"The Sicilian pepper. What else?"

"Looks like Landau's got his teeth sunk into the neo-Nazi idea like a pit bull."

"He'd be delighted if we found out that white supremacists were behind this. Or at least influenced Boggs. Landau's an old antiwar activist who never got over the sixties. He sees right-wing conspiracies everywhere. And for a guy who's ambitious—he'd like to be sitting in Eileen's chair one day—neo-Nazis are an easy target. It's neat, simple, politically correct."

"Yeah, but that thing about the shotgun . . . "

"Coincidence," Heartwood said with annoying certitude. "I spent the entire weekend reading everything in the public record about Boggs. In one sense, he's like every mass murderer I've dealt with in the past twenty years. A loner honked off at the world. Those types aren't joiners. They can't take orders. They don't get along with anybody, not even with neo-Nazis."

"And in another sense, he's what?" asked Gabriel.

"Different. Doesn't completely fit the mass-killer profile, which is why I agreed to do this autopsy. Boggs intrigues me."

Gabriel switched on the car radio. He'd forgotten that he'd turned the volume to full in his acoustical duel with the rap-loving homeboys. A startling blast of electric guitar made the speakers rattle, the air vibrate with refracted sound. He turned the knob and the music faded to a slow, smoky blues, each note speaking of humid sex, the ache of lost love, some guy hugging the pillow where his baby used to lay her pretty head. God, he wished he could play like that. Half as well would do.

"'Last Night.' Larry Carlton," Gabriel said. "Heard of him?"

"I have now," Heartwood said, wriggling in his ear a finger that bore a class ring with a blue stone. "You like it loud."

"No, I . . . "

"I'm a classical fan. To me, this stuff is kind of primitive."

"Primitive? Hey, Wynton Marsalis can play classical with the best of them *and* flat wail on a Monk tune. Listen to that and tell me he's primitive."

He realized that his anger was less a reaction to Heartwood's views on music than to Heartwood himself. So far, he couldn't find anything to like about the man. Even the way he sat was irritating: his back straight, knees joined to make a platform for that monogrammed briefcase, over which his fingers curled tightly. The posture made him look prim, tense, and secretive, like some well-bred courier for the CIA.

"Sorry if I struck a raw nerve, Gabriel," he offered, though in a tone that hinted he wasn't sorry in the least. "I didn't realize you were so committed to jazz. Do you play?"

"Hack at it. Guitar. Helps round the corners. So what is it between you and Landau?"

"A rape case four years ago in Contra Costa. Black guy out of Oakland assaulted five women. Landau was in the prosecutor's office back then, and it was a big case for him. The defense entered an insanity plea and asked me to testify for Driggs. He had the mental development of a thirteen-year-old. In his mind, it wasn't rape, it was lovemaking. Screwing was screwing. Landau had me on cross for four days. Quoted me articles and studies from psychiatric and legal journals I'd never heard of. And I rebutted every one. It was like a duel. Made the front page of the *Oakland Tribune.* People were coming into the courtroom on their lunch hours just to watch us go at it. Our side won. Gates hasn't forgotten that. Or forgiven it."

They stopped at a traffic light.

"I'll bet those women haven't done much forgetting or forgiving, either." Gabriel turned and leveled on Heartwood a look he'd perfected over the years, through a hundred interrogations: the Gabriel Glare. It said that he'd heard every alibi, excuse, and rationalization invented by the devious human mind and wasn't going to settle for anything less than the full truth. "You can't tell me that you really believe that guy didn't know what he was doing."

"He didn't know that what he did was wrong."

"So what?" The light changed, and they turned onto J Street, the Ford gliding through light mid-afternoon traffic. "I could show you a dozen gangbangers who've tapped out a dozen guys each, *pop*, right between the running lights, and not a one will say that he thought he was doing wrong. Just taking care of business."

"There's a difference between thinking you're not doing wrong and not knowing it. You were in the Navy, weren't you?"

"How'd you guess?"

"That expression. 'Between the running lights.' I was a sailor, too—'70 and '71. Medical corps psychiatrist. I was with Charlie Med, attached to the Marines up in I Corps."

"You must have been the busiest shrink in the world or didn't have a damn thing to do, 'cause Marines are either completely crazy or they don't have enough brains to go crazy with."

Heartwood's slender lips drew into a smile, a small, tentative smile, true, but Gabriel felt that getting any kind of a smile out of him was an achievement.

"I was brownwater Navy," he offered. "Gunner on a PBR in the Delta, I got some shrapnel in the breadbasket, lost a third of it on the operating table, which is why I'm still one-fifty-five instead of middle-age fat. That's all I'm going to say about my Navy days. The only thing that bores me more than telling war stories is listening to them."

"My point, Gabriel, isn't that we can tell war stories. It's that we're going to be working together. So let's try to find some things we can see eye to eye on. Ex-sailor to ex-sailor."

"You weren't a sailor."

The remark somehow came out more harshly than he intended.

"Not in the military sense," Heartwood said, appearing to shrug it off. "When you're a Navy doctor, the only thing they teach you is how to salute and how to wear the uniform. I used to dodge enlisted men whenever I could, so I didn't have to salute. Made me feel like I was impersonating an officer. But don't tell me I'm no sailor. Sailing's my sport. After my divorce, I single-handed my thirty-two-footer to Ensenada and back. That's over a thousand miles round trip."

"Back where?"

"San Francisco. I've got an apartment in Pacific Heights."

Pacific Heights. The guy's divorce hadn't completely cleaned him out. Gabriel hurried through the intersection, punched the gas, and swept up an entrance ramp to the Sacramento-Placerville freeway, Highway 50, the same route the bus traveled toward its collision with Duane Leonard Boggs. Why did those Okies always go by their first and middle names? Billy Lee and Jimmy Joe. Out of the corner of his eye, he caught Heartwood looking at him.

"Something on your mind, Doctor?"

"Lee will do. And yes, there is. I get the impression I rub you the wrong way. Not unusual. I rub a lot of people the wrong way."

"Put it like this. I've got a problem with psychiatrists. Seen it over and over. One of you testifies for the defense that the defendant's nuts, another one testifies for the prosecution that he's sane. Flip a coin. Heads he's crazy, tails he's not. Guys who ought to be locked up or gassed get off because of an opinion, not a fact."

"But a psychiatrist's opinion is one based on facts. It's an informed opinion."

The city fell swiftly behind and they rushed through a stark exurbia. Warehouses. Office towers with reflecting windows that looked like copper foil wrap.

"It's what criminals do that counts," Gabriel said brusquely. "Not what they think about what they're doing. There's no way to know for sure what's going on inside a guy's head."

"My whole profession is predicated on the idea that we can know what's going on in here"—he pointed at Gabriel's temple—"or we can at least make some pretty educated guesses."

"Cops don't deal in guesses. Evidence. Witnesses. Facts."

"We're going to be doing a lot of guess work on this one, unless Boggs left a secret diary somewhere. Sometimes guessing's all you can do, sometimes it works. Know the Redlands Ripper case?"

"Serial rapist and murderer four, five years ago."

"Four. I'm the guy who drew a psychological profile of him. I did a lot of guessing, based on the facts of what he did and how he did it, about what kind of guy he was. The guy they caught fit my profile like a custom-made suit."

"Way I heard it, they caught him because of some acrylic fibers they found on one of the victims. I know the lady in the crime lab who analyzed them. Jean Sheldon."

"I know the story. The cops who made the arrest were in that neighborhood because *I guessed* the guy was going to strike there next, okay?"

Gabriel decided not to disagree. In the interests of their sailor-to-sailor relationship.

"You and my father would get along," Heartwood said. "He was a general practitioner in Green Bay before he retired to Florida."

"That's where you're from? Home of the Packers?"

"Yes. But don't start talking football. I hate football. Something else my father and I didn't see eye to eye on. Anyhow, he doesn't think psychiatry is real medicine. Mending a broken bone, heart surgery, curing fevers, that's real medicine. Last time I saw him he told me that a hundred years from now people will look on psychiatrists the way we look on witch doctors today."

Gabriel offered a crooked smile.

"Oh, hell, I don't think you guys are that weird."

"My father does, and you know, in a way he's right. Take this psychological autopsy. What's my job? To come up with an explanation for a senseless act because people do crave explanations when a Boggs does what he does. Landau was right about that. I'm like a medicine man ten thousand years ago. A volcano blows its top, half the tribe is wiped out, and the survivors send the medicine man out on a vision quest to find out why. He comes back with a story. The mountain gods were angry about some offense or other. So you could call this a kind of vision quest and me a kind of shaman for a secular age that doesn't believe in gods. People want a story, but it has to sound, oh, psychologically right."

"A story?" Gabriel asked, a little incredulously. He was uneasy with the turn the conversation had taken. Vision quests and shamanistic ritual were not a cop's native waters.

"I'm not talking about a story as fiction. A coherent narrative. I'm supposed to make a coherent narrative out of Boggs's life. The key is to get inside his head, get behind his eyes, and see the world as he did. If you can do that, then everything else follows with the inevitability of Greek drama."

"That's what you do? Get inside these crazies' heads?"

"In a way, yeah."

"Ever afraid you'll crawl so far inside you can't find your way out?"

"That's TV-movie-of-the-week bullshit. Shrink tracks down serial killer, discovers that he's a psychopath himself. Forensic psychiatry isn't method acting. You don't have to become a psychopath to figure one out. They're human beings, after all. I use the word *monster* all the time, but the fact is, guys like Boggs are human beings."

Gabriel left the freeway at the Rancho Cordova exit and went down a wide street lined with sterile corporate parks.

"I don't think so. Not for a New York second," he said, braking for a road-repair flagman. Ahead, smoke coiled from an asphalt truck and from the pitchy lumps shirtless workmen tamped into potholes with the flat sides of their shovels. "I believe in monsters. You know, like those goofy headlines you see in the supermarket papers. 'Woman Gives Birth to Alien Baby.' I believe things like that happen, only the aliens don't come from outer space. Mr. and Mrs. John Q. Normal give birth to a sonny boy who's an evil son of a bitch. Born bad to the bone."

The flagman waved them through. As they passed the truck, the smell of hot tar blew into the car. Pollen swirled and sparkled in the air, like spangles in Brownian motion. Heartwood sneezed violently. Gabriel watched him pull a bottle of nasal spray from his pocket, lean his head back, and with a kind of fussy precision, spray each nostril three times.

"Allergies," he said. "This Central Valley air in the spring is hell." Turning off the street, they cruised down an asphalt byway, its surface as unrippled as a slough on a still afternoon as it wound between bone-white curbs through the shadeless backlands of light industrial parks.

"Remind me to give you a book," Heartwood said. "It's by a nineteenth-century Italian psychiatrist, Lambroso. He had a theory that criminal brains were anatomically different than normal brains. That idea was discredited. Now it turns out Lambroso might have been on the right track after all."

Gabriel glanced at him quizzically, then pulled into a lot behind a long row of offices and parked in front of the last one. Heartwood looked at it, a puzzled frown on his face. Without a sign or lettering on its door, it appeared vacant.

"We don't advertise. Get all the business we want without it."

Buttoning his suit jacket, Heartwood opened the car door. Gabriel stopped him with a gentle pressure on his shoulder.

"Wait one minute. Finish up what you were saying about the Italian guy. I'm enjoying this talk. Haven't had one like it in years."

"Glad you're amused. Ever hear of Robert Alton Harris?"

"The guy on death row? Got a stay of execution a few months ago?"

"Him. Neurological defense, a brand-new, cutting-edge thing. Brain scans turned up evidence that a part of his brain that we think controls violent behavior was damaged. Childhood trauma. His father beat the hell out of him regularly, okay?" Sitting with one foot on the pavement and the other still in the car, Heartwood seemed to have his attention on an attractive, red-haired nicotine junkie, crushing her smoke outside the mortgage company next door to the field office. "I do consulting at a brain research lab. We're starting to discover amazing things. We're actually learning how the brain is organized, or, in a case like Harris's, disorganized. One of these days we may be able actually to see what makes a psychopath's brain different from a normal one. We may be able to demonstrate derangement in an objective, scientific way. No more coin tosses. Heads insane, tails sane. We'll show it like an X ray of a fracture, okay?"

"Rrrrrroger," said Gabriel, climbing out of the car. He stood with his elbows on the roof and squinted against the dry glare of the parking lot. "But if I remember right, Harris wasted a couple of teenagers. Hijacked their car to make a getaway from a bank robbery. And then killed them. Said something like, 'God can't help you now, boys, 'cause you're gonna die.' You're saying Harris didn't do that because he's a lowdown, mean, cold-blooded murdering son of a bitch but because he's got a damaged brain? You're saying that all we gotta do is call in a surgeon and zingo, a bad motherfucker becomes a child of God? Talk about dizzy bullshit."

"I can tell I haven't converted you."

"I'm a real heathen when it comes to that." They went up a short sidewalk to a blank brown door, which Gabriel opened with his key card. "Evil is what evil does in my book."

"You're Old Testament. You've even got a biblical name."

"Right. I blow the horn on Judgment Day."

Inside, two female dispatchers sat in a glass cage behind a bank of lit-up phones and radios. Gabriel opened a second door by tapping its code on a keypad.

A sense of homecoming washed through him as he entered a large room where one agent in undercover dress sat talking on the phone, his sneaker-shod feet up on his desk, and another with a holstered Glock jabbing his ribs peered at a rap sheet on a computer screen. Otherwise, the room was empty, its spare furnishings and bare walls giving the impression that it had been moved into that morning and could be moved out of that night. He supposed it looked fly-by-night to Heartwood, like a boiler room operation, but the atmosphere suggested to Gabriel a dedication to a task too serious for frilly touches like pictures and indoor plants. Until now, he hadn't realized how deeply he missed these ascetic surroundings, the soul and center of his working life. It seemed like months instead of three weeks since he'd been exiled from here, the rogue cop. That he was returning on a facsimile of an official mission seemed to imply that he'd been forgiven. Still, he hoped not to run into Croydon and kept on the lookout for him as he led Heartwood down a corridor, past the library with its thick blue volumes of the California Criminal Codes. Croydon was Special Agent in Charge of the Sacramento office and Gabriel's judge and benefactor, the one who'd banished him but saved his career by keeping his misstep within the family. He wasn't sure he was ready to look Croydon in the eye, difficult under any circumstances: the man stood six-six.

They walked into another big, Spartan room, the Department of Organized Crime and Criminal Intelligence. Heartwood paused to gaze at the titles on the file drawers braced against one wall: GANGS,

VIETNAMESE . . . GANGS, BLACK . . . GANGS, HISPANIC . . . GANGS, CHINESE . . . GANGS, CAMBODIAN. . . . He said he was amazed by how many there were. A gang for almost every color and nationality. Showed how divided the country had become. Even organized crime had become disorganized. It was enough to make you nostalgic for the Cosa Nostra, with its medieval hierarchies, its codes of honor and *omerta*, its elegantly dressed capos and dons.

In a glassed-in office in a far corner of the room, Krimsky sat beneath historical lithographs of U.S. Marines battling various enemies of the Republic. With the flick of a finger thick as a cigar, he signaled Gabriel to come in.

"Welcome home, prodigal son."

"Hey, Bob. You don't know how great it is to be back. Thought I'd introduce . . . " He paused and sniffed the air, which smelled of stale cigarette smoke and pine-scented air freshener. "Hope Croydon doesn't get a whiff of this. What kind of example are you setting for us peons?"

Krimsky stood up. An aging 1950s football star. Brush haircut, barrel torso divided from slender hips by a gunbelt shiny as a patent leather purse.

"Listen, anybody can quit smoking, but it takes a real man to die of lung cancer," he said in a golden, resonant voice that predicted throat cancer instead. "These chickenshit rules. Making me sneak puffs like a kid in a bathroom."

"Now that I'm partners with a medical professional, I'm concerned about your disgusting habit. Bob, this is Lee Heartwood, excuse me, *Doctor* Leander Heartwood."

"Lee will do." He extended his hand.

"Bob Krimsky. I'm Gabe's C.O., so to speak."

"Lee was with the Marines in 'Nam. A Navy psychiatrist. Told him he was either real busy or real bored because Marines are either completely crazy or don't have any minds at all."

"That's hilarious, you scumbag swab jockey." Krimsky turned to Heartwood. "I read about you somewhere."

Heartwood straightened his shoulders, cocked his head a little to one side, and gave a short but definite nod, a gesture that seemed to congratulate Krimsky for recognizing his name.

"The L.A. *Times* the other day. They interviewed me when Ruggerio announced the task force. Or maybe you're thinking of *People*. They did a piece on me a while back. The Redlands Ripper case."

"Yeah, I think that was it. Outstanding piece of work," Krimsky said, and Heartwood acknowledged the rave with a smile. "So how'd things go in the holy of holies?"

"We got the idea that some people will be happy if we can connect Boggs up with neo-Nazis," Gabriel said.

"Sounds too pat for me, Gabe." Gabriel winced and Krimsky folded his arms across his chest. "Sorry. *Gabriel.*"

"We'll need a little help with something. While we're running around, could you get someone to run a check on the kids on the bus? I'm—we're—looking for gang affiliations. One of the kids might have been an apprentice gangbanger." Gabriel, gripping the back of a chair, inclined his body forward. "I've been wondering how Boggs knew the kids were going on a field trip that morning. How he knew where—"

"Asked myself that same question," Heartwood interjected. "The school might have published an announcement in the local paper. Boggs could have seen it there."

"Or the source of this vital information was someone inside the school." Gabriel leaned harder on the back of the chair, raising the front legs a few inches. "A gangbanger or the kid brother of one."

Krimsky remained expressionless except for a furrow in his jutting brow. Above his head, Marines with fixed bayonets glinting in a winter moon counterattacked across a Korean mountainside.

"Okay, I'll get somebody. Could take a while."

"How about my picture-taking session?"

"You don't get to be a recruiter's pinup. This is your job now. We got Wong to replace you."

"This place smells like a Christmas wreath in the smoking section."

"Charlie Chin, the poor man's Chan. Keep me informed. This is a politically motivated investigation, affecting our boss's political future, so I want to know what the fuck is going on."

Gabriel signaled Heartwood to follow him into the outer office, where, for old time's sake, he ducked into Armstrong's cubicle and moved the perfectly squared desk pad half an inch off center. Post-it notes were pasted to a partition wall so neatly they looked like tiny windowpanes. He removed one and replaced it slightly higher than the others in the row, then, with a mischievous laugh, shuffled two of the alphabetically arranged books, a Mandarin-English dictionary changing places with *Methods of Interrogation.* "That'll drive Armstrong up the wall. He'll be talking to himself. I like to mess with his mind. He's a neatness freak. You guys have a word for that?"

"Obsessive-compulsive disorder," said Heartwood, trailing Gabriel to his cubicle, the second to last in the row. "Of course, I can't make a real diagnosis without examining the patient. It's possible the guy is merely organized. Who is he?"

"My partner. You know a funny thing? They put us together because he speaks Mandarin and Vietnamese and I don't know a word of either. Except *hoydoy*—that's bad boy in Chinese, but I don't know if it's Mandarin or Cantonese or whatever. It's weird when we go to turn some gangbanger and Armstrong starts rapping in the guy's language and there's me, having this Anglo translate my questions."

"Weird for who? You or the gangbanger?"

"Both."

Gabriel sat at his desk, feeling like a kid returned to his own room after a month at summer camp. With a jab of his head he indicated a straight-back chair in a corner of the cramped enclosure. Heartwood took off his suit coat, hung it carefully over the chair, and scowled with irritation at a smudge on one of his French cuffs.

"Okay, Doctor, I belong to you from here on out. What do we do?"

"Let's start by deciding what we aren't going to do. And that's spend a lot of time chasing those wild geese Landau talked about. It's the only thing he said that made any sense. I mean this gang angle. It's interesting, but I'd be generous to call it a long shot."

Tilted backward in his swivel chair, hands clasped behind his head, Gabriel looked on with a steady neutral gaze. Heartwood coughed nervously.

"It's natural to try to fit the massacre into a framework we're familiar with. Landau's got his Hitler Youth fixation. You're used to investigating gangs. That's what makes sense to you. You're used to solving crimes, but this isn't a cops and robbers story. The mystery isn't out there. It's whatever was going on inside Boggs's mind."

"All right. Are we going to get to work or what?"

Pulling his chair up to the desk, Heartwood opened his briefcase, its interior exhaling a breath of warm leather, and took out a legal pad and a folder of press clippings.

"In the best of all possible worlds, I'd interview his family first, but his sister's somewhere up in Idaho and we don't even know where his mother and half-brother are at the moment."

"Finding them won't be a problem. There's employment records, driver's license records, Social Security records, records up the gump-stump. I can handle that." Gabriel swung his arms down to the desk and shuffled through the clippings. "People still think this country's big enough to disappear in easy. It isn't. Not anymore. All right. I find Mom and baby brother. Then we talk to them? What are we after? What do we ask them? If we were looking for a live Duane, I'd know what to do. But what was going on in his mind . . . ?"

"This'll save a lot of explaining."

Heartwood handed him a sheet that said: "Psychological Autopsy. Shneidman and Farberow. Sixteen-step procedure."

Gabriel scanned it: Step one—Identifying information about the victim. . . . Step two—Details of death. . . . Step three—Outline of victim's life history. . . . He chuckled when he came to Step thirteen.

"I never thought of that as droll," Heartwood said. "What's so funny?"

"This." He snapped a finger against the paper. "Step thirteen. 'Assessment of intention—role of suicide victim in his slash her own demise.' That's easy. Boggs's role in his own demise was to stick a nine to his head and pull the trigger."

"Now you've had your fun. What we need to know is why he pulled the trigger. Unless I'm missing my guess, his suicide's the key to the murders. If we can figure out his reasons, we should be able to answer why he wanted children for company."

"Saw some guy on the tube. Professor type. He said something about killing kids being the ultimate revenge on society."

"That was Tom Renfro. Criminologist from Stanford. Smart guy and he's probably right. But Renfro doesn't know any more about Boggs than we do. Maybe less. Okay, okay. What are we after? Boggs's state of mind at the time, as near as we can come to reconstructing it."

"His state of mind at what time?"

"At the time he crossed the threshold between thinking about doing something and taking the first concrete steps toward doing it."

Gabriel's gaze flitted erratically around the cubicle, as though he were tracking the flight of a trapped hummingbird.

"Gabriel, believe me, capturing that moment can be just as rewarding as capturing a suspect," Heartwood said earnestly. "And when it comes to Boggs's state of mind, we've got plenty of mysteries to solve."

"Yeah? Seems to me his state of mind was easy to figure out. Fucked up to the max."

"Yes and no. 'Actions are sometimes performed in a masterly and most cunning way, while the direction of the actions is deranged.' Dostoevsky."

"What the hell are you getting at?"

"A guy does something irrational but does it rationally." He pointed at Boggs's photograph in the Saturday *San Joaquin Dispatch*. "Here's why this creep intrigues me. Serial killers like Bundy or Gacy are usually smart, adept at covering their tracks. Cunning. The typical mass murderer—the guy who kills a lot of people in a single incident—usually goes off like your human time bomb of popular cliché. They're commonly impulsive, they seldom plan their crimes carefully, they usually pick easy targets, like a crowded restaurant. If the media has it right, Boggs fits that profile, but he—"

"Had to do a lot of planning," Gabriel interrupted. "He had to figure out how long it would take the bus to get to his ambush site so he'd be there to meet it. Or he followed the bus from the school. But even then, at some point he would have to have gotten out ahead of it, given himself time to set up, be ready to go. He must have clocked distances."

"Right. Next point, since most of these killers are white trash losers, boys with deep cravings that demand instant gratification, they usually choose very public targets that they know will draw immediate attention. Even if they intend to kill themselves, they want to die knowing the TV cameras and reporters will be there ten seconds after the smoke's cleared."

"But Boggs ambushed the bus way out in the boonies," Gabriel said.

"Right again. You might say that he chose a crime with deferred gratification. More facts. He bought his suicide weapon at Ray's Gun Shop in San Joaquin, waited out the fifteen-day waiting period, and picked it up a week before he turned it on himself. Another fact suggesting deliberation and self-control. And so is the evidence of a pipe bomb the El Dorado County sheriff found inside the truck. A small pipe bomb. That's what blew up the truck, not the gas tank. A homemade pipe bomb. Now why that?"

"He knew he wasn't going to need the truck anymore," Gabriel quipped.

"School bus doors open from the inside. You can kick them open or try to pry them open from the outside, but it isn't easy. And while you're doing that, your intended victims will be crawling out the windows, running out the rear emergency door."

Gabriel had stopped fidgeting. He was becoming interested, and he looked more closely at the photo. It gave him the same chill he'd felt earlier. That frosty breath from a morgue freezer. Boggs's eyes were unnaturally pale and bright, but it was the brightness of a doll's eyes or the eyes in a hunter's trophy. He had seen that malevolent vacancy before. Boggs was another mutant, a carrier of the alien evil.

"So he set his truck on fire, figuring the bus driver would open the doors as a safety measure in case the gas tank blew up and threw burning fuel on the bus," Gabriel said. "Kids have a way out, but now Boggs has a way in."

"And the bomb?" Heartwood said. "Maybe for shock effect, but probably for insurance. If the fire doesn't convince the driver to open the doors, the explosion will. And what's the first thing Boggs does? Kills the driver, which disables the bus and gets rid of the only adult male, the one person most likely to give him trouble. So what does this tell us about him so far?"

"A planner, organized, calculating."

"He even wore ear protectors. Is a guy planning to kill himself going to worry about hearing loss? Maybe the earphones were a screwy detail, but I think he wore them so he wouldn't be distracted by his own gunshots, by screams and cries."

"In so many words, Boggs doesn't fit the profile you were talking about."

"But he *does* fit the profile, at least from what we know so far."

"What the hell are you saying? That he couldn't have committed the crime he did?"

"I see Boggs as like the outline the evidence techs drew around his body. We have to fill it in. He fits the profile, his crime doesn't. That's one of our mysteries to solve. Match the criminal to the crime."

"So . . . "

"So we start here." Heartwood thumbed through the color-coded tabs of a report whimsically titled "Duane's Progress: July 1992–April 1993" and pulled out a couple of pages. "Here's what we know. Boggs worked at the United Foods cannery in San Joaquin from May till mid-July last year. At the end of July, he turned up in Fontana, living with half-brother Jacob and his stepfather, one of his four stepfathers, Wilson Tipton. Then he was arrested for that caper in the San Bernardino National Forest, tried to commit suicide in jail, served forty-five of a sixty-day sentence, and by late October was living with his sister and brother-in-law in Idaho. Left there a few days after

New Year's. His sister said that Boggs and her husband got into an argument. Her husband told Boggs to move out of the house, Boggs wanted to stay. That's interesting. We'll want to get the details on that squabble. Okay, okay. Duane next appeared in Florida, renting a trailer at Mangrove Mama's Trailer Court in south Dade County. Mangrove Mama's? I'll bet that's a charming spot. Employed as a laborer by the roofing company, repairing Hurricane Andrew damage. Late February he quit, and on March fourth registered at the Camino Real in San Joaquin. Four days later, he visited the county mental health clinic to find out if he qualified as disabled due to drug and alcohol dependence. Other than the examiner, we know of only two people who had contact with him recently. One was a waitress in the Howard Johnson outside San Joaquin. She saw him on the morning of the massacre. The other was Ahmad Khan, the motel owner, who told the press that Duane died owing him two weeks' rent."

"He had other things on his mind than paying his bills."

"Boggs's mother's last known address was Homestead, Florida. Apparently, she left sometime this year. Did they see each other when he was down there? Did something happen between them that pushed him over the threshold? He could not have known about the field trip when he left Florida, but maybe the seed of an idea formed in his mind. Some dark, dark desire to do something terrible. But if that was the case, why did he drive all the way across the country to act on it?"

Gabriel pointed at himself.

"You're asking me? How would I know? How would *you* know? Maybe we should call a medium because there's no way we're ever going to know that without talking to Boggs."

"Not necessarily."

Gabriel paused, biting his lips as he thought of various possibilities.

"He was from California. He knew it."

"Exactly! You're getting the hang of this. Mass killers almost always pick a place or situation they're familiar with. It makes them feel more comfortable."

"Then again, he could have headed back here for some other reason."

"Possibly."

"I'll contact the Dade County sheriff and ask him to put a trace on Mrs. Boggs."

"It's not Boggs." He consulted the summary. "It's Ortiz. No . . . that was her third husband. Sutcliff. Ralph Sutcliff is her latest husband, unless she's found a replacement. Last known address 124 312th Street, Homestead. According to the press, the house was destroyed in the hurricane, so who knows where she's gone."

"We'll find out." Gabriel wrote down the address. "While I'm at it, I'll ask Dade to run down what'shisname. Willy Owens. Not trying to make a cops and robbers thing of this, but I'd like a talk with Owens. It'll be mighty interesting if this redneck Klansman sold Duane the shotgun. Or gave it to him as a going-away present."

"That wouldn't prove anything."

"Didn't say it would. Said it would be interesting. How about baby brother? A last known on him?"

"Just Fontana, but the media haven't been able to find Tipton, either."

"Fontana's a sweetheart of a place. Birthplace of the Hell's Angels. Did two years there when I was in Narcotics. I'll call our field office down that way. See if they can find the Tipton kid."

"Okay. For now, we go through the press reports, make a list of everybody who had contact with Boggs. Then we divide it into an A- and B-list, just like a hostess planning a party. A-list—everybody who knew Boggs intimately. B-list—people who knew him casually. A or B, we'll want to pay close attention to anyone who saw him or spoke to him during the week prior to the crime. He might have dropped a few words that could be the key to what we're looking for."

"His state of mind," Gabriel snickered, and said in a singsong falsetto, "'The city of happiness is in the state of mind.' I had a great-uncle who used to say that. He was an extortionist with one of the Tongs."

The roster turned out to be depressingly short; only six made the A-list.

Heartwood shook his head. "Pretty scant. Four people on the B-list in San Joaquin. The Pakistani motel manager, Boggs's foreman at the cannery, the examiner, and the waitress. I suggest we talk to them first, get that out of the way, and then we can concentrate on his family, if you can call it a family."

"Nearest ones are his grandparents in Walnut Grove. Clovis and Adelaide." Gabriel entwined his fingers and stretched his arms overhead and couldn't keep a sneer from playing across his lips. "I'll bet that's a pair of real old-time Okie-dokies. He probably calls her Addy. 'Addy, y'all cook me up some greens an' chickin-frad steak, ratnaow.' "

"Clovis and Addy didn't have much to say to the media. Only that they were shocked and sorry, then it was all no comment."

"Yeah, so I'll bet they'll open up when they see us at the front door. A gook cop and a shrink with a big Jew nose. 'Why, howdee-doo,' they'll say. 'Y'all come in and set a spell and we'll tell y'all ever'thing 'bout our grandson.' "

He saw Heartwood frown with disapproval, but couldn't quite contain the rancor that had risen in him out of nowhere. It seemed to lower the barometric pressure, bringing a tension to the air.

"I'll mention this only once. These interviews are going to be exactly that. Not interrogations. We take it easy on people," Heartwood counseled. "We gain their confidence so they speak candidly."

"Gotcha. I can be sweet as a powdered sugar donut when I have to be." He looked at his watch. "Four o'clock. We can head down to San Joaquin now and be there in forty-five minutes. Or are you a nine-to-fiver?"

"No, except for today. Have to call my son between five-thirty and six. Connecticut. He's in school there."

"What college is he going to?"

"Prep school."

"Oh, a preppie . . . "

"No reverse snobbery, okay? Anyway, it was my ex-wife's idea to send him there. Her father's alma mater."

"So how long are you two split up?"

"Two years."

"We're still together"—Gabriel pointed to Adrienne's photo and rapped his knuckles on the desk—"eighteen years this August."

"These days anything over five is an achievement," Heartwood said, and put the files back in his briefcase.

As he rose and pulled his suit coat off the back of the chair, Gabriel noticed him pausing to stare at a photograph pinned to the wall. It showed Trinh, scowling under his mane of black hair. Shirtless, his lean torso was tattooed with a rising moon and a fire-breathing dragon with a coiled tail and claws that drew long gashes across his chest, the blood from the gashes flowing down to form the words *Moonlight Dragons* across his abdomen.

"Who—or what—is that?"

"Pham Van Trinh. Vietnamese gangbanger. He's the reason you and me are working together."

"Oh?"

"That story I told? About the gangbangers boiling a kid alive?"

Heartwood grimaced and nodded.

"We had information that Trinh was one of them. Solid information, but the kids' parents were too scared to come in and finger him at a lineup. Brought him in for a little conversation. Wise guy. No idea what I was talking about, and he's smirking and talking jailhouse lawyer jive and all the time I'm thinking, 'A baby, they boiled a baby like a goddamned lobster and this asshole couldn't give less of a shit.' I went out and got a hot plate and filled up a kettle and brought the hot plate and the kettle into the interrogation room and put it on a boil, and when that kettle started whistling, I said, 'Trinh, my man, this isn't for a tea party. Ever wonder what it feels like to get doused in boiling water?' More jive. Didn't think I was serious. Wrong. Somebody outside heard him howling and opened the door and Trinh runs out, falls down on the deck screaming, just when the Special Agent in Charge is coming through, giving a tour to some Explorer Scouts earning merit badges in law enforcement. And there I'm standing, with this fucking scalding kettle in my hand. Six-month suspension from regular duties. I should have been canned, maybe put on trial myself, but . . . well, for a lot of reasons, the boss decided to keep me on and keep the incident within the family. Anyway, Krimsky called me this morning and told me if I worked with you on this autopsy thing, I'd be off suspension when it was done."

Heartwood did not say anything at first. Then he asked, "That's the only reason you're doing this?"

"Nope. I'd like to know if this Boggs bastard was after Asian kids or not. Just for my own satisfaction."

"I'm wondering why you told me that story."

"Thought you should know."

"Really?" Heartwood said it in a way that implied some deeper, more complicated motive. "Why do you keep his picture there?"

"Are you putting me on the couch?"

"Hardly. What happened to Trinh?"

"There is a God in heaven and justice in this world." Gabriel opened a desk drawer and withdrew another photo, a police Polaroid that made Heartwood shut his eyes.

"Got mixed up with some real pros. Chinese gangs smuggling in heroin and Vietnamese boat people. Trinh got greedy, overreached. Guys like him always do. This is him after a three-week swim in the bay. Looks like a shark got his legs."

"Gabriel, thanks for a pleasant and productive afternoon. How about a lift back to my car? We'll get started first thing tomorrow."

Tuesday, April 20th

IN THE EARLY MORNING DARKNESS, LEANDER HEARTwood sat in his room in the Camelia House, his face lit by a Steuben glass desk lamp and the pale iridescence of his laptop's screen. He yawned, stretched, wriggled his toes inside his flannel-lined slippers, and stared at the screen, which seemed somehow expectant, as if it were eager for him to begin work. He might as well. He didn't have a lot of time until he had to pick up Gabriel, and these hours before the intruding world awoke were the best time for undistracted thought.

He put on his reading glasses, opened a file folder bulging with print-outs, graphs, and eerie images that resembled time-lapse photos of summer lightning. These were MRI scans of a brain belonging to Lamont Crewes, an itinerant carpenter who had raped and murdered five women in Arizona, then cut off their breasts and hung them from a pegboard in his van, right above his skillsaw and belt-sander.

Heartwood began to enter information about Crewes's life and neurobiology, building a new file for the lab's database. It was painstaking work, and an hour of it brought a crick to his neck. He got up and paced the room, touching his ears to his shoulders, shaking the kinks out of his fingers. His mind began to wander, diverted by the thought that the laptop could perform as many operations as the furnace-size IBMs that used to spit out punch cards when he was in premed at Marquette University.

He supposed he was getting old if he could remember vacuum-tube computers. For that matter, he could remember when there weren't any kind of computers, a time for which he felt nostalgic because the world seemed so much saner then. A lot of people seemed to be feeling that temporal homesickness, even those too young to remember vacuum-tube computers, Studebakers, and Harry Truman moving jerkily in grainy newsreels. The disarray of the present, with its daily birth announcements of beasts spawned out of the American id—CARJACKERS MURDER GERMAN TOURIST IN MIAMI . . . BROOKLYN TEEN SHOOTS WOMAN AT AUTOMATIC TELLER . . . WACO CULTISTS DIE IN HUGE BLAZE—was corroding hope for the future and causing the nation's collective eye to look toward a past that hadn't been as virtuous or innocent as it seemed in retrospect. People had forgotten the dark side of yesterday's moon—segregation and Joe McCarthy and the quiet suburban desperations that had whispered of a serious design flaw in the engine of postwar prosperity. It hadn't generated the complete happiness it promised. And yet, maybe life *was* better then. At least there wasn't this dread that things were spinning dangerously out of control, toward some Hobbesian state of unpredictability, when random gunfire would echo everywhere, sea to shining sea.

Heartwood's dread was perhaps stronger than most. His arcane calling had made him all too aware of how terribly out of control people could get. For twenty years he'd explored the forbidding backwaters of the human mind, seeking the rookeries where monsters with unnatural appetites were hatched. He'd been credited with finding two or three previously unknown species and had won a sober renown among his peers, a small circle of criminologists and psychiatrists who specialized in analyzing the freaks of the criminal world—the spree killers and child molesters and sadists who did not do what they did for conventional motives like greed or jealousy but were prompted by the things that squawked and hissed in the swamps of their interiors.

There had been a time, not too long ago, when he believed that such people were the psychological correlatives of the bodily deformed, their minds bent by the absence of love in their hearts. Because nature abhors a vacuum, the space where love should have dwelled became filled with hate and anger. Those mass murderers and serial rapists hated themselves, hated the parents who had beaten and savaged them, denied their longings for the nurturing breast, the embrace, the comfort of a gentle hand or word. Anyone maimed by so much brutality cannot live normally in the normal world, so the normal world and normal people become hateful to him and deserving of the punishment he himself has suffered. His thirst for retribution is so fierce that he doesn't care whose blood he sheds to slake it—the blood of those who'd refused him love or of innocent strangers.

An elegant theory, but Heartwood was no longer confident of its truth. It didn't explain why there were now so many monsters roaming the land, exacting their random vengeance. They weren't freaks anymore, the two-headed men and alligator ladies of the criminal carnival. The sideshow had moved into the main tent, the abnormal had become normal. It seemed you no longer had to be a clinical psychopath to commit a psychopathic act, and Heartwood had begun to wonder if some kind of plague were spreading across the land, an AIDS of the spirit, striking even hearts with love in them. The horror in Waco was a new chapter. It had pushed Boggs's atrocity off the front pages and the nightly news. A whole community of people from ordinary walks of life had been turned into fanatics yearning for the apocalypse—and they had gotten it from FBI agents garbed in black, like Ninja warriors.

He had not been entirely candid with Gabriel yesterday. Yes, he was the shaman the tribe sent forth to tell why the mental volcano exploded, but he was a shaman who'd ceased to believe in the old myths—the theories of Freud and Jung and all their disciples. Classical psychiatry was sufficient when it confined itself to treating bundles of Woody Allen neuroses, but when confronted by the truly dangerous acts, he had to admit that it was what his father had called it—witch-doctoring, all masks and ritual dances, gourds rattled at the terrors of the night. Heartwood had grown impatient with such psuedo-science, and that impatience was among the reasons he was awake at this hour, entering data into his laptop.

Looking out the window, at the streetlight falling on the roof of his Porsche, he recalled the phone call that had brought him into the Imaging Systems labs in San Jose as a part-time consultant. It had been from Walt Apetheker, an old classmate from Yale Medical School, whom he hadn't seen in several years. Walt had taken leave as chief of neurosurgery at Stanford Medical Center and had gone to the I.S. labs on a research grant. He was one of a handful of people working on the most spectacular research in neuroscience: mapping the topography of the brain with fast MRIs and PET scans.

Nearly two years ago, he'd asked Heartwood to join him in a special project, which would best be discussed in person. Lunch would be on him. They met at the Fairmont—being a neurosurgeon with grant money in his pocket, Walt could afford the sticker shock. Heartwood noticed that his classmate had taken on the appearance and the persona of a medical éminence grise since they'd last seen each other. A tall, handsome man handsomely dressed in a houndstooth sport jacket and raw silk tie, his face had gone craggy, his thick, straight hair prematurely white, while his manner had become aristocratic. He seemed to make a point of not looking at the maitre d' when he asked for his table, or at the waiter when he gave his order, as if these people weren't substantial enough to merit even a passing glance. Beside him, Heartwood felt shabby, peasantlike, uncomfortably aware of his prominent nose—like an anteater's, as his father, who had the same nose, used to say.

Walt maintained an air of mystery, mentioning nothing about the project while they ate. They traded small talk, caught up on each other's lives, Walt's successes at Stanford Medical, Heartwood's divorce from Paula, his media prominence. "Heard there was a story about you in *People* a while ago," Walt said, the "heard" signaling that he didn't read the magazine himself, the arch in his silver brows that he considered that sort of publicity not entirely appropriate.

He didn't get around to the subject at hand until after they'd taken a long walk to Aquatic Park and then out to the end of the pier, where he leaned against the railing, his back to the windy bay. When he commented on the splendid fall weather, Heartwood said, "Is your grant from the CIA, Walt? Am I going to be asked to perform dubious experiments on unsuspecting subjects? Why all this obliqueness?"

"Oh, it's just my way, just my way. You must remember that from when we were at med school."

Heartwood in fact remembered Walt as being direct, even brusque, and he said so.

"Very well, you're right. I've become a little paranoid about the work we're doing."

"Afraid of industrial espionage?"

"Partly. Mostly it has to do with a conference that I helped organize last year. On the biological and neurological roots of violence. There was some advance publicity and the next thing I knew, yawps of protest. To the effect that the conference wasn't scientific, but ideological. That we were going to say that violence is genetic, particularly prevalent in blacks. I was publicly accused of being a racist, even got a couple of nasty phone calls from politically correct Stalinist types at Stanford. Anyway, we had to cancel. Some of this bears indirectly on the project I want to bring you in on. I've decided to call it the Gage Project. For old Phineas."

Heartwood laughed. Phineas Gage, the nineteenth-century railroad man whose conscience literally had been blown out of his head, had been studied as a curiosity by generations of neurologists and psychiatrists.

"Don't chuckle yet," said Walt. "How up to speed are you on the stuff we're doing? Not a great deal published yet."

"I've read what's been published."

A few yards down the pier, a Chinese fisherman in a crushed cap grinned to a friend as his spinning rod bent and twitched.

"I'll give you a quick overview," Walt said. "What we're doing is nothing less than the complete exploration of inner space. The advancements we'll make in treating strokes, amnesia, speech and motor-control impairments, will be unbelievable, but I don't have to tell you where the most exicting developments will come from."

"Psychiatry," Heartwood said.

"It will become, and soon, a hard science. It will become real medicine, as real as neurosurgery."

"You sound like my old man."

"Maybe so," Walt replied, and then delivered, with a passion more suited to the missionary than the physician, a sermon on his research. He and his colleagues were making movies of the mind as it worked! They'd come up with objective proof that the mind was not some abstract entity equivalent to the soul, free-floating in the inner ether; it was organic! An astonishingly complex network of neurotransmitters within the *brain.* Different sectors of the brain lit up when someone was asked to look at an object, or listen to a piece of music, or speak a noun or a verb. Dreams had been filmed, even thoughts had been captured and photographed. Human thinking, like perception, was at its root a matter of neurochemistry. Dizzying stuff. The visions of the prophets, the songs of the poets, even Einstein's sublime equation—all were born from minuscule discharges cracking through the cranial soup.

Heartwood resented Walt's tone; he was speaking as if he, Heartwood, were a layman, unaware of the latest advances in brain research. His glance roved to the World War Two blockhouse in which cannons once pointed seaward, prepared to fire on Japanese warships. Odd, he'd been a toddler in a time when archaic guns guarded San Francisco Bay, and now he was talking about making movies of human thoughts. He was no layman, and yet he had a sense of history and technology moving faster than he could keep up with them.

Walt sidled out of the blockhouse's shadow into the sunlight and his pale hand traced a line just above his ear.

"The amygdala. It begins there."

"Repository of primitive memories," Heartwood said. "The scaly beast in us all."

"And what is it but a tight bundle of neurons swimming in a pool of chemicals? Not as poetic as the scaly beast, but the hell with poetry. We think we're on to something. We're doing some fantastic work, Lee. Diagramming the biology of human emotions. Finding the centers of emotions in the brain. Figuring out why people feel the things they do. We've gotten Vietnam vets with PTSD to volunteer, guys who experience complete flashbacks at the sound of thunder or a backfiring car or a door's slam. In other words, we're starting with that most basic and powerful emotion—fear."

"And . . . ?"

"It looks like PTSD is resistant to conventional psychotherapy because it's a neurological disorder. It's organic. It has nothing to do with the old mumbo-jumbo."

"I haven't seen anything published on this . . . "

"Because nothing has been. We're hoping to soon in the *Archives of General Psychiatry*, but I'll give you a preview. The sense is that a traumatic event like combat can cause an unusual strengthening of nerve connections to the amygdala and hippocampus. I'm talking about observable, measurable changes in neuroanatomy caused by extreme *emotional* stress, not any sort of physical trauma."

Heartwood watched a big sloop tack in front of the buff walls of a vacant Alcatraz, then sail off close-hauled. Sea breeze washed over him, sea smell tingled in his nostrils. This was exciting stuff, but also a little disturbing, a contradiction of cherished assumptions about how the mind and the heart worked.

"And we have the whole spectrum of emotions to deal with," Walt went on. "Poets have been trying to tell us what they are and why we feel them for centuries. They've had their shot. Three thousand years of it. Now it's our turn, science's turn. By sometime early in the next century, we might be able to define love with precision. Diagram it. We might be able to show the biochemical reactions of jealousy."

Heartwood raised both hands, appealing for silence.

"Walt, do you want me to consult on this PTSD research?"

"No. I've been thinking about the work you've done all these years. The people you've dealt with are the embodiments of abnormality. Some were born that way, I imagine, but I'll bet most of them were made that way by experiences. Neurologically changed by childhood emotional traumas, maybe by experiences later in life, like the vets."

"I don't know about physiological. Anatomical. I don't know about that."

"Look, if fear causes changes in neurochemistry and neuroanatomy, what about two other powerful, primitive emotions, two other waste products of that scaly beast? Rage and hate. Do they cause similar changes? Make these changes extreme enough and you get abnormal reactions, you get insanity, bizarre compulsions, you get rape and bloody murder. The gravest sins of a fallen world, Lee."

"The serpent in the garden is a short-circuited neural network?"

Walt cocked his head to look at him earnestly, and again with that faintly rueful smile, and Heartwood immediately regretted the flipness of his remark. Walt's theory made sense. Men are disturbed not by things but by the view which they take of them. That quote from Epictetus hung in Heartwood's office. It was his professional Bible, compressed into a few words. If thought and perception were at their roots neurochemical reactions, then disturbed behavior was the child of disturbed perceptions that were in turn the progeny of bad chemistry, miswired neurons.

Clouds had begun to scuttle across the sky and Walt seemed to be staring at some distant object on the Marin headlands, green then gray-green in the mottled sunlight. As he turned with an upraised hand, his pewter-colored hair rose in a gust and the disheveled gray and the hand uplifted gave him, for an instant, the look of an obsessed prophet. "We've established that there are neural pathways that mute fear and that sometimes these networks become blocked, as in the case of the Vietnam vets. I recently came across a case of a guy in Massachusetts. This is your sort of stuff, not mine, but it's interesting. A rape case, a guy with a German name."

"I'm familiar with it. Meinholz. Raped and murdered his neighbor's daughter. Scans indicated that the part of his brain thought to moderate sexual impulses was abnormally formed. Also found abnormalities in his brain's ability to control arousals. Got convicted anyway. A lot of this stuff isn't accepted in the legal or forensic community."

"I don't give a damn what's accepted. We are on to something. What if there are neural networks to mute rage, hate, lust, just as there are networks that mute fear? What if these moderating systems are what we've called conscience all these many centuries?"

"It's an intriguing notion."

"Come work with us, Lee. We old Elies have got to stick together." This was actually delivered with an old-boy jab on the shoulder. "We'll see if we can't scientifically define rage and hate. Find the neurological and biochemical causes behind the greatest wrongs people can do to each other. In a way of speaking, we'll try to find the equation for evil."

That was in September of ninety-one. Since then, Heartwood had been traveling to San Jose two nights a week and on weekends. He loved the lab, loved the analysis rooms cluttered with control boxes and computer terminals, the examining rooms agleam with the high-tech polish of the new EEG and MRI machines. A hard, clear, quantitative edge to everything, an atmosphere intolerant of ambiguities and vague assumptions. He thought of Caesare Lambroso, measuring craniums with his calipers in rat-infested nineteenth-century jails, and imagined the Italian psychiatrist looking over his shoulder as he worked and crying out, "*E nel cervello! Nel cervello!* It's in the brain, in the brain! I was right all along!"

An equation for evil.

So far, Heartwood and his assistant, a Cambridge clinical psychologist with the parodic name of Percival Worsthorne, hadn't come near to formulating one. Over the past nineteen months, they'd studied more than forty murderers and rapists but hadn't found any definite links between their brain chemistries and neuroanatomies and the awesomely bloody deeds they'd done. Still, Heartwood was convinced that one day he would make an image of a violent thought or impulse, track the glowing transmitters of murder as they signaled a hand to pick up a knife, club, or gun. He would no longer have to guess or use his intuition or make imaginative leaps. Yes, there it is, ladies and gentlemen of the jury. We have found it at last, the heart of darkness, and it's a neurochemical glitch!

His laptop, its microcircuits alive but idle, called him back to work. He opened the next file: Dave Pierpont, another volunteer who'd agreed to have his brain literally picked at the lab. He'd come off death row in San Quentin, a killer more typical of the ordinary guy turned psychopath than Lamont Crewes, the amiable necrophiliac. Pierpont had been a machinist, a husband and father, and one day three months after he'd been laid off, he'd sauntered into the San Diego Zoo with a handgun and shot three people to death at a snack bar.

Heartwood entered the data. Brain weight. Patterns of neuron firings. Levels of serotonin, dopamine, and norepinephrine. Graphs and images of neural activity in the thalamus. He relished the precision of it all, and the hope that lay within the precision, the hope of finding an answer that philosphers and theologians and Freudians and neo-Freudians couldn't find. His hands fluttered over the keyboard until light fell through the window of his snug Victorian room and the smells of fresh coffee and frying bacon rose from the kitchen. Time to quit. He switched off the computer. The instant its screen went dark, he felt the same desolation he did many years ago, when his father shut off the TV and marched him to his room to do his homework. He was cast out of his laptop's electronic space, back into the world of quotidian dimensions. In other words, he had to shower, dress, and go out to earn his billable hours. His first full day of trying to figure out why one Duane Leonard Boggs murdered fourteen schoolchildren with a semiautomatic shotgun.

"What in the hell is that?"

Gabriel never had heard such music: a masculine choir singing a cappella, though it didn't sound like singing to him. More like a droning, a mournful droning in a weird language.

"Gregorian chant." Heartwood leaned forward against his seat belt and reached toward the cassette player. "I'll change it if it bothers you."

"Doesn't bother me exactly," Gabriel said, though in fact it did. He wasn't much of a morning person and could have used something more stimulating. A hard Charlie Parker bop. "It's eerie. This is some kind of classical?"

"Preclassical. Medieval. Goes back to the eighth century. What's playing now is the Requiem. A solemn high funeral mass."

"Sounds like a funeral. So they're singing in what?"

"Latin."

Heartwood looked out the car window at a band of migrant workers clustered beside a farm truck and walls of wooden produce crates. In the distance, irrigation pipes on huge metal wheels spat water over a field.

"I listen to it, usually, last thing at night, first thing in the morning. It relaxes me."

"You nervous about something?"

"What I meant is that it helps me keep a clear head."

It's the austerity of it, Heartwood thought. The monophonic lines clean and bare as monastic tables, the melodies of order, appealing to the intellect and the soul instead of the senses, a good antidote to the glandular cacophonies of rock and rap. The Jesuits who'd educated him, first in the seminarylike confines of Campion Academy and then at Marquette, had given him an everlasting distaste for the church and all her unbending doctrines, her Latin mysteries. But as the choir began singing *"Gloria in excelsis Deo et in terra pas hominibus bonae voluntatis . . . Laudamus te . . . Benedicimus te . . .* " he remembered with longing the cowled priests chanting vespers at Campion, the stately rhythms of psalm and antiphon, the fragrance of incense in the chapel.

"Not to get personal, but you're a Catholic?" asked Gabriel.

"Born one. I'm the fallen-away kind. An excommunicant."

He preferred the severity of that word, with its suggestions of exile and banishment, to the insipid "fallen-away."

"Heartwood doesn't sound like a Catholic name."

"What's a Catholic name sound like?"

"Like the guys I went to high school with. Fanelli, O'Mara, Sanchez. You know, ethnic."

"Heartwood was French originally. Some ancestor of mine was a French fur trader in the upper Great Lakes way back when. Jean-Baptiste Coeurdubois, meaning 'heart of the woods' in the sense of 'middle of the woods.' Somehow it got mistranslated into heartwood, meaning the 'wood in the center of a tree.'"

"Hey. Ask a simple question, get a simple answer. Shit, working with you is like going to school. So what happens when you're an excommunicant? That you can't go inside a Catholic church or what?"

"I can't take the sacraments. Not that I feel a need to. If I've got a religion, it's medicine. Medicine and science. What about you, as long as we're on the subject."

Gabriel picked up the coffee cup steaming in the drink holder and sipped and didn't answer right away. He watched the Delta lands roll by, shining with the brightness of a promise fulfilled, the eucalyptus-shaded levees looking as though they'd been there forever, though they'd been built when his grandfather was a small boy. Built by Chinese labor. How many of those Anglo farmers out there knew that the levees and dikes and canals had been built by a hundred thousand coolies? He himself had not known until last night, after dinner, when he'd gone to listen to Ellington in his typical American family room with its sliding-glass door and BarcaLounger and bookcase of unread books. He chose *Indigos* from the row of CDs. Something drew his eye to one of the books; its title, *Paper Sons into Native Sons: A History of the Chinese in California*, impelled him to draw it out. One of Adrienne's college texts. Her name and the course and some page notations written on the flyleaf. So that particular book hadn't gone unread. Gabriel turned to the marked pages and educated himself about the Tideland Reclamation Company, which had hired idled Chinese workers after the railroads were done and the mines played out. A hundred thousand men were put to work transforming an immense tule marsh into farmland. A dull, unfamiliar resentment sneaked into him as he read, and stayed in him. He woke up with it. Why hadn't someone told him about what his people had done, their sinewy yellow backs aching as they dug canals by hand and raised the levees and dikes without which those fields and orchards now rolling by with the brightness of a promise fulfilled would still be swamp?

"Bet you think I'm a Buddhist," he replied to Heartwood's question. "Or a Taoist. That I read Confucius and mumble weird shit to my ancestors' spirits."

"What are you being so defensive about? I didn't think anything of the kind."

There was something about Gabriel that made Heartwood tense and guarded. He didn't raise his voice or act threatening, yet his exterior calm seemed disturbed by a hidden anger, as a quiet river's surface is creased by a submerged snag.

"Religion-wise, I'm not anything in particular. Neither was my dad. Him and my mom were married by a justice of the peace during the war. Adrienne and I got married in a Lutheran church." At the edge of his vision, he saw Heartwood draw back in surprise. That usually got white people. A Chinese Lutheran. "Why not, Lee? A lot of those blond hippie-dippies from the sixties turned Buddhist, ringing gongs and shit, so why not me and Adrienne in a Lutheran church?"

"So you're a Lutheran, then?"

"Nah. That church just happened to be available on the date we'd set. Hell, we would have gotten married by an Amtrak conductor, we were so hot for each other." He smiled inwardly, remembering last night, after the kids were asleep. "Still are."

"Yeah? You're a lucky guy, then. The problem I found with marriage is that it turns lovers into relatives."

"How long were you married?"

"Sixteen years."

"I'm going to get personal again."

"What now?"

"You had an old-fashioned divorce. Blood on the decks. Your ex socked it to you, probably because she caught you cheating on her."

"That isn't personal. It's downright invasive. All right, I may not look it, but I'm a man with large physical appetites. I have a problem with fidelity. I broke Paula's heart. I got what I deserved."

"You were used to living pretty well. Champagne tastes, but now you've got a beer wallet. Alimony, your kid's tuition at the fancy school. You're busting butt to keep this ten-year-old sports car running."

"Eight years old. Is there a point to this line of conversation, or are you just nosy by nature?"

"Testing to see if I've gotten rusty sizing people up."

Heartwood shot a glance at him and decided to come up to his weather side and block his wind.

"Now it's my turn to get personal. You're pissed off at something. You like to think of yourself as an all-American guy, you live in a perfect little whitebread neighborhood, but you can't forget you're different. It's there in the mirror every morning. You were probably the butt of racial slurs when you were a kid, but you didn't fight back. You swallowed the insults."

Gabriel did not say anything. He couldn't remember anyone calling him "chink" or "gook" in school.

"I saw those photos and trophies in your den. Martial arts. You'll never swallow an insult again. Somebody says something wrong, *wham,* you'll be on him like Bruce Lee in those karate epics."

"Put it this way. Most people think that the Chinese in this country are nice and polite and passive. That we aren't dangerous."

"But *you* are. I'll bet you flirted with juvenile delinquency. Tried to prove what a badass you were. Ever wonder why you poured boiling water on that Vietnamese punk?"

"Told you yesterday."

"Righteous indignation? You were the avenging angel, meting out a kind of frontier justice? Bullshit. One thing I've learned is that most people's self-portraits are flattering fakes."

"I did it to find out if the son of a bitch had a human nervous system."

"You poured boiling water on yourself. Once upon a time you wanted to be like that punk, a super badass with a dragon tattooed on your chest. Dangerous. But the respectable, suburbanite somebody you are now won't accept that side of yourself and needs to punish it, so out comes the kettle and the hot plate."

"All right. Truce."

"I won't try to be more of a cop than you, don't you try to be more of a shrink than me. I'm better at it."

The "Sanctus" was being sung as they entered San Joaquin's ragged fringes. *Sanctus, sanctus, sanctus, Dominus.* Tawdry motels, gas stations where you paid attendants in bulletproof booths before pumping, convenience stores where signs courteously warned robbers that the cashiers had no access to the safes and the cashiers kept hidden revolvers for use against criminals who'd be happy with the small change in the registers. *Plenisunt caeli et terra sua gloriam . . .*

"There it is," Gabriel said as they crested an overpass.

Heartwood looked below at a horseshoe-shaped building with a clay tile roof and stucco walls the color of a citrus-flavored soft drink. A semitrailer was parked on the frontage road, the cab in the motel parking lot, along with half a dozen cars. A neon crown topped a sign like a theater marquee. CAMINO REAL—LOW RATES DAY WK MO—XXX MOVIES.

The parking lot's asphalt was cracked as a dry river bed, grass sprouting through the cracks. On the left leg of the horseshoe, near the office, was a door with two strips of yellow tape crossed over it. The door to Boggs's room, no different than the others, yet the police tapes crossing over it like the X in a tic-tac-toe square made it look mysterious and forbidding. CRIME SCENE, read the black letters on the tape. NO ENTRY. *Benedictus qui venit in nomine Domine.*

In the office, under dusty fluorescent tubes, sat a pudgy man wearing a patched sweater and glasses so thick they made his eyes look as big as bottle caps. He stood and bared gold-capped teeth in a smile like an idol's.

"I can tell you gentlemen are not wanting a room in this place. Allow me one guess. You are from a newspaper or TV station wishing to interview me about my former guest, Mr. Duane Boggs."

"Close, but no cigar," said Gabriel, flashing his badge and ID card. "You're Ahmad Khan? The owner?"

"Yes. I've told the police all I know."

"We're not on a criminal investigation. This gentleman is a forensic psychiatrist, Dr. Lee Heartwood. The attorney general's asked us to look into why your former guest did what he did. His motives, that's what we're trying to figure out."

Folding his hands, Khan leaned over the counter. His magnified eyes, moving side to side, reminded Heartwood of a fish in a tank, watching for predators.

"We want to ask you a few questions about your impressions of him," he said, taking a notebook and tape recorder out of his briefcase. "How he behaved while he was here. Okay? Did you notice anything strange about him when he checked in? Any change in him between then and later on?"

"He never talked to me or to nobody, not even to say good morning." Khan tugged at a loose thread in his sweater. "He was in his own world. Once, when I took the night shift for my assistant supervisor, I saw Duane Boggs walking up and down that road out there. Up and down, all alone, late at night."

Heartwood jotted that down.

"We want to know what he said to you. Did he ever cause any problems when he was here? You were quoted in the papers as saying that he owed you a week's rent."

"Two weeks, but the only other problem I had with him was that girlfriend he brought here."

Something leapt in Gabriel's chest.

"What girlfriend? He had a girlfriend?"

"I don't know if they were, oh, you know, sweethearts. Maybe ten days ago, I was again taking the night shift for my assistant, and, oh, I think it was five in the morning when I saw Duane Boggs walk out of his room with this girl. I have strict rules. I don't mind if some fellow brings a girl to his room for what we in Pakistan call jigjig, but if she stays the night, then she must sign my visitors' book, and the person renting the room owes me for double occupancy for that night. So the next time I saw Duane Boggs, I told him I saw him coming from his room with this girl, holding hands, and that he owed me for double occupancy. And he acted, oh, you know, very upset and said it was his business who stays with him. He said some nasty word, but in the end he paid me what he owed."

Gabriel asked, "Ever see him with the girl again?"

"No."

Heartwood scribbled in his notebook. This female, whoever she was, had been with Boggs only a week or so before the massacre. He must have known his plans by then, most of them anyway. Would he have kept them from her?

Gabriel folded his arms on the counter and leaned over it.

"How's your vision, Mr. Khan?"

"So now you'll ask what did the girl look like? I don't remember very well, except that she was tall, maybe as tall as Duane Boggs. Thin. Maybe blond, and she was wearing a shiny jacket, you know, like satin. Not real satin. Like those shiny jackets street girls wear."

"How sure are you that it was a girl you saw?"

A stiff smile broke across Gabriel's face. It reminded Heartwood of Chou En-Lai, exchanging mirthless grins with Richard Nixon.

"What do you mean?" Khan plucked a string of worry beads from his pocket and a thin ingot showed between his lips. "You're saying possibly Duane Boggs was, oh, you know, a Nancy boy?"

"Nancy, Jane, Sally. He was popped in L.A. for homosexual prostitution. How do you know you didn't see a guy with long hair?"

Clack clack clack went the beads.

"Why, because . . . well, no, I cannot be sure. She, or he, was in blue jeans, so maybe . . . "

"So, let's move on. A reporter quoted you as saying you saw Boggs that morning. He said something to you."

"I was on the phone, speaking to my daughter in L.A., then I saw Duane Boggs through the window. I put down the phone, going to the door and calling out to him, 'Duane Boggs, you're owing me for two weeks!' And he called back, 'There's nothing to worry about.' And then he got in his truck and drove away."

"Alone, right?"

"Why of course. Alone."

Heartwood, fuming, switched off his tape recorder. Goddamned Gabriel had taken over the interview.

"I'd like to have a look at Boggs's room, if that's all right with you," he said to the motel owner.

"It's very fine with me, but not with the police. They told me no one is allowed in the room until further notice."

"I'm the police, so consider this the notice," Gabriel said.

"Very good." Khan pulled a key from the wall rack behind the desk. "Does this mean I can take those tapes from the door? Very bad for business, you know. People drive in here, wanting a room, and what do they see? 'Crime scene. No entry.'"

"Oh, hell, I'll bet the kind of people you get here are used to that," Gabriel said, smirking.

"My customers are not the best, that is true." At arm's length, he held the room key delicately between his thumb and forefinger, as if it were something long dead and smelly, and dropped it into Heartwood's palm. "But they are not murderers, no, mister, they are not the murderers of children."

"You had one that was."

Outside, Heartwood said, "Thought I made it clear about how we're going to handle things. This is a psychological autopsy. Don't try turning it into a criminal investigation."

"It's a little of one, a little of the other, if I heard Ruggerio right."

"*If* we dig up evidence of white supremacist involvement is what she said. When we talk to his sister and mother, I'll lead the questioning, okay? I know what to ask, what to look for. We can't waste time grilling them like you did that guy. All that *Dragnet* stuff."

"Gotcha. But wouldn't you like to find this girl, or guy?" he asked amiably, though he was thinking, It wouldn't take much for me to break this guy's nose. Plenty of nose to break.

"Sure. But I don't see how without a name and a better description than Khan gave."

"Like you said, I won't try to outshrink you if you don't try to outcop me."

Across the parking lot, a potbellied guy exited a room with a wide-hipped woman in snug jeans, the both of them clomping in cowboy boots toward the cab of the semitrailer. A ma-and-pa trucker team on the road. Wondering if they'd watched one of the XXX movies last night, balling each other while Debbie did Dallas on TV, Gabriel saw Adrienne's buttocks round as fruit thrust up to receive him. She liked it that way sometimes, the position she said had been called horse-on-horse in the ancient Chinese brothels. Adrienne knew goofy little facts like that. And big, not-so-goofy facts like a hundred thousand coolies transforming the Delta from a swamp to an Eden. Horse-on-horse. Heat rushed into his groin as he recalled his plunge into her, her vagina like wet, warm silk caressing him. Still hot for each other. Not relatives yet.

When they came to the room—its number, 102, was barely visible under layers of paint—Gabriel tore the tape from the door. Heartwood paused before inserting the key. He needed to be alone in the room, but he didn't want to explain why.

"How about you talk to the Howard Johnson waitress while I check things out in here," he said.

"You don't want to talk to her, you, the guy who knows what to ask?"

"Talk to her. Find out if she's got something to add to what she told the media. If it looks like she's worth a follow-up, I'll interview her. Meet me back here, say, in an hour."

"Rrrroger, commander. I always wanted to drive a Porsche. Who are you going to be talking to in there? Boggs's ghost?"

The curtains were drawn and Heartwood's eyes took several seconds to adjust; then the details began to reveal themselves one by one, like objects in a developing negative. The juxtaposition of the bizarre with the banal, the deadly with the commonplace, was disorienting: a photo calendar on the wall beside a camouflage tarp that hung like a deranged tapestry, with the cartoon character, Calvin, drawn on it, his sprouts of hair haloed by random squiggles, swirls, and lightning bolts, the word *Hezbollah* painted in yellow, uneven letters beneath his chin. An empty box of shotgun shells beside a stick of underarm deodorant. A small Styrofoam tray of 9-millimeter bullets, a dozen of them missing, nestled next to a Westclox windup alarm. Toy soldiers everywhere—on the rug, on the bureau, atop the curtain rod, inside the mini-fridge, where six were deployed around three beer bottles.

Picking a path through a squadron of plastic tanks, Heartwood wondered if there might be something to the mystical belief that those who die suddenly and violently linger on earth for a time. He seemed to feel Boggs's presence, as if his evil had not died with him but had soaked into the cement-block walls, the bristly red carpet. He turned to look at the objects on the bureau and his breath caught when he saw, in his peripheral vision, a shadowy figure standing in the doorway. But it wasn't Boggs's spirit incarnate, only Heartwood's own reflection in a dressing mirror bolted to the inside of the door. Scared by his own image. He opened the curtains to dispel the gloomy, haunted atmosphere, then raised the window to get rid of the smells of unwashed clothes and a fumigator's insecticide. Scents of oleander and honeysuckle blew in on the breeze, mingling with the odor of exhaust fumes drifting down from the overpass. Across the overgrown vacant lot next to the motel, cars were filling up at a mini-mart gas station. GAS 4 LESS.

He moved away from the window and surveyed the room, trying to get some sense of the killer who'd inhabited it. Dirty laundry, a duffel bag at the foot of the rumpled bed, with a shirt and a pair of bluejeans hanging out of it, a pint of yellow paint on the nightstand, a Magic Marker tossed on the pillow. Odd. The crime suggested a calculating, systematic personality, this disarray pointed to someone who was anything but. Possibly, though, it wasn't all Boggs's mess. Over the weekend, at Heartwood's request, Ruggerio had told the San Joaquin police to leave the room as they had found it, but the detectives, looking for evidence to link Boggs to white supremacists, might not have been too scrupulous about restoring the room to its original condition.

In the bathroom, a dirty towel lay on the floor, a razor and a can of shaving cream were atop the toilet tank; water filthy with lather scum and black bristles filled half the sink. Another contradiction. Someone who planned to kill himself in only an hour or two would not have bothered to shave unless he were habitually well-kempt, but a personality like that also would have drained the sink, hung the towel, put the razor away. In fact, he would have made it a point to tidy up, ritual neatness being an important prelude to suicide for such people. People like the general. Heartwood's first psychological autopsy, twenty-three years ago. The general had shaved, washed, polished his boots, made his bunk, and cleaned the .45 that he later stuck in his mouth.

Heartwood drained the sink, and watching the water suck and swirl, pondered alternatives. Possibly Boggs had spruced up on the last morning of his life for reasons other than habit. Die young and leave a good-looking corpse. A notion forming in his mind, he went back into the room and began to rifle through the bureau drawers.

The waitress was young, no more than twenty-five, but varicose veins already marred her calves, muscular and white above her white sneakers.

"Can't think of anything I didn't tell the reporters and the cops," she said in an Okie drawl that, Gabriel thought, should have been bred out of her generation, smoothed and softened into California bland.

"Mind going through it again for me?"

He straddled the counter stool, his notebook open beside a cup of undrinkably weak coffee.

The waitress's glance sidled toward two customers at the far end of the counter, her hand reached up to straighten the name tag above her left breast. CLARE.

"Okay. He came in here ten-fifteen, no later than ten-thirty, dressed up like a soldier, you know, like those soldiers back in that Persian Gulf thing?"

"Desert camouflage."

"If that's what you call it. I figured him for a soldier when I seen him out there." She pointed lazily at the entryway, where the phones and the cigarette machine were. "We didn't have a lot of customers, six or seven was all, all of 'em but one at the tables. So I didn't have much to do. I was hanging out? Trying to look busy? And I noticed him right away 'cause I thought he was, well, you know? Kinda cute? That black hair. Thick and black, like yours. He was getting cigarettes and I guess something went wrong with the machine 'cause he started to bang on it, then he kicked it, all pissed off. Then he walked in and right away I knew he wasn't a soldier, knew there was something right strange about him."

Right strange. Okie for sure.

"What made you think that?"

"He was too messy to be a soldier. His shirt? It wasn't tucked in, but hanging out, and it didn't match his pants. Pants were brown and tan and the shirt was green and black. My older brother was in the Army and I know no soldier would go around like that. He came up to me and said the machine screwed him out of two seventy-five and he wanted his money back or a pack of Marlboros. He was just so weird. Not cute at all, like I first thought. His eyes? I never seen eyes that color before. Didn't look real. Like they'd been bleached or something?"

A customer summoned her for a check. Turning on the stool, Gabriel looked out the window at the traffic on Calaveras Avenue, the cars in the right lane slowing down to make the freeway entrance ramp. The school bus had gone up that ramp between ten-fifteen and ten-thirty Friday morning, when Boggs was in this restaurant, bitching about a bandit cigarette machine. Idly stirring his coffee, he heard the buzzing in the back of his brain that always went off when things were not adding up.

Heartwood felt against all reason that he was violating Boggs's privacy. Finding nothing in the drawers, he lifted the duffel bag from off the floor and emptied it on the bed. A packet of colored pencils and a sketchpad fell out with the dirty clothes. The pages were blank except for one that bore another likeness of Calvin—possibly a preliminary sketch for the larger version on the tarp—and again, the word *Hezbollah.* That ought to have settled the question about Boggs's white supremacist leanings before it was asked. No self-respecting neo-Nazi would invoke the name of a Muslim terrorist group. But did he, in some convoluted way, identify with them and their suicidal violence?

He fished in the jeans' pockets and pulled out three identical wallet-size photographs—duplicates of the one found on Boggs's body, the one that had appeared on the front pages. Moving to the window, he held the photographs up to the light. They hadn't been taken in an instant photo machine; the quality was too good. The edges were uneven, as if they had been cut by hand from a proof sheet. He stepped over to the wastebasket and dumped it, spilling on the rug an empty six-pack carton, a paper sack and Styrofoam containers from Wendy's, wadded tissue paper. The basket in the bathroom contained only the discarded head of a razor.

He sat on the edge of the bed and gave the trash a little kick with his toe. A roach scurried out of the greasy Wendy's bag.

A pall settled over him, part revulsion, part weariness, part disappointment. A graduate of Yale Medical School, a fifty-year-old psychiatrist of some repute, picking through a killer's garbage in a run-down motel. What could he learn from this? Was it ever possible to know what was written on the mind and heart of even an ordinary human being, let alone a mind and heart like Boggs's? He wished he were in the lab, drawing conclusions that could be measured, graphed, charted. That hard quantitative edge. He thought about something Diana Cahill had told him a few months ago. Diana, the Caltech astronomer whom Paula and David blamed for breaking up their marriage. "I don't see how you can do what you do, how you can sit in jail cells and talk to those creeps. I'd rather be out there," Diana had said, pointing heavenward. "It's pure. A void at two degrees Kelvin. No bats in the attic." He missed her. With her living in Pasadena and he in San

Francisco, they seldom saw each other more than once a month, and now she was in Hawaii, stargazing atop Mauna Kea.

But we're both looking for black holes, he thought, and picked up the Wendy's bag and emptied it. Out fell a couple of moldering french fries, hamburger bun scraps, and the thing he was looking for: the remains of the proof sheet, crumpled up but intact. He unfolded it and smoothed it with his hand. On the back of the bottom edge was a hand stamp with the name and address of a San Joaquin photo shop.

He tore it off, put it in his pocket, and returned to the office to ask Khan if the Camino Real had maid service. Of course! Khan replied. The Camino Real was a legitimate establishment, in good standing with the San Joaquin Chamber of Commerce. When was the last time the maid cleaned Boggs's room? Thursday morning.

"Can I use your phone?"

Khan gestured to him to come around the counter.

"Refill?" asked Clare, returning with a pot of coffee.

"Only if that's got more lead in it than the colored water you poured the first time."

"Hey, what do you expect? This is a HoJo's, not one of those fancy-dancy ex-presso places." She raised the pot and squinted at it. "This does look a little stronger, though."

Gabriel made a pouring motion over his cup.

"So you were telling me he wanted his money back."

"Yeah. I couldn't give him a refund, so I got Jack—he's the manager and he's got the key to the cigarette machine. Jack went out with the creep, got him his Marlboros. I thought that was all he wanted. The cigarettes? But he came back in and sat down and ordered a cup of coffee."

"How did he act? Calm, collected? Jumpy?"

She thought for a moment, screwing up her small, bowed mouth.

"Little of both? He kept looking around, behind him, to the side, out the window, all over, like this . . . " She twisted her head back and forth, turned to look over her shoulder. "Like he was afraid he was being followed or something. 'Course, I realize now he was looking for the school bus to come by so he could follow it . . . "

"How do you know that? Did he say something?"

Clare shook her head, an ash-blond wisp falling across her face. She brushed it back with flair.

"They said so on the TV. They said maybe he followed the bus on down the freeway and out to where he ambushed it. That was on the TV."

"Just tell me what you saw him do, heard him say. Forget TV."

"Already told you. He was drinking a cup of coffee, smoking, looking around, jumpy and nervous."

"But didn't I read something that Boggs talked to you? Something about his name?"

Clare nodded. A bell rang three times and, with an athlete's practiced movements, she spun on her heel, went to the kitchen counter, picked up a steaming plate, and delivered breakfast to a customer. The thick morning reek of frying bacon, onions, and eggs made what remained of Gabriel's gut tumble. He couldn't understand how people ate that greasy stuff first thing in the morning. His breakfasts were light, usually a bowl of dumpling soup, his grandparents' favorite dish. At his last annual physical, the doctor complimented him on his cholesterol level—182. "Wish I could convince some of the other agents to eat the way you people do," the doctor had said. *You people.* Funny. That phrase hadn't bothered him then; he'd paid no attention to it. Now it came back to him, slapping him softly, a velvet-gloved insult. *You people.*

Clare returned, a charming bead of sweat on her upper lip.

Heartwood reentered the room and sat on its only chair, a vinyl chair with pitted chrome legs, and contemplated Boggs's face while he waited for Gabriel. Men are disturbed not by things but the view they take of them. What went on behind those pale green eyes? How did those prisms distort what they saw, bending and twisting the light of the world into a scheme to slaughter innocents? "I think I'm beginning to get an idea, I think I'm on the track of what made you do what you did, you sick, sick son of a bitch," he said out loud. Have to use my imagination. Make the leap, using the artist's agility rather than the empiricist's plodding, rigorous logic. Sometimes you landed on the right spot.

"So, right, Boggs did talk to me. I was staying away from him, down at the other end, but then I had to go to the register to make change and when I passed by him, he said, 'Bet you don't know who I am' in this, oh, kinda voice like when people smoke too much. You know? I didn't say anything, so he asked me again, 'Know who I am, miss?' I just shook my head and then he said, 'Well, you're going to find out real soon.' "

"And that's all?"

"Except that he left five dollars. Biggest tip I ever got for a cup of coffee. He sure was right, though, wasn't he? About finding out who he was?"

"Something to tell the grandkids around the fire." Gabriel rose and left two dollars on the counter. "Hope you don't mind, but I'm not as generous."

Clare said, "Do you know what? When I did hear what happened, I put five dollars back in the register. Felt like if I'd've kept it something awful would happen to me. Like it was blood money or something."

"One other thing. Did you see the school bus pass by?"

"No," she answered. "I wasn't paying attention. It might have. Must've. The TV said it came right by here, but the only bus I saw was the city bus."

"So how come you noticed that?"

" 'Cause it stops here. Eastbound stops in front, then it goes to the university, turns around, and it's the westbound and makes a stop across the street. Boggs got up and left right when it stopped."

The buzzing in Gabriel's head grew slightly louder.

"See him get on it?"

She shook her head.

"Got in his truck . . . I mean, he must've got in his truck . . . "

"Because it said so on TV. But you didn't see him get into the truck?"

"Mister, you sure do ask some nitpicking questions. A lot more than the local cops did."

"That's why they're local cops and I'm a special agent," he said with a half-grin.

"Well, la-tee-da. Aren't you the big deal? All right, no, I didn't see him get in his truck. Saw him walk out, is all."

There was a knock at the door.

"Yoo-hoo, Mrs. Boggs?" came a falsetto voice from outside. "Can Duane come out and play with his new AK-47?"

"Come on in, Gabriel."

He entered, admitting a trapezoid of light that fell across the toy soldiers, the tanks with their guns pointed at the door.

"How'd your séance go? Any messages from beyond the grave?"

"No. And not too many from this side, either."

Gabriel looked down at the tanks, then, frowning, picked up one of the soldiers, a red one charging with fixed bayonet.

"Weird, huh? A guy his age with these things. How do you analyze that, Professor?"

"Some military fixation," Heartwood answered distantly. "Gave him a sense of power, I suppose. The more interesting things are these." He showed the photographs to Gabriel. "He had these taken the day before the massacre. A photo store downtown that does ID cards, passports. Mostly for migrant laborers. Boggs put one in his wallet and left these here."

With a look, Gabriel begged an explanation, but Heartwood decided to withhold giving one for a while. Tease him a little, get some mental leverage on him and hold on to it. He stood and jabbed his head at the door.

They drove back to the freeway and headed south, toward the cannery and the interview with Boggs's old foreman, Joshua Somers.

It lay on flatlands a mile off the highway: a big building of corrugated steel, a water tower, a steel smokestack bearing the name United Foods, smaller stacks venting steam.

Gabriel asked, "What was so interesting about those photos of Boggs?"

"Wondering how long you'd hold out," Heartwood said. "He had the pictures taken the day before the massacre and made sure to put one in his wallet. He wanted it to be found on his body, wanted it to run in the papers and on TV, okay, okay? He wanted to look his best for his great moment."

Gabriel was silent. He hated this psychological bullshit. They should have given this assignment to Watts, the headshrinker cop.

"The waitress confirmed what she'd told the media, right? He said she was going to find out who he was?"

"Right. Okay, he wanted to be famous. So what? That's what most of these jerks want. To be somebody."

"But Boggs wanted to be a *special* kind of somebody. He crafted a scenario so spectacularly awful no one would forget his name for a long, long time. You see, I think Boggs probably knew he had a problem with precedent. Guys like Manson and Bundy and Huberty at the Burger King—"

"It was a McDonald's," Gabriel said as they pulled past the loading dock. A Mexican in a yellow slicker stood with a pole beside a sloped conveyor belt pouring tomatoes into a chute.

"I meant McDonald's. But there's my point. I specialize in this stuff, but even I got the place mixed up." Explaining his theory aloud was making Heartwood more confident in it. "So, you're Boggs. You know people have gotten used to things that would've brought the whole country to a screeching halt in the past. Twenty-one people blown away in the middle of their Big Macs and the next day everyone's back to work, back to school, eating, drinking, fucking, like nothing much has happened. The intolerable has become tolerable, the unthinkable commonplace. How are you going to get everyone's attention? The bar of outrage has been set pretty high and you're going to have to do something really spectacular to vault over it . . . Well, you get the idea. How's it sound?"

"Like you should write it up, send it to Ruggerio, and we're done in one day. Then I can go back to chasing live bad guys."

The plant supervisor, a squat man wearing a pocket pen holder, led them past a line of checkers in latex gloves and plastic hairnets, then through a thunderous cavern, tin cans marching by the thousands through steel tracks overhead, and finally into the warehouse, where boxes stacked on pallets formed cardboard canyons fifteen feet high. The noise and the pungent smell of brine took Heartwood back more than thirty years, to the summer he worked in a cannery outside Green Bay. The job had been his father's idea, one of Dad's attempts to make a man of him by teaching him what hard, dirty work was all about.

Joshua Somers occupied an office far too small for a man his size. When he stood up in the tiny cubicle papered with waybills, shipping invoices, and inventory sheets, he had to hunch down to avoid hitting the hooded light fixture above his head. His hand, as he shook first Gabriel's, then Heartwood's, felt as big and leathery as a first-baseman's glove.

"Last few days, I've spent more time answering questions about Boggs than anything else," he said in a slow, soft voice out of phase with his bulk. "Making a career out of it." He sat down, the swivel chair squealing under his bulk. "So you guys want to know what? Why he did this? Damned if I know."

"We don't expect you to," said Heartwood, looking around for a place to sit but finding none. "We're trying to get a picture of him, what kind of guy he was."

"He was a lazy son of a bitch, I can tell you that. Ask that college guy he worked with, he'll tell you."

"What college guy?"

"Kid from San Joaquin State. Summer help. Weight-lifter type. Had one eye. Think his name was Withers. Payroll might still have a record of him. I'll call up if you think it'll help."

"Anything would be a help at this stage."

Payroll came through with the name a few minutes later. Somers had gotten it wrong. It was Weathers. Mace Weathers.

"Talk to him. He loaded ten pounds to Boggs's one. Pissed him off. Weathers couldn't stand that bum."

"Did Boggs ever say anything to you, did you ever hear him say anything that might give you an idea why he did this?" Gabriel asked, propping himself on the corner of the desk.

"Just what I told that reporter from the *Dispatch*. You musta seen that."

"Refresh our memory."

The foreman scratched behind his ear and expelled a breath hard, as if he were tired of answering the question.

"He didn't like, well, you folks," he said, looking sideways at Gabriel, who shifted his weight, a heat rising swiftly in his face. *You folks, you people*. "One time I heard him talking to a couple of guys in the cafeteria. He was bitching about him being a red, white, and blue American boy, and why was he doing nigger work in a cannery? Then he said something about his grandparents coming out to California back when from Texas or Arkansas or someplace and they chopped cotton and picked oranges and didn't go on no welfare. But now these gooks . . . " Somers, looking at Gabriel, showed his palm and spread his fingers. "His word, not mine, Detective. Boggs was saying they came here from Cambodia and Veetnam, and first thing they do is go on welfare, but he's gotta bust butt in a cannery. That was a laugh. That son of a bitch couldn't spell *work* much less do any."

"This doesn't have a damn thing to do with anything. It's for your information," Gabriel said sharply. "I'm not Cambodian or Vietnamese. I'm Chinese, and there's as big a difference between us and the others as there is between Italians and Swedes. My family's been in this country since they started building the railroad, and we've never taken a dime in welfare, not even in the Depression."

Somers rolled backward in his chair and raised his arms in mock surrender.

"Whoa, there. *Whoa*. I wasn't giving you what I think. I'm saying what Boggs said." He lowered his voice, injecting a hint of threat. "You got that, Detective?"

"He knows," Heartwood said in apology. That submerged anger, surfacing again. "What was your impression of the men Boggs was talking to? Did they seem to agree with him? Fair to say that Boggs might have felt he had an audience here for what he did?"

The foreman gave an exaggerated shrug. "We've got a few guys here who might have. You oughta talk to that college guy. Worked with Boggs eight hours a day six days a week for six, seven weeks. Musta known Boggs good as anybody. They played chess once in a while."

"Chess? Boggs played chess?"

"If there was a breakdown on the line and they had some time, they'd set up a board and play."

Heartwood made a note to ask Weathers about Boggs's skills. What was known about him so far did not suggest someone who could play gambits or knew a Sicilian Defense from a Lopez Variation. A small missing link that would match criminal to crime? If he was any good, then he had a mind that was inventive and methodical, able to foresee contingencies and anticipate pitfalls.

A forklift driver parked outside the office. He came in, wedging himself between the door and Heartwood, and handed the foreman a form to sign. When he left, Gabriel got up off the desk, his lips drawn between his teeth. The buzzing started in the back of his head again, like the old-fashioned doorbell in his parents' house.

"Thought you said Weathers couldn't stand him," he said a shade too aggressively. Somers drew back.

"Right. Had a hard time working with him. It's hot, sweaty work on the dock in the summertime, but that Weathers, he'd come in every morning in a clean T-shirt, clean pair of blue jeans. Boggs wouldn't change three, four days running. He stunk besides being lazy."

"But Weathers played chess with him, buddy buddy?"

The foreman rubbed his temple. "Look, what do you think I do around here? Make notes on how my workers relate to each other? Maybe Weathers was trying to get along with him, like I told him to. See, one time Weathers asked me to move him to another job or to move Boggs. I told him I couldn't be changing jobs around just to suit him. He was only summer help, didn't have to work with Boggs the rest of his life, so he should try to get along."

"And did he?"

"I guess," Somers said, exasperated. "Toward the end there, Boggs was kinda Weathers's trained puppy. Weathers'd say, 'Doo-wayne, get me a Coke,' and Boggs'd fetch him a Coke. Or 'Doo-wayne'—that's how he called him, sarcastic-like—'Doo-wayne, get me a candy bar,' and Boggs would run to the canteen and buy him a candy bar. Funny. Anybody else had asked Boggs to get him anything, he'd've told him, 'Go fuck yourself, I ain't your nigger.'"

"We may need to practice your social skills," Heartwood said, breaking a silence of fifteen minutes' duration. He and Gabriel were stalled on a bridge; it was being repainted and traffic was reduced to one lane.

"What did I do wrong now?"

"That screed about your ancestry. You were practically yelling at that guy."

Gabriel looked below at a freighter loading wheat piled on a wharf in sulphur-colored mounds. The river ablaze in the sharp noon light, the ship seemed to be floating on a sheet of molten pewter.

"Thought I'd let him know that Gabe Chin no greenhorn Chinee boy, but wan hunna pahcent Melican, long time Californ."

"Fine. Established." Heartwood stifled a sneeze, started to speak, and then cupped his nose as it exploded three times. "Sorry if I'm being a pain in the ass, but one more time—this is not, repeat not, a criminal investigation."

Gabriel was no longer so sure about that. As traffic moved again, he debated whether to confess his doubts and suspicions. The trouble was, he had nothing to support them: no evidence, witnesses, facts. Only a hunch, a detective's instincts, a noise in the back of his head.

"Let's eat," he said, entering the semidisaster area around downtown San Joaquin. "Hope you like Chinese. I know a pretty good Szechuan place near here. Couple of blocks from the city P.D."

After Heartwood tucked his precious car safely in the police headquarters lot, the two men walked past a pasture of rubble—some urban renewal project gone bust—then down a street of flophouses with windows thrown open, exposing iron bedsteads and gauzy curtains drawing in and out on the breeze. PLAY CALIFORNIA LOTTO, urged a sign on a liquor store window, but the bum sleeping beneath it on yesterday's headlines did not look like he expected his number to come in soon. A drunk merchant sailor stumbled from a curb, hooked a tattooed arm around a broken parking meter, and spun in circles, spewing on the pavement the whiskey in his belly.

Someone had tagged a wall in bright colors: VERT EROC MERLIN.

"Christ, this is a depressing town." Heartwood longed for the cool mists and sophistications of his San Francisco.

"Detroit's supposed to be worse," Gabriel said. What the hell, he thought. I'll try it out on him. "Listen, some things aren't adding up. And don't tell me I'm making a criminal investigation out of this."

Heartwood said nothing. He slung his sport jacket over his shoulder.

"Didn't we agree that Boggs planned this out to even the small details like wearing ear protectors? And didn't you say that this was his big moment, his one and only chance at being a somebody? In his mind, anyway. So I can't figure why he stopped in the HoJo, made a big deal about losing a few quarters, sat down to have a cup of coffee. What was he doing there?"

"Probably waiting for the school bus to come by," Heartwood answered as they came to a traffic light that commanded DON'T WALK.

"On the way back from talking to the waitress, I timed the drive between the school and the HoJo. Going the speed limit, which I figured was what the bus would have done, it took less than twenty minutes. Seventeen to be exact."

WALK flashed the light. They crossed, heading toward Chinatown.

"What's the point, Gabriel?"

"From what we know, the school bus left McKinley about ten A.M. That teacher, the DeLuca woman, said she was positive it was Boggs's truck she saw, circling the school just before the kids got on board. Throwing a lot of smoke. We don't know for sure what Boggs did then, but we can assume he followed the bus, down Oak Street to Calaveras, Calaveras to the HoJo at the freeway entrance."

"Or he watched the bus leave, then, because he didn't want to risk being spotted following it on city streets, drove to the Howard Johnson to intercept it."

"The waitress told me she saw him between ten-fifteen and ten-thirty and that he spent around ten minutes inside. To leave the school area about ten and get to the HoJo ten minutes *ahead* of the bus he would have had to have driven at almost twice the limit. The guy's already risking getting stopped for a pollution citation. Is he going to add to the risk, take a chance of getting stopped for speeding with a pipe bomb, a semiautomatic shotgun, and a nine in the car? After all the planning he's done? Don't think so, unless he was twice as screwy as we think."

They turned into Chinatown: a few restaurants, a couple of Oriental groceries, and half a dozen curio shops on narrow streets once dense with carts and stalls and tangy smells, now sterilized into pedestrian malls. At the House of Hunan, an elderly waiter escorted them to a rear booth and asked what they wanted to drink. Gabriel ordered a Beijing beer, Heartwood an extra dry Bombay martini, straight up with olives, thanks. The waiter smiled at him blankly.

"Bombay," Heartwood repeated. "Gin, you know?"

"Oh no gin no whiskee. Beer wine only."

"Try the beer," Gabriel advised. "Better than our weak tea stuff. Should be. East Germans built the brewery."

"So go on," Heartwood urged after the beers arrived.

"Whether Boggs followed the bus from the school or not, it's a mathematical fact that it had to be on the freeway while he was hanging out in the HoJo. So whatever he was there for, *if* he was there for anything but coffee and cigarettes, it wasn't to wait on the school bus. He knew where it had gone, but why did he let his target get out of sight? Why would he take the chance of losing track of the bus just for a pack of smokes and a coffee break and a little chitchat with the waitress?"

"Not very likely on a freeway. A big, yellow and black vehicle. And with a load of children on board, it wouldn't be going eighty. Why did he let it go on in the first place? If he did his homework, as we presume he did, he would have known it had only one direct route to the state park. The freeway to Highway 50 east, then 50 to Route 49 north. So he could have had his ten-minute coffee break, then took off, passed the bus up, proceeded to his ambush site, and waited for it."

The waiter arrived with soup and a steaming plate of fried rice. Heartwood removed from their wrappers a pair of chopsticks and a ceramic scoop. Gabriel picked up the tableware, dipped a fork into the rice, and smiled at Heartwood's puzzled look.

"Wan hunna pahcent Melican, long time Californ. Gabe no usee chopstick. Chopstick for white boy trying to go native. Knife, fork much betta!"

"This white boy will use 'em."

"Listen, I still say that if I was in *that* white boy's shoes, I wouldn't have let that bus out of my sight unless it was for a real good reason."

"We don't want to put ourselves in the guy's shoes. Try to see things the way he saw them," Heartwood lectured with emphatic jabs of the chopsticks. "This crime was well thought out, sure, but it was still the product of a deranged mind. My guess is that the key to his interlude in the Howard Johnson was his comment to the waitress."

"'You're going to find out who I am real soon.'"

"There you go. If my idea about fame is right, there you go."

Heartwood's moo shoo pork and Gabriel's ginger chicken were delivered with a plate of wafer-thin pancakes.

"You put the meat and vegetables in the pancakes," Gabriel instructed. "Fold it over. A kind of Chinese taco . . ."

"I'm from San Francisco, remember?" Heartwood said.

"So explain to this dodo. Boggs knows he gonna be on every anchor's lips from L.A. to Boston if he pulls it off. Why does he have to make an announcement to some roadhouse waitress?"

Heartwood, struggling to assemble the pancake, did not answer. As he bit into it, the filling shot out one end as from a toothpaste tube and splattered grease on his perfect shirt cuffs.

"White boy from San Francisco velly crumsy. Here. Let Chinee boy make for you." Gabriel filled another pancake, neatly folded it lengthwise, then tucked in the ends. "I show you how to eat, you teach me stlange rogic clazy mind, hokay?"

"You can overdo that, you know." He took another bite. "Here it is. Boggs knows he'll be on the anchors' lips, but that's too abstract. He wants, he needs a flesh and blood audience who'll remember him and what he said. You might say Boggs wanted to speak a few last words and he picked the waitress to hear them."

Gabriel's pager beeped. As he reached for it under his jacket, Heartwood caught a glimpse of his holstered pistol, and the sight of that big black gun seemed to speak volumes about the gulf between them. Gabriel was the warrior, he the seeker.

"It's Krimsky. Better see what he wants."

Heartwood followed him to the phones, went into the adjoining booth, and looked up Mace Weathers in the book. A woman answered, an elderly voice. He heard her calling, "Mace, oh, Mace."

Weathers, who spoke in the slightly lazy, drawn-out tones of Southern California, was reluctant to be interviewed. He'd dodged the press so far, he said. Didn't want his name mentioned in the same breath as that filthy creep's. Heartwood assured him their talk would be confidential, and after some hesitation, he agreed to meet at four at his off-campus apartment.

"Lotta news, Professor," Gabriel said when he finished talking to Krimsky.

"Me, too. Weathers will see us at four. By the way, let's make an arrangement so we don't get into bad habits. You don't call me 'Professor' and I won't call you 'Gabe.'"

"Like you'd say, don't be so defensive. The news is, Ruggerio got the psychiatric reports on Boggs released. Copies waiting for us at the city P.D. along with the other stuff. Ballistics, autopsy, Boggs's arrest record, photos."

"The Sicilian pepper works fast when she needs to," Heartwood said, signing the check.

"There's more. Heard from the Dade County sheriff. Mrs. Boggs, or whatever her name is now, left Florida last year. Blown out by the big hurricane. She left an Oakland forwarding address."

"You work fast, too. Anything on the half-brother?"

"Nothing yet. One of our agents in the L.A. field office is trying to track him down." He paused, hiding his lips between his teeth in the way he did, making himself look like an old man with missing dentures. "Funny, the way that kid's vanished into thin air."

When he was an intern and reading Freud, Heartwood often had asked himself, "Does anyone really believe this nonsense?" But there was one Freudian axiom he believed in then and still did: the things that happen to a child affect him all his life. A long time ago, his outdoorsman father dragooned him into a canoe and fishing trip with his friends and their sons. During a long, uphill portage in a thunderstorm, drenched, bitten by black flies, the canoe's gunwales stabbing his shoulders, thirteen-year-old Leander dropped his end and started bawling. His father, who'd been a battlefield surgeon with Patton's Third Army, called him a weakling, and when he wouldn't stop crying, slapped him hard in front of everyone. That moment in the Ontario wilderness had made him forever afraid of appearing weak or soft in the eyes of other men. He'd been that way among the Marine officers in Vietnam, most of whom considered psychiatrists the accomplices of malingerers and cowards. He'd never confessed to those captains and colonels how his heart ached for the boys who were brought to him, trembling or twitching, or stock-still and staring from sights of blood too red, too thick for their minds' absorption.

Sitting with Gabriel in a briefing room in the detective division of the San Joaquin Police Department, he made himself look at the photographs of the massacre when every cell in his being begged him to turn his eyes away. He forced himself to betray no emotion, when every cell in his being begged him to cry out. He assumed Gabriel was all case-hardened steel inside and would hold him in contempt if he did. But when Gabriel looked at the first set of photos, of the fourteen children who lay dead on the steps of the bus or on the road outside the door, he cupped his hand over his mouth to choke back a sob or nausea.

"God almighty," he said in a near whisper, and looked at Heartwood with black and penetrating eyes that seemed to pierce his charade and to reprove him for it. "To get on the bus, he had to . . . "

"I know."

"Walk over them, right over them . . . "

"I know."

"He must have stepped in . . . "

"I know."

"Do you, Lee? I look at these and see my own kids with this done to them. My kids, like this." He gathered the photos from the tables and put them back in their folder, tying its fastener tightly, as if it contained secrets too obscene for revelation. "You know, I've been thinking about what you said, and you were dead wrong. I really did want to find out if Trinh had a human nervous system. Because I think a guy who did what he did couldn't have been a human being. Like this fucking Boggs couldn't have been. They're mutants."

As he usually did when confronted by people with passionate opinions, Heartwood sought refuge in scientific detachment.

"I've got a colleague who'd almost agree that they are mutants," he said. "That something is different about them, neurologically—"

"That brain damage bullshit?" Gabriel interrupted, and suddenly picked up the folder and flung it into a wall. In the corridor outside, two patrolmen were escorting a handcuffed prisoner. One of the cops said, "Phoenix'll take it this year."

"There I go, all pissed off again," Gabriel continued. "Wanna analyze me? Listen, there must be an epidemic of brain damage going on because I've been one kind of cop or another for twenty years and seen my share of shit and every year the shit gets worse."

"I think you finally hit on something we can agree on," Heartwood said, and in that moment saw Boggs as Gabriel did: an alien being. The picture of him walking over the small bodies and stepping in their blood to climb on the bus and claim more victims was as appalling as the picture of him actually murdering the children. It mocked Heartwood's faith in science. Could such savagery be explained by defective chromosomes, depleted levels of serotonin or norepinephrine, or an absence of the MAO-A enzyme? The heart of darkness as neurochemical glitch? Evil's equation? At the moment, the image of evil painted by his Jesuit teachers seemed more true than any equation—scarlet Satan, roaming the earth to seek the ruin of souls.

"So we agree on something. Good," Gabriel said. "I even think my great-uncle Tommy Chin would. He was the one bona fide gangster we had in the family, a real bad actor, my dad told me. But Uncle Tommy wouldn't even have thought of boiling a kid alive to scare some people into forking over. Forget doing it. Put it in the bank, he would've been skinned alive and hung from the highest lamppost in Chinatown if he did. People didn't gave a damn about the why of it back then. They weren't real interested in explanations. There was certain shit they wouldn't put up with, so the shit didn't happen. You said outrage. That's what they had then. Outrage."

"Blame it on the age. It's tough to be outraged when you can turn on *Oprah* and see stuff that would have made the Marquis de Sade nervous."

"*Oprah,* shmoprah." Gabriel rose, picked up the photo folder, and slapped it back on the table. "Okay. Your patient's okay now, Doctor Lee. Got it out of his system. Let's get back to work."

They divided the box of documents according to their specialties. Gabriel took Boggs's arrest records, the El Dorado County sheriff's report on the massacre, and the coroner's autopsy. Boggs's psychiatric history went to Heartwood.

He skimmed the evaluations, and, as he'd expected, they were superficial, forming the equivalent of an explorer's first, tentative sketch of an unknown coast, its contours merely suggesting the shrouded terrain that lay beyond. He began to study the crude charts in detail, noting the prominent features, the bays and headlands, the mouths of the rivers that snaked into the interior.

Thus he learned the details of the child neglect charges filed against Karen Ortiz née Karen Tipton née Karen Boggs in 1985 and 1986. Neighbors told police that her three children had not seen her or her husband, Angel Ortiz, in days. Ortiz was later booked on child abuse and sexual assault charges. Young Duane had returned home from school early one afternoon to find Karen and Angel "engaged in oral copulation on the living room floor." Drunk, enraged at the interruption, Ortiz first slapped the boy in the face, and when Karen tried to stop him from striking him again, hit her with his fist. Duane ran to the kitchen and grabbed a knife, but Ortiz disarmed him; then, pointing the knife at his throat, "forced the boy to commit an act of oral copulation with him." Boggs, his sister, and younger half-brother were taken into protective custody. The two older children were later placed under the care of their paternal grandparents in Walnut Grove, Jacob sent to his father in Fontana. Duane ran away after three months, was picked up for public drunkenness and possession of a dangerous weapon, a knife, and brought to a Sacramento clinic for psychiatric evaluation. He told his interviewer that he wanted to kill his stepfather for "turning me into a gayboy. . . ." Diagnosis: "Strong sociopathic features, homicidal ideation, Boggs appears to be seeking a strong father figure to restrain or guide him. . . ."

Heartwood went to the next report and the next. The shabby chronicle enveloped him in a cloud of disgust and depression. On his legal pad, he compiled statements that Boggs had made to various clinicians, a monotonous litany, but he detected in it a slowly rising curve of fury.

—I never fit in with anybody else.

—I just can't think right. I can't hold on to a job, I'm just not good enough.

—My father was a good guy and my mother's an asshole but she's a lot smarter than my dad ever was. My dad was a retard. His whole family are retard hicks and hillbillies.

—I tried to kill myself last week taking pills, but I guess I didn't take enough. I even screwed that up.

—I've got a bad temper and I'm a violent person, but I'm nowhere's near as violent as I'd like to be.

His tirades against Karen attained the level of a venomous poetry.

—That slut abused and neglected me and my sister and my brother, she's a no-good cocksucking bitch of a child abuser and a cruel, torturing, blackhearted whore, mean and evil.

—I've had to live under bridges and eat out of garbage Dumpsters and suck dick for money on account of that Witchbitch, but I'd rather live under bridges and eat out of Dumpsters and suck dick than live with Dearest Mom.

The last two reports glowed with warnings of the coming firestorm that would engulf Boggs's mind. The first was made after he was arrested with Jacob for the incident in the San Bernardino wilderness. In jail, he attempted suicide by cutting his wrists with his fingernails and, when that failed, by fashioning a noose from his T-shirt. A guard cut him down.

"Despite disassociated thought patterns and evidence of auditory hallucinations, Boggs is capable of understanding the charges against him and is competent to stand trial," the first report concluded. "He should, however, be considered extremely dangerous. He must be kept on a suicide watch as he is a risk to himself, albeit ambiguously; that is, he appears to be a greater risk to others. . . ."

Weren't you right, thought Heartwood. He scanned the last report, written by the Evaluation Division of the Social Security Administration, San Joaquin office:

> Boggs entered this facility on this date (3/8/93) to apply for disability benefits. . . . He stated that he went to live with his sister and brother-in-law in Idaho. He was told to leave their house shortly after New Year's because of his drinking problem. . . . He was fired from a construction job in Florida in late February for drinking on the job. Boggs stated that he had been straight and sober while at his sister's but had begun to use alcohol, Valium, and marijuana afterward to "help me forget my fucked-up life" and to drive "evil, violent thoughts out of my mind." He was arrested for public intoxication two days ago by the SJPD and referred to the D.A.C.O. (Drug and Alcohol Counseling Office). . . .

Heartwood wondered how Boggs would have turned out if those things hadn't happened to him. The drunken stepfather coming at him, and the final degradation at knifepoint. He sifted through other documents, attempting to find a connecting thread in Boggs's itinerant life. Up and down California, a cross-country bolt to Texas, where he enrolled in an auto mechanics course, worked in a repair shop for a few weeks, then ricocheted back to California, enrolled in another mechanics course in a San Joaquin vocational school, dropped out, and went to work in the cannery.

A now-familiar character in the American theater of blood: a loose, lone electron created by the social atom smasher, careening about the country aimlessly, nurturing his resentment and rage, seeking some other human particle to collide with. I am here, at the edges of your town, I am here, unknown, unknown, full of hate, a loaded gun in my pocket or in my car. I am ready and waiting for the moment . . .

Why children?

Heartwood started to make notes.

"Childhood the template for adulthood. That which is endured passively by a child reenacted actively as an adult . . .

"Boggs in San Bernardino jail . . . slashed wrists with fingernails . . .

"If imagination is the only light into Duane's interior, then try to imagine yourself slashing your wrists with your fingernails. That vein is so deep. I've seen patients who failed to kill themselves that way with knives and razors, so what would it take to draw blood with your fingernails? Hate. The depthless self-hate that resides in the schismatic mind. Duane became two people in his cell. Here's an equation.

"Boy victim = adult victimizer. Duane as Duane = Duane as Ortiz."

He paused and turned toward Gabriel, who with his forehead resting on his knuckles, was reading and taking notes of his own. They were like dormmates studying for an exam, an arm's length from one another yet miles apart. Miles apart. White man, yellow man. Chinee boy wan hunna pahcent Melican long time Californ. Yes, but still a foreigner to some. The Other. Heartwood's feet grew warm as the threads of an idea began to weave themselves together. . . .

Why children?

Why Asian children?

Why suicide?

The threads twined and raveled and the warmth rose through his legs.

"Was massacre same act as one in jail, acted out on a bigger scale, bigger stage? Children = foreigners," he wrote. "As foreigners, the children are not like me, as I was not like Ortiz. But as children, the children are me, little me's. Now with my semiautomatic shotgun, I have become the all-powerful, furious father, inflicting pain, meting out punishment on—*myself*. In this act, I become both abused and abuser, the one who bleeds and the one who draws blood . . . "

He lifted his pen and paused. The strand of suicide remained unknit. In the psychopathic suicide, forget conventional logic, find the deranged logic. Of course! If Duane was Ortiz, then Ortiz had to be executed for his crime. I destroy him by destroying—myself. Of course!

His theory had a nice ring, but did it explain Boggs's evil any better than defective chromosomes, depleted serotonin levels? Was this autopsy merely an attempt to make an irrational mind appear rational so people could comprehend? A false imposition of order upon disorder?

He was concentrating so intently that he flinched when Gabriel broke the silence, saying that he needed to check something out.

"When are we supposed to talk to the college guy?"

"Less than an hour."

"I'll be in the Homicide division. Down the hall."

Gabriel had worked with several of the Homicide detectives in the past and they were happy to let him use a vacant desk and to bring him what he wanted—strong coffee and a Triple-A road map of central California.

He sat down, and feeling at home in this noisy room where witnesses were questioned and evidence collected, put his feet up on the desk and spread the map across his upraised legs.

With a ruler he marked off the distance between the Howard Johnson and the junction of Highway 50 with Route 49, then the distance between the junction and the crime scene.

He wrote the mileages down beside his notation of the approximate time of the massacre, 11:50 A.M., and posed himself a problem that reminded him of a school exam. A simple problem, but it soon tied his brain in knots. He phoned Willow, master of chaos theory and blood-spatter analysis. Willow did not sound pleased to hear from him and was downright irate when Gabriel explained what he wanted.

"Do you mean to tell me that you called me away from one of my classes to solve some time and distance problem an eighth-grader could figure out?"

"Hey, Roger, I flunked eighth-grade math."

"Speed equals distance divided by time in minutes multiplied by sixty. Distance equals speed multiplied by time divided by sixty, et cetera. You don't remember how to do that?"

"Listen, this could be important."

"Better be. All right, run the problem past me."

Gabriel did. After a pause of some fifteen seconds, Willow said, "Here's your answer. If Boggs left Point A, the freeway entrance at the Howard Johnson, ten minutes later than the bus, yes, he could overtake the bus and arrive at Point B, the crime scene, ten minutes ahead of the bus without seriously exceeding the speed limit. The truck's average speed on the freeway portion of the trip would be about sixty-five miles an hour, on the secondary road portion about thirty miles an hour. Why is it so important to get the truck there ten minutes ahead of the bus?"

Gabriel raised his eyes toward an acetate board displaying unsolved homicides. A phone rang.

"That's kind of arbitrary. It's what I figure Boggs would have needed to get himself set up. He might have needed a little less, maybe a little more. The main thing I needed to know is that he could leave later than the bus but get there ahead of it without having to do, say, seventy-five or eighty."

Willow's breath in the phone sounded like wind in a seashell.

"What are you trying to prove with all this?"

"Roger, you've been a big help."

He hung up and, thumbing through the record of Boggs's and Jacob Tipton's adventure in the San Bernardino wilds, asked himself, What am I trying to prove?

He put his thoughts on rewind, reeling them back to the incident that had set off the buzzing in his head: Boggs's peculiar coffee break. He could not dismiss Heartwood's explanation; it was plausible. Or Boggs took the break on impulse. Also plausible. He was careless and impulsive, like most petty criminals. Gabriel had formed that impression while studying Boggs's rap sheet: four years ago, he and another street rat committed a purse snatching in Modesto in broad daylight and made their getaway in Boggs's car, which had expired tags. A traffic cop stopped him and his accomplice only minutes later and saw the woman's purse, nestled between them on the front seat. A twelve-year-old would have known better. Boggs was not only careless, he was stupid, he lacked foresight; and those flaws suggested that the explanation growing in Gabriel's mind was as plausible as any other. All the physical and forensic evidence did not support it, but—if Mother Teresa tells you what time it is, check your watch.

He thumbed through the San Bernardino file, coming to the six-page transcript of a sheriff's deputy's interrogation of Jacob Tipton. Most of it was routine stuff, but an exchange on page five had caught his eye in the briefing room. He read it again.

Q: Jacob, you seem like a pretty bright young man. Are you still in school?
A: Yes, sir. I'll be a senior next year. Doing okay, I guess. B-minus average.

Q: So why did you go along with Duane to take target practice with the AK-47?
A: Excuse me, sir. But I didn't take target practice. I never fired the rifle.

Q: My question to you is, what were you doing with Duane in the first place?
A: Well, sir, Duane has always had this thing about firearms. And since he came down from San Joaquin to stay with my dad and me in Fontana, he's gotten mixed up with some rough guys. Bikers. Meth dealers, and—

Q: Jacob, what was your role in this expedition, that's my question.
A: Role? Well, sir, I guess— Duane's older than I. Four years. But he's never been completely right. The times we've been together, recently I mean, it's like I'm the older brother. I have to rein him in.

Q: You're a restraining influence? From what?
A: Duane dreams things up. Scenarios. Like sometimes he's talked about making incendiary devices that can't be traced. Self-destroying I mean. One time, he cooked up this plan to sniper a traffic cop from a bridge. Crazy stuff like that. If I'm there, I poke holes in these ideas.

Q: You mean you stop him from acting on these scenarios, or you help him refine them?
A: Refine them? No, sir. I just tell him that the stuff he's thinking is crazy shit and that he'd be ten times crazier if he ever tried to do any of them.

Q: How about this thing? Was this one of his scenarios? Let me tell you, as a restraining influence, you fell on your ass.
A: Guess so. But Duane's been acting real weird lately. Talking about missions and shit, like he's a commando. When he told me he was going to take target practice I went along to make sure, you know, that he didn't do something really nuts. You never know what Duane's going to do, one minute to the next. Don't think he knows.

Q: So without you there he might have shot up someplace? I see. Tell me, have you ever been arrested before?
A: Four years ago, yes, sir. Vandalism. Duane and I broke the windows in our mother's new car. Duane's idea. She stole Duane's insurance money from his father's death and bought the car with it.

Q: You weren't much of a restraining influence then, either. Anything else on your record?
A: Okay. Solicitation. This summer. A month ago. I went to L.A. for the weekend—

Q: We're talking solicitation for prostitution?
A: Yes, sir. Duane used to do that to get by and I—For spending money was all. For the weekend. I'm not gay and neither is Duane.

Among other things, Gabriel underlined the correct grammar and phrases like "rein him in" and "incendiary device." No double digit IQ under that skull. He turned back to the first page and to the photograph of Tipton clipped to it. A mugshot taken at the San Bernardino substation. It showed a slender young man with shoulder-length hair, dark blond or light brown in color, standing with his head just below the six-foot line on the height chart. Someone with poor eyesight who saw him at night, leaving a motel room hand in hand with a man, might have mistaken him for a tall female. A brief shiver went across Gabriel's back. He supposed he was more liberal than most cops about homosexuality, but he drew the line at homosexual incest. Was he jumping to conclusions? Krimsky would say he was making quantum leaps, yet he was almost certain that it was Tipton whom Khan had seen, one night about ten days before the massacre. And that and Tipton's disappearance and the tantalizing hints in the transcript had all conspired to amplify the doorbell's buzz to a Klaxon's blare.

He studied a diagram of the massacre site, then telephoned the El Dorado chief of detectives, Phil Youngblood, and asked if they could meet at the scene in an hour. Gabriel withheld his suspicions, wishing to avoid starting any rumors that might find their way into the media. The raspy-voiced Youngblood sounded guarded at first. What was Gabriel looking for? All evidence had been gathered and filed. The case was closed.

"Thought it would help this autopsy thing if I walked the ground myself. That's all. I'm not out to second-guess your department's work," Gabriel replied, figuring out the reason for the detective's wariness. "No Monday morning quarterbacking."

"All right. When did you say?"

"Give me an hour. That should give me a good two hours of daylight."

"Might want to use every minute," Youngblood said mysteriously, and hung up.

A few seconds after Gabriel put the phone down, Heartwood hurried in and said it was time to leave.

"Can't make it. Just got a call from Adrienne. Been in a fender-bender. Car's been towed. Needs me to pick her up."

Heartwood looked at him skeptically.

"Nobody hurt, I hope."

"Nah. Only a couple of dents, but Adrienne's a little shook up. You go on ahead. I know the chief. He can loan me one of the department's vehicles."

"Gabriel, what the hell are you up to?"

He didn't answer.

■ ■ ■

He and Youngblood avoided the wide, dark smears that looked like oil or grease spots. Gabriel had seen that in the war—how men would not walk where people had been wounded or killed, as if ground stained by blood violently shed was sacred, cursed, or both. There had been no rain since Friday and the silhouettes of fallen bodies, chalked in blue, showed vaguely on the asphalt. He looked at them and saw the photographs again: the blasted windshield, the sieved fenders, the children sprawled. *He* had walked in their blood, the ground had been neither cursed nor sanctified for *him*, that murdering mutant. Could it get any worse than the massacre? Yes, and it probably would.

"Take you through it from the beginning, near as we were able to reconstruct the sequence," said Youngblood. Listening to his clipped abrasive voice on the phone, Gabriel had imagined a veteran nearing retirement, but Youngblood was indeed young blood, still under forty, with thick, dark brown hair combed straight back, a trim mustache, and a chiseled Anglo-Saxon face that gave him the appearance of a British inspector.

He stepped off the road onto a widened part of the shoulder, hedged by underbrush and sapling oak, Gabriel beside him, breathing in the floral exhalation of the early evening woods.

"Parked here facing the road. Didn't choose this spot on the spur of the moment. Had to reconnoiter. Not many places on this stretch of road where you can pull off." Youngblood motioned at the remnants of tire tracks in the sand-colored earth. "We took casts, matched them to one of his tires that survived the fire. Looked to me like he peeled out of here when he blocked the road. You can see where his rear wheels dug in."

"Any way of telling how long he'd been here?" Gabriel asked, kicking at the tire marks. A stream rushed far below.

"Can't say for sure. Can't say a lot of things for sure. Got here late. When I got the call, I was at the other end of the county. Some campers found a body, badly torn up. Guy who'd been missing from South Lake Tahoe. Suicide. Bears had been gnawing on him by the time the campers found him." Youngblood snorted and smoothed with two fingers the Scotland Yard mustache. "Funny place. This kind of thing going on at one end of the county, black bears eating somebody at the other end."

Gabriel nodded to say yes, it sure was a funny place.

"It's like there's some message in that, damned if I can figure out what. Anyway, when I got here, I saw that my people didn't do the best job of securing the scene. Pandemonium. Paramedics and firemen running all over the place, evac helicopters kicking up the dust, the usual ghouls who show up when something like this happens, a few do-gooders beating the bushes, looking for wounded kids."

"So you might have lost some evidence."

"Might've. Had one guy on the ball. One of my sergeants found two butts on the ground here, right next to each other. One smoked almost down to the filter, but you could make out the brand. Marlboro. Other one smoked halfway. Also Marlboro. Boggs's brand. Butts looked pretty fresh. Could have been his, could have been someone else's, tossed there earlier. If they were his, then figure he waited long enough to smoke one all the way, the other halfway. Ten minutes maybe."

That fits nicely, Gabriel thought. He said, "If they were his, the fact that the second was smoked only partway . . . "

"Suggests that he didn't have the time to finish it. Knew the bus was coming, had to get set. The cigarettes could be kind of key here."

Gabriel, taking two steps to where he estimated the front of Boggs's truck had been, looked south toward the bend in the road some half-a-city-block away. By raising his eyes slightly, he could see the top of the bluff above the bend, but if he held them level, the road was masked by webbed leaves and branches.

Wondering if it were visible from the height Boggs had been sitting at, he looked around for something to stand on.

"Don't bother," Youngblood said from behind him. "To see over that stuff, your eyes have to be about eight, ten feet above the ground. I came out here and experimented myself, the next day."

A little startled, Gabriel turned and met Youngblood's gaze, level and cagey. Realizing that he had a probable ally, he considered dropping the pretense that he'd come here only to get the lay of the land, but he held off. Let things unfold in their own time.

"He could have stood on the roof," he said.

"Awkward. Main thing's the time factor. . . . Look at this."

Gabriel followed him out to the centerline, where he stood in the scorch marks the burning truck had left.

"Three hundred and twenty-two feet to the curve. Sorry for being a master of the obvious, but you'll notice that you can't see around it from here. And of course nothing on the other side can see you. So let's say Boggs got out of his truck, stood at the roadside to see what was coming. Probably left the engine running. The teacher said she smelled fumes just before everything happened. The wind that morning was blowing out of the north, northwest, about down the axis of the highway. Soon as the bus rounded the bend, Boggs would have had to have jumped back into his truck, pulled out to block the road, jumped out, set the truck on fire, and hid himself before the bus driver knew what was happening."

"Have to be a real criminal athlete."

"More like Superman. Saturday, when I was out here, I simulated all that with a deputy timing me with a stopwatch. Best time was eighteen seconds. But in eighteen seconds, figuring the bus was doing around twenty miles an hour, it would have gone roughly five hundred and thirty feet from the curve. Even if it was doing only ten, the driver would've spotted him. Plain language, mathematically impossible for Boggs to pull this off if seeing the bus round the curve was his first warning that it was coming."

Clearly, this detective with the voice that sounded as if his throat were lined with roofing shingle was no back-country Okie lawman.

"You wouldn't happen to know a guy named Willow, would you?"

"No. Why?"

"Just wondering. Okay. Now I'll be master of the obvious. We need to know how Boggs knew the bus was coming before it reached the bend."

The cagey look again cloaked Youngblood's face. He said nothing and walked quickly up the highway, Gabriel alongside, and stopped about five yards short of the curve. A horn warned them off. A maroon car with Utah plates went past. Dad in a floppy, short-brimmed hat behind the wheel. Mom next to him, three kids in the back, all going to visit the mill in whose tailrace a Mormon carpenter long ago saw nuggets glimmering. Off in the woods a crow called raucously.

"Right here, you can see where the bus driver hit the brakes. Soon as he came around. These skid marks are the only physical evidence that shows that the truck was already blocking the road and on fire when the bus made the curve. We've also got the teacher's statement. She said the truck was burning pretty well, but no sign of Boggs until he came out of hiding and started shooting."

Gabriel looked up and down the winding road, dim in the shade of the crowding trees and the vine-trellised bluff that rose on one side.

"How much advance warning do you think he needed?"

Youngblood dropped his eyes to the skid marks and worked his jaw as if he were chewing gum.

"Thirty seconds. No less. Arson went over the truck. Gasoline was the combustible. Best guess is that it was in a flammable container of some kind. Probably a plastic gallon jug. Sort of a Molotov cocktail. A device like that would get a pretty good fire going pretty quick. Bottom line is, Boggs could have done everything I've described with half a minute's warning. He might have wanted a little more, but half a minute would do it."

He frisked himself for a cigarette and muttered, "Damnit, left them on the front seat."

They walked without speaking to where their cars, listing like boats, were parked beside a culvert. A squirrel leapt noisily through the oaks that fell away toward the invisible, rushing stream. Youngblood found his pack, lit up, and leaned against his unmarked cruiser.

"I'm glad you did all this work. It's going to save me a lot of time."

"Wouldn't think you'd need all this for what you're doing."

"Might as well tell you that I didn't come out here for the reason I said."

"Hoping that. Could use a friend in high places."

"I could use a pal or two myself. What is it? You've been muzzled?"

"Not exactly. Sheriff Knowles doesn't buy my idea, doesn't want me to try selling it to anyone else."

"Boggs wasn't alone."

"*Probably* but not *necessarily*. There's another possibility." Youngblood took a shallow drag and crushed the cigarette underfoot, mumbling to himself that he couldn't quit the damned things. "The other scenario, let's call it scenario one, goes like this—Boggs tailed the bus up this road for a distance, clocked it to get an idea of its speed, then pulled out and went just fast enough to put a thirty-second interval between him and it. But he probably built in a safety factor. Gave himself a little buffer. Put a minute between him and the bus. It's averaging twenty, he averages twenty-five. Got to the ambush site, backed in, counted down, then peeled out and . . . "

"Which is why the cigarette butts could be key."

Youngblood gave an exaggerated nod. "That's scenario two. If—*if*—they were his, then he'd been waiting for roughly ten minutes. Maybe longer . . . "

"Unless," Gabriel started to say.

"Unless he'd been smoking one while he was driving. The one smoked down to the filter. Pulls in, tosses it out, lights up the second. Tried to put myself in his place. Smoking while driving a winding, up-and-down road with a Molotov cocktail and black powder pipe bomb in the car. Might not want to risk blowing myself to hell before my time. Now if it had been me, I wouldn't have lit up even with the truck parked, but could be he gave himself a last cigarette."

"Could be. Let's look at scenario two."

"Thought about it till my brain hurt. How could he have known where the bus was during those ten, twelve minutes? How could he have known when it was close enough for him to make his move? He couldn't have blocked the road and everything else five minutes ahead of time. Probably not even three minutes. Suppose another vehicle was between him and the bus? Suppose another vehicle came up from the opposite direction? They'd see the roadblock first and that would have screwed the whole thing up."

"Hell, that's obvious."

Youngblood straightened up, his eyes narrowing.

"Yeah? Talk to Sheriff Knowles. Not so obvious to him. Or maybe it is, but he wants to pretend it's not. If scenario one, yeah, then Boggs could have done everything on his own. It would have taken some fine timing, but it was possible, especially if he'd come out here beforehand and did a dry run or two. A lot of school buses make that field trip, so he could have practiced. But if scenario two, I can't see how he could have sprung it without an accomplice who signaled him."

He made a stabbing movement at the low, jutting bluff, crossed the highway, then climbed a faint trail to the crest of the bluff and stood on a granite slab the size and smoothness of a driveway apron. All around were the Sierra foothills, forested in places and in places opened by fruit orchards in full blossom or by grassy meadows rising toward stands of sequoia and fir. Westward, thin clouds wore striated colors of peach, pale rose, and lavender. It seemed impossible that a crime so awful had been committed in a landscape so beautiful.

"See down there, that's where Boggs hid his truck," Youngblood said, gesturing. "You were there now, you'd be able to see me up here. Also, notice that we can see a little ways beyond the ambush site, we can see if a vehicle is coming up in the southbound lane from the direction of the state park. Now have a look that way." Gabriel's eyes followed his hand as it pointed in the opposite direction, at a straightaway that sloped gently downward for a distance before it ended in another sharp turn. "From the curve below us to that one yonder is a little over three hundred yards. And we can see every yard. All right, the bus appears, the accomplice gives Boggs the signal. How long does it take for the bus to cover three-hundred-plus yards?"

"Don't ask me."

"If it's doing twenty miles an hour, fifty-five seconds. At twenty-five, forty seconds, at thirty, thirty-five seconds."

"Just enough time."

His glance roving freely over the panorama of forest, orchard, and meadow, Gabriel tried to picture the so far theoretical accomplice standing up here, signaling.

"Could he have acted as his own lookout? Spotted the bus, then ran down the trail we just came up, then down the road to the truck, and so forth?"

Youngblood shook his head. "Considered that, tried it myself. If Boggs was an Olympic sprinter, he could have pulled that off. But a second guy would sure have made things a lot easier for him. Hand and arm signal, maybe waving a shirt or a rag. Like Indians in a movie."

"Some Indians these were."

"Some movie. Show you where it ended."

They scrambled down the trail, pushed through a fence of vines and brush, and came into a clearing violet with lupine. A very old tree, knotty and scaled, flung branches thick as young trees over the round, stained top of a partly buried boulder. Where blood had been spilled, the ground was cursed, sacred, or both. Here it was cursed. Gabriel did not have a fanciful imagination and no belief in the occult, so he attributed the chill on the back of his neck to his recognition of this spot from the photograph Landau had shown. If he didn't know what had happened in this clearing, it would seem no different than any other patch of woods. Nevertheless, he couldn't quite convince himself that something wasn't here, some malevolent spirit, hovering in the air. Ten years ago, when he and his father went to the Chin family association to fulfill his granddad's wish for a traditional funeral, an old man versed in ancient ways told them that someone not in mourning would have to ride in the hearse and throw out devil's money to keep demons from molesting the departed soul. "What're you telling us, that we gotta make a payoff, like to a building inspector?" Gabriel's father asked. "Who'm I gonna find to bribe devils? I don't know anybody who believes in 'em." And the old man said, "Oh, I'm not surprised. That's the trouble with everybody in this country."

It certainly was easier to believe in them here, where a tree too old to live lived nonetheless, casting its crooked branches over the rock marked with a mass murderer's blood.

"This is the part that's got me confused," said Youngblood, returning Gabriel to more immediate concerns. "Makes me doubt my doubts Boggs was alone."

"How's that?"

"First, I would've thought the other guy would've opened fire, too. But the ballistics is clear. Nothing but buckshot. And Boggs had two twelve-round magazines and we recovered eighteen shells and found six unfired in the second magazine. Second, seems out of whack to have one perp who kills himself, while the other one gets away. Doesn't make four in my math book. Would've thought they both escape or die together. Suicide pact maybe. Third, no evidence, not a damn dime's worth that anyone else was here, up on the bluff, anywhere around. No footprints, fingerprints, loose change, clothing fibers, matchbooks, cigarette butts, nothing. Nothing that didn't have a good explanation."

"You mean there were plenty of footprints and whatever, all belonging to the people who were running around here. The medics, the do-gooders."

Youngblood's face colored.

"Like I said, my people didn't do the best job of securing the scene, so who the hell knows what got lost? Searched the area for about a hundred yards around looking for prints. There's a hiking trail leads off back to the park. I would have used that for an escape route. Footprints all over it, probably from a hundred different hikers. Never be able to trace whose was whose. If there was another guy, he knew what he was doing. Got away without a trace. If I had *something* . . ."

"Make it 'we.' You and your friend in high places."

Moving closer to the rock, Gabriel could see the faded outline an evidence technician had drawn around the corpse. The outline Heartwood wanted to fill in. Match the criminal to the crime. Poor match so far, but a second man made things fit. Boggs had fallen with his head facing away from the road, his right arm flung outward. Between the head and arm was the long bloodstain, dried now to a coffee color, broadening as it flowed down the side of the rock and into the dark earth. Landau's photograph flashed in his memory again. Boggs lying like a fallen soldier, rigored fingers half-closed, the nine on the ground about a foot away. Something not right, out of place. Like one of those puzzles. What's wrong with this picture? Gabriel hadn't worked on enough suicide cases to say. Three in his career and only one with a firearm.

"I know what the coroner said, the ballistics tests. Know his prints were on the piece. How about you? You sure he did it to himself?"

Youngblood again made an overdrawn nod.

"On top of all that, we've got the teacher's statement. She saw him put the piece to his head, like he'd meant to kill himself out on the road. Then he lowered it, ran into the woods, and bingo. Bye-bye Boggs. Now why he did it that way beats me. But there's no doubt in my mind that he did it. The way the gun fell, the powder residue on his hands."

Gabriel stared at the outline. Fill in the blanks.

"So what are we, a bush-league Sherlock Holmes and Dr. Watson with a goofy idea?"

"You be Holmes."

"Not you? You look like one of those Brit detectives."

"Rather be Watson. He doesn't take the heat when things go wrong. Far as my boss is concerned, case is closed. Only thing we haven't got is the motive and he figures you and your team will come up with that, for whatever it's worth at this point."

"What is it with him? Is he dumb or lazy?"

"Politician."

"And without something to go on . . . "

"Yup. The chances of finding the other guy are slim to none. And the crime the media keeps calling the worst of its kind in California history goes unsolved on Knowles's watch."

"So I'll get to work trying to find something to go on. Boggs's clothes, personal effects. Who's got those? You or the coroner?"

"They're in our evidence locker."

"No problem turning them over to me? I know a gal in the lab who could find the pubic hair on a mosquito. Trace evidence specialist."

"No problem," Youngblood said. "Didn't know mosquitos had pubic hairs."

"If they did, Jean would find them. And if anybody can help us find the other guy, it's her."

"You sound more convinced than I am that there was another guy. How come?"

"A funny noise in my head."

"Knowles would love to stake his rep on that."

"What about you?"

A songbird trilled in one of the branches twisting above them. Youngblood turned and began walking back toward the road, his hands in his pockets, his cagey eyes on the ruined shine of his shoes.

"I like the way you handle yourself," Gabriel said when they returned to their cars. "We could use people like you. Not that I'm recruiting, but think about it. We don't get calls about bears."

"I *like* getting calls about bears. I like bears and woods, working a jurisdiction where the trees outnumber the people thousand to one."

"The trees and the bears didn't stop Boggs from coming in. There's nowhere to run anymore. No place the bad stuff won't find you when it wants to, so you might as well stare it in the eye."

"Any more bad stuff like what happened Friday, I'll move to Alaska. Last frontier. The bears there are grizzlies." He watched a dump truck crawl past, its engine howling as the driver downshifted around the oxbow bend. "You know, the sergeant who found the cigarette butts broke down when the excitement was over and he had time to think. I had to give him three days off. It's different when something like this happens to kids."

"Different, yeah. It's different, all right. That's why I'm going to find the filthy son of a bitch, and when I do, I hope and pray the scumbag makes a run for it, or better yet, tries to draw down on me."

Youngblood pulled a card from his wallet and handed it to Gabriel. "If you need a hand. Strictly when I'm off duty. It would have to be like a hobby."

"Hey, I'm told everybody needs one."

"He told me he'd be late, but I didn't think it would be twenty minutes," said Mrs. Van Huesen with a fluttering of her liver-spotted hands. "Why, he's so prompt you can set your watch by his comings and goings." She was so apologetic about Weathers's tardiness, so eager to praise his virtues—best tenant she ever had, rent always there first of the month, not like most of the college kids she rented to—that Heartwood was ready to believe she was Weathers's grandmother instead of his landlady.

She offered another cup of tea. His kidneys bursting, he turned her down with a wag of his finger and asked if he could use the bathroom.

"Of course you can!" Mrs. Van Huesen declared, her ancient hands clasping tightly the wings of her armchair. "Down the hall. First door on the right."

He went into the hall through a square arch trimmed darkly in walnut. Vintage family photographs covered one wall: sepia portraits of women in lace-collar blouses and men with long whiskers; a black-and-white of a brother or husband or cousin in the uniform of the old

Army Air Corps; color snapshots of teenage grandchildren. This house with its sense of generational continuity, its somber moldings and twelve-foot ceilings depressed him; it was too much like the one on the cold shores of Green Bay, where he'd spent his comfortable but unhappy boyhood, the only boy in a family of five ruled by a troubled mother and a father who believed that true manhood was nurtured in duck blinds and deer camps.

He flushed the toilet, dried his hands, and carefully combed a kinky lock over his bald spot.

Outside, the front door opened and closed, and he heard Mrs. Van Huesen's voice, Weathers's cool, level baritone. He stepped out and saw in the foyer a tall, tanned young man with hair the color of freshly cut maple and a torso that strained against his oxford shirt. Except for the patch worn over his left eye, he looked like a Laguna surfer who'd ridden a freak wave a hundred miles inland.

Smiling, Mrs. Van Huesen introduced them. Heartwood felt puny beside Weathers, conscious of his fifty years, his waning powers that no amount of jogging or calisthenics could restore.

"The detective couldn't make it?" Weathers asked.

"He had a problem at home to take care of. I'm pretty sure I can handle things on my own."

"From what I've heard about you, I'll bet you can."

"What have you heard?"

"A lot, a lot." Weathers's lips parted, showing two pointy, slightly protruding eye teeth that spoiled what would have been a perfect smile. "I'm from Redlands. I was a senior in high school when that rapist was going around. The girls in school were scared to go out. I didn't know you're the guy who caught him until I told my criminal psych teacher that you were going to interview me."

"I didn't catch him," Heartwood offered in a not altogether successful effort to sound modest.

"My teacher's jealous. She said she'd like to talk to you. Or have you address our class. She said you're one of the foremost forensic psychiatrists in the country. It's an honor to meet you. I'm flattered you think I can help you out."

"Well, thanks for that," said Heartwood, somewhat perplexed by the formality of the testimonial. No one under forty spoke like that anymore. "Maybe we could get started."

"Sure. My room's upstairs."

It was in the turret of the house: a small but sunlit room with a sloped ceiling that made it seem smaller. Weathers kept it neat to a fault. The Marine sergeants Heartwood had known in the war would have given a good conduct medal for the bed, its cover drawn so tautly that it almost quivered from the vibrations of footsteps on the swept, varnished floor.

"You can sit over there."

Heartwood ducked under the slanting eave and sat down, balancing his legal tablet and writing pad on his lap. With a tug at his trousers, Weathers sat at the desk, crossed his legs, and ever so carefully pulled at his cuff to straighten his crease.

"Did you go to military school?"

"My mother and father's training. Mormons."

"Sorry. I don't get the connection."

"Ever been to Salt Lake City? Spiffiest town in America. Mormons are so clean they squeak."

They killed five or ten minutes getting acquainted. Weathers said that he was a senior, a psychology major, and that he would graduate after the next term. This semester should have been his last, but he'd been set back because of . . . well, call it an accident. He pointed to the eyepatch and hesitated a beat, inviting questions about it.

"Car accident?"

"No. It's kind of a long story. Here, this will tell you quicker than I can."

He opened a desk drawer and pulled out a copy of the story that had run in *State Lines,* the college newspaper. Heartwood glanced at it, put it in his briefcase, and then explained how a psychiatric autopsy worked. He went to some pains to point out that anything Weathers told him would be kept strictly confidential.

"Why are you making such a big deal about confidentiality? I don't have anything to say that's confidential."

"You seemed concerned about that on the phone." For reasons he could not quite identify, Weathers made him a little uncomfortable. Possibly it was his cramped, overly organized room, where even the dust seemed to have settled in regular patterns. "I like to make sure that the people who were close to Boggs or who knew him fairly well feel free to speak their minds."

Weathers turned away and lightly ran his fingers over his computer keyboard. "Close to Duane? Where did you get that idea? Boggs and I weren't friends, and if you read that story you'll know why." He pointed to his eye patch. "A racist pig like Duane did this to me."

"I meant that you might have known him better than most people. Your old foreman, Somers, suggested to us that you had a better fix on Boggs than he did."

"Suppose that's true. So who else do you talk to on this kind of thing?"

"Duane's mother, his sister, and half-brother, if we can find them. Maybe to his grandparents, if they're willing to talk to us."

Weathers stared, blinking rapidly, and Heartwood noticed that he had exceptionally long lashes. They gave his eye an almost feminine quality that made a jarring contrast with the brutal body.

"You go pretty deep, then, talking to grandparents. I'm asking because I know my abnormal psych prof is going to ask if I learned anything."

"Usually, I don't go beyond the immediate family, but Duane's grandparents had custody of him when he was thirteen or fourteen." He uncapped his pen and slouched a little, trying to relax in the hope it would help Weathers loosen up a little. Compared to David and his prep-school friends, with their baggy khakis and mismatched blazers and sloppy postures, this guy was as well-dressed and rigid as a window dummy. "I'm going to get to Duane's racism in a minute, but . . . This might strike you as off the wall, but what kind of chess player was Boggs?"

"Chess player? *Boggs?*" Weathers scoffed.

"You and he did play chess at the cannery, didn't you?"

"A few times, but that didn't make us great buddies."

"That isn't why I asked. I know you weren't great buddies. Somers made that pretty clear. Said you couldn't stand Boggs."

"He did?"

"Yes, he did. Why, are you surprised?"

"No. I just didn't think he would have mentioned that."

"You'd asked not to work with Boggs anymore. He was lazy. Apparently, he had an aversion to baths and changing his clothes."

"He was a mess!" With startling, sudden animation, Weathers pitched forward in his seat. "A filthy, stinking mess! I can't stand messes or messy people."

"I can see that. So, back to the chess."

"You know, I don't understand why the way Boggs played chess . . . What's that got to do with what you're after?"

"Why do you keep answering my questions with questions?"

Weathers, with a strained smile, bared again the sharp, protruding eyeteeth. He'd had orthodontic work when he was young, a shoddy job. The two teeth, misaligned with the front, looked like incipient fangs.

"Are you trying to analyze *me*?"

"Yeah. In a way. My fault for not explaining to you earlier. When you do a psychological autopsy, you have to get an impression of the people who knew the victim, so you can learn how he struck different people. What you look for is a consistency or inconsistency of report. Did Boggs strike different kinds of people in different ways? Or different people in the same way? Okay, okay?"

From one side to the other Weathers crooked his massive neck corded with muscle and tendon. Heartwood was unable to tell if this movement signaled a readiness to go on or was some sort of sitting calisthenics.

"I can understand why this makes you uncomfortable. It's disturbing to be reminded that you once worked side by side with a guy who turned out to be a monster. Right?"

"I didn't realize that I seem uncomfortable."

"Yeah, you do. Relax. This won't hurt."

"I guess you're right about wanting to . . . to put some distance between me and him. You know, a few reporters came around wanting to interview me. 'What was Boggs like? Do you think he was racist?' I just had to tell them 'No comment.' I figured it would embarrass my parents if my name got in the papers or I was on TV. You know. People start asking, 'Were you that guy's *friend*?' Like he and I knocked back brews together after work or something. Knowing Boggs isn't exactly what I'd like to be known for."

"That's my point about confidentiality. By the way, *did* you ever have a beer with him? Ever an occasion when you two just talked about things?"

"Are you kidding? You spend eight hours around him, the last thing you want to do is drink with him."

"Yeah, I can imagine. So now can we get back to your chess matches? What kind of a player was Duane?"

"How do you mean?"

"Seems simple enough. Was he good or bad? Did he ever beat you?"

"Oh, come on! Duane?"

"Don't take it as an insult. There are idiot savants."

"He never beat me, but then I'm pretty good. I taught Duane a few variations, you know, to get him to a level where playing him wouldn't be a bore. I was in the chess club in high school. No points or anything like that, but I'm a lot better than your average player. Do you play?"

"Used to. College, the service. So you'd say Duane was average?"

"Do you mean how he handled his openings? His endgame? If you could be more specific, I could . . . "

"Mace, don't complicate things. I simply want to know what kind of player he was. Was he thoughtful and deliberate? Did he plan his moves ahead? Or did he play one move at a time? Was he impulsive? When you beat him, did you do it easily? Or did he give you a good match? Specific enough for you?"

Weathers turned toward the window and looked out at the fading, late afternoon light. He was a very handsome guy, though in the unremarkable, unmemorable way of a male fashion model. Without the eye patch, he would leave a pleasing but fleeting impression. There was something undistinctive about his jaw, his slender mouth, and aquiline nose. Even his eyes were neutral: a hazel that shaded more to gray than green. And his voice went with his appearance; he spoke in the uninflected tones Heartwood would have pegged as a chronic depressive's. His mother had spoken like that during her episodes.

"Deliberate, thoughtful," Weathers said finally. "Almost too deliberate. He'd take too much time figuring out his moves. You could tell that he knew the moves, you know, if black bishop's pawn two to pawn four, then white knight takes pawn. But where somebody like you or I would figure that out in seconds, it would take Boggs longer."

"So he wasn't impulsive? You'd say he had a capacity for logic, planning?"

"Oh, yeah, definitely. Far as chess went anyway."

"Can you think of any other time he displayed this trait?"

Weathers donned a pensive frown.

"One time, yes. Not something he did but talked about doing. There was one thing about Duane. He didn't talk much. We'd go two, three days on the job and hardly say a word to each other. But sometimes he'd get high and blabber a mile a minute."

"He'd get high on the job?"

"He'd come to work buzzed. Coke, speed. I don't know. One of these times, he started talking about this plan he'd worked out to ambush a carload of Mexican illegals from some bridge. In Chula Vista I think it was. He told me he'd been down there once and he'd watched a van coming up from Tijuana on I-5. It pulled off and a bunch of illegals jumped out and ran for it. That pissed him off because nobody did anything, nobody tried to stop them. He was really pissed off. He said, 'Those fuckin' wetbacks, they're like invaders, like an army invading the U.S.' Something like that—"

The click of the tape recorder interrupted him. Heartwood flipped the cassette, then motioned to him to go on.

"His idea was to get on that bridge some night with a gun and a load of firebombs. He was going to drop one of the bombs on the first vehicle he saw with Mexican plates. Like a mini–napalm bomb, he'd said. Naturally, that would stop the traffic behind it. He was going to toss more bombs at the stalled vehicles and then start shooting when people came running out of the cars. When the cops came, he was going to throw the rest of his Molotov cocktails at them, surround himself in a ring of fire. He was going to shoot through the flames until he ran out of ammunition or the cops brought him down."

"Fantastic!" Heartwood set down his pen and loosened up his fingers. "What was your reaction to all this?"

"My reaction? My reaction, right." He rose from his chair and took two steps to the window, his leather soles creaking on the bright oak floor. As he stood there, his tall, dense body did not seem to block the light so much as draw it into himself. "My reaction was pretty much what you'd expect. I didn't take him seriously, thought he was just spouting off some nutty fantasy."

"Did you say as much to him? Did you ask him why he wanted to stage this one-man Götterdämmerung?"

"He said everybody would remember him. Everybody talked about beaners and boat people taking over California, but nobody had the balls to do anything about it. He was going to do something and go down in flames doing it. Be a hero. Be famous."

"He actually *said* that to you? That he wanted to go down in flames and be famous?"

"His exact words were, 'Everybody's gonna remember who I am.'"

Heartwood had not expected a vein so rich. What he was hearing now was the next best thing to interviewing Boggs himself. He saw the vectors converging: Duane's racial hatreds, his lust for fame, his compulsion to be both victim and victimizer.

"I want to make sure of one thing. Boggs definitely said 'going to'? Not 'If I did that, everyone would remember me,' but 'Everybody's *going to* remember me'?"

"Remember it clearly."

"So would it be your impression that he'd made up his mind to do something as long ago as last summer? Maybe he didn't know what precisely, but that he'd decided on some course of action?"

Weathers stiffly shrugged his football player's shoulders. "I can't say. You're asking me to read his mind."

"And you never mentioned any of this to anyone?"

He cranked his body around in a half-turn, smoothed a wrinkle in his shirt.

"Do you mean *should* I have mentioned it? Yeah, looking back. It should have been obvious that Boggs was going to do something awful some day. Inevitable. But I didn't realize it until he actually did something. So, yeah. I should have mentioned it. Maybe to the cops—keep your eye on this guy. He's dangerous. But I didn't, so now fourteen kids are dead."

"Mace, there were people in authority who should have done something. You can't blame yourself," Heartwood said, though he didn't know for sure if Weathers did. There was something impenetrable about him, something that took in light but let none out. The handsome but wooden face, the automaton's speech. He'd noticed that Weathers seemed aware of the deficiency in his voice; once in a while, as he had in his last comment, he tried to vary his monotone, but always managed to stress the wrong word. So instead of "And now *fourteen kids* are *dead*," it had come out as "And *now* fourteen kids *are* dead." It was as if he were tone deaf, unable to match his vocal notes to the emotions he wanted to convey.

"Ask you something? Do you think any good will come of this?"

"The attorney general thinks so. Her office is going to issue a report when I'm done. It'll be full of recommendations. Like all the other reports full of recommendations that nobody ever acts on."

"I didn't mean what you're doing. I meant the massacre."

"I fail to see what good could come of that."

"But doesn't some good come out of the worst things? Like World War Two. What could have been worse than that, but look at all the good things that came out of it."

"I don't think you can make a comparison between the war and what happened Friday."

"I was just illustrating that sometimes it takes evil things to make the good things happen. It seems to me, well, that . . . Don't you feel sometimes that Chaos's hour is near?"

Heartwood was nonplussed by the portentous phrase and the textureless voice that uttered it. He might have been asking, "Don't you think it's time for lunch?"

"Never thought of it that way. But I suppose anyone who reads the papers, watches the news, and doesn't think something's gone way off track would have to be . . . "

"Blind!" Weathers half-rose off his seat in one of his fits of animation. "Exactly what I think. People are blind. You'd think something like the massacre would help make them see and, and . . . "

"And what?"

"I don't know," he said, turning to stare for a long minute at the blank screen of his computer.

"I have to move on to other things. Your opinion of Boggs is no mystery, but how do you think he felt about you?"

The broad shoulders rose up and down as if drawn by pulleys. His whole body seemed a thing powered by pneumatics and hydraulics, projecting not a supple, animal power but mechanical advantage.

"I'll put it another way. Do you think Boggs might have looked up to you? Respected or admired you?"

He smiled weakly and shook his head. Heartwood flipped through his legal pad.

"Here it is. Somers told us this. 'Boggs followed him around like a trained puppy. If Weathers wanted a Coke or a candy bar, Boggs would fetch it for him. Anybody else had asked him to do that, he'd tell him to fuck off.' "

"I'm not sure what you're getting at."

"I am trying to see things through Boggs's eyes, best as I can. In this case, I'm trying to get a picture of your relationship from his point of view."

"Relationship? We didn't have a relationship. What're you talking about?"

There was a knock. Weathers opened the door a crack. A young black man peered inside and said, "Sorry, didn't know you had company," and patted his pocket.

"Later, Pickett," Weathers told him in an undertone. Before he could shut the door, a cat slipped between his legs into the room.

As soon as he saw the animal, a long-haired mixed breed with a bushy black tail and black and white markings that made it resemble a miniature, furry dairy cow, Heartwood reached for his handkerchief. His eyes welled up burning, his nostrils prickled, and he sneezed so hard his glasses slipped from the bridge of the nose. He sneezed twice more and gestured to Weathers to put the cat out.

"Here, Spats, c'mere," he cooed, bent at the waist, stalking. The cat leapt onto the desk, scampered across the computer keyboard, jumped back down to the floor, then cowered in a corner. The creature was shedding even as it crouched, motionless. Black and silvery hairs ascended shimmering in the windowlight. Heartwood sneezed again.

"You little son of a bitch, I said, c'mere!" shouted Weathers.

He lunged, and with a swift stab of an arm, snatched the cat by the scruff of its neck. As he held it, writhing and twisting and hissing, he shoved the door aside with his foot and slung the animal into the hallway. It screeched and fled, its claws making against the bare floor a noise like branches scraping a windowpane. Mrs. Van Huesen called from the floor below, "Oh, no, Spats! Have you been in Mace's room again?"

"I told you to keep him away from here!" Mace called down.

"Yes, Mace. I'm sorry."

He came back into the room and, with a disgusted look, brushed hairs from his shirt.

"Damned little son of a bitch. Sheds all over the place. Look at this stuff! Look at this mess!"

He pulled a Dustbuster from the closet and crept around the room, tracking down hairs, and when he was done, stripped off his shirt, revealing biceps and chest muscles that bulged unnaturally, then pulled a fresh shirt from a closet where clothes hung as systematically as in a men's store. Calm and composed again, the wooden mask back in place, he returned to his desk chair and resumed his cross-legged posture.

"Sorry about that. I try to keep her out of here. Sounds like a bad allergy you've got."

"Cats are my worst, with pollen second."

"You were asking me?"

Heartwood said nothing, studying him for a moment or two. The outburst had been a little disturbing, though it wasn't atypical of the obsessive-compulsive personality. They lose it when anything is out of place or a speck of dirt appears.

"You were doing the asking. You wanted to know what I'm getting at. It's what I said before. A consistency or inconsistency of report. The different ways Duane reacted to different people. Apparently, if most people asked him to do something, even a little thing like getting a Coke, he'd tell them to buzz off. But he didn't with you. So I'm wondering if you could shed some light on why that was so."

"No," he answered coldly. "I don't even remember Boggs following me around like a trained puppy dog." He turned toward his desk clock. "Are we about wrapped up? I have to meet my lifting partner at the gym."

"One last thing. After Duane quit the cannery, did you ever see him or hear from his again?"

Weathers appeared to examine a spot on the otherwise spotless floor. He crooked his neck, three times to one side, three times to the other. When he raised his head, the single gray-green eye began to rapidly blink again.

"Are you talking about D.A.C.O.?"

"The rehab place Duane was signed up at? Dropped out after a couple of weeks, the files said."

"The files?"

"On Duane. The records of his psychiatric treatment."

"Oh, those. Yeah. I work part-time at D.A.C.O. Clerical stuff mostly. I get credit for it for a course I'm taking on the psychology of addiction."

"Duane . . ." Heartwood said.

"Yeah. Well, what they really use me for is kind of like a bouncer. To make sure none of the people that come in there get out of hand. I drive them home if they need it. The cops bring drunks there sometimes instead of jail. A lot of drunks and druggies in this town. That one night, I think it was in early March, who came in, trashed to the max, but Duane? I didn't even recognize him at first. He had long hair and didn't have a mustache when I worked with him. But he recognized me. 'Mace!' he said, like I'm his long-lost brother. After he straightened out a little and a counselor talked to him, I took him back to that fleabag. The Camino Real."

This was getting interesting.

"Helluva coincidence, I'd say."

"How so?"

"You don't think it was a coincidence, the two of you crossing paths again?"

"If you believe in coincidences, I suppose."

"You don't?"

"Things happen for a reason. Most times, we don't know what the reason is, so we call it chance or an accident or a coincidence."

"Did you guys talk about anything after not seeing each other for nine, ten months?"

"It wasn't a reunion, Dr. Heartwood."

"You two didn't say a word? He must have said something. What was your impression of him?"

"He wasn't real coherent. Still pretty trashed. I think he said something about living with his sister and that it didn't work out. Something about a job in Florida that didn't work out either. That's Boggs for you. One of those dirtbag losers nothing ever works out for."

"Did you see him after that?"

Weathers studied the spot once more and rubbed it with his fingertip.

"Like you said, he dropped out of the program."

"How about on the street? Run into each other?"

"Why would we?"

"Why don't you tell me."

"Damn. I told you. I couldn't stand him. And I kind of sensed that he was, oh, at the end of his rope. Needy. Yeah. Needy. That was my impression of him. Needy, like a starved, stray cat that shows up at your door. You could tell that if you ever let him in, you'd never get him out. Maybe I should have. I've wondered the past few days if he did what he did because he felt cut off from everything and everybody." He looked at the clock again, grabbed his gym bag, and stood. "Got to go . . . "

Heartwood flipped through his notes, then rose, bumping his head against the sloping ceiling. Weathers let out a short, mechanical laugh.

"Took me a year before I learned not to do that." He extended his hand. "Well, if you think of anything else . . . "

Heartwood handed him a business card. "In case you do. Call collect. Won't be at that number for the next three, four days. You can reach me at the Camelia House in Sacramento."

They went downstairs to the front porch, where a bench swing hung from rusting chains. Weathers pointed at the Porsche.

"Yours?"

Heartwood nodded.

"I might get one of those someday. But my Camaro looks pretty good, doesn't it? For a '78?"

It looked in fact brand-new, its cream top and pale yellow body unblemished.

"This really is the last thing," Heartwood said, going down the steps. "If you had to describe Duane with one word, what would it be?"

Weathers paused, exercising his neck again. Three times to the left, three to the right.

"Feral," he said.

They made a tableau as they stood in a semicircle by the front door: Jack Crenshaw and his slender wife, Marge, then Theresa, wearing a loose dress over her voluminous bosom and hips, white-haired Estaban, and finally Joyce's mother, ponderous and dour, thick calves showing between her pleated gray skirt and the clumsy shoes that midwestern women seemed to fall into the day they reached sixty-five.

Alex pulled the Volvo wagon into the drive. With the alacrity and some of the awkwardness of a boy on his first prom, he got out, opened Joyce's door, and offered his arm. She hesitated. Getting into and out of cars and climbing up and down stairs, acts once as unconscious as breathing, now required forethought and effort. Think of them as *challenges*, the hospital's repulsively upbeat physical therapist had said when teaching her to use her new crutches. More like a royal pain in the ass, Joyce thought. She clapped the crutches together, clutched the grips, and, grasping Alex's forearm, pushed herself upright. Step one. Standing with both crutches under her right arm, she got her balance, then transferred one crutch to her left arm, and hopped onto the lawn to give Alex room to shut the door. Step two.

"How're you doing, hon?"

She nodded to say that she was doing fine. Her injured leg, its throbbing dulled with Percocet, was in a brace from the knee down. She held it rigidly in front of her in a suspended kick.

"All right, then." Alex attempted to look solicitous, but the lines in his long, lank face made his expression more mournful than considerate, as if she were a wife declared terminally ill and sent home to die.

Alex beside her, Joyce swung herself across the lawn, past a bright girdle of poppies and snapdragons, and beneath the cherry trees that had been fully blossomed when last she'd seen them, a mere four days ago. Now they were past peak, and the wind swooping down from the Sierras raised a bunch of white petals to send them flurrying past the faces of the people awaiting her at the front door.

She looked at them and at the house, its stone walls blued in the dusk. Theresa's old Ford and Estaban's truck, with the name of his landscaping service hand lettered on its doors, were parked alongside the house. Those two good hardworking people had delayed going to their homes to welcome her back to hers, which made her feel ridiculous and unworthy, as if she were impersonating a returning war hero. She did not consider herself any sort of hero, regardless of what the papers called her. It wasn't courage that had impelled her to rescue Paul Lim; a courageous act was performed when you were aware of the consequences, but she'd reacted as an animal does, without a thought. And there had been a touch of banality about her injuries. The doctor told her he'd fixed limbs hurt worse in falls from ladders and in skiing accidents. Of course, he was a repairman of the human body and didn't realize that the real damage had nothing to do with bones, ligaments, and joints.

"Do you need a hand going farther?" Alex asked.

"No. I'm okay, really. How's Ghost? I'd like to see her."

"Ghost is fine. I've fed her, exercised her, mucked out her stall and she's fine."

"I'd like to see her. Now."

"But . . . " With a frown, Alex motioned to the five people, who suddenly struck her as a gauntlet she had to run.

She couldn't do it, not quite yet, and pinning a smile to her face, she called out in a falsely cheerful voice, "Hello, everyone! Go inside and make yourselves comfortable. I'll be right along." Then quietly to Alex, "Look after them, will you?"

He nodded. Had she been hurt in a fall or in a skiing accident, he would have lectured that it was an insult to greet her horse before she did those who loved and cared for her, but she had touched and been touched by the Great Mystery and was to be indulged in her whims.

He went to see to the guests while she propelled herself down the road to the barn, the dusty road she'd ridden or walked on countless times but now seemed to be treading for the first time. The barn lay fifty yards ahead, down a little slope. The old vineyard marched up the hillside behind it, the pruned, dry-farmed vines gnarled and leafless, like November trees. Dry farming stressed them. Dying of thirst, the vines sent forth one final burst of life and poured their distilled essence into the grapes, producing a small berry with an intense flavor. Anyone who drank the DeLuca old-vine zinfandel therefore tasted the fruit of a viniferic death throe, a great beauty created by a great anguish. After harvest, the vines were irrigated and brought back from the edge of extinction, only to be subjected to the same torment the next season.

Pausing to gaze at them in the gathering dusk, she could almost sense the panic that rose, year after year, from the parched roots to the trunks, from the trunks to the canes and spurs. She identified with them, for as she lay bleeding in the culvert, thinking she was dying, her own life forces created that intensity of consciousness, that beatific instant when she felt that she had become almost pure consciousness, released from the material world and her corporeal self. Oh, to experience that again! She had seemed so near to understanding . . . what? Some great truth. That was the only way she could express it, though she had in the past day or two wondered if it had been an apprehension of God. Then why had it slipped so swiftly away?

She entered the double dusk of the barn and drew in the odors of hay and manure, of old wood, old leather, and Ghost's musky flesh. The mare, recognizing her mistress, snorted and pawed in her stall. Joyce leaned against the stall gate for support and rubbed Ghost's face and petted her neck, loving the suedelike smoothness of her skin, feeling through her palm the pulse of life, warm and quick.

"How's my girl? How's my big temperamental girl?"

Ghost pawed again, thinking they were going for a ride. Joyce explained it would be at least a month before she could.

With one big oval eye, aglow in a sliver of twilight seeping through a crack in the wall, the mare looked down and seemed to ask what was wrong.

And Joyce told her of all that had happened. She spoke of her wound and her luck. Had she been a mere five yards closer to *him* (she could not bring herself to utter his name, as if it were an evil incantation that would summon him up), she certainly would have bled to death out there, died with her children in the Motherlode Country. And why hadn't she? What had given her the five yards that made all the difference? Blind luck or Providence, and if Providence, then what was she to do with the gift of years it had granted her?

Ghosts flapped her lips—an answer more succinct but no less satisfactory than the one Joyce heard from the psychologist Fran Bigelow had sent to her bedside yesterday afternoon. Fran thought she could use some counseling before her release. The psychologist, a fortyish woman with frosty blond hair lacquered to the point that a hurricane could not have mussed it, had been among those dispatched to the McKinley School to administer emotional first aid to the surviving students. These days, school districts all over the country kept such paramedics on call.

The woman was bright and well-meaning—they were all bright and well-meaning—and she'd answered Joyce's question with a long oration about post-traumatic stress disorder and methods of coping with survivor's guilt. Joyce listened with growing resentment and at last cut the woman off with a chopping movement of her hand and said that she did not want to learn to cope. To cope with the horror would be to diminish its horror. It wasn't the sort of event that ought to be coped with. Would the psychologist have counseled a Jew to *cope* with the Holocaust, or a woman like Sokhim to *cope* with Khmer Rouge genocide? She couldn't listen to the woman's psychobabble, the dead language with which people sought to tame the wild, dark turmoils of the human soul. She wasn't going to allow anyone to trivialize what had happened by squeezing it into a bland category of emotional trauma.

"You're talking to me like I lived through a plane crash or something," she'd said. "I saw a bright, curious, wonderful boy named Billy Pate die with his arm blown off. I saw a sweet twelve-year-old named Rose Ortega nearly blown in half by a maniac with a shotgun. Her guts were lying in the road like a dead animal's, do you understand? *I saw that.* This might surprise you, lady, but I don't feel guilty that I survived all that. Not the slightest. I'm glad I did. All I want to know is why I did. Was it for some purpose or not? Answer that and then I'll consider this visit worth the time."

The woman fingered one of her earrings; she was as nonplussed as a telemarketer interrupted in the middle of her spiel by a question for which she had no prepared answer.

"You're angry, Joyce. Very angry," she replied finally. "And that's understandable, that's natural, that's *good* . . . "

Joyce raised herself up.

"Of course I'm angry. Know what I keep thinking? I could have killed him if I'd had a gun. There was a second or two there when he ran out of bullets and he was reloading. I could have killed him right there if I'd had a gun. I mean this, nothing like that will ever happen to me again. Soon as I'm on my feet again, I'm going to buy a gun and learn how to use it."

"Violence is the mother of violence, Joyce."

"That sounds like something you get out of a fortune cookie."

"We can't make any progress if you fight me every inch of the way."

Joyce reached to the nightstand and picked up the magic marker lying beside her paper pill cup. Tranqs in it. Painkillers for the spirit.

"Why don't you sign my cast and leave me alone."

"It looks to me like you have quite enough signatures."

"More than the Constitution and the Bill of Rights."

"In case you need to talk to me." The psychologist drew a business card from her purse and laid it on the nightstand. "And you might."

As soon as she was out the door, Joyce ripped the card in half.

Angry. It's natural, it's good. Ha! She wasn't angry at *him*. There wasn't a name for the emotion that burned through her when she thought about *him* with his soulless eyes, green and cold as fish scales. She was angry at herself for failing to heed the warning scrawled on the school's wall, for being unprepared and unarmed, angry for having lived thirty-eight years under a delusion: that the grand mechanics that fixed the sun and stars in their places and kept the planets spinning in their immutable orbits also governed her own small existence. Until last Friday, she'd awakened each morning more or less sure of what the day would bring, as if its events were as scripted as her lesson plans. She and Alex read about the violence and anarchy in Los Angeles and other places but had been sure it would never touch them. They planned their holidays a year in advance, they spoke of the times to prune their vines and harvest their grapes without ever considering the possibility that they might not be around to perform those tasks. Such confidence would have been excusable in the rural Minnesota of her girlhood, or in some stable country like, say, Switzerland. It was unforgivable in end-of-the-century California, land of unforeseen catastrophes, manmade and natural. The whole state could be split in two without warning by one great shrug of the earth's tectonic shoulders.

Anything could happen to her any moment. That was how she saw her life now, and it had altered her vision of all creation. In place of the fixed sun and stars, the planets that turned like the gears of some magisterial clock, she saw solar flares bursting with the power of a million nuclear bombs, errant meteors scattering like immense shotgun pellets to collide with worlds and blast them from their orbits. And beyond all that? A void. Chaos surrounded by darkness. That a murderous moron had caused her outlook to change so radically was almost funny. From now on, nothing would surprise her. She could thank *him* for that.

Ghost nuzzled her. Holding on to the stall gate, she bent down carefully and plucked from a burlap feedbag a fistful of chopped carrots and apples. The mare lowered her head with its blue-black forelock, drew back her lips, and snacked pleasurably, wetting her mistress's palm. Joyce looked toward the back wall, where her saddle was draped over a sawhorse with one stirrup and a fender thrown over the seat, and the saddle and its rawhide lacestraps hanging from silver studs and her bridle figure-eighted to a peg above the saddle filled her with her desire to ride. In her mind, she cantered Ghost up the road. The air was cool on her face, the mare's flanks rippled between her knees. Saddlecreak and hoofclatter and then a quick kick and Ghost stretched her neck, gathered herself and lengthened her stride to a gallop, and it was just the two of them, a woman and a blue roan mare running fast and free under the first evening stars. In her mind, they ran all the way back to the mesa beneath the Mogollons, where she dismounted, unsaddled Ghost, and turned her loose to see her again as first she had—a spirit horse out of some Apache myth.

"Joyce?"

Silhouetted against a violet sky, Alex stood in the barn door.

"Are you all right? What's been keeping you? We're all waiting for you and everyone else is going to be here in half an hour."

Everyone else included the neighbors, the DelAssandros, two other couples who owned nearby vineyards, and Alex's lawyer, Pete Spotswood, who was looking into the feasibility of filing a class action suit against the school district. For what? As if a lawsuit would make sense of everything and set everything to rights.

"I'm okay. I told you I was okay," she said irritably and with a secret shame that his concern got on her nerves.

"The fact is you're not okay. You're just out of the hospital and you're walking around on crutches in the dark and you've got a houseful of people worried about you."

Ah, now he sounded more like his true self: impatient and commanding. Alex DeLuca, successful wine grower and real estate baron.

"I don't know why you had to have this get-together tonight. Couldn't you have waited a few days?"

"Honey, it's for you."

"Is it really?"

■ ■ ■

In the weight room, loud with snorts and groans and the clang of barbells big as boxcar wheels, Mace Weathers stood alone before a mirror and admired his splendid body, three years in the sculpting. Shoulders that rose like ramps to meet his neck, lamp-tanned torso so plated with muscle it did not look quite like human flesh but as if he were wearing a bronze breastplate stolen from the prop room of a biblical epic. Maybe he ought to go into competition. He wouldn't stand a chance in L.A., where guys devoted their lives to getting just the right cut to their calves, the perfect flare to their lats, but in these Central Valley hick towns he might win a contest or two, at least take a runner-up's trophy. He thought of Schwarzenegger in *Conan the Barbarian*, Stallone in *Rocky*, and clasped his hands in front of him and pressed hard, making blood vessels pop in his biceps, his laterals swell into huge triangular slabs.

The symmetry wasn't right. Lats out of proportion to his pectorals. He ought to do a few more bench presses, go for the burn and pump up the pecs. But it was seven P.M. and he always wrapped up his workouts precisely at seven. More important, he had to phone Heartwood and propose an idea that had come to him as he was driving to the gym. He'd thought of making the call before he began lifting, but decided to put it off till after. He didn't want to appear pushy or anxious.

So now he was faced with this dilemma: to phone immediately or continue his workout a little longer. Three more sets of fast reps with light weights would do it. He was convinced that if he didn't, not only would his pectorals fail to grow in proportion to his lats, they would turn to fat and sag into those mock male mammaries known to lifters as "bitch tits." The sign of the steroid abuser. Mace did not use steroids, so he knew that his fear of acquiring bitch tits was irrational, but the knowledge gave him no power to control the fear.

He could put the call off another ten or fifteen minutes. After all, he hadn't told Heartwood he was going to phone at seven. And yet an inner voice warned that he would miss Heartwood if he delayed, and if he missed him tonight, he would continue to miss him, and then the entire tapestry he'd woven during the interview would begin to unravel. This, too, was an irrational fear his reason could not overcome.

Caught between his opposing dreads like a nail between two equally powerful magnets, Mace stood still in front of the weight-room mirror, his splendid body before him, clad in sneakers and a pair of sweat shorts stenciled SJS-ATHLETIC DEPT.

Got to do something, got to act. He cricked his neck three times rapidly to the left, reciting to himself, "Celestial, terrestrial, telestial," then three times to the right. "Telestial, terrestrial, celestial." Three was a powerful number, and the ritual worked its magic. It released him from his paralysis, told him that he could extend his workout for a short while without running the risk of missing Heartwood.

He grabbed his dirty towel and wiped the sweat from the bench, then laid his clean towel over it. Couldn't be too careful. This was the age of AIDS. Tuberculosis was making a comeback. Deadly viruses and bacteria on the rise, another sign. The millennium only seven years away. Chaos's hour approaches.

He pulled two quarters off the bar resting in the uprights, leaving two discs on each side. Two hundred twenty-five pounds total.

"Hey, Ronkowski, you look idle. C'mere and spot for me," he called to the nose tackle.

Ronkowski, a great slab of two-seventy, ambled over, huge square head swaying side to side. He stood behind the bench while Mace lay on it, arms upraised. He took in a breath, hefted the barbell, did ten quick repetitions, then sat up and rested. Celestial, terrestrial, telestial. The three kingdoms of the Mormons' post-resurrectional world revealed in the golden tablets dropped off at Joseph Smith's front door by the Angel Moroni, heaven's very own UPS delivery boy.

"How's Pickett?" Ronkowski asked.

"In what sense? His attitude? His health? His grades?"

"You're such a wise-ass, Weatherman. You know what I mean. King Kameakamea needs a new cycle."

"Why don't you say it a little louder, Ronkowski? Put it up on the bulletin board. Jesus."

"The Raiders are giving him a look. He doesn't want to go back to chopping bananas off a tree in Samoa. He wants to play for the Raiders. He needs to bulk up. Fast. Decas."

Mace looked across the room, where girls in color-coordinated tights were pulling on Nautilus machines, riding stationary bikes, climbing Stairmasters while reading magazines spread across the instrument panels that told them how far they'd climbed. Asses looked cute in those tights, even the fat asses. Bend them over and take a trip up their dirt roads. Make it hurt. They never cried rape when you did that. Too humiliating. He lay flat and did a second set of ten.

"Injectables, pills if Pickett can get them," Ronkowski whispered in his ear as he rested before the third set. "Quiet enough for you?"

"Anybody told the King what that stuff will do to his heart, his liver? He'll be dead before he's forty."

Mace said this to satisfy his conscience. He had a conscience, but he also had an uncanny ability to freeze it when necessary.

"He doesn't want to chop bananas. He wants to play for the Raiders."

Mace pretended to mull over the request. So what if a Samoan brute died at forty? Or lost his mind in a 'roid rage? He'd play for the Raiders, he'd make more than he could in ten lifetimes of banana-cutting, right? And Mace needed the money. Lewis and Anne, those good Mormon drones, were saving up for the operation that would restore their only child's face to its former handsomeness. The work was to be done by a plastic surgeon in L.A. who specialized in rejuvenating and reconstructing the movie stars' faces. He was very expensive, and Lewis and Anne could not afford the twenty percent of his fees not covered by their medical insurance. They were saving every penny and had nothing left over to send Mace for spending money. Even if they had it, Lewis wouldn't send any. Mace's part-time job didn't cover half his frequent laundry and dry-cleaning expenses. He never wore a shirt twice without having it washed, couldn't bear trousers without knife-edge creases in them. He needed the money, the King needed to bulk up for the Raiders' scout, everyone benefited.

"I'll talk to Pickett. Shouldn't be any problem," he said. "How about you?"

"I'm all right."

Mace finished the last set, then did a negative, slowly counting down from ten as he lowered the bar with its wheel-size discs to his chest, then counting up to ten as he raised the bar, his arms trembling, rockets of pain shooting through his shoulders.

He sat up, a pleasurable agony scalding his chest. He crooked his arms into wings and touched his swollen pecs.

Symmetry. He felt more confidence in himself. He could make the call now.

"Take a break. Spot for me," Ronkowski said.

The clock read seven-fifteen.

"Got to go," Mace said, looped the towels over his neck, and headed for the men's locker room, passing the girls in their clinging tights and brightly colored knee socks. Pulling, pumping pedals, climbing to nowhere. Celia had threatened to go to the dean of students and cry "Rape!" He'd known the threat was empty. She, repressed little Korean that she was, had been too humiliated to admit what had happened. And what if the story got back to her old-school father? He wouldn't hold her blameless. Besides, she knew that Mace had a right to her in any way he wanted; if it had not been for her, he would today be seeing with two eyes. She'd been hot and tight and creamy there and she'd cried that it hurt, pretended not to be enjoying it, because she wasn't free to acknowledge her dark things as hers and make friends with them. She was incomplete. She had to bow to her cramped immigrant upringing and pretend that she didn't enjoy it, that it hurt, that she'd been raped. She didn't realize that none of that meant anything. *What's happened to you, Mace? You didn't used to be like this*.

What happened? That moment of white pain in a Bakersfield gas station last year had drawn an indelible line of before and after through the course of his life. He'd lost half his sight but had gained a clearer vision. These were the latter days, though not the ones Joseph Smith had said they were; these days were the prelude to the hour of Chaos, when all the snakes in the mud would hatch out. Mace saw that now. There'd been other changes: that moment of white pain had liberated him to become completely himself. He'd made friends with his other half, the familiar he'd always sensed at his side but had been too timid to embrace.

Leaning against a wall by the pay phones outside the men's locker room, he wiped off the receiver with the cleaner of his towels and asked directory assistance for the Camelia House number.

Let all the snakes in the mud hatch out. Where had he heard that?

He dialed. A ring, two. His heart beat faster, his confidence ebbed. He was nervous about sounding nervous, nervous that he wouldn't come off natural, relaxed, self-assured.

"Camelia House," a woman answered.

Mace could not believe that he was afraid to speak, that his mouth had a strange, unpleasant taste, a little like the aftertaste of stale coffee. What was the matter with him?

"Camelia House," the woman repeated. "Hello?"

"This is a bad connection. I'll try again," he said, and hung up.

He hated this anxiety and couldn't understand why he felt it.

He called again. One ring. The same woman answered.

"Dr. Heartwood, please."

"Just a moment."

A psychological autopsy. Pick the lame brain of Duane the Pain, give voice to a dead man and let him tell his tale. What tale could he tell?

Another phone rang. Once, twice. Panic flashed through him again. Know the board, anticipate your opponent's moves. Four rings. Heartwood picked up the phone and said, "Hello," and in that instant, Mace's anxiety flew out of him, his pulse rate slowed, like a trained athlete's when the game begins.

"Dr. Heartwood?"

"Yes?"

"This is Mace. Mace Weathers? Did I catch you at a bad time?"

"Just drying off from the shower. I'm getting ready to go to dinner."

"Oh, sorry. I'll let you go, then."

"That's all right. The Capitol Grill's been recommended to me. What do you think?"

"I don't get to Sacramento much, but I've heard the Capitol's terrific. It's a little out of an undergrad's price range," he said, though in fact he'd never heard of the Capitol Grill. This was wonderful. Nice and relaxed, like a jock playing in the zone. "I called because I remembered something Boggs said to me the night he showed up at the rehab center. It probably won't help you much, but I thought I'd mention it."

"Well . . . ?"

"He said 'Something's going to happen, something's got to happen.' I had the impression he was kind of talking to himself more than to me. Like I said, he was pretty trashed."

"That's all? Nothing more specific?"

"No, sir. I thought I should let you know because a comment like that, it sort of suggests that he had something in mind."

"I suppose so. Anything else, Mace?"

"Well, yes." He paused. He had to strike just the right note—hesitant but not too. "I ran into my abnormal psych teacher and she asked me how the interview went. I've got a final paper due in a month, and, well, she suggested that a paper on psychological autopsies would be a great topic. Original, I mean. She thought if *I* interviewed *you* and found out how you do one, the kinds of questions you ask, the conclusions you draw and how you come to them . . . not just in general, but specifically tied to Boggs. She thought that I have a real opportunity here for some firsthand, original research."

He heard Heartwood's breathing.

"I'd be happy to talk to you in a couple of weeks, Mace. Consistent with confidentiality. I couldn't identify the people I talk to or give you my impressions of them by name. I could give you a general idea, perhaps."

"I see." And even though Heartwood could not see him, he put on the broad, open smile with which he'd greeted people when he was a young Aaronic priest, going door to door with Lewis on domestic mission work. Peddling latter-day salvation to the unregenerate in Redlands and San Bernardino. "Would it be possible for me to go along with you on one or two interviews? Sort of as your assistant? Then you wouldn't be violating anyone's confidence."

"I'd be sailing under false colors. You're not my assistant," Heartwood said coolly.

"I'm sorry. I wasn't thinking. It's just that I want to ace this course. Do you think if you told them I was a psych major, doing a paper, that . . . "

"You're persistent. Look, these interviews are official and confidential."

Mace, holding his smile, hesitated. He knew he could persuade Heartwood if they were face-to-face.

"Well, okay. Two weeks, you said?"

"About that. You have my office number in San Francisco. Call me first week in May. We can set something up."

"It'll be tight. The paper's due finals week. Third week in May."

"Take some No-Doz and pull a couple of all-nighters. It's an old undergraduate tradition. Meantime, I can recommend some books on psychological autopsies to get you started on your research. Got a pen handy?"

"Just a second." Mace cupped the mouthpiece, counted to five by thousands, then said, "Okay. Go ahead."

He stood, drumming his fingers on the cool, cement-block wall while Heartwood rattled off half a dozen texts. To add a little realism to his fakery as well as to amuse himself, Mace asked him to repeat a title.

Let all the snakes in the mud hatch out. Or was it let all the snakes hatch out in the mud?

"That should keep you busy for a while," Heartwood said. "Good luck on the paper."

"Thank you, Dr. Heartwood."

Well, damn. Hadn't worked. He walked to his locker, stripped, and sat on the bench with a vague uneasiness lumped in his belly and his chin cupped in one hand.

"Thought you were in a big hurry."

Mace looked up.

"Got to go. Can't spot for Ski," Ronkowski said, and straddled the bench with his hands between his enormous thighs.

"Had to make a phone call." Mace removed his eye patch and put it in his locker and slammed the door shut. He spread a towel on the tile floor, slipped on his shower clogs. The floor looked clean but had to be crawling with bacteria.

"Couldn't you have put it off for a couple of minutes to spot for me? That's how it's supposed to work. One guy spots for the other guy, the other guy spots for him."

"I know the etiquette. I had to make a call."

"Who? That Korean girlfriend? Heard you two broke up. That she broke it off with you."

Mace wrapped a towel around his waist, enjoying the feel of his abdominals, a series of rock-hard ridges.

"We're back together. True love conquers and forgives all."

Ronkowski looked up at him, his eyes like holes in a box. He motioned for Mace to sit down, to come closer. A secret to be shared.

"Heard she was going to blow the whistle. Heard she broke up with you because you took a drive up her Hershey highway. That what she forgave?"

A conspiratorial look. A c'mon-you-can-tell-me-just-between-us-guys look.

Mace rose again, and one of his spells suddenly came over him. A deadly cold that sometimes frightened even him. This was how assassins felt when the knives were drawn: not hot with fury but like glaciers inside.

"Where'd you hear that?" he asked, in a voice level as ice on a pond.

"It's been going around. That you did a couple of other bitches like that."

There was a time when he would have feared Ronkowski, who was probably as strong as a small grizzly bear. A bashing, crippling nose tackle. But Mace was complete now, and he said nothing, gazing down on the hulking man with his one good eye, the lid of the other drawn over the vacant socket and sewn shut to form a slit in a bulb of scar tissue the size, color, and texture of a squashed plum. He'd learned from the scrawny savage who'd disfigured him what it meant to be a complete man, without doubts. He'd even learned from Duane. When Doo-wayne talked about his mother, he was complete. His rage and hate filled the empty places where doubt could flourish.

"I was just wondering if you did," Ronkowski said. "You know, if it was true."

"Don't ever ask me that again."

"Hey, no big deal." Ronkowski blinked. "I always wondered myself what it'd be like to do that."

"Go to San Franscisco. A thousand guys there would be happy to teach you."

And then Mace smiled his wide Aaronic priest's smile and turned off the deep freeze. He could not turn it on at will, but he could switch it off.

"Fuckin' Weatherman," Ronkowski said, shaking his head. "You're a piece of work."

Skin tingling from the scalding shower, hair armored against mussing with firm-hold spray, Mace Weathers crossed the campus with long deliberate strides and counted the cracks in the sidewalks. Sodium vapor lights bathed Mission-style classroom buildings, ranks of royal palms, and groves of white oak in an artificial noon. The old lamps, with their soft charm, were no longer sufficient. Dangers lurked in the shadows between the buildings, creatures of the night hid in the groves. A girl had been abducted from campus two years ago and was found raped and murdered. There'd been a couple of muggings near the credit union and an assault or two, so now sodium vapor lights glared, erasing the shadows. Yellow emergency phones stood ready to offer assistance. Each had a number that lit up automatically on a display screen in the campus police headquarters as soon as the receiver was lifted. You didn't even have to cry, "Help!" Only lift the receiver and a cop would be dispatched. They rode to the rescue in golf carts. But were they enough, the phones, the cops, the great, arcing electric suns? Could they stop the clock from ticking toward Chaos's hour? People were blind to what was happening. They put their faith in lights, in emergency phones, cops in golf carts. They didn't realize that these things were not solutions, but signs, like AIDS and a resurgent TB.

There were one hundred and six cracks in the sidewalk between the fieldhouse gym and the statue of Commodore Stockton, Anglo conqueror of Spanish California. Four feet ten inches between cracks. Call it five hundred and thirty feet total. Mace passed beneath Stockton, his stone arm cradling a stone sword. From the statue to the library steps was seven hundred and ten feet. One hundred forty-two cracks. His head was a repository of such numerical facts. State's campus covered two point two square miles. It was three point six miles between campus and his room in Mrs. Van Heusen's rooming house. Commodore Stockton's statue was twelve and a half feet tall.

The numbers gave him a sense of power and control. There was a power in numbers, but people had forgotten how to tap into it.

Yodehyod means "let" in Hebrew. *Yod* equals ten, *eh* five, *yod* ten. Ten. One-zero. One is the Hebrew masculine number, zero the female. Let there be light. God mates with himself to create the world. Yahweh. I Am Who Am.

A hermaphroditic deity. No weirder than a delivery-boy angel with an Italian name. Please sign for these golden tablets, Mr. Smith.

Three kingdoms in the post-resurrectional world. Celestial, terrestrial, telestial.

Twelve gates to the City, four times three, and three archangels, and the number of the Beast was six sixty-six. Rome was the Beast. *Veni vidi vici.* VIVIVI. Six six six. Twice three twice three twice three. John got a look in Revelations. He'd tapped in to the power of numbers, big-time.

One hundred forty-two cracks. Confirmed. He climbed the library steps, fourteen of them, then walked down a long corridor bearing murals of Frémont at Morgan's Hill, U.S. Marines accepting the surrender of a tiny Spanish town called Pueblo de Los Angeles—what might the Marines have said if they'd known what that would lead to? In the periodical room—racks and stacks of newspapers, magazines, and journals, microfilm and microfiche, information by the kilobyte, megabyte, yard, ton—diligent students stood by the Lexis-Nexis terminals, looking up references for term papers and theses. Mace waited for several minutes before one was free.

There are sixty-four squares in a chess board. Know your opponent, anticipate his moves.

TYPE SUBJECT OR NAME AND PRESS ENTER, the green, glowing screen instructed. IF NAME TYPE LAST NAME FIRST.

He hunched over the keyboard and typed:

HEARTWOOD, LEANDER T.

Wednesday, April 21st

EVIDENCE. WITNESSES. CLUES.

Gabriel stood on the trestle above the American River, thinking of how little he had in the way of the detective's trinity. The river below slid over its gravel bottom, the same river that had washed the pans of gold-dazed placer miners, eyes peeled for the glitter that promised everything a man could ask for. Old Coloma, and the replica of Sutter's Mill, with its decked sawlogs and paddle wheel, were clustered along the western bank. The air had a crisp, dry taste, the rimrock crowning Mount Murphy glowed like rose quartz in the early morning light, and there were no sounds but birdsong and river-rush. He'd never been one for small towns and rustic living, but he could see the appeal it held for someone like Youngblood. San Francisco, only a three-hour drive away, seemed in another country, L.A. in another universe.

His brain and body pleaded for a cup of coffee. He'd slept badly, roused at midnight by a terror that some copycat killer would take a shot at Leland and Eleanor. In the darkness, he tossed for an hour, thinking of ways to rearrange his and Adrienne's schedules so they could escort the kids to and from school, calculating the costs of installing an alarm system. After drinking a glass of warm milk and reading a little more of *Paper Sons into Native Sons,* he returned to bed and dozed fitfully until the alarm rang at four-forty-five. "Christ!" Adrienne groaned, wrapping the pillow over her ears. "This is like the good old presuspension days. You're home after dinner, out of the house before breakfast."

Evidence. Witnesses. Clues.

He'd driven to the scene and by flashlight found his way back to the place where Boggs died. The venerable tree in its static writhing looked as if it had sprung out of some Gothic folk tale. Small animals scratched and rustled in the semidarkness, and when a hawk or owl flapped loudly from a branch at the clearing's edge, his heart jumped and his hand went reflexively for the Glock. Give him a dark alley anytime; at such an hour the woods reminded him too much of the Delta, another place where ghosts and demons dwelled. He searched for footprints, clues of any kind. He knew it was futile this long after the crime, yet he felt compelled to try. Working westward for about half a mile, he came out of the woods onto a road that paralleled Route 49 for the eight miles between Coloma and Placerville. Cold Springs Road, according to the map. He walked it southward for a few hundred yards, returned to his starting point, searched northward about the same distance, then repeated the process on the opposite side, looking for tire tracks. If the accomplice had escaped by car, he might have parked the getaway vehicle on Cold Springs.

He found nothing that looked useful, and now, on the bridge above the American, he flipped pebbles into the water and considered various possibilities. Functions of complex variables. Plenty of variables to work with, too many. *If* the accomplice had fled by car and *if* he and Boggs had left San Joaquin in separate vehicles, they would have rendezvoused at the Howard Johnson, then gone separate ways at Placerville, Boggs up Route 49, the accomplice up Cold Springs. He would have parked at a predetermined spot and cut through the woods on foot to stand lookout on the bluff.

Another possibility was that Boggs picked up his partner at the Howard Johnson, and they rode together in the truck. Boggs stayed in it, the accomplice got out and went to the lookout spot. But how did he get away? Had he left a car somewhere nearby? Would he have done that, say, on the day before the massacre? Leaving a strange car overnight in such a small town would have been risky; it could have been tagged and towed, or some nosy type might have taken down its license number. Still, the son of a bitch had to have some way to get out without leaving a trace. This killer was like the ones he used to pursue. He hadn't acquired an immunity to fear of punishment. He'd done everything possible to make sure he didn't get caught. Gabriel laughed to himself. Listen to me, now I'm psychologizing.

But all the psychology on earth wasn't going to help without something concrete to go on. The confidence he'd felt yesterday was waning. He'd even begun to wonder if he'd invented the idea of an accomplice to spice up a boring assignment.

A car pulled up in front of the park entrance station, across the road from the replica of the mill. A figure in ranger brown went inside. As he walked toward it, the ranger, a broad-boned girl, came out and raised the Stars and Stripes and the Bear flag of the California Republic. Gabriel approached her and identified himself with a flip of his ID wallet.

She said she'd been on duty when the massacre happened, but no, she hadn't noticed anything or anyone unusual in the park that day. Had she seen a car that might have been left overnight? No, but he might check at the RV and trailer campground across the river. He thanked the ranger, and skirting a display of nineteenth-century mining equipment, went into the visitors' center. A short, gray-haired woman greeted him with practiced cheerfulness.

"You're here bright and early! How can I help you?"

Her clear, dry eyes switched back and forth, inviting him to browse among the racks of postcards, the shelves of Gold Rush histories, the display cases aglitter with trinkets and souvenirs.

Gabriel once again flashed his badge and ID. Instantly, the grandmotherly face composed itself into one that recalled a photograph of a frontier woman, its expression simultaneously keen, hard, and sour. He saw that this look came more naturally to her than her trained smile.

Her answers were the same as the ranger's. Nothing suspicious, nothing out of the ordinary, not that she saw. Came as a complete surprise. No one in Coloma had heard the gunshots, even though the shootings occurred only two miles down the road. Hills must have muffled the sound, she offered, as if the townsfolks' deafness needed explaining.

"Why, we didn't realize anything was wrong until we heard the sirens." She attempted to reassert her smile. "All I can say is that that young man must have been terribly, terribly angry to do what he did. That's what the TV said and they're right."

A week ago, Gabriel would have paid no attention to the remark; now it drilled into his ear.

"About what?"

"All these *people* coming into this state. Millions of them, and we have to take care of them. We're all angry about that."

"What people?"

"Why, Vietnamese, Cambodians, Mexicans. Who do you suppose I mean? Too many people in California and the wrong kind. It's really bad down in L.A. and San Diego, what with all the illegal Mexicans they've got." She laid her white, wrinkled hands on a display case, and spreading them over a necklace of fool's gold, went on. "California is dying under a burden of welfare. And the government keeps letting more and more of them in, so the federal government should take care of them." She sighed in resignation. "But I suppose that would just be our tax dollars too. Affects us in other ways, you know. Take the Bay Area. Folks from there are moving out this way in droves because there are too many minorities where they are. But when they come out here they want all their modern conveniences, like shopping malls, and that's just marring up our beautiful country."

And pursing her lips, she concluded with an emphatic nod, as if to underscore the indisputability of everything she'd said.

Gabriel stalked out without a word and surprised himself when, with a savage sidekick, he splintered one of the informative signs by the display of antique machinery. Embarrassed, he picked up the half that lay on the ground and carefully refitted it to the piece still on the post. "California Stamp," said the sign. "When miners discovered gold in underground quartz veins, mills were brought in to process ore . . . " Yeah, thanks. He had learned new facts from Adrienne's book. Chinese forty-niners had been ambushed and murdered for their gold by Anglo miners whose luck had played out or who were too lazy to work their own claims. No doubt the blue-eyed bitch in the visitors' center would have approved. Damned minorities, digging up *our* gold. Got what they deserved.

That she'd tried to justify Boggs was incomprehensible; that she could have said the things she did to Gabriel's face was not. Like the Oroville cop who'd told him, "Don't mind those folks, they're not used to seeking chinks up here," the woman didn't realize she was offending him because she hadn't seen the color of his skin or the shape of his eyes. His complexion had been bleached and his eyes rounded by his mannerisms, by the way he walked and dressed, above all by his tongue, which never had uttered a word of Mandarin or Cantonese. He'd achieved assimilation's goal—invisibility—and that made him angrier than any racial slur, intended or unintended.

He needed to get this poison out. He had some serious work and thinking to do.

Striding across a picnic ground, he climbed atop a granite shelf at the edge of the woods, removed his gun belt, windbreaker, and shirt, and assumed the ready position. He began to execute *Koryo*, a first-degree form, starting slowly, careful of wrenching his back. Pivot left, right back stance, double knife hand block, double sidekick . . . Maybe I ought to start wearing a pigtail and a skullcap. Maybe I ought to go to night school, learn the language. Block, spinning backfist, straight kick. Maybe I ought to bring offerings to my grandfather's grave. Too many minorities in the Bay Area. Warmed and loosened up, he glanced down at his midriff, slashed by a long scar. A sudden explosion of gunfire and recoilless cannons from the tangled mangrove and trees on the riverbank, Gabriel firing back with the quad-fifties, the gun turret swiveling back and forth, then the shrapnel boring like a hot drill bit into his belly. Dad fought for this country in Italy, I fought for it in Vietnam and lost a third of my guts for it, who the hell does she think she is? He went into *Cheon Kwan*, the difficult "Heavenly Fist" form of the fifth degree. Right front kick, right body punch, right back stance . . . Blue-eyed bitch, my ancestors probably were in the Bay Area before yours ever heard of it. Great uncle nearly stoned to death by a white mob the minute he set foot on the mainland. *Stop thinking about this shit* . . . Horse stance, leap . . . And for an instant Gabriel was no longer a middle-aged cop with part of his stomach missing, but a deadly ballet dancer, soaring, turning full circle in midair, his leg snapping around in a crescent kick. He landed and resumed the horse stance. He became completely absorbed in the movements, thought of nothing. Then, adopting the meditative stance, he spread his arms wide as eagle wings, exhaled, and forced his anger to flow out of his fingertips.

That was when, for no discernible reason, he remembered what was wrong with the photograph.

He quickly dressed, jogged to the bank of pay phones by the visitors' center, and called Jean Sheldon at the crime lab. She was a tall, plain, and plainspoken woman, one of Gabriel's favorite people. Besides a genius for analyzing trace evidence, she possessed a doleful wisdom. When she'd worked a district lab in Southern California, she'd been called to many a messy scene of murder, suicide, and murder-suicide in Palm Springs and other preserves of the rich and famous. She'd seen them lying in undignified positions in puddles of blood and urine. "They end up just like us," she'd said to Gabriel one day. "I've seen a lot of it and it's never pretty. Y'know, if people could see the way they'll look when they die, maybe they'd live their lives differently."

"Sheldon," she answered.

"Hey, Jeannie. Gabriel Chin. Whatcha up to?"

"Looking at some fibers we peeled off a sixteen-year-old rape and murder victim. How about you?"

"Want to verify something. Suicide with a semiauto handgun. You'd find what?"

"Powder residue on the victim's gun hand. Trace residue on his face and shirt, maybe in his nostrils if it was a head wound. Blood blowback in the barrel."

"And the gun would be stovepiped, right?"

"In all likelihood."

"And if it wasn't stovepiped?"

She paused. He pictured her—mousy brown hair worn long, lanky farm-girl body. Sexy in an odd way. Her plainness said, "Here I am, no frills, no glamour, no speed, your basic female utility vehicle, but I last."

"Hard to say, Gabriel. A stovepiped semiauto is a strong indicator of suicide. If it isn't? Could be a peculiarity in the weapon that allowed the slide to complete its rearward motion, despite relaxed trigger pressure. Could be death wasn't instantaneous and the victim maintained pressure just long enough to prevent stovepiping."

"How about homicide?"

"It wouldn't be definite evidence of homicide, no."

"Fishy?"

"Depending on circumstances. If there was some other sign that the wound was not self-inflicted then a nonstovepiped weapon would make me start thinking murder."

"Suppose everything—powder residue on the victim's hand, et cetera—pointed to suicide, but not the gun? What would that tell you?"

"I remember an unusual case from a few years ago. A woman got AIDS from a blood transfusion and blew her brains out. Cops talked to her husband, the guy wasn't answering right. They held him on suspicion, called me in. He'd washed his hands by then, but I got trace residue off the shirt he was wearing when she died. And I used a British technique and found residue in his nostrils. Good thing he hadn't sneezed. We had arguments with the coroner. He said suicide, we said maybe homicide. Turned out to be a little of both. The husband confessed. The victim held the gun to her own head but didn't have the nerve to pull the trigger. So the husband wrapped his hand around hers and helped her do it. Murder, but you could call it a mercy killing, or an assisted suicide. Help you at all?"

"It might. Listen, sometime today you should get a bundle of evidence from the El Dorado Sheriff's Department. The school bus massacre case. Appreciate it if you could get to it soon as you can."

"Sure . . . but isn't that one closed?"

"Jeannie, thanks."

He hung up, then called Krimsky to see how the backgrounding of the victims was coming along. Nothing yet, he said. The chance that the massacre was part of an Asian gang war was beginning to look pretty remote. A message had come in for him overnight from the Southern California field office. They still hadn't any luck tracking down Tipton. He was absent from school yesterday, and his father had said that he hadn't seen Jacob since he'd come home from school Thursday afternoon. He thought the kid might be in L.A. Jacob had been doing that a lot lately, cutting school and going to L.A. on weekends.

"The message definitely says Thursday afternoon?" Gabriel asked.

"Does. What'd you suppose?"

"The kid likes long weekends."

He put the phone down, then crossed the bridge and knocked at the doublewide trailer that served as the office and residence of the campground's owner, a tough old bird with a mole on the tip of his nose. Before Gabriel could produce his badge, the old man said he had two sites available, both with full hookup, so much per day payable in advance each day, and no credit cards. He plucked at his mole and frowned when Gabriel told him what he was there for. No, didn't see nothin' that looked funny, and no, didn't remember nobody checkin' in on Wednesday or Thursday and checkin' out on Friday, but then he saw lotsa different people everyday and he couldn't be expected to remember any of them, 'less there was somethin' strange about 'em, and he didn't have no recollection of anyone strange-lookin' or strange-actin', no sir. Gabriel persuaded him to let him examine his registration list for the previous Wednesday and Thursday.

It was not very thorough—only signature cards with license plate numbers. That would do for a start. The old man did not have a copy machine—this ain't a Holiday Inn, he said gruffly—so Gabriel, deciphering the signatures as best he could, recorded the names and tag numbers in his notebook. Twenty-two altogether. Thirteen from out of state, two from Canada.

"Can you tell me which of these checked out on Friday or Saturday?" he asked. "You have a record of that?"

"Sure as hell don't," the man snapped. "Folks pay each day in advance. Don't give a damn when they leave long as I got their money. What you'd have to do is check my Saturday records of which cars was here. Match those against the other days, see which plate numbers is still there, which ain't."

And for the next forty-five minutes, that is what Gabriel did. He narrowed his list down to seven people. Four who left on Friday, three the next day. Then, from a brochure, he took down the names of motels in the area. Maybe Youngblood could compile a list of their guests during the week of the massacre.

Heartwood, awake at four-thirty to begin entering more data on his laptop, had fallen asleep at his desk when he'd put his head down to rest his eyes. He dreamed that he and Diana were making love among the galaxies and spiral nebulae. His lips fast to hers, they twirled through a void, where at two degrees Kelvin their flesh could not corrupt and they could truly be lovers till the end of time.

He was quick-cut from this vision of eternal copulation to a courtroom scene. He had been called to the assizes of heaven to testify as an expert witness in the trial of his mother's soul, accused of the gravest sin. The defense attorney rose from his table and spoke on direct examination. "In your opinion, Dr. Heartwood, did the defendant, Catherine Heartwood, commit despair on the morning of February 16th, 1971?" At the opposite table, scowling and robed like Torquemada, the prosecutor, Gates Landau, waited for his turn on cross-examination. Heartwood glanced at him, at a gender-balanced jury of six male and six female saints, and finally at his mother. She wore the martyred expression he knew so well, that look of suffering virtuously endured, and he imagined how she would shriek were she shut out of heaven forever.

He could not bear to hear those cries and answered, "She did not. She was not suffering from a spiritual affliction but one as physical as cancer. Unipolar depression of the manic-depressive cycle, which is caused by imbalances in the brain's neurochemistry. Someone with this condition suffers a mental anguish as bad, if not worse, than the most acute physical pain. The patient is sure it cannot be relieved, as indeed is often the case, even with the best therapy and antidepressant medication. My mother did not give up hope; rather, her ability to experience hope had been taken from her." The saints nodded gravely, but Heartwood wasn't sure if he'd persuaded them.

"You are excused," said the judge, an archangel, and Heartwood was instantly transported back to earth, where a phone was ringing.

His eyes opened to the full light of morning and he realized that the ringing was from the phone in his room. He pushed away from the desk and answered with a drowsy "Hello?"

"Heartwood?" asked a rough male voice. "You Dr. Heartwood?"

He mumbled that he was.

"Woke you up, huh? Tried to reach you yesterday, but no luck. Figured I couldn't miss you at this time. Was I right or was I right?"

He rubbed the sleep from his face, shook the last webs of the dream from his mind.

"Who is this?"

"Never mind who I am. Got some information might help you out."

He was unable to place the voice.

"There's a guy in Fontana knows something about Boggs. Name of Mike Thor. Like the thunder god." The caller hummed a couple of bars from the "Ride of the Valkyrie." "That thunder god. Real name's Mike Silva, ex–W.A.R. skinhead who graduated to the neo-Nazi majors. He can tell you a lot about Boggs."

"And this tip is going to remain anonymous, I'll bet."

"Are you right or are you right? Mike works night shift at CSI. That's California Steel Industries. Usually hangs out at Rick's Empire Bar or the Truck Plaza on Cherry Street after work. Don't find him there, he'll be at home. Fontana."

The line went dead. Heartwood looked at the phone as if it and not the caller had been responsible for waking him. He padded into the bathroom, urinated, and farted with gusto through his silk boxer shorts. One of bachelorhood's advantages, that. No need to contain yourself. He showered and shaved in the faux-Victorian pedestal sink. Must be quaint little factories somewhere, turning out these reproductions for the B & B trade.

Mike Thor?

He supposed there would be more such tips as the nuts emerged from their hideyholes, and he supposed he would have to follow up on some. Mike Thor. Encore neo-Nazi nonsense, Norse runes, prophecies of the coming Aryan revolt. He dressed, and was about to head down to the dining room when the phone rang again.

"Lee? Gabriel. What the hell are you doing?"

"On my way to breakfast. How's your wife? How's her car?"

"Nothing the matter with either of them."

"What a surprise."

"I'm at the state park. Been poking around here since before dawn. Like you to take a run with me to the scene. There's something I think you ought to see before we take the next step."

"We're playing cops 'n' robbers, aren't we?"

"We're a long way from robbery."

"I had other plans for today, such as setting up interviews with Boggs's sister, his grandparents. Like finding Jacob Tipton. Have your people had any success on that?"

"They're working on it."

"They're working on it and you're nosing around the scene of the crime. What the hell is this? You are supposed to be assisting me, remember?"

"If I didn't think this was important, I wouldn't bother you."

"You swear this isn't going to waste our time?"

"Chinee boy sweah on ancestuh grave no shit."

He shaved, dressed, and, foregoing breakfast, drove off in a state of aggravation heightened by his growling stomach. Breakfast this morning had been one of his favorites. Blueberry pancakes. If Gabriel was off on some screwy tangent, he would call Eileen and demand that she assign someone else.

As he headed east, toward the hazy blue wall of the Sierra Nevada, the radio scanned among rock stations, country-music stations, Christian stations promising salvation, all-news stations crackling with reports of Waco's aftermath. No salvation there. He put in a tape of chants and listened to a Benedictine choir sing the "Confiteor."

Credo in unum Deum, omnipotentem paternam, factorem terra et caeli, omnium visibilium et invisibilium . . .

A music out of time. The monks' voices, swelling, falling, swelling again, calmed him and he found himself analyzing his strange dream. Everyone in it had been some aspect of himself: the defense attorney, Landau, the jury of saints gravely nodding. There had been no verdict because the jury was still out in his own mind and, at this late stage, probably would remain so. A hung jury. He did not condemn his mother, yet he could not forgive her for taking herself from him, she who'd given him in his youth a love of literature, learning, and music, she who'd protected him in childhood from his father's *Sports Afield* machismo.

He recalled that his father had not even tried to hide his disappointment after his failure of manhood on the Ontario canoe trip. At last, his mother rose to his defense. "Oh, will you stop it, Ron. He's only a boy. So what if he couldn't carry a canoe through a wilderness that's a wilderness only because no one with an ounce of sense lives there."

Mother was from near Chicago—River Forest, a reservation for lace-curtain Irish and other well-off Catholics. She had certain pretensions toward cultural refinement, an avid subscriber even in her college days to operas and concerts and poetry readings. It was she who'd encouraged Heartwood to apply to Yale Medical School, she who'd thrown the party for him when he was accepted. All his father did was to hand him a beer and say, "Don't let any of those Ivy League snoots make you forget where you come from, bucko." Good Lord, all Heartwood wanted to do was forget Green Bay and its paper mills and canneries and all its midwestern burghers, hiding their kinks under the gowns of their Rotarian sensibilities.

The telegram had been delivered to him at Camp Pendleton Naval Hospital, where he'd finished his Navy tour. MOTHER DIED SUDDENLY THIS A.M. PLEASE COME HOME. FUNERAL SATURDAY. DAD. Not, "Love, Dad." Just "Dad."

He knew what had happened, as if the truth of his mother's death had been written on the wire in an invisible ink only he could see. So when he phoned Julia, the elder of his two younger sisters, he wasn't surprised to hear that Catherine Heartwood had died of an overdose of Seconal. She'd acquired the fatal dosage over a period of three months, using forged prescription pads from Dad's office to buy the drug at three different pharmacies. She'd planned it out like a murder, which, of course, it was. Self-murder.

He'd often wondered what he would have turned up if he had performed a psychiatric autopsy on her. Really, he was glad he hadn't, because he suspected that neither despair nor chemical imbalances had drawn her hand to the bottle of big red pills.

She'd always considered herself above Green Bay's provincial vulgarities, and endured them as a sentence in purgatory. But nothing had been as mortifying as her loveless marriage. Surely love and passion had burned within it once, but her husband had come home from the war a bitter man at twenty-eight, bitter as the Ardennes winter in whose snows he'd performed trepannings and amputations on eighteen- and twenty-year-old boys. His wartime experiences made it impossible for him to take emotional disorders seriously. They weren't real illnesses, as the treating of them wasn't real medicine, and he made no exception with his wife's depressions.

Mother must have secretly and quietly raged against him and the narrow world he made her live in, against his frequent absences as he went with his friends into camps reeking of whiskey and wood-smoke, wet bird dogs and wet boots.

Heartwood could still see her so clearly, her long hair disheveled, her small face so wan in the northern light streaming through the living room window that looked out on Lake Michigan, and she sitting there sinking into some endless night of the soul. He wanted to believe that the bottle of big red pills had been nothing more than an escape from an anguish that could not be relieved. But he feared it was the instrument of a prideful spite toward everyone in her life. She would show them all. Husband, kids, neighbors. You're gonna miss me when I'm gone. No one ever would know if she had taken a moment to reflect on the pain she would cause those who did love her. She didn't leave a note.

"Credo in unum Baptisma, in remissionem peccatorum," sang the Benedictine choir. The forgiveness of sins. Yes, to love truly was to forgive, and Heartwood knew in the innermost vaults of his mind that his failure to love Paula as he'd promised rose from his failure to forgive the first woman he had known and loved.

Gabriel sat on the front porch of a reconstructed frontier cafe, sipping coffee served by a rangy woman got up in a bonnet and long gingham dress. The whole damned country's turning into a theme park, he thought, looking at her *Wagons West* outfit. He turned and saw the red Porsche idling up the main street, Heartwood looking out the side window. Gabriel waved and watched him pull over and cross the street with that cocksure walk of his. Didn't even look to see if any cars were coming, as if he expected them to stop for him. Another white boy who thinks who the hell he is.

Two hours later, after he had taken Heartwood over the ground and explained his theory, they were back at the cafe. Heartwood listened without comment, then briefed him on the interview with Weathers. It didn't sound as if he had missed much, although he would have liked to have heard with his own ears the story of Boggs's screwy plot to firebomb illegal aliens. Fit in with what Tipton had said about him: always cooking up off-the-wall scenarios.

Now Heartwood was devouring a breakfast of pancakes and poached eggs as if he hadn't eaten in days. How did the guy keep from turning into a blimp? Probably jogs a lot.

"Do you jog a lot, Lee?"

He nodded.

"If I ate the way you do, I'd be two-fifty."

"It's not the jogging. Metabolism. My father could put away more calories than a lumberjack, never ran when he could walk, and he never went over one-seventy."

"Well, I didn't waste our time, did I?"

Heartwood wiped his mouth with his napkin and signaled the pioneer woman for a refill of his coffee.

"To sum up your thesis, you think the mystery man was the brains behind this. He planned it, did all the time and distance calculations, etcetera. He parked a getaway vehicle in the campground or at a motel nearby the night before the crime, somehow made his way back to San Joaquin, rendezvoused with Boggs at the Howard Johnson Friday morning, acted as his lookout, and then pulled the trigger for him by holding his hand over Boggs's gun hand, so none of his prints were left on the weapon. Then he left the scene by way of a hiking trail, returned to his vehicle and drove out."

Heartwood tore open a packet of sugar and dumped it in his cup, stirred thoughtfully.

"I guess an assisted suicide isn't altogether fantastic. Boggs blew his previous attempts. Maybe he asked for help to make sure this time, and the accomplice would have been only too happy to oblige, Boggs being the only person who could have identified him."

Gabriel glanced at a nearby table, where two tourists were reading glossy brochures and discussing what they should see first, the monument to James Wilson Marshall or the sawmill.

"Right. This was a guy who not only wanted to make sure he hid his own tracks, he wanted to make sure that this crime looked like it was committed by one man. He didn't want people to even wonder if somebody else had been in on it."

"We're not back to the Benedetto fantasy, are we? White supremacists make it look like the work of a lone psychopath to create an atmosphere of random terror?"

Gabriel shook his head.

"If this was a terrorist operation, the neo-Nazis would have made their point a lot better by making sure no one survived. You do that best by having more than one shooter. Two, maybe three guys. Crossfire. Wipeout. Then they disappear into the woods."

"Gabriel, I've got to admit that the possibility that somebody masterminded this massacre arouses my scientific curiosity."

"It oughta arouse more than that."

"Pardon the detachment, but the fact is, mass murderers are the least examined of all psychopathic criminals because nine out of ten do exactly what Boggs did. I myself have never interviewed one. A monster like this. It would be something to . . . "

"Christ, we're not talking about capturing some kind of rare animal. A Sasquatch or whatever."

"I almost *want* him to exist," Heartwood said.

"Know the feeling. I've been wondering if I'm just dreaming this up."

At the next table, the woman tourist remarked that James Wilson Marshall had died a penniless drunk. Her husband said that he'd needed a good portfolio manager.

"I want him to exist, you do," said Heartwood. "The desire to believe often leads to belief itself. Ask any UFO enthusiast. So I feel compelled to poke a hole or two in your scenario."

"Go ahead."

"Why the elaborate logistics for one thing? Good plans are usually brutally simple."

"Hey, you use your imagination to figure out why. I use mine to figure out how. Sometimes how can help me find who. But the scenario I gave, that's just one possibility out of maybe half a dozen. Main thing is, I've got three reasons why I think there was somebody else. One, Boggs was too damned dumb and impulsive to plan and pull this off on his own. Put it in the bank. I don't care what Weathers told you about him being okay at chess. All that proves is that he could play chess. Boggs was a guy who fouled up a penny-ante purse-snatching."

Heartwood rang his spoon against his cup, clicked his tongue.

"Had doubts about him on that score, too. As soon as I saw that mess he lived in. A disorganized guy. But let's not get carried away. This wasn't *all that* sophisticated a crime. It took brains to plan, but not some criminal genius, not some evil Dr. Moriarity."

"Okay. Let's give him the brains for now. He still had to be warned, *probably* had to be warned that the bus was coming. And that's all the other guy did, besides planning the whole thing. He didn't fire a shot. Like I said, he didn't want to leave any evidence, and bullet holes from a second gun would have done that."

"What's your third reason?" Heartwood asked.

"The gun."

"Run that past me again. Guns aren't my métier."

"Your what?"

"I don't know much about guns."

"The way a semiauto works . . . Here, I'll show you."

The tourists looked a little startled when Gabriel leaned over and displayed his badge.

"Excuse me," he said, "I'm a state special agent. We're looking into what happened here on Friday."

The woman's mouth formed an O. Her husband said that it was a pretty awful thing, they were driving through Kansas when they heard about it on the radio. They almost didn't come to California.

"Welcome to the Golden State," Gabriel said pleasantly. "I have to demonstrate something to my partner. Don't be alarmed."

They were alarmed nevertheless when Gabriel drew the Glock from under his windbreaker, ejected the magazine, and pulled the slide back to make sure the chamber was clear. The tourists swiftly packed up their things and brochures and fled toward the parking lot.

"Gabriel, for Christ's sake, this isn't the place for . . . "

"I get bored easy. Perking up a dull morning. C'mon, this is how I think it happened."

Heartwood nervously glanced at the waitress, standing frozen in the doorway with a pot of coffee. He assured her that what she saw was not what she thought; it was merely a demonstration, official state business.

"So if this gun was loaded, this is what would happen when you pull the trigger." His hand jerked the slide quickly backward and forward. "The spent cartridge would be ejected, the next reloaded into the chamber, because pressure is being maintained on the trigger for a split second. But if it's pulled by a suicide's finger, pressure on the trigger relaxes instantaneously. The slide opens to eject the spent cartridge, but won't go all the way because there's no resistance. The weapon falls. The cartridge jams cockeyed in the ejection port. Sticks out like a stovepipe. Boggs's gun wasn't stovepiped, which indicates that somebody else had it in his hand. Indicates. Not proves."

Heartwood looked at the waitress, who remained motionless, staring at them.

"We'll take a refill," he said cheerfully.

She hesitated. He motioned to her and she approached the table cautiously and poured. Gabriel reloaded the magazine and holstered the weapon.

"An AIDS test was run on Boggs's blood samples, wasn't it?"

"You've got a weird way of perking up dull mornings," Heartwood remarked.

"Hey, Doctor. AIDS."

"Yeah. It was negative. That isn't why he killed himself. Or had somebody help him kill himself. Or whatever. I can't picture it. This mysterious accomplice helping Duane pull the trigger. All planned out ahead of time. It's too contrived somehow, too artificial. Unless . . ."

He studied the tablecloth, chimed the cup with the spoon again.

"Let's back up some. What kind of man would be able to put Boggs up to this? Someone who knew him intimately. Boggs once told a counselor something interesting—that he was violent but not as violent as he wanted to be. So this somebody would have known that about him and might have shown him how to be as violent as he wanted. Also he would have known that Duane was self-destructive. They would have had a close relationship. They would have come to an understanding, made a pact, like the husband and wife you told me about. Given Boggs's history, it could have been a homosexual relationship."

"How about a homosexual and a blood relationship?"

Heartwood looked at him.

"I'm wondering about Tipton. The Southern California field office says that he dropped out of sight Thursday afternoon. That's the big surprise I've been saving."

"Interesting."

"Tipton's smart enough. He was with Boggs on that San Bernardino incident. And if you look at his picture, you can see how somebody like that half-blind motel owner could have mistaken him for a tall girl, especially if he was holding hands with a guy."

"And you're proposing what?"

"We don't leave finding Tipton to the Southern California office. We do the looking. Go to Fontana and trace him from there. Maybe take an hour to check out your tip. Could be a connection between this skinhead and Tipton. Kinda coincidental, them coming from the same place. Then we go to Tipton's old man and see if we can't get more out of him about where sonny boy's gone to."

"When?"

"We can catch a commuter flight out of Sacramento this afternoon."

Heartwood hesitated.

"I'll need you on this," Gabriel said quietly.

"For what? I thought you were working for me."

"Solving your everyday murder is damned hard without eyewitnesses. This one, we'd be trying to prove murder and conspiracy to commit murder, fourteen counts of it, without witnesses and next to zero evidence. Not even circumstantial. It's damned near impossible."

"You need me to help you pursue the impossible?"

"We find Tipton, but we don't interrogate him like he's a suspect. All the kid would have to do is yell 'Lawyer!' and we'd be done. We tell him we're doing this autopsy thing on Duane. You do most of the questioning. You told me you know what to look for, how minds like his work, right? Every now and then I slip one in from left field. We see how he reacts. Make him nervous, make him sweat. Between the two of us, maybe we'll get him to trip himself up."

"If he's guilty."

"If."

"A confession."

"Best evidence in the world," Gabriel said

Interlude

The People of the Neighborhood

THE SCHOOL BUSES WERE LATE. WHAT WAS KEEPING them?

Standing on their front porches and lawns, the people of the neighborhood cast expectant glances up and down the street, or tried to see past the white vehicles labeled with bold, bright logos and slogans. NEWSACTION-6. LIVECAM-3. ACTIONCAM-7. A few people got bored with waiting and crossed the street to be closer to the action that was being video-recorded by NEWSACTION-6, LIVECAM-3, and ACTIONCAM-7. Mrs. Frances Bigelow, principal of the McKinley Intermediate School, was being interviewed on the question of whether or not the school should have been opened today.

Suddenly, the crowd around her turned and, as one, began to move swiftly across the school grounds toward the street. The school buses were approaching, led by a minivan.

The mass of reporters and cameramen broke up into pieces, each piece attaching itself to one or another of the buses. But when five Buddhist monks climbed out of the minivan, the pieces coalesced again into a single mass that attached itself to the monks. One was quite old, the others were young. With their shaved heads and flowing saffron robes, they reminded some people in the neighborhood of the ones they'd seen on television years ago, setting themselves on fire in Saigon.

Surely these monks were not going to do something like that?

No. The old monk led a procession; the younger ones walked behind, ringing small golden bells. All began chanting. Reporters thrust microphones at the old monk. *Excuse me, sir, could you tell us what this ceremony is all about . . . ? Do you speak English . . . ? Excuse me, I'm from NewsAction Six, could you tell our viewers the meaning of this ceremony . . . ?* Nimble cameramen leapt in front of the procession and, walking backward, filmed the monks as they moved solemnly down the line of buses, chanting and ringing the tiny golden bells. The reporters tagged alongside and continued to jab microphones, but the old monk ignored them.

Does anybody here know what the hell's going on? one reporter asked another. *Why aren't the kids getting out of the buses?* The reporters and the people of the neighborhood wondered why the monks hadn't appointed a spokesman to explain what they were doing. How could there be sense, structure, and order if these strange clerics conducted a ceremony of obscure meaning in a language no one understood?

The monks walked on, sandals shuffling on the pavement. They rang their bells and chanted in Pali, which is believed to be the tongue in which Buddha preached. This is what the monks were saying:

"May all suffering and fears of every kind disappear before they come near you. May all dangers, May all bad omens, May all that is not conducive to peace not come near you . . . "

Ken, sound up on this, okay? It sounds good anyhow . . . Jimmy, tight on the old man, then pan up to the kid's faces in the windows . . .

"May you live long, May you be prosperous, May you be popular and well known, May you be strong and vigorous, May your physical form be beautiful and attractive . . . "

Anyone have a name for the old monk . . . ? Excuse me, could we have your name . . . ? Janice, did you get an advance release that they were going to do this . . . ?

"May all despair and lamentations and such sorrows disappear from you, May the enmity be destroyed before it approaches you."

Jim, go long, get in the monks and the buses . . . Right . . . Right . . . We've got to get a translation . . . What is this?

The monks circled around the line of buses. Then they stood off to the side and continued chanting. The doors opened and the reporters and cameramen surged toward the buses, pointing cameras and boom microphones on long poles. The faces of the children and mothers pressed against the windows. A woman and a boy climbed off the first bus. A reporter shrieked, *That's one of the kids who was there! The kid the teacher saved!*

This was Paul Lim and his mother. She froze and pulled him close to her as the wave of newsmen and women rolled toward her, the microphone poles aimed like spears.

"Stop! Please! You're frightening them!" Mrs. Frances Bigelow called out.

Hand in hand, Paul Lim and his mother fled across the school's playground, toward the baseball diamond. The mob chased them, yelling at them to stop, shouting questions on the run.

What was it like you were there why did you come back to school are you scared what's your name what were you thinking when . . .

Paul and Mrs. Lim reached the baseball diamond and ran hand in hand down the second base line with reporters and cameramen on both sides. Mrs. Lim tripped over second base and fell in the infield dust. As Paul stopped to help her up, the crowd descended on them.

Go tight on him, Kenny. What made you decide to go to school today . . . Can you tell us what happened and what about the teacher who rescued you . . . Are you getting any of this, Jim?

Paul started to cry.

Move in on him, if everybody gets this kid and we don't, our ass is grass . . . I'm from WCIX from WCBR from Channel Six Seven Eight . . . What's your name and can you tell us why you're in school today?

Mrs. Lim sat on second base, holding Paul close to her. She was crying too. None of the people of the neighborhood could see her and her son, only the clot of jostling reporters and cameras and microphones. What had been an orderly rite of coverage had become chaotic and confusing, but the people knew that everything would make sense when they turned on the news tonight.

IT LAY A THOUSAND FEET BELOW THEM, SPRAWLING with exuberant chaos under tattered skeins of smog.

Like many San Franciscans, Heartwood detested L.A., though he often tried to look beyond the city's gargantuan flaws and see its virtues. If San Francisco had charm, L.A. had magnetism; if San Francisco was elegant and European, L.A. was glamorous and uniquely American in its booming incoherence. Those were the views he occasionally expressed when he was far from the city, but his opinions became as conventional as everyone else's when he was in it, or as was the case on Tuesday afternoon, above it. Looking down from the commuter plane, all he could see was what he hated about L.A.: its artificiality—a city conjured out of nothing by swindlers and speculators—its horizontal jumble and poisonous air, the plaque of traffic clogging its concrete arteries for miles on end. And something else that he couldn't see but could feel, even from a thousand feet up—the fraudulence of its promises. It was the Vatican of Illusions, promising the satisfaction of all needs, the gratification of all desires, the fulfillment, at the New World's farthest edge, of the New World's boundless hope, the perfect place in the perfect climate: the City of Angels. Pilgrims had come to it for the sunshine and the scent of oranges, for the role, the deal, the big defense plant contract, the beach-front condo, the Beverly Hills mansion, the house with swimming pool in the Valley; and what black depressions descended, what resentments were stirred when they didn't get what they'd come for, or discovered, if they did, that it wasn't enough and there was nowhere to go for more but the gray and vacant sea.

Descending toward LAX, the plane ran into turbulence and shuddered, intensifying Heartwood's moderate fear of flying into existential dread. Clutching the arm rests, he underwent a sudden reconversion and began reciting Hail Marys to keep at bay visions of the aircraft cartwheeling across the runway, his own sweet flesh flambéed in burning jet fuel.

Half an hour later, he and Gabriel were driving westward on the San Bernardino Freeway. In the near distance, against the dirty sky, the towers of Century City looked like the bars of an immense bar-chart drawn on a brown background. South Central sprawled in the opposite direction. It seemed indicative of how things were going in the city that a special agent armed with a seventeen-shot semiautomatic made sure to stay clear of those gutted neighborhoods where the most recent boosters' bandwagon—Los Angeles as multiracial capital of the Pacific Rim—had been stopped in its tracks by the riots of '92. Heartwood recalled a front-page photograph he'd seen last April: two Korean shopkeepers firing pistols into a crowd of black and Latino looters. The picture had the quality of stark prophecy: the multiracial capital of the Pacific Rim as a future Sarajevo.

Looking southward, across rooftops stretching as far as his eye could see, it occurred to him that the L.A. ganglands had become proper fields for his exploration of the psychopathic mind. The violence in them used to be inhumane rather than inhuman. Crimes of passion, barroom knife fights, a gun drawn at a crap game. Now the absurd, once kept out by faith and the communion of shared struggle and suffering, had penetrated the ghettos and barrios, making them prolific monster rookeries where sixteen-year-olds planned their funerals instead of junior proms. What bitterness must enter such young hearts, forced into an intimacy with death before they'd begun to know what life was all about. Out of the bitterness rose rage, out of the rage, the mindless brutality that made the early funerals all but inevitable. A closed circuit of murder begetting murder. How different was a Robert Alton Harris or a Duane Leonard Boggs from the Vietnamese thugs Gabriel had told him about, or the black carjacker who isn't satisfied with stealing a car but must kill its owner, or the Latino assassin who sprays a street corner on a drive-by with no concern for the innocent bystanders he slaughters? White, black, or brown, some awesome howling emptiness had entered them all, some . . . The term "spiritual void" came into Heartwood's mind, but he evicted it immediately. For if the source of the plague was spiritual, its cure did not lie with people such as himself and Walt Apetheker any more than it did with the social reformers or the law 'n' order crowd.

INTERSTATE-10

CHRISTOPHER COLUMBUS TRANSCONTINENTAL HIGHWAY

The sign appeared at the city limits. Nearly three thousand miles away, I-10 ended in Jacksonville, Florida. The plague seemed to have struck worst in the two states joined by the Christopher Columbus Transcontinental Highway. Disney World in the one, Disneyland in the other, sunshine and random violence in both. Perhaps there was some mysterious connection between overbright skies and Mickey Mouse, some evil synergy between warm climates and fantasy that drove young men to kill without reason.

Thousands of cars and trucks choked the highway named for the Great Navigator. Heartwood wasn't sure if Columbus would have appreciated the honor. Mile after mile, beneath a sky that grew more embrowned with each mile, linked suburbs reached into the industrial interior of Southern California, the Inland Empire. If he loathed the city, these ghastly outlands stirred in him a primal revulsion.

He was, besides, uneasy and uncertain about the wisdom and legitimacy of this adventure. On the plane, he'd read the interrogation transcript that had awakened Gabriel's suspicions of Tipton. Using the autopsy to set a trap for him, assuming they found him and he had something to hide, seemed out of professional bounds. But Heartwood's curiosity overruled his qualms.

A tangle of overpasses and underpasses marked the town limits of Pomona. That fell behind, then Ontario. Gabriel began to reminisce about the two years he'd spent in this infernal region as a narcotics agent, assigned to tracking down methedrine labs. He spoke of good old boys thrown out of work when Kaiser Steel shut down its huge Fontana mill, "Okies" who set up the labs in the outlaw tradition of their fathers' and grandfathers' whiskey stills.

"Turned out crystal meth, ice, croak, and wholesaled it to motorcycle gangs who put a walk on it and retailed it to long-haul truckers," he said with a hint of admiration for their entrepreneurship. "I think the depot in Fontana is supposed to be the biggest one in the country, probably the planet. So they had a helluva market." He gave Heartwood an almost imperceptible sidelong look. "Bikers' old ladies sometimes peddled their asses to the truckers. All of that right out in the open. Yeah, this was the goddamned Arizona territory if you were a narc, especially if you were a narc with any skin but white. . . . And here we are at the OK Corral."

He turned off at the Cherry Avenue exit. A water tower above a lumberyard carried an inspiring message: IF YOU THINK THIS WORLD IS BAD, YOU OUGHTA SEE HELL! JESUS SAVES!

The depot where Mike Silva was said to spend his off-hours was called "Trucktown" and it appeared to be the mother of all truckstops: Kenworths, Macks, and Peterbilts in a dozen colors, coupled to single- and double-reefed trailers numerous as boxcars in a switchyard. Inside, in booths and on counter stools, long-haul drivers stoked up on breakfast before hitting the road, hollow-eyed steelworkers from CSI slurped coffee before starting their shifts. Heartwood wished he'd dressed for the occasion; in his corduroy sport jacket and khaki trousers, he looked like a lost college professor.

Sitting at the counter, Gabriel cocked his head at a booth where a redheaded woman and a man in a ten-gallon hat were in quiet, earnest discussion with a biker whose wrestler's torso was naked except for a leather, chrome-studded vest. His bicep bore a tattoo of a swastika.

"Ma and Pa truckers," Gabriel whispered. "Probably laying in a supply of Mollies for the next trip."

"Mollies?"

"Speed. There's enough amphetamine around here to keep everybody in China awake for a week."

They ordered coffee from a harried waitress. Gabriel asked if she'd seen Mike Silva. As expected, she answered that she'd never heard of him.

"We're told he hangs out here."

"Ask him. The manager," she said, motioning sullenly at the cashier's booth, where a thickset man, talking on the phone, hulked behind the girl at the register.

"Wait here," Gabriel said.

As he waited, Heartwood became aware that a man three stools down was staring at him. In his mid to late twenties, his gaunt, unshaven face brought memories of Marines Heartwood had treated for combat neuroses.

"You guys cops, right?" he asked in a voice neither hostile nor friendly.

Returning his gaze to his coffee cup, Heartwood said nothing.

"Yeah, you're cops, all right. That Chingchong Chinaman you're with spells cop. C-O-P."

He sprayed the air on the last letter.

"Actually, I'm a psychiatrist."

The young man said by his look that he couldn't have been more dumbfounded if Heartwood had declared that he was an exotic dancer. Then he laughed.

"A psychiatrist? Hey, that's good. I like that. Me, I'm a brain surgeon."

"I really am a psychiatrist."

"Hey, dude, if that's what you are, you come to the right town. Overheard you. Mike left half an hour ago. And don't ask me where he went, 'cuz I don't know."

"Sure about that?" Gabriel asked, coming up on him from behind. "No idea at all?"

A long look sizing Gabriel up.

"Musta gone home. Mike plays it straight since he got out."

Gabriel moved closer, pressing his shoulder into the other man's.

"Folsom? Soledad? San Quentin?"

"You don't know?"

"This is a quiz to test your knowledge."

"The Q. Did three of a nickel. Him and a couple of skins cracked a nigger on Sierra Avenue back in '89. How's that, dude? Now you don't gotta ask me the details."

"But I do gotta ask you where he lives and you gotta tell me because nobody else in this greasepit seems to know and he's not in the book."

"Who the fuck are you?"

"Charlie Chin, the poor man's Chan. Special Agent, Department of Justice." Gabriel then grinned with the humor of a Red Guard interrogator. "Otherwise known as Chingchong Chinaman."

The young man reached across the counter, took a napkin from a dispenser, and wrote down the address.

"Thanks for your cooperation." Gabriel folded the napkin into his pocket and bent down and whispered into the man's ear, "I ever hear you say Chingchong Chinaman again I'll kick you so hard it'll hurt your mother *and* the customer she's fucking."

On the way to Silva's house, Heartwood decided that Fontana was the ugliest and strangest town in California. Blocks of new subdivisions, so shoddily constructed they were deteriorating even as they were being built, alternated with blocks of shanties whose front yards had become auto graveyards. Sheep grazed in a meadow near an enormous junkyard where old RVs and trailers, their last miles driven long ago, rusted away by the hundreds. A cemetery for dead road graders and construction cranes crowded up against a derelict fruit orchard amid whose blossomless trees smudge pots corroded, their smoke and warmth no longer needed against killer frosts. Like obedient sentries guarding an abandoned installation, they possessed a steadfastness at once ridiculous and noble. Gabriel made a couple of turns, passing a ghost chicken ranch, a defunct outdoor theater, the back of its screen smeared top to bottom with graffiti a brigade of semiologists could not have decrypted, then the vastest ruin of all in this town of ruins, the Kaiser mill. Heartwood would not have known what it was if Gabriel hadn't told him, for the stumps of smokestacks scattered across the mile-square wasteland and the skeletal blast furnaces silhouetted against the shrouded sky looked like a photograph of Hiroshima. At the fringes of the desolation, behind chain-link perimeter fences, scrapyards thrived. Scrap metal, scrap automobiles, black mountains of scrap tires. Aways off, atop a weed-covered rise, a trailer bore two signs large enough to be read from the road: WILLIAMS BAIL BONDS and DIVORCE/BANKRUPTCY/STOP EVICTION—CALL 856-9500.

A great ugliness awes no less than a great beauty, and Heartwood was awed. He felt as though he were touring the scene of some holocaust whose survivors peddled whatever was left. Laid-off steelworkers turned junk mongers or meth dealers. Bikers with swastika tattoos. Skinheads beating a black man on the main street. Here the rending of the social fabric was almost audible.

Gabriel turned away from the forsaken mill and entered a neighborhood of clapboard bungalows that had been more or less kept up. The mown lawns, looking ashen in the toxic air, the painted and repainted houses, the repaired and re-repaired fences evidenced a brave if futile defiance of the second law of thermodynamics.

In the middle of the block, in a front yard slashed by the diagonal shadow of a Washingtonian palm, a man in late middle age sat on a rusting lawn chair and stared at the street. He didn't move a muscle as Gabriel and Heartwood opened the gate and came up the walk.

"If you're here about the orchard, you shoulda called first," he said, squinting up at them from under a baseball cap.

Heartwood said they had not come about the orchard.

"Got one for sale. Was my father's. Grew lemons. Prime development land. Know anybody who's interested, tell 'em to call me. Jim Silva. I'm not in the book, my number's . . . "

Stifling a sneeze, Heartwood said, "We're here to see Mike. Is he home? We didn't find him at Trucktown."

His squint deepened. "Parole officers? Mike hasn't violated his parole. I can tell you that. Stayed put, kept his nose clean, hasn't missed a day of work since he got out."

"Hey, it makes me feel warm and cuddly all over when I hear about a rehabbed con." Gabriel produced his badge. "We need to talk to Mike about a case we're working on."

Jim Silva studied the badge and whistled through his teeth softly and said, "Department of Justice? Special agent? What the hell's that boy done now?"

"Nothing. We just need to talk to him. Is he home or what?"

"Asleep. Works the graveyard shift at CSI. He'll be up around five, six. Come by then."

"My friend was waked out of a dead sleep this morning by somebody who said we should talk to Mike. We've flown down from Sacramento just to do that, so how about you get his ass up."

Silva hesitated briefly, then rose and went inside.

"I give up trying to teach you a bedside manner," Heartwood said to Gabriel, and then sneezed twice.

A short time later, Mike Silva alias Thor came out with his father. Like the older man, he had pale eyes that did not match his olive complexion. He stood only five-eight at most, but his chest was broad and his arms, exposed by the tank top he was tucking into his jeans, had long, tightly woven muscles that looked like bunched electrical cables.

"So what the fuck is this? What the fuck is so important you got to get a working man outta the sack for?"

He cocked his jaw. Heartwood tensed, waiting for Gabriel to explode, and was delightfully surprised when he explained the reasons for the intrusion in the most civil way.

"I don't know no Boggs. Hear what I'm sayin'? I didn't have nothin' to do with shootin' up those kids, and I don't talk to cops without my lawyer here," a still feisty Silva answered, but his defiant manner wasn't what impressed Heartwood. As he half-turned, as if to go back into the house, he showed his left shoulder; it bore a tattoo of a circled cross.

"I'm not a cop, I'm a psychiatrist," Heartwood said. "You're not under suspicion of anything."

"A *headshrinker*? Well, you're with a cop and that's one too many for me to talk to without my lawyer here. Hear what I'm sayin'?"

Gabriel's meager fund of patience was exhausted.

"You hear what I'm sayin', dickhead. It's got to be in the terms of your parole that you're not to hang with any skinheads or known felons. Make you a bet that you do anyway. Make you a second bet that I'll get the particulars, report them to your parole officer, and then your sweet young white ass is back to the Q to make the black boys happy who missed it. So how about you give us ten minutes of your time?"

"For chrissake, Michael, talk to these guys."

Silva alias Thor flexed his prison gym muscles while sullenly gazing at Gabriel.

"I didn't make no jungle jerkoffs happy in the Q or anywhere." He pointed to the tattoo. "They didn't mess with us."

"It's great to meet a virgin. Now tell us what you know about Boggs and his baby brother, Tipton."

Silva shoved his hands in his back pockets and contemplated the ground for a moment.

"It ain't a lot," he said.

And it wasn't, but what he did know was enough to cause Heartwood to begin rethinking his theories, which he found painful. He tended to marry his theories and didn't divorce them easily. Inside the bungalow's dim and shabbily furnished living room, he put down his pen and wondered what to make of Silva's account of meeting Boggs and Tipton at an Aryan Youth rock concert outside Fontana the previous summer, of befriending them and then putting them in touch with a recruiter for the W.A.R. skinheads. It sounded a little too neat, it violated what he knew about people like Boggs: they tended not to be joiners. He looked at the young ex-convict, drinking a Coke and slouching in a threadbare chair, and tried to think of a reason why he would lie or embroider the truth. But his prison-hardened face, far older than its twenty-four years, was unreadable.

"Mike, I'd like to go over a couple of points to make sure we understand you correctly." He hoped to catch him in an inconsistency if not an outright contradiction. "You said it was your impression that Tipton talked Duane into joining the W.A.R. skins? That Tipton seemed to be the one calling the shots?"

"Play back your tape. That isn't exactly what I said. Duane had the newsletter he picked up at the concert. Told me he'd been in some training program in San Joaquin—auto mechanics, I think—with a bunch of gooks and beaners and that they got better treatment. He said the stuff in the newsletter was right."

"White men built this nation, white men are this nation. That stuff."

"He said that was right on."

"But Tipton made the proposal to join."

"*Proposal?*" He smiled sarcastically and a mean twinkle came into his eyes. "That's a word. Proposal. Yeah, Tipton made the proposal and Duane didn't have no objections. Hear what I'm sayin'? They were into it, both of them. They were into the music. Skrewdriver."

"That was the name of the group?"

"Spelled with a K."

"Do you have one of their tapes?"

"It ain't no fuckin' Christmas album."

"I'd like to hear it."

Silva swaggered into another room and came out with a boombox.

The first song was a bizarre fusion of heavy-metal rock and Germanic marches. Guitars struck ominous reverb chords and death-knell notes; stomping boots provided percussion. Heartwood could make out only snatches of the lyrics. Some anthem to Teutonic gods, promises of Valhalla to skinheads who died fighting for the Aryan cause, prophecies of a coming racial apocalypse. "Lightning strikes, thunder roars, cloven hooves storm the shores!" *Boomstompboom.* "Hail The Order! Hail The Order! Life's a struggle! Life's a struggle!" *Boomstompboom.* Silva put on a little show, possibly to outrage Gabriel. He lip-synched the words, kept time with jerks and bobs of his head. The happy tune ended with a crash of drums. "We are on the frontlines! Skinhead! Skinhead! Skinhead!"

Heartwood gestured to Silva to shut the boombox off. He got the message, understood its appeal to people like Boggs and Tipton.

"That garbage reminds me of the fart on the crowded elevator. It oughta be kept in the asshole, where it belongs," Gabriel said.

"Ain't no worse than gangsta rap," Silva said. "Folks eat up songs about niggers killing niggers, niggers most of all. So what's wrong with songs about whites killing niggers?"

"I want to get back to what happened after Boggs and Tipton failed their initiation ceremony," Heartwood said. "They failed it because of Boggs, right?"

"It's there on your tape, man. Listen to it and lemme get back to sleep."

"Tell us again, Mike," Gabriel said. The elder Silva looked in for a second and went back outside. Silva alias Thor swigged from his Coke and set it next to a small box on an end table on which cans and glasses and cups had left marks like the linked rings of a paper chain.

"Fuck. Okay. They had to pass the test same as we all did. Got to whack on a minority, preferably a nigger 'cause they're the most trouble, to prove you got the balls to be one of us. So the way I heard it . . . Hear what I'm sayin', I heard this, I wasn't there because my parole says I can't engage in no movement activities. Violation of my rights, my lawyer says, but that's the fuckin' ZOG for you. ZOG bends over backwards for spades and spics but not white dudes . . . "

"ZOG?" Heartwood asked.

"Washington fucking D.C.," answered Silva. "The Zionist Occupied Government. So the way I heard it, some guys in The Order brought Duane and Tipton to the south end of town, the other side of the freeway, pointed out a nigger, and told 'em to whack him. Tipton was set to go, but Duane about pissed his trou. So two of the guys went out and whacked the nigger, they came back to the car, told Duane, 'See, that's how you do it, you chickenshit asshole.' They whacked on Duane hard and told him and Tipton both if they ever saw their sorry asses again, they'd do 'em both for good."

Heartwood said, "And then Duane and his brother came to you."

"It's on the tape."

"Duane was crying. Said he fouled up everything he ever tried, that he wasn't good enough. Tipton wanted to know if they could have a second chance, what would they have to do to prove they had what it takes."

"On the tape."

"And you said you couldn't help them, but your advice was that they would have to, quote, blow up a church full of niggers, gooks, or beaners, unquote, before anybody in the movement would so much as look at them."

"It's on the tape, man. I didn't advise them to blow up a church, or to do anything. Just my way of sayin' that they couldn't have no second chance. Don't go tryin' to say I encouraged Duane to shoot that fuckin' bus up."

"Do you know the proverb, 'The guilty man fleeth when none pursueth'?"

"You sound like a faggot with all that 'eeth ueth' shit. Hear what I'm sayin'?"

Heartwood shut off the tape, stood, and thanked him for his time.

"Hey, no problem. Wake me up whenever you feel like it."

It was Gabriel who noticed that the small box on the end table was a portable chess set.

"You play?"

Puzzled, Silva looked at the set.

"What is it? Playin' chess is a parole violation?"

"No, wiseass. I asked if you played."

"Learned how in the Q. Helped pass the time."

Heartwood asked if he had had any matches with Duane, a question that drew a sharp, derisive laugh.

"What is that supposed to mean?"

"Just funny you asked me that, 'cause Duane bugged me to teach him, the whole month I knew him, it seemed like."

"He didn't know how?"

"Said he did. Said some buddy of his he worked with up in San Joaquin taught him. But the first time I played him, I kicked his ass in about six moves. So then he kept buggin' me to teach him. Imfuckin'-possible. Whaddya call it when a dude can't remember shit you showed him how to do two days before?"

"Short-term memory loss," Heartwood said.

"Yeah. That was him. Drugs, his brother said. Another good reason we didn't have him in the movement. Don't need no speed demons and potheads who can't remember shit. I'd show him, you know, a queen's pawn opening, or a king's pawn, or a two knights and two days later have to start all over again."

Gabriel said, "Any idea where Tipton is now? As of last night, he hadn't been home for four days."

"Soon as he checks in with me, you'll be the first to know."

"Mike, I'm glad that bending over for the homies in the Q didn't ruin your sense of humor."

They rode in silence across town toward the Tipton house. Gabriel scanned through the country music stations until he found a jazz program, then hummed quietly to a Count Basie tune. They were on Sierra, passing an acupuncture clinic and a coin-operated laundry, when he said,"A plug nickel for your thoughts, Dr. H."

"About what?"

"About the situation in Bosnia. What do you think about what?"

"All right. Maybe we've, or you . . . maybe you've got a live, warm suspect and maybe you've got a motive."

"Oh, yeah. I think so. Tipton staged the massacre to prove his mettle to his Aryan brothers, got rid of his fuckup brother in the process, and didn't leave a fingerprint."

JESUS LIVES! proclaimed a handbill on a telephone pole.

"They're big on Jesus out this way."

"You lived here, you'd be too. I asked about the chess because that seems important to you. Proving that Duane had a systematic mind even if he was dumb as a post. Looks like his playing level didn't impress Silva at all. Doesn't square with what the college kid told you. Guess he wasn't as good a teacher as he thought."

"He didn't say that Boggs was tournament caliber. Only that he could play well enough."

"Not that I thought Boggs's chess playing made any difference one way or another."

"Just an angle I was pursuing. Trying to get some picture of the guy."

Gabriel watched Heartwood pop open his briefcase and take out a newspaper clipping. He sat back to read it, massaging his forehead with his thumb and forefinger.

"What's that?"

"Nothing," Heartwood said distantly. "A clip from the college newspaper Weathers gave me."

He finished reading, then replaced the clipping and sat in that prim, secretive way, the briefcase on his lap, fingers curled over the locks. He seemed preoccupied about something. Gabriel was going to ask what was on his mind when he saw the Tipton house, a tidy stucco ranch east of Sierra.

No one was home. A neighbor said that the elder Tipton could be found at work, a chicken ranch at the south end of town; his son would be at the high school.

But Jacob still had not returned to school. A severe, dark-haired woman in the administration office confirmed that he had been absent without excuse since last Friday. Had he attended classes on Thursday? Gabriel asked. The woman checked her attendance records and nodded.

At the chicken ranch, manure from a hundred thousand clucking hens made little hills that resembled termite mounds. Heartwood and

Gabriel could hardly breathe for the stench. They found Wilson Tipton on a bulldozer, pushing the piles from one end of the ranch to the other. Somewhere in his mid-forties, he had a sparse, hay-colored mustache and a lean face whose youthful handsomeness was wearing away under the wind of mounting years. Gabriel had come prepared to battle another sour, sneering racist like Silva, but found himself drawn to Tipton almost immediately. It might have been the Navy tattoo on his forearm, with the name of his ship on a banner, that inclined him to look upon the man favorably. Or it might have been his softspoken manner as he looked down from his seat atop the bulldozer, rattling at idle.

He said his son had not dropped out of school, he was merely lying low for a while, avoiding reporters who wanted to talk to him about that goddamned half-brother of his. Lying low where? L.A. That was a big place. Tipton apologized for not being more specific; Jacob hung out in L.A. a lot, mostly on weekends, but he didn't know where exactly. Truth was, he'd lost control of the boy the past year. And had he last seen his son after he came home from school on Thursday? Yes. Said he was going to L.A. Gabriel gave him a long, appraising look, judged that he was telling the truth, and decided to tread easily.

"Has his own car, I take it."

"Yeah. I went through this the other day with some other cop. What the hell's going on? Is the kid in some serious trouble this time?"

Heartwood assured him he was not and explained about the autopsy. Tipton laughed harshly.

"I can tell you why Duane done it. He was flat crazy. Crazy as his mother. The single worst decision I ever made in my life was marrying that . . . Shit, there ain't a word for what she is."

"See you were on the *Galveston,*" Gabriel said, gesturing at the tattoo burned into Tipton's arm in some forgotten parlor in some forgotten port.

"Gunner's mate second class."

Gabriel mentioned that that had been his rate, and for several minutes, they engaged in salty reminiscences, Gabriel of riverine patrols in the Mekong Delta, Tipton of shelling North Vietnamese shore batteries and being shelled in return. He seemed almost nostalgic for the days when his life had some drama and poignancy, his cruiser's eight-inchers sundering the still sticky nights in the Gulf of Tonkin.

"Sometimes I think I should have stayed in. Be a retired chief by now, sitting on a beach and drawing a full pension. You been by the old mill?" he asked, raising with a finger the bill of his baseball cap.

Gabriel said they had been.

"Used to work there. First job I had after I come home from 'Nam. Casting mill. Got laid off when they shut her down. Took me two years before I found this job. Shoveling chickenshit on the last chicken ranch in Fontana, California. Life does put you 'round some damned funny turns, don't it?"

And leaning with his palm flat against the bulldozer, Gabriel agreed that life indeed did that and had Tipton heard from his son since last Thursday? No. He hated asking the next question, for he truly liked the former sailor.

"The massacre happened on Friday. Why did you say your boy went to get away from reporters?"

Tipton raised the bill another inch and looked at Gabriel squarely and steadily.

"Now wait a second, you don't think that . . . "

"No," Gabriel said. "Just a cop's habit, asking questions like that."

"Didn't say that's why he *went.* Said that's why he's staying."

"How would you know that if you haven't heard from him?"

Frowning, Tipton rubbed his arm with a thumb.

"I don't know. I'm guessing that's why he stayed. Maybe he's got some other reason for staying this long and no word. He's been . . . He's . . . " His voice trailed off and the sadness in his look deepened into one of real sorrow, of a private suffering.

Gabriel sensed that he was not withholding information but was merely keeping his pain secret. It would be impossible for a man like him to admit, even to himself much less to others, that he knew what Jacob had become.

"If we were to look for him in Hollywood. Sunset. Santa Monica Boulevard . . . "

"You might find him around there."

"Any particular place he hangs around? A bar, a restaurant, a corner? I know this isn't easy for you, but you'd save us a lot of time if you know."

"There's an old viaduct under the Hollywood Freeway. A lot of kids, runaways, hang out there. Hustlers and, you know. Some asshole, some ex-con is kind of their leader. I had a go-round with him a couple of months ago, when I went there to get Jacob the hell out of there." He cupped his hand over his mouth, coughed. "Cops picked the kid up there a couple of times, too. You got a map of L.A., I'll show you about where it is, but you'll need to ask around."

"If we find him, you want us to tell him you'd like to hear from him?"

Tipton gave a quick nod, and feeling an ache of sympathy, Gabriel hoped not to discover that Jacob was something far worse than a male prostitute.

▬ ▬ ▬

Yawning, Mace looked up at the ancient tintype ceiling, its scrollwork almost invisible under layers of gray paint. Half an hour to go. He lowered his gaze to the young man who sat across the table from him, finishing up an admissions questionnaire.

"Are you about done, Mr. . . . ?"

"Pickering. Ben Pickering. I'm close to," the young man said in an adenoidal voice. The tip of his tongue curled over his upper lip as he wrote, in a childish scrawl, the history and nature of his dependencies, his employment record, his arrest record—the rough outlines of a useless existence.

A fluorescent light sputtered overhead and voices murmured in a nearby cubicle, where a counselor told a junkie about his course of treatment: acupuncture five days a week, Narcotics Anonymous meetings twice a week. Pretty easy, Mace thought. Probably a pothead.

"A couple more questions," Pickering said. His hair had been dyed a bright blond and was cut in a modified Mohawk, and he wore a leather vest over a denim shirt with cut-off sleeves baring gaunt, tattooed arms, the one proclaiming that he'd been born to raise hell, the other that he'd been born to lose. How much hell-raising he'd done was open to question, but he surely must have lost; otherwise he wouldn't be here.

He passed the questionnaire to Mace, and sat back in a slouch, managing to make his sloppy posture look insolent. His fingers beat quickly on his knees, his eyes, in sockets blued from lack of sleep, roved randomly over the bare walls, seeking something to fix on, finding none. He brought a pack of cigarettes out of a vest pocket.

"There's no smoking here, Mr. Pickering."

The counselors could address patients formally or informally at their discretion, but Mace and other part-time help were required to call them "Mr.—Ms.—Miss—Mrs." to help them regain a sense of self-esteem. What a joke! Only way to build their self-esteem would be to feed them hallucinogenic mushrooms and let them think they're Napoleon or Joan of Arc.

A cigarette between his fingers, Pickering asked, with a note of recalcitrance, if it was all right to hold one. Or did the rules say that he had to keep his cigarette in the pack?

"Just don't light up," Mace answered amiably.

He studied the questionnaire. The usual wretched biography. Father's address unknown. Mother's address unknown. Have you ever been convicted of a felony? Yes. If yes, note in the space at right the dates and charges. The litany of petty crimes, with the expected misspellings. Felany poseshun of marauana. Poseshun of a dangerus weapin . . . Mace noticed, however, a greater than normal number of violent crimes: two purse snatchings as a juvenile, two third-degree assaults, one attempted armed robbery as a juvenile, possession of an illegal assault weapon when he was nineteen. Interesting. Profession . . . welder . . . last employer . . . Sandy Point Tank company, Portland, Oregon . . . What kind of substances do you use regularly? Drinking (a lot of beer), marauana, coke (if I can aford) . . .

"Have you drunk any alcohol or used any substances today?" Mace asked, turning the form over to the box labeled "For Staff Use Only."

Pickering looked on silently, with a sullen expression on his spade-shaped face that reminded Mace of history book photographs of Lee's army at Appomattox: lank, exhausted men, defeated yet still restive. Mean.

"You might as well tell me because the next step is a urine test."

"Okay, I had a couple beers, did some coke."

"How much coke?"

"Not much."

"Powdered or rock?"

"I look like a nigger to you?"

"What do you mean by that?" Mace asked, though he knew perfectly well what was meant.

"Crack is a nigger drug."

Mace reached into a box and gave him a sample bottle.

"I'm required to watch you."

Pickering stood, his hands jammed into the side pockets of his vest. Long and bony, a body that was all sharp angles. He wore a key ring on one side of his belt, a holstered jackknife on the other.

"You're gonna *watch* me take a *piss*, that's what you're sayin'?"

A loser, but a loser still capable of attitude. A possibly dangerous loser.

"It's so no one uses someone else's urine sample. It's only a precaution."

"You get off on that or what?"

A little too much attitude, Mace thought. Asking for it. The type who picks fights he knows he can't win. Asking to get hurt. Asking to lose.

He got to his feet, expanding his chest as he moved around to the other side of the table. Pickering drew back half a step, slumping in submission; in the next instant, his pride took over and he straightened his shoulders and put on a cocky grin. No big bruiser was going to intimidate him.

"A little advice, Mr. Pickering. I'm only a part-time assistant around here, so if you've got smart-assing to get out of your system, I guess it's best you get it out on me. But after you give the sample, you're going to be interviewed by a drug rehabilitation counselor. She's going to ask you a lot of questions, give you a test to fill out, and if she decides you're too much of a smart-ass for us to bother with, you're not going to be admitted to this program and that means no checks from Social Security. If that was too much information in one gulp, I'll put it this way—you're going to be shit out of luck if you don't watch your mouth and how you act. The men's room is this way."

He brought him into the back hallway and opened the men's room door. The top panel was a one-way window.

"So now what? You goin' to hold it?"

He had golden brown eyes. Feline. Another feral human.

"Don't screw around with me, Mr. Pickering."

"Just gettin' it outta my system."

Pleading for it, that's what he was doing.

"Go on inside, Mr. Pickering."

This is what I do for spending money, he thought, peering through the window as Pickering unzipped his trousers, then looked back at the door with a stupid grin and pointed at his penis. This is what I do because Lewis is angry and won't send any money. *I'll go the tuition because that's my responsibility, but everything else, you're on your own, and it's about time anyway.* So this is what I do. Watch losers piss, like some faggot voyeur in a bus station.

Pickering walked out, affecting a swagger. Mace escorted him to Susan Sexton's office, then returned to his table to wait for the next hopeless case to come in from the waiting room. This is what I do. He heard Sexton begin her catechism . . .

How long have you been using cocaine and marijuana, Ben? Why did you start . . . ? In another office, a woman howled, *He's makin' me come in here for tests so's I can keep the kids, him, which gets himself so goddamn drunk that he can't even see his dick to pee straight?* Then the counselor's soothing voice: *Please, keep your voice down, Betty. It isn't him, it's the court, it's a court order . . .*

This is what I do, all because Lewis doesn't get it, or if he gets it, can't accept it. That I'm me now. That it's over, all that traipsing door to door with the Book of Mormon, ringing doorbells, telling people about Joseph Smith and Brigham Young and all the prophets who sought to build New Zion out where the buffalo roamed. Hello hello, may we have a moment of your time to tell you some good news? Hello hello, did you know that we are in the Latter Days and when they're over, do you want to wallow in the Telestial Kingdom with adulterers and liars, or live in glory as gods in the Celestial?

Mission work had interested Mace for a while because it gave him the chance to practice one of his skills: he was a natural dissembler with an uncanny knack for saying one thing while thinking its opposite or for expressing one emotion while feeling another without giving the slightest clue that he was masquerading. Most of the conversions that Lewis and he effected were his doing. Lewis could move Macs and IBMs out of his store, but he wasn't much as a salesman of eternal life. Mace, on the other hand, was persuasive. He loved to exercise his ability to preach a doctrine he did not believe in, to manipulate people's emotions and turn their minds into believing that his faith was genuine. People mistook his enthusiasm for zeal; even the most skeptical at least agreed to read the literature in Lewis's briefcase, while the more gullible were ready to sign up for Adult Baptism. He was a master of illusion, a magician of sorts, but unlike the stage magician, who loves his audience for accepting his sleights of hand, he felt only contempt for his.

Mace had never experienced love in any of its forms. The bronze breastplate of his torso shielded a heart made of the same metal. It could be pierced by fear, lust, and rage, but love, compassion, and pity bounced off it without leaving a mark. Even as a child, he'd had difficulty showing affection for Lewis and Anne. He forced himself to hug and kiss them and to say kind things he didn't mean. He made sure to remember their birthdays and to give Anne a card on Mother's Day. He mastered the outward show of love, and in truth, he'd done this partly in the hope that going through the motions would somehow generate love itself. But in the flow of time, the sham began to leave a sour taste in his mouth, and the joy with which his parents received his empty words and embraces turned the sour taste to acid. How gullible they were to believe that he had given them the real thing instead of an imitation. But then, anyone who thought that an angel named Moroni appeared to Joseph Smith with a set of golden tablets was likely to believe anything.

He knew that his bland good looks also helped to lull them. Like the people he'd met on his missionary treks, his parents assumed that he with his fine but unremarkable face and hair hued like grain was as pleasant and honest as he appeared.

He'd made the same assumption. He could deceive people easily because, until that moment of white pain in a Bakersfield gas station, he'd deceived himself about who and what he truly was. He'd behaved as a creature of his image: the image others had of him, the image he had of himself, which were one and the same. Yet he'd been aware that another personality dwelled within him, a secret Mace, a darker, more interesting Mace, whom he'd wanted to get to know better but had been afraid to.

Until the moment that changed everything.

In the weeks afterward, as he recovered in the hospital, waited in the office of the surgeon who fixed film stars' faces, or lay in his room at home in pretty Redlands, he'd silently asked, "Why did this happen to me?" and received for answers the hum of air conditioners, the whisper of traffic outside his hospital window, the dubbed laughter of daytime TV. He'd consulted trendy books that claimed to reveal why bad things happened to good people. Maybe he wasn't good. Maybe his loveless heart was a sign that he was evil. But how could that be? He had not made it that way. It was the heart he'd been born with and could not be any more evil than a withered arm, or the nerve disorder that made some people incapable of feeling heat or cold.

One afternoon late last May, he was lying on the living room sofa, crippled by one of the headaches that struck him periodically. The missing eye, still sending messages of pain to the nerves. Phantom pain, though it felt real enough, it sure did. His father came in and asked how he was feeling. Mace answered that he had a bad headache and then asked Lewis if he could answer the question that seemed to have no answer. He was a tall, thin, earnest man, and he stood without speaking, furrowing his earnest brow. A kind of emotional static electricity crackled in the air. There was a tension between them that went back three years, when Mace declared that he was going to college instead of on a mission abroad. Looking for converts in Redlands and San Bernardino had been amusing, but the picture of himself preaching to Amazon Indians was appalling.

Lewis sat down, his hands folded. Perhaps the awful thing was a sign that he was being called, away from the secular world of college and to a mission. Mace looked at him. And then there was, Lewis went on . . . Ah, this is difficult . . . the matter of who . . . that girl . . . Mace continued to stare and waved at his father, telling him he need not go on. He did not want to hear that an interracial couple, who would have drawn no attention in L.A. or San Francisco, was asking for trouble in that part of the state.

He got up off the sofa. That's all you have to say? Then Lewis: I don't know, son. Maybe the answer will come in God's own good time. Mace laughed harshly. That's all your goddamned Mormon wisdom can come up with? Maybe you ought to send a fax to the Italian angel. Yeah, maybe if you fax old Moroni, he'll come on down with the answer on one of his golden tablets. Lewis stood trembling, a knobby hand on his knobby hip. I can't believe I'm hearing that kind of talk from you. Mace told him to believe it because he never believed any of that bullshit. Lewis pointed at him, the picture of the stern outraged father. You watch what you're saying! What happened to you doesn't give you the right to talk blasphemy, son. Then Mace, still laughing while the jolts of pain lit with neon sparks the darkness where his eye had been: Stop calling me son. I'm not your son, you pious asshole. Anne burst into the room. Mace! You, Mace! Don't ever say such things . . . Oh, Mace, darling . . . She came toward him, reaching out to touch him . . . Darling, you're not yourself . . . He backed away and said joyfully, Oh, yes, I am. Yes, I am.

. . . well, okay, yeah, it's a court order, but his lawyer got the court to issue that order . . . Betty, please . . . It's only twice a week you have to come in . . . Ben, this armed robbery, did you commit that to get money for drugs? . . . Yeah . . . How would you describe your relations with your parents? One word—shit . . .

This is what I do. Watch them pee, listen to human trash talking their garbage in this toxic waste dump for toxic people. Three hours a day three days a week for spending money. Dry-cleaning money. Laundry money. Gas money for the Camaro.

Ben, was there anything in your relations with your parents that caused you to start drinking and taking drugs . . .

Jesus, thought Mace, why do people like this exist? It offended him that they breathed the same air he did, walked on the same earth as he walked.

Were you ever sexually molested, Ben? . . . What? . . . Were you ever sexually molested? . . . By who? . . . Anyone. A stranger, a neighbor. Did either or both of your parents sexually abuse you when you were a child? . . . You mean like my father? What're you askin'? My father wasn't no pervert and I'm not neither . . . I didn't say that, Ben. I'm only asking to determine the causes of your early drug and alcohol abuse. You said you started drinking when you were twelve . . . Well, it's a bullshit question. Sexually molested, shit . . . Please cooperate, Ben. . . .

The cocaine talking, thought Mace, handing a questionnaire to his next customer, a scrawny girl in a torn flight jacket. The cocaine talking, the cocaine fueling the belligerence, and it probably had been only five percent cocaine that went up his nose, the other ninety-five percent a brain-bending recipe of walks. Linocaine and crushed diet pills and maybe a few milligrams of boraxo. The girl began to fill out the form with trembling hand. Blotches on her cheeks. AIDS? This is what I do.

. . . okay, a nigger did once. In prison. This nigger thought he was the bull of the block, said he got to sample new wares first. Said it was quality control or some cute shit like that . . . Silence . . . *You were raped, Ben? . . .* Silence . . . *Ben? . . . Yeah.* The answer came almost inaudibly, the voice breaking. *Was that a cause of your starting to use harder drugs like cocaine? . . . Ain't no fuckin' nigger goin' to get me on drugs. Did it all on my lonesome, like everything else I done. . . .*

Here it came. The downslide from the high. Self-pity.

Very well, Ben. Incidentally, if you have a problem with minorities, please keep them to yourself. There are a lot of minorities in the program, and you'll have to get along with them . . . Got no problem with minorities, they got a problem with me . . .

The words, so close to those a skinhead had spoken to him—*You done got a problem, surfer boy, because I got a problem with you*—caused Mace to sit up.

I understand what you're saying, Ben . . . Susan Sexton's sexy sibilance . . . *Please sit down* . . . *Listen, I'm sayin' the big problems is theirs with me, and know what? They're goin' to have a big problem* . . . *Please sit down or you're going to be forced to leave. Are you intoxicated right now?* . . . *Fuck yeah I am* . . . A thump, then the shudder of the partition wall as Ben drove a fist or a shoulder into it.

"Mace!" Susan called.

This is what I do. Mace jumped up from his chair. Cool their jets when they get unruly, and if they really get unruly, hustle them out like a bar bouncer.

I come to this town because I heard about what that guy done here. That Boggs guy, and he had the right idea and I'm goin' to do what he did, then you'll see who's got the fuckin' problem!

The words stopped Mace cold for a moment.

"Mace! Get in here now!"

Counselors and patients were coming out of the cubicles to see what the commotion was all about. Mace ran into Susan's office. She was braced against a wall covered with diplomas certifying her competence and Pickering was waving a pistol in the air.

"What're you doing?"

He kept his voice low, unthreatening.

Pickering blinked and looked at the revolver, a palm-size Saturday Night Special, as if he didn't know how it had gotten into his hand. He wasn't pointing it at Susan, only showing it to her as proof that he was a dangerous man.

"Better let me have that," Mace said.

"Oh, man," Pickering groaned. "I wasn't . . . "

"I know, Ben."

Mace advanced to within a foot of him, holding his hand out. The idea of touching Pickering repelled him; who knew what alien bacteria crawled on that pasty skin?

"Do I get it back?"

"No."

Pickering slipped the gun back into his vest pocket and raised his hands.

"Okay, man? I'm good. No problems. I was just showin' off."

Mace stood fast, his hand still extended. He was completely focused, his blood flowed through his veins like freon through copper tubes.

"Ben, if you don't give me that gun right now, I'm going to break every bone in your body."

Pickering whipped his head to one side and cried out, "Fucked up again!"

He drew the pistol and handed it over, as Mace had known he would.

Susan sighed audibly and sank into her desk chair.

"Thanks, Mace. I'm glad you're here."

She was in her early thirties, with wavy chestnut hair and thick, sensual lips. He would have her one of these days. Might as well get something more than six-fifty an hour for risking his neck and his health in this Dumpster.

"Happy to be of service. It's what I do," he said with a mock bow, then turned to Pickering. "You'd better do as Miss Sexton asked and sit down."

"That won't be necessary," she said sharply, and wrote a note and clipped it to Pickering's file.

"I don't think we can be of any help to you at the moment, Ben. I'm recommending that you be examined first at the county mental health center. If they determine that you're suitable for this program, then we'll try again. Maybe you'll behave yourself next time around."

She handed the file to Pickering and glanced at Mace.

"I suppose we'll have to install metal detectors next. Ben, do you have money for bus fare or a taxi?"

"Got my own car," he muttered.

"It's our policy not to allow patients we know to be intoxicated to leave here and drive themselves home. That's for our own protection as well as yours and other people's."

"I can take him back," Mace volunteered.

Susan looked up at the clock.

"But you're off now. You don't have to."

"It's another thing I do. I'll get cab fare back out of petty cash." He faced Pickering. "Okay, Ben, you gave me your gun, now I'll take your car keys."

He unclipped the key ring from his belt, slapped it into Mace's palm, and went toward the door.

"Mace, you really shouldn't. He's . . . "

"Nothing I can't handle," he said with a casual gallantry, then, placing his hands on her desk, brought his face closer to hers. A good smell. A whisper of cologne and soap. "But I wouldn't mind if you mentioned to the director that I deserve a raise." He smiled to distract her from his gaze, wandering down her blouse. A satiny blue bra. A warmth rising from there. Early thirties. They were really hot at that age, he'd heard.

A little flustered by his nearness, she brushed back a lock of her hair.

"I'll be sure to mention it."

"I really appreciate that, Susan."

Pickering's fifteen-year-old Buick was not quite the wreck Mace had expected. Why these drifters, with their marginal incomes, favored eight-cylinder gas-guzzlers mystified him. No thought to the future, live for the moment. Die for it too.

"When you goin' to give me the gun back?" Pickering asked diffidently. The coke with its grant of exaggerated self-confidence was wearing off quickly. He was heading for the ditch in which he would see himself for the nobody he was; then he would need another blast as an antidote to despair, another blast to get him through the rest of the day.

Mace passed the revolver to him. He hesitated, then snatched it before Mace changed his mind.

"Well, you got some balls. I could waste you right now."

"Could, but won't."

"How come you're so sure?"

"Call me a good judge of character. Put it in your pocket, Ben. No sense keeping it out in plain sight, is there?"

Pickering did this.

"Now you owe me one. Two, as a matter of fact. I could've called the cops, then you wouldn't have to worry about making room and board."

"I can make that okay. Got some money saved up from my last job. I was makin' eleven-fifty an hour."

"That's more than I make."

"You don't believe me?"

"I believe you."

"You don't believe me, look at this."

He reached for his wallet and pulled from it a rumpled pay stub, which he shoved under Mace's nose. Mace drew back, fearful that it would touch him.

"You were doing pretty well, then. But you couldn't hold it together, could you? You couldn't stand the idea that you might actually make something of your life, so you smarted off to the boss, started showing up late, then didn't show up at all one or two days and got yourself fired."

"Laid off."

"Fired, Ben."

"Laid off because they hired a gook. Some slant-eye that could hardly speak no English. Some kinda affirmative action shit."

So predictable, thought Mace. The loser's invincible sense of grievance.

"Ben, let's speak honestly to each other. You lost your job for the same reason you've gotten booted out of the program before you even started. You said it yourself. You fucked up. And you fucked up because that's what you are. A fuckup."

"How do you know so much? Only thing you know about me is what I put on that paper, and you don't even know even if I made it all up."

"I take one look at a guy like you, listen to you say ten words, and it's like the words to a song I know by heart."

Pickering looked out the side window. The spring sun was falling, the sky shedding a weepy blue light over downtown and over the old San Joaquin Palace, in a time long past a hotel for senators and important visitors who arrived on the California Zephyrs and danced to big bands in the ballroom that was now a warehouse for the county welfare department, as the rooms where the senators and important visitors slept and fornicated were now offices for caseworkers, cluttered with the paperwork of misery. Beneath the hotel's arcade, with its mission arches, homeless men lay on flattened cardboard boxes.

"Next stop, is that what you're thinking, Ben?"

Pickering said nothing.

"Up till now it's been flops and fifth-rate motels, maybe the back of this car once in a while. Next stop is the sidewalk. Snuggle up inside some appliance box."

Pickering doubled his arms across his waist and half-bowed, as if he were carsick.

"How come you're talkin' to me like this?"

"Like what?"

"Like you are."

"Bother you?"

"No. Just that nobody never has much to say to me, one way or the other."

Pathetic, Mace said to himself. All I've done is insult him and yet he's so starved for someone to take an interest, he'd rather listen to insults than nothing at all.

"I'm in rehab work, Ben. I'm studying psychology at the college here. It's my work to talk to people the way I am to you."

"So what's next?"

"I just told you. An appliance box."

"I mean, what do I do?"

"You go to county mental health and convince the headshrinker that you're not a psychopath but merely disabled due to drug and alcohol dependencies and therefore qualified to enter the rehab program. That won't be fun. If you think Miss Sexton asked you embarrassing questions, wait'll you hear what that shrink is going to ask. Or you can forget the whole thing and look for a job. I wouldn't advise that. There's no work around here, unless you want to pick asparagus with the Mexicans and Hondurans."

"You kiddin'?"

"Of course. I wouldn't do that, and I wouldn't want to see you doing it."

"So you don't think I'm so much of a fuckup?"

"Wouldn't want to see any white man doing that kind of work, even a fuckup. By the way, did a nigger really rape you?"

He nodded weakly. "I need a drink."

"It's good that you're being honest with me, Ben. That's a very good start."

Three blocks up, Mace pulled into the back lot of a package store and handed Pickering a five-dollar bill.

"Get me a Diet Coke."

While he waited, Mace pondered if Pickering had fallen into his lap for a reason. Wanted to emulate Duane the Pain. Why would a remark like that have been made in his presence if not for a reason? Perhaps he was standing too close to see it. Destiny's designs were like those in a pointillist painting: stand right up to it and all you saw were chaotic dots; step back a few feet and the pattern and meaning became manifest.

"So tell me about yourself, Ben," he said after Pickering returned with the Coke and a twelve-ounce malt liquor wrapped in a paper bag.

"You interested?" He lit a cigarette.

"Sure. You're an interesting guy."

"I am? Even if I'm a fuckup?"

"You're an interesting fuckup."

Through the aging residential districts, then through the new developments and the ring of malls, Mace forced himself to listen to the dreary tale. Twenty-four years old. Born in Eureka. Moved to Oregon as a kid, moved back to California. Father a sometime millworker and a full-time drunk. Mother became one to stay with the old man. Fights, beatings, dropped out of school at fifteen, drifted, hustled on the streets, arrested, two years in juvenile prison for the armed robbery attempt. Learned welding in prison. Got a welding job when he was released. Lost it. Drifted to Texas, because the union said there was work in the oil fields. None. Drifted to Tennessee, swept floors with niggers in a Memphis machine shop, him a qualified welder sweeping floors with niggers. Back to California. Bought an AK-47 and got busted . . .

"What were you going to do with an AK?"

"Dunno."

"Were you going to use it on anyone?"

Pickering shrugged. They were on the freeway now, passing through the wilderness of strip malls, cut-rate motels, and truck stops, neon signs just coming on in the gathering dusk. The branches of the date palms, spread against a reddened sky, looked like the legs of huge, furry spiders climbing a blood-smeared wall.

"I think you were *thinking* about it," Mace said. "I think you're the kind of guy who'll take just so much shit before he starts giving it back."

He sensed Pickering looking at him.

"Life goes to work on you, then one day, you go to work on it."

"Never thought of it like that, but yeah. Yeah, I like the way that sounds. Go to fuckin' *work* on fuckin' *it*." He lit another cigarette, tipped the malt liquor to his lips, then wiped them with his sleeve. "Yeah, that sounds pretty good. And I got the tools to go to work. Got another AK."

"Where?"

"My room."

"You know, there are a lot of people in this town who think the way you do."

The exit was ahead. Mace glanced in the rearview mirror, then flipped the turn signal to change lanes. The signal gave off a startling buzz.

"Somethin' wrong with that thing, ain't nobody could fix it," Pickering said. "Think like me how?"

"About what you said at the clinic. A lot of people think Boggs did, well, not the right thing exactly, but they understood why he did what he did. They're fed up to here, just like he was. You know, he was in a job-training program and got bumped off to make room for minorities."

"Like I lost my job at Sandy Point."

"*Is* that how you lost it? No bull now."

"No bull, man. They hired a bunch of, I don't know whats, and I'm out on my ass. My *white* ass. Ain't that somethin'?"

"I believe you now, Ben. A lot of people here have had experiences like that. Up to their necks with it. The difference between Boggs and them was that he *did* something about it. He's a hero to them. And the difference between you and them is that they don't have the guts to say what they feel. That's why you interest me. A guy who's not afraid to speak his mind."

"Well, yeah." Pickering squared his shoulders. Build their self-esteem, Mace thought, and not by calling them *Mister.* "I always been that way. Which is why I can't hold a job. Boss gives me shit, I don't take it. I give it back or I walk."

"Seriously, now, how are you fixed for cash?"

"You offerin' or what?"

"Not exactly."

"Got a week's paid in advance, got enough for one more week, somethin' to eat. Then . . . "

Mace drove slowly down the frontage road. The Valley View's sign flickered a couple of blocks away, two letters darkened: V—LLEY VI—W. The red clouds westward darkened toward purple. The color of a squashed plum.

"Then it's the appliance box. You really need to get into this program."

"Yeah, fuck yeah."

"Now a guy like you might have a problem with the program. The meetings. You have to stand up and say that you believe in God and that your problem is in God's hands and then confess to all sorts of shit in front of all kinds of people."

"Like the lady said. Minorities and what all."

"Yes. And I can tell, Ben, I can tell just in the past half an hour we've been talking that that's not suitable for you. You're a loner, a lone-wolf kind of guy. Kind of like those old-time mountain men. You're not the kind of guy who'll stand up in front of a bunch of strangers and tell them what a fuckup you've been and that you need God's help."

Pickering shook his head vigorously, smoke coiling from his nostrils. Mace parked in the motel's potholed lot and, putting his arm across the back of the seat, turned to look squarely at his passenger. Pulling his strings was easy, almost too easy, but Mace was having fun. It was fun to do stuff like this for its own sake. He wondered if ever he could pull it off with someone who had an IQ over, say, eighty-five.

"No promises, but I think I can help you out. Get you into the program so you get your money without the hassle."

"No shit?"

"No shit that I'll try. But no promises."

"Well, what the hell. How come you . . . ?"

"I'm interested in this kind of work, but . . . let's say I've got unorthodox ideas about how to help people like you. Give them a sense of purpose and direction. I'll see what I can do." He flipped his wrist, looked at his watch. "Six-fifty and I've got to pick up my girl at seven. Jesus, you've made me late for a date."

"Sorry." Pickering made a vague gesture, then held out his hand, thumb extended.

"Thanks, man. For the talk, the beer, whatever you can do."

Mace gritted his teeth and took the loathsome hand in his and locked thumbs.

"You take care, Ben."

■ ■ ■

The Vatican of Illusions looked its most promising at this hour, evening's dawn, with buildings great and small aglow against a violet sky and the lights along the endless freeways burning like beacons through the smog.

The sign stood high on the hillside above in hopeful white letters. HOLLYWOOD. Here's where all your dreams come true. Bad dreams, too.

Heartwood's eyes burned as he watched crackheads, bag ladies, and bikers treading over the bronze-gilt stars embedded in front of the Chinese theater, teenage girls in tight shorts negotiating curbside with potential tricks, punks panhandling tourists scurrying to answer the tour bus drivers' calls of, "Movieland excursions will be leaving in three minutes." He supposed that he and Gabriel, cruising slowly eastward on Hollywood Boulevard, must look like a couple of middle-age out-of-towners, hunting for a quickie, but they were only looking for someone to guide them to the viaduct where Jacob Tipton hung out with other runaways. His father's directions had been off.

At a street corner east of Highland, Gabriel identified the tag of the Eighteenth Street Crips sprayed on a wall. Greasy smells rolled out of a pizza joint next to an S & M leather shop. A boombox boomed. This wasn't an ambience of faded glamour, this was implosion. The vacant dreamland was collapsing into the hollowness that had always been at its core.

"Don't look like cheerleaders to me," Gabriel said, pointing at three girls, patrolling in stiletto heels the sidewalk in front of Hollywood High. He made a U-turn and pulled to the curb in front of the school.

The girls, awkward as prepubescents dressed up in Mommy's shoes, wobbled over in reponse to his wave. Two came up to Heartwood's side, one with short-cropped lime-green hair, the other with orange. The colors reminded him of Popsicles.

"Hi!" said the green-haired girl, who might have just graduated eighth grade. A ring glittered in her nose and the yellowish street lights gave her skin a jaundiced tinge. "Vice, huh?"

"I'm a psychiatrist."

"Yeah, right."

"Wanna listen to my problems?" asked the orange-haired girl in a twang that sounded like Texas. "Whatchyall charge?"

"Hundred eighty-five an hour. How about you?"

"Don't I fuckin' wish."

The oldest of the three—all of fifteen—went around the car to Gabriel's side and, sticking her rear end in the air, leaned over to rest her elbows on the door. The smell of her perfume almost made him choke. He reached into a folder on the seat beside him and pulled out the mug shot.

"Know this guy? Jacob Tipton?"

"Whaddya want him for?"

"Interesting conversation. How about it? Recognize him?"

She shook her head, the tip of her tongue appearing between lips that looked as if they'd been painted with blackberry jam.

"Mandy, Jennifer, you know this guy?" she asked her two friends.

Gabriel turned the photograph toward Mandy and Jennifer. They shoved their heads through the open window, forcing Heartwood to draw his back.

"Nope," said the one with orange hair. "Kinda cute, though."

She and her friend shrugged and Heartwood gazed past them and the royal palms motionless in the still air toward the names of Shakespeare, Pythagoras, and Newton inscribed in a lintel on the school wall. A different kind of graffiti, he supposed. Western Civ's tag. The Dead White Male gang. The names looked as out of place in this setting as they would in the Rock and Roll Hall of Fame or in one of those Fontana scrapyards.

"Tipton hangs out under a viaduct somewhere around here," he said to Mandy and Jennifer. "A bunch of kids led by some ex-con."

"That's gotta be Daddy Grand," Orange drawled.

"That's the name he goes by? Daddy Grand?"

"Yeah. He's a pimp, a sicko. Leader of the Trolls. That's how they call themselves. Because they live, you know, under a bridge."

"So where's this bridge?" Gabriel asked.

She cocked her hip, stuck her tongue in a cheek, frowned. The child showed briefly through the hard little street broad. She might have been trying to think of the answer to a test. "West of here a couple of blocks. Left side of the street."

Not three years older than Eleanor, Gabriel thought, pulling out into traffic. Could she wind up here, like this? Crazy to think so, she came from a good home. But the malignancy, the malignancy . . .

Heartwood looked ahead, at the huge movie billboards bathed in floodlights for the benefit of studio execs heading westward to Beverly Hills, Westwood, and Brentwood. This is what *we're* doing, what're you doing? The smog looked like sulphur fumes in the streetlights and a theater marquee's neon shone garishly on the striped Mohawks of two boys, sauntering down the sidewalk, hungry eyes seeking contact.

"This place scares the hell out of me," he said, thinking out loud.

"You don't have to tell me," Gabriel said. "Your kid, right?"

"Right. I picture him here."

"You wonder what these kids' homes were like that they'd rather be here than there."

"Count on some deep domestic pathology for, say, eight out of ten. The other two? Figure this is where they'd want to be no matter how good things were at home."

"Know what I've noticed? None of these punks look Chinese."

"What's that supposed to mean?"

"Nothing. It's an observation."

"No, it wasn't. It was a commentary. Do you think Chinese kids are immune to this kind of thing?"

Gabriel felt a flash of temper. Can't say anything to this guy without him analyzing it.

"I don't know, immune. You grow up in a Chinese family, you know who your parents are, grandparents, even great-grandparents. You're taught not to let the family down, and you've got six thousand years of history to fall back on when things get tough. These American kids, it's like they're floating around in the middle of the ocean. No compass, no rudder."

He glanced sidelong, noticing a troubled expression cross Heartwood's face. A barrier seemed to rise suddenly between them, transparent but hard, like the window between a taxi driver and his passenger.

"I didn't mean your kid, Lee. I was just talking in general."

"I didn't peg you as the ethnocentric type."

"As *what*? What're you . . . " Gabriel cut himself short as it dawned on him that he'd used the word *American* in a way he never had before.

The Trolls' home was a cavern formed by two prefab concrete walls, its roof the freeway above. Flames guttering in a fire-pit cast a nervous light. Eight or nine kids sat around it on frayed sofas and cafeteria chairs, their shadows moving hugely across the walls as they talked and passed a gallon of jug wine. Off to one side, two figures lay side by side under the rent canopy of a canopy bed. The floor at its foot seemed to be in motion. Rats foraging for scraps. The two men crossed a patch of dirt and pushed through clumps of wild chapparal that had begun to reassert itself, covering the scrap lumber and tie-rods left by a highway construction crew. Heartwood imagined the stuff sprouting on Sunset Boulevard in some post-apocalypse Hollywood, coyotes coming down from the hills to howl in ruined mansions.

The kids around the campfire stopped talking and looked up warily at the two approaching figures. The two people on the bed sat up suddenly, like a sleeping couple alarmed by a strange noise in the house.

"Yo! Trolls! No need for an alert. We're friends."

"Drink?" one kid asked, hospitably holding the Riesling jug out to Heartwood and Gabriel. They shook their heads. A hideous rag doll, hanging from a cord at the entrance to the cavern, caused Heartwood to suffer a sudden and severe attack of California culture shock. Breakfast at a fake frontier cafe in the Motherlode Country, lunch on the plane, an afternoon spent amid the industrial wastelands of Fontana, now this . . .

"That's our mascot, the Troll doll," the kid explained. He wore an earring and had dyed his hair to within one shade of an egret's wing. "Sure you guys don't want a drink?"

"They look like they're on duty to me."

This came in a throaty voice from the man who'd been lying on the bed. He was thin and sunken-cheeked, with a black Zapata mustache and long hair that seemed to flow out from under his cocked beret. He looked like a half-starved Central American revolutionary. Beside him, a wan girl of about eighteen was putting on a pair of gold scorpion earrings.

"So who the fuck are these guys?"

"A couple of cops," the kid said.

"It's not that way exactly, Daddy," said Gabriel

"Exactly what way is it?" Daddy Grand pointed to a framed scroll on one wall. It bore the legend: *The Ten Troll Commandments.* "First Commandment, 'What Daddy Grand says, goes.' And I say Trolls don't talk to no cops, no social workers."

"Bye-bye, Daddy. Got to get to work," the girl said, putting the finishing touches on her lips with black eye-liner.

"Yeah, okay, babe. Take care now." He gave her bottom a quick, lewd pat, then turned to three boys sitting on one of the tattered sofas. "Tee, Motown, Bobby, you walk her to the boulevard. Stay close. She gets hassled, you know what to do."

The boys rose, proud of their protective role but feigning the grim reluctance of veteran warriors called again to dangerous duty. One, wearing a silver-studded dog-collar, slipped a switchblade from his back to his side pocket. The weapon was an artifact out of *West Side Story* and seemed, in these days of Uzis and Tec-9s, to possess an archaic charm. Might as well bring a bow and arrow to D-Day, Gabriel thought, and then, as the boy passed a yard in front of him, recognized Tipton. The same face as in the mug shot—slender, light-eyed, the lower lip fuller than the upper—but now it was topped by a Mohawk instead of a rock musician's shoulder-length mop.

"All except you," he said, taking a step forward and grabbing Jacob by the shoulder. "We need to talk to you."

Startled, Jacob turned and gazed down at Gabriel from his six-foot height.

"What the fuck is this?" Daddy Grand made a little movement, as if to interpose himself between Jacob and Gabriel, then raised one hand, spreading fingers asparkle with street-vendor rings. "You can't just bust in here. We know our rights. This is like somebody's house."

"This isn't a bust, so take it easy. We need to talk to Jacob about his brother. In private."

"Brother? Tee got no brother I know of. Hey, whoever you are, maybe I better see a badge. I'm responsible for these kids."

"You aren't responsible for shit. What you are is a worthless scammer hustling kids out of a few bucks and balling underage pussy while you're at it."

Little rats' paws scuffled in the dirt, out of Gabriel's vision. The freeway overhead trembled slightly from the passage of a loaded truck and Daddy Grand's black eyes glistened with manufactured outrage.

"Man, have you got that wrong. Have you ever got that the fuck wrong." His ringed hands went to his hips and he shook his head, the motion a little bit of stage business to say that he was tired of being misunderstood but would forbear it once again. Hollywood, Gabriel thought. Everybody here has an act. "I *give* to these kids. Give and give. You think I'm here 'cause I wanna be? I give my time, I give myself." He turned to the children, watching with a mixture of confusion and suspicion. "Hey, Trolls, tell him, does Daddy Grand give or what? Does he give his time? Does he give of himself?"

As three or four heads nodded to confirm the man's self-sacrificial nature, Jacob broke his silence.

"It's cool, I know what they want to talk about. Something I've been dealing with all my damned life." His voice was low and carried an undertone of lament.

"Something you can talk to these guys about, but not me?" Daddy Grand sounded hurt—a father who's discovered that a son's been keeping secrets. "Hey, Tee, I didn't even know your name's Jacob."

"I don't know your name, either."

"Let's go," Gabriel said, and turned and led Jacob to the car, Daddy Grand calling to their backs:

"They ask about me, you set 'em straight. You tell 'em Daddy Grand's a giver, not a taker."

When they were back on Sunset, Heartwood said, "Sorry if we almost blew your cover. We didn't think you could keep it a secret, all the coverage there's been."

Jacob sat alone in the backseat. That was part of the plan. Don't make him feel crowded or pressured, let him think he could get out anytime he wanted.

"They don't know who I am," he said in the low voice that made him sound much older than seventeen. "Nobody around here knows who anybody else is. Can we keep this private, whatever the hell it is? I don't want anybody to know Duane's my brother. Here, I mean. They know at school. I can't hide who I am at school. Oh, man, I go back there, they'll be looking at me like I'm a freak."

"That why you dropped out?"

"Didn't drop out. Just taking a vacation till, you know. So what's this all about?"

"There's been a lot of speculation in the media about why your brother did this, about what kind of guy he was. They painted a pretty dim picture of Duane. What was he really like, what really happened, what factors influenced him to do what he did, that's our search. This isn't a homicide investigation," Heartwood said, concluding his prepared speech.

Slumped in his seat, arms folded across his narrow chest, Jacob listened expressionlessly. Glancing at him in the rearview mirror, Gabriel's suspicions rose. He'd long ago become literate in the body language of suspects, the signs that someone had something to hide.

"Hungry?" Heartwood asked.

"Sure."

"Any preferences?"

Jacob turned to look at a row of storefronts that seemed to have been put there as a display of L.A.'s multicultural mix. A Pakistani news agency was flanked by the Bucharest grocery and the Pearl of Siam restaurant. "No weird foreign shit."

They chose an ersatz fifties diner on Hollywood, an oasis for those whose palates had tired of dishes like pumpkin ravioli and drooled for thick burgers with greasy french fries.

Inside, all the props were in place—the jukebox selectors at the tables, golden oldies by Elvis and the Platters, chrome napkin dispensers, waitresses in saddle shoes. Nostalgia for Eisenhower's America.

Heartwood slid into a booth, Gabriel across from him, Jacob beside him, on the outside. In the bright light, the adolescent blemishes on his nose and cheeks were plain to see, but there was no spark of youth in his eyes and a stoniness in his expression that added a couple of decades to his face. So many of these street kids looked that way; the flame that leaned toward the future had been snuffed out in them. They stared at you like forty-year-old convicts serving life without parole.

"How come you think I know what made Duane do it?" he asked, looking at the menu.

"We don't think you know. We're hoping you might help us figure that out. We're asking for your cooperation. You don't have to talk to us. You can walk out right now if you want," Gabriel said.

"Do I get warned of my rights and all that shit?"

Gabriel could have thanked him. He'd been wondering how to give the Miranda warning without alerting Jacob to his suspicions.

"It isn't necessary. Like Lee said, we're not conducting a homicide investigation, but I'll give you the warning if it makes you feel more comfortable."

He didn't wait for a reply, but recited the litany—you have the right to remain silent, the right to counsel, anything you say may be used against you . . .

A waitress appeared, gyrating to Chuck Berry's "Maybellene" as she stood with pencil poised over her check pad. If Jacob was nervous about the interview, his appetite didn't show it. He ordered a salad, two cheeseburgers, and fries.

"Where were you when you first heard about the massacre?" Heartwood asked after the food arrived. Looking disconsolately at his own salad of wilted iceberg lettuce and unnaturally red tomatoes, he thought: I'm in a diner, eating a lousy salad with the possible author of the worst crime of its kind in California history.

"Here. Hollywood, I mean," Jacob replied, pouring French dressing over his lettuce. "Friday night. Saw it in the newspapers at a newsstand. Duane's picture. Front page."

Oh, Maybellene, why can't you be true? Ohhh, Maybellene . . .

"I'm a little confused. You mean you took this vacation from school before you knew about what your brother had done?"

"I was taking a vacation from my father. We don't get along. He thinks he's still in the Navy. Always on my ass. Shape up or ship out. Get a haircut."

"See that you did," Gabriel said. "How long have you had that?"

You started back doin' the things you used to do . . .

"Got it Thursday."

Jacob rubbed his Mohawk and allowed himself a little smile, his glance moving to Gabriel for a moment, then down to the cheeseburger in his hand.

Normal eye contact was thirty to sixty percent, that's what the book said.

Heartwood asked, "What did you think when you saw your brother's picture?"

"I was hoping it wasn't true. I was hoping it was some guy who looked like him."

. . . heat went down . . . and that's when I heard that highway sound.

"It wasn't something you could see Duane doing?"

"Duane had a bad temper. Go off like a rocket. I could see him blowing up one day, getting mad at the boss, killing him. I could see him doing like that guy did in that cafeteria, where was it?"

"Killeen, Texas."

"Like that. Wham. But he had to be planning what he did for a while. You don't just wake up in the morning and say, 'Hey, I think I'll find a school bus of kids on a field trip and then blockade the road it's on and ambush it.' "

"Why? Because it's children or because of the planning involved?"

Why can't you be true? Started back doin' the things you used to do.

"Maybe both? Duane didn't hate kids any more than he hated grown-ups."

"But he had a grudge against Asians."

"My brother had a grudge against everybody. Duane could hate like nobody I've ever seen."

Jacob said this with a direct look at Heartwood, his voice dipping to deeper register, almost to a groan. Then he went to work on his cheeseburgers, gulping like someone who hadn't eaten a square meal in days, and maybe he hadn't.

"So you couldn't see Duane planning this thing out? That wasn't the Duane you knew."

"He'd think up shit. All kinds of scenarios, but anybody with half a brain could tell that he didn't think them all the way through. Like fantasies, you know?"

"Am I getting the right impression from you, Jacob? Are you saying that your brother probably didn't plan this crime? That he couldn't have?"

There was a long pause, Jacob pushing his fries around with his fork. Watch for the pauses, Gabriel thought, those moments when a suspect began to weigh his answers. He glanced out the window, at the neon-drenched freak show passing by, then back at Jacob, and asked himself, Why would this kid suggest that his brother wasn't likely to have planned the crime? If he'd been in on it, wouldn't he want us to think the opposite? Yeah, unless he's smart enough to realize that and is deliberately endangering himself to show us how innocent he is. The plan was to change the venue to the Hollywood police station if the kid's responses started to come up wrong. An interview room. Confessions were best obtained in settings more private than a diner. The timing would be key, and the timing wasn't right, yet.

Heartwood said, "I had a look at Duane's psychiatric records. The last two times he was tested, his IQ came out an eighty and an eighty-three."

"Duane fried his brain. He did a lot of speed and uppers. Mollies, diet pills, whatever. He'd pop 'em like M&M's."

"What I'm getting at, are you telling us that Duane was a little too dumb or fried or whatever to have planned this?"

Another few seconds of silence as Jacob squeezed catsup on the fries.

"I don't know. Can't say. He must've been smart enough because he did it, right?"

The answer Gabriel had expected. Time to raise the heat a little. Only a little. Like the frog in the pot. Toss a frog into boiling water, it'll jump out. Heat it gradually and its body will adjust to the temperature until the next thing it knows it's dead.

"What do you think of this stuff that's been in the papers about the neo-Nazis?" he asked offhandedly. "That they put him up to this? Maybe helped him plan it?"

"Sounds like bullshit to me. Kind of shit they put in the papers."

"Know a guy named Mike Silva?"

He shook his head.

"We talked to him. He says he knew Duane and you. Met you both last summer at an Aryan Youth rock concert in Fontana."

Jacob waved a french fry in the air, nodded, swallowed.

"You mean Mike Thor? Yeah. I knew a guy by that name. Not Silva. He tried to recruit Duane. Duane was hot for the music, the message. You know, kill the niggers, send the gooks back to Vietnam. And Thor says, 'We could use guys like you.' Something like that."

"And . . . ?"

"Duane was hanging with some badasses then. Bikers and meth dealers. I think he wanted to show them how bad he was, so he took Thor—Silva, I mean—he took him up on the offer. Went to some kind of meeting, I think. Told me he didn't like those skinhead dudes. They wanted him to shave his hair and he didn't want to. Told him he couldn't smoke weed, that he had to be disciplined, that he'd have to follow orders. That wasn't Duane. He wouldn't let anybody tell him what to do."

"Silva has a different memory of what went on. He said that Duane and you were hot to sign up. The swastika boys put you both to a test. You were supposed to beat up a black guy, but Duane chickened out. After that, Silva told you and Duane that if you still wanted to join, you'd have to make up for Duane's cowardice. You'd have to blow up a church full of niggers, beaners, or gooks before the neo-Nazis would even give you a second look. Now why would Silva tell us that story?"

"You'd have to ask him. The guy's got a great imagination. Okay if I have dessert?"

"We're on expenses."

Jacob turned and signaled the waitress. While she took his order for apple pie and ice cream, Gabriel spun the jukebox selector. This kid is either innocent or a great pretender, he thought. Might as well have a little fun. He dropped a quarter into the slot and punched the button for "The Great Pretender" by the Platters.

"See, if Silva's version is right, then we have to wonder if your brother was making up for his screwup in a very big way. Proving to those skinheads and Aryan Resistance guys that when it came to putting the hurt on minorities, no one could touch him."

Oh-oh, yes, I'm the great pretender, just laughing and gay like a clown . . .

"But Duane killed himself. Doesn't make sense. He wanted to be this big-time skinhead, why did he kill himself?"

"That's exactly what we've been wondering," Gabriel said, putting a point on each word.

I seem to be what I'm not, you see . . .

"Did it surprise you, your brother committing suicide?" Heartwood asked.

Jacob shook his head, looking—or pretending to—for the waitress and his apple pie à la mode.

"He'd tried it before. He always talked about doing himself. Those fantasies? They always ended with him dead. Either he'd kill himself or he'd fix it so the cops would have to kill him."

Jacob's dessert appeared, the waitress lip-synching the song as she delivered it. Another great talent awaiting discovery.

Too real is this feeling of make-believe . . .

Heartwood scowled at Gabriel to tell him that he thought his musical psychological warfare was silly.

"Back there under the bridge, you said something about something you've been dealing with all your life. You meant Duane, didn't you? We're not keeping secrets. We're being open and aboveboard with you and we hope you'll be the same with us. We saw a transcript from when you and Duane were arrested in San Bernardino last summer. You told an arresting officer that although you're four years younger than Duane, you're more like the older brother. That you had to watch out for Duane, rein him in, I think is what you said. There was a suggestion there that you felt responsible for him."

Too real when I feel what my heart can't concee-ee-al, oh-oh, yes . . .

"Sara Jane and I. We both had to watch out for him," Jacob answered, in what sounded more like sorrow than anger, his voice creaking like old leather.

I'm the great pretender . . .

Heartwood moved a little closer and felt the table vibrating as Jacob pumped one leg up and down.

"That must've been difficult, being your older brother's keeper."

"I guess."

"Reminds me a little of *Of Mice and Men*."

"What's that?"

"A novel by John Steinbeck."

"Who's John Steinbeck?"

"A writer. Set most of his stories in California. Don't they teach him in school anymore?"

The boy pushed his dessert away, leaving it half-eaten, and leaned back, both hands folded on his stomach.

"Man, I'm stoked."

His leg pumped like an organist's.

"*Of Mice and Men* is a sad story. It's about two men, George and Lenny. George is an ordinary guy, a ranch hand. Lenny's a huge, dumb halfwit, and George ends up responsible for him. Lenny's always getting into trouble because he's so stupid and so strong and George is always having to bail him out of it. To make a long story short, one day George shoots Lenny in the back of the head with a Luger. It's kind of a mercy killing."

There was a momentary stillness that seemed much longer than momentary.

"You can sympathize with George," Heartwood went on, almost in an undertone. "He was doing Lenny a favor, but I've always felt that possibly George's motives weren't all that pure. George did himself a favor. Got rid of a millstone around his neck." Heartwood slid an inch closer to Jacob, leaned his head toward him, as if to let him in on a secret. "Listen, I can understand how you felt. How you feel now. It's natural. I'd feel the same way if I were you."

"Feel how?" Jacob asked. That croak again, as though he had laryngitis. A sadness had come into his indifferent eyes.

"It's nothing to feel guilty about," Heartwood said with deliberate ambiguity. "Duane was going to do it sooner or later. He'd tried it before."

An atmosphere of privacy had formed around the booth, so that the counterman and the waitresses and customers in the background seemed like figures on a movie screen with the sound turned off. Jacob's hands fell between his legs, his shoulders pulled in toward his neck. If he was going to reveal anything, it would be now, but all he said was, "I don't feel glad that he's dead. No shit, I don't. What makes me feel like hell is that he could've called. Y'know, said goodbye. We used to be tight. And maybe I could've talked him out of doing what he did."

Heartwood drew back, his nerves strained. He wasn't sure if Jacob's sorrow was real or contrived, but knew he'd sailed this tack as far as he could and passed the questioning to Gabriel.

"Could you stop that, Jacob? You're shaking the table."

He sensed it still—the boy was hiding something.

"Stop what?"

"Whatever you're doing with your leg. It's shaking the table. It bothers me." An old trick. Don't let them siphon off their anxiety with movements and gestures, make them feel as if they're in handcuffs. "Two questions. Did Duane say anything to you about what he was planning to do when you saw him at his motel, oh, I think it was around a week before the massacre. And did he talk about killing himself then?"

Jacob's leg began to move again. Gabriel reached under the table and touched his knee to stop him. Jacob's gaze slipped off toward the counter, then moved to the window. He rubbed his chin with the back of one hand and tugged at his dog collar.

"Didn't you say he liked to sketch out these scenarios? That they always ended with him killing himself or forcing the cops to kill him? He must've said something to you about what he was planning to do. It was only a week before. His plans must've been pretty firmed up by then."

"What motel are you talking about?"

"The Camino Real. You spent the night in his room. Left around four or five in the morning. The motel owner saw you leave. We had a long talk with him the other day, before we searched your brother's room." Gabriel put his elbows on the table, leaned forward, his own eyes manacling Jacob's. "You and Duane must've talked about something in all that time. Or were you two just getting it on? Is that why you went to visit him? Maybe he wanted a little and was afraid to hustle around San Joaquin. That's one tough valley town. Not what I'd call a gay rights kind of place."

Jacob stiffened, looked ready to bolt.

"I'm no fuckin' faggot, man. I didn't go up there to blow my own fuckin' brother, man. What is this? What do you think I am?"

"You were popped for solicitation. So was your brother."

"We don't do that shit because we're into it. It's easy money."

"But there had to be some reason you two were together in a motel room all night. Am I wrong, Jacob? Was the motel owner having hallucinations? Did he have an overactive imagination, like Silva? Help us out."

"I wasn't there all night. It's a long drive from Fontana. Didn't get there till ten, eleven, left around two or three."

"Holding hands. The motel owner saw you two holding hands. That's brotherly love, all right."

"Who's this motel owner?"

"Ahmad Khan."

"Some sand nigger told you I was shacked up with my own brother, holding hands?"

Gabriel smiled secretly. He'd found Jacob's button all right.

"He didn't know you were brothers, but he described you and your car. What were you doing there that time of night?"

"Duane called me. He wanted a jacket. A camouflage jacket he'd left at our house after he went to Idaho. It had been his father's when he was in the Army. Duane was big on all that Vietnam shit."

"Tilghman Boggs was never in Vietnam," Heartwood said. "I've seen the records. He got a medical discharge before he was sent. Medical-psychiatric. He stole a pistol from the Fort Ord armory and was going to shoot somebody when the MPs caught him."

"He was going to shoot the guy he'd caught Karen in bed with. Duane's dear old mom. My dear old mom. Maybe he was going to shoot her too. Should have."

"If he had, you wouldn't be here."

There was a library in Jacob's look.

"So you're trying to tell us you drove three hundred miles in the middle of the night to bring him an old army jacket?" Gabriel asked.

"Duane's toy soldiers? You seen those?"

Gabriel nodded.

"When he played war games with them, he'd put on his father's old uniform. We used to—when I was a kid, I mean—we used to play these war games to see who'd get the brave guy and who'd get the cowards. The brave guys were the guys standing up with bayonets and the cowards were the guys laying down. Duane would dress up like he was some kind of general."

"Okay. The jacket meant a lot to him. What else to make that drive for?"

"Duane owed me some money. Two hundred."

"For what? The jacket?"

"I never did find it. Duane was real upset. . . . You said this wasn't an investigation."

"Right. But you're going to make it one if you keep forcing us to pull answers out of you. He owed for what?"

He switched on the Gabriel Glare and watched Jacob's shoulders slump—that relief and relaxation that came over even hardened criminals when they decided to come clean.

"Okay. For the P-39."

Gabriel was barely able to conceal his surprise at hearing this. "A Ruger?"

"That's who makes it."

"He already had a Taurus and a Street Sweeper. What was he starting? A gun collection?"

"He called me up, maybe a week before I went up? He'd put money down on the Taurus, but he didn't have it yet because of the waiting period. He was worried that the gun store was going to find out about his record and not let him have the gun. He asked me to talk to some dudes in Fontana. He wanted a nine. Cheap as I could get it, quick as I could."

"When was this conversation?"

"First week in April maybe. So I scored the piece. Hundred bucks."

"Hot," Gabriel said, screwing up his eyes.

Jacob shrugged. "Look, you make a street score, you don't ask how the guy got what you're buying. Okay, I ran the piece up to him on a Friday, right after I got out of school. Damn if Duane didn't have the Taurus. Everything had gone through, he'd picked it up that afternoon."

"So we're talking April ninth? Exactly one week before the massacre?"

"I guess that was the date. I wanted two hundred from Duane, hundred for the Ruger, hundred for my time and trouble, but Duane said he'd laid out three-sixty for the Taurus and didn't have any cash. We got into an argument . . . "

Gabriel brought his face closer to Jacob's.

"Look, I can understand Duane being dumb, but I'd figure a smart kid like you would've waited till Duane knew if he'd got through the record check okay. If he didn't, then you'd score the Ruger."

"He said he needed it quick. I got the chance to score, I took it. I figured there was no way Duane was going to get the Taurus, not with his record."

"And you never once asked him why he was in such a hurry?"

"I figured . . . " Jacob looked off. "I don't know what I figured. I didn't ask, no."

"All right," Gabriel said wearily. "So you two had an argument. Then what?"

"Duane told me he had a buddy he could sell the Ruger to. Said he'd charge the guy two hundred, give me the money. I said, 'Hey, bro, if you've got a guy you could sell the gun to, then you must know people in this town and could've made a street buy yourself, don't give me any shit.' Swore he had this buddy. Said this guy had given him the three-sixty for the Taurus and was taking care of him. He'd be good for the money."

"What friend?" Heartwood looked quickly at Gabriel. "Taking care of him how?"

"Didn't say who. Some guy who worked at the rehab clinic. See, the way it works with that disability program is first thing, you have to have a shrink certify that you're disabled because of drugs or alcohol, and then you have to be enrolled in a drug and alcohol rehab program or you don't get your check."

"We know that. Except Duane wasn't in rehab. Social Security screwed up. Kept paying him anyway."

Jacob looked askance. "Y'know, that's just what I figured. It was a screwup. I didn't believe that other bullshit about his buddy, that's why I said no way to the deal and kept the Ruger."

"What 'other bullshit'?" Heartwood demanded.

"Duane told me he was getting his checks because his buddy filled out some paperwork to make it look like he was still in rehab. And when Duane had to come in to give a urine sample, this guy would substitute his for Duane's. Then all he had to do was sit on his ass, do his drugs and beer, and collect. He was bragging about it. Thought it was funny."

"This is what he told you that night?"

"Bragging about it. Like he was some big-time scammer, you know, trying to prove he wouldn't keep the two hundred for himself if he sold the guy the gun. Didn't impress me. See, Duane said this friend was a guy he'd worked with the last time he was in San Joaquin. The college guy he'd worked with at the cannery. I figured he was bullshitting because no college guy I know of would be a friend of Duane's. No college guy would stick his neck out, phonying urine tests, and then just give Duane three hundred and sixty bucks. Like I said, Duane dreamed up a lot of stuff."

Heartwood felt a dampness under his arms, a tightening in the back of his neck. The waitress, swaying to another golden oldie from the Fabulous Fifties, "Unchained Melody," interrupted, asking if they wanted anything more. He waved her off and gestured for a check.

"A college guy he'd worked with? You're sure that's what he said?"

Jacob, pushing out his thick lower lip, thought for a second, then nodded.

"Think it was the same guy I met last summer."

"Where?"

"Some bar near the cannery. It was Duane's last day there and I'd gone up to San Joaquin to give him a ride down to Fontana because the car he had then blew a head gasket and he junked it. So we were having a couple of beers before we took off and the college guy came in and Duane called him over, asked him to have a brew with us."

"Did you hear a name? What did he look like?"

"Big dude. Like a football player. I don't remember what Duane called him."

"That's all? That's it?"

"The guy was wearing a patch over one eye. Like a pirate. Couldn't miss him."

Heartwood swapped glances with Gabriel, then gestured to Jacob to go on.

"So he came over and Duane bought him a brew. The guy drank it, then left."

"Duane didn't introduce you? You never found out who he was?"

"Duane never did polite shit like introduce people. And the college guy, he acted sort of stuck-up, you know, like he was doing us both a great big favor by having a beer with us. He acted like I wasn't even there."

"Do you remember what he and your brother talked about?"

"Hey, man, we're talking about ten, fifteen minutes in a bar nearly a year ago. The only thing I remember is that when the guy left, he punched Duane in the shoulder and said something like, 'Doo-wayne'—yeah, I remember that, he called him Doo-wayne in this sarcastic way. He said, 'Doo-wayne, guess I'm gonna have to find somebody else to get my Cokes for me.' Something like that. Then he left."

"Nothing more to it?"

"Nothing. Maybe I asked Duane what happened to the guy's eye, I don't remember. What's this have to do with what Duane did?"

"Maybe nothing," Gabriel said.

"Whatever you guys say, this is starting to sound like an investigation to me."

"It's turning into one. And I'm going to ask you a real, direct, investigation-type question and I expect a real, direct-type answer. Where were you Friday morning, when your brother was murdering those children?"

"Been waiting for that one. I wasn't with him. I was here."

"And I'll bet you've got Daddy Grand and all the little Trolls lined up."

"Got better witnesses than that. But"—he dropped his voice again—"listen, I'm no fuckin' faggot."

"We're not interested in your sexual orientation. You can screw sheep for all we care."

Jacob ran his finger under his dog collar and turned to face the window.

"I was in the Hollywood jail. Propositioned an undercover vice cop Thursday night. Daddy Grand bailed me out noon the next day. You can check it out yourself."

"We're going to, Jacob. And you'll come with us."

"Okay if I go to the bathroom first?"

"Don't take too long. We might get worried."

"I'm not going anywhere," Jacob said, standing.

From the freeway, the city looked like a lava flow, rivers of light pouring down through the canyons and valleys to form a great bed of light, spread flat across the basin that lay between the coast and the Hollywood Hills. The Hollywood police had confirmed Jacob's alibi, and now Heartwood and Gabriel were headed for Santa Monica and Heartwood's favorite hotel, the Sovereign. He wanted to spend the night away from all this smog and congestion. He wanted sea air, the sounds of surf and gulls.

"Right now I feel like a goddamned rookie," Gabriel said. "Did you see the smirk on that kid's face when the desk sergeant pulled his records up?"

"No way for you to know he'd been arrested. And I liked the way you ran that bluff about the motel owner. That wasn't rookie. Would've never known we had any doubts about who Khan had seen."

"Thanks. And I'll give you a commendation for that George and Lenny story. Just for a second there, I thought it would be like the movies, Jacob would break down and say, 'I did it.'"

"Truth-teller or not? What's your judgment?"

"I don't think we got a hundred percent truth, but we got enough. We'd better take a closer look at Weathers." And a thought that had been skulking at the back of Gabriel's mind stepped to the front. "How's this sound? What if the teacher heard Boggs wrong? Suppose what he yelled when he ran into the woods wasn't 'Race! Victory!' but . . . "

"Now that's pretty good," Heartwood said. "Weathers called me last night. Said he was doing a thesis on psychological autopsies and asked to go along with us. Research."

"You didn't tell me."

"It didn't seem important then."

"Does now. What do you make of that, Professor?"

"The innocent request of an innocent man, or he's got something to hide, *Gabe*. Not necessarily complicity in mass murder, but something, and he's trying to insinuate himself into the investigation, find out what we're up to, what we know."

"Ever run into anything like that before?"

"A colleague of mine did in Seattle. A serial child abductor case. Next to no forensic evidence. The bad guy was a carpenter who hung out in a bar where the detectives on the case unwound. Bought them drinks, told them he was a father—which he was, by the way—and that he was concerned about his kids. He'd ask them how the investigation was coming along. The guy looked as ordinary as white bread toast and they gave him regular reports. Kept him right up to date on their progress."

"Catch him or what?"

"More or less by accident. My colleague was called in to draw up a profile of the kind of guy the cops were after. It fit, oh, say ten thousand middle-age males, but when the cops mentioned the profile to the carpenter, he panicked. Like I told you, men are disturbed by their perceptions of things, and this guy thought, mistakenly, that the cops were getting warm. All of a sudden, he stopped showing up in the bar. One of the detectives had something on the ball and looked into the guy's background. Solid family man, good worker, Little League coach, and he'd disappeared overnight without a trace. Seattle PD put out a nationwide be-on-the-lookout-for. Three months later, the carpenter was stopped in Atlanta for running a red light. The traffic cop remembered the bulletin, brought him in for questioning. He confessed. If he'd stayed put in Seattle and kept his cool, he probably never would have been suspected."

"I like happy endings," Gabriel said. "What did you tell Weathers?"

"No."

"Okay, if Duane told Tipton the truth and Tipton told us the truth, then Weathers lied to you."

"But Duane could have lied to Jacob. It could have been that he was still getting his disability because of some clerical foul-up, but wanted to impress his smarter younger brother, telling him it was really a scam between him and Weathers."

"Lee, why do you have to complicate things with all this psychologizing?"

"I learned from the Jesuits how to argue both sides of an issue. Everybody's impression has been that Weathers couldn't stand Duane. We've got Somers's statement, we've got Jacob himself doubting that Duane and a guy like Weathers would be friends. Does it make sense that Weathers would commit fraud on Duane's behalf? Give him three-sixty to buy a gun?"

Gabriel bit down on his lips, his face bright then dark then bright in the sweep of passing headlights.

"Nope. So for right now, let's stick to Weathers's drinking habits. You said he told you he never, but never had so much as one beer with Duane. Looks like he bullshitted you about that too. If a guy bullshits you about one thing, even a little thing like that, bank on it, he's bullshitting you about something bigger."

"How about Silva?"

"My hunch is that Silva was somebody's talking dummy. Somebody who wants us to come to the conclusion that Boggs was at least under the spell of the neo-Nazis, even if they didn't order him to do it."

"Benedetto."

"There could be a connection between him and Silva. Could be Benedetto was your anonymous tipster. He wants us to back up his conspiracy theory, so he gets Silva to give us that story. Probably an exaggeration of something that really happened. No way for us to prove it or disprove it."

"That would work in our Mr. X's favor as well," Heartwood said. "Figure he's smart enough to anticipate that some people might wonder how a moron like Duane could have schemed out this crime. So he set up a false trail. For all we know, Mr. X sprayed the graffiti on the school wall, or had someone do it."

They left the freeway and went north on Lincoln, the seedy side of Santa Monica, where bar signs flickered and shoals of used cars lay under flapping pennants, terse come-ons waxed on the windshields. LIKE NU-$4300! . . . LOW MI STEAL! Across Santa Monica Boulevard, the neighborhoods grew sedate, the streets lined with blooming bottle brush and sycamore with their lower trunks booted in whitewash.

"Speaking of X's, mine lives here now, two blocks from here," Heartwood said, thinking aloud again and picturing, with a faint jab of jealousy, the ocher Spanish house where Paula lived with her new husband. "Got remarried six months ago. A guy who owns a couple of art galleries."

Gabriel could not have cared less. His mind was elsewhere. He made a left on Washington and said, "Let's do some supposing. It's Weathers waiting back in the trees. Duane yells, 'Mace! Victory!,' runs into the woods to join up with him."

"And then what? Mace says, 'Okay, time to kill yourself, Duane. Here, I'll help you.' "

"Youngblood said something that got me to thinking. A suicide pact. Weathers, or whoever our Mr. X turns out to be, has a handgun, somehow convinces Duane that they'll go out together. Each guy holds his own gun to his head, but to make sure nobody chickens out, each guy holds his free hand on the other guy's gunhand. One two three bang. Only Weathers's gun isn't loaded."

"Imaginative," Heartwood said dryly.

Gabriel stopped in front of the Sovereign, an art-deco relic of old L.A.—if anything in L.A. could be called old—its walls steeped in an atmosphere of spoiled romance, film noir intrigues.

"We've got a lot of blanks to fill in, Lee. We start by finding everything we can about Mr. Weathers. I want to know what kind of skivvies he wears. I want to know more about him than maybe he knows about himself. If and when the time comes, I want to be ready for him."

Thursday, April 22nd

WITH BACH'S *TOCCATA AND FUGUE IN D-MINOR* PLAYING on his Sony Walkman, Heartwood jogged through Palisades Park, high above the Pacific, on a foggy morning.

It felt good to run again, cleansing. Questions that had troubled him during the night were temporarily silenced by the rhythm of his feet against the dirt path that led through avenues of palm and past Australian tea trees with limbs whorled like hawser. Beneath one of these, four homeless men were packing up their belongings, like broken soldiers preparing for another day's retreat. Loosened up, Heartwood broke into a sprint, easily overtook two white-haired retirees, flopping along on wizened legs, and then a bronzed California youth in tank top and nylon shorts. Rewarding himself for that achievement, he slowed to a walk. To his right, a cliff plummeted to the beach, and wild sage on the ledges scented the air. *Toccata and Fugue* swelled in his ear, elegant as mathematics. Finally, he reached the Santa Monica Pier, cluttered beyond its arched gateway with small arcades and seafood shacks. A short walk brought him to the end, where anglers wet their lines in an ebbing tide that made creases around the pilings and signs warned against the taking of white croakers.

The questions began to trouble him again. In a manner of speaking, we'll be looking for the equation for evil. How did Weathers fit into that algebra? Did he fit in at all? Gabriel had taken the early flight back to Sacramento to begin finding out. Heartwood had remained in L.A. to deal with a parental problem.

Last night, after checking into his room, he'd phoned his answering service for messages. One was from Diana in Hawaii and warmed his libido; the second, from Paula, struck him like a cold shower. David had gotten into trouble again at school. She wanted to speak to

Heartwood right away. Though it was late, he called her from the Sovereign, and was grateful when she answered instead of her new mate, the artworld maven. How convenient that he was in Santa Monica, she said. Now they could talk this problem over face-to-face. She had a closing at nine tomorrow, but could make lunch at twelve-thirty. A little place she knew in the Third Street Promenade. Heartwood demurred, citing the pressures of work. She insisted. Too burdened by the divorced father's guilt, he offered no further argument. Lunch would be fine.

Then, at eight this morning, she phoned his room: lunch was off. There were complications with the closing; she didn't know how long it would take; and Arnold, her new husband, didn't like the idea of her and Heartwood lunching together. She would fax the headmaster's letter to the Sovereign from her office; after he read it, they could talk on the phone.

The fax should be there by now. He started to run back, loping down the beach, hardened and paved smooth by the receding tide. The dense fog offshore shrunk the Pacific to the width of a lake, and the sea rose and fell in the windless air as gently as the breath of sleep. Long-beaked wading birds, digging for snails at the water's edge, scurried up the shore when a swell washed in, down again when the sea slipped back hissing.

Do the black waters flow within us all, Dr. Heartwood? Yes. Checked by the dams of social convention and the levees of our personal inhibitions, but no one can say for certain that some stress, some great stress like war or a quotidian one like losing your job, won't cause the dams to burst, the levees to break. But isn't it true that the black waters flow deeper and stronger in a sick few than in the rest of us? Yes, madam. Yes, yes. We don't know why, but perhaps . . . *e nel cervello!* Phineas Gage was a railroading man, a terrier who blasted rights of way through mountains with dynamite, and one day in 1848 a tamping iron three feet long and an inch in diameter was blown through his skull, taking out his left eye and a portion of his frontal lobe. Phineas Gage recovered, he was perfectly normal in every respect except that he could no longer make moral decisions. A religious, hardworking man before his accident, he became irreligious, profane, dishonest, and lazy, a drifter who flouted all the many social conventions of his day. Gage had ceased to be Gage, madam. His conscience, or a part of it, had literally been blown out of his head, and he has been studied by neurology and psychiatry students ever since, and now we involved in the Gage Project at the Imaging Systems labs are looking into the possibility that he suffered damage to the neurocircuits that control ethical reasoning. It may be that people who can do all the things normal people do but are psychopaths or sociopaths have had frontal lobe damage such as his, so you see that questions of moral actions, previously the speciality of priests and philosophers, will soon become the province of scientists and physicians.

Heartwood stopped short, pulling the earphones from his ears. Weathers was religious, a Mormon. Weathers had lost his eye to a blow. A sawed-off baseball bat studded with bent nails, the newspaper article said. What if . . . ? Christ! For an instant, he wondered why he hadn't thought of it before, the idea seemed so right. An instant later, it seemed absurd. Weathers, the Mormon Jekyll, becomes Weathers, the mass-murdering Hyde, all because of a whack on the head? Gabriel jeered in his imagination. Not that brain-damage bullshit again.

He finished his run when he came abreast of a staircase that scaled the almost sheer palisades, choked with brush, pocked by swallows' nests. Halfway up, as he paused on a landing to catch his wind, a wildman sprang out of the dense brush on a ledge, shrieking,

"Asswipe!"

He stood on the step above, and he was very tall, impossibly thin, and had long, greasy gray hair and a long, stained, gray beard.

"Asswipe!" he shrieked again, revealing a mouth missing half its teeth. His arms flailed like ropes in a wind. "Block nordu, you fuckin' asswipe. I know you!"

Heartwood's breath stopped in his throat. Was this maniac someone he'd helped send to prison? He tried to place the face, couldn't, and then realized the man wasn't some escaped or paroled killer out for revenge, but merely one more screwball loose on the streets. Maybe not a harmless screwball, though. This morning's L.A. *Times* reported that police were still looking for a homeless man who'd strangled an elderly woman in Palisades Park only two weeks ago.

"Asswipe! Block nordu!"

The man glared down on him, blue eyes burning from deep within his narrow skull. What did those eyes see to make him act the way he was? Maybe he'd been a football coach before he went crazy. You asswipe, I told you to block Nordu!

"All right now, it's all right. I'm coming on up and I won't bother you," Heartwood cooed, knowing the man's brain, like a malfunctioning decryption machine, would scramble his assurances into gibberish. It was the tone of voice that mattered.

"Do you know what a fart is, you asswipe?" the mad hermit snarled, bending at the waist and thrusting his wild-maned head forward. "Air passed through shit!"

"Thanks for sharing that. All right. Quiet now . . . "

Heartwood climbed cautiously up a step, pressed the hermit's skeletal ribs, and gently pushed him aside.

"Goddamn," he said, now in a sad, defeated voice, and his bones almost rattled as he slumped onto fleshless buttocks. "It's only air passed through shit, so why's everybody make a big deal about it? Answer me that, asswipe."

Heartwood stepped around him and bolted up the rest of the stairs.

Back in the park, he bowed, palms on his wobbly knees. It had been a while since he'd had a scare like that. The guy could have had a knife or gun. That elderly woman must have been jumped on in the same way.

He changed tape sides and plugged the Walkman back into his ears and jogged along Ocean Drive toward the Sovereign, staying clear of the trees and dense gardens in the park. Never know who or what else might be in there, poised to spring. No safe rear areas anymore. Got to keep alert, even in Santa Monica. Traffic rushed past, the occasional car peeling off from the stream to glide down the incline to the Pacific Coast Highway. He couldn't hear the traffic, nor the radios blaring in the cars, nor the silvered jet, coming in on a final approach to LAX, a few miles south. *Alleluia, alleluia, laudate Dominum.* The racket of his own dreadful century was drowned out by the songs of medieval cloisters, cold and serene. *Venite, exultemus Domino . . .*

Evidence. Witnesses. Clues. Facts.

Cases were made or unmade by small facts.

A thread. A drop of blood. A bullet was smaller than a thumbnail.

The first thing Gabriel did after landing in Sacramento was to drive to the San Joaquin State campus and ask the chief of the university police to find out if Mace Weathers had attended classes on Friday. He kept the true reason for his inquiry to himself and said that he was looking into a ring smuggling steroids out of Mexico to California campuses. Somers's description of Weathers as a weightlifter had been the inspiration for that cover story. Fiction met fact. It turned out that the campus cops had their eye on Weathers, suspected him of dealing steroids to the football team, but so far hadn't found any evidence. Thrilled to be called on to assist a special agent, the chief couldn't have been more cooperative. An hour later, he came through with disappointing news, news that made Gabriel's elaborate theory fall into pieces, like an ice sculpture struck by a hammer.

He drove back to Sacramento through the Delta lands where the pickers' straw hats resembled in the distance dull yellow flowers and the mobile irrigators flung streams across the fields, black and green and golden through the eucalyptus on the levees his ancestors had raised out of the mud. Charlie Christian strummed sweet chords on the tapedeck, but only one thought kept running through Gabriel's head: If not Weathers or Tipton, then who? Who was waiting in the woods? Whose name did Boggs call out? Mace! Victory! Couldn't have said that. Weathers had been in classes between nine A.M. and one P.M. on Friday. A small fact.

He walked slowly across the Department of Law Enforcement parking lot, like an old man lost in thought or memories, and went inside and climbed a flight of stairs to a corridor walled on one side by windows, the windows looking out on a courtyard where file clerks, fingerprint analysts, ballistics experts, biochemists, and arson specialists ate lunch under a pollen-hazed sky. He glanced at them, still thinking, if not Weathers or Tipton, then who? Maybe there wasn't anyone. Or . . . yes, or. There was one other possibility, but he didn't want to think about it and all the difficulties it would make for him.

He passed through double doors with round windows like portholes into another corridor that had the look of a passageway, and his mind wandered momentarily to his last ship, an old World War Two Liberty ship converted to a spy vessel for monitoring French A-bomb tests in Eniwetok, where Gabriel had seen the apocalyptic flash, the mushroom cloud spreading its radioactive cap over travel-poster seas and palm-belted atolls. Not many people had seen that sight and lived to tell about it. A sneak preview of the end of the world.

The serology lab was a large room, a zone of mysteries where blood and semen stains were analyzed and DNA chains were made to yield up their secrets. He recognized, from his brief career as a wandering scholar of police science, a device called an electro foresis tank; otherwise, the equipment and the computer screens inscribed with the scientists' hieroglyphics made him feel like a time-traveling refugee from the fourteenth century.

In the trace evidence section, Jean Sheldon, raw-boned and lanky, stood by a wide table on which she'd piled Boggs's clothes. In her lab coat, she reminded Gabriel of his high school chemistry teacher, Mrs. DeHoog. That stern old Dutchwoman used to give him bad marks for his deportment. Did they still worry about deportment in high schools? Not likely. Teachers were happy if students showed up for classes unarmed. Even at Leland's suburban school, there now were discussions about installing metal detectors. From spitballs to bullets in a generation.

"Well, Jeannie, what've you got for me?"

"Not a whole lot," she said. There was something sad about her. Even her smiles were sad, suggestive of some deep disappointment in life, a loss that couldn't be forgotten.

Gabriel leaned against the table.

"I was hoping you wouldn't say that."

"But then, I don't deal in the 'whole lot,'" she said. "The micro not the macro, your friendly particle picker of dust motes and powder residue, that's me. Here's what we have. Three to four different kinds of synthetic fibers, red, blue, and brown, some cotton fibers, acetate fibers, tobacco residue, hair follicles from two different people, one young, the other probably middle-aged or young and prematurely gray, and finally, cat hairs. Ran chemical tests on a couple of swatches from his shirt and trousers. Found fairly strong concentrations of petroleum naphtha in the shirt. Dry-cleaning solvent to you."

"Tell a story?"

"I can't say without comparative samples. What kind of story are you looking for, Gabriel?"

"One with a happy ending."

"I'm not a broadcaster, you know that."

"All right. We don't think Boggs was all by his lonesome. No idea who his partner might have been. We had two possibles, but I alibied them out. Nowhere near the scene when it went down."

Jean cocked her hip, picked up a slide, and locked it in a microscope tray. With a movement, she invited him to look at it.

"Those red fibers are a synthetic. Easy peasy. The size and shape tell me that they're carpet fibers. Ditto for these."

She removed the first slide, inserted another, containing blue fibers, and a third with brown.

"Boggs's motel room had a red carpet," he said, squinting at the threads, magnified to about the width of a straight pin. "Blue and brown I don't know. Where'd you find these?"

"The red ones were embedded in the pocket seams of his trousers. Lots of them. That means the trousers spent a lot of time in an environment where there was a red carpet. To say that it was the one in Boggs's motel room, I'd have to see samples from there. I was looking for major themes," she said, pointing at a plastic tray filled with glass slides and plates. "There were some brown carpet fibers in his trousers, a lot of tobacco residue, which suggests to me that he carried his cigarettes in those big side pockets. There were no blue fibers. Now these"—she took one of the slides and placed it on the microscope's tray—"came from the collar of his shirt."

Gabriel did not see anything. Jean, her hand lightly brushing his cheek as his head bent to the eyepiece—the brief touch brought a warmth to his face—turned two rings to increase the magnification and adjust the focus. Several strands came into view, some dark, the others neutral-colored, like monofilament.

"Those are human hairs. Black and gray. I found very light concentrations of the black hairs, but a good deal of the gray hairs, and those were embedded under the collar."

"Tell me a story."

"The coroner's report said Boggs had black hair. Again, I'd need samples to confirm that these are his, but assuming they are, I'd say he hadn't worn this shirt very long, but the person with the gray hair did. I'd say he was middle-aged not only because of the color but because of the numbers of hairs—he was losing his hair."

"He? Definitely? You can tell the sex of the hair?"

"A guess. Those folliciles have been cut short, almost in a crew cut. Also, the hair loss suggests male-pattern baldness. Anyway, male or female, the shirt spent a lot more time on the back of that person than on Boggs. Now we change species."

A new slide was inserted and Gabriel looked again and saw dark and light strands that resembled those on the previous slide.

"Those are cat hairs, found on the shirt but not in the trousers."

"None?"

"Not a one. The cat was some kind of long-haired breed, like a bushy-tailed Persian, or a mongrel with Persian strain. Can't pinpoint the color. That's always hard with some kinds of cat hairs. Either gray and white, black and white, or black and gray."

Gabriel raised his head.

"Did Boggs have a cat?" Jean asked.

"Not that I know of."

"Smoker?"

"Yeah. Hey, Jeannie, here's a challenge. What brand?"

She winked.

"Marlboro."

"Lucky guess."

"Guess, but not lucky. Over there"—she gestured at a drawer under a counter crowded with power supply units and test-tube racks—"I've got tobacco samples from all major companies, plus information on the blends they use. There were a few grains of tobacco in Boggs's shirt and they looked like the ones in his trousers. I did a comparison. Philip Morris Company. No guess there. Their most popular brand is Marlboro. That was the guessing part."

"And . . . ?"

"So for a brief period he had an open pack of Marlboros in the left breast pocket of the shirt."

"Bought a pack about an hour before he did it. Four cigarettes missing from the pack."

"Okay. Otherwise there was no tobacco residue in that article of clothing. That reinforces my opinion that the shirt had not been in his possession for very long. A day or two."

"Wouldn't the dry cleaning have taken a lot of stuff out?"

She shook her head.

"Fingerprints, sure. The only prints on it were Boggs's. Surface lint, sure, but not the particles that get embedded in pocket linings, in seams, and under the collar. You want to run an experiment, take a dirty pair of trousers to a dry cleaner's and then cut open the pocket seams with a razor. You'll find all sorts of particles, some of which have probably been in there for years."

"Put it all together for me."

"Sure. With the understanding that the shirt could have been contaminated at the morgue and in the sheriff's evidence locker."

"Understood."

"A previous owner of the shirt was a middle-aged male with short, thinning gray hair. He was a nonsmoker. He lived in a house or apartment with a blue carpet and kept a cat. The shirt did not have a lot of interim owners, because if it did, there would be more major themes. At some point, it did spend some time in a place with suits or sport jackets or both, suits or sport jackets made of wool and cotton."

"How do you tell that?" Gabriel asked, mesmerized by such detail gleaned from stuff you could barely see.

"I found some woven fibers. They're very distinctive. Also acetate threads, the sort used in suit and sport jacket liners. Not in great quantity, indicating that this old army shirt didn't spend a long, long time in such fancy company. It also spent a brief time in some place where there was a brown carpet, possibly, *possibly* two different kinds of brown carpet. Observe, Gabriel."

He squinted at two more slides.

"The size and shape are both consistent with a synthetic, but you can see that the ones on the first slide look lighter and longer than the ones on the second. Almost gold. I'm guessing, but they could come from a quilt or bedspread. I'd really need samples for comparison and do some further tests."

"Any idea when it was dry-cleaned?'

"Recently. Can't pin it down any more precisely than that."

"Kinda funny, dry-cleaning an old fatigue shirt. It's the kind of thing you'd toss in the wash. And Boggs, he's living hand to mouth. Why would he spend the money to dry-clean when he could have washed it for a few quarters?"

"That's out of my line," Jean said, shrugging. "The trousers hadn't been dry-cleaned. Not even washed." She picked them up and held them by the waistband. "Don't have to be a trace-evidence specialist to see the grease and oil stains. Ordinary motor oil, by the way. The guy must have worked around cars a lot."

At the other end of the room, a technician removed with tongs a rack of testtubes from what looked like a microwave oven. Two more were questioning each other about the degree of biodegradation of semen found in a rape victim's vagina.

"I'm thinking out loud," Gabriel said. "Boggs's kid brother told us he wanted his father's old army shirt. He asked Tipton to bring it to him, and a nine-millimeter handgun. The kid said he couldn't find the shirt, but he told us he did bring the gun."

Jean looked at him questioningly. The sadness was deepest in her brown eyes. Some loss or disappointment. Gabriel imagined a bitter divorce, or a lover who'd died before his time.

"If Tipton was willing to admit that he brought Duane a handgun, why would he lie about a lousy shirt?" he said, to explain his out-loud thinking. "And anyway, I don't think this would have been the shirt Duane's old man had in the Army."

"Why not?"

"Standard GI issue was plain green or mottled green camouflage. You can buy imitation tiger stripes in surplus stores, but the real thing was issued only to Vietnamese Marines and airborne troops and their American advisers. Duane's father wasn't in Vietnam."

"The brother was one of your possibles?"

"Yeah. But he was in the Hollywood jail when the massacre went down. You can't get any more airtight than that. The other guy's a college student, and he was in classes."

"How does the shirt relate?"

"If Boggs bought it himself, say at an army surplus store, it doesn't relate at all. But if someone gave it to him, I'd like to talk to that guy. Find out what made him give old Duane the shirt off his back. Especially after what you've told me. That the shirt probably hadn't been in Duane's hands for very long. That would at least mean the guy saw Duane, talked to him only a few days before the crime. It could mean more."

"I'd tend to favor the gift idea." Her large hands, reddened and cracked as a cleaning woman's, spread the shirt out wide against Gabriel's torso. He thought he smelled something, a lingering ghost of an odor, and had to force himself not to leap back so the cloth wouldn't touch him. Walked in their blood. Stepped right over them and went on shooting.

"You look like a medium, and I'd call this an extra-large," Jean said. "The autopsy said Boggs was five-eleven and one-forty. A drain pipe. Of course, this isn't my line. Maybe Boggs liked this shirt so much he didn't care about the size, maybe he liked the baggy hip-hop look."

"Boggs wasn't a hip-hop kind of guy."

"Then we've got this."

She showed him a thick gold ring, with a plastic eagle's head on its face.

"The coroner's autopsy said he was wearing it on one of his toes."

"We're told Boggs had a Vietnam hangup. Over in 'Nam, guys sometimes wore their rings on their toes to hide them from the VC in case they were killed and their bodies not recovered right away. That eagle looks like the symbol of the 101st Airborne. He could've picked it up at an army-navy store or a pawn shop."

"Maybe. But . . . this doesn't mean we're in love," Jean said, slipping the ring on his middle finger. It was loose and when he turned his hand upside down, the ring slipped off and fell on the floor.

"He might have worn it on his toe because it was too big for his fingers. One last thing. This shirt was worn over a black synthetic and cotton knit. There were a fair number of knit fibers on the inside seams, along the button line."

He tried by force of imagination to fill the shirt with a body, to picture a face and neck above the faded collar.

Then he noticed something on the collar and asked Jean if she had a good old-fashioned magnifying glass. She produced one from a drawer under the table.

"You look like Sherlock Holmes. Like Sherlock Holmes in those old movies," she said.

"I am. Reincarnated as Chinee boy. Charlie Chin, the poor man's Chan."

He thought he'd heard an affectionate teasing in her voice, not entirely innocent, and was a little taken aback to find himself excited by it. She wasn't much to look at and two inches taller than he, but there was that old allure, that forbidden allure of white women, and an archaic, reckless desire to break his grandmother's taboos. You gotta girlfriend, Gabriel? Better be good Chinese girl.

He moved the glass up and down, getting the right perspective and focus, then handed it to Jean.

"See those two small dark patches on each side of the collar? Darker than the material around it. Shaped like a peaked roof? Chevrons. Rank insignia. The shape tells me they were buck-sergeant chevrons. You look carefully, you can see the holes where they were pinned on."

"Yep."

"What's that tell you?"

"These chevron things . . . "

"Small metal rank insignia, worn in the field, black so they don't reflect sunlight, so they can't be spotted by the enemy."

"It tells me they must have been pinned on and taken off frequently, for the holes to be worn through enough for us to see them with only a magnifying glass," she said. "You'd take them off when you washed the shirt, pin them back on. But they must have been on a lot more than off. That's why the material underneath isn't as faded and weathered as the rest."

"Right."

"Very good, Gabriel. Very Sherlockian of you."

He spread the shirt flat on the table under the fluorescent lights.

"See that? Don't need the magnifying glass." He laid a finger just above the right breast pocket.

"That dark, rectangular patch?"

"That's where the name tag had been sewn on. The cloth underneath looks almost brand-new. At least a full shade darker than the cloth around it. That suggests the name tag had been taken off fairly recently."

"Think I can answer that one in a few minutes. Let's do a little tape lift."

She pulled from the drawer a roll of wide, clear tape, cut off a strip of about six inches, carefully laid the strip over the spot where the name tag had been, then peeled it off as delicately, placed it clean side down on a glass tray, and with that tray, went to an electron microscope with dual eyepieces like binoculars, switched on a light, and slid the tray under the lenses, her wide knobby shoulders hunched as she bent her neck and fitted the rubber eyepiece hood to her face. She peered for three or four minutes, then stood up straight and said, "Probably it was taken off recently."

Gabriel looked down into a pale light and saw three dark threads in a row at the top of the tape, two more at the right side, also in a row.

"I can run tests to determine what those strands are made of, if you want. But they look like fragments of sewing thread. Notice that they're aligned, at the edges. Neat, strong stitching with heavy-duty thread, probably done by machine. Whoever took the name tag off was pretty meticulous about also removing the tag ends of the threads, but he missed these. If he'd done it a long time ago, the material underneath would blend better with the rest, and these surface threads would have worked themselves out. Especially in the dry cleaning. Most of the fragments he'd missed would've peeled off and been left on the press. These stayed. How's this help your story? Got a plot yet, a main character?"

"Plot, maybe. Character? Not so sure. My guess is that the original owner of this shirt was a non-com, a junior adviser to a Vietnamese paratrooper outfit. My next guess is that he wasn't the one who gave it or the ring to Boggs, if they were presents."

"Why not?"

"Up in my attic I've got the pair of jungle boots I was wounded in. They're cracked, dried-out, bent way out of shape. Useless. I've probably gone to throw them out twenty times since I got back, and I can never do it."

"They mean something to you."

"Yeah. So we're fairly sure that up until recently, the name tag and the rank insignia were still on this shirt. Now who would keep them on for twenty-odd years? The guy who'd worn the shirt in Vietnam. He valued it, like any old soldier does his uniform. He wouldn't be likely to give it away to anybody, or to sell it to a surplus store for resale, or donate it to the Salvation Army. That's as far as the story goes so far. What do you think, Jeannie? Sherlockian or what?"

"I suppose . . ."

She hesitated, offering him her doleful smile. Maybe that expression didn't come from an unforgettable loss or some disappointment in love but from her years of peeling trace evidence off the corpses of the Palm Springs rich as in their own blood and piss and shit they lay on the floors or on the beds and sofas of their pricey houses flooded with merciless desert light, picture windows boxing views of fairways and dry mountains.

"I can give a telephonic deposition if you think what you've got here justifies a search warrant. Then we can collect comparison samples."

"Not ready for that yet."

"You haven't got any evidence that there was another guy?"

"None. I'm on a fishing trip."

"You know if you catch something, if you find that some guy did give this shirt to Boggs a couple of days before it went down, all he has to say is, 'Oh, yeah, I remember now. He asked me for that thing,' and then all this particle picking goes down the drain."

"I don't expect to find conclusive evidence here. I'm looking for arrows to point me in the right direction."

"Am I out of line asking why you think there was another guy?"

He told her about the theory he and Youngblood had constructed and about the small facts that had shattered it, at least for the time being.

"I still think it's a valid idea," he went on. "It's a question now of finding another possible. I need something to place another guy at the scene."

"Say the word and I'll drop everything and go there. I've got a kid in school myself and I'd do anything to help crucify a guy like that."

"Six days have gone by and those Okie sheriff's deputies did a lousy job of securing the scene. A hundred people stomped around there. Helicopter rotor blades blowing everything to hell and gone. Do you think you could find anything?"

"I'd need a miracle, but you know, it could be you need to rethink your theory. As a trace-evidence specialist, I can think of one absolutely foolproof way for this mastermind of yours not to leave a trace of evidence at the scene. Talk to any Mafia boss, he'll tell you."

"Been in the back of my mind, but, Christ, that would make an almost impossible case really impossible."

Heartwood read the fax, and its words stung.

". . . estimates of the costs of repairing and re-erecting the statue come to $6,250 . . . Each of the seven boys involved to be assessed equally . . . Received written apologies from all . . . but David, who is now on final disciplinary probation . . . I have spent too much time handling faculty complaints about his conduct in the past two years, and his disrespect for . . . Attempts to counsel him not only have failed to alter his behavior but have been singularly ineffective in persuading him that his behavior is inappropriate . . . Unfortunate that David's positive qualities haven't been harnessed to a firm moral character, but turned instead toward . . . Sincerely Yours, T. Wilmont Bellamy, Headmaster."

He gazed out his window on Second Street, where an octogenarian Jewish woman, her head probably cluttered with memories of extinct Brooklyn ghettos, clutched a walker as she shuffled along, a stout black nurse at her side. Then he picked up the phone and called Paula at her office.

"How did the closing go?"

"It didn't yet," she answered. That well-bred voice, every vowel speaking of old Yankee money. "When it does, another two-hundred-thousand-dollar bungalow sold for half a million because it's on the west side, where your eyes don't sting at high noon. Or anytime."

"L.A. real estate's not as bad off as the papers say?"

"Five years ago, the place would have gone for seven-fifty."

"I read T. Wilmont Bellamy's letter. Some name that guy's got. Never liked him. It's like he's read every description of the anal-retentive Wasp schoolmaster and decided to imitate them."

"One, I am getting tired of people saying things about us Wasps they wouldn't dare say about Jews or Latinos. Two, an attitude like yours is only going to encourage David to keep behaving like a jerk."

"Mr. T. Wilmont Bellamy is telling us, in his snide way, that we've been lousy parents. We've failed to instill a firm moral character."

"You're saying that. Your Catholic guilt is rearing its boring head again. What's boring about it is that it never stopped you from unzipping your pants in the wrong bedrooms. Speaking of which, are you still boffing the ingenue stargazer?"

"She's an astronomer and she's thirty-two. Past the ingenue stage," he said, calmly refusing to rise to the bait. "Look, I'm not trying to make light of what David did, but that letter made it sound like those kids committed murder. It was only a prep-school prank that got out of hand."

"Sixty-two hundred dollars out of hand. If he and his gang had done that off-campus, they'd be in jail. And it's David's attitude about what he's done that bothers me even more. When I look back, we always had problems getting him to accept reponsibility for his acts. There was always an excuse. It was always someone else's fault."

"That's common these days."

"Lee, I'm not interested in the human condition, all right? This is our son. It's like we've got a disabled child on our hands. He can't seem to feel shame or remorse."

Her voice had become cool and objective now.

Heartwood, still looking down on Second, watched a blond roller-blader, her muscular ass rippling under lycra shorts as, on skates with Day-Glo laces, she nimbly weaved around pedestrians.

"So what do you think we should do about this disability?" he asked.

"That's rich. You're the shrink. You're supposed to know."

"There's something ridiculous about being a psychiatrist and the father of a problem kid. It's like being a cardiologist whose kid eats smothered pork chops."

"Then I'm proposing the nonpsychological approach. One, we split the eight hundred and ninety down the middle and we make David pay us back out of his summer job. Two, we both tell him to write that letter of apology and get off final disciplinary probation or we don't pay one cent toward his college tuition. He'll be on his own. I'll be damned if I'm going to see him turn out like some of those preppie brats I grew up with. They'd screw up, but Daddy's connections would get them off the hook. I won't have that."

"No worries. I'm very unconnected."

"You know what I mean. So this is the plan. I talk to him, lay down the law. You talk to him, lay down the same law. No chinks or cracks for David to wriggle through. A solid front."

He loved her when she got like this, clear-headed and firm and unsentimental.

"I've got a flight to catch. I'll call David tonight from Sacramento."

"Don't let him bamboozle you."

▬ ▬ ▬

A pink message slip lay under his door at the Camelia House. Gabriel phoned. Urgent. Call back.

Heartwood set down his overnight bag and dialed the number. After a dozen rings, a dispatcher answered rotely, "Law Enforcement Division, Sacramento Field Office." She rang Gabriel's extension, then paged him when he didn't answer. Finally he announced himself with an officious "Special Agent Chin."

"I'm glad this wasn't an emergency," Heartwood said. "I'd be dead by now."

"We don't handle nine-one-one calls here. Where've you been? Your kid's problems straightened out yet?"

He bristled at the flippant tone, as if David's trouble were an unimportant diversion.

"They're not problems you straighten out in one afternoon. What's so urgent?"

"Does Weathers have a cat?"

"*That's* urgent? No, but his landlady does. Its name is Spats if that's any help."

There was a pause, the sound of Gabriel's breathing.

"Long-haired? Sheds a lot? Black and white or gray and white?"

"Black and white. Spotted like a cow. Weathers doesn't like it. He's the fastidious type. All the signs of someone with O.C.D."

"With what?"

"Obsessive-compulsive disorder. A neat freak, remember, like your partner? The cat gets into Weathers's room and sheds. It did when I was interviewing him. The guy actually went around picking up cat hairs with a Dustbuster. Tell me, how did you guess it was a long-haired cat with dark and light fur?"

"Remember how to get here?"

"Sure."

"Get here."

Gabriel ushered him through the stark corridors to a desk where a man with short brown hair and a carefully barbered mustache sat before two computer terminals. He wore a suede jacket with arrow-tipped slash pockets, Levi's, and cowboy boots, and a revolver instead of a semiauto was buckled to his hip. It was as if, in the age of DNA tests and computers, he were trying to maintain the image of the mythical western lawman.

"Lee, this is Phil Youngblood, El Dorado Sheriff's Department."

"You're the co-author of Gabriel's script."

A braided whip of a man, Youngblood stood and shook hands.

"Making a few changes," he said in a voice that sounded like a file scraping on wood.

"Phil's taking some sick leave he's got on the books to give us a hand. That makes him one of two things—dedicated or dumb."

Heartwood sat on the edge of the desk, across which five or six print-outs containing lists of names lay scattered.

"I await enlightenment."

Gabriel filled him in on the crime lab's findings and on his own suppositions about where the tiger-stripe fatigue shirt might have come from. Was Weathers a smoker? No. Did he have a blue or brown carpet in his room? Heartwood couldn't recall. He seemed to remember bare hardwood floors, but there might have been an area rug under the bed. How about suits and sport jackets in his closet? Yes, a couple.

"I called Jean right after I talked to you. No way to determine for sure that the cat hairs on the shirt came from the same animal that got into Weathers's room. We're not talking evidence here."

"Then what are we talking?"

"Indicators." Gabriel pointed at a spot on the wall and moved his finger to one side tick by tick. "Little facts pushing the arrow away from Tipton toward Weathers."

"We already ruled out Tipton."

"Under the old script, yeah. We could rule Weathers out, too. I checked this morning. He was on campus, in classes when it all went down."

"Enlightenment still eludes me."

"Here's a simple riddle. If somebody orchestrated this crime, what would be the best way for him to leave no evidence at the scene?"

After a few seconds' pondering, Heartwood replied, "Not to be at the scene in the first place."

"There it is. He's miles away, like the mob boss who's eating linguine in white clam sauce while his hitman's whacking out some guy on the other side of town."

"So all that stuff about someone signaling Boggs, about the assisted suicide, all that's out the window?"

"Could be. Could be we came to the right conclusion—there was another guy—but for the wrong reasons. Boggs was a kind of human weapon, operated by remote control."

Heartwood mused on this new hypothesis. It was not without appeal, but it seemed that Gabriel was piling theory upon theory, raising a scaffolding of speculation into ever-thinner air.

"What makes you so sure?" he asked. "You start from the premise that Duane was too dumb and impulsive to have been in this by himself. But you don't have any evidence, so you invent a theory explaining the lack of evidence. The methodology's not scientific."

"Does this look like a laboratory to you?"

"I'm saying that instead of testing the accomplice theory by trying to disprove it, you guys are turning circus tricks to prove it, and all over a few cat hairs and an old army shirt."

Gabriel's expression clouded.

"Got to go on the wisdom of the intestine. And we've got more than cat hairs. We've got Weathers lying to you. We've got the possibility that he falsified records to keep Duane in disability checks."

"I wouldn't take Tipton's word on that."

"Not going to. I've got friends in the fraud division. They can check the Social Security and drug rehab records. Also, Phil turned up something while we were away."

"I'm Santa Claus. Make the lists to find out who was naughty or nice." Youngblood snapped a sun-browned finger against one of the printouts. "Slow crime day yesterday in El Dorado. Me and three deputies compiled lists of everyone who stayed in the park campground and in motels near the scene. Sat up till midnight at our RAN terminals, running the names through the criminal history data system."

"Go easy on acronyms," Heartwood said. "What's a RAN terminal?"

"Pretty new thing. Remote Access Network. Gives us backwoods men access to the state's criminal information databases. Fingerprints. Criminal histories. Tap a keyboard, you've got a guy's rap sheet in seconds. The wonders of and all that shit. We were looking for guys with major felony records, violent crimes, guys who might have teamed up with Boggs in the past. Weren't half done when we found this." He pointed at a list on which three names were highlighted: Leonard Best, R. K. Cannon, and William Cass. "All three of these guys stayed at the Gold Hill Motel in Placerville the night of Wednesday, the fourteenth, and were checked out before noon the next day, the day before the crime. Nothing special about that, but I remembered, from when I'd checked Boggs's arrest record, that he was popped on a possession charge in L.A. County back in '91. Used 'Lenny Best' as an alias. So I had one of two possibilities. Either some guy who happened to have the same name as Boggs's alias stayed at the Gold Hill that night, or—"

"Or," Heartwood interrupted, with some impatience, "it was Boggs."

"It was. Went to the Gold Hill first thing this A.M. with a criminalist and dusted the registration card, room he stayed in. The room had been occupied since, so we had a few sets of prints to deal with. We got our cleanest off the card. Two sets. One belonged to the owner. Criminalist went back to our office, accessed Boggs's prints, did a latent print match. His."

"So he spent a night near the crime scene . . ."

"Gold Hill's only a twenty-minute drive from it," Youngblood said. "And it's Boggs's kind of place, all right. Don't get asked for credit cards because if you're staying there, you aren't likely to have one. Cash up front, sign in under any old name you choose, get your key. And incidentally, the rooms are all carpeted in brown."

"And all that suggests that he was making a reconnaissance the day before, which suggests that he did plan the thing carefully, which further suggests that we've been underestimating his brain power."

With a slight incline of his head, Heartwood asked the detective to explain what further significance Duane's overnight stay might hold.

"Lee, Boggs could organize a snowball fight and not much more," Gabriel said and then turned to Youngblood with a sly grin. "Get to the good part."

"Yeah. Had a thought. At no time between Boggs's return to California and the massacre did he try to hide his identity, except that one night. Stayed at the Camino Real under his real name. Used his real name and ID to buy a gun. The guy's not shy about that, why is he using an alias to stay at a motel?"

"With a personality like his . . . " Heartwood began to say.

"A possibility. A screwball, he was playing some kind of cops and robbers game with himself. But I thought of another possibility. Duane was *told* to use an alias. Somebody else, a John Doe, didn't want it known that he'd stayed there, didn't want a record."

Bowing his head and rubbing his temples, Heartwood said, "Because this John Doe stayed at the Gold Hill on the same night. By hiding Duane's identity, he helped hide his own. He didn't want attention called to the place. Am I with you, Phil?"

"Little ahead," Youngblood replied. He sat back and gave his mustache a quick brushing with his fingertips. "Mr. Doe would've picked that motel because it was a low-rent, anonymous place. He might've driven around Placerville, looking for the worst dump he could find. And the Gold Hill had an extra advantage—the owner's a sixty-odd-year-old alcoholic, not a guy with what you'd call sharp powers of observation and a terrific memory. Figured Mr. Doe would've thought this way—the chances that this old juicehead is going to remember Duane's face are pretty minimal. He'll see Duane for a very brief time, when he checks in and pays in advance, maybe for an even briefer time when he drops his key off, if he sees him then at all. Duane would have to behave himself and not do anything to call attention to himself, which I imagine Mr. Doe coached him to do. Maybe there was a partial disguise, nothing outlandish, maybe a cap to hide the color of his hair. But—"

"Boggs's name is going to be more well known than the president's after the massacre goes down," Heartwood said, cutting him off. "And there's a chance that all that publicity will jog the memory of even an old drunk, okay? And the owner might go into his records, find that Boggs was his guest for a night, and call the cops or the media and say, 'Hey, guess what?' Then you've got swarms of cops and reporters asking questions, poking around, and maybe, just maybe someone will ask the owner about who else he rented rooms to that night. Hence, the alias became extra added insurance of anonymity. Still with you?"

"Yeah. While the guys were doing the print match, I drove back to the motel. Asked the owner if he remembered anything about Cass and R. K. Cannon. He pulled the registration cards and stared at them for a while, and the old guy stunk like a redneck bar at closing time. I noticed that Cass left a complete address in Oregon, even filled in the space that asks for your license tag number, but Cannon didn't even leave a full name. That looked funny."

"Did the owner remember anything?" Heartwood asked.

"Yeah, after I offered to buy him a breakfast cocktail. Seemed that one of those guys—he couldn't say which one—was on the big side, wearing sunglasses when he checked in. It was after eight o'clock at night and the guy was wearing sunglasses, those one-way kind, and he was carrying a camouflage jacket over his shoulder in a plastic bag. The owner remembered that because it reminded him of the kind deer hunters wear and he'd asked the guy if he was going hunting and told him he ought to know that opening day was six months away. Guy didn't say anything that he could remember, just took his key and went to his room. At that point, I didn't know what you guys had turned up in L.A. Didn't know anything about this Weathers guy, I was just looking blindly for Mr. Doe. Didn't think I had anything interesting until I talked to Gabriel a couple of hours ago."

"Another little fact, a couple of little facts." Gabriel, leaning against a wall, drew his lips between his teeth and made a popping noise. "We checked Cass. He's clean in California, and half an hour ago, we linked with Oregon. Clean there, too. Address he left was authentic. He's sixty-five years old, five-ten and one-seventy. Not a likely possible."

Heartwood asked if the room rented to "R. K. Cannon" had been checked for fingerprints. Youngblood shook his head. The criminalist team had been called to another crime scene after they matched Boggs's prints.

"So I went out on a limb—this is a closed case for us—and secured Cannon's and Boggs's rooms, pending further investigation."

"That's my man!" Gabriel said.

"Now we're looking to see if Cannon has a record. 'R. K.' is insufficent data for the system, so we got this." He held up a baby's name book, shook out a cigarette, then put it back when Gabriel pointed out the No Smoking sign. "Been looking up every masculine name beginning with R, Randolph to Ryan, Raleigh to Rupert. Check driver's licenses on one terminal, criminal histories file on the other."

"So far, we've got driver's licenses for a Rawl K. Cannon, a Rhett K. Cannon, and a Roger K. Cannon. No criminal records or felony arrests for any of them," Gabriel said. "And personally, I don't think we're going to find anything anywhere under that name."

"Because you think R. K. Cannon doesn't exist. Weathers is R. K. Cannon. He wore no-peek sunglasses to hide his bad eye and to avoid wearing the patch," Heartwood said.

Gabriel spread his hands as if in blessing.

"Did you run Weathers's name through your fabulous system?" Heartwood asked.

"Of course. *Nada,*" Gabriel replied. "No record, never been fingerprinted. But I got off the phone to my campus cops just before I called you. Weathers has only one class on Thursdays. At one P.M. He had all last Thursday morning free."

Rising from his seat, Heartwood paced, and pacing, said, "Let's have some fun and assemble a plausible narrative if we can. Let's start last Wednesday night at the Gold Hill Motel and assume that Mace Weathers, under the name of R. K. Cannon, is staying there with Duane Leonard Boggs, alias Leonard Best, to check out the crime scene the next morning."

"More than check out," Gabriel said. "Put yourself in Weathers's moccasins. You're not going to be around to supervise Duane. You're worried that he'll foul the thing up if he isn't taken through it by the numbers, one-two-three. You decide to hold a dry run twenty-four hours before the real thing. You want to give yourself plenty of time to do this, to work out any bugs, get the fine points down, make sure Duane knows what he's doing. Bright and early Thursday, you're out practicing . . ."

"And you might be practicing following real school buses," Youngblood interjected. "Schools run field trips to the park nearly every day. Sometimes two or three a day."

"Two to three hours later, you're done. You head back to campus and go to your one o'clock class, just like always."

Gabriel mimicked turning a steering wheel and Heartwood pictured the scene. Two young men on the road, dress-rehearsing in the pearlescent dawn the terrible drama to unfold the following day. A plausible narrative, but was it true? He looked at the two detectives.

"Chekhov once said that if you introduce a gun in Act One, it had better go off by Act Three."

They regarded him expressionlessly.

"How does the fatigue shirt fit into your new script? Or is it just a prop?"

"A present for Duane," Gabriel offered. "Also the Airborne ring. He's got this Vietnam hangup, thinks ambushing a busload of schoolkids is some kind of mission. He wants to dress up for it. Weathers has the uniform, gives it to Duane to humor him."

"Not bad for a guy who says he hates psychologizing. How about your profile of the Vietnam vet you think the shirt and the ring first belonged to? Does that have any bearing here?"

"Probably the gray hairs on the shirt belonged to him. Probably there's a connection between him and Weathers. His father maybe, maybe an uncle."

"You're also not bad at guesswork, for a guy who says he doesn't deal in it."

Gabriel raised his eyes toward the ceiling, seeming to implore the heavens for patience.

"Goddamnit, Lee. You're the one Weathers lied to. Don't you want to find out why and what he's hiding? Why are you fighting us on this?"

"Testing your narrative so we don't waste a lot of time chasing after some figment of the imagination."

"Figment? Jesus Christ. You goddamned shrinks."

"Please don't start to delaminate."

Heartwood, a hand fussily patting into place the disobedient remnants of his curly hair, began to pace again, gathering his thoughts.

"The cannery foreman suggested some sort of master-servant relationship between Weathers and Boggs. Let's look at the master. College student, squeaky-clean son of the Mormon middle class, and, I'd say, a rigid obsessive-compulsive personality. What are the underlying causes of O.C.D.? Usually forbidden impulses or desires that are suppressed or displaced through repetitive rituals."

Youngblood frowned and pressed his thumb between his eyebrows, and Gabriel patted him sympathetically on the shoulder.

"You'll get used to this, Phil. Dr. Lee likes to lecture." He looked toward Heartwood. "Sorry for interrupting, Professor. Go ahead."

"Thanks, *Gabe*. We know that Duane was a male prostitute off and on. Okay, you don't have to be gay to be a male whore, but it helps. We also know that Weathers goes out with girls, but what if he had a relationship with Boggs that was closer than he's willing to admit? Is it possible he's bisexual and has a powerful, forbidden desire for other men? He's a *Mormon*, okay, okay? He's ashamed of these feelings and afraid of acting on them because that would risk his being found out by his girlfriend, his family, his macho weight-lifting buddies. He keeps the desires under control by keeping his environment under control. Everything in his life has its place, and I'll bet he has a few other tics I haven't seen, classic O.C.D. tics."

"You're saying those two were an item?" Youngblood sounded incredulous.

"Maybe. All I'm doing is creating an alternative narrative, another way of explaining why Mace lied, why he might have forged records for Duane's benefit. I believe him when he says he couldn't stand Duane. Duane was everything a guy like him despises. But suppose Mace became irresistibly drawn to that which he despised? In Duane he found someone who hero-worshipped him, who would do whatever he wanted, who could provide an outlet for his secret desires without grave risk of discovery. The very qualities that made Duane disgusting also made him attractive. A loser and drifter like him wasn't likely ever to run into someone from, oh, call it Mace's daylight life. Duane was the homosexual equivalent of those teenage hookers we saw getting picked up by good suburban dads looking for something they're not getting from the mothers of their children. Mace would have been disgusted with himself, not only for surrendering to his hidden lusts but for doing it with a degraded and degrading partner like Duane. And all his fears and conflicts would have become heightened after his lover committed the crime of the decade. Then Mace would have an even stronger motive for keeping the truth of their relationship under cover. End of lecture."

A phone rang insistently in a far corner of the room, accentuating the silence that followed Heartwood's speech.

"Lover boys," Gabriel said, stiffly grinning. "But if that was true, Weathers must've known what Duane was planning to do. At least known."

"Possibly, but that wouldn't make him a co-conspirator."

"Could make him an accessory. You know someone's gonna commit murder and you say nothing, do nothing about it, you could be in trouble. At the very least, you're a material witness."

"And I'll bet Weathers is aware of that, too. Still another motive for denying any close involvement with Duane. Anyway, a first-year law student could knock that accessory charge out of the ballpark. His client had heard Duane's violent fantasies before, dismissed them as ravings, and put his talk of killing schoolkids in the same category. No one could have been more shocked by what happened than his client."

"Well, if Weathers is the devil, I guess you're the devil's advocate, all right," Gabriel said.

Heartwood remained silent for a moment, rubbing the tiny hairs that sprouted from the tip of his outsize nose. Another sign of age. Falls off your head, grows on your nose and in your ears.

"Of the two, I'd say mine is the more plausible story. Yours has a couple of holes in it I could fall through without touching the sides on the way down. One of them is the same hole that's in Benedetto's version."

Gabriel flagged him into silence.

"We're a couple of dumb cops, but we thought of them all by ourselves. First hole is based on the Hell's Angels principle of confidentiality—'Three can keep a secret if two are dead.' If Weathers was Mr. Doe, his safety would depend on making sure Duane pulled the trigger on himself."

"And how could he be so sure?" asked Heartwood rhetorically. "More to the point, why would someone so thorough, so careful, and clever enough to leave no tracks take a chance like that? Answer—he probably wouldn't. He'd most likely be there to make sure Duane died. And that leaves Weathers out."

"And the second hole is a motive, right, Lee? Why would this—what did you call him? squeaky-clean Mormon?—why would he commit an atrocity like this?"

"Any ideas?"

"Screwball motives are your department."

"I don't know enough about Weathers to even guess."

"So I go back to what I said last night. We find out everything we can about him, down to the kind of skivvies he wears. Boxers, briefs, bikinis."

"We ask him to drop his pants?" Heartwood quipped, and Youngblood laughed a laugh that sounded like nails spilling into a tin can.

"I've got some better ideas." Gabriel's gaze hardened. "I've got no illusions that we'd ever find enough forensic evidence to charge this guy, but . . . your whatchacallit—narrative. Yours and mine agree on one thing—Weathers is hiding something. We're going to get him to tell us what by committing mental fornication on that white boy, and you, Lee, are going to be the main man for that job. We search his room, you rummage around in his head, find out what kind of head we'll be screwing with before we start screwing with it."

"What do you suggest, Gabriel? That I put him on the couch?"

He shook his head once and slowly.

"Weathers has already opened the door. All you've got to do is step through and see what's on the other side."

■ ■ ■

As he contemplated his mangled eye in the mirror on his dresser drawer, Mace noticed that the glass was smudged. He got a bottle of Windex and a paper towel from the closet shelf and wiped the offending smear. But now the part he'd cleaned was brighter than the rest, which compelled him to spray and polish the entire mirror until it shone uniformly.

His left eye, the slit in the scar tissue that looked like a squashed plum, stared back at him. The Los Angeles surgeon who repaired film stars' faces was going to rebuild his occipital bones, then do skin grafts and fit him with a glass eye that would duplicate God's original except, of course, it wouldn't move or see. The surgeon had promised that all traces of the injury would be removed. No one would be able to tell the difference. "It'll be a long process, Mace, but when it's done you'll be yourself again," Anne had said in the breathless voice that sometimes sounded ethereal and sometimes spooky. She hadn't said that he would look like himself again, but *be* himself, as if his very nature and identity were functions of his appearance. There was a lot of truth in that, which was why he'd begun to have doubts about undergoing the operations.

He put on his patch, adjusting the band to slant across his forehead, carefully brushed his grain-hued hair, then straightened his room. The Segovia and Montoya CDs he'd listened to while studying for his history final were returned to their rightful niches. His albums took up the two lower shelves of the bookcase over his desk and were arranged alphabetically and by category. Pop and Rock. Jazz. Classical. He slid his pencil holder, with its uniform beige Pentels and green number twos, into its spot beside the desk lamp, squared the draft of his senior psychology thesis so its bottom edge was even with the edge of the desk, and centered his computer keyboard against the system unit. That done, he slipped his blazer, a fresh shirt, and a tie into a garment bag, and stood by the door for a moment, drawing satisfaction from the neat room. He recalled his freshman year, when he'd nearly gone mad, living in the dorm with a pig who never kept anything in its place. Joe Fermin. Fermin the Vermin. A worse pig than Duane the Pain.

He started to go out, but couldn't open the door. An invisible force froze his hand to the knob. Half his mind was sure he'd left something out of place. The other half, the rational side, knew full well that he hadn't. He checked his desk, bed, and bookcase, then his closet. Shirts in dry-cleaning bags hung with two-inch spacing between them, trousers ranked according to color, dark on the left, light on the right, shoes lined up on the rack.

All was in place.

He returned to the door, a rivulet of nervous sweat trickling from each armpit, spoiling his shirt. Now he would have to change it. *No*. Got to get control of this.

He twitched his neck to the right three times . . .

Celestial
Terrestial
Telestial

then three times to the left . . .

Telestial
Terrestial
Celestial

. . . and the door swung open, like a fairy tale gate opened by a magical incantation.

He stepped into the hall just as Pickett Greene emerged from his room, carrying a leather dobkit the same calfskin color as the hand that held it. Walking toward the bathroom in his billowing maroon robe, he bore himself like a royal Moor of old until, a yard short of Mace, he tucked the dobkit under an arm, faked left, faked right, then spun and burst open the bathroom door with a stiff-arm.

"One more astonishing TD run by the amazing Greene," he said, leaping triumphantly back into the hall. "What speed, what grace, the man's a phenomenon."

"Too bad he's not on the football team," Mace said, moving to the head of the stairs.

"A shame, a pity, a crime!" Pickett hung and shook his head in feigned dismay, playing it broadly. Then he looked up, squinting with one slightly bloodshot eye, opening the other wide. "Ar-har, there, Cap'n Kidd, lemme look at ye and give yer appearance my imprimatur afore ye go out to plunder the Spanish Main. Oh, fine, real fine," he went on, nimbly changing accents. "The picture of suburban Beaver boy. Pleated trou, Brooks Bro shirt, and he's carrying a blazer and a tie! And, oh, those loafers! My, how they do shine!"

Mace laughed and Pickett laughed with him.

"There's my man. Shit, I don't think I've seen a smile out of you for a couple of weeks. What awesome responsibility has been weighing you *down*?"

"My psych thesis," he said to explain his peculiar demeanor.

Pickett pulled a pair of nail clippers from his dobkit and made the movements of a surgeon cutting into a patient. "Should have gone into premed, like me. No thesis, just four thousand years of school and interning."

That reminded Mace of a business matter.

"King Kameakamea needs a new cycle. Ronkowski told me the other night."

Pickett shot a nervous look past Mace's shoulder and down the stairs. Mrs. Van Huesen was rattling utensils and singing to herself in the kitchen below.

"Your powers of dissimulation need work." Mace turned on one of his frigid smiles. "You're looking so guilty it's like we're dealing rock. Frosty, Pickett. Past frosty. It's only that ditsy old bitch down there. Say 'Decadurabolin' to her and she'd think you're speaking a foreign language."

"It isn't rock, but it isn't exactly legal either. For damn sure the way I'm getting it for your jock consumers would at the very least end my academic career."

Mace held the smile.

"The Raiders have been giving him a look. He knows he needs to bulk up big time if he's going to have a shot."

"What does he want?"

"Pills if you can get them."

"Doubt it."

"Injectables, then."

Pickett skewed his lips.

"Payment in advance this time. And you can tell Ronkowski that he's way past his grace period."

"I'll be seeing him in the weight room tomorrow. He's supposed to settle then."

"Forget 'supposed to.' *Will*. Risk, reward, you know? No reward, I don't take any more risk. If the clinic finds out I've been . . . "

"They won't."

"Glad you're so confident. Where you going with a blazer and a tie? A country club?"

"Celia's parents are taking us out to dinner. I think it's their way of thanking me."

"Little late, aren't they?"

"Taken them a while to accept things. That she's going out with a white guy."

"Fun to see a Caucasoid on the receiving end. Hey, is it impri*mater* or imprimachur?"

"The first, unless you want to sound British."

Mace walked briskly to the bus stop, resisting the compulsion to count cracks in the sidewalk. No time to waste. He'd brought his Camaro in for a tune-up this morning and had to get it out of the shop, put in his three hours at D.A.C.O., then pick Celia up for dinner. Lanny's Service Center was a long bus ride away, out by the new mall that had been asparagus and tomato fields when he'd started at State four years ago. He liked Lanny's. They washed and vacuumed your car after servicing it, didn't just leave it with grease-stained paper mats on the seats and floor.

He settled into a backseat, under two grim ads for an AIDS testing clinic and a suicide crisis hotline.

A disheveled edition of the *San Joaquin Dispatch* lay on the seat beside him. He straightened it and folded it lengthwise, whetting the crease between his thumb and forefinger, and noticed that for the first time since Friday there wasn't a word about *it*. But there were two big stories about Waco. He went through the paper section by section. No, not a word. Less than a week and it was out of the news altogether, as if nothing had happened. Things had returned to normal. He felt dejected; it was as if something special had passed out of his life, something that had given a quickness and a sharpness to each moment of the past weeks. He'd drawn satisfaction from reading about *it*, and clipping the endless speculations about Duane's motives. Amusing how wildly off the mark some of that stuff was—all those reporters interviewing all those analysts, and everybody throwing out theories like physicists trying to explain some phenomenon that defied the known laws of science. He'd felt a little godlike. He alone knew the secrets to Duane the Pain's bleak, bent little mind, he alone was keeper of the mysteries.

The bus went east on Calaveras, passing under oak arches that shattered the waning sunlight into fragments. It came to a stop and three women climbed on, two Asians and one Mexican. The bus jerking into motion again, the Asians lurched into a bench seat and sat side by side, like matched figurines. Vietnamese? Cambodian? Lao? The racist cliché was true: you couldn't tell them apart.

So kill 'em all and let God sort 'em out. On that T-shirt Riley was wearing. A death's head suspended from a parachute, the skull's jaw resting on a scroll that bore the legend "Airborne," and arced over the chute, the noble exhortation, "Kill 'em All and Let God Sort 'em Out." Building a new life for himself, he'd said to Mace on that hot bright afternoon last September. Some new life Riley was building in that cramped, cluttered garage apartment on the wrong side of Riverside. You got your life and I got no place in it and I'm building a new life for myself and you got no place in it, don't want to set eyes on you again. His exact words. All those years of searching and when I'd found him, what does he say? That he was building a new life and didn't want to set eyes on me again.

And as he recalled that brief, painful reunion, something keen rended Mace's heart and the waters of an icy rage poured into its chambers. It would have flooded them if he had not been distracted by the older of the two Asian women, who was giving him quick, uneasy glances. With his piratical eye patch and the harsh expression anger had brought to his face, he must look menacing to her. When she glanced again, he offered his sweetest smile, the counterfeit smile he used to switch on like a light when he went door to door with Lewis, peddling tickets to Mormon heaven. The woman didn't appear to be reassured. She had a big straw bag on her lap and clutched it tightly to her chest, as if she were afraid he was going to snatch it. Couldn't blame her. The papers said the Asians in San Joaquin were terrified.

Too bad. They didn't need to be shown that the world was a deadly kingdom of the absurd. Duane's sermon in blood was not supposed to be preached to the converted. Mace would rather have seen uneasy looks from the other passengers, particularly from the white couple across the aisle. Blue-collar types, judging from their discount store clothes. Maybe in their late twenties, early thirties, but already going to fat from a fast-food frozen-dinner diet, beers emptied in front of the boobtube every night. Dull-eyed and complacent, like a pair of overfed dogs.

WHAT DOES IT TAKE TO WAKE YOU PEOPLE UP? he bellowed in his mind, though his pleasant smile never changed. It could happen to you or yours, you know. No, you don't, I can tell by the way you're sitting that the world must still seem to you as safe and sensible as once it did to me, when I was growing up in pretty Redlands. The world where effect follows cause as night does day. BULLSHIT! I am half BLIND FOR THE REST OF MY LIFE but I see better than you that Chaos's hour is coming, its dark demented gods to rule the land. You should know that, fat faces, if you read the papers and watch the news. Why don't you? Is it because most of those kids didn't look like you or your kids so you think they were singled out and that you and yours are safe? I'm here to tell you you're not. I know better than anyone.

Spring break last year. He and Celia were bound for Laguna's beaches, but left campus an hour later than planned, held up by her last-minute packing and then a phone call from her mother in Los Angeles.

Two hours later, on I-5, they ran into a big traffic jam caused by an overturned trailer truck. Low on gas, irritated by the delays, Mace detoured down a state road that led to Highway 99. Celia grew neurotic about running out of gas and badgered him to stop. Finally, he did, pulling into a station where three bikers were filling their Harleys. Two were finished and had already started their engines. The third was inside, paying the attendant. He stepped out, paused, and stared across the apron to the island where Mace stood, pumping gas. The biker wore boots with red laces, jeans, and a black flight jacket emblazoned with double lightning bolts on the shoulder. A German army helmet hung from his hand by the strap, his skull bristled like a Marine recruit's.

Skinhead.

He bent his knees to peer through the passenger window of Mace's car and said, "She belong to you?"

Mace pretended not to hear. He looked at the flashing dial on the pump. He would always remember that the day was clear and hot for March and that the wind was blowing out of the hills eastward and that the dust it raised on the khaki flats between the station and the hills swirled and sparkled like plankton in sunlit water.

"Hey!" The skinhead took a couple of steps and paused again. His two companions, leaning on their rumbling bikes, watched him from a far island. "Didn't I ask you something? Didn't I ask if the gook bitch belonged to you? Swore I did." He grinned horribly and pushed out one ear with a forefinger. "Swore I did and I swear I don't hear no answer."

"She doesn't belong to anybody."

"Well, she oughta. Way I see it, everybody oughta own one. How do you see it?"

Again Mace did not say anything. Celia once had told him he looked like a guy who could handle himself when things got ugly, but he wasn't so sure about this situation. It would be three against one. He remembered the time in eighth grade, when a kid challenged him to a fight after school. He accepted, but when he went to meet the bully, his guts heaved and he retreated to the boy's room and threw up and then ran home to Lewis and Anne.

The skinhead moved another pace closer, still pushing his ear.

"Man, you talk soft, y'know? That's the second time I asked you a question and didn't hear no answer."

He looked to be eighteen or nineteen. Six feet tall, but skinny. Mace knew he could handle him easily, but the completeness of his rage and the purity of his hatred granted him a power and a leverage. He was like some feral dog, ready to die, ready to kill, and Mace was neither.

"We're not looking for any problems. Just getting some gas and then we're out of here."

"I don't give a fuck what problems you're not looking for. You've done found a problem, and I'm it because I got a fuckin' problem with you, surfer boy."

Mace was getting angry, growing cold and calm. Eighth grade was a long time and lot of muscle ago.

"I don't surf," he said. "Do you see a surfboard? You see an ocean?"

"Hey, whaddya think? Doin' pushups on some fuckin' beach makes you bad, or what?" He swung his helmet across his front, smacking its black crown with the palm of his hand. "Listen up, here's the problem. If she's your old lady and you're havin' little two-tone babies, you're a traitor, surfer boy. A traitor to the race."

"She's not my old lady and we're not making any babies."

"Uh-huh, uh-huh." The skinhead glanced quickly toward his

friends and turned to look in the other direction and then back to Mace. "So if she ain't your old lady, guess you wouldn't mind sharing. Looks like you got too much lemon cake for one dude." His voice fell into a singsong and he bounced merrily on his toes. "Maybe me and my buddies can help you lick off some of the frosting, whaddya say?"

Celia was sitting with her eyes straight ahead, her face blank. She seemed to be trying to make herself invisible. Mace took a second to picture what he was going to do, and holding the picture in his mind, dropped the nozzle and snatched the steel fisherman's billy he kept under the front seat in case he ran into trouble when he worked nights at the rehab center. The thong looped around his wrist, he charged swinging, and the skinhead threw up his helmet as a shield and Mace knocked it from his hand. The skin ran toward his bike, the other two were leaping off theirs to help him; then the attendant, a burly man with treelike forearms, came out from the station and made two long strides across the apron. He held a big wrench in one hand.

"What the hell's goin' on here?"

"Motherfucker wrecked my helmet."

"I think you're lucky he didn't wreck your head." The attendant tapped him on the shoulder with the wrench. "Okay, you pick up your helmet and you and your pals roll on out of here now or I'll see you looking like a road kill."

The skinhead hesitated to let everyone know he wasn't going to be hurried, then spit to the side and picked up his helmet and walked slowly toward his Harley with an exaggerated swagger.

"Assholes," the attendant said, and went back inside.

The bikers ran their throttles up and down, making the engines sound like a giant clearing its throat, before they rode off in single file. Last in line, the skinny one gave Mace and Celia the bird and the mirrors and chrome on all three bikes seemed to flash signals in the sun.

Celia, a hand held between her breasts, watched them leave.

"Get me a pack of cigarettes," she said without looking at Mace, and went to the ladies' room.

Inside, he paid for his gas and asked the attendant to make change for the cigarette machine.

"Good thing it wasn't the other way around," he said, spilling quarters into Mace's palm.

"What do you mean?"

"Her white, you whatever she is."

"Korean."

"Would've had all three of them on you then and there wouldn't have been no conversation beforehand."

Mace dropped the coins into the machine. He was pleased and proud of the courage he'd shown, but now the reaction was setting in. His hands were beginning to shake.

He walked around to the side, where the bathrooms were. A mountain of used tires rose from behind the station. He knocked at the women's door.

"Ceal? Are you okay? I got the cigarettes."

"All right. Just a little sick. Thanks, Mace. Thanks for what you did."

He could hear the terror in her voice, mixed with admiration and gratitude. Because women never had made a difference to him, he was surprised that winning her esteem mattered as much as it did, that it mattered at all. He went into the men's room and emptied himself and noticed, as he washed his hands, that they had grown steady again. He heard the toilet flush in the ladies' room, then the sound of the door opening, then Celia's scream and the slam of the door.

"Mace!"

He rushed outside and the skinhead was there, waiting for him.

"Gook sucker!"

He feinted with his left, and as Mace jerked his head aside to slip the punch, swung with his right a sawed-off baseball bat studded with bent nails. A mace for Mace. It and the flash of chrome and glass from behind the mound of tires were the two last things he would ever see with both eyes. There came a much brighter flash, as if a magnesium flare had burst in his head, a light white and hot, and then a jet of pain as hot as the light.

Heartwood was back in his room by six-thirty. He loosened his tie and spread his files on the desk, intending to make notes, but he was distracted when a young couple pulled up across the street and exited their car arm-in-arm and walked toward their front door. Its screen half-veiled another woman's face—a nanny or baby-sitter, he supposed, as two kids came running to jump at their parents like puppies.

His spirit's mainsail drooped, for in this becalmed interlude between workday's end and dinnertime—misnamed "happy hour"—the air always grew stifling with memories and regrets, the loneliness of middle-age bachelorhood closed in on him, and he saw the coast of his life's likely next destination: a quirky old bachelorhood, dentures soaking on a table beside an empty bed, the TV on for company. The scene of domestic happiness outside only made him feel worse.

He went down to the Camelia House's empty kitchen, where he'd stowed his road supply of Bombay and vermouth, and mixed a martini. It occurred to him as he climbed the stairs, greeting another guest with a nod, that this was his third of the day. He'd downed one at the airport, still shaken by his morning encounter with the mad hermit of the Palisades, and then another on the plane. Do I have a drinking problem? he asked himself, returning to his room. No. My problem is that I grew up in Wisconsin in the 1950s, so I can remember a time when you could walk down a beach without some maniac jumping out at you and calling you an asswipe. My other problem is that I was educated by Jesuits, who beat all that Aristotelian logic into my young head, so I keep trying to make sense of things that probably can't be made sense out of.

He promised himself not to have any more martinis for the next three days, knowing he wouldn't keep the pact, then tried to work until it was time to call David. Concentration was difficult. While part of his mind rehearsed the lecture he intended to give his son, another part dwelled on the conversation with Gabriel and Youngblood. He'd agreed to play his role in the plan, though it would take him into uncertain ethical ground. He was in the end a clinician who was supposed to employ his skills to analyze killers, not capture them. That was the investigator's job. But if Gabriel was right about Weathers and they succeeded in pulling a confession out of him, the publicity would outdo the Redlands Ripper case by a factor of three. This was not a seemly consideration—Walt would disapprove—but in a society so obsessed with fame that it had made a shrine of the mansion where the drug-addicted king of rock and roll died of a stroke while moving his bowels, one ignored the power of celebrity at one's peril. A profile in a magazine, a mention on TV, a radio interview—all helped to bring those extra lecture dates, those seminar chairs, those visiting professorships without which Heartwood's up-and-down income would have more valleys than peaks.

No income, no tuition for David, which reminded him to call his son, ringleader of the iconoclasts who'd toppled a one-hundred-and-eighty-year-old cast-bronze statue of the Reverend Increase Marshall, congregational minister, friend of Samuel Adams, and founder, in 1803, of the Dunwich School. The call lasted only a few minutes, long enough for David to explain that it had been a senior-class prank, that the statue's fall was accidental, the intention having been to move it, not to knock it down. He refused to write an apology to the headmaster until Heartwood delivered the ultimatum: no apology, no money for college.

He hadn't liked wielding the weapon of the purse strings, but his affair with Diana and the divorce had robbed him of moral authority over the boy. Economics was the only power left to him. Maybe, though, there was a chance for him and David to begin anew, a chance to become a real father again instead of an occasional Santa Claus, a sometime policeman, an accountant who paid the bills. He cautioned himself against excessive optimism. The continent between them was more than geographical and a five-minute phone conversation wasn't going to bridge it. Also, David might not deliver the apology. The kid could screw up yet. He had a genius for it.

After hanging up, he undressed, hung his suit on the wood valet—a nice old-fashioned touch, that—and got into a pair of jeans and sneakers. Work was out of the question. He was going to take a long walk. Talking to David had made him feel like an emotional pinball machine on tilt. Old, old, I'm getting so old, he said to himself. There are no pinball machines anymore, only video games.

How he wanted to see David graduate, how he wanted to be there at commencement next month with all the other parents! Outside, a sentimental snapshot of the campus flashed in his mind. The embracing hills of northwestern Connecticut. Budding oak and elm, forsythia throwing out sprays of buttery yellow, frame and redbrick buildings where you could almost see the shades of the Enlightenment's sons walking in knee-breeches, ghostly Transcendentalists writing their reasonable essays. But this image dissolved when he saw an exquisite brunette walking with a silver-haired man who was old enough to be her father but obviously wasn't. Heartwood tried not to picture the old coot boffing the young beauty, he tried not to think of Diana, the home-wrecking bitch of Paula's dark fantasies. But what a wonder in bed she was! He figured that the hours she spent in cold observatories, her sea-gray eyes peering across interstellar seas toward the farthest shores of time, witnessing the births and deaths of distant worlds, had made her greedy for every pleasure she could squeeze from her nanosecond of earthly existence. Diana made love the way people do in wartime.

Envy and lust, deadly sins, warned ancient Jesuit voices in his memory. He walked briskly to Capitol Park, and then around it, admiring the flower beds, fountains, and tall trees encompassing the capitol building, as ocher as the fading sun it reflected. Such a hopeful structure, raised up at a time when it was possible to believe that virtuous architecture would inspire virtue in a horde of gold-fevered rabble.

He cut through the park on his way back to Camelia House. The paths and walkways were lightly trafficked by the last whey-faced bureaucrats heading for their cars and home. The gin was sweated out of him, yet he did not feel tired and his emotions were still careening like pinballs, and then he found himself at the Vietnam memorial: a miniature rotunda, roofless and white, that resembled an ancient Roman shrine. It hadn't been his destination, but something seemed to have drawn him to it. He went inside and sat on a stone bench to regain his wind: a survivor surrounded by the carved names of the thousands of Californians who had not survived. The brave and the cowardly, the brutal and the gentle, the weak and the strong were all together now and equal, fused by the common dignity that death in battle confers. Names in stone that a century from now would have no power to evoke feelings of loss and grief because no one would be alive to remember the faces and the voices and the stories that went with them.

He was beginning to feel haunted by memories, of five men who had lived but had been destroyed in another way. As he stood to leave, he saw coming up the walk an underfed man wearing a yellow windbreaker, soiled trousers, and sneakers bound with duct tape. The sun had set but a last fan of light, spreading over the cloud tops that rose above the buildings westward, angled through the trees onto the man's sparse, gray hair. One of the homeless arriving early to claim his bench or patch of grass for the night? Another madman like the hermit of the Palisades? He didn't walk with a vagrant's shuffle. His arms swung vigorously, his tread was measured, purposeful. He was in fact marching, and as he drew closer, Heartwood heard him softly calling cadence to himself. Two paces from the memorial, he came to a smart halt, whispered, "Present arms," and raised his right hand in a salute that would have done an honor guardsman proud. This appeared to be a daily ritual. Faded eyes staring directly ahead, scarlet capillaries tangled on his cheeks, the man held the salute for a full minute, and he was beautiful and heartbreaking, a lone pilgrim to war's shrine standing straight and still in the pale evening light. Heartwood felt as if he were intruding upon some private ceremony of honor and remembrance and fidelity. He dropped his gaze, waiting until he heard the hushed command, "Order arms." Looking up, he saw the aging warrior lower his hand, execute a crisp aboutface, and then march back the way he had come. When he reached the sidewalk, his soldierly bearing fell away and he slipped immediately into the aimless, floppy-legged gait of a derelict, and something pushed through Heartwood, sweeping him clean of his own confused emotions, something like a river, slow and powerful and sad.

Mr. Kim, with a magician's flourish, plucked a gold lighter from the pocket of his linen trousers and lit the cigarette he'd twice tapped against his thumbnail. A well-manicured thumbnail, Mace observed. White and smooth as a pearl onion. The lighter gleamed in the candlelight; so did the collar pin and monogrammed cufflinks of Mr. Kim's monogrammed silk shirt; so did his straight clean teeth as he bared them, lightly clamping the cigarette's filter.

"Well, I decide, no, I'm not going to buy gun. No pistols, no machine guns, like other guys in the community. Like everybody in L.A.," he said in English almost accentless, almost flawless except for the occasional lapse in tense, the occasional dropped article. He'd emigrated to the U.S. when he was fourteen, a couple of years after the Korean War, and now, sipping a postprandial scotch, he was talking about his experiences in another conflict—the Los Angeles riots. "I pay taxes for cops to play Dirty Harry. Why should I shoot out with looters. What d'you reckon, Mace?"

Assuming this was a rhetorical question, Mace did not say anything.

"What's wrong? Got a cat on your tongue?"

"Cat got your tongue, Dad," Celia said. "You always get that one wrong. Mace played Dirty Harry just the other day. He disarmed a crazy man at work!"

"Guess you're some brave guy. How did that happen?"

"I didn't disarm him, Mr. Kim. He wasn't trying to shoot anyone. He was only showing off his pistol at the rehab clinic where I work. I asked him to give it to me and he did."

"And you didn't have gun?"

"No."

"That's what I mean. What d'you reckon?"

A busboy began to clear away the dessert plates. He noticed that half of Mrs. Kim's cake remained and asked if she was finished. She answered with a nod and a weak smile, her lips seeming to struggle against their natural, downward set. She was a stout woman, so quiet and self-effacing as to be practically invisible.

"I'm not sure what you're asking me, Mr. Kim," Mace said.

"We pay big taxes in L.A. A lot of those taxes pay for cops. Does it make sense for everybody to arm themselves? What are cops for? So you don't have to arm yourself. This is like Wild West days in L.A., only it's today."

Mace pictured gunslingers sauntering down South Central's mean streets, quick-draw duels with Uzis instead of Colt Peacemakers. *High Noon* meets *A Clockwork Orange.* He held his breath against the smell of the cigarette, and was grateful that they'd gotten a table on the deck outside.

"I suppose you're right. People feel they can't count on the cops. Take care of themselves."

"You're right on money there. Know what I did during the riot? Drove up into Hollywood Hills and watched. No fooling!" His small hand planed upward with a twisting motion to simulate a winding ascent, and his eyes widened as if his flight to high safe ground had been an astonishing feat. "Other guys in the community, grocery guys mostly, they stick it out, in their shops with their pistols. I ask myself, 'A few heads of lettuce, they're worth playing Dirty Harry for?' No way! Okay, I don't have groceries, I've got electronics stores, but it's the same thing. A TV set, boombox, this is worth taking risks with my life, playing Dirty Harry? No way. Anyhow, I have only one store in South Central, smallest one of the four, so I drove up and watched everything burn. Other people up there, too. We're all watching L.A. burn. And I'm thinking, 'Burn baby burn!' That's what those black guys all said in sixties. Burn baby burn. Okay, burn baby, and when it's over, I still got my three biggest stores and what do the blacks have? Ashes. That's what they want, that's what they get. So lazy! Except when there's riot. Then they got all kinds of energy."

"Dad, I wish you wouldn't get on this. I hate this," Celia said.

Her father shook his head and exhaled a cloud of smoke over the deck railing. Below, floodlights sparkled on the main shipping canal, wind-ribbed and dark except for the floodlights and the reflected cabin lights of a cruiser, moored to the restaurant's dock. Its rubber bumpers squealed against pilings.

"She thinks I'm racist guy." Mr. Kim gave a dismissive shrug.

"Sometimes you are," Celia said.

Mace looked down at the yacht and the inviting glow of its cabin, slatted by partly drawn blinds, and pictured himself inside with her. The coppery curves of her naked ass.

"But you know what I tell her? How can I be racist?" Mr. Kim asked, without looking at his daughter. His thin, dark brows rose, like shadows of crescent moons "Me, I been a victim of racism. Black guys don't like Koreans, white guys, they're not too hot on Koreans. And if I'm a racist guy, how come I'm letting her go out with a white guy, how d'you reckon, Mace?"

"Oh, *Dad.*"

"Old-timers from Korea, they wouldn't let a daughter go out with any guy but a Korean guy. Sam Kim, he's not like that." He paused, stubbing out his cigarette. "Now I gotta admit, black guy, that'd be different."

"Please."

Celia's gaze rose toward the striped awning, then slid sideways along its slant to its fringed ruffle, the strands jiggling in the breeze. She was wearing her Mom-and-Dad outfit: a calf-length skirt, a modest blouse. When she went clubbing—to what few clubs there were in San Joaquin—she wore tight halter tops, tight sweaters, tight jeans, and danced like a woman out of her father's worst nightmares. Mace was an awkward dancer, but he liked to watch her and her long, straight, black hair flying wildly. She was full of snakes dying for her to say yes to them.

Mace turned to her mother and, his hand on the small ceramic pot, asked if she cared for more tea.

She regarded him silently. She wasn't accustomed to having anyone do anything for her, and didn't seem to know how to react. He turned on his smile and asked her again with a slight motion of his head.

"Why, yes, thank you," she answered hesitantly.

He poured the tea and watched her in the candlelight flickering inside a colored-glass mantle.

"The riots must have been frightening for you, Mrs. Kim."

She stiffened, looking at her husband.

"Oh, not too. Riots don't come close where we live. Our old place, Koreatown, near Western, they come close there but not our new place."

"But you must have been frightened for Mr. Kim."

Again she regarded him with blank-faced silence, and Mace realized that she wasn't used to hearing and speaking English, perhaps even to hearing and speaking any language. Locked up alone in the house all day. This is what became of you when you denied too much of yourself, when you did not embrace all that was within you, the darkness with the light. You became less and less complete, you disappeared.

"Mr. Kim was at the store in South Central. Weren't you scared that he might not get out?"

"Oh, yes! I try call. No good. I worry a lot when he not home for dinner."

"She didn't know I hightailed it for the hills," said Mr. Kim with a laugh. He called the waiter over, ordered another scotch, specifying Johnny Walker Black, and waved a pistol formed by his thumb and forefinger at Celia and Mace. She shook her head, Mace asked for a beer and turned back to Mrs. Kim.

"You must have felt happy when he did come home."

"Oh, yes! Happy!" She wrested another smile from her downcast lips. "A little bit angry when he tell me he is not where riots are. Why you don't call me, Sam Kim? I worry sick!"

Mace smiled back at her. He wanted to charm her. He liked to exercise his powers now and then, just to see if they still worked. Besides, Celia would appreciate it if he paid attention to her mother, and maybe not put up too much resistance later on.

"You know, Sam is right one thing. Black people hate Korea people so much. It's like that where you live?"

Her glance switched swiftly side to side, as if she were making sure that everyone approved of her offering an unsolicited opinion.

"There aren't very many blacks or Koreans in Redlands. It's mostly white."

"You know, I got theory about those riots," Mr. Kim said, leaping back into the conversation.

"Which I've heard at least three times already, so I'm going to the ladies' room."

Celia rose and Mace rose also, to show the Kims that he respected their daughter and knew his social graces. After he took his seat again, Mr. Kim expounded on his ideas.

"You know, papers said the cops screw up, that they could've stopped the riots before they start. But I think the chief told them to screw up. Screw up on purpose. I think he wanted riots to happen. You know him, Mace. Gates."

"Yes. Darryl Gates." Mace leaned toward Celia's father. These were the first interesting words he'd uttered all night. "What makes you think he did that?"

"Number one, LAPD look like hell after that Rodney King thing. Like LAPD is one more street gang, only wearing uniform. So Gates let the riots happen to say to ordinary people, 'Hey, you need LAPD, this is what happens when you don't have LAPD.' You get big, big disorder."

"Chaos."

"Yeah, that's the word. But number two, this Gates, everybody knows he doesn't like black people. He doesn't like minorities period. Now who got hurt in riots? Black people, Spanish people, Asian people. You see anybody from Brentwood getting hurt? Beverly Hills? Nah. Black people, Spanish people, Asian people, all burning each other's business, all fighting each other."

Celia returned, wrinkling her nose when she heard that the topic hadn't changed. Mace stood and helped seat her.

"So how d'you reckon, Mace?"

"My opinion of your theory?"

"Yeah."

"I don't agree with it, if you'll excuse my saying so."

"You're excused. Lotta people I know don't agree."

"It's what comes from growing up in a country like Korea," Celia said.

"What d'you mean?"

"If something bad happens, then it has to be a conspiracy," she said.

Celia's hands vanished under her hair, which she raised in a mass with a languorous movement that made the baring of her neck seem provocative, and then she let it fall and crossed her legs. Mace mentally parted them, mentally turned her over and heaved her copper buttocks toward him, his fingers untying the tight pink knot of her rectum, seal to her moist cave and the only virginity a man could take from a woman over sixteen in these latter days.

"Like this country not that way? What about Kennedy assassination? More conspiracies that you can shake a wand at."

"Stick, Dad. Shake a stick."

"Actually, Mr. Kim, I don't completely disagree with your idea," Mace said.

The older man made a movement with his head and hands.

"Okay! I have ally."

"But I think Gates's only role was to make sure no one stopped the reaction from happening. He was an agent of mass psychology. I'm taking a course in that, right now. I think almost everybody in L.A. wanted the riots to happen. I think everybody knew, way down deep, that they had to happen, and Gates was only supposed to not stand in the way."

Both Mr. Kim and Celia were giving him bemused looks. He'd never spoken of these matters before and debated if he should go on. He didn't want to come off as some nut. Were they, these little Korean bourgeois, ready for his message? Was anyone, anywhere?

"Something big is getting set to happen in this country. A lot bigger than the riots. Those were only a sign. There are other signs everywhere," he continued, aware that he was speaking a little too fast.

"Like what?" asked Mr. Kim.

"Epidemics like AIDS. Did you know that even tuberculosis is coming back? A new strain, resistant to modern medicine?"

"Yeah, I suppose I read that somewhere. What's that gotta do with thousands of people burning stores, looting?"

Mace pushed his chair from the table, leaning it against the deck railing, his arms spread across its back. He'd gone this far, might as well go the whole way. But he had to be careful of speaking too fast, sounding like some nut.

"'To follow and honor the right and have nothing to do with the wrong, to follow and honor those who secure good government and have nothing to do with those who produce disorder shows a lack of acquaintance with the principles of Heaven and Earth. It is like following and honoring Heaven and taking no account of Earth, like honoring the yin and taking no account of the yang.'"

Mr. Kim laughed.

"That sounds like that Chinese bullshit."

His wife, as if to assert her existence, gave his choice of words a rebuking hiss.

"It *is* Chinese. Chung Tzu." A certain superciliousness had crept into Mace's voice. "Taoist philosopher."

"Well, hasn't this all gotten just too weird," Celia said, and Mace felt a quick searing burst of hatred. Smug, stupid little middle-class bitch. Isn't this all just too weird.

"The Taoists believe that human action should be spontaneous, that it has to be in harmony with nature and with one's own true nature. Nature in general and your own individual nature are made of good and evil, light and dark, angels and demons, and you have to make friends with your demons and not just your angels."

A perplexed silence fell over the table. Mace looked long at Celia and knew by her expression that he was going to have a very hard time getting her to understand the meanings of things with arguments such as the one just made. We must suffer to know the truth, and he would make her suffer, go up into her hard, bring her screaming to that point where pain's half-circle fused with pleasure's to make the full circle within whose circumference such distinctions did not exist. Maybe then she would see the light he had, white-hot as a magnesium flare, illuminating the truth that they had not run into the three skinheads by chance, for life was not the chronicle of accidents it appeared to be. That encounter was meant to happen—a rendezvous arranged by nature to introduce them to those who produce disorder so they in turn would look within themselves to see the disorder there, and seeing it accept it, and accepting it become complete. Yes, the skinhead had stolen the light from his eye, but had brought him a purer light. A devil in a leather jacket and Nazi helmet, yeah, but Lucifer means "light-bringer."

"Well, do you want me to tell you how all this relates to the riots or should we change the subject?"

"Whatever," Celia said, with a bored shrug.

What a waste, he thought, if all she ever does is get married and fuck in the missionary position in some stainless suburban bed and raise a brood of kids and never see the circle made by pain and pleasure, never, never look straight into the cold, yellow, unblinking eyes of her serpents and invite them to twine themselves around her. Yes, I accept you all.

"Okay, the riots were spontaneous action. A mass of people instead of one, acting in harmony with nature. What's going on in this country is that . . . it's the snakes hatching out in the mud. We're all making friends with disorder, we're stepping right up to it, and shaking its hand and saying, 'Hello!' We've got to because the old harmony's broken down and before there can be a new harmony, we have to have disharmony. Like Chung Tzu says, 'No Heaven without knowing the Earth.'"

"Mace is a Mormon, Dad," Celia said, as if apologizing for him. "They believe that the end of the world is the next feature coming to your local theater."

"Oh, so that's it!" Mr. Kim reached into his shirt pocket for his Dunhills and tapped another against his pearl onion thumbnail. Again the flourish of the hand, the gold lighter, the tobacco stink.

"I'm not a Mormon," Mace said angrily to Celia. "You know damn well I'm not."

"You were raised one. Your parents are Mormons."

She was asking for it.

"That doesn't mean I'm one anymore."

"The Church of the Latter-day Saints. Spooookeee. The end is coming. Repent."

Practically begging for it.

"Hey, Ceal. I'm not some right-wing religious fanatic."

"C'mon, you two. Know saying? Never argue politics or religion? Your family got a business in Redlands, Mace?"

It was a pointed question, a father checking on the background of his daughter's boyfriend. Also Mr. Kim's way of steering the conversation back onto familiar terrain.

"Computers."

"Make 'em, sell 'em, what?"

He tipped his scotch glass to his lips and shook it like a dice cup, the ice rattling and the light reflected by his watchband twitching on the wall behind Celia as his wrist turned rapidly back and forth.

"They sell them. Mostly to offices. They set up office networks, Mr. Kim."

"Sam."

Mace understood, from the way this was said, that few people were allowed to call Sam Kim "Sam" and he nodded graciously.

"The business to be in nowatimes in Southern California is security. Alarm systems. Been thinking of expanding into that myself."

"Why not open a gun store, Dad?" Celia shook her head in dismay. "Import those AK things from China."

"Nah. No good. People don't want to play Dirty Harry. Only play because they feel they must. But everybody *want* to feel safe. Whole secret of successful business is very simple. Give people want they *want.* They don't know what they want, make them want something. Video cameras every corner of the yard. Windows doors wired up. Movement detectors in the house. You know, every man's home is a castle? Now every man's home is a bunker. Like on thirty-eight parallel back in Korea. This is what people want and we don't need to make them want it. The black people, Hispanic people, they make them want this stuff. White guys, too. Take that guy who killed all those kids. Now he makes everybody feel crazy because what kind of stuff gonna make your kids safe from nuts like him? You know him, Mace."

Misperceiving the sense of Sam's last statement, Mace felt as if colonies of inchworms had suddenly fallen on him from the branches of some invisible tree. They wriggled in their thousands down his neck and spine, across his shoulders and over his chest, the sensation so tactile that he had to beat back an impulse to leap up and claw at his shirt. In the next motion, he understood perfectly well that Sam's remark was harmless, was really a question, and still the creatures spawned by his imagination humped their tiny cold bodies over his flesh.

"C'mon, what was his name?" Sam, speaking to himself, snapped his fingers two or three times. "Biggs, I think."

"Boggs."

Now Celia lit a cigarette and the stench doubled. It made Mace queasy and the worms tunneled into his nostrils. He unbuttoned his collar, loosened his tie.

"How d'you reckon that guy? There's nothing nobody could do to protect their kids from guy like that. So people, they got to control what they can. Make their homes secure at least. Alarms. Movement detectors. That's the future."

"Mace, are you all right?" Celia asked.

"Sure."

"You're sweating bricks all of a sudden."

"Sweating?"

He touched his forehead and it was wet and a necklace of sweat had formed under his collar though it was open to the breezes blowing down the canal.

Mrs. Kim looked at him with concern.

"You not sick, Mace? Maybe fish bad?"

"I'm fine. Just got a little warm is all."

The cruiser's bumpers squealed like dying rats. The sound went right through him.

"Lotta bad stuff in fish these days," said Mr. Kim. "Mercury, PCBs. Hey, Mace, you Mormons think those are signs too?"

Celia leaned forward and laid the back of her hand against his forehead.

"I'm all right, goddamnit!"

His arm responding not to his will but to the command of some other faculty whipped up and swatted her hand away, hard enough to propel it back into her mouth. He leapt to his feet with a movement just as involuntary. Celia rubbed her wrist and lips, and she and her parents looked at him as they would at a rude and violent stranger who'd barged in on them from out of nowhere.

He stood in silence, a little short of breath and mortified by his own actions. He was always, always in control of himself. Well, not always. Most of the time. A couple at a table across the deck were watching him, and so was their waiter, holding as in freeze frame the bottle he was about to pour into their glasses.

"It's the cigarettes," he said. "The smoke. The smoke makes me sick."

Mr. Kim gave him a long look and then snuffed his cigarette.

"Didn't know that."

"I didn't, either," said Celia, crushing hers. "First time I've seen this reaction." She turned away to daub her mouth and then her eyes with a napkin. "That hurt, Mace. My wrist is numb."

"Ceal, I'm sorry. Really. I didn't mean it. I was . . . "

"Celia, you got pain?" her father asked.

She shook her head but her eyes continued damp and her lower lip was bleeding and beginning to swell and Mr. Kim turned toward Mace with a face gone to stone.

"Hey, Mace, you see this woman here?" He gestured at his wife. "Twenty-seven years married and not once do I hit her."

"Excuse me, Sam."

"You don't hit a daughter in front of her father, mother. You do that, makes me wonder what you do when father, mother aren't around."

"Sam," he said, activating his Aaronic priest's smile. "I really didn't mean to."

"No, not 'Sam.' Back to 'Mr. Kim.'"

"Excuse me, I'd better . . . "

And then he walked off quickly toward the men's room, not certain what it was he'd better do. He knew he had to escape for a moment, get away from that nerve-wracking cry of rubber against wood, from Mr. Kim's stony stare that his bright smile had failed to soften. Touchy Orientals.

He took off his shirt, tie, and jacket, removed his eye patch, and splashed his face in cold water. This was ridiculous, and worse, he was disappointed in himself for experiencing such anxiety over a misunderstood phrase. This was not how a complete man behaved, a man in tune with all his selves and his true nature. Was he less than complete? He was acting . . . guilty. But of what? He'd done nothing. He hadn't for chrissake even seen anything. All he'd done with Duane was to talk. Was there some law against talking? They'd talked, thrown ideas back and forth, and what Duane did with that talk and those ideas was Duane's business, Duane's responsibility.

He turned on the hot water and filled his hands with soap from the dispenser and scrubbed them, his chest, and shoulders. Then he rinsed himself in cold, and imagined the invisible worms swirling down the drain like shipwrecked passengers in the whirlpool of a sinking vessel. His shirt felt fresh when he put it back on, and he left the men's room restored and confident. The spell had been no more than that—a passing fever of a sort. He stepped out on the deck, beaming, but the table was empty. He surveyed the outside dining area for Celia and her parents, then looked inside but still did not see them, and he stood in the middle of the dining room, amid strangers, smiling the frozen smile of a man who'd died instantly while laughing at a joke.

Interlude

Inside Duane Leonard Boggs

CORONER'S AUTOPSY
WILLIAM MACBRIDE
SHERIFF-CORONER, COUNTY OF EL DORADO

Name:	BOGGS, Duane L.
Sex:	Male
Age:	21
Race:	Caucasian
Date and time of death:	4/16/93 @ 11:50 A.M.
Place of death:	State Route 49, approx. 5 miles N. of Placerville.
Date and time of autopsy:	4/17/93 @ 8:00 A.M.
Place of autopsy:	ECFPF
Identification:	Coroner's I.D. tag, left wrist
I.D. number:	026
Height:	71"
Weight:	142 pounds
Witnesses:	Det. Youngblood, Sgt. Tomlinson, ECSD

POSTMORTEM CHANGES: Well-developed rigor mortis, posterior lividity.
EXTERNAL DESCRIPTION: The unembalmed body is that of a slender white male who looks the recorded age. Scalp hair is dark black. He is clean-shaven except for a trimmed black mustache. Nasal bones are intact, eyes are light green without conjunctival petechiae. Teeth are natural. There is abundant blood smear on the right side of his face and bright red blood in the right ear canal. There is no blunt trauma to the

nose, lips, or neck. Thorax has normal configuration, abdomen has no palpable organomegaly, external genitalia are normal. The lower extremities exhibit no injuries. There are four horizontal, resolving bruises or abrasions, approx. 6" long and ½" wide and spaced approx. 1" apart on the buttocks.
GUNSHOT WOUND: There is a perforating gunshot wound of the head. The entrance is in the right temple, 3" below the right vertex, 3" above and 1½" anterior to the right external auditory meatus. It is a gaping 1¼" hole with radial splits and a partial automatic muzzle imprint. The exit wound is in the left temporal region. It is a gaping 1½" x 5¾" defect centered 2" below the vertex and 4" above and 2" anterior to the left external auditory meatus. There is evisceration of brain tissue and bone fragments.
NOTE: I failed to mention the presence of a large gold ring on the right 3rd toe. The face of the ring has a likeness of an eagle's head.
INTERNAL EXAMINATION:
ORGAN WEIGHTS IN GRAMS: Brain, 1320; heart 310; left lung, 330; right, 480; liver 1405; spleen 140.

PSYCHOLOGICAL AUTOPSY: DUANE LEONARD BOGGS

PREPARED BY LEANDER T. HEARTWOOD, M.D., M.P.H.

Partial Transcript of Interview with Sara Jane Pittman, 25, Boggs's Sister. Conducted at Mrs. Pittman's Home in Elbow Creek, Idaho.

. . . You said, Dr. Heartwood, that I should tell you the things I remember about my brother and not to worry if they mean anything or try to organize them. Just as they come to me, okay. One thing I keep remembering, and I don't know why, is that he didn't want me to paint our mailbox yellow. That was back in the fall, when he came up here to stay with Jim and me. It hurts me down in the pit of my stomach to think back on that, because Duane almost put it together up here. I swear if he'd stayed, he might have straightened out and those kids and him would be alive today. He came up here because he was lonely and things just didn't work out for him in California. They never did anywhere for him. You know, I think lonesomeness was Duane's biggest problem. He couldn't really talk to anyone unless he was on drugs or drinking and then he talked too much. But most times he was shut up inside himself, like he was in solitary confinement, and let me tell you, those bars that you couldn't see were just as hard as the iron ones you can. Before Jim got Duane the job at the mill . . . you must have seen it coming into town, that big Louisiana-Pacific mill, they turn sawlogs into construction lumber there. Jim's a foreman down in the power plant in Idaho Falls and he belongs to the IBEW and he used his pull in the union to get Duane the job in the mill. Electrician's assistant. Before that, Duane tried to be real helpful around the house. Did odd jobs, helped me with the housework, I never saw him like that. I liked to think he'd changed his selfish ways, but when I think back on it, I realize that he was scared that if he didn't make himself useful, me and Jim might not let him stay.

One thing you need to know, Jim wasn't real happy about Duane staying on with us. Jim's fourteen years older than me and he'd been married before, had a real bad divorce, let me tell you, Dr. Heartwood, and then got laid off from Lockheed down in L.A. That's where we met. I was waitressing down there. Well, after the union told him about the job in Idaho Falls and we moved up here, we decided it was going to be a new life, a new start for both of us. I've got just the most awful memories of California and Jim too. The other thing, we're both Christians. What you'd call born again? Jim didn't like it that Duane had done so much drinking and drugs, and he laid down the law. No drugs and only two beers for Duane a day. And as soon as Duane got on his feet moneywise, he'd have to find his own place. Maybe that was unfair, considering that Duane didn't have a soul besides us, but . . . I want you to know, Dr. Heartwood, that me and Jim, we're no fanatics about religion and living right. We do believe that if you don't open your heart to our Lord Jesus Christ, you're in for misery, but we're not holy-rolling crazy, like my grandma. . . .

I'm sorry for that. Her and grandpa, they were good to me and Duane when they took us in. Tried to be anyway. . . . Oh, this is so hard. . . . It's more than I can stand sometimes. You know, I've had folks in town come up to me and say, "Oh, you're that California killer's sister! Why it's like he's famous." And we had a TV movie guy, two of 'em, bothering us, offering us money for Duane's story, but Jim, he said that if we made money off those kids being murdered it wouldn't set right with the Lord and we'd be in for it. I've prayed to our Lord Jesus Christ for strength and not to send me any more trials for a while. I'm sorry. I forgot where I was . . . oh, yeah, the mailbox.

Well, I wanted the mailbox painted yellow and Duane thought that was stupid. Whoever heard of a yellow mailbox? he asked me. And I told him that he knew how I always liked bright colors and anyway, the mailman could see it better, and . . . You know, I just thought of why I remember that. Couple of reasons. I told you it was in the fall, October, and you ought to see this country that time of year, with the aspen all going golden and shaking in the wind on the mountainsides. It's really a paradise. Duane loved it. And that day, when we were standing out by the mailbox, he looked at the mountains and said they looked like the ones in those big, lighted up photographs that advertise Coors in bars, except that these here were the real thing, the real and true Rocky Mountains. Then he said something beautiful, Dr. Heartwood. He said that when the aspen moved in the wind, they flickered like a million candles, like a million pilgrims were walking along the mountainsides with candles in their hands. Now it seems to me that that showed Duane had a real appreciation of nature and beauty, and more than that, that he had a soul. But someone who did what he did couldn't have a soul, couldn't really be a human person. I've had such a hard time putting the two together, how someone who could say that the aspen flickered like pilgrims' candles could go and murder children. The only thing I can think of is that sometime between that day up here and the day he . . . How long was that? Seven months? That sometime in those seven months, he lost his soul. Doesn't it seem like that to you? If you've got a better explanation, I sure would like to hear it.

Saturday, April 24th

THEY'D HAD ONE OF THEIR RARE ARGUMENTS LAST night, after Gabriel, returning home from the field office, looked at the three suitcases in the front hall and asked who was going away.

"Oh, you know, Daddy," Eleanor said, thinking he was teasing. She swung lightly off a counter stool in the kitchen and stretched out her legs to show off her new sneakers. "Mom got these for all the walking around."

"Walking around? Where?"

Adrienne, chopping breasts and thighs for his favorite dish, General Tsao's chicken, glanced up and smiled.

"You shouldn't joke around with her," she said. "She's been looking forward to this weekend for a month. I played old-fashioned wife and packed for you. Your connubial valet, sir."

"Toontown, yay!" Eleanor did a little pirouette.

He was so tired, frustrated, and distracted that he did not react immediately even to this unambiguous reminder. He'd spent the better part of the day trying to persuade Croydon to reopen the case. While Heartwood was picking Weathers's brain, Gabriel wanted agents from the Southern California office to go to Redlands and, as surreptitiously as possible, check into his background. Family life. School history. Any juvenile delinquency problems that had not made it into official records. Criminalists should pick through the rooms in the Gold Hill and Camino Real, a team of Sacramento agents should be on call for a twenty-four-hour covert surveillance of Weathers, if that became necessary. Krimsky was behind him, but Croydon was reluctant to commit such resources because Gabriel heard a funny noise in his head. And, like Youngblood's boss, Sheriff Knowles, he was afraid of a press leak. All that activity would be bound to generate attention, and raising public fears of a second killer still at large, with such slender chances of catching him, would be risky. Gabriel suggested that the media could be taken care of by putting out a cover story that the intensified activity had been caused by the discovery of new evidence of white supremacist involvement. That would also serve to deceive Weathers—or whoever the mastermind was—and thus make him feel comfortable and off his guard. Croydon relented a little: that was not a bad idea. He would need authorization from the Director—the case would have to be transferred from El Dorado County to state jurisdiction. Once that was done, all the help Gabriel needed would be his for the asking.

"But I can't go to him with what you've got so far," Croydon said. "If you could find something a little more solid, something a little more incriminating, it'll make things a lot easier."

It was the typical bureaucratic kiss-off.

He'd driven home, his brain a nursery of ideas, one of which seemed worth nurturing. Croydon knew no judge would approve a search warrant on the basis of a hunch. By telling Gabriel to find "something more solid," he'd practically given prior approval for other measures. And Saturday, when Weathers would be with Heartwood, would be the ideal time to try them out. That's what preoccupied him when he'd walked in and seen the suitcases.

After Eleanor's exclamation, he went to the refrigerator for a beer. Adrienne set down her knife on the cutting board and leaned against the counter, her fingers curled tightly around its molding.

"You aren't joking around, are you?"

He shook his head.

"I'm having a beer is what I'm doing."

"Eleanor's Easter vacation, remember? Disneyland? Your idea? You made hotel reservations a month ago? I've taken Monday off so we can have all day Sunday there?"

He banged his forehead on the refrigerator to say that he'd forgotten.

"The absent-minded detective. Good thing you have a heads-up wife. I confirmed at the Marriott. They're also holding entrance tickets for us. And, let's see. I filled the tank after work, and, to repeat, packed for you. All you have to do is point the car toward Anaheim."

He sat on a stool with the guilty look of a schoolboy who'd forgotten his homework and muttered, "We can't go."

Now, on the morning when he should have been exploring the

illusory lands of the Magic Kingdom with his wife and daughter, he was taking part in an illusion of his own devising. He was driving a van loaned by the State Environmental Protection Agency and wore a dark green shirt and name tag that identified him as an inspector in the lead abatement department. His companions, Youngblood and Sheldon, were similarly costumed, and the back of the van cluttered with equipment that would give their masquerade a veneer of verisimilitude.

"I've got a friend who worked as a Disney character right after she got out of college," Jean was saying.

Gabriel had been telling them about the aborted trip and that he was now in the doghouse. Last night's spat had gotten nasty. He'd accepted his verbal lashings like a penitent, hoping that the lack of resistance would mollify Adrienne, but it only inspired her to lay on the whip even harder.

"How do you work as a character?" he asked. "You mean a voice for the cartoons?"

"Who do you suppose is inside the Mickey and Minnie getups at Disneyland? People. That's what my friend did. I forgot which character she was. I know she had her sights set on being Goofy the dog. She was as tall as I am and they needed tall people for Goofy."

"You mean it's like a career? You work your way up?"

"You start as a minor character, you know, maybe you're the old man who carved Pinocchio, what's his name . . . "

"Gepetto," said Youngblood hoarsely.

"That's it. So let's say you apprentice as Gepetto. Eventually you get a tryout for Goofy or Mickey or Donald Duck. Those are the big roles."

"How tall are you, Jeannie?" Gabriel looked into the rearview mirror to gauge if this was a sensitive question.

"Five-eleven and a half."

That was two and a half inches she had on him. He was struggling to fathom his attraction to this forty-something woman who looked as though she'd walked into California off some Nebraska farm. Last night, as he bared his back to Adrienne's verbal cat-o'-nine-tails, Jeannie popped into his mind with the thought, *she* wouldn't beat up on me like this.

"Left the next block," Youngblood said with a glance at the city map. "Then four blocks up, third house on the right."

Gabriel made the turn and said, "Well, I've got a confession to make. I'm glad I'm not taking the kid to Disneyland. I don't like any kind of theme parks and I hate Disneyland. I brought my boy there when he was six or seven and I hated every minute of it."

"Un-American," Jean said with a flip of her hair. "I'm surprised that this state employs a man with your subversive feelings."

"That's it up there." Youngblood pointed to a house two doors ahead. A wraparound porch on peeling posts, a turret with clapboard sides blemished by the acids leached from the clotted leaves rotting in the gutters. "So let's all get into our characters."

"Never done this before on the sly. Always on the up-and-up," Jean said, sliding the van's rear door open.

Gabriel grabbed a clipboard, a big black case of testing equipment, and what looked like a *Star Wars* ray gun.

"You said you'd do anything to help crucify the guy. Okay, here's a bucket of nails."

"What do you do if we find something? It'll be tainted."

"Come back with a warrant."

"Makes me nervous."

"This isn't illegal, Jeannie. Only unconstitutional."

"What we call nonstandard law enforcement measures," Youngblood said, which did not reassure Jean.

As they'd planned, she rang the doorbell. A female inspector might look out of the ordinary, but a woman would put Mrs. Van Huesen more at ease.

The door opened, revealing a grandmotherly figure with wide hips and stout arms. She stood behind the locked screen door and listened passively as Jean explained the multitudinous dangers of lead-based paint and then asked Mrs. Van Huesen if she would allow them to test her home as part of a statewide program to determine the extent of this grave problem. Subterfuge wasn't Jean's game. She spoke with some nervousness and stiff gestures, and the older woman appeared unmoved.

"George Wong. How are you today, Mrs. Van Huesen?" Gabriel said, stepping forward with a honed smile. He took out his ID wallet and, covering his badge, flashed his identification card just long enough for her to see his face and the words STATE OF CALIFORNIA but not long enough to read his name or the smaller print that said DEPARTMENT OF LAW ENFORCEMENT.

"Pleased to meet you, Mr. Wong. Why has my home been picked?"

"We're looking into older structures. They're the ones most likely to contain lead-based paint. As a matter of fact, I can give you an idea of how your home stacks up right now, simply by pointing this testing gun at one of your walls. It's state-of-the-art, gives us a rough lead content level instantly."

"Oh, my . . . " She unlatched the screen door. Before she had second thoughts, he opened it and stepped inside and stood in the foyer. Aiming the gun at a wall, he switched it on, and it made a weird noise that sounded like pigeons cooing under a viaduct.

Gabriel looked at the digital read-out window and shook his head.

"Look at that, Mrs. Van Huesen. Hazardous levels."

"Oh, my. What does lead do to you again?"

"Brain damage. That's the main danger. Now we can't go based on this alone. We'll have to inspect every room, take samples for laboratory testing. We'll be about an hour."

Mrs. Van Huesen's pet stole into the foyer from another room and sat on its haunches at its mistress's feet, its forepaws together, like a figurine of a cat.

"She's adorable!" Jean said.

"Oh, yes. That's Spats. Say hello, Spats."

"It looks like a kid's fantasy of a cat. All those little spots, like a dalmatian's." Jean squatted down and petted its black and white head and then picked it up and held it to her shoulders. "She's friendly too."

"He," Mrs. Van Huesen corrected.

"He's friendly. Listen to him purr."

"Yes, Spats has a very pleasant disposition. Does lead cause brain damage in cats, Mr. Wong?"

"Sure does. Makes 'em crazy."

"Oh, dear."

"So we'd better get to work right away." Gabriel looked up the staircase with its handsomely carved newel post and rail, in need of a new coat of varnish. "I hope we won't be disturbing anybody, Mrs. Van Huesen."

"I have two tenants, boys from the college, but they're out."

"If their rooms are locked, we'll need you to let us in." Gabriel holstered the ray gun, feeling like Luke Skywalker after a tough laser duel with Darth Vader's storm troopers. "Lead levels can vary from room to room in a house this size."

"Lead levels vary from room to room? Where did you come up with that?" Jean asked after Mrs. Van Huesen admitted them to Weathers's room and then went downstairs to show Youngblood the kitchen.

"Same place I came up with the idea that lead drives cats insane."

"That was mean."

"It was an inspiration."

"Trusting old soul. She's a rape or a robbery waiting to happen."

"Maybe not. I like to think it was my acting skills that did it. Bet I could be a Disney character."

A swift, acute ache lanced Gabriel's chest when Jean playfully pressed the tip of his nose.

"Not Pinocchio. His nose got long when he lied."

He softly shut the door, an act suggestive of intimate possibilities. He had to get these thoughts out of his head. This was no time to be distracted by messages from the groin, or whatever part of his anatomy was speaking to him. Also, he didn't want to spoil his record, stained by only one night of infidelity. The cause of that brief transgression had been a narcotics snitch, a half-Irish, half-Korean wild woman.

Jean opened the small bag she was carrying and took out a roll of the clear tape and laid a strip of it on her shirt, where she'd held the cat.

"That was pretty good, the way you got those samples. You'd make a good street cop."

"My own inspiration."

"But I thought you said you couldn't match these hairs to the ones on the shirt."

"Not conclusively, right. Nothing I could testify to in court, but I couldn't testify to a damn thing I'm doing today. What I can do," she said, pulling the tape loose and then folding it into a plastic bag, "is give you a fair idea whether the hairs came from the same animal."

"Every little bit helps. Okay, remember that if you move anything, put it back exactly the way you found it. If it's off an inch, Weathers'll notice."

Jean broke out her fingerprint kit and began to dust the desktop and doorknob, Gabriel warning her to make sure she wiped up every trace when she was done. He searched the dresser, where he found the answer to one of his questions about Weathers: a pair of red boxer shorts perfectly folded beside a stack of seven more, each a different color. The bottom pair were also red.

"Christ, this guy color-codes his skivvies. A color for each day. He's got a two-week supply."

"So what's he wearing today?"

"Dark green. Saturdays are dark green, Sundays red, Mondays white, and so on."

"Take a look at this closet." Jean made a sweeping movement at Weathers's clothes. "Shirts face the same way, trousers go dark to light from left to right. This boy's screwed down tight."

As she began to collect fiber samples with tape and tweezers, Gabriel went to the desk, shoved up against a wall and facing one of the turret room's two curving windows. A bookcase alongside contained textbooks and a collection of CDs—some rock, some classical, a good deal of jazz, alphabetically ordered. Blakey . . . Brown . . . Carter . . . Corea . . . Ellington . . . Flanagan . . . Hawkins . . . Henderson. Good taste in music anyway, though the absence of Coltrane seemed an unconscionable omission.

The stuff in the desk drawers—notebooks, paper clips, and staple boxes—were arranged with such exactitude he was afraid to touch anything, as though the entire room would fly apart if the smallest article were moved out of place. He usually felt a twinge of shame on covert searches, but he felt nothing amid all this obsessive order. There was no sense of a life lived in this room; it seemed as sterile and organized as an operating room.

He went through the desk, looking for an address book, but didn't find one. That surprised him—surely a guy like Weathers would keep an up-to-date address book. He opened the bottom drawer, which contained a pile of file folders, also color-coded, and in each folder were photographs of Weathers. Class or yearbook pictures. The first was marked "Freshman Year—Redlands North H.S.—1984," the last "Senior Year—SJSU—1993." Gabriel got his first look at the object of his suspicions, and flipping through the folders year by year, watched him change from a slender boy to a bull-necked young man, saw what Weathers looked like without his eye patch and how he looked now. He removed one of the photos from 1992's folder, taken before Weathers lost his left eye, and slipped it into his shirt pocket. This was a chance—Weathers might know how many prints were in each folder—but Gabriel needed a picture. Get a police artist to draw on a pair of sunglasses and he would have something to show the manager of the Gold Hill Motel.

In the same drawer with the photos were Xeroxes of stories from the college newspaper. *Skinheads Assault Two State Students on Spring Break . . . Injured State Junior Will Lose Sight in One Eye . . .* One of the copies showed side-by-side photos of Weathers and his girlfriend, Celia Kim. *Anti-Asian Racism Blamed for Assault . . .*

"Hey, Jeannie, what do you make of all this?" he asked in an undertone."The guy keeps pictures of himself from every year he was in school."

She moved over from the closet.

"Ask your shrink friend what to make of it. Not my long suit," she said, writing something on a sticker attached to a small, plastic evidence bag. "Offhand, I'd say he's vain, a narcissist, and I'd say he's got a reason to be. Good-looking guy. Very good-looking."

Needles of jealousy and resentment pricked Gabriel.

"Also, would a guy with a Korean girlfriend, a guy who'd been attacked by skinheads because he's got an Asian girlfriend, would a guy like that be involved in a crime against Asians? Doesn't fit."

"Way out of my territory, Gabriel. Give me a dust mote, give me a powder grain."

"If you find an address book, give that to me. None in his desk."

Jean smiled that rueful smile of hers and tapped the filebox of floppy disks beside Weathers's computer.

"He's part of the MTV generation. They don't write anything down if they can help it."

He rifled through the disks and found one labeled "Addresses & Phone Nos."

"There you go," she said, giving the copy to him. "Need anything else, just whistle. Know how to whistle?"

"Put your lips together and blow. I saw the movie too."

He wanted to believe there was something behind this reference to Lauren Bacall, that it was an encrypted admission of attraction.

He turned on the computer, opened up the address disk, and recorded the names and numbers in his notebook. There were only fifteen, a few in San Joaquin, a few more in Redlands, and one in Washington, D.C. An organization of some kind. The Mender Foundation. Mender Foundation, he thought. The name was remotely familiar, but he couldn't place it. Jean, on both knees, was meanwhile emptying a footlocker she'd hauled out of the closet. A pleasant scent rose from the footlocker and two of the cedar eggs that had been inside rolled noisily across the hardwood floor, like petrified Easter eggs. Gabriel was bending down to pick them up when a knock froze him and Jean, she holding in midair the tape she was about to apply to the sweaters piled beside the footlocker, he crooked at the waist like an old man. They looked at each other. There was a second knock and then a gravelly whisper:

"Gabriel? You in there?"

He let Youngblood in.

"You two about wrapped up? I fooled around downstairs long as I could, entertaining the old lady with tales of lead poisoning. I think she might be starting to wonder if we are who we say we are."

"Maybe not so trusting after all. Jean, how far along are you?"

"I'll just do these and . . ."

Her eyebrows drew together, her head cocked to one side.

"These were piled so high inside the top was ajar," she said, and with her thumb and a finger measured a four-inch gap between the top of the trunk and the top of the piled sweaters.

Reaching inside the trunk, Gabriel rapped his knuckles on the bottom. There was a hollow sound, but the bottom panel was securely nailed, the paper lining undisturbed. He closed the lid and turned the locker upside down and heard hidden objects moving inside, felt their weight shift.

"Well, well . . ."

The outside bottom was loose along the rear and side reinforcement strips. He slipped the big blade of his Swiss Army knife under the strips, popping the brass fasteners, and raised the bottom piece, exposing within the space between it and the false bottom a scrapbook, a Bible, the Book of Mormon, a paperback called *The Thought of Chung Tzu*, a clear plastic bag containing a pair of tiger-stripe trousers and a black T-shirt, and an old leather case dried and shriveled like the hide of something long dead and exhaling a trace of an odor familiar yet faint, more the memory of a smell than the smell itself. He held the case to the light and noticed, stamped on a bottom corner of the cover, a symbol whose gold embossing had been worn away almost entirely, though enough remained for him to recognize the profiled eagle of the 101st Airborne. This recognition stirred a recognition of the half-remembered aroma: that mixed effluvia of mud, mildew, and mold that impregnated the jungle boots now stored in his attic.

He shook the case. Something rattled inside, but the brass hasp, corroded like the brass hinges to a lichen-green, was locked. He gestured to Youngblood, who passed to him a ring of picks. After a couple of minutes, he succeeded in springing the lock. Taking a quick look at the contents, he said, "I'm proud of myself. My Sherlockian powers. Look at these."

Jean fingered the two black metal objects in his hand.

"Those are the chevrons?"

"Right. E-5 chevrons. Buck sergeant. And this must be him."

He held out a Polaroid sun-bleached almost to the brightness of an overexposure but with enough definition to show a tall, broad-shouldered man in tiger-stripe camouflage towering over two smaller men in identical uniforms and red berets.

"Vietnamese paratroopers," Gabriel said, and turned the print over and saw the date written on the back in smudged ballpoint: 1971.

Jean pointed at the double-decked ribbon bars. "Those are his medals, I take it."

"Yup. That red, yellow, and green one is the Vietnamese campaign ribbon, the purple one's a Purple Heart, and the one next to it—this guy was an authentic hero—is a Silver Star. They handed Bronzes out over there like candy, but a Silver, you had to earn that. And these"—he picked up a silver parachute flanked by outspread wings—"are his jump wings."

There were half a dozen more photos: two more of the tall man in Vietnam; one of an exceptionally beautiful young woman with long, tawny hair, the print undated and speckled in places, probably from sticking to the plastic inserts in the paratrooper's wallet; another of the same woman holding the hand of a towhead toddler, dated 1974, and a last undated one showing her sitting on a bed, wearing only a pair of black bikini panties, her superb legs tucked under her, something in the style of an old-fashioned calendar girl, though there was nothing old-fashioned about this girl.

"Sweet Lord," Youngblood said with a half-whistle, half-hiss as he leered over Gabriel's shoulder. "Looks like the young Cybill Shepherd. You know, in that movie, what was that movie about Texas."

"*The Last Picture Show*, and I'd say Cybill Shepherd could be this gal's ugly sister," Gabriel said, feeling now that he was intruding on a life, discovering secrets, though the nature of those secrets eluded him.

He looked at the back of the photo, on which a tantalizing message had been written in a flowing feminine hand—"This is what's waiting for you when you get out!"—and beneath that another message tantalizing in a different way, one word printed in capitals so hard that the pen had made deep impressions in the paper: WHORE!

"Charlie Chin, poor man's Chan, say this getting velly intelesting."

"Yeah. Whore or not, if I'd been over there and got a picture like that, I'd've taken Hanoi single-handed," Youngblood said.

"Not so sure this was sent to him in 'Nam. That phrase, 'when you get out.' "

"Get out of the Army, she must've meant," Jean said.

"Or prison."

"So if I'd been in the slams and got that picture I'd've broken out."

"Christ, Phil. It's his mama."

"How do you know it's Mama?"

"Who else?" Gabriel raised the Polaroid of the woman with the toddler. "The kid looks two or three. Weathers was born in '71. Gotta be him."

"A guy would keep a picture of his *mother* bare-breasted, in black bikini underwear? A picture somebody wrote 'whore' on?"

"Better do some work while you two slobber over that cute patootie," Jean said, and unfolded the T-shirt. It was one of those novelty-shop things, emblazoned with a death's head and the cheery slogan, "Kill 'Em All and Let God Sort 'Em Out."

As she plucked threads from it and the trousers with her tweezers, Gabriel opened the scrapbook. Pasted inside were cuttings from the *San Joaquin Dispatch* and the *Sacramento Bee*, all about Boggs and the massacre, all in chronological order.

"Velly, velly intelesting," he said, and then heard footfalls in the hall outside, a light knock.

"Yoo-hoo, inspectors?" said Mrs. Van Huesen through the door. "Are you finished yet?"

"In just a few minutes," Jean answered, quickly refolding the trousers and shirt.

"I have to leave very soon. Seniors' bingo at the Methodist church."

Youngblood gestured that he would go out and keep the old woman occupied. He slipped out the door and began talking to her. Gabriel fanned through the three books, finding passage after passage highlighted, pages marked with folded corners, and a slip of paper bearing a telephone number inserted in the Bible, in St. Paul's

Epistle to the Romans. He copied the number. There was no time for anything else. Then he and Jean repacked the trunk exactly as they'd found it, lifted it to avoid scratching the floor, and put it back in the closet.

■ ■ ■

The levee rising high above the wheat field masked the canal from view, so the freighter they saw sailing slowly eastward, its stack and V-shaped booms and tiered white decks rising high above the levee, appeared to be voyaging across dry land.

"Strange-looking, isn't it?" Heartwood said to make conversation. "A ship where you'd expect to see a train."

Mace, silent, looked out across the field at a combine slashing wind rows through the stalks and at the chaff shimmering as it blew away from the combine and over the levee in a cloud like gold dust pounded from some enormous nugget.

"How come you decided to let me go along?" he asked, for he wanted to know if it had been mere luck or his talent for persuasion that had changed the psychiatrist's mind.

"I think you could be a help to us. You're a smart guy, you've studied psychology, you knew Duane. Seemed like a winning combination to me."

"I didn't know Duane all that well."

Heartwood, downshifting his Porsche to make a tight turn in the two-lane road, heard a note of forced humility in Mace's voice, but the way he sat up straighter, his shoulders spreading beyond the width of seat, said that he was more flattered than anything else. And that was the idea. Flatter him whenever possible, let him think he's smarter than we are.

"But you knew him better than Gabriel or I. So maybe you could offer some insights. A unique perspective."

"I'll try. I guess we could start with how you go about one of these autopsies." He took out a notebook, opened it on his lap. This performing was fun. He was the eager student, working on a thesis.

"Basically, I follow Shneidman and Faberow's procedure," Heartwood answered.

"Shneidman and . . . "

"One of those books I recommended, Mace. The procedure's laid out right in there. Didn't you read it?"

"Didn't get a chance."

"How about the others?"

"The library didn't have two or three of them and I've been busy with another paper."

Out of the corner of his eye, Heartwood noticed Mace looking directly at him. That, he'd observed, was what he did when he wanted you to believe him.

"You're going to have a lot of work to do if the thesis is due in two weeks."

"Then maybe we could start by you telling me how you got into forensic psychiatry. I read somewhere that it was something that happened in Vietnam. You were a Navy psychiatrist in Vietnam."

"How'd you find that out?"

"There's all kinds of references about you in the library. You're a real celebrity in the field."

Mace himself wasn't bad when it came to flattery, and this time, his voice carrying more inflection than it had during their first interview, the praise sounded less rehearsed.

"You looked me up."

"Nothing wrong with that, is there? I figured that as long as you were letting me go along, I ought to know something about you. I think it was in *People* magazine. Some kind of war crime you looked into."

That story, Heartwood thought, would devour all the time they had before they reached Clovis Boggs's farm. Yet it could be a good start. For now, Weathers should be made to think that he was getting more information than he was giving, that he was learning more about Heartwood than Heartwood about him.

"You know," he said, "sometimes when I look back on my life, it's like everything before Vietnam was a childhood. Premed, med school, my first year interning in New York. When I look back on all of that, it seems as if I wasn't a fully conscious human being."

He came to an intersection. A sign for Walnut Grove pointed left, and he made the turn and clattered over a drawbridge, below which boys were leaping into the canal from the roof of a houseboat lashed to overhanging trees.

"So what happened?"

"Five Marines led by a twenty-year-old corporal, five exemplary Marines—perfect records, the corporal and one other bona fide medal-winning heroes—committed an atrocity in a friendly village not far outside the Marine airfield at Hue. The battalion those

Marines belonged to had been pulled out of combat for a rest. They were guarding the airfield, the kind of work security guards could do, so there wasn't the heat-of-battle excuse for what they'd done. Not a shot had been fired at them when they came into that village. People waved at them. Kids asked for candy and cigarettes. There were buffalo in the fields and farmers plowing and ducks in the pens. Everything peaceful, and they murdered eight of those villagers, including two children. In as cold a cold blood as you can imagine. It wasn't five men exploding in some collective fit of blind rage. It was all horribly calculated, deliberate, fiendish. Okay? The kind of thing some Nazi extermination squad would have done. Two of the villagers were tossed off a bridge with live hand grenades tied to their legs.

"The Marines were court-martialed and sent to Portsmouth Naval Prison for life," Heartwood continued, his right hand falling from the wheel to the gearshift, where it rested, an inch from Mace's left knee. Mace moved his leg slightly and pressed himself against the door, as if he were afraid that Heartwood was going to grab him suddenly.

"They pled guilty. Their defense counsels read their fine military records to the court, they read a few letters from commanding officers saying what fine, brave men they were, a few letters from parents and ministers and schoolteachers saying what fine, good boys they'd been as civilians. And they had been. These weren't delinquents who'd been given a choice between jail and the Marine Corps. The defense counsels did what they could, but when it came time for sentencing and the president of the court asked if any of the Marines would like to make a statement in extenuation, not one said a word. The court sentenced them to death. There were seven officers on it and they were angry because they'd wanted to hear at least a word of explanation, at least a word of repentance or remorse, and all they got was silence. So they handed down a death sentence. In those days, that meant a hanging or the firing squad. The commanding general later commuted their sentences to life, but that's another chapter. The Marines stood at attention, heard their sentences without a show of emotion. It was uncanny, but these were combat Marines. Action was their language. It was as if they'd done what they'd done to make a point, to make a statement, and having made it, they saw no reason to say anything more and they didn't. Like Duane, I suppose. Duane was making a statement. He was an inarticulate guy, full of unexpressed emotions, and so he'd made a statement with an act, don't you think?"

An unpleasant sensation came suddenly into Mace's chest. It felt as though a gas bubble had formed in his sternum and was slowly expanding, squeezing his lungs.

"How would I know?"

"I'm looking for those insights, those special insights you might have."

Mace laid one hand on the dashboard, and then, noticing that it was dusty, removed his hand and rested it back side down on his trousers. He began to squirm and asked if Heartwood had a clean rag or towel in the car.

"There's some paper towels in the glove compartment."

He wiped his hand, scrubbing each finger individually, and with a fresh towel dusted off the dashboard.

"You ought to keep a car like this cleaner."

"Well, I try, Mace. You know the remarkable thing about those five guys? *One* of the remarkable things, I should say. It was that all of them entered into this conspiracy of silence and stuck to it. You would've thought one at least would've copped a temporary insanity plea, begged for the court's mercy, blamed the others, pled some excuse when the president asked them to. But they were unanimous in their silence. As though they were one being, one single mind with five faces.

"The investigating officers weren't able to find a shred of evidence or corroborating witnesses that they'd planned the monstrosity before they left the perimeter that morning. Matter of fact, they didn't even know they were going on a patrol until the last minute, so it was safe to say that they didn't leave the air base with criminal intentions. But somewhere between the air base and that village—it was only a thousand yards or so, a lousy little kilometer—something happened to them. Something evil struck them, like a kind of psychic lightning. Do you believe in evil, Mace? In a spirit of malevolence that can strike any one of us when we're least expecting it, or that any one of us can tap in to?"

He hesitated. Why was he being asked a question like that? "There are no negatives in the subconscious," he remarked confidently, pulling a phrase from one of his textbooks.

"The great craving amoral id, right. The neurobiological school would say that what we call evil is right up here"—Heartwood went to tap his forehead, but an unexpectedly tight curve in the road caused him to return his hand to the wheel—"a sequence of neurochemical reactions in certain neural pathways. Chemistry. Good an explanation as any. Or maybe it was the heat, something as simple as that. The day they went out on patrol was unbelievably hot, even by Vietnam's standards. One hundred and twelve degrees. Ask any big city cop what happens to the homicide rate when the temperature gets over ninety-two. That was the best explanation I could give the general—it was just too damned hot—but that wasn't the answer he'd hoped for. He killed himself."

In his peripheral vision, he caught the sudden turning of Mace's head toward him.

"General Bartholomew Taylor, the division commander. The atrocity shook everybody up in the division, even the guys who hated Vietnamese, but it shook Taylor right down to his black shiny boots. It upset his ideas of how the world was supposed to be ordered. He assigned me to look into the incident. Not unlike this case. A whydunit instead of a whodunit. Taylor wanted some rational explanation for the Marines' behavior. Those were my marching orders. I remember that Taylor kept saying to me, 'Heartwood, each one of those boys, each damn one of them was an outstanding individual. He was *one of us*.' The 'us' didn't include me, by the way. The general meant the Marine brotherhood.

"I think he realized that if those five 'outstanding individuals' could do what they did, then anybody could. Or to put it in other words, that whatever happened to them could happen to anyone, that medals and exemplary records weren't vaccines against certain deadly afflictions of the spirit. In so many words, the world was ceasing to make sense for General Taylor, and I could tell that he was suffering when I was in his headquarters.

"I still remember that night, it was in one of those old French colonial buildings in Hue, one of the few that hadn't been blown to bits in Tet, and bugs were swarming around the light overhead, and they threw magnified shadows on the walls. Mosquitoes looked as big as moths, moths as big as bats, and I suppose if a bat had flown in there, its shadow would have looked like a vulture, and way off in the distance you could hear artillery thumping, sometimes a machine gun going *chatchatchat*.

"Normally, Taylor looked the way a Marine general should, except for his ears. They stuck out comically, but otherwise you could picture the guy staring at some enemy-held ridge, ready to take it or die trying. But there was all kinds of doubt in his eyes that night. He wouldn't look at me, he seemed to be transfixed by those magnified shadows on the walls. He said, 'Heartwood, I want you to find out what made them do it. Something's happening . . . ' And his voice trailed off and I said, 'Sir?' I wanted him to finish the thought. Was something happening to him? Something happening to all of us over there? I felt a little sorry for him, but at the same time—got to admit this—I took some satisfaction from his confusion and doubt. Those steely-eyed, jut-jawed types, like my father, get on my nerves. I was, well, *happy* that Taylor had encountered something in life he couldn't explain or look in the eye without flinching. He'd called on me to help him hold on, to help him maintain his faith in the validity of shiny buttons, shiny boots, and medals as manifestations of virtue. In his mind, there could be only one of two logical explanations. His five Marines had gone clinically crazy, and I was supposed to prove that. Taylor even suggested that my findings could lead to the establishment of new psychological tests to determine if recruits had hidden pathological tendencies and reduce the chances of such atrocities happening again. Well, I didn't find out a damn thing and there's no Heartwood Test today to take its place along the Rorschach and TAT and Millon Personality Inventory.

"I was in the States for thirty days, interviewing the Marines' families, their ministers, schoolteachers, the hometown police chiefs. All Midwestern boys, by the way. One from my home state, Wisconsin. I was looking for domestic pathologies, and sure, I found some. The divorce here, the alcoholic father there, but we were sending kids to that war from really dreadful backgrounds, and compared to them their backgrounds were fairly *Reader's Digest.* To say that Lance-Corporal Bendix—that was the Wisconsin kid—tied up two people and rolled them off a bridge with live grenades taped to their legs because his father was an occasionally abusive drunk would be like saying that someone contracted leukemia because he'd suffered a cut knee when he was thirteen. I interviewed him and the others in Portsmouth. Very polite, still very much disciplined Marines. Always called me 'sir,' or, if they said something they thought disrespectful to my exalted rank, they'd say, 'Begging the lieutenant commander's pardon.' The thing was, they were so absolutely, boringly ordinary. No lunatic gleams in their eyes, no bizarre gestures, no savage talk about killing gooks because the only good ones were dead ones. I was almost disappointed. I wanted some outward sign of monstrosity. They were polite and respectful, but not forthcoming. Didn't tell me anything more about the why of it than they did at the court-martial. I was begining to think that possibly they themselves had no idea why until I interviewed the last one, the corporal, Darryl Adams. He started the whole thing off when they were on the outskirts of the village. Saw an old farmer plowing a rice paddy behind a water buffalo, and he asked a little kid nearby who the guy was. Adams could speak some Vietnamese. And the kid said, 'That's my uncle,' and Adams walked up to the man and shot him dead. Then Bendix, without an order being given, a word spoken, shot the kid. Just a ten- or eleven-year-old kid, and the others opened up on the water buffalo and killed it. How would you explain that?"

"That a rhetorical question?"asked Mace.

"No."

"Brief Reactive Psychosis," he answered, in the same sure way he answered oral quizzes in classes. "What they did sounds like B.R.P. You look into their backgrounds for predisposing factors."

"B-plus for being half-right. I was looking for an impulse control disorder, but not that one."

"Intermittent Explosive Disorder. An aggressive act grossly out of proportion to the precipitating stressors. How's that?"

"Now you get the A," said Heartwood, pleased to have a chance to flatter him again. "Not all the diagnostic criteria were there, but intermittent explosive disorder seemed the closest to what happened. Except for one thing. It's a zillion to one that five guys are going to be suffering from the same disorder and that it's going to manifest itself at the same moment. So I was grasping at straws by this point, I was getting desperate to come up with explanations, not just for General Taylor, either. For myself. The deeper I looked into the case, the more the answers eluded me and the more I wanted to find one. I knew that Adams had lost his father when he was eight or nine. Some kind of farm accident down in southern Indiana. A couple of years later, his mother got remarried to her brother-in-law and he took over the farm. Darryl's uncle became his father and they didn't get along. I suppose if they'd been some aristocratic family, you could've made something Shakespearean about it all. The son embattled with the usurper to his father's rightful place. Add a touch of Oedipal jealousy exacerbated by the fact that it wasn't Dad in the marriage bed with Mom, but Uncle Art. That was his name. Arthur Adams. It was an interesting starting point, the only real starting point I could find. I think you see what I mean."

It was another innocuous comment, like Sam Kim's, and it shook the same colonies of inchworms down on Mace, they in their thousands slithering across his skin, rubbery and alive. Was Heartwood toying with him? Did Heartwood know? But how could he? And even if he did, what difference would that make? *Don't want to set eyes on you again.* And Riley didn't and all the records were confidential, locked up in a vault somewhere. Mrs. Mender was the only one who knew and she was out of the picture. Jailed for fraud on the other side of the country.

He opened the glove compartment and patted his damp forehead with a paper towel.

"I don't know what you mean, no."

"Archaic rage," Heartwood replied. "A rage ignited in childhood, sometimes in infancy, often suppressed, and the cause of which becomes forgotten in the conscious mind while the emotion remains in the subconscious. Like an artillery shell that buries itself in the ground without exploding, just waits there for something insignificant—a vibration or a footstep or corrosion—to set it off. Ka-boom!"

Mace lowered the window, though the air conditioner was on. Heartwood asked him to put it back up.

"I'm a little warm in here. Think that AC is bumming out on you."

Pearls of sweat chained across his blond brow, and Heartwood, aware that something he'd said had provoked this reaction, made a mental note.

"The AC was just fixed," he said. "Please roll the window up. I'm allergic. That pollen starts blowing in here, I'll be sneezing for the next hour."

Mace pressed the button. Asshole. Dr. Hayfever.

"Adams's uncle was a farmer and he hated him. The little kid pointed to the old farmer and called him 'Uncle.' That was the trigger, okay? Not much, but then the trigger on a gun isn't much. A little kid can pull it, but my archaic rage theory didn't stand up to its wind tunnel test. Oh, I suppose it could've explained the killing of the old man and maybe you could explain Bendix killing the kid to get rid of the witness. But it didn't explain what happened afterward. The patrol entered the village and very methodically rounded everybody up, old people and children mostly, maybe twenty-five altogether, and made them sit down in a cleared area near a buffalo pen with their hands behind their backs and their backs facing the Marines. The

Marines sat down, ate their C-rations, smoked a few cigarettes, shot the shit. Then one of them, a Silver Star winner from Cleveland named Lugarno, made a mudball and shut his eyes and threw the mudball at the villagers. It hit a woman. Adams said, 'Her.' That was all. As if everything that was supposed to happen was understood in that single word. 'Her.' He and Lugarno and a third Marine, O'Neill, took her into a hut, stood her on a chair, tied a rope around her neck and tossed the rope over a beam. Adams interrogated her. Where are the Viet Cong? She didn't know. How many Viet Cong had she seen? She hadn't seen any. What kind of weapons were they carrying? She didn't know because she hadn't seen any VC. This was a village loyal to the government, they never saw any Viet Cong. And then Adams said something interesting. 'We know, but that doesn't make any difference anymore.' And then, once again without an order being given, Lugarno kicked the chair out from under her and they stood there, watching her strangle. She was taking too long dying, so O'Neill knelt down and grabbed her around the knees while Lugarno took the free end of the rope and O'Neill pulled down while Lugarno hauled away like a sailor and they broke her neck. She was the third victim and they picked the other five the same way. Closed their eyes, picked up a stone or a piece of mud and threw it and whoever it hit, that's who died."

Heartwood glanced covertly at his passenger and looked for a reaction. If there was one, it didn't show.

"I tried to pry the why of it out of Adams in every way I knew. Interviewed him for three days. Nothing. I asked him what he'd meant when he said, 'We know, but that doesn't make any difference anymore.' And he answered, 'Because it didn't, sir.' I got pretty exasperated. What the hell was he talking about? Of course it made a difference.

"Finally, I tried my archaic rage theory. I figured that business with his uncle, my knowing about it, would surprise him and touch a sensitive spot and get him to open up. But he just looked at me with these Corn Belt cornfed cornflower-blue eyes of his and said, 'Begging the lieutenant commander's pardon, but that is so lame, that's so pathetic.' And I got angry and asked what the hell was so damned lame and pathetic about it? He was serene, Mace. His calm almost seemed to be mocking my anger. In the end I was reduced to asking him flat out and straight ahead, 'Corporal Adams, why did you kill those people?' Again I got that serene stare and his voice came almost in a whisper, a gentle whisper. 'If you have to ask that, sir, then you'll never understand the answer.' And that was the end of it. I suppose I got into this funny line of work because I'm still trying to figure out what made those men do what they did. Maybe it wasn't psychological any more than it was organic. Maybe it was . . . I don't know . . . metaphysical. They'd killed without a shred of conscience and with complete randomness. The war didn't make any distinctions about who it killed and didn't. Old ladies, soldiers, infants—all the same. I think that's the answer Adams said I couldn't understand. Those five men had *become* the war."

"You're wrong," Mace said with a self-confidence that he knew bordered on pomposity. He couldn't help it. He felt so much better now. The legions of inchworms had withdrawn, the gas bubble in his sternum had shrunk to the size of a pea. He realized that those reactions had been caused by an awe of Heartwood's intelligence and skills. An unjustified awe, for if the man couldn't see the why of that long-ago incident, then he wasn't as perceptive or smart as his press made him out to be.

"Am I really? You have an answer, Mace?"

"Sure. Adams was a complete man, Dr. Heartwood," he replied, picturing the Marine's eyes of cornflower blue and imagining the sound of the tranquil voice. "That's why he was so self-possessed. Good and evil had become united in him. One thing. I'll bet that's what he meant about there not being any difference. Straight out of the Tao. Not that there's no difference between good and evil but that they can't be separated."

"Somehow, Mace, I don't think Adams would've been so philosophical about it. Do you believe that? Good and evil are Siamese twins?"

He drew in a deep breath, delighted at the opportunity to deliver his opinions on these deep questions, opinions he considered well thought out and original. What most men call order in the universe, he expounded as they approached Walnut Grove, is really a construct of their own limited imaginations to make sense of the vast forces whose true nature and order they are incapable of comprehending, and so the sense they make of things is false, an illusion, a magic trick by which they deceive themselves into a *trompe l'oeil*—he enjoyed using such phrases—of understanding. And that included the codes of behavior and conduct that compose the so-called moral order. What most minds, and most were mediocre, called morals were in truth *mores* that varied from place to place and age to age. There were cannibal tribes still living in New Guinea, and who were we to tell them that the eating of human flesh was a crime? The Vikings, whom we today admire for their daring, were once so dreaded that priests in coastal villages ended their masses beseeching God to spare them from the wrathful berserkers who leapt from their high-prowed ships to sack and slaughter more cruelly than the five Marines had on that very hot morning in Vietnam.

"You sound like you've thought about this quite a lot," Heartwood said. There was something in his voice Mace didn't like.

"Sure. I'm in college. That's what you do in college," he remarked, striving for a light-hearted tone. "Think about stuff you won't have time to think about when you're out of college and busting your tail."

He saw the town of Walnut Grove huddled below the levee, clapboard buildings seemingly braced against the flood that could come at any moment, and he listened to Heartwood's riposte. What men call the order of the universe may indeed be illusion, but it is not necessarily false. Cartographers have drawn across the earth and its seamless seas fraudulent lines called latitude and longitude and have strapped around its belly a make-believe girdle called the equator; yet without these fabrications no mariner far out on the ocean could know where he was, nor where he'd been, nor where he was bound. And as for the moral order, Mace, compare it to a compass or sextant or satellite navigation system, which are themselves inventions to interpret the meanings of those fanciful lines on the globe and so tell the sailor how to get where he wants to go. We can know the truth through fiction, and the truth is that when we lose the will and the vision to impose order on this world, however mythological our imposition may be, we become lost, utterly lost, as we are now becoming lost in this land of endless murder.

The word *bullshit* begged to fly off Mace's tongue, but he suppressed it. Talk about lame and pathetic. The old "moral compass" metaphor. Now he felt disappointed in Heartwood; he would've expected something more original out of a man who'd been written up in so many magazines and newspapers.

"Taylor got lost," Heartwood droned on. "I still feel a little responsible for what happened. I could've, should've given him the narrative he wanted. A complete fiction, not the kind that leads to any truth, but a story he could've clung to. But I came back and handed him a four-page report, double-spaced, that said in so many words that his five fine lads had committed a motiveless crime. Or at any rate a crime whose motives could never be ascertained. What happened indeed could've happened to anyone. There were no immunizations. It was just too damned hot that day.

"He brooded for a while, or so I'd heard through the scuttlebutt in the officers' mess. Had good reason to. The incident got into the news. He'd tried to keep it out, that was one of the reasons he'd commuted the death sentences. There hadn't been an execution in the Marine Corps for decades and he knew if five were carried out on his watch it would make very big headlines. Made headlines anyway. Some stuff got nasty. There was one columnist in the *Washington Post*—a prominent guy, one of those smug pundits who's never seen the trapdoor open and gotten a good look at what's down there, never had to make a decision involving people's lives, never faced a moment of danger to his body or soul—called for Taylor's head. Said he should be relieved of command at the very least. Pointed out that in World War Two, we'd executed a Japanese general in the Philippines because a few of his privates and corporals had committed atrocities. Did we hold our own generals to lesser standards? That got to Taylor, because it had a ring of truth. It was part of the officers' code after all. A commanding officer is responsible for everything his men do or fail to do. The Marine Corps backed him up. The commandant himself gave a press conference and announced that Taylor had acted properly, but Taylor had been in the service twenty-six years and knew the service game. When the board met to consider him for his third star, when the names for chief of staff were tossed into the hat and his came up, the incident at the bridge would be recalled. The adverse publicity would be remembered.

"Then the monsoons came. Rain every day, sometimes twenty-four hours a day. Misty rains, drizzling rains, driving rains that cracked on tent canvas like buckshot and made so much racket on the tin roofs of the hospital that I sometimes had to shout at my patients. Every shrink should try that. Administering therapy to some shell-shocked rifleman at the top of your lungs. I heard that Taylor was taking his meals dressed in a helmet and flak jacket, with a loaded pistol on the table, alongside his knife and fork. That he'd sit at his desk dressed like that, reading the court-martial transcript over and over, as if he could force it to give the answers. That he'd doubled the guard around his quarters and ordered it ringed with a double layer of wire. The poor man was fighting back in the only way he knew how, with men and rifles, but the enemy was inside himself.

"It was late December, 1970, just a week before Taylor was to rotate back to the States. But he knew he couldn't go home. He packed up his uniforms and photographs and all those mementos of a soldier's life bravely and honorably lived, and he addressed the trunk to his wife in Pennsylvania. He polished his boots, cleaned his pistol, shined all his brass. He took his sword from the wall and polished it and buckled it on. He took the medals out of the case and pinned them on his battle-dress uniform, the right way, too, personal decorations and campaign medals in their correct order. Then he stood up, stuck the muzzle of his Colt in his mouth, and blew every thought and memory and hope he'd ever had all over the peeling walls of those old French barracks. And that, Mace, became my first psychological autopsy. I knew the answers before I began. In my own way I helped put that Colt in his hand and I still have bad dreams about it now and then."

An expectant silence fell, broken only by the flat whisper of the air conditioner. Mace felt that he was supposed to make a comment, and he tried to think of one as he watched a cone of moving dust that marked a tractor's progress.

"I don't see why you do. I don't think I would," he said, but saw by a stiffening in Heartwood's posture that he'd made the wrong choice of words.

"You don't understand that I feel as bad about Taylor as a surgeon would about a patient he lost on the operatating table? You don't see that?"

"You didn't say he was your patient."

"He wasn't, but he . . . " Heartwood stopped himself, spotting an opening. "Let's get off this. Let's talk about Duane."

"Okay. Let's do that."

"I seem to recall you felt the same way about Duane. The night you drove him home from the clinic. You said there was something needy about him. That he seemed isolated, was reaching out for someone. At the end of his rope, and that maybe if you'd extended yourself things might have turned out differently."

"How you go from that, to thinking that I feel like I put a gun in that dirtbag's hand, beats me. Blaming myself for what other people do—I'm not into that."

"I'm sure you're not. So tell me, what gave you the impression that he was needy?"

They were passing a pear orchard, row after picket-straight row flashing by, the budding fruits hanging like ornaments from the dark green trees. Mace took a few moments to edit his memories of that night, deciding which scenes to censor, which would be safe to show.

"I had to call the clinic to tell them that I'd got Duane back okay. We're required to do that. Lawsuits. I asked him if I could use the phone in his room, he said yeah, but there wasn't a phone in it. So I went to a pay phone outside and he followed me asking me to hang out. He wanted to rent some porn flicks from the motel and invited me to watch them with him." Mace's tone changed from the reportorial to the contemptuous. "It was the way he was asking me, 'C'mon, hang out for a little while, we'll watch the movies, hang out.' Like I told you before he was like a starved alley cat that shows up at your door, meowing for a saucer of milk. It was pathetic. 'C'mon, whydoncha, Weatherman? Hang out for a little while.' "

"Weatherman?"

"The guys at the cannery used to call me that. Duane picked it up," he explained.

"How did that make you feel? The invitation."

"How do you suppose? That room stunk! Piles of dirty laundry all over. It stunk like the inside of a washing machine when somebody's left damp clothes inside for three or four days. That and the roach spray they used in that shithole. Jesus, I'm going to sit in there watching X-rateds with a speed freak?"

"Yeah, we had a look at that room. It made me wonder. Organization, neatness, it's a way of life, permeates everything somebody does. Like you, Mace."

"What about me?"

"Your room was very neat and organized. You dress neatly. I imagine you're that way in everything you do. Your Mormon training."

"You were saying about Duane?"

He could feel the keenness in Mace's gaze as he slowed for a crossroad. On the left stood the remains of a service station, its rusted pumps displaying prices that hadn't been paid in thirty-five years, most of its white tiles missing, the green and melancholy neck of the Sinclair dinosaur on the toppled sign bent groundward, as if the beast were grazing on the weeds upthrust through the broken asphalt. Heartwood glanced at his odometer. Clovis said his farm was four and a half miles from the intersection.

"Everything we've found out about Duane says that he was a sloppy, haphazard, impulsive guy," he replied to Mace's question. "The one exception to this pattern was the crime he committed. There, all the facts point in the opposite direction. An important point for your thesis. The temptation to soar into pop Freudian poetry is very great in forensic psychiatry, so you have to stick to the facts whenever you can. Fact. Duane arrived in California in possession of an Alley Sweeper—"

"Street Sweeper," Mace corrected. "As long as you're being a stickler."

"Well, by any other name it's still a twelve-round semiauto shotgun that's very effective on crowds of people in enclosed spaces. If Duane came back to California with the intent of simply slaughtering a lot of people, he had the means to do it right away, like, say, Huberty at the San Ysidro McDonald's. But he waited six weeks."

He went on, mortaring fact to fact, building an edifice of Duane's unusual deliberateness.

"And finally, we've got the particular bus he attacked. Full of Asian kids. It happens that schools run field trips out there all the time, okay? If Duane's intent was to kill children, he could have done that most any day, but he waited for that particular one, further supporting the supposition that this crime was as calculated as an assassination—"

"Hold up a sec, let me catch up," Mace said, scribbling in his notebook.

Heartwood leaned over a little, toward his passenger's blind side, and bagged a look at what he was writing.

"So Duane must've wanted to get minority kids. I wasn't sure about that a few days ago, but I am now," he said, now also sure beyond all doubt about the purposes of Mace's research. Some thesis it was going to be if all it contained was the name "Mace Weathers" repeated over and over.

"Are you saying you think the neo-Nazis might have been in on it? That Duane wasn't capable?"

Heartwood sensed that Mace was probing him as much as he was probing Mace. All right, for now let him believe that the neo-Nazi herring hadn't lost its smell.

"That's still a possibility. Gabriel's looking into that, but I've never been convinced Duane belonged to any organization. He was a loner, so more likely, Duane had, call it a hidden talent—"

"The chess! *That's* why you were asking me those off-the-wall questions! You couldn't figure out how somebody like Duane could have planned the crime. You were looking for some . . . some evidence that he had a capacity for organized thinking, for thinking ahead."

Heartwood was aware of a not entirely successful attempt to feign a note of excited discovery, but Mace was betrayed by his emotional tone-deafness, that inability to match sound to feeling.

"Exactly," he said, thinking, *You didn't figure that out just now, you divined it four days ago in your tidy little room and told me what I wanted to hear.*

Ahead was the barn Clovis had described, one wall bearing an advertisement, faded almost to invisibility, for Quaker State motor oil. He pulled into the gravel drive. A dog barked.

"By the way, we talked to another of Duane's chess partners. He said Duane was lousy, that he whipped him in half a dozen moves."

Pleased that this news did not upset his composure, Mace said, "Really? That's strange. Duane was about average, I thought."

"But I suppose that guy's a top player, maybe a lot better than you—and don't take offense."

"None taken. I'll bet I'm better than you think. We'll have to play sometime."

"Be glad to." Heartwood got out of the car and breathed in odors of silage and fertilizer. "Doubt I'd be much of a match."

■ ■ ■

Up here, winter still tinged the wind, blowing down from higher elevations where old snows clung in the crevasses and to north-facing slopes, and rivers invigorated by the spring melt-off bellowed through the sequoia and lodge poles that gave voice to the wind, the boisterous duet of moving air and moving water reducing to a petty *pop-pop-pop*, the discharges from the rifle and pistol ranges just up the road.

"The smell reminds me of Minnesota, that pine smell," said Joyce, walking with a cane, her knee still in a brace. There were only three other vehicles in the clearing that served as a parking lot: two Broncos and a Landcruiser with Ducks Unlimited and NRA stickers on their windows. She'd wanted to come up before the crowds arrived, so she wouldn't embarrass herself in front of experts.

Alex opened a gate and they continued down a wide, well-tended path hemmed by tall trees throwing quilled shadows, trees and shadows trembling in the wind.

"Helluva day for this," Alex said. "Not that I think there's any good day for it."

"I know your feelings, I know you're humoring me. I know, I know."

He bestowed upon her his most lugubrious look, the one that made him resemble some melancholy Florentine prince. "There's something I need to talk to you about when you're through."

"What?"

"When you're through."

They passed under a wooden arch with the words AMADOR ROD AND GUN CLUB burned into it and a sign spelling out safety precautions attached to one of its posts. Before them were a stand of covered bleachers and a row of shooting stations. Targets. Range markers. Downrange a berm, and beyond the berm, an alpine meadow so thick with poppy it looked as though someone had spilled a vat of melted butter over it. Two men occupied two of the stands. They wore baseball caps, ear protectors, vests with club and competition patches, and their extended arms jerked as they fired their pistols, the reports louder now. Will Drake approached them, his head cocked slightly to one side, as if he had a sore neck. He smiled and thrust out his hand, a man of infectious good cheer.

"Hey, Joyce! Alex! How are ya! All set to punch some paper?"

An East Coast voice that rang harshly in their western ears. Drake was a retired airline pilot originally from New York. He kept himself occupied by running a gun and sporting goods store in Amador and giving shooting lessons to neophytes. Joyce had bought the Smith & Wesson from him. She'd wanted a Walther PK semiauto, attracted by its compact size, but Drake advised that a revolver was more accurate and a better weapon for self-defense. The .25-caliber Walther didn't pack the punch. Today he would give Joyce her second lesson. She'd gotten the first yesterday, at the indoor range attached to his store.

She donned her ear protectors and tinted shooting glasses, and they stepped into one of the stands, where she laid the revolver on the bench and sat on a stool so she could shoot without putting weight on her leg. Drake reviewed yesterday's instructions, then said, "Lock and load."

She opened the cylinder, and with slightly shaky hands, loaded the wad-cutters into five chambers, then locked the cylinder, leaving the hammer on the empty chamber.

Drake stepped sideways to look through a spotting scope. Joyce's heart was beating fast, more from a fear of looking foolish or incompetent than anything else. She glanced over her shoulder at Alex, seeking encouragement, but he was up in the bleachers, his eyes seemingly on the mountain crests far beyond the meadow.

She raised the revolver, cupping her right wrist in her left palm, cocked the hammer to fire single-action, sighted, and held on the midsection of the human silhouette target twenty-five yards downrange. It looked so close it seemed impossible to miss.

Breathe . . . aim . . . squeeze . . . The trigger seemed stuck . . . *Squeeze*. Then a crack, the pistol jerking off to her right.

"Maggie's drawers," Drake said, pronouncing the last word "drawse." He meant that she'd missed.

Breathe . . . aim . . . squeeze . . .

"Better, you're in the white at least, but you're high and to the right."

"Should I aim lower and more to the left, then?"

Drake shook his head and said, "It's not your aim, it's your triggah squeeze. You're flinching. Anticipating the shot and jerking the triggah."

He stood alongside her, instructed her to aim, but not to squeeze the trigger.

"You just relax and let me do that," he said, enveloping her hand in his, a great paw of a hand she could see grasping the throttles and wheel of a 747.

"Okay. Breathe . . . that's it . . . let out a little breath . . . that's it . . . and squeeeeze . . ."

The pistol bucked, her arms twitching on the recoil.

"Surprised ya, didn't it? Like it had gone off by itself?"

She nodded.

"That's to give you an idea."

They fired the next four shots in the same way. Then the rangemaster called out through a microphone, "Cease fire! Shooters may go downrange to check your targets."

She got her cane and accompanied Drake, who patched the holes with little squares of black tape. He pointed out the last five, bunched tightly beside his group.

"All ya gotta do, relax and concentrate."

She did feel more relaxed and confident when she returned to the stand and settled back onto the stool; and when she raised the .38, the scenery that had intruded into the edges of her vision was no longer there; she saw the target only, and then *he* suddenly rose in its place, *him* with his plaster-white face and fish-scale eyes and the bright gun at his side, his form vivid and three-dimensional, as if through some unconscious necromancy she'd summoned him from the grave. Her first emotion was terror, but it darted through her, drawing a chill anger in its wake. She cocked the hammer and fired, and she knew without seeing that the bullet had struck its mark.

"Abdomen," Drake called. "Wouldn't kill an attacker, but it definitely would slow him down."

Kill an attacker. Could she pull the trigger if that were a human being in front of her?

Yes, if it were *he*. Or anyone like *him*.

She fired the next four with a smooth rhythm, with a sense of oneness as when she and Ghost were in tune with each other's movements, horse and rider united into a single being.

Drake, hands on his bent knees, continued to peer through the spotter as she opened the cylinder and shook the spent cartridges into her hand. Then he straightened up and looked at her, inclining his head in a way that made him look sly.

"Comeah and take a look at what you did."

She squatted behind the scope and saw four holes grouped within the span of hand in the center of the target.

"I missed one."

"Uh-uh. Take a closer look at the lowest one."

She looked again.

"It's bigger than the others."

"What's called a figgyah eight. Your last round hit right next to the fawth. Incredible. You're one fast study, Joyce."

"My father," she began, warming with pride, "when I was a girl, I learned to shoot. Not a handgun. A shotgun, a little twenty-eight gauge. I shot my first pheasant when I was twelve."

He went downrange and taped the holes, telling her, when he returned, to fire another ten rounds, to test if her feat of marksmanship had been luck.

Although she put all ten in the black, the grouping wasn't as tight; nor could she recapture that cold calm and sureness, that sense of union with the weapon.

Alex came down from the bleachers, and like a duelist's second, loaded the pistol, glasses, and earphones into the bag.

"She's learning quick!" Drake said jovially, clapping Alex on the shoulder. "I'll have her on pop-ups at the combat range in no time!"

Alex winced.

"You're sure you won't take anything?"

"After what she's been through, hell no!" Drake paused and looked off toward the meadow. "Tell you what. Heard that old-vine zin' you've got is terrific. Take a couple of bottles of that after the fifth lesson. Awright?"

Alex shook on it, then escorted her down the path to his dusty Blazer.

"That's really nice of Will," she said.

"And the combat range is next. The *combat* range." He shook his head in a way that was belittling: a father indulging a daughter in some frivolity he didn't approve of. "I want you to imagine something, Joyce. You're in a parking lot, a guy assaults you, the gun's in your purse. What are you going to do? Tell him to hold on a second while you get your makeup out and then surprise him? Jesus."

"Yes," she said, getting into the car. "Yes."

They rode in silence out of the high country wind, the road unraveling like a black thread through meadows painted with spring wildflowers, through piney groves, and as the elevation dropped, through stands of black oak mixed with pine. Alex drove slowly, and with a fixed look, his knobby shoulders raised as if he were hunched against rain. He'd fallen into one of his pensive moods, shut up into his thoughts so completely he was as impenetrable as a bank vault.

After a quarter of an hour, they turned onto Route 88. Beside the road, the Consumnes sparkled in its long tumble from Lake Tahoe to the Sacramento. She saw the slate roof of the DelAssandros' place, and to fill up the silence, observed that the DelAssandros were using quadrilateral cordons.

"Yeah," Alex said distantly. "On his sauvignon blancs."

"Well?"

"Might try it as an experiment. Tom's enthusiastic about it."

"Well, when does the mystery of what you wanted to talk about get cleared up?"

Her knee was beginning to throb, and she pushed the seat all the way back and raised her leg to rest it on the dash.

"Called the doctor. Canceled."

He said this quickly and without nuance. She couldn't tell if he was happy or bitter about it, and so did not know what to feel herself. She sat quietly for a few moments, remembering the day she'd first seen him, in the office of the LaJolla cemetery where she'd worked as a temp, typing deeds to cemetery plots while she waited for her California teacher's certification to go through. It was called the Vista del Mar, a name more suggestive of a beachfront condo than a graveyard. Alex's father, retired in San Diego, was dying of lung cancer. Alex had come in to see about a gravesite on that warm afternoon when the smoke from the crematorium arched across the clean coastal sky as a reminder that there was one thing no one could escape, not even in California. He was tanned from working outdoors, and his hair, dense and black then, was combed straight back, the tan and the hairstyle combining with his angular features to give him the antique handsomeness of a 1930s matinee idol. What drew Joyce to him, though, was the solemnity of his expression: a look of great gravity that his father's impending death had not caused but only deepened. She did not know why that recollection should occur to her now, but it touched her with a pressure almost physical.

She brushed Alex's shoulder and allowed her fingers to fall down along his arm and then over his hand lightly, but he did not sense the remorse in that gesture.

"I didn't decide because . . . It wasn't to make you feel better. Charity or something. It wasn't . . . "

She did not say anything, but continued to look at him, regretting life's capriciousness, its uncannily bad sense of timing.

"Something like this happens to someone you love, you start to thinking about what's important. I asked myself, is it really important that we be free to go to San Francisco on weekends, Tuscany in the summers? Is that why we're together?"

"Tony's engaged," she said, mentioning his eldest child. "You could have a grandson who's half-brother to your son."

"Or a granddaughter who's half-sister."

"Those sound more like family knots than family ties." She paused. "Last week, when you told me it wasn't accidents you were afraid of, that you were afraid of yourself. What did you mean by that?"

"That. Yeah, I did say that." His face colored and he glanced obliquely at the river. "When I think about us having a baby, making love to have a baby . . . I'm not good at this kind of talking." He dropped a hand from the steering wheel and began to play with the radio buttons, the heating and air-conditioning lever, as if he were literally fumbling for the right words. "When I picture you pregnant, I get excited. All right? Makes me feel like I'm nineteen again. Like nature's telling me, 'Go on, Alex, do it, be a father again. And I'm—was—afraid I'd give in to that some night."

She said, "I don't want a baby, Alex," and saw him blink. "I've thought things over, too, and I don't want one. Not now, not ever."

"I would've thought that after . . . that you'd want one even more."

"I read it in the papers every day, hear it on the news. Infants shot to death in their cribs from stray bullets, first-graders going to school shot to death by drug dealers or God knows what. And these fourteen kids . . . If I had a child and what happened to Billy"—she swallowed—"Billy Pate or Rose . . . I think that having a kid now, the way things are, I think it'd be almost criminal."

■ ■ ■

The guilt that gnawed at him as he sat with Jean Sheldon in the Jolie Jelly jazz club seemed both perplexing and quaint. This was the age of the talk-show confessional. If Woody Allen didn't mind telling the world that, yes, he'd slept with his teenage stepdaughter, why should Gabriel Chin's conscience nag him merely for sitting in a club with another woman? It was like driving the freeway in a Model-A and feeling nervous about speed traps. Nothing had passed between him and Jean, not a touch, and the conversation was strictly professional; yet the hour—it was nine o'clock, time for him to be tucking Eleanor into bed—and the music and such cornball effects as cigarette smoke swirling in the filtered stage lights created an atmosphere illicit and intimate. Jean had shed her lead inspector's costume and had changed into a white blouse and navy-blue skirt that just touched her knees. She had long, muscular legs, and his thoughts, liberated by two bourbons, had turned adulterous. He'd already betrayed Adrienne by lying to her, telling her that he and Youngblood would be working late, following up on leads and waiting for some results to come in from the crime lab. Youngblood was home in Placerville, and the results came in two hours ago, Jean having done a preliminary analysis of the fibers and particles purloined from Weathers's room and the Gold Hill Motel.

She'd lived up to her reputation as a specialist who could make a case out of almost nothing. Though they were still a long way from making a case, Gabriel was excited by her findings, but he didn't end the day with a satisfied feeling of accomplishment. After they finished up in the lab, a restlessness seized him, something like the kind that used to grip him in high school and led to trouble, or to what was considered trouble in 1965. It was a discontent bound up with expectancy—a sense that something dramatic was going to happen, and if it didn't happen of its own accord, then a way would be found to make it happen. The covert entrance into Weathers's room, the discovery that Boggs's shirt had come from him, and that a long, brown polyester thread lifted from a pair of Weathers's jeans matched the fibers in the motel's bedspreads had put Gabriel on a high. He wanted to maintain it, didn't want it dulled by the domestic rituals of his suburban brick ranch.

"He seems like a really good cop," Jean said, speaking about Youngblood. "Meticulous. You don't see that very often. Surprises me he made a mess of the scene."

"If he'd been there, it wouldn't have been. He was halfway to Nevada when it went down."

"I like the way he noticed that the cleaning lady hadn't dusted the radio. The way he figured that Weathers would have set the alarm to get up early for his reconnaissance. That was good solid police work."

"Yeah. Surprised a dump like that had a clock radio," Gabriel said, not too surprised to find himself jealous of these praises. He thought they'd all done a fine job, assisted by luck, almost too much luck. Although Cannon's room had been occupied by only two people in the past week, the Gold Hill's maid service wasn't up to Hilton standards. Besides the ones on the radio, Jean lifted prints from at least six other people, which the experts would have to sort out tomorrow and try for a match with the prints lifted from Weathers's room.

"I'll be even more surprised if any of them turns out to be Weathers's. He wouldn't have been that careless. Would've wiped off everything he'd touched, and if he'd watched enough cop shows, he might have worn gloves. Why the hell hasn't Heartwood called in yet?" Gabriel wondered, with a glance at his pager.

"Worried?" Jean's finger went around and around the rim of her wine glass. "Heartwood riding around with a possible psychopath?"

"Nah. If that's what Weathers is, he's a special kind of psychopath. Gets somebody else to do his killing for him. Doesn't like to get his hands dirty."

She looked off toward the stage, where the bass player, in a dim blue spotlight, went into his solo. He wasn't bad, Gabriel thought. No Buster Williams, but not bad, his big hands plucking round, full notes from the instrument.

"Well, enough shop talk," Jean said abruptly, moving her gaze back to Gabriel.

He felt a stirring of hope, and at the same time, a wariness of plunging into a more intimate conversation, but when he saw her steal a worried look at her watch, he realized that he had nothing to be worried about, nor to hope for.

"Sixteen-year-old daughter and it's Saturday night," she said.

"Mind if we stay the set?" he asked timidly. "Can't be more than another ten minutes."

"Okay, if it's only that."

He restrained himself from asking if there was a husband at home. The quintet's leader, a young sax player with a butterscotch complexion, announced that the next tune had been written by the great Billy Strayhorn. He sounded a bit too reverential, but Gabriel forgave the piousness when he heard the opening bars of "Lush Life." He lost himself in that haunting melody, closed his eyes, and pictured himself in the guitarist's place.

"Not bad, not bad," he said softly, admiring the arrangement.

Jean leaned over and murmured in his ear, "All this sounds somehow the same to me. Sorry if I sound like a Philistine."

"A what?"

"A dope."

"How can this stuff sound the same? Rock, yeah, but . . ."

"I meant I can't tell what makes it good or bad."

Despite their subdued voices, a young woman at a table next to theirs turned to them scowling, a finger over her lips.

"The interpretation . . . it's . . . okay, this part . . . not so good . . ." Gabriel whispered as the bass and drums, borrowing from the original Coltrane arrangement, went into the double-time Chambers and Hayes had played so subtly. "Too much. Should be just a hint, an accent. What these guys are doing is hiding that they can't sustain a ballad. It's good hiding, but it's hiding. . . ."

The young woman's date now shot them a nasty look, mouthing a silent and offended, "Quiet!"

Though Gabriel had himself issued such imperatives to talkative patrons, he felt a flash of anger. It was the guy's snippy manner and soap opera star looks that annoyed him. A perfect fair-haired yuppie, probably some upcoming Sacramento lawyer who'd been messing his diapers when Coltrane first recorded the tune and who wouldn't know a chord change if it poked him in his blue eyes.

The sax, bass, drums, and piano backed up the guitarist on the last number of the set—Wes Montgomery's "Monterey Blues," another of Gabriel's favorites.

Over Jean's protests, he insisted on paying the tab and walking her to her car.

"It can get funny only a couple of blocks from here," he argued and she shrugged an okay.

His gallantry struck even him as absurd when they stood to leave. Wearing low heels, Jean reduced him to the stature of a fourteen-year-old.

The yuppie, throwing them a quick, disdainful glance, made a few comments to his date, "Pretentious . . . thinks he's a jazz critic . . . "

Gabriel's anger grew, but he contained it and maneuvered around the closely packed tables, Jean a step behind him.

Outside, it was a splendid spring evening. A northerly breeze had blown the pollen and haze from the air, the sky had a violet tinge, and a few bright stars managed to shine through the light pollution.

"Those assholes," he muttered as they left the Capitol Mall and walked down a side street toward the parking garage.

Jean gave him a questioning look.

"Those yupsters back there. Shushing us like we're in church."

She put her arm in his then, and he liked the feeling it gave him, though he knew it meant nothing, was merely a gesture.

"I didn't realize you knew so much about music."

"I don't."

A short distance ahead, two young couples strolled. Vietnamese kids, one of the girls wearing her hair in the traditional style, its dark cascade evoking memories of girls in filmy *ao-dais* cut away to the waist, silk trousers underneath. How they seemed to flow in those dresses, through the marketplaces, across the sparkling paddies.

"Well, then, you talk a good game," Jean said.

"So what's your husband do?"

"Don't have one, Gabriel. Never did. Marrying Nora's father

would have added one mistake to another. Not that she's . . . Not that I think she's a mistake. I almost gave her up for . . ."

The car roared up from behind, shot past them, and swerved toward the curb. A kid in the front seat leaned out the window and tossed a full beer can over the roof. It struck the long-haired girl in the head, the kid yelling, "Cat-eyed motherfuckers!" as she went down and a paper bag sailed out the rear window. The car squealed away, the kids inside whooping, kicking their legs and waving their arms out the windows with monstrous glee.

Something seemed to explode in front of Gabriel, like the powder flash in an antique box camera, and he was running after the car, faster than he thought he could run. Five or six white boys. A banged-up old gas-guzzler, a white-trash cruiser, probably from the Okie lands west of the river. The driver had slowed, unaware that he was being pursued. Gabriel pounded down the street, weaving and pivoting through the traffic like a two-back dodging a secondary, his eyes focused on the big, vertical taillights ahead. He was hoping for the traffic signal half a block away to turn red, but it didn't. He vaulted onto the hood of a parked car, drew his gun and held down with both hands, aiming square at the back window, waiting for a clear shot that never came. The car vanished into the darkness of the streets beyond the intersection.

He leapt off the car to the stares of a couple of frightened passersby and ran back to Jean. A small crowd had gathered around her, kneeling on one knee beside the Vietnamese girl, who sat with her legs spraddled. She looked about sixteen or seventeen and she was sobbing and the blood that flowed down her forehead in a single rivulet branched at her eyebrows, then branched again, tributaries forming tributaries so that she looked like a fractured image of herself.

"There, honey. There. It's all right. You'll be all right."

Jean pressed a handkerchief to the girl's scalp. The blood spread through it like ink through a tissue. The beer can lay against the wall of a shuttered store, mustard and catsup and food scraps were splattered across the sidewalk from the paper bag. Wendy's.

"Somebody's calling an ambulance, but she'll be okay. Looks worse than it is. Get their tag number?"

Winded, mute in his rage, Gabriel shook his head. Jean made a quick movement with her hand, and he realized that the Glock was still drawn, held along the side of his trousers. He holstered it.

"God, you weren't . . . ?"

He shook his head again—his second lie of the night. He was alarmed that he had lost all control; he would have fired if the shot presented itself, killed somebody over what amounted to a third-degree assault. Slowly, as though awakening from a trance, he became aware of himself, of a dangerously fast pounding in his chest, of a burning sensation in his sciatic nerve—he'd wrenched his back leaping onto the hood—and of a familiar, bitter taste on his tongue, like old coins soaked in vinegar. He'd sampled it on riverine patrols in the Delta and on high-speed pursuits, known it while busting methedrine labs around Fontana, but now it wasn't Viet Cong, murderers, or drug dealers that brought it to his mouth.

■ ■ ■

Drowsy from heavy doses of antihistamines, Heartwood sat in his room, swaddled in a flannel robe. His eyes were bloodshot, his nostrils raw, and when he breathed, he heard an asthmatic wheezing in his chest. The attack struck shortly after he and Mace left Clovis Boggs's farm. Unable to see the road for the flood in his eyes, or to steer for the sneezing fits that shook him head to foot, he turned the car over to Mace while he waited for a double dose of Seldane to take effect.

A true California son, Mace loved fast cars and handled one with ease. Driving the Porsche thrilled him, and there was such a boyish charm about his excitement that Heartwood almost began to like him. When he asked, during a respite in his fits, how Mace was allowed to drive with only one eye, he laughed and said that "allowing" had nothing to do with it. The Department of Motor Vehicles didn't know about his disability, he "allowed" himself to drive, and could do it as well with one eye as most people with two. By way of demonstration, he accelerated, downshifted smoothly, and took a curve as if the road were a banked track. *Better* than most people.

Behind the wheel, and with Heartwood rendered almost speechless, Mace was more relaxed and talkative than he'd been as a passenger, offering unsolicited impressions of Clovis Boggs. It was plain to see that Duane got that chip on his shoulder from his grandfather. That attitude that he deserved more than he had, that he'd been cheated, that the world was against him. Chip, ha! It was a boulder. Heartwood mostly agreed with this assessment.

Clovis was barely stooped by his seventy-four years, his hair gone to the color of ashes but still thick, and his eyes were the same strange green as his grandson's, but where Duane's were without life or dimension, Clovis's shone with the fire of the poor white southerner, a tricky combustion that was fueled by anger and pride, self-pity and contempt, and burned with a fierce, perverse beauty. In the two-hour interview, he devoted perhaps twenty minutes to Duane and the rest to the saga of his flight from the droughted cottonlands of western Arkansas to the California garden that proved a purgatory where the rich ranchers and growers who called themselves "native sons of the Golden West" scorned Clovis and his kind. They who had picked their own cotton bowed and stooped for the stranger in the stranger's fields, they who'd never seen an orange climbed ladders to pick oranges in the orchards of the rich man, shook walnuts from the trees in the groves of the native son.

"So that's what we was, migratory workers, goddamned Dust Bowl refugees, all right, me and Addy." He gestured at Adelaide, as frail and confused as he was vigorous and alert, though not so confused that she failed to admonish his frequent invocations of the Creator's name in vain. "We worked hard but we didn't complain and demand our rights, we were not that way. Me and her, we saved every penny. She drove a school bus for extra money . . . "

"And the gospel bus on Sundays, don't you forget that," she said, interrupting the lament she'd been humming in a worn chair across the room. "I drove the gospel bus to Assembly!"

"You didn't get paid for that."

"I will be paid in other ways. In the riches of His Kingdom," she responded in a thin voice, then resumed her humming and Clovis his tale.

In 1949, a decade after they arrived in California, they bought the farm they now were on, and so reclaimed what had been lost to the dust-darkened winds and stingy skies of western Arkansas.

Heartwood found himself moved by this story. Yet he was put off by Clovis's belief that his victory over hardship was a triumph too meager won at a price too high. He ought not to have suffered so for a mere three-hundred-twenty acres of corn, walnuts, and pears. He ranted against today's refugees, "Messicans and Asiatics and what-all," not because they came expecting things to be handed to them but because things *were* handed to them, whereas he and Addy had had to consider as found money every dime of profit from the farm, and a lot of years the profit could almost be counted in dimes. Life had levied other taxes. His eldest son . . . not right, put away in a state home when he was but fourteen . . . and his middle son, Tilghman, Duane's father, marrying that . . . And there Clovis's anger grew so deep it robbed him of the power of speech. And then Tilghman getting killed in a car wreck. Only his youngest had escaped this awful destiny. Went to school, graduated U.C. Davis, degree in agriculture. Now right up there with the State Agriculture Department.

Duane's crime fell into the category of the wrongs life had done Clovis. To give him a grandson to bring such disgrace to his good name, to make him afraid to show his face in public, or answer the phone because it was likely to be some reporter asking questions was a cruelty to a man who'd worked so hard for the little he had.

He and Addy had tried hard to straighten Duane out during the few months they had him, and they did not spare the rod, no, sir, there's no man could say Duane turned out a killer because he hadn't been disciplined.

The old man rose from his chair, went into a closet beneath the stairs, and brought out what looked like a hardwood hiking stick. "Used this. To save the soul, chastise the flesh!"

He stood in the middle of the room, fiery as a tent-meeting preacher, and brandished the instrument of salvation and chastisement. Mace, who had been sitting passive and bored up to that point, appeared to take a sudden interest in the conversation—and not a benign one. He leaned forward, milking his hands between his knees, and turned his head slightly to fix on the old man the frigid stare Heartwood had noticed earlier. In her corner of the room, Adelaide began to sing her ancient lament.

"Wish to the Lord I'd never been born, died when I was a babe, my lord, died when I was a babe . . . "

"Hated to do it, swear I did," Clovis said over the singing. "But Addy and me was coming onto sixty-six years when we took charge of Duane and Sara Jane—now there was a good child—how else was a pair of old folks to handle a boy like that?"

"I wouldn't be eatin' this cold corn bread, sloppin' this greasy gravy, my lord, sloppin' this greasy gravy . . . "

"Always truant from school. In one kinda trouble or t'other. So it was four times crost the backside with this, but it didn't do no good anyway . . . "

Four. The number jogged something in Heartwood's memory. Something about Duane, something from the reams of reports and clippings he'd read in the past week. Four what? He struggled to summon it up, but was distracted by Mace, who looked coiled, as if he were about to spring from his seat and break the stick over Clovis's head.

The old man, becoming conscious of him, stopped talking, turned, and said, "How come you're looking at me like that?"

"Like what, sir?" Mace asked, his voice going toneless.

"Like you are now. Like that. I s'pose you're one of them people don't believe in whupping!"

There was no reponse to this comment, only the steady, glacial stare.

"Mr. Boggs—" Heartwood started to say.

"Would you get me a Coke, please," Mace interrupted. His upper lip curled in a half-grin, baring his sharp, protruding eyeteeth.

"Coke? We got no Coke."

"Then any kind of soft drink, Mr. Boggs. Or a glass of water, please."

There was the barest suggestion of threat in the final word.

"Addy, get this young man a soda."

Adelaide sang on and did not move.

"Goddamnit!"

Clovis returned the stick to its place, went into the kitchen, and came back with a can of Dr Pepper.

"There y'are, young man," he said, but much subdued. He held the can at arm's length, as though he were afraid to get too close.

"Thank you, Mr. Boggs."

Mace's expression changed instantaneously, his coldness thawing as his predatory grin broke into a brilliant smile as welcome as sunlight after an ice storm. Clovis smiled back. He seemed relieved.

It was a moment Heartwood found interesting. He did not want to make too much of it, yet he thought a door had cracked briefly, offering a glimpse of something essential in Mace's nature, something powerful and intimidating.

Other glimpses had come during the drive back to San Joaquin, and now, in his room, he was writing down his impressions.

A car door slammed outside. He looked out the window and in the half-light of the corner streetlight saw Gabriel crossing the street.

Putting his slippers on, he went downstairs to the front door.

Gabriel looked strange, his cheeks flushed, his face a little wild.

Heartwood took him into the library, a cozy room where cloth and leather-bound classics democratically shared the shelves with soft-porn romances, and switched on an hourglass table lamp, its glow diffused through frosted glass. Gabriel lowered himself delicately into a wing chair beside the window.

"Looks like you need a drink. I've got gin in the fridge. Otherwise, the only thing they have here is sherry." He motioned with his head at a decanter and glasses set out on a table.

"Sherry."

Heartwood poured two glasses and sat down. He wanted to think of them as two gentlemen, sipping sherry in the library, but Gabriel's pistol, visible though his open sport jacket, spoiled the effect.

"Glad to see that Weathers didn't eat you, Lee. Why didn't you call?"

"Haven't heard that question since I was married. Didn't get the chance. I plead a severe allergy attack. Mace had to drive me back to San Joaquin and I just barely made it from there to here on my own."

"Mace? You two on a first-name basis now? Guess you got acquainted pretty good."

"Are you all right? You look a little . . . "

"Yeah, yeah," Gabriel said with a wave.

"Well, was the day productive?"

"Weathers is wearing dark green boxer shorts today. Red tomorrow."

He then related some of the more interesting results of the day's forensic work, beginning with the fabric samples found in the Gold Hill Motel.

Heartwood felt relieved. It wasn't much—a case literally hanging by a few threads—but it was at least tangible.

"I showed a photo of Weathers to the motel owner," said Gabriel. "Got the artist from the San Joaquin PD to draw sunglasses on it. The old juicehead couldn't make an identification. What we need for proof positive that Weathers was in the Gold Hill is going to be in our print match. We're bringing the impressions in tomorrow."

"If they're not good enough, I volunteer to try to get a fresh set tomorrow when we go to Oakland. Maybe off a soda can, a glass. I'm starting to like cops and robbers."

"You've seen too many cops and robbers movies. We needed fresh prints, we could get 'em off your car right now. So you interview Duane's mother at what time tomorrow?"

"Noonish. When we're done, I'll ask Mace to take a sail with me, maybe have him over for dinner, all in the way of winning his confidence. I suspect he'll accept, because if I read him right, he wants to win my confidence. Or, putting it another way, to make sure he has nothing to worry about. It's going to feel real good to be back in the Bay Area."

Gabriel tossed back his sherry and held out the glass for a refill.

"Aren't you still on duty?" Heartwood asked, pouring.

"This stuff couldn't make a chipmunk drunk. Got a bullshit psychology question for you. A guy keeps a picture of his mother in a trunk. Buck naked except for a pair of bikini panties. The word *whore* is written on the bottom of the picture in block letters. What does that say to you?"

"Off the top of my head, that it's not a normal, healthy mother-son relationship."

"C'mon, Lee, it's late and I'm tired and my back hurts. We found a Polaroid in the false bottom of a trunk. Dated 1974. A blonde. Good-looking isn't the word. The kind of honey who'd make the Pope leave the Vatican. There were a few other pictures of her and a guy in the tiger-stripe uniform in 'Nam. And one more of her in '74, holding a little towhead by the hand, two or three years old. Don't know for dead certain that it's Mace and his mother, but you figure it's gotta be."

"Any other pictures for comparison? More recent ones of his mother and father?"

"That's the funny thing. None. Only ones I found were pictures of Weathers himself. School pictures going back to eighth grade, in chronological order."

"What else?"

"The Book of Mormon, a Bible, with a scrap piece of paper with a phone number for a bookmark, and a scrapbook full of clippings about the massacre."

"What? Why didn't you tell me that right off the bat? A detail like that tells me more than a basketful of threads, a wall of fingerprints."

Gabriel sucked his lips between his teeth, then mouthed a litany of silent obscenities.

"What is it?"

"You've got some incredible talent for pissing me off, that's what. I break my ass getting the little bit we got, I violate the Fourth

Amendment of the fucking Constitution of the U-fucking-nited States of America to get it, and then you say it doesn't tell you anything."

"All right, all right."

"Not all right. I gotta be thinking about what story will sound best to a district attorney because he's gotta think of what'll sound good to a jury, and a D.A. is gonna hear a lot better story in fibers and fingerprints—forensic fucking evidence—than in a scrapbook. Listen, Weathers isn't some kind of case study for me, he's not some kind of Sasquatch that I'm gonna examine for brain damage or whatever." He rose part way from the chair, jabbing his finger. "I *want* this son of a bitch, Lee."

As Heartwood gestured frantically to him to keep his voice down and the obscenities to a minimum, Gabriel grimaced and pressed his hand to the small of his back.

"Shit!"

He got down on the floor, lay on his back, knees bent, and began a series of pornographic movements with his groin.

"May I ask what you're doing?"

"Threw my back out tonight. I'll be okay in a sec," he grunted, then locked his arms around his knees and brought them doubled to his chest. "Sorry for blowing my cork, but you know where I'm coming from on this. Same place I always did."

"Right beside you. No experiment, no case study, no Sasquatch, okay, okay? I'm not as interested in making a medical or psychiatric point as I was a few days ago. Not sure what kind of point I want to make. Maybe a moral one. My opinion, what we might have in Mace Weathers and Duane Boggs is a Charlie Manson with a cult of one."

Gabriel stood cautiously, seemed to test his back for reliability, and then sat down again.

"Cult of none, thanks to a Taurus nine. What did you find out? What kind of guy are we dealing with?"

"One, Mace is definitely not writing a thesis on pyschiatric autopsies. No big surprise there, but it's the third lie he's told me. Two, Mace is no longer a practicing Mormon, he despises the religion, which has put him and his father on a bad footing. His old man's a lord high something or other in the Mormon church. When Mace turned eighteen, he was supposed to go on a foreign mission. I gather that's de rigeur among Mormons. Mace refused. He kept his father happy for a while by going to B.Y.U. Lasted one semester. Transferred to San Joaquin State. Three-six-five average, so we aren't dealing with an idiot. By the way, he told me all this on the drive back, when he was at the wheel. I didn't pump him because I could hardly speak. That tells me that he's most off his guard and relaxed when he's in control, or thinks he is. Whether it's a car or an agenda. Let's remember that."

"Say anything about his old man being in Vietnam?"

Heartwood shook his head. Trying to formulate his next thought, he rose, walked across the room to a bookcase, his glance roving over the titles, everything from *Moby Dick* to *Love's Passion Regained*.

"Go back to Thursday and our two narratives. I don't think they have to be mutually exclusive."

"Boyfriends?"

"Maybe. And if they were, it wasn't a sweet and loving relationship. There was a curious moment this afternoon. The whole time we were there, Mace was bored. The one time he perked up was when Clovis started to talk about how he'd beaten Duane with a hickory stick. Straight out of the good old days. The damn thing was just this side of a billy club. Clovis would crack him four times across the rear end every time he screwed up. It's really hard to describe the way Mace reacted. Looked like he wanted to kill the old man with it, but there might have been something else working there. He was—cold, somehow. Scary. No kidding. I wouldn't want that big guy staring at me the way he stared at Clovis. Whatever, it was the only topic that excited his interest. I happened to remember from the coroner's report . . . "

"Oh, yeah . . . "

"Four bruises on Duane's buttocks," Heartwood went on. "Duane lived with his grandparents when he was thirteen. My first thought was that the old man must have cracked him damned hard as well as often to leave marks that were still visible eight years later, so when I got back, I looked at the autopsy and there it was, four horizontal, resolving bruises or abrasions, six inches long, half an inch wide, one inch apart. *Resolving*. A fact. Four facts."

"Love 'em. Recent, you're saying."

"I'm saying. Anything else strike you?"

Gabriel's eyebrows came together in a black ridge. "Inch apart. Regular, methodical."

"Sure. And four and no more. So even if marks did last eight years, imagine you're a stern old grandfather, at your wits' end with a delinquent kid who's been dumped in your lap. Can't do anything with him. You're mad as hell and you beat his butt and don't pay much attention to where on his butt. And if you're whacking on the kid every other day, there'd be more than four. The kid's whole ass would be a bruise."

Gabriel said, "A whipping boy."

"Maybe. Was he Mace's? No way to tell yet. But if, I stress the 'if,' it was Mace, we have to ask why. Did Duane represent some aspect of Mace himself that he needed to hurt?"

Gabriel raised both hands and made a pushing motion.

"There you go again. Off into the never-never. We've got to relate this to nailing the son of a bitch or it's just a lot of . . . "

"No need to say it." Heartwood sat down again, and feeling a tickle in his nostrils, took a spray bottle from the robe's pocket. "I think it could relate. Facts first, now imagination. If they had such a relationship, I would imagine it came first and that the conspiracy grew out of it. Somehow, someway, they went on to mass murder. One controlling, the other being controlled."

"I should hear something from the people in Fraud next week. Be nice if we could actually pin something on Mace, wouldn't it? Shit, now you've got me calling him Mace."

"Duane's price for playing the whipping boy," Heartwood said with a nod. "'Beat me, punch me, kick me, whip me, Mace honey, but get me out of those Narcotics Anonymous meetings and those weekly urine tests but keep those checks coming in.' If that's what was going on."

"If. I'm getting damned tired of that word," Gabriel said.

A heavy silence fell. Heartwood stared at his toes. Gabriel tapped the sherry glass with his fingernail, making the glass ring.

"I'm getting worried that maybe there isn't any key to cracking him," he said, expressing Heartwood's very thought. "When I was in his room, I got the feeling that this is one *cold* fish. And what you've told me confirms that."

"Not the type to rattle easily. Or rattle at all."

"So let's pretend that by tomorrow we can prove he was in the Gold Hill the same night as Duane. We confront him with that and the lies he told you, and we start to jam him. What do you suppose would happen?"

Heartwood stood again, the seed of an idea sprouting in his mind. "He'd look at us and say, 'Whoa, guys, do you think I was in on this?' And then his next move . . . "

"The L-word," Gabriel said with disgust. "And the lawyer asks Mace to explain what was going on. Why the shirt? Oh, I forgot. I loaned him one. Were you in the Gold Hill Motel? Very worst case for him, he admits he had a relationship with Duane that he was ashamed of, and that's all he was hiding. So we still need a helluva lot more."

"A lot, a lot," Heartwood replied distantly. The idea was beginning to flower, but it needed some light and nourishment. "Trouble is, there really isn't a lot we can get."

Another silence fell. He looked out the window and saw something fly past the streetlight so swiftly he could have believed it was a particle of dark matter from some remote corner of the universe, made visible for a sliver of a second. There it was again, and a third time, the object sharply changing its direction, swooping up, swooping down with black wings bent in their middles to form a boomerang. Then it was gone: a nighthawk or shrike flown from its roof or chimney nest to hunt what prey the city offered. The floor above creaked as a guest turned over in bed. The grandfather clock in the living room solemnly counted eleven, and in the stillness that followed, he imagined he could hear Gabriel's thoughts as clearly as his own.

"You mentioned Manson. I remember right, the Tate-LaBianca murders were supposed to be kind of a kickoff for a whole series of mass murders."

"Helter-skelter," Heartwood said.

"Where he screwed up was sending out his happy little family to do them. Too many people. He should've hired the Hell's Angels as consultants."

Gabriel turned slightly, his head moving part way out of the table lamp's light so that his face became divided like a half-moon. Its illuminated side had a brutal look: the hollow cheek, the acute cheekbone like a ridge, the smashed nose.

"You should continue. The fingerprints, trace evidence, whatever else," Heartwood said, leaping far ahead, as though everything had already been discussed.

"I'm going to, tomorrow. Check out some phone numbers . . ." He stopped in mid-sentence and, turning again, looked at Heartwood with fixed attention, eyes like the bores of a side-by-side derringer. "But what we really need is for the son of a bitch to make a move. We need for him to *do* something."

"To betray himself through action."

"To do something we can pin on him or use to pin him against a wall, and not something penny-ante like dealing steroids. We haven't got much, but I'm pretty sure it's enough to reopen and get authorization to put him under twenty-four-hour surveillance. If you and me decided that that's necessary . . . "

He did not put a period on the last sentence, leaving another thought unexpressed. It seemed to hover in the air, a presence as real as an electromagnetic field.

"You mean if we decided there was a likelihood Mace is going to try again," Heartwood said.

"My experience has been that a one-time criminal is as rare as a whore in church. Guy gets away with something, he's most likely to try again."

"So we put him under surveillance and wait to see what he does? How long?"

"Guess that depends on . . . What is it you keep saying? About perceptions? Guess it would depend on Mace's perceptions."

"Which could be"—Heartwood sat down, conscious that his breathing had grown more rapid, and said in a voice hardly more than breath—"manipulated."

"By somebody with the skills," Gabriel replied just as softly. "Old saying is that the easiest man to con is a con man, so maybe the easiest man to manipulate is a manipulator."

And so the idea blossomed, and it did not need light. A cereus opening its petals to the darkness. Two men, quietly talking in a quiet room, he thought. My God, it might have begun just this way with *them.* Two men talking in a room. All traces of his drowsiness had fled, replaced by a quickening not entirely pleasant. He could not name the emotion he felt at that moment, formed as it was of repulsion and anticipation. What do I want? he asked himself. Only to make a moral point, bring the criminal to justice? No. He wanted to confront Mace, and to know, to *know*. That room in Portsmouth naval prison, so long ago, and the statement that struck him like a slap, insult, and challenge all at once. *If you have to ask the question, you'll never understand the answer.* It began then, this craving to see into those black holes of the mind where all light was imprisoned.

"Gabriel, I'd have to be . . . " He sought the proper word. Subtle? No. Circumspect? No again. "I'd have to be conscientious. He did say a few things to me in the first interview. Odd things. I could find a way to bring those up. It would have to come up in the course of, in the context of . . . exploring those ideas. It couldn't be a . . ." He paused once more to thumb through his mental dictionary. A suggestion? A little push in the right direction? A prod? His vocabulary failed him. "We're talking something bordering on entrapment. It's not a question of practicalities, not even of professional ethics. I couldn't live with myself if . . ."

"Way I see it is that we wouldn't let it go too far," Gabriel said. "Wouldn't be like a sting operation that you take right down to the wire. Not to the point that a lot of lives are endangered. Just far enough."

"What if it doesn't work? What if it turns out that what he did *was* a one-time thing?"

Gabriel's lips stretched, his clamped teeth showed whitely in the frosted light, but no one could have called that expression a smile.

"Just what I've been thinking. Let's call what we were just talking about Plan A, so we need a Plan B. But I'm fresh out of ammo and ideas."

Heartwood helped himself to another sherry and stood staring at the bookshelves.

"Weathers is the kind of bad guy I haven't run into in a while. Moved through this whole operation like a ghost," Gabriel said to his back. There was a note of admiration in the remark. "He's no Manson. He's sane enough to know how not to get caught. Sane enough to know that even plain vanilla homicide is tough to prove without corroborating witnesses. Two can keep a secret if one is dead."

Heartwood turned around. "Thank you, Gabriel, thank you. Weathers doesn't know that we've talked to Tipton, right? Doesn't know that we know where he is? He doesn't know anything about Tipton except what's been in the papers. That Jacob's disappeared."

Gabriel looked at him with a squint.

"And he doesn't know that Tipton saw Duane for four or five hours, a week before the massacre. That Tipton came up to San Joaquin to deliver a Ruger."

"Well, we're pretty sure Mace doesn't know that. Duane might have told him he'd seen his brother."

"Even if he did, this still could work. Because Mace wouldn't know what they talked about that night, unless he was right there in the room, and we know he wasn't."

"I'm following you. Hey, Professor, you're pretty good at this. He'll think he's in danger like that Seattle carpenter you told me about. He'll think, at least he'll worry that Duane told Tipton that Mace was the brains behind the whole thing."

"And then it becomes a question of how Mace acts on that perception. Critical. Because if all he does is run, like the carpenter . . . "

"Don't think he will. He'll try something else. Because smart guys like Mace always think they're smarter than they are. He'll think he's smart enough to get away with it."

"Smart, that's right. Smart, smart." Heartwood walked across the room with a preoccupied air. "Look, he's bound to weigh one thing against another. He's bound to wonder what the chances are that Tipton knows everything and if those chances are great enough to warrant taking the risk of going after him."

"He's got to be convinced that Tipton knows everything," Gabriel said.

"And the way to convince him of that is to convince him that Tipton's disappeared for a very good reason," said Heartwood, picking up the thought. "A better reason than merely knowing what Duane was planning to do."

"I've misjudged you, Lee. You've got a nasty mind."

"Mace must have had doubts about Duane's ability to carry it off on his lonesome, no matter how much he practiced. We play on those doubts. We lead him to believe that Tipton actually took part in the crime, get him to think that Duane, without his knowledge, enlisted Tipton's help one week before the massacre."

"Yeah. *Yeah.* And the beauty of that is that'll make Mace think we're off on the wrong trail. He'll feel—"

"Emboldened," Heartwood interrupted. "Okay, okay, now we don't tell him outright that we suspect Tipton's the accomplice. He'd wonder why we were letting him in on such privileged information. We drop hints, we let a few, oh, suggestions float in the air, and let him draw his conclusions."

"A calculated news leak. No one identified, only that we're looking for a suspect. I know just the guy we can use."

"Good, good. Great, in fact. It'll lend credibility. But we'll need Tipton's and his father's consent. Their cooperation. Tell him to stay out of sight until we're ready for him to reappear."

"I've got to go along with you two tomorrow. Youngblood can take care of the other stuff."

"Gabriel . . ."

"I'll behave myself. Too much at stake here for me to blow my cork."

Though he'd thought of it, the enormity of the scheme, and all the things that could go wrong with it, rose up horribly before Heartwood.

"I want to sleep on it, assuming I get to sleep tonight. You'd better, too," he said. "Because if somebody gets hurt or worse, we'll be . . ." He almost said "in trouble," but that was far too mild. "We need to think this all the way through."

"Thinking's got nothing to do with it," Gabriel remarked mysteriously.

"That wife of eighteen years must be wondering where you're at."

Gabriel said nothing, getting to his feet, wincing with pain.

"How did you do that?" Heartwood asked, showing him to the door.

"Running. I was . . . some guys . . . Ah, nothing. Running. Threw it out running."

He hesitated in the doorway, a palm on the door post, eyes cast down.

"Hey, Lee. You know I hate psychological bullshit."

"You've made that abundantly clear."

"Right. Guess so. I got a . . . Let me ask you something. Have you ever been afraid that there's something inside . . . have you ever been afraid of yourself?"

Now Heartwood paused. For Gabriel, this guarded question was tantamount to a baring of the soul.

"Until tonight, no."

Gabriel gave the slightest nod and walked out on the porch. As he started down the steps, Heartwood called out, "Got something you want to talk over?"

Without turning around, he shook his head, made a fluttering movement with one hand, then crossed the darkened street and got in his car. Heartwood, closing the door, saw again the quick darting in the streetlight. Nightbirds here then not here, almost too swift and dark for the eye to catch, winged incarnations of all things obscure, uncertain, unknowable.

Sunday, April 25th

BAREFOOT, IN HIS PAJAMAS, GABRIEL PADDED DOWN the hall licking the dryness from his lips and holding his head as if it were a crystal vase. His house was quiet, and he was grateful; a loud noise could very well shatter his skull. He had never been a world-class drinker, but suffering this fragility because he'd downed two bourbons and a couple of sherrys seemed indicative of middle-age decline. Of course, he'd also put in a fourteen-hour day and covered almost two hundred miles driving from Sacramento to San Joaquin, San Joaquin to Placerville, and then back to Sacramento.

It was bright in the kitchen, too bright for his liking. The white cabinets and countertops blazed like ski slopes. He made coffee, then went into the family room to do his exercises. His back was feeling better, but he was cautious, practicing *Koryo* as slowly as those old Chinese he'd seen doing t'ai chi in TV documentaries. Pivot left, right back stance, double knife—hand block. It might be a good idea to do these forms every morning; such a discipline might help him keep himself in check. Last night, drawing his gun, he'd felt taken over; some force had overwhelmed his brain like a commando team seizing a presidential palace. Double sidekick, block, spinning back fist. Block, straight kick. All these people coming into this state and all the wrong kind. Blue-eyed bitch. Easy now, easy. Got to stay in control today. Pivot right, left back stance, double knife—hand block.

He returned to the kitchen when he was finished. Adrienne was on a counter stool in her maroon robe, sipping coffee and surfing through the Sunday *Bee*. Her hair shone blue-black in the light and he kissed the top of her head, filled a coffee mug, and sat beside her.

"Dumpling soup or something all-American this morning? Pancakes?"

"Soup," he said, and opened the sports page. The coffee and the exercises eased the delicate feeling in his head, the pain behind his eyes. He caught up on the NBA playoffs.

"Y'know, if there is reincarnation, I'd like to come back as a basketball player."

"Thought you'd want to be a jazz musician."

"That's in this life. Maybe after I retire. The Joe Blow Quartet, featuring Gabriel Chin on guitar. Next life, basketball."

"You're too short," she said, looking at the magazine section.

"There's five-nine pros," he said. "There's even one who's five-three. Anyhow, if I got reincarnated, I wouldn't be five-nine. I'd have to duck to get through doorways."

"When did you ever play basketball that you want to come back as one?"

"Chinese school."

"All you did was break the hoop."

"*Hoydoy.* The slider on the back deck was unlocked last night. Anybody could've walked right in here. Next thing, you'll start leaving milk and cookies so the burglars or rapists can have a snack."

She closed the magazine, slapped it against the counter, and went to the freezer for the dumpling soup.

"Sorry," he said. "I was just trying to keep it light."

"We're in the suburbs. In a *gated* community in the *suburbs,*" she said, sliding the soup into the microwave.

And the gate isn't guarded by Marines but by guys who ought to be in old people's homes, he thought. They can't keep the malignancy out.

"I'm asking you not to be mad at me."

"No need to. I'm not mad. I'm just being distant."

"I called. Said I would be late last night." He cleared his throat, fighting back a strange impulse to confess his white lie. Well, kind of off-white, cream maybe. "Can I change my order to pancakes?"

She turned around and leaned against the counter with her arms crossed. "Today, no. Next Friday is the last day of Eleanor's spring vacation. I've changed our reservations. We are going Thursday night. We will spend Friday and Saturday at Disneyland and come home Sunday morning. If you can't make it because you're hot on the trail of the evil Joker, she and I are going. Leland has volunteered to give up the last weekend of his spring vacation to help with the driving."

"I don't want you going without me. The way things are. All

kinds of people out there. Last night, I saw a carload of Okies toss a full beer can out the window and hit a Vietnamese girl in the head. Right downtown, in front of God and everybody. Knocked her down, blood all over her face."

"My God, she wasn't . . . "

"No. Looked worse than it was. An ambulance took her to the emergency room."

Adrienne looked at him with a kind of alertness.

"When were you downtown? Thought you were at the crime lab. At D.L.E."

"After we wrapped up," he explained, recovering instantly from the slip. "Phil and me went downtown for a couple of drinks. We were walking to the car when we saw this happen. Right in the head. Those rednecks wouldn't have had the guts to do that to blacks or Hispanics, but they figure Asians are passive and polite, that we don't fight back."

"Are you just discovering bigotry, Gabriel?" she asked. "That kind of thing's been going on here for about a hundred and fifty years. Doesn't mean we've got to live like prisoners. Doesn't mean I've got to look over my shoulder to go to Disneyland."

"I won't argue about it. I'll go. Promise."

"Do you absolutely, solemnly swear?"

He nodded and raised his hand.

She opened the microwave, returned the thawed soup to the freezer, and took out mix and milk and began to whip pancake batter with a wooden spoon.

"Talking about a hundred and fifty years ago, I've been reading that old college book of yours. *Paper Sons into Native Sons*. A history of the Chinese in California."

"Oh, that. I haven't seen that since Sac State."

"It says that paper sons were these peasant Chinese who weren't allowed to come over to the States because of some act of Congress. The Exclusion Act. They couldn't come over unless they could prove they were the sons of Chinese born in this country. Rich guys mostly. Businessmen. So these peasants got falsified birth certificates, paid a fee to the rich guys, who'd become their fathers on paper. Kind of adopted them."

"You didn't know about that?"

"The Exclusion Act, yeah. I remember hearing my dad and grandfather talk about that. But this paper son thing, that'd mean there's a whole bunch of Chinese in this country descended from illegal immigrants. Chinese who don't have the names their ancestors were born with. I wonder if I'm . . . "

Adrienne shrugged. "No way to know at this point. And what difference would it make now?"

"None, I guess. Just seems like it would if my real name isn't Chin. You know, if I'm really a Yuen or a Lee or a Jeong."

"I'm a Jeong. So that would be okay. If you were a Jeong."

"Damn right," he said, and rising, came up behind her and embraced her waist. Memories of other mornings rushed past his inner eye, too quickly for him to grasp anything more than fleeting images torn loose from their places in the ordered pages of time. It was like flipping through a family photo album assembled without any regard to chronology: a picture of Leland eating breakfast in this house in his wrestling sweater, another of him as a clowning eight-year-old, entering the kitchen of their apartment in San Diego dressed as a ghost in a bed sheet; a snapshot of Adrienne making coffee as a young bride, another of her last winter, looking through this kitchen's window at a tule fog that shrouded the neighborhood. And these swift glimpses of the near and remote past filled him with happiness. I'm happy, right here in this Sunday morning kitchen with this woman, he thought, and kissed her neck.

"This is affection?" she asked, craning her head to brush his throat with her lips.

"Little bit of lust, too. I changed to pancakes so I could watch that gorgeous ass of yours shimmy when you mix the batter."

"You are so retro, Gabriel," she said but without rebuke, and pressing her hips against him, she made a slow, sinuous movement that would never have been shown on the Christian Broadcasting Network.

"That was to inspire you to hurry back."

"From where?"

"You're working today."

"I didn't tell you."

"Eighteen years did."

"Going to Oakland. Late again tonight and I might have to stay overnight. I'll call."

"I envy you."

She flipped the pancakes, the batter crackling.

"For going to *Oakland*?"

“Christ, no. The way you love your work, the way it obsesses you. Me? Five days a week, eight hours a day, I look for gingivitis, cavities, plaque. Did you know that dentists have one of the highest suicide rates? I can understand why. Mouths. Wide ones, narrow ones, straight teeth, crooked, white, yellow, tobacco-stained, crowned, capped. Eight hours a day.”

“Well, you’re not a dentist. You’re a hygienist.”

“Honey, don’t worry. I don’t have a window ledge picked out.”

She handed him a plate with three large pancakes. He watched the pad of butter slip and melt atop the stack, the syrup trickle down the sides.

“When are you leaving?”

“About an hour. Heartwood’s picking me up.”

He began to eat. That remark about high suicide rates had been a way of getting his attention. Her work was a job and nothing more; it wasn’t her life, as his work was his. He would have to curb his obsessions; a marriage, like any other living thing, needed sustenance, and more than he was giving.

Passing through the doors of City Hall and between two ionic columns, Joyce came to the edge of the staircase, paused to reconnoiter the steep steps, then started down, one hand on the copper handrail, the other on her cane. Little jets of pain burned up her leg—nothing crippling or agonizing, just sharp enough to make her sympathetic toward the disabled people who kept lobbying for ramps and kneeling buses and other conveniences to help them through a world built for the healthy and the whole. Just sharp enough to bring a flash of irritation at the optimism that had moved the city’s founders to design such a huge, heroic structure, with a staircase that belonged on some monumental edifice in Washington. “So now I have met mayor!” Sokhim said when they came to the car.

Joyce got in and cinched her seat belt tightly. Sokhim’s driving did not inspire confidence.

She backed out with a jerk, pulled into traffic with a cheerful obliviousness to the cars and delivery vans circling around Sutter Square, then turned down Pacific Avenue and headed south, toward the Buddhist temple for a meeting with its leader, the Mahtera.

“Mayor did not seem happy with our plans.”

“He’s worried about security.”

“The W.A.R. people?”

"Who knows."

Yesterday, after she'd come home from her pistol practice, Joyce found a long message on the answering machine: a woman named Alice McFadden, executive director of the Concord House, which was some kind of nonprofit church group that worked with Asian immigrants in San Joaquin. McFadden was organizing a memorial service for the massacre victims. It would be held at the city's Buddhist temple. She would love it if Joyce and Sokhim helped enlist support from the mayor and priests and pastors. "We want this to be ecumenical!" The woman's fervor came through even on the machine. "We want every race and religion to be there."

Alex, still smarting from their conversation in the car, smarting like a rejected suitor, was against it. Those do-gooders had their nerve, asking this of her and Sokhim.

"I can't really say no," Joyce replied. "How could I say no?"

"Because they're using you, that's why. They figure that no one will say no to you."

And no one did. Hers and Sokhim's efforts had been successful beyond expectations. They'd enlisted two Catholic and three Protestant churches, as well as San Joaquin's small Jewish temple and the AME Zion church. The mayor had agreed to provide police protection and bleachers from the municipal auditorium to accommodate the overflow; yet Joyce felt only a letdown on this glowing afternoon. Maybe things had gone too smoothly. She'd anticipated reluctance from the pastors and the rabbi, resistance from the mayor. She'd in fact *wanted* it, had girded for battle, fantasizing herself as a warrior who would cross swords with the powers of bigotry and timidity and emerge triumphant through force of will and the righteousness of her cause. Instead she'd encountered an outpouring of goodwill and compassion. The mayor even agreed to meet with them on Sunday.

The walls had crumbled without a shot; in truth, the walls didn't exist except in her imagination, and the sense of anticlimax dropped on her like a shroud, darkening the fits of depression that had begun to plague her.

The oddest things triggered it. Last night, browsing through *Time* before she went to bed, she came across a story in the science section about the apocalypse that was to come in 1.2 billion years, when the sun was going to expand into a red giant and boil all the seas on earth to steam and incinerate everything on land. As it cooled and diminished into a black dwarf star, all that steam would condense into a mantle of ice four hundred miles thick. She'd fallen asleep while reading, woke up around three in the morning, the hour of despair, and—she couldn't describe the sensation precisely, but it was as if she'd been propelled into another temporal dimension. She seemed to see things from God's point of view; the life of Methuselah winked before her more briefly than a firefly; the planet she now lived upon was one moment green with life, the next an ice-coated cinder, spinning pointlessly around a dead, dark star.

She obsessed on this bleak image, couldn't get it out of her head, and went down to the kitchen to warm some milk. She drank it enveloped in a sense of gloom and mourning she'd known in her junior year in high school, after her father's life was ended by the accidental discharge of his beloved Winchester over-and-under, the gun he'd taught her to shoot. Then she would think to herself, "What's the use of getting up to go to school? Of worrying about who'll take me to the prom? Of learning quadratic equations? We're all just marching to the grave." And in her kitchen early this morning, she perceived that the entire human race and the whole damned solar system were proceeding to the same end. *What's the point? What's the point of any of us doing anything?*

Alex came down in his robe. What was the matter? What was she doing up at such an hour? She resented the intrusion, resented the mere sight of his face, so long of bone and expression, and those big somber eyes, and his thinning, silvering hair. What was wrong? Come back to bed, honey . . .

She showed him the article and told him what was wrong, and he looked at her as if she were mad, which was not to be discounted.

"Don't you see?" she asked. "Even if the human race survived another billion years, everything it accomplished . . . It's like all of this is one big pointless joke."

He laughed nervously, and though she could see how comical she must seem—a grown woman driven into depression by an event more than a billion years in the future—she did not feel comical.

"I've got a feeling you're going to tell me that what I need is a baby. That I need a child to care for, aren't you? That all I need is a good fuck and to get pregnant."

She was normally fastidious of speech, so the vulgarity struck him like a slap and at least made his grin vanish.

"No, Joyce, I wasn't going to say anything like that," he remarked tiredly, and walked out. As the door shut behind him, she had a sudden feeling that her head was going to separate itself from her neck, that her arms were about to fall off, that she was already a shattered mirror still in its frame and the frame about to break.

Pacific Avenue dipped under a viaduct, then rose again to pass by the derelict John Deere works. A huge banner ran along the top floor: THIS BUILDING FOR SALE. Ahead, railroad crossing lights winked in warning and a gate dropped. The question was in her mind again. *What's the point? So we have a memorial service for the kids, so what?* A slow Union Pacific freight rumbled by, the great yellow engine pulling half a mile of ore cars.

She turned to Sokhim.

"How old was Prith when you and Pandra were escaping?"

"One year and three months."

She tried to form a picture of this flight: the man and the woman with an infant strapped to her back, walking through nighttime jungles. Piled corpses, pyramids of skulls, and always the dread that the Khmer Rouge would appear around the next twist in the trail. Had that all been pointless?

"And your daughter was born here?"

"No, no. In Thailand refugee camp, was two years when we came here. Liem was born here. Salt Lake City, when we live with my uncle."

Dih-dih-dih-dadum, dih-dih-dadum, the ore cars rolled on hardly faster than a walk.

"After you got out of Cambodia . . . did you ever think that you didn't want to have any more children?"

"I have two more. Of course I want them."

"Why?"

Her hand rose to her hair, upswept and fastened with a glittering barrette, and she turned toward Joyce with a puzzled frown.

"*Why?* I am wife. Married woman. You marry, you have children."

"You mean the natural thing?"

"Everything does something. Seed falls from the tree in the forest, another tree grows."

The last car clattered by. Sokhim punched the gas, then hit the brake, then punched the gas again.

"Sorry, Joyce. Still learning."

"The question I was asking. Maybe I didn't ask it right. After the things you saw in Cambodia, did you ever think it would be wrong, a mistake to have another child? That if you brought another child into the world, it would be just one more human being to suffer for no reason. Did you ever think that?"

"We are supposed to suffer. Buddha teaches that. Life is a sea of sorrows. You are asking me funny questions, Joyce. I don't know how to make an answer. I never think about such questions."

"Maybe that's the answer."

Heartwood read pleasure and relief on Mace's face as he looked down from the dock at the scrubbed cockpit deck, at the roller-reefed jib wound tightly as a window shade, the bowlines flemished off on the foredeck.

"And I promise you, she's as bristol inside as out," he said, a hand on Mace's shoulder.

"Bristol?"

"Trim, squared away, everything in its place, clean. No messes on the *Keewaydin.*"

Mace gazed away from the marina and out toward the bay, white-capped and speckled with sails, the city climbing the hills southward in great blocks and rectangles dominated by the spired cone of the TransAmerica Building.

"I'd gotten as much as I needed from her. You didn't ruin the interview. Don't feel embarrassed. That pigsty was about to drive me and Gabriel nuts," Heartwood said, and knew it was the wrong thing to say when Mace turned toward him, his eye icing over.

"Is that what you think, Dr. Heartwood? That I acted nuts?"

"No! Not at all. Did you bring sneakers like I asked?"

"In my car."

"They won't do any good there."

As Mace walked away, toward the parking lot, Heartwood climbed aboard. Gabriel followed him, clinging to a piling and grimacing as he swung his leg over the lifeline.

"Back still bothering you?"

"Yeah. Those seats in your car . . . " He examined the cockpit, the teak decks, the tiller and mahogany cabin door mirror-bright under their coats of varnish. "Pretty nice, Professor. What did you make of Mr. Weathers's temper tantrum?"

Whistling tunelessly, Heartwood took the padlock off the door.

"I think we learned that the guy can be rattled."

Mace wanted to count the planks in the dock, but there were too many. He counted instead the pilings between Heartwood's boat and the end of the dock, and there were twenty-two. His age. Did that signify anything? He took his sneakers from the trunk and started back, irritated by the chime and clatter of halyards against wooden and metal masts, the snapping of flags in the fierce wind.

Nuts. He hadn't gone nuts, though he might have if he'd stayed in Karen Boggs's apartment another ten seconds. It was the basement apartment in an old frame duplex on the fringes of a Hispanic neighborhood. Inside, it looked as if it had been ransacked by crack addicts desperate for cash. The disorder, the dimness, and Karen herself, sitting in blue jeans with one leg thrown over the arm of a lumpy chair, chain-smoking, the ashtray mounded with lipstick-smeared butts, had made him short of breath. An old black-and-white movie was on the television, with the sound off. She kept glancing at it while she answered Heartwood's questions, gowning herself as the modern heroine—a struggling single mother. She could've gone on welfare but didn't, she'd worked and went to night school to improve herself, and with three kids and a schedule like that, she needed to *par-tee* sometimes, and okay, sometimes the *part-ee-ing* went on too long but who were those goddamn neighbors to call the cops on her for child neglect? When Heartwood asked about the time Duane had intruded on her and her third husband, and about the time, after Duane's father's death, that she'd spent the insurance money meant for him on a new car, her glare sparked like a welder's torch. *Are you accusing me of something? All right, sure Angel and me were—y'know. What the hell, we were married, and I tried to defend Duane against that animal, got hit in the face for it, and he never showed no gratitude for that. None of that is any of your goddamned business anyway. Duane was bad to the bone, that boy hated me from the day he was born, and you wanna know the truth, I came to hate him, but don't you go blamin' me for the way he turned out. . . .*

You did it, you made what he did inevitable, you whore! Mace shouted in his mind; then a fear loomed in him that he was going to shout it aloud.

Oh, I can tell what you're thinking. What kinda woman is this? I mean . . . she musta been a Monster Mom. Witchbitch is what Duane called me, and Jacob?—to him I was Megabitch. Isn't that just sweet? That new car you were talkin' about? Those two got together and smashed the windshield with a lead pipe! A brand new Honda Civic! When Duane was ten, a ten-year-old child, he made a spear out of a stick he found somewheres . . . think we were livin' in Modesto then and I was workin' a night shift at Butterball, guttin' turkeys. . . . Cops caught him threatening littler children with the spear, makin' them give him money! A ten-year-old extortionist!

Mace was standing, his back against a brown wall, because he wouldn't sit on her furniture. The fabric had to be a breeding ground. His foot tapped the carpet, stained with a hundred stains—rusty rings, drink stains, stains that looked like inkblots, and, he imagined, the stains of cheap sex.

Celestial   Telestial
Terrestial   Terrestial
Telestial   Celestial

The old ritual didn't work, failed to bring him ease and calm. He was sure that he was going to do something terrible any second. Shout into her booze-bloated face, slap her into wisdom and make her see that she'd mothered a feral child.

Now what was I supposed to do with a son like that? I mean . . . all those social workers, those cops, and those drug rehab people couldn't do a thing with him, so what could one woman do who was guttin' turkeys for a livin' and going to school to improve herself? Let me ask you something, Doctor. . . . I raised Sara Jane, and she was a fine child and she's a fine woman now, married to a good man with a good job, a qualified electrician, and if she turned out all right, how can anybody say that I had a damn thing to do with Duane being what he was?

She stopped and stared at Mace, her face like a lump of risen dough with two slits for eyes and two holes for nostrils, her dyed hair a reddish brown snake's nest. Yet he could see that she'd been good-looking once, ten-thousand cigarettes and ten-thousand drinks ago. A woman of devastated beauty.

Why are you standing like that, moving your head around? You're making me uncomfortable. Sit down. Relax. I won't bite. She grinned, showing diseased gums; they'd been scraped, giving her teeth the elongated look of skull's teeth. Maybe you'd like something to drink to help you loosen up. No? Well, I'm gonna have one and I never drink alone. . . .

She rose, and as he watched her pass through the filmed light slanting through one of the ground-level windows, he saw another woman turning her back in another dingy room in another time. The image possessed in its faintness the quality of a fragment recalled from a dream, but he knew it was the memory of a moment that had happened in real time. He knew, now, that that woman had been uncommonly beautiful (was her beauty ruined, as this woman's was?) because he'd seen her in the pictures that had arrived in the mail in February, along with Riley's other things. Vague as the memory was, it seized him powerfully, and that other woman, no less than the mute figures flickering on the TV screen, was with him in Karen's living room. He could almost smell her, hear her breathing, even as he heard the clink of ice cubes falling into glasses in the kitchen; he saw her back turning on him, her figure receding down some long, half-lit hall, and feelings of fear and desolation rushed into him, as if he were being abandoned in a wilderness. Those were not remembered emotions, but the very emotions themselves, reaching out across the chasm of time to clutch him with a cruelty and a power the years had not diminished. Then Karen returned carrying four glasses and an iced vodka bottle on a tray.

So let's all have a drink and relax so I can talk about this shit, it isn't easy for me, y'know. She poured a shot into each glass, then, sipping from hers, brought one to Mace. He shook his head, pleading his Mormon faith. *Oh, c'mon, I've known a few Mormons to take a drink. The lurch of Saturday night saints. Ha!* She poked his shoulder. *Oh, man, aren't you built like the old brick outhouse . . .* and took another sip, her puffy eyes looking up at him over the rim of her glass with a barfly's repulsive coquettishness, and he shouted into her face, "I don't want a fucking drink, you fucking slut!" and knocked the glass from her hand. Then he bolted outside, where he gulped the sooty Oakland air like someone who'd been tear-gassed.

"All set?"

He nodded to Heartwood, sat on the dock, and changed into the sneakers. Heartwood started the engine and tossed him a couple of ropes.

"Stern and spring lines, Mace. Bend 'em around a piling and then get aboard."

Why was he going on this stupid sail? All right, he'd lost control, embarrassed and humiliated himself, but no real harm had been done. He had nothing to fear from Heartwood, and less than nothing from that detective, a real "dese and dose" kind of guy. He'd learned what he'd set out to learn: the psychological autopsy was that and nothing more.

"Go up forward, Mace, and cast off the bowline."

He moved cautiously alongside the cabin and knelt on the foredeck and uncleated the line. He'd gone this far. Might as well see the thing through. Maybe he really would write a thesis on the subject. He tossed the line on the dock. The boat bumped forward, causing him to stumble, but he caught his balance and went astern. Heartwood stood by the tiller: a somewhat comical figure with his sparse, windblown curls dancing on his otherwise bald skull. Looking at him, Mace felt a strange letdown, as when he'd played chess with opponents he'd thought his equals and then discovered that he'd overestimated them. He still took care to win, but the challenge was gone, the edge off.

They motored out of the harbor into open water, the boat hobbyhorsing on the wake of a big cruiser. The sky directly overhead was pristine, and only faint, feathery clouds had gathered southward, over the city. It really was a beautiful city, all whites and pastels on the hills. Maybe he'd move to San Francisco after he graduated, rent an apartment on one of those hills, and watch the great ships of the world, like the one now steaming under the Golden Gate, sail in and out of the bay.

In fifteen minutes, they were more than a mile out. Sitting alongside Mace on the high side, Gabriel watched with mild apprehension the *Keewaydin*'s lee rail vanish under a silvery stream of rushing water. He cringed as the sloop seemed to spit froth from her bow and fling it over foredeck and cabin into the cockpit and his face.

"Oh, she's got a bone in her teeth now!" Heartwood cried out, standing at the tiller, balancing himself on the canted deck, his sight fixed on some point on the eastern shore, where gritty Oakland clustered beneath the hills. "Bet you never buried the lee rail on that brown-water stinkpot over in Vietnam, Gabriel!"

"You did and she'd be on the bottom."

"Were you in Vietnam too?" Mace asked.

Gabriel licked the salt spray from his lips.

"Yeah. The Navy. Your father was there, wasn't he?"

Do they know something? They couldn't.

"My father?"

"He'd be the right age."

"He's forty-five, but he wasn't in Vietnam. Where did you get the idea he was in Vietnam?"

"Lee told me. I thought Lee told me." He looked up at Heartwood. They had worked out their routines during the drive from Sacramento. "Hey, Lee, didn't you say that Mace's father was in Vietnam?"

"Nope. Must have him mixed up with someone else."

They don't know. It was just an innocent question, like Sam Kim's.

"My father was doing mission work in Central America after he got out of high school. Turning Catholics into Mormons. Lucky for him. My father's such a . . . He wouldn't have lasted long over there."

Looking at Mace's profile, Gabriel could not read his expressions and gauge his honesty. He had to judge from his voice, and the contempt in his last comment sounded genuine. If he was telling the truth, then who was the paratrooper in the photograph and why was it kept hidden in the trunk?

Close-hauled, they ploughed across the bay for another twenty minutes. Angel Island, pale green speckled with dark green, passed on their port side, and Gabriel pictured his ancestor incarcerated there for a month, then transported to the mainland to be stoned by a white mob. A paper son, journeying to the New World under another man's name? Another sheet of spray swept into his and Mace's faces, and then another. Mace lowered his head and lifted his patch to wipe the saltwater that had trickled into it.

"I'll come about in a second, give us a little easier ride. Ever sailed before?" Heartwood asked Mace, who replied that he hadn't.

"Give you a lesson. You handle the jib. Do it right, I'll let you take the helm. Okay, when you hear me say 'hard alee,' take the starboard jib sheet—that's that rope there on the right side, behind you—let it go quickly off the winch, then bend the port sheet around that opposite winch clockwise and trim the jib—I mean pull on the rope till I say to stop."

Mace mimicked a salute, and the gentle mockery in the gesture bothered Gabriel; it suggested that he had a sense of humor, which suggested further that he was a human being, and Gabriel did not want him to be.

"Ready about . . . hard alee!"

A ratcheting noise as the sheet wound off the winch, and a sensation of being caught in a whirlpool as the sloop turned smartly into wind, the lee rail rising. Gabriel was nearly pitched to the port side by the sudden change of direction, the lurch of the boat as she righted.

Mace moved agilely, for so big a guy in such a confined space, and the jib flew outward, snapping in the wind.

"Too far!" Heartwood called out. "Luffing! Bring it in about halfway . . . Here, you'll need this"—he reached down, picked up what looked like a big socket wrench—"I'll tail for you . . . "

Mace paid no attention, and with one powerful haul, pulled the jib in, his back flaring to the breadth of a card table; then he cleated the sheet and sat down again. Heartwood stood looking at him for a moment.

"Pretty impressive. In a wind like this, most people would've needed the winch handle."

"I can bench three-eighty," Mace said matter-of-factly.

"Take the helm?"

"Got to do something first. Hope you guys are ready. This isn't pretty."

He removed the wet patch, and, no, his mutilated eye wasn't pretty. It transfigured him completely, but he didn't turn away to conceal the disfigurement; he paused to look at each of them, almost as if daring them to react.

Then he put on a pair of mirrored sunglasses, and Gabriel was much more interested in those than in the scars they masked. A small fact.

He and Heartwood exchanged glances as Mace positioned himself alongside the tiller.

"Keep her on this heading. Pick a point on the horizon and steer for it. Don't manhandle the tiller, a little push or pull in either direction will do it."

"*Keewaydin.* What kind of name is that?"

"Indian. Ojibwa. It's the Ojibwa name for a northwest wind. Comes from the 'Song of Hiawatha.' First big boat I ever sailed on was called the *Keewaydin.* Forty-four-footer one of my parents' neighbors owned. He taught me to sail. By the time I was fifteen, I was crewing for him in the Mackinac race on Lake Michigan. Loved it. If I was sailing, I didn't have to go with my father on his fishing trips. I didn't get along with my old man, either."

"Why was that? . . . What the hell?"

The sloop, seemingly of its own volition, had suddenly turned toward the wind, and Mace didn't know what to do. Heartwood reached over, shoving the tiller steadily to bring the boat back on course.

"Lifter," he said. "A strong gust that points your boat to windward. She's got a weather helm anyway, she'll point up with the least excuse. To answer your question, my father was a big-time outdoorsman, never happier than when he was shooting or hooking something, and I wasn't and he never forgave me for that. I suppose that's how it is with your father and your not going on mission work?"

"I never said that. I never said that my father didn't forgive me."

"I didn't, either. I was just asking."

Mace tossed a glance at Heartwood, and his entire face became as opaque as the sunglasses.

"Practicing your psychotherapy on me?"

"Oh, hell no! I gave up private practice years ago, but old habits die hard." Heartwood rose to a half-crouch and spied under the jib for oncoming vessels. Off in the distance, racing boats were rounding a mark for a downwind leg. "You haven't told me if you can go to Idaho to interview Duane's sister."

"You didn't tell me when you're planning to go."

"Day after tomorrow. It would take a couple of days. After her, there's only Duane's half-brother, but we haven't been able to track him down."

Heartwood left it at that for the time being.

"I've got a good idea how you do these things, Dr. Heartwood. I'd better start writing the paper."

"Good enough. Fall off a little."

"Fall off?"

"Fall off the wind. Go that way. Port. Left to you lubbers. That's it. I'll let out the sails some . . . okay, now we'll let her run, a nice easy run home."

The sloop's glistening bowsprit rose and dipped and she left a straight, white wake on the green seas running toward the horizon, split by the vast spans of the Golden Gate. Heartwood settled back. He reveled in the salt-seasoned wind, so refreshing after the pollen-laden airs of the Central Valley, and in the feel of the *Keewaydin* beneath him, her hull vibrating with life. But he wasn't here to enjoy a sail, no, he was here to play a couple of roles: psychological confidence man, swindling Mace into revealing secrets of his personality; a provocateur who would use the stolen goods to prod him into making an incriminating move. Neither part—impostor or provocateur—came naturally, and the fraudulence of this exercise, to say nothing of its potential dangers, continued to trouble him. Yet he wasn't troubled enough to put a stop to it.

"Y'know, Mace, you said something when I interviewed you that's been going through my mind ever since. I don't know why, but I can't seem to get it out of my head."

Now what? "What did I say?"

"That you were wondering if any good would come out of what Duane had done. It baffles me why you would wonder that."

"Wouldn't anybody wonder that? Or want something good to come out of it? Like what you're doing. This report is supposed to do some good."

"That's what the attorney general is feeding the public. It's really bullshit. There must be thousands and thousands of guys like Duane out there, ticking away, waiting for their time, and no way to stop them when they're ready to go off."

Mace asked, almost with a playfulness, "Still looking for insights, Dr. Heartwood?"

"Why not?"

He wants insights, give him insights. "It's for sure Duane couldn't have been stopped. Not in a thousand years."

"Go on."

"All you've got to do is read the stories. If you *decided* to turn somebody into a mass murderer, you'd give him a life like Duane's. And then look at how he got away with everything. He was actually declared a danger to himself and others and nothing was done about it. Nothing, not a damned thing!" An intensity had come into his voice. "It's like it was inevitable, almost like it was *meant* to happen. Doesn't it seem that way to you?"

"I don't know about the workings of fate, Mace."

"You've never felt that something's already happened, like in another dimension, and that all it takes for it to happen in this dimension is for us to catch up with it?"

"No. So if it was all inevitable, what good do you think could come out of it? Oh, we've had the ritual hand-wringing editorials, the politicians calling for tighter gun-control laws, stiffer prison sentences, more careful monitoring of people with records like Duane. The usual boilerplate that comes after a horrific crime. Is that what you meant?"

Mace threw his head back and laughed. There was something stiff and mechanical about the movement, and the laugh sounded artificial. The more Gabriel thought about it, the more everything about him seemed artificial, the one exception having been his outburst in Karen's ratty apartment. That had been authentic.

"I said something funny?" Heartwood asked, feigning an injured tone.

"No. I'm sorry. I know that I'm only an undergrad, but I hope you don't think I'm stupid."

"Not at all. Maybe I'm stupid. Because I can't figure out what you meant."

Rather than a swindler, Heartwood now felt like a cat-burglar, tip-toeing into Mace's mind without, he hoped, setting off any alarms. I want to steal as many of his perceptions as I can and make them my own. I want to see the world as he sees it.

"I wonder if you'd get it. No one else does."

There were notes of grievance and arrogance in Mace's voice: the bright but misunderstood undergraduate.

"Try me."

Mace sat on a vinyl cushion, cradling the tiller under his arm, and asked if he were familiar with the Tao. Heartwood shook his head, casting a quick, wary glance astern and slightly to starboard. The fleet of racers, sped by their brilliant spinnakers, was bearing down on them.

"The Tao says there is a constant flux between harmony and disharmony, chaos and order. A flux and an interaction. Can't have one without the other. Light, dark, pain, pleasure. What Duane did was an act of disharmony. Everything that's going on in this country is disharmonious. What happened to me. This, *this*," he said, jabbing angrily at his hidden eye. "This happened out of nowhere, for no damned reason. Did you read that clipping I gave you?"

"Sure," Heartwood replied, but he was distracted by the fleet, spread out over a front of a hundred yards, and really cracking on, much faster than he'd calculated. Distracted by the conversation, he'd allowed Mace to come up somewhat into the wind, causing their course to veer at a diagonal across the racers' course.

"Fall off," he ordered. Perhaps he could outrun them, keeping a safe gap between them and the *Keewaydin*.

"That's the disharmony I'm talking about, the chaos. But if people become awake to it, if they could see it, then a new harmony can rise out of the disharmony, order from chaos. Do you get it, Dr. Heartwood? Get it?"

"*Fall off*, I said." Heartwood shoved the tiller and looked warily astern. The sloop was on a line closer to the right edge of the fleet than to its center. The spinnakers had doubled in size in less than a minute: huge, striped triangles, taut as drumskins in the wind, now blowing hard enough to make the rigging hum. There was no question of coming up and attempting to cut across the fleet's bows on a close reach, nor of tacking: he'd tack right up into them.

"Maybe I didn't make myself clear," Mace continued, oblivious to the cause of Heartwood's concern. "Things like what Duane did, all these things, maybe they're meant to happen. They have to happen."

As often happens at sea, a crisis developed quickly. What was cause for concern fifteen seconds ago was now cause for alarm. The *Keewaydin* was too slow, the distance narrowing rapidly. That armada of swift boats, sleek and sharp as daggers, would be on them in no time, the chances of a collision too great to risk remaining on the present course. Already, foredeckmen on the lead vessels were waving angrily, telling the *Keewaydin* to give right of way.

A jibe, Heartwood thought. We'll have to jibe.

"I'll take the helm," he said calmly, to avoid panicking anyone.

"I'm doing okay," said Mace, totally absorbed in himself and his philosophy. "Did you understand what I'm getting at?"

"Give me the goddamned helm!" Heartwood bellowed, and snatched the tiller from Mace with one hand while the other sheeted in the main.

"We're going to jibe! Get the jib! Quickly now!"

Only then did Mace see the danger. He lunged for the jib sheet and uncleated it as Heartwood brought the boat hard off the wind, hollering, "Jibe-O! Watch the boom! Duck!"

There came a clatter and banging of rigging, a loud slam as the boom swung across the cockpit like a huge metal arm and sent a shudder through hull and mast. Gabriel tumbled from one side to the other, his curses muffled by the jib, flapping like some immense, maddened ghost.

"Sheet that jib home!" Heartwood yelled, then heard a faint yell come back at him. Fifteen yards off . . . now twenty . . . now twenty-five . . . Mace was flailing in the water. A blue-hulled racer passed within five yards of him; another, spotting his upraised, waving arms late, corrected its course and veered at the last second, but a third was coming straight for him. His legs rose briefly out of the blue-green chop and he dove out of sight.

"Jesus Christ! Gabriel! Life preserver! That compartment right by you!"

Heartwood hauled in the jib and tacked up as quickly as he

could. What a tenth-rate piece of seamanship that had been, and a man overboard, their prime suspect overboard. Good thing the jib—the sloop's power sail—had not been sheeted home; if it had been, they would've shot away at six knots.

The fleet had gone past, trailing sparkling wakes. Mace reappeared, his blond head looking not much larger than a lobster pot. Dragged by the weight of his clothes, he looked as though he were struggling against the current. Gabriel hadn't gotten the life preserver. He seemed as indifferent as the sea itself as he watched Mace thrashing.

"Get the thing! Now, you son of a bitch!"

Gabriel wouldn't have thought this was in him—the capacity to stand idly by and allow a man, even a man he thought guilty as the devil, to be swept away in a tide. Then, without making a conscious decision, he opened the compartment, pulled out the life preserver, and hopped on the gunwale, ready to throw. This Heartwood was a good sailor all right, he thought, as the boat came trimly alongside Mace and within a few yards of him. Gabriel tossed the bright orange ring, watching the safety line uncoil. Heartwood simultaneously uncleated the mainsheet, and bringing the sloop into the teeth of the wind, hove to. Mace swam to the preserver, his arms bashing the seas, his sunglasses gone, his ropy, purple scars resembling some sucking sea creature that had fastened itself to his eye.

A little more than two hours later, at the time of evening when San Francisco looked its most magical, its electric constellations beginning to gleam along the ecliptic of its bay, Heartwood was in his kitchen, preparing dinner. He'd calmed himself after the near-disaster, but it had been too close a thing. If you're going to sail, then pay attention and sail; otherwise stay ashore.

The impromptu swim had made Mace moody. He'd been subdued on the sail back to the marina, as anyone would have been after being knocked by a boom into a body of water reputed to be a vast shark pen. Later, in his car (Gabriel drove the Porsche to the apartment while Heartwood accompanied Mace in the Camaro), he turned alternately sullen and caustic. Traffic had been diverted because the San Francisco Marathon was being run, this year to benefit AIDS research, and looking at the panting runners, Mace laughed acidly, muttering something about the plague being yet another sign—of what he didn't say. Sullenness changed to envy when he entered Heartwood's Pacific Heights apartment and stared admiringly out the front window, the city falling away in a cascade of brick, stone, and trees toward the waterfront, the bay, and the bridge beyond. He murmured, a shade resentfully, that it must be nice to live in a place with such a view, and asked if the 'quake had done much damage to the neighborhood. No, Heartwood answered, not much, nowhere near as much as to the neighborhoods below, though it had knocked him out of bed, dropped pictures and mirrors, and broke the very window Mace was looking through. Living on a fault line gave a certain piquancy to life, gave you a perspective on the impermanency of things. Mace showed a flash of anger. He didn't need fault lines to remind him of how uncertain things could be; all he needed was to look into the mirror. Then he asked if he could shower and use the washer and dryer to clean his sea-soaked shirt and trousers.

Having neither clothes nor bathrobe that came even close to fitting him, Heartwood handed him a bed sheet. He emerged from the shower cloaked in it, and observed that "this must look a little kinky, you know, *San Francisco*, two older guys in an apartment with a naked young guy walking around in a bed sheet." After assuring him that no one was watching, and that no one would care if anyone was, Heartwood concluded that for all of Mace's contempt for his father's faith, some Mormon censor still resided in his head.

Now, looking somewhat mythological in his makeshift toga, he was poking around in the study while Heartwood chopped basil plucked from the herb pots on his back terrace. "Anything in there he shouldn't see?" Gabriel asked quietly. Drinking a beer, he sat at the butcher-block table, performing his assigned task—shredding mozzarella.

"There's my briefcase, but it's locked." Heartwood sampled his Bombay martini and said, "Ambrosia."

"This stuff's sticking to the shredder."

"Don't use so fine a shred. Long, slender strips, that's what the dish calls for. Hope you like Italian."

"I'd rather have sweet and sour soup, shredded beef in a hot pepper sauce, but Italian's okay. You did all right out there, Professor. Guess you are a sailor."

"That never should have happened. Wasn't paying attention."

"You were cracking orders like Captain Bligh."

"Bligh would've hung me from the yardarm for that screwup."

"Well, you've got some balls after all—for a shrink."

Heartwood laughed and scraped the basil into a simmering skillet of butter and crushed plum tomatoes.

"I assume that's your idea of a compliment. Sorry for calling you a son of a bitch."

"That's what I was being at the time. Okay, finished."

He spread his hands like a TV chef over the mound of shredded white cheese.

"We add that in the last minute," said Heartwood, shaking salt and pepper into the sauce. "Okay, start the water . . . pop the garlic bread on warm . . . Ready in half an hour or so."

"Likewise the basketball game," Gabriel said. "I'll watch while you go to work."

He went into the living room to turn on the television. Heartwood entered his study, where he startled Mace in the midst of reading a transcript on his desk.

"Oh! Sorry, Dr. Heartwood, I was . . . "

"It's okay. Nothing super-secret there. Interesting case, isn't it?"

"I just glanced at it."

He'd conducted many informal seminars in this room for postdocs in clinical psychology and criminology, and instinctively fell into a pedagogical tone.

"Case of William Baird, age seventeen, who'd confessed to shooting two people with a high-powered rifle in front of a porno theater in downtown Fresno."

"What happened to him?" Mace tugged at the bed sheet. "I feel stupid in this. My clothes about dry?"

"A few minutes. We'll hear the buzzer." He sat in his favorite chair, of tufted burgundy leather, and faced the wall upon which an ancient photograph of Cesare Lambroso hung surrounded by pictures of human brains, imaged on the MRIs at the San Jose labs. "The Baird case hasn't gone to court yet. That's the transcript of a mental competency hearing I testified at earlier this month. Baird was raised by religious fanatics who beat him silly everytime they found a *Playboy* under his bed or thought he was masturbating in the bathroom. He told the cops that he was going to become the phantom sniper of porno houses so nobody would patronize them anymore. He wasn't a stupid kid, and he wasn't crazy. An artful rationalizer. He'd shot those people out of impulses buried deep in his own subconscious—his rage at his parents for beating him so severely and, at the same time, a paradoxical need to win their approval by starting his own vendetta against the sins of the flesh. But to make the act of murder acceptable to himself, he concocted this high-flown idea that he was eradicating an evil from his neighborhood, that he was doing good."

"Kind of like those anti-abortion nuts who shoot abortion doctors?"

"Kind of," Heartwood answered, thinking, *Kind of like you! You justified mass murder in your own eyes with some muddled, sophomoric philosophy, while underneath, way underneath, other forces moved you.* "Kind of like Duane, too, I suppose."

"Duane!" Mace scoffed. "I don't think that idiot could have had any such idea in his head."

"He might have thought he was striking a blow for white guys like him. There are a lot of pissed-off white boys out there, and he might have thought they'd remember him when he was gone."

"He only wanted his name in the papers."

"Another insight?"

"It's yours. You told me that's your theory."

"I don't believe I did."

His chin, lips, and nose illuminated by the desk lamp, his patch, obscured in the dimness beyond the flute of lamplight, resembling the eyesocket of a skull, Mace cricked his neck to the right and left. Three times each side.

"Must've read it, then. This is a really interesting room." His arm rose slowly and, enfolded in the sheet, cast a sepulchral shadow on the wall. He made a sweeping gesture that took in Heartwood's diplomas, FBI certificates, and awards, the black lacquer bookcases crammed with psychiatry and pathology texts, the glass case that contained murder weapons ranging from a semiauto pistol to a German hunting dagger, and an original edition of Lambroso's first monographs, published by the University of Turin. "There must be a thousand books here."

"Seven hundred and ninety-six." Heartwood rose, and to muffle the sounds of Gabriel's basketball game, switched on his CD player, turning the volume low. Faint as a distant choir, monks began chanting the *Agnus Dei*. "You'll notice that they're grouped by topic and subgrouped alphabetically by author." He offered a coy smile. "So you aren't the only one with a blessed rage for order."

"*Blessed* rage?"

"Wallace Stevens. A poet you probably haven't heard of."

Agnus Dei, qui tolis peccata mundi . . .

"It just so happens that I have," Mace replied indignantly.

. . . misericordi nobis . . .

"Apologies. I take a dim view of what passes for education these days. 'Oh blessed rage for order, Juan Fernandez. . . .'"

"Look, I . . . "

"Mace, why are you so touchy? See that?" He pointed at one of the MRI images. "That's a picture of the brain of an OCD sufferer. We did an experiment on her at the labs where I consult. As soon as we put a dirty towel in her hands, her brain lit up like a freeway at sundown. It's as much neurological as pyschological. It's not a character defect." He sat down again and lifted his martini glass to watch the play of light through the gin. Enough of psychiatric swindling. It was now time to change roles, time to cross the line. "By the way, you didn't read anywhere that I think a desire for fame was one of Duane's motives. I haven't said anything to the press."

Agnus Dei, qui tolis peccata mundi, misericordi nobis . . .

Mace sat down and glanced at a desk photograph of David. "Your kid?"

Heartwood nodded. "The other one's my girlfriend. An astronomer. But to stay on the subject—you guessed about fame and you guessed right. Not hard to figure out, except that Duane wanted a particular kind of fame, a lasting fame, which is why he committed such a heinous crime. Ring true to you?"

"Maybe. You keep forgetting, I hardly knew the guy," replied Mace, his voice falling into its default mode, a monotone.

"Of course. Only bouncing ideas off you. But I'm almost positive that Duane had it in his head to get his name right up there with Charlie Manson. He failed, though, didn't he? Here we are, only nine days afterward, and do you see a word about it in the papers, hear a word on TV? Nope. He got knocked out of the running by Waco. Now, even that's off the air. What you hear is what you hear in the living room. Basketball games. Or talk shows. Or game shows. Sitcoms. Idiocy. I'd bet that if you polled every adult in this state, most couldn't even remember Duane's name."

Mace showed a sudden agitation. He began to pluck the pens and pencils from their holders, turning the pencils point-side up, the pens on their caps. "You should keep fountain pens like this. Otherwise they'll clog up. . . . My girlfriend's father . . . the other night, he was talking about the massacre and he kept calling Boggs 'Biggs.'"

"There's my point. Nobody calls Manson Janson or Hanson, do they? *Manson.* Now there's a killer with a kind of immortality."

Agnus Dei, qui tolis peccata mundi, dona nobis pacem . . .

"And yet, and yet, if the Manson family did today what they did twenty years ago, I wonder if it would have the impact. Doubtful. It would get, oh, absorbed. Like firing a bullet into a hot-air balloon filled with Jell-O. You were right, Mace, in what you said. That everyone's numb these days."

He'd begun to rearrange the objects on the desk, moving David's picture to form a V with Diana's, lining up the letter opener alongside the address book.

"Let's take another of Duane's probable motives—terrorize society," Heartwood pressed on. "That's where I think all that 'Hezbollah' stuff came from. Duane saw himself as a terrorist. His need was to inflict on society the pain and suffering he believed society had inflicted on him, and how better to do that than by killing kids? Children are to be loved and nurtured and protected, children are society's hopes for the future."

Mace straightened the stack of three books beside the lamp.

"So what Duane did was far worse than Manson. Manson scared hell out of everybody. But did Duane? Did he really terrorize society? Has it suffered, is it suffering now?"

"Basketball games, talk shows," Mace murmured, and aligned the phone with the answering machine.

"Exactly. Duane failed in life, he failed in death. He's forgotten already and the revenge he sought lasted maybe a week. The threshold of pain is too high now."

Mace's hands moved randomly about the desk, seeking something out of place to put in place; finding none, he popped out of the chair as if in response to some alarm.

"I'd better get in some dry clothes," he said. "Do you have an iron?"

"Sure. Don't take too long. Fettucine scuie-scuie needs to be served piping hot."

They ate from trays arranged in front of the TV. Mace, in creased shirt and trousers, picked at his food. Gabriel asked if he'd played basketball. The postgame analysis was just wrapping up.

"No. Soccer. Played soccer in high school. I had a partial scholarship to B.Y.U., another reason my old man got so fried that I left there."

The news came on, but Gabriel continued talking in a chatty tone, to make it appear that the TV was on only for background noise. Soccer was catching on in this country, he said. World Cup would be played here next year. . . . On the TV, shells burst amid the ruins of Sarajevo, then a handsome face appeared in front of UN headquarters in New York . . . commercial break . . . Heartwood professed disappointment with Mace's appetite, or didn't he like pasta? . . . The anchorwoman again, then . . .

"Locally, there's been a dramatic new development in the investigation into the motives of the killer who murdered fourteen schoolchildren near Placerville. For details, we turn to Drummond Aikers, of our Sacramento affiliate. Aikers filed this exclusive report only hours ago."

Gabriel gestured for silence. He'd known Aikers for several years, had used him before for calculated leaks, as Aikers had used him for unsourced exclusives. This time, though, Aikers had no idea that he was being used, nor what for. He stood on K Street, with the Justice Department building behind him.

"WCJV has learned that state investigators are now certain that the killer, who committed suicide immediately after the crime, did not act alone. Earlier speculations that he was ordered to commit the murders by a white supremacist group have been ruled out, but evidence gathered at the scene now shows that Boggs had an accomplice. Justice Department officials have refused to comment, but sources close to the investigation have told me that they have a suspect in mind . . . not yet in custody . . . whereabouts unknown . . . no further details . . . "

"Shit!" Gabriel switched off the TV with what he hoped was a believable show of surprise and outrage. "By tomorrow morning, this'll be in all the papers, all over the state, maybe the country. He'll take off for Mexico, who the hell knows where. Shit!"

He kicked a hassock, Heartwood signaling him with his eyebrows to watch the overacting. Mace looked perplexed, but betrayed no emotion as he twirled strands of fettucine around his fork.

"I'd best call Youngblood and see if I can track down the leak."

"Phone's in my study. When you're done, we'll need to work out damage control," Heartwood said, playing the calm and wise counselor. "We'll need denials. I'll call Ruggerio, ask her to go on record that the story's inaccurate. There is no suspect."

Gabriel went into the study and shut the door.

Heartwood, refilling his wine glass, sat silently for a few moments. He was disturbed by Mace's nonchalance. He'd expected that the mere disclosure of a suspected accomplice would provoke a reaction. Sweat, anxious gestures, an apprehensive look. There was nothing. The guy was so disengaged. Either he wasn't guilty, or he wasn't guilty-*minded*, was even colder and more controlled than Gabriel and he had thought: not a criminal who believes that he's covered his tracks too well to be caught, but who believes that he hasn't done anything wrong. A guy with a freak conscience, or none at all.

"Well, Mace, as you see, we've got a problem."

"I'm getting the idea that I've been hearing things I wasn't supposed to hear," he remarked whimsically, and chomped into a piece of garlic bread. That was the only change Heartwood observed—his appetite had improved.

"You and two or three million other people. It'll be thirty million by tomorrow."

"I know you can't tell me, but *do* you have a suspect? I'm a little confused."

"Of course. Why do you think we're trying to find the leak?"

"And you don't know where the guy is?"

"If we did, he'd be in custody. Mace, I hope you appreciate that you've been privileged to come along with us so far. You've learned some things that are confidential and I'm trusting you to respect that confidentiality. I can trust you on that?"

A vigorous nod.

"Our suspect's disappeared, not as a result of our suspicions. He went into hiding earlier. His dropping out of sight, along with a few other things, was what led us to suspect him in the first place."

Heartwood stopped there. If Mace remembered the stories in his scrapbook, he would realize who they were talking about.

"How did he help Duane? Help him plan it, or what?"

Heartwood didn't answer right away, pretending to be distracted.

"Excuse me. I was just thinking of what I'm going to say to the attorney general. What did you ask?"

"The accomplice, did he help plan the thing?"

"Probably. What we're more sure of is that the other guy helped him carry it out. That he was right there."

"You actually know that?"

"Yes. That's all I can say. I'm proceeding with the autopsy, but Gabriel and the detective he's working with are handling the criminal investigation. Comes to that, I'm kind of like you, along for the ride. I'd better get these plates."

"Let me," Mace offered.

"Dishwasher's on the fritz."

"Then I'll be it, Dr. Heartwood." He gathered up the plates and silverware and went calmly into the kitchen.

He had good manners anyhow.

Gabriel cracked the study door and gestured. Heartwood went in, softly closing the door behind him.

"Talked to Phil. Prints don't match," he whispered. "If he was in there, he must've worn gloves."

"Right out of the movies. *Damnit.* So all we've got to put him in that room is a thread? What about the phone numbers?"

"*Nada.* Friends, relatives. One on the scrap of paper was for a currency exchange and photo ID place in downtown San Joaquin. The Washington one—Mender Foundation? Out of service."

"Then all of this—a waste of time . . . ?"

Gabriel shook his head.

"No, it's not. We'll talk later. Better call Ruggerio."

Gabriel returned to the living room, where he stood by the window, taking in the view of the sparkling city and the Golden Gate, lit up as if for a festival. He would have loved to have placed Mace in the motel beyond all doubt; at the very least it would have been a fine weapon in an interrogation. And a good district attorney could have made something out of that small fact in court. Why were you there on the same night as Duane? Why did you register under an assumed name? Okay. No print match. All the more reason to play this hand out. If Mace made one of the moves Gabriel expected, then they would know, would have something on him; if not, okay, they'd have to try another tactic.

"Man, wouldn't you kill for a place like this?"

Gabriel turned around. Mace was drying his hands on a dishtowel.

"Nope, how about you?"

"You could get laid every night. Twice a night in this town. All the faggots, the women have got to be desperate."

There was something totally false in this attempt at locker-room banter. He's talking like this because I'm a cop and wants to prove what a man's man he is. Asshole.

"Sit down a sec, I want to ask you a couple of questions."

Mace dropped into an easy chair angled to the small fireplace.

Remaining on his feet, Gabriel turned his eyes into little onyx stones just for the practice.

"Did Duane ever talk to you about his friends, his relatives?"

"He didn't have any friends. The only relative he talked about was his mother. He hated her."

"I've got different interests than Lee. I don't give a damn about that potty-training stuff."

Mace looked off into the middle distance.

"I think he might have mentioned his brother once or twice. Something about them getting together to . . . what was it? They did something together, something they got in trouble for . . . "

Probing, thought Gabriel. Trying to find out if Tipton is our suspect.

"Shooting an assault rifle in a national forest?"

"No . . . I read that. That happened after he quit the cannery, didn't it? So he wouldn't have mentioned it to me."

Got his chronology down pat. Won't be easy to trip up, Gabriel thought.

"Maybe you're thinking about the time the two of 'em vandalized their mother's car."

"Could be."

"Never heard him mentioned after that?"

"No."

Gabriel paused, allowing himself time to make a few rapid guesses and judgments. The small fact of Tipton's late-night visit to the Camino Real, with some amendments, was critical to the fiction he and Heartwood were weaving. It would work even if Mace knew they'd seen each other, but it would work better if he didn't. The revelation would come as more of a shock.

"You're sure about that?" he asked.

"Never heard him mention his brother again. I wouldn't even know his name if I hadn't seen it in the papers."

He focused on the ruined face like an air-traffic controller on a radar screen. His reading was that Mace was telling the truth.

"Ever see Duane with anyone else? He was a loner type of guy, so if he was with anybody, that'd be unusual, right?"

Again the gaze off into the middle distance. Gabriel didn't know chess, yet he sensed in Mace a chess player's shrewd concentration. How should I answer this question? How much of the truth should I tell? Or should I lie and how much? What will benefit me the most?

"I think I do. Yeah, I do remember now. It was in a bar, where most of the guys from the cannery went after work. I was in there one night, and Duane was with a guy. He called me over, asked me to have a beer with them."

"Did you?"

"Hell, no. Work with that guy, the last thing you'd want to do is drink with him."

"What did the guy look like?"

"Long hair. Like a hippie. Like somebody out of the sixties. Maybe skinny."

Gabriel stepped across the room and opened his briefcase as Heartwood came out of the study and sat down opposite Mace.

"Eileen is damned unhappy, but she'll hold a press conference tomorrow. Issue a categorical denial."

"Good," said Gabriel, striding back across the room with a folder. He opened it, revealing an eight-by-ten blow-up of Tipton's mug shot, his name blacked out. "Look like the same guy?"

"May I?" Mace asked, extending a hand.

"Sure."

He took the photo and turned it this way and that.

"I'd say so. Yes."

"How sure? Sure enough that you'd testify in court it's the same guy?"

"Testify?"

"Would you testify?"

He nodded. "I take it that he's your suspect?"

"A thin young man with long hair was seen entering and leaving Duane's motel room approximately a week before the massacre. We've got information from other sources that he came up with a handgun, a nine-millimeter Ruger. He probably dropped it off with Duane for safekeeping."

He let that sit for moment. Weathers didn't move, didn't blink.

"All right, you may have to testify. We're trying to build a conspiracy case and that's tough. One way we do it is to show previous associations between two conspirators, previous crimes they . . . Nevermind. We try to build links in a chain. You testify that you saw this guy with Boggs last summer, that could be a help."

"Can I ask who that is?"

As he took the photo back, Gabriel looked sidelong at Heartwood, who said, "He says we can trust him, and if it comes to him testifying, well . . . "

"Nope. Sorry. This damned case has been badly compromised already, can't risk it. Soon as our boy hears that broadcast, he's going to bury himself so deep we'll need a quarry crane to dig him out." Immersed in his role, to the point that he almost believed it himself, Gabriel leaned on the arms of the chair and practically rubbed noses with Mace. "But I'm warning you, Weathers, I pick up a paper tomorrow or the next day and I read a description of this guy, I'll know where it came from and you'll find your college-boy ass in the defendant's chair because I'll charge you with obstruction of justice. That clear?"

"It is, Detective Chin."

"Agent. Agent Chin."

"It's Duane's brother, right? That's pretty obvious."

"Jacob Tipton."

"That's who it is?"

"No, that's Duane's brother's name," Gabriel replied sharply. "Told you, we can't say. All I can tell you is that we've got physical evidence another guy was at the scene. Know anything about chaos theory?"

"Excuse me?"

"Chaos theory."

"It has something to do with mathematics. Probablities and predictabilities."

"We use it in blood-spatter analysis. Nowadays, we can look at the blood spatters at a crime scene, and using plain old high school trigonometry, we can determine how a victim was killed, what sort of weapon was used, and where the assailant was," Gabriel said with authority.

"But . . . the news stories . . . the witnesses never saw anyone else."

"Because they couldn't see him when he opened fire. He was in the woods. He'd picked up his empty shells, but the blood spatters and the ballistics told us where he was. Number two, we're ninety-nine percent sure that assailant helped Duane kill himself. An assisted suicide. What do you think of that, Weathers?"

He said nothing, lifted a hand to make a gesture, lowered it to his lap.

"See, when a semiauto is used in a suicide, it does what we call stovepiping. The empty cartridge jams in the ejection mechanism. Duane's Taurus wasn't stovepiped, which told us that in all likelihood someone else had his hand wrapped around Duane's and made sure he squeezed the trigger and didn't miss. Pretty interesting."

"Yes."

"The theory we're working on is that Duane probably got this idea on his own and started to plan the crime," Heartwood said. He was now reveling in the theatrics, drawing a certain creative satisfaction from them. Perhaps Mace had drawn a similar satisfaction as he molded Duane's clay. Crime could be creative, after all. "But somewhere along the line, he got just smart enough to figure out that he wasn't smart enough to pull it off on his own. For one thing, he needed someone to signal him when the bus was coming. At all events, he called someone in for help at some point. Someone brighter than he was. The guy probably took over from there."

"This guy paid another visit to Duane," said Gabriel. "The owner of the Camino Real saw him entering and leaving Duane's room late on the night before the massacre. Thursday night."

"Really?"

"Really." Gabriel turned to Mace with his most humorless grin. "You're now the man who knows more than he should, even if you don't think it's much. You hadn't been here when that broadcast came on, you hadn't ID'd this picture, you'd be as ignorant as everybody else. Anyhow, thanks, Weathers."

He held out his hand. Standing, Mace took it in a crushing grip. Don't want this guy to get a hold of you.

"Glad I was of some help. Maybe I could . . . If I can help you out any more . . . I don't know how . . . help you some way to find him, I'd be glad to do that, too."

"Possibly, Mace," said Heartwood. "You possibly could help us. We'll see. Stay in touch. Meantime, Gabriel and I have our damage control to work on and you've got a long drive home."

He took Mace's elbow and maneuvered him toward the door, but then felt a resistance.

"I was thinking. The thesis. I could really make something out of it if I could . . . I know it's a lot to ask . . . if you could tell me when you've found him, and say I went along. . . ."

"On the *arrest*? Mace, *I* won't be there when that happens. Police work. I'm sure I'll interview him afterward. Get at his psychopathology. Maybe you could accompany me on that. Stay in touch."

Thursday, April 29th

A SHADOW PLAY.

His shadow, sitting on the shadow of the couch; her shadow standing, the shadows of her hands vanishing as her hands vanished beneath her hair, and her arms as they bent to lift her hair drawing ellipses' curves on the wall, and the shadow of her hair rising like smoke.

"So I'm forgiven?" he asked.

"Forgiven."

He did not see her hair fall, only the smoky plume on the wall, falling beside the shadows of the candles and their flames.

"Then let's play our game."

"It's your game," Celia said, a pout in her voice.

"I did what you wanted, now you do what I want. Our game."

"Please. Say please."

"You have something to be forgiven for. Taking off on me like that. Stranding me."

"You hit me."

"I didn't mean to. I asked to be forgiven for doing what I didn't mean to. Now you have to ask to be forgiven for doing what you meant to do."

"Will you forgive me?"

"No. Game. Forgiveness is in the game."

"Please."

"All right. *Please*."

A shadow play. Her shadow, flowing across the wall to eclipse the shadows of the candles and their flames. The shadows of her legs, bending before him in genuflection.

"Where are we?"

"In a hot, steamy Asian country."

He watched the shadows of her moving lips. Her profile on the wall looked like the black construction-paper cutout of the whore's profile. It had been among Riley's meager things. A shadow-drawing, Riley had written on the back, made on his honeymoon in Hawaii. Riley had gone there on R & R and she met him and they got married.

"And who are you?"

"I'm an Asian prostitute."

"Whore."

"Whore," she said.

"Where are we?"

"We're in my house on a hot night. It's lit by oil lamps. Lizards cling to the walls."

"Like the game?"

"Sometimes."

"Is this one of those times?"

"You did what I wanted, I'm doing what you want. We forgive. Don't do that other thing this time. Don't hurt me."

"Now you say 'please.'"

Inside a delivery van from American Beauty Florists, Gabriel sat and yawned. Surveillance was an activity he generally found only a little more interesting than waiting for a bus.

"How long now?" he asked.

"Two hours, five minutes," answered Youngblood. "Man, wish I was that age again. Last all night."

Gabriel looked across the rain-puddled parking lot, awash in a yellow glare, to Mace's car, then raised his eyes to the third-floor apartment. A faint and flickering glow showed through the curtained window.

"I don't know if they're screwing up there or holding a goddamned séance."

"Whatever, this guy isn't behaving like a worried man." Youngblood gripped the steering wheel and leaned back, working the kinks out of his muscles.

"He's not like the impulsive idiots we're used to dealing with. But I'd put it in the bank that he's convinced that dumb-ass Duane called Tipton in for a helping hand. He's convinced himself that he can't just sit back and hope Duane didn't tell his half-brother that

Weathers planned the whole damn thing, gave him the money to buy the Taurus."

"Three hundred sixty bucks. A lot for a college kid to give away."

"Weathers's steroid sideline, that's where it came from."

"Sure or bet?"

"More sure than bet," said Gabriel, because he'd been called on Tuesday by the chief of campus police, who told him they'd questioned Weathers's partner and housemate, Pickett Greene, a premed student with a part-time job at a sports medicine clinic in San Joaquin. Greene eventually admitted that he obtained the steroids by writing false prescriptions on the clinic's stationery and filling them at pharmacies all over the city. Weathers was in charge of sales and marketing. Pretty good at it—he'd expanded the business off-campus to two private weight-lifting gyms and a high school. Greene confessed because he was unhappy with his colleague, who hadn't paid him his share of their fifty-fifty split for three months. The campus police were ready to go ahead, but, the chief said, he thought he'd better check first. Gabriel thanked him profusely; a wider investigation was in fact under way. It would be jeopardized if the university were to move against Weathers now. Could its investigation be suspended for two or three weeks? The chief agreed.

"And it's more sure than bet that Weathers has been looking at his chess board the last three days, working out his moves."

"That's about all. The logs aren't exciting reading," Youngblood said, referring to the reports filed by the agents who'd followed Weathers on Monday and Tuesday. "Goes to class, goes to the gym, goes home, goes to the library, goes to the post office, goes to the rehab center, now he's getting laid. Y'know, I'm getting too old to work my sick days and off hours, and my wife is real unhappy."

The rain had stopped an hour ago, but the tree they were parked beneath continued to drip maddeningly on the van's roof.

"Patience. The phone calls."

"Yeah, those."

Weathers had been observed entering a pay phone near the rehab center at 5:07 P.M. on Tuesday. Twenty minutes later, Wilson Tipton, as he'd been instructed to do if he got any unusual calls, contacted Gabriel, telling him that he'd just got off the phone with someone claiming to be a solicitor for a credit card company. He asked to speak to Jacob. When Tipton answered that he wasn't home, the solicitor said that Jacob qualified for his company's card, and where and when could he get in touch with the fortunate young man? Knowing that no credit card company would consider his son an acceptable risk, Tipton answered that he had no idea where Jacob was.

Gabriel had flown to L.A. first thing Monday morning to enlist the Tiptons. Obviously, that ought to have been done first, but there hadn't been time. Persuading Jacob, who'd returned home from Troll-land, to act as bait hadn't been easy. He refused unless Gabriel got the prostitution and a misdemeanor drug charge against him dropped. This Gabriel did, though it required several hours' haggling with the Hollywood police and district attorney's office.

There had been no calls to the Tipton house after Tuesday's, but Heartwood had reported in from the wilds of Idaho yesterday. Mace had contacted him on his cellular phone, eagerly—but not too eagerly—inquiring about the progress of the manhunt. Heartwood replied that it was still going on; certainly he would be kept abreast of developments.

"Put it in the bank," Gabriel said to Youngblood. "He's asking himself, can I get to Tipton before the cops do, but if the cops can't find him, how can I? Should I let the cops find him for me, figure out some way to silence him before he can talk to them? And if that doesn't work out, he's wondering what he'll do, what he'll say if he gets called in. . . . Jesus, do I have to take a leak."

He slipped out and ducked behind the tree, relieving himself in the darkness. His watch glowed twelve-twenty. Twenty minutes into Thursday. By late this afternoon, he'd be on his way to the Magic Kingdom.

Mace entered the bathroom, where he removed the filthy condom and flushed it down the toilet. After washing himself in as hot water as he could stand, he returned to the other room, where she lay on the sofa bed, her face in a pillow, her back heaving.

He looked no longer at the shadows. Game over. Play over. Her coppery back heaved in the light of a dozen candles: fat Christmas candles, slender dinner candles, stubby candles bearded with melted wax.

"Baby? Celia?" he said, dressing.

She did not say anything. He finished dressing and sat beside her, stroking her back, her long black hair, the hair like a shadow.

"Baby, I didn't hurt you, did I? I tried not to."

"Get the fuck away from me," she said into the pillow.

"You have beautiful hair."

He lowered his head to kiss the back of her neck, but as soon as his lips touched her, she leapt up and ran into the bathroom and locked the door. He felt a burst of anger, thought of kicking the door down and slapping her. He controlled his temper. He had things to do, important things that must not be jeopardized by losing it over some ignorant middle-class bitch. He knocked softly.

"Celia? Baby?"

"Get the fuck out, Mace!"

"Celia, you're forgiven."

"About time," Gabriel said, sliding down into his seat.

"Surprised the guy can walk."

They watched Mace, clad for anonymity in a plain gray sweatshirt, plain blue baseball cap, jeans, and sneakers, come down the stairs and get into his car. They waited until he pulled out of the lot, saw in which direction he turned, then drove out and followed at a discreet distance.

Twenty minutes later, they were on a two-lane road on the fringes of the suburbs, the Camaro half a mile ahead. To the north, the city slept under a hazy dome of its own lights. Southward, all was in darkness on this cloudy night, save for farmyard lights that shone across the Delta like the lights of ships across a waveless sea. A road sign appeared: an intersection ahead. Hangtown Road. The Camaro's right turn signal blinked.

"He obeys the traffic laws anyway," Youngblood said.

"He might be taking us on this ride because he thinks he's being tailed. Don't turn. Cross the intersection, then make a U. We'll pick him up again."

Passing through the junction, Gabriel looked down Hangtown Road and saw the Camaro's taillights growing smaller. Youngblood made the U-turn, but Weathers's car had vanished.

"The boy must've stomped on it."

"Better catch up," Gabriel said, and as the van surged ahead, switched on the reading light and opened a San Joaquin map.

"There's another intersection about two miles up, Phil. He might've turned there."

"Yeah, but which way?"

The desolate urban outskirts rushed by: a farm field, a warehouse, another field, a billboard promising that affordable homes were coming soon to this site, a pasture strewn with boulders—no, the backs of sleeping sheep—a pole barn. Gabriel's vision was blurred. He would be too exhausted to drive this afternoon; Adrienne and Leland would have to take turns at the wheel, he thought, with an edge of resentment. The trip couldn't come at a worse time; Weathers was finally breaking the routine of the previous three days and nights. He was up to something.

Near the intersection, reflectors glittered like a row of red eyes on a gatepost marking a farm road. Passing it, Gabriel caught a quick, dull gleam of glass or metal: a car was backed into the road.

"There he is! He pulled off. He's parked on that access road back there. Keep going, but slow down."

Gabriel looked into the rearview mirror, waiting to see if the Camaro pulled out. There was no movement.

"Whatever he ducked in there for, it wasn't because he's on to us. Kill the lights, turn around, go about halfway back, pull over."

As Gabriel reached to the floor for the night-vision binoculars, Youngblood hid the van behind a low, block-brick building: RYERSON'S PLUMBING AND ROTO-ROOTER SERVICE said the sign painted on a side wall, IT'S S— TO YOU, BUT BREAD AND BUTTER TO US! Cute, thought Gabriel. There's a slogan that won't make it onto a TV commercial. On the other hand, these days it might.

They got out, into a darkness scented by rain, damp earth, and honeysuckle, and by the acrid stink of chemical fertilizer in an asparagus field between the plumbing shop and a clump of buildings half-hidden by a line of cypress trees.

Squatting behind a fifty-gallon drum, Gabriel raised the binoculars, in whose pale green light he saw that the buildings were a trailer park: two doublewides back to back, like barracks, and four more that had been joined into one and put up on a foundation. He scanned the park, scanned back to Hangtown Road, spotting the gatepost and the Camaro's roof, then back to the park, where someone moved out from under a cypress into the lesser darkness beyond the trees. The figure walked with long, slow, deliberate strides, then turned sharply to the right and continued pacing. Gabriel couldn't see his face, but made out the baseball cap, the breadth of the shoulders. Weathers was carrying something small and square in one hand. He stopped walking.

"Your eyes are better'n mine. What's he doing?" Gabriel whispered, passing the binoculars. He noticed a pinprick of reddish light where Weathers was standing. He was alert now, all senses awakened, though his tiredness had not been overcome, only suppressed. It was lurking under the quickness, waiting to reassert itself.

"Looks like he's writing something, maybe drawing something," Youngblood said. "On a clipboard, I think. Holding something up . . . must be a penlight . . . "

"With a red filter," said Gabriel.

"Busy boy tonight."

"He likes this part of the week, remember? Thursday he gets to sleep in till noon."

"Okay, he's moving again . . . Real slow . . . stretching his legs out . . . looks like he's pacing off distances."

"Let's try and get a little closer. Got a feeling we're looking at Weathers's next target."

"A two-bit trailer park?"

They stalked across the field, trusting in the darkness to conceal their movement. A dog barked from one of the trailers, went silent. They crept on, Gabriel fighting his impatience to get over the open ground quickly. He was excited and troubled at the same time. He had expected Weathers to attempt another crime, especially after Heartwood's subtle manipulations; but he had not expected the attempt to come so soon. He thought Weathers would work overtime to eliminate the threat of being exposed by Tipton. Had he realized the falsehood of the threat? Or was he confident that the secret of his complicity had died with Duane?

The dog barked again, as Gabriel and Youngblood reached the cypress. Both men lay down in the pitchy shadows of the trees, and cringed as they felt the wet grass soaking through their shirts. A man called out from one of the trailers, but Gabriel couldn't make out what he'd said. The dog barked in earnest now: the chest-deep, menacing snarls of an attack dog. He couldn't see Weathers, and was drawing the binoculars from their case when he heard a car start. Headlights swept swiftly across the park, revealing for an instant walls painted in brilliant oranges, yellows, and reds, two weirdly shaped posts or pillars flanking the entrance to the four attached trailers, and men running out of the trailers behind. As a gong rang with an eerie reverberation, the car roared away. Youngblood called out, "Shit! we're gonna lose him!" Gabriel and he leapt up, began running across the yard toward the road, and were stopped cold by the sudden, blinding glare of stadium lights and the sight of a half-naked Asian man with a shaved head, standing behind an enormous rottweiler straining at its leash with bared fangs and ears laid back. Ten or twelve other young men, hair shorn, barefoot and bare-chested, were advancing toward them from the side, clubs in their hands.

One of the men yelled something in a singsong tongue Gabriel couldn't understand.

"It's okay, okay!" he shouted back. "Call the dog off!"

His vision adjusting to the blazing lights, he saw that the pillars were shaped rose and oleander bushes, growing around two miniature temples, each with its curvilinear roof and tiny statue of Buddha.

The men stopped advancing and formed a line like a riot squad, their long clubs at their sides, their naked skulls gleaming, and the rottweiler as black as a panther making a low rumble in its throat like a panther's purr. The handler said something in the lilting language and the dog sat on its haunches, raised its ears, and dropped its lips over its teeth, but its eyes never left Youngblood and Gabriel.

"It's okay, okay," Gabriel said. "Is it okay now? We're going . . ." He leaned forward, taking half a tentative step toward the phalanx of monks.

One of them squinted at him.

"Chin?" he asked in English. "Special Agent Chin?"

His stocky torso was covered by a tattoo: the letters *AK*, an assault rifle forming each leg of the K. The Angkor Killas, one of the more vicious Cambodian street gangs.

"Vann Ong," Gabriel said, recognizing the broad, round face. He'd arrested Ong a year ago on extortion charges, but a sympathetic Superior Court judge had released him on condition that he enter a Buddhist monastery.

"You got it!" Ong said. "The Mahtera's right. The wheel of life takes its turns." Then he turned and spoke in Khmer to his fellow novitiates, whose stony faces broke into laughter as, Gabriel guessed, he informed him that they were looking at the cop who'd arrested him.

"This is some coincidence, Agent Chin. So whatchya doing here at two in the morning?"

"Investigating."

"What?"

"Can't tell you yet."

Youngblood lit a cigarette and inhaled greedily. The rest of the monks crowded around them, a few begging smokes, others making little bows, patting Gabriel on the shoulders, taking his hand.

"They're apologizing for scaring the sh—, for scaring you," Ong said. "Didn't know you're cops. They're okay, they're great, they turned me around, man, and that's no sh—, no lie, I mean. I'm learning self-discipline, I eat nothing but veggies, I do without nothing. No women, no children, no money"—he rubbed the stubble on his head—"no hair. Not no drugs or guns."

"I'm really inspired, Vann. What's with the clubs, the attack dog?"

"Taking care of ourselves," Ong replied, with a look back at the other monks and the rottweiler. "Ever since that school bus thing? We've got phone threats, high school punks driving by throwing rocks, rotten vegetables. That's not just the monks' temple," he said pointing. "It's for all the Buddhists in the area. We're thinking of calling it off. Couple days ago, the Mahtera himself got a call. Some bad shit."

"The who?"

"The Mahtera, Bante Dharmawara, kind of the main monk."

"What bad shit did they say?"

"Cat-eyes eat dog meat and W - A - R eats cats. That's him now."

Ong backed away and, clasping his hands, bowed. The others were doing the same as a short, frail figure with a skull like an ocher egg emerged from one of the trailers. Wrapped in saffron robes, with a red cloak pinned across his shoulders, he seemed almost to float over the ground, commanding the monks with subtle gestures to raise their heads. Then he stood before Gabriel and Youngblood, peering at them through thick glasses. There was no kindly wisdom in that gaze; it was hard and concentrated, and despite the old man's age and stature, he exuded an intimidating presence.

He turned to Ong and asked in English what had happened, and when all was explained, faced Gabriel again.

"My apologies for so much trouble," he said in a powerful voice so disproportionate to his size it seemed to be coming from somewhere else. "Apparently there was an intruder. We must be careful. There are people who wish us great harm on the dark of the moon."

"There are, ah . . . Ong, what do I call him?"

"Bante."

"There are, Bante. You ought to ask for police protection."

He interrupted with an upraised hand that turned to point at the two miniature temples flanking the temple's entrance.

"We have faith in ourselves and in the protection of those guardian spirits. Please excuse us. As we have been awakened only one hour before our morning prayers, we will say them now."

And he swung on his bare heel, his robes swirling, and led the monks away. Gabriel held Ong back by the shoulder.

"What's he mean? The dark of the moon?"

"That's one of our worship days. Next one's a week from Saturday. That's when it was scheduled for, but we don't know now. Maybe not here."

"What the hell are you talking about?"

"You don't read the papers?"

"Sports page."

"Hey, read the news." Ong looked anxiously toward the temple. "Got to go."

Under the bus's harsh interior lights, a tall, wasted black man in a scratched leather jacket slept with his head thrown back and his mouth open like a corpse's. Another man, short-legged, brown and seamed of face, sat near the forward door: a Mexican migrant on his way to some highway junction where a truck would pick him up for a ride to orchards or fields.

Mace sat in the rear, wearing a clean pair of examination gloves. He always carried several pair. Microbes had to be hatching on the bus seats, a new generation every twenty minutes. Incredible. He'd worked out the numbers some time ago. In less than three years, microbe generations equaled all the generations of mankind since the first Australopithecus rose off its knuckles and said, "Look, Ma, no hands!"

He was through with Celia. She was hopeless.

Microbes would win in the end. Numbers were important. A hundred thousand generations in under three years.

Streptococcus A ate you alive.

Legionnaire's disease dropped cruise ship passengers into sickbeds on tropical holidays.

Tuberculosis was rising with renewed power. Invaded these shores from Vietnam. Riley's war hadn't ended, but merely taken on a different form: Mycobacterium tuberculosis, Viet Cong germs, small, silent, and deadly, brought here by a refugee, striking first in Westminster High School, where Mace would have gone if Riley had not gone to prison.

Why had Riley turned his back? Building a new life for myself and you got no place in it.

Poor Riley. His lawyers pled insanity. They claimed that Riley had gone mad, thinking that night on Westminster's streets that he was roaming the jungles, killing 'em all and leaving the sorting out to God.

Riley wasn't crazy; he was a loser, living a loser's life in that cramped, cluttered garage apartment on the wrong side of Riverside. Riley was a loser; that's why he got caught.

Mace pressed the buzzer, the bus pulled to a stop. The frontage road was utterly deserted at this hour, half-lit by the neon of its motels and gas stations and all-night convenience stores, where derelicts stocked up on Mad Dog and Twinkies. He removed his sunglasses and tucked them in the pouch pocket of his sweatshirt. No one knows I'm here, no one will ever know, I move through this wasteland, leaving no tracks, I move through here as do all the faceless inhabitants of this marginal world, anonymously. Yet I am not of it. Only a night traveler, a brief sojourner.

The broken sign burned on the next block. V–LLEY VI–W. Beneath an overpass across the frontage road, a homeless band's campfire guttered. Your next stop, Ben Pickering, unless I save you from it.

Of course the vectors of his life and of Pickering's had crossed for a reason. His mission was becoming clearer now, revealed to him by degrees, like a secret too big to be comprehended all at once. Looking back, it seemed this clarity had begun when he dove to avoid being hit by the racing boat, dove deep into the chill opacity of the bay and felt a piercing in his temples, as when you swallow something cold too quickly. Then, with a couple of strong kicks, he rose into the warmer waters of the surface, into the light.

He'd been chosen to hasten that dread hour when all the snakes in the mud would hatch out, giving birth to the dark, demented gods who would rule the land until the hour of the new harmony was struck. He was an agent of order whose tools were disorder.

No artful rationalizing that, Dr. Leander Heartwood.

There was only this problem of Duane's half-brother. Half-brother to a halfwit. Had to be who they were looking for. Mace had researched the clippings—thank God he'd kept those stories!—and could not see any other conclusion. Too bad there wasn't a photograph of Tipton in the newspapers that he could have matched to the one Chin had shown him. Well, he didn't need a photograph. He was sure that the moron had enlisted his brother. Secretly. Kept it from me. Mace wouldn't have thought him capable of such duplicity. But now the questions were, what does he know, and if he's caught, what will he say? Worst comes to worst, it would be my word against his, but . . . *I don't want to be in that position.* So the next question is, what do I do? Stay frosty, past frosty, find out what I can, move deliberately and cautiously. As he walked, he reminded himself to trust in his destiny. It was like the graffiti and the history of Duane's shotgun. Coincidence that someone had sprayed those messages on the school wall only the night before? That Duane's gun had been stolen in the Klan robbery in Florida, so that, when some people started wondering if Duane had acted alone, their attention was turned toward white supremacists? Why, it was as if those things had happened expressly for Mace's benefit. No, not "as if." Possibly this business with Tipton was more of a blessing than it appeared, for if he knew nothing, then he would be the one to go to prison. The idiots would think they had the case solved. But if he does know? An opportunity would present itself. Just be ready for it when it does.

"It's three-thirty in the fuckin' mornin'," said Pickering, clad only in briefs, his white belly sagging under a sunken chest.

"Light was on."

"Watchin' TV."

Pickering coughed: a deep-down, rib-shaking hack. God, did he have TB?

"I knew you were the night owl type. That's why I'm here now. Your report from county mental health came in yesterday. Thought you'd like to know."

"Good news or bad news?" he asked, an alert look coming into his sallow face.

"Little of both."

"C'mon in."

Mace stepped across the threshold, surprised to find the room neat as a barracks, except for the bed Pickering had been lying in while watching a rented video. On the screen, a woman's throat was being slashed by a madman with a stiletto.

"Wild shit," Pickering said, flopping on the bed and lighting a cigarette. He clicked the TV off, took a swig of a beer. Beside the can was a prescription bottle of Elavil, and under the bottle a rumpled story cut out of the *San Joaquin Dispatch*: CHURCH GROUP URGES SAN JOAQUIN TO MOURN 14 WHO DIED. *Memorial service to be held at Buddhist temple here . . .*

The focus of Pickering's anger and frustrations. On Monday, jumped-up on an overdose of the Elavil county mental health prescribed for him, he came to D.A.C.O., asking about the results of his examination. Though he'd behaved himself, his jittery mannerisms made Susan Sexton uneasy. She'd asked Mace to speak to him. He took Pickering to a corner coffee shop, bought him a piece of pie, and told him the results weren't expected until Wednesday. Only to kill time, he'd asked what Pickering had been up to since last week.

His major activity had been to drive aimlessly around the city for hours, he'd said. Over the weekend, his random travels took him beyond the subdivisions and strip malls and past the temple. He was furious at what he'd seen and heard: bald-headed dudes in what looked like yellow hospital gowns, gooks coming and going, weird gongs and bells. What was a gook church doing here? Were there so many slants in this town that they had their own *church*? he'd asked, and pulled the clipping out of his leather vest pocket. He confessed that he looked up the temple's number in the phone book and called in a threat, just to put a little fear of the real true God into them.

"What did you say?" Mace had asked.

"Cat-eyes eat dog meat . . . y'know, Boggs's tag."

"Nobody knows if Boggs tagged the school."

"It's a good tag anyhow. Eat them cat-eyes."

That was the moment when Mace had stepped back, as it were, and saw the *design* of things. His spine prickled. It was so eerily similar to what had happened with Duane. Pickering had not passed by the temple by accident; he'd been guided there, as Duane, one day in the latter half of March, had been guided to drive past the McKinley School at the moment when it was letting out, at the still more precise moment when a kid crossed the street against the light into the path of his truck. At the screech of his brakes, the kid spun around and dropped a folder. The papers inside fell out and blew over the street. Duane cursed, he gave Duane the finger, and Duane cursed him again; then another boy, older, tough-looking, with gang tattoos on his arms, yelled, "Fuck you, that's my little bro," wadded one of the papers, threw it through the open window of the truck, and ran off, sneering back at Duane, his middle finger raised. Duane was almost crying with rage when he talked to Mace later. Slant-eyes talking to him like that, giving him the bird, throwing stuff at him. Should have run the little gook over. One less. The whole school crawled with them, hardly a white face to be seen, and look at this, Weatherman, they don't even read American. He opened the crumpled bulletin, which announced the field trip in English, Vietnamese, Cambodian, and Lao. *I oughta blow 'em away, blow 'em all away . . .*

Accident? Coincidence? The punk could've thrown any one of a dozen pieces of paper, but picked that one. He could've missed the window, but no, it sailed right inside and bounced off Duane's forehead to land in his lap. Guided.

Mace sat in Pickering's only chair, careful not to touch anything. The place really was tidy: a pair of sneakers and a pair of combat boots side by side by the bed, clothes hung in the alcove that served as a closet, toiletries lined up on the dresser. Pickering could be the best of both worlds—a disgruntled moron with a sense of organization, a little self-discipline. He would not call for help at the last minute.

"How come you're wearin' sunglasses? You doin' some shit yourself or what?" Pickering asked.

"I don't do anything."

"Whatchya lookin' at?"

"You keep a neat room. Most people like you are pigs. I like neatness, Ben. I like it that you're neat."

"You do?"

"Sure."

"Prison," he said proudly. "That slam I was in, it was like the Army. Make your bed, shine your shoes. I was in the Army too."

"Really? You didn't put that down on the questionnaire."

"I don't like to brag about it." He coughed again and shook a capsule from the bottle, twisted it in half, and poured the contents into the beer. "A little up with a little down," he said, raising the can in toast. "Wanna beer? Six-pack in the fridge."

"Get it for me, Ben."

"Get it? You're right next to it. Just reach over and . . ."

Mace stood and moved to the bedside and loomed over Pickering.

"Now I'm not next to it. Listen, it's the middle of the night, I came here especially to let you know right away what the shrink said. To help you out. I'm damned tired. The least you could do is have the manners to get the beer you offered me in the first place."

"Okay, man, okay. Be cool, all right?" He got up and went to the fridge, ripping the pop-top off.

Pickering had potential, but he was going to be difficult, more difficult than Duane.

"There it is. Open and all. What did the shrink say? What's the good news?"

Before answering, Mace got a fresh washcloth from the bathroom and wrapped it around the can.

"Helps keep it cold." He sat down again. "He thinks you'd benefit from the program, that you're not a candidate for the bin. Bad news is, you'll have to follow the program. Acupuncture treatments. Urine test three times a week. N.A. meetings five nights a week."

"With the niggers and what-all."

"Right. Plus . . . the way this program works is that your checks won't be made out to you."

Pickering looked at him.

"They have to be made out to your nearest next of kin."

"What for?"

"This is taxpayers' money. Everyone knows what losers like you would do with the money. Instead of rent and food, it'd go to drugs and booze, so it's paid to your nearest relative, who cashes it and puts you on an allowance. But I don't suppose you have any relatives around here."

"What the fuck!" Pickering cried out. "Nobody told me about this!"

"They'll get around to it the next time you go into the Social Security office. Most of our patients are in your situation, so what they do is find a friendly bar owner or the owner of a package store who's willing to take the checks. Funny, isn't it? Because then the bar owners sell them booze, taking it out of their checks, with a little more taken out for services. It's like owing your soul to the company store. And there our patients are, spending the money on the very thing we're trying to cure them of. That's how I can help you out."

"So how?"

"I've got a friend, a really good guy, an older guy who had some rough times and likes to give guys like you a helping hand. He'll be the recipient of the checks, won't take a dime for himself."

"How do I know that?"

Mace leaned forward. "I just said he's a friend of mine, didn't I? You trust me, you trust him. I like helping guys like you out, too. Why the hell do you think I'm here now? Why the hell do you think I work at the clinic? Because it'll make me a millionaire? Christ, you got any brain cells left?"

"Why you always soundin' pissed off at me?"

"Because you piss me off. I'm giving you a chance to get around a problem, and you throw it in my face. It pisses me off to see guys like you think of ways they can mess themselves up. I saw the psychiatrist's report. You tried to commit suicide after you lost the job in Oregon."

"Wasn't serious . . . " Pickering said, staring blankly at the blank TV, his voice thickening.

"I know you weren't. Otherwise, you'd've used your gun instead of an overdose of downers." Mace moved to the edge of the bed and rested his hand on Pickering's bony shoulder. "I know you weren't serious because you didn't want to die like that, a nobody in some public hospital emergency room, nobody to remember you. No way to go. If you're going to go out, go out big. Make a splash, right?"

"Like that Boggs done."

"That was big, all right." He began to knead Pickering's shoulder. "What you did up there was what everybody in clinical work calls the 'cry for help.' Nobody, not your mother, not your father, not the teachers in school, not the jerks you worked for, ever gave one damn about you. We know the syndrome. And so you do something desperate to tell the world, 'Here I am, Ben Pickering, I'm a human being and I hurt bad inside but nobody gives a damn.'"

His dull eyes still fixed on the screen, Pickering made a quivering movement with his head.

"And even then, I'll bet nobody gave a damn. Did anybody come to the emergency room to see you? Anybody?"

"What the fuck do you think?"

"So you could've died a nobody, with nigger crackheads, spics who'd been knifed. Do you feel like crying, Ben? I get the feeling that you'd like to."

"Nah . . . nah . . . I . . . "

"It's okay to cry in front of me. I'm here to help." His fingers dug deeper into Pickering's spare flesh, working their way around to the back of his neck. "There are a lot of ways I can help. I do give a damn. I take my work seriously. Why else would I be here at four A.M.?"

Pickering twisted away and went into the bathroom without a word. Too proud to shed tears in front of another man, thought

Mace, glancing at the newspaper clipping. Different than Duane, who could break into sobs of self-pity almost on cue.

"What else can you do?" Pickering asked when he came out, his composure regained.

"I can see to it that you get what's coming to you without you having to go to the meetings, the bullshit."

"How're you goin' to do that?"

He opened the minifridge for another beer and fell into a coughing fit. Was it TB? Mace felt a flash of panic.

"Let me handle it. I've done it before."

"So why you botherin'?"

"You expect people not to bother, don't you? But I'm not like other people. And like I told you, I don't like to see white guys mixed in with niggers, getting needles stuck in them by these chink acupuncturists."

"That's what they do? Stick you?"

"And I hate to see that," Mace said with a nod. He hesitated for half a moment, then pulled his sunglasses off and Pickering flinched.

"Yo! Man, what happened . . . "

"A Vietnamese street gang did this to me."

"Man, that is bad. I was wonderin' why you wore that patch. Bad."

Pickering went to the nightstand and lit another cigarette from the pack there. He exhaled, coughing. Mace figured it was the cigarettes. There was no bloody spittle. A dry smoker's cough.

"A Vietnamese gang? Them little gooks and a big dude like you?"

"Do you think I'm lying, Ben? I hate lies."

"No."

"There were eight of them and one had a shotgun, so there wasn't much I could do. The one gook stuck the shotgun in my back, another one hit me across the eye with a club. A club with bent nails in it."

Pickering grimaced and sat down.

"Real brave fuckin' guys," he said, and hacked into his hand.

Mace put the sunglasses on again.

"Enough of that. We're not here to talk about me. About you, Ben. Y'know, that cough you've got, you ought to quit smoking before you even think about quitting anything else."

"It ain't cigarettes."

"Sounds like it to me."

"Smoke annihilation."

"Inhalation."

"That's what I'm sayin'. From when I was in the Army? The Persian Gulf."

That was the second time Pickering claimed to have been in the Army. That these morons had their absurd fantasies was one thing; that they expected someone of his intelligence to believe them another thing altogether.

"Ben, I have to ask you not to lie to me. I don't bullshit, don't like to be bullshitted."

"I ain't."

"I can't help you if you bullshit me. You weren't in the Army."

"No bullshit!" he yelped, with something close to honest resentment. "Remember when them Eye-rakis blew up them oil wells? I was in a special unit that got sent in to put the fires out and I breathed all that shit in. That oil well smoke. Fucked up my lungs."

Mace admired the creativity of the falsehood, but Pickering was asking for it.

"With a record like yours, the Army wouldn't have taken you. Now c'mon, Ben. I'm not some loser on the street you can bullshit."

"A special unit. They drafted guys outta prison because they figured we had nothin' to lose."

Couldn't he read the signs? No, these morons were illiterates when it came to that.

"One last time, or I'm going to hurt you bad for lying."

"Don't get pissed again. I'm just sayin' I got smoke annihilation from them oil . . . "

Mace reached over and backhanded him across the mouth, and watched with cold glee as Pickering cowered against the headboard, covering his lips.

"I'm sorry, Ben. But we've got to play straight with each other. Now tell me, yes or no, were you in the Army in the Persian Gulf?"

Blinking rapidly, he shook his head.

"I'm really disappointed. I thought you might be worth . . . " He half-turned as if to leave, turned back again. "Listen! My best friend from high school was killed in the fucking Persian Gulf!" he said with a low-voiced intensity. "So when somebody bullshits me . . . "

Pickering dropped his hand. His lower lip was swelling, a sliver of blood glistening at the corner of his mouth.

"Was just rappin', man. I didn't know about your buddy."

"Niggers rap, Ben." Mace drew a breath, waited until the calm flowed in like freon: that feeling of being a honed athlete playing in the zone. "All right. Either I walk out and you never see me again and get through things on your own, or you take your pants down, turn over, and take your licks like a man."

Panic struck Pickering's face.

"Hey, wait a minute, I ain't no . . . "

"No what? Faggot? Do you think I'm a faggot?"

He shook his head.

"You'd better not. I know you're not one." He jabbed his thumb under Pickering's collarbone and pinned him to the headboard. "You're a goddamned liar is what you are. A liar and a loser. So what is it? Maybe you'd like another smack in the mouth. Your choice."

Hesitantly, his frightened gaze held by Mace's cold one, he pulled his briefs to his thighs and rolled over. A flat white bottom where only hours ago there had been Celia's curves. Mace stood over him, pulled off his belt, wrapped half of it around his hand, and shook the other half at his side, jingling the buckle. He raised the belt, then something arrested his arm. Duane used to practically beg for it, and suffered his discipline in silence. Pickering was a little different; maybe he didn't need as much discipline—and he might yell and someone would call the cops and that would be disastrous. Besides, Mace had learned what he needed to know. Pickering had rolled right over for him, like a dog that expects a whipping. *I can get him to do things he doesn't want to do, so imagine what's possible with the things he wants to do.*

He laughed sharply and gave Pickering's buttocks a locker-room slap.

"Get up," he said.

Pickering lay rigid, then, turning slowly onto his back, covered himself. Fear, relief, and then gratitude played across his face like light on water as a weak smile fluttered at the corners of his bruised lips.

"Man, you had me fooled."

"Wasn't fooling, Ben. Don't even think of lying to me again."

■ ■ ■

Re: your note of the last week—a complex variable is a mathematical function of a complex quantity of the form x + iy, in which x and y are real variables and i is the imaginary square root of minus 1. Hope that clears things up.

All best, Willow

"Sure as hell does," said Gabriel under his breath as he checked the office mail before beginning the pilgrimage to Anaheim. He was relatively fresh after only three hours' sleep, though he knew he was running on the dregs of the night's adrenaline. As soon as it was exhausted, he would be, too. He opened the next envelope as he walked toward his desk.

Inter-Departmental Memorandum

From: J. R. Higgs, Bureau of Medi-Cal Fraud and Patient Abuse, Criminal Law Division

To: G. A. Chin, Bureau of Organized Crime and Criminal Intelligence, Division of Law Enforcement, Sacramento Field Office

Pursuant to your request of 22 April, this Bureau opened an investigation into allegations of fraud involving Duane Leonard Boggs, enrolled in a drug and alcohol rehabilitation program administered by the U.S. Social Security Administration, San Joaquin office. We have determined that no state employees or state funds are involved in the program, which is funded solely by the federal government; therefore, we have no jurisdiction in the case. We have forwarded your request to the appropriate federal authorities . . .

"Oh, for Christ's sake! Took you a whole goddamned week to figure that out!" Gabriel said aloud, drawing a startled glance from a passing file clerk.

The second paragraph told him which federal authorities to contact, explained how payments in the program worked, with the checks going to a third party. It was otherwise uninformative, except for its last sentence:

Our investigation did disclose that Boggs designated a Riley B. Kincannon, POB 426, 1237 Pacific Street, San Joaquin, CA 94133, as the recipient of his checks. We were unable to find any other address for Kincannon in San Joaquin; however, a CLETS system check of DMV records disclosed a driver's license issued on 4 June 1991 to a Riley B. Kincannon residing at 2345 Vallejo Street, Riverside. This information was forwarded as a courtesy to the above-named federal authorities.

"Kincannon, Kincannon, Kincannon," Gabriel muttered to himself, hurrying toward his cubicle, where he began to rifle through his files on the Boggs case. Had he and Youngblood misread the Gold Hill Motel registration card? Riley Kincannon. R. K. Cannon. He found a Xerox of the card, squinted at it, held it up to the overhead lights, then, with a magnifier, moved toward the back windows, and studied the signature in the natural light. He was looking for an *i* and an *n* after the *K.* No, the two letters weren't there, but he could not ignore the similarity of the names.

Files in hand, he went to his bureau's CLETS terminal, typed in his access code, and drumming fingers impatiently on the monitor, waited for the system to verify his authorization. After it did, he switched to the Department of Motor Vehicles file, then to the vehicle registration and driver's licensing subfiles, and pulled up Kincannon's birthdate and registration and driver's license numbers. Electronic paths led him from there to the Criminal Justice Information system, and on to the criminal history file. "Don't tell me insufficient data," he muttered to the computer as it hummed and clicked. The screen went blank for a shaved second, and he felt something like a low-grade electrical shock travel down his arms when the screen filled with the case history of Riley Barnes Kincannon, born November 19, 1948, male Caucasian, six feet, 220 pounds. The code words and acronyms that followed would look like a foreign language to the layman, but Gabriel could translate them easily enough: Kincannon had been arrested in Westminster in May 1974, charged with two counts of first-degree murder. Charges later reduced to second-degree. Convicted March 1974, sentenced the same month to seventeen years. Then came his long itinerary through the prison system. Receiving at Chino, transferred to San Quentin, ten years there, transferred to Vacaville, and finally to Tehachapi . . . working his way down, as he grew older and behaved himself, from maximum to minimum security. . . . The payoff came at the end: paroled March 9, 1990 . . . no parole violations, no subsequent arrests . . . off parole effective March 10, 1991. . . .

But that might end real soon, Gabriel thought as he printed out the history.

Krimsky's office no longer smelled of stale cigarettes and air freshener. As he sat beneath the lithograph of U.S. Marines charging at fixed bayonets through Korean snows, he chewed a wad of gum that made his cheek bulge like a squirrel's. Two boxes of Trident sugarless gum sat atop a file cabinet.

"What gets me is that there's a warning on those. That the artificial sweetener causes cancer. Can't win!" he grumbled. "All right, Gabriel. So Weathers isn't prime anymore? You want the surveillance to continue?"

"Hell, yes. Did some research. Buddhists worship four times a lunar month. The two eighths of the moon, the full moon, the dark of the moon. Next Saturday, May the eighth, is the dark of the moon. That's when they're going to hold a memorial service for the kids at the Buddhist temple."

"Oh, shit."

"He wasn't sneaking around that temple because he's a Hari Krishna. Kincannon's off parole, free to travel around. A conspiracy of three. The uniform and all. That fits, too. Six feet, two-twenty. Only thing that bothers me is that signature. He wouldn't have used his real name, but as an alias 'R. K. Cannon' is pretty lame for a San Quentin grad. Would've thought he'd use something less obvious."

Krimsky reached for another stick of gum.

"So you need what?"

"First, the case needs to be officially but quietly reopened."

"No problem now."

"Next. Prints. See if Kincannon's match any of the ones we lifted from the motel. Second, somebody should check with the post office where he had a box. Third, whoever we've got keeping tabs on white supremacists should check Kincannon out."

"Back to that?"

"He might've gotten mixed up with the Aryan Brotherhood in prison. Fourth, somebody from the San Diego office could get hold of a trial transcript."

"Case nearly twenty years old, doubt it," said Krimsky, frowning. "We'll try."

"I've worked with the deputy chief in Westminster before. He used to be their Asian gang expert. He's been there forever. Maybe he was around when Kincannon was collared."

A bodiless voice summoned Gabriel to the dispatcher's desk.

"That's Adrienne and the kids," he said, standing. "I'm bound for the Magic Kingdom. There's no way out of it. Hey, did you know that people make careers out of playing Disney characters? You start off as one of those chipmunks, work up to Mickey and Minnie."

Krimsky spat the golfball-size wad into a tissue.

"Thinking of a career change?"

"If those prints match, I'll want a warrant. We'll search his place in Riverside, so I'll want a senior criminalist with me. And back up. If this guy gives me one funny answer, I'm going to pop him. Murder, criminal conspiracy."

"Let's see what more we can get before we start talking busts. This is no different than Weathers. Prints only prove that he happened to be in the same motel at . . . "

"I know. I'll take him in and sweat him."

"What happens to Disneyland?"

"Anaheim's close enough to Riverside."

Neither his gaze nor his attention was on Walt Apetheker; his gaze was outside, on the groves of power transformers and boxy concrete buildings that formed the technological orchards of Silicon Valley, and his attention was a thousand miles away, in the Idaho valley where Sara Jane Pittman lived with her electrician husband. There was a gravity and a depth in that thin, dark-haired young woman that had moved Heartwood. It was as if she'd assumed the burden her mother ought to have borne, drew all the shame and hurt into herself, like those surrogates of medieval legend who assumed another's sins.

Recalling her and the words she'd spoken as their interview drew to a close, he wondered what she would think of what was being said in this conference room in the Imaging Systems labs. Five people were sitting across the table from him and Percy Worsthorne: two doctors from the Centers for Disease Control, and a woman and two men from the Revere Institute, a social policy foundation that doled out large grants for studies of criminal behavior.

All five sets of eyes were on Walt, pointing with tapered finger at a videotaped image of a brain. He didn't look like the medical éminence grise this afternoon but, in his dark Italian wool suit and St. Laurent tie, like the CEO of some high-powered electronics firm. The corporate appearance was not accidental, for the purpose of this meeting was more promotional than scientific: a sales pitch to the assembled ladies and gentlemen that the Imaging Systems lab was doing work most deserving of government and private funds. Walt was, in his indirect and patrician way, asking for cash and lots of it.

... *looking for what one might call the biological plastique that causes certain people to explode in mortal rage* ..., he was saying. *Elementary, my dear Watson, the neurotransmitters did it* ... laughter ... *found that brain wave patterns shift into a chaotic state with certain mental functions ... Is it possible that something like this occurs with the impulse toward violence? Chaos of one kind producing chaos of another kind ... In a phrase, this is a quest for the equation for evil....*

Heartwood's own thoughts journeyed back from Idaho down winding pathways to Mace Weathers. He hadn't spoken to Gabriel since yesterday and wondered, with some trepidation, if they'd set forces in motion they might not be able to control. As his mind traveled, so did his eyes, drifting outside again, first to the buildings with their tinted windows afire in the light of a falling sun, then farther to the Diablo range, which made a blue, craggy horizon miles to the east. His gaze stopped there, but his thoughts jumped the mountains and all the vast distance beyond, flying to the campus in northwestern Connecticut. Yesterday, after he'd returned from Idaho, he found in his mailbox a thick envelope bearing the scroll and cross of the Dunwich School. He opened it fearing the worst and was relieved to discover an engraved invitation to the 1993 commencement exercises. Relief turned to delight when he noticed David's name on the list of graduates, and alongside it the words *cum laude.* A handwritten note from the headmaster was inside: David had submitted his written apology, taken responsibility, and so was off final probation. All he needed to do was behave himself for one more month. Heartwood's mental travels then became temporal, taking him to the campus on May thirtieth. He saw himself posing for a photograph with David and Paula in front of the chapel with its white steeple and clean Puritan lines. They would replicate, for the camera, the family they'd once been. Better than no replica at all.

Dwelling on that image, he only half-heard Walt finish up, and then the buzz of questions and answers.

Walt looked to him and asked if he had anything to add. He hadn't prepared any comments and started to shake his head, but seeing Sara Jane Pittman's face before him, he abruptly changed his mind and stood.

"Just a few cautionary words," he said, looking directly at the three people from the Institute. "Dr. Apetheker mentioned the case

I've been working on at the beginning of this session. I know you came here hoping to discover that we are on the track of some clear, objective answers for problems that so far have defied all other attempts to solve them. All the violence in this country . . . it does seem like a plague, and so we're all turning to science to cure it. Like a Salk vaccine against murder, but maybe we're looking in the wrong place, because in the past couple of weeks I've begun to think that this pestilence can't be found in neurotransmitters or genes or chemical imbalances. It's a pestilence of the spirit. The soul, if you will. And that's not science, that's not progress. Dostoevsky said it, 'the soul is retrograde.' "

He hesitated, surprised by the words pouring out of his own mouth. Actually, they'd been simmering inside him for several days and Sara Jane had somehow brought them to a boil. *I think Duane lost his soul. If you've got a better explanation, I'd sure like to hear it.*

But, he thought, Boggs didn't *lose* his soul. He surrendered it. If he lost anything, it was his conscience. Conscience! That's retrograde, too.

His long pause was making everyone nervous. Walt coughed, Worsthorne was running his fingers through his hair.

"Personally, I don't think there is an equation for evil, not in any sense," he said at last. "Think about what Boggs did and then ask yourselves what could have driven him to it. Too much vasopressin? Too little serotonin? Well, we've demolished a lot of myths, so now we want hard science to make sense of things. But is it possible that the scientific facts we seek are themselves myths, a kind of superstition, pretending to objectively measure what can't be? Or charted? Or graphed? Or imaged on an MRI machine? The horror of what a Boggs or a Gacy or a Manson does mocks any medical or biological facts that try to explain it. You might as well try to describe what happens to people in a plane crash with physics and chemistry—"

"Very well!" Walt interrupted, his pallid face gone red. "Provocative questions, I'm sure, but we cannot allow too many value judgments to—"

"Oh, but we should," Heartwood interrupted in turn.

■ ■ ■

The car was safely hidden in a clump of eucalyptus beside the old levee road Mace had discovered. Hatching insects dimpled the stagnant slough behind it, while, in front of it, across a fallow field two hundred yards wide, the orange and pale yellow trailers were clearly visible behind the sheltering picket of cypress trees. Cars were parked at the side of Hangtown Road, worshipers and robed monks were moving about the temple grounds. Something of a disappointing sight. A Buddhist temple ought not to be a collection of trailers but a structure of exotic grandeur, with swooping roofs, gleaming spires, plaster dragons. Mace leaned back against the oak that shaded him and Pickering, and, sipping his Coke, admired the fairness of the day. The air was so clear this afternoon; everything was becoming so clear.

"Burger King's better'n McDonald's or Wendy's," Pickering said, after gulping a bite from his Double Whopper. A gob of catsup clung to his upper lip. Mace wanted to slap him, hard, backhanded.

"I didn't know you were a connoisseur of fast-food franchises."

"A what?"

"You can tell the difference between Burger King and McDonald's? All the same to me."

"Big difference. Burger King's better."

"Wipe your mouth, Ben."

Pickering used his hand, then licked the catsup off.

"God, you're a pig."

His shoulders drew together and his ragged teeth showed in silent laughter. How he loved to be insulted. It meant that someone recognized his existence.

Mace turned his gaze back toward the colorful trailers. "So that's it. That's what's got you all bent out of shape."

"That's it. How'd you find this road?"

"How'd I find this road. Jesus, what do you think you've got to be to find a road? Christopher Columbus? I was driving along, I saw the road from the highway."

"This is pretty cool, this road running right back of that fuckin' place."

"What's so cool about it?"

Pickering, hunched over, like an animal guarding its food, bit into the Double Whopper again.

"Are you keeping secrets from me, Ben?"

"Nah."

"You aren't planning to do something, are you? Is that why you think this road is so cool? It fits into your secret plans?"

"What plans?"

"The story you clipped from the newspaper. About the memorial service they're going to hold out here next Saturday. Are you thinking about doing something then?"

"If I was, I wouldn't tell you and not nobody else neither."

"Why not?"

"'Cause if you're thinkin' about doin' something, you keep it to yourself and then you just do it."

"I'm taking risks for you. I filled out your paperwork. I took a clean urine sample and submitted it to the lab with your name on it. Come Monday or Tuesday, your first check'll be delivered to my friend and he'll cash it and give the money to me and then I'll turn it over to you. Seems I'm owed some thanks here. Seems that you could tell me your secrets."

"So thanks, all right? I got no secrets."

A breeze had sprung up, ruffling Pickering's dyed hair, and the splinters of sunlight falling through the leaves speckled it with spots almost as white as ermine. Mace struck him just above the ear with the heel of his hand.

"Goddamnit, man!" he yelped, shying away. "I ain't lyin'. I got no secrets. I just cut that thing outta the paper, I . . . I don't know why."

The feral little eyes looked at him without blinking, and Mace sensed that he was telling the truth. Brains like Pickering's didn't make plans, didn't think in terms of ideas, but, like primitives, in murky images and inchoate thoughts. It was his mission to bring those thoughts up out of the subconscious, to give them shape and make the images clear.

"Only making sure, Ben. Only making sure you're not lying to me again."

They sat in silence for a while. The temple grounds were empty, monks and worshipers gathered inside. The sound of a gong rung three times rose toward them on the breeze, and then the screeching of wind instruments, the faint rise and fall of chanting voices: sounds as alien to this landscape as Mormon hymns would be to the rice fields of Asia.

"Listen to that," he said.

"Yeah, fuckin' weird. A gook church. How do the people who live around here stand it, listenin' to that shit?"

"They have to, Ben. There's nothing they can do about it. Or maybe I should say, they *think* there's nothing they can do."

"Chickenshits."

"You know, I listen to that, right now, listening to that, do you know what I see?" Mace asked, working himself into a show of rage that was not, he realized, entirely a show. "I see those eight bastards who did this to me." He jabbed at his eye patch. "For all I know, some of them are in there right now, singing away."

"Yaaah yaah yaaah uuum uuum," Pickering mimicked the chanting.

"The same people who knocked my eye out."

"Yeah, yeah. *Yaaah yaah yaaah uuum uuum."*

"Same people who put you out of work."

"Takin' over. Takin' over everything. *Yaaah yaah yaaah uuum uuum."*

"Yaaah yaah yaaah," Mace chanted.

"Uuum uuum," Pickering responded.

They made a game of it for a few moments, *Yaaah, yaaah . . . Uuum, uuum,* and then Pickering said, "We oughta do somethin' to shut them the fuck up."

"What?"

"Dunno. Shit, if some gooks put out my eye, I'd sure do somethin'."

"What would you do?"

"Dunno. You tell me. You're the smart dude. You're the one's goin' to college."

"They don't teach stuff like that in college. You've had a different sort of education. I think you know more about stuff like that than I do."

"I do? You think so?"

Break them down, raise them up, thought Mace.

"I think so. It's for sure you'd have the nerve to do it. More nerve than I've got. I don't think I'd have the nerve."

"You ain't sayin *you're* chickenshit?"

Mace gave an evasive shrug and Pickering crumpled up the Burger King bag and tossed it down the levee embankment, into the brush on the shore of the slough.

"For Christ's sake, you pig. Pick that up."

"What for? Nobody can see it."

"I'm trying to help you get your shit together. And step one is to teach you not to be a pig. Not to leave stuff lying around."

"You think you can order me around."

"Pick it up."

He didn't move for half a second, then got to his feet and clambered down the embankment and retrieved the bag.

"Here it is," he said sullenly, dropping it at Mace's feet. "Now I ain't no pig."

"Sit down, Ben. Sit down and tell me what you'd do to shut those people up."

"You mean like right now?"

"Right now. Tomorrow. Anytime."

Pickering's eyes moved across the black furrows of the field below, his eyebrows, several shades darker than his hair, puckering. Orange-clad monks came out of the temple, towing a procession of men in white shirts, women in brightly printed dresses, and a party of pallbearers carrying a red and gold coffin on a platform. The cortege snaked around the temple grounds, a drum thumped every so often, and a hundred pair of feet raised a moving veil of dust.

"A fuckin' funeral," Pickering said, standing up to watch the train shamble out behind the temple and toward a swale of bare earth covered with mounds that looked, at this range, like anthills. "Maybe that's what I'd give 'em all. A fuckin' funeral."

"With what?"

He patted the side pocket of his vest. Mace sprayed the air with Coke as he burst out laughing.

"Your Saturday Night Special? You'd walk up to more than a hundred people with your little six-shot popgun?"

"Yeah. Walk up to 'em, open up, waste as many as I could, wham-bam, and then I'd take off. Run back to the car, and then I'm gone, man, in a cloud of dust. Hit and fuckin' run. Wham-bam. You think I'm chickenshit to do it?"

"What if they chased you? A hundred gooks running after you."

"I could outrun them little short-legged slopes."

"Not with the cigarettes you smoke. You wouldn't get fifty yards before you were blown out, and then they'd be on top of you, a hundred gooks, all those slimy little yellow hands tearing you apart."

"No fuckin' way. That happened, I'd save a last bullet for myself."

Mace looked long at him, gauging if this was pure bravado.

"You think you'd have the nerve to do that? Blow yourself away?"

"If I had to. I ain't afraid of dyin'. It's livin' that scares the shit out of me sometimes."

"Well, there they are, and your popgun's in your pocket. Let's see you do it."

He rose up on his toes, his hands opening and closing, and one side of his mouth twitched into a half-grin.

"What's this? Like some little kids' game? I dare you, double-dare you?"

"Killing people is no kind of game, Ben."

"If you think gooks is real people, I guess not," Pickering said, turning his head to look at the mourners, clustered around the new grave. He bounced on his toes, beat a rhythm against his legs with his hands. "I know I ain't chickenshit."

"Then stop talking and *do it.*"

"What kinda game you playin', man?"

"No game. I'm only trying to figure out when I can believe you and when I can't. Are you lying to me again? Are you chickenshit after all?"

"You're just fuckin' with my head."

Pickering sat down, clutching his knees to his chest. Mace rose and sat down beside him, hooking an arm around his reedy neck. One good jerk and I could snap it, he thought.

"Ah, Ben, Ben, Ben. I knew you wouldn't, but not because you're chickenshit. Because you're too smart."

"I am?"

He could feel Pickering's cartoid artery throbbing repulsively against his bicep, and the urge to lock both arms around his miserable neck grew stronger, to the point that he feared he might actually throttle the life out of this useless piece of human flotsam. Celestial terrestial telestial. He wasn't useless, that was the point. The purpose had to be fulfilled, and if all went as he foresaw, Pickering would remove himself from existence.

"That's right," he said, pulling his arm away. "Too smart. You're as dumb as a stone in some ways, but in other ways you're smart. If I didn't think so, do you suppose that I'd waste a second of my time on you? Would you like me to tell you a few things about yourself? Things that you yourself probably aren't aware of?"

"Like what?" Pickering asked with a sneer.

Interesting how he could act like an insecure child one moment and turn surly and mean the next.

"You didn't take me up on the dare because you knew it would be a waste. Maybe you'd off three or four or five people, maybe you'd stop all that *yaaah-yaaah uuum-uuum* shit for a day or two, maybe you'd get away, maybe they'd catch up to you and then you'd have to off yourself. What a waste. It would prove nothing."

"I suppose."

In the distance, the crowd of mourners was breaking up and knots of people were moving away from the cemetery toward their cars.

"You didn't come here all the way from Oregon for something small like that. You had big things in mind. You still do."

"What did I come here for, then? I thought I come lookin' for a job."

"That isn't what you said not too long ago. That isn't what I heard you tell Miss Sexton."

"I was just fucked up, I was just talkin'."

"Were you, Ben? Then why did you cut that article out of the newspaper? I assume you can read."

"Hey, man, I almost got my G.E.D. in prison. I ain't no fuckin' illiterate."

"Look at me, Ben." Pickering raised his head from his folded knees. "Since you studied for your G.E.D., I guess you know what psychotherapy is."

"I've talked to headshrinkers. Yeah, I know what it is."

"Well, that's what I'm studying. I'm a student of what goes on between here," Mace said, clamping both hands on Pickering's temples. "The whole purpose of psychotherapy is to get somebody to see the truth about himself, to understand why he does what he does, why he wants to do what he wants to do. That's all I'm doing right now. Trying to get you to see the truth of why you drove hundreds of miles from Oregon. You know it'll only be two weeks tomorrow and Boggs has been forgotten already."

"Not by me."

"No, but by a lot of other people. Kind of tragic. All that he did and only a few people remember. He didn't do enough, I suppose."

"He sure did put the fear of God into them gooks for a while, though."

"Ben, you didn't come all this way just to do what he did. It was to outdo him, to do better."

"You askin' or tellin'?"

"Little of both."

Mace's companion stood and walked off a foot or two, then kicked a divot of grass with one of his Doc Martens.

"I suppose when I seen that story, yeah, I suppose . . . They said they was goin' to have this remoralizing service for the dead gook kids and that white people, niggers, gooks, Catholics, Protestants, even the fuckin' mayor, everybody was goin' to come. So I suppose I thought, man, all them people crowded in . . . " He spun on his heel and a cunning expression spread across his sallow, rodential face. "Hey, how do I know you ain't some kinda cop?"

Mace threw his head back in laughter.

"Right. I go to college, I work for six bucks an hour in a crummy rehab clinic, but I'm really an undercover cop assigned to figure out what morons like you are thinking. Goddamnit, just when I think you might have something going on in your skull, you turn around and act like an idiot. If I were a cop, I would've busted you when you were waving your popgun in Miss Sexton's office."

Pickering scuffed his boots.

"Listen, if you want to stop talking, that's fine with me. Just give me a lift back into town."

"Nah," said Pickering. "I was only bein' careful."

"So go on. But only if you want to, Ben."

"I was sayin' . . . white people goin' to a thing like that remoralizing service . . . "

"Memorial."

"Yeah, right. Y'know, they're no better'n gooks or niggers themselves. They're like, y'know . . . "

"Traitors?"

"Yeah. Traitors. So I was thinkin', man, I'd take my AK, double-taped magazines, maybe a couple of spares"—he moved off a yard or two and picked up a fallen oak branch, and bracing it against his hip, bent his knees, one hand at the back of the stick, the other at the front, and swept it back and forth—"like this. Assault rifle on semi-auto, you got to hold the barrel down because the barrel climbs when you fire and you shoot high, so you hold it down like this, and you let go, right into 'em, man it'd be righteous. *Dadada-boom, dadadada-boom.* Righteous, I'm sayin'."

"A righteous slaughter," said Mace, fascinated by the transformation the mere imitation of the act had wrought in Pickering. His movements crisp and economical, his gaze concentrated. A completeness. Like watching a good hitter when he picks up a bat and takes a few practice swings. You *know* he's rehearsing the one thing he's meant to do.

"I think like that sometimes. A lot of times. A lot of times I start thinkin' like I know I ain't supposed to be. Not thinkin' right. I told that to the shrink last week."

"How do you know it's not the right way? How do you know it's the way you're not supposed to be thinking?"

"That's what everybody says."

Mace laid his hands on the other man's shoulders, holding him an arm's length away.

"But what do you say? That's the important thing. Listening to your own voices. What do your own voices tell you?"

Pickering half-turned, wound up, and sent the branch twirling into the air, twirling through the leaf-broken sunlight and into the slough, where it rested like a sleeping snake.

"You sayin' I should be thinkin' like that?"

"Nope. It's not my role to tell you how you should or shouldn't think, what's right, what's wrong. There are no negatives in the subconscious, Ben."

"What? That some kinda shrink talk?"

"It only means that way down deep in your mind, my mind, everybody's mind, there is no should and shouldn't, no right, no wrong. It's all one thing."

"It is?"

"There is only the truth of the way you do think."

"No shit? You learn that in college or what?"

"Let me put it like this. There are a lot of people who think like you do. But unlike you, they don't have the balls to say what they think. I told you that before. They're afraid of their own thoughts. And they're ten times more afraid of acting on those thoughts. They're not men of action, like you."

"Like who're you talkin' about for instance?"

"Like me for instance. When you were describing how you'd open up on those people, do you know that I saw myself doing something like that? To get back at the gooks for doing what they did to me? But . . ." Mace caused his voice to trail off, dropped a disappointed look over his face.

"Chickenshit."

"I don't even know how to handle a gun. The way you were showing me how to hold the barrel down. I didn't even know that. So you see, in some ways, you're smarter than me."

"Yeah, sure," Pickering said, bobbing his head in assent. "They don't teach you how to handle an AK in college, you're sayin'."

"I'm saying. But if I did have the guts to do something like that, I'm not sure I'd do it the way you said you would."

"Yo, man! An AK, double mags, big crowd, you could fuck up the whole day for a whole lot of people."

"We're just talking, right, Ben?"

"Yeah," he answered, shrugging. "That's all we been the last hour."

"Talking. Just two guys batting a few ideas around."

"Yeah. Talkin'. Right."

"C'mon up to the road. I want to show you something."

Mace squatted, smoothed the dirt in the shoulder, and drew with a stick a diagram of the temple.

"It's two hundred fifty feet from the highway to the back, and a hundred and fifty feet wide."

"How d'you know that?"

"I can tell by looking."

Pickering cast his eyes across the field.

"Yeah. Yeah. You're right. That looks about right."

"And these are the cypress trees, on all four sides," said Mace, poking dots into the ground. "Like a natural fence. Now at that memorial service . . . *me-mor-i-al*, Ben . . . "

"Right. Memorial."

"They'll be packed in there real tight."

"Like fish in a barrel."

"Maybe fish in a net would be better. A net with holes in it. A lot of people would be able to get away, just by running through the trees. So if I were to shoot at them with an AK, there's no doubt I'd get quite a few, but a helluva lot more would get away, and I wouldn't do any damage to the temple. After a while, gooks would be coming back to their church and ringing their gongs and chanting."

"Yaaah yaaah uuum uuum."

"I'd want to see that temple burn."

"Yeah."

"And I'd waste a whole lot of people at the same time."

"Fuckin' *righteous.* Yeah."

"We're only talking."

"Yeah. Talkin'."

"Here's what I'd do. I'd create an explosion and I'd be firing into the crowd at about the same time. You know what I'm thinking about right now? Hezbollah. Do you remember Hezbollah, Ben? You're old enough to remember when the Marine barracks were blown up in Beirut about ten years ago. Hezbollah did that. Two guys, only two guys willing to die drove a truck full of high explosives right through the Marine sentries and into the Marine barracks and blew themselves and three hundred Marines up. Two guys only. Willing to die. Three hundred Marines. The Marines never lost that many killed in a single action in their entire history. And to this day those two terrorists are remembered by their people. Heros. They're dead, but not dead. Their names are still living in the minds of thousands of people. Hezbollah."

"Sand niggers, you're sayin'. A couple of sand niggers done that."

"I'm saying. Now if you wanted to do something like that against that gook church, what would you do?"

Standing over him, Pickering stared down at the diagram, pursing his lips and brow in thought. He struck Mace as a little smarter than Duane, but he was still true to type: impulsive and an egotistical misfit. His limited capacity for premeditation had to be nurtured, not forced out of him; his impetuosity and destructive passions had to be managed but not curbed, and he had to believe that he would be carrying out a plan of his own devising, not one imposed on him.

"I'd use my car," Pickering said. "Like them sand niggers used a truck. I'd . . . Shit, where you goin' to get explosives? Not like you can go to a store and buy 'em."

"That'd be a problem, all right. What about plain old ordinary gasoline?" Mace suggested. "Five or six jerry cans of gas in a car."

"Yeah, *yeah.* And . . . I was in a prison with a dude. Blew up another dude's car with a pipe bomb. Told me how he made it. Real simple. Take the powder from a couple boxes of shotgun shells, pack it real tight inside a pipe. Cap the pipe. You got you a hole drilled in the pipe, and a firecracker with the fuse stickin' outta it. That's what he done to set off the bomb. Simple old firefuckincracker." He dropped to his knees and looked down at the diagram, and Mace could see the transformation coming over him again. That wholeness. "I got it, man. I tape the pipe to one of the jerry cans, I got a twisted-up rag soaked in gas tied up to the pipe bomb. I bust in there top speed, like in the movies, I light the rag. It's long enough for me to get outta the way before it sets off the firecracker. I jump out, open up with the AK, I'm flat hosin' 'em down and then the bomb goes off, *babafuckinboom,* man, like a napalm bomb. Spray burnin' gas all over, cookin' 'em up good. Righteous."

A beginning, thought Mace. It needed considerable refinement.

"That's pretty good, Ben. It's better than what I would've thought up."

"It is?"

"Yes. But I can see a couple of problems you'd need to work out."

"What problems? Man, wouldn't that look like somethin'?" Pickering asked feverishly.

I've blown on the coals that have been smoldering in him, nothing more, Mace thought. I've raised the flame of a vision. For now, it's merely a fantasy. The task, and the trick, is going to be to convince him—no, to get him to convince himself—that what he imagines happening can be made to happen, and, finally, that he needs to make it happen. Everybody needs a purpose in life. Really, it's all a matter of getting him to see what his is.

"Would you like to hear what some of these problems are?" he asked.

"Yeah, why not?"

"What're we doing, Ben?"

"Talkin'. We're just talkin'."

▬ ▬ ▬

It was a pink bungalow in a neighborhood of pink and white and ocher bungalows, illegal apartments added on to garages or to the backs of the houses. TVs and radios were tuned to Spanish stations, Mexican love songs crooned onto the street. Light-headed from exhaustion, Gabriel climbed out of the squad car, and flanked by two Riverside patrolmen, went up the short walk to the front door. Old-time police work. Shoe leather. Knocking on doors in the middle of the night.

"*Quien es?*" a man asked from inside.

"Senor Alvarez? Emiliano Alvarez?" said one of the patrolmen, a stocky young Mexican.

"*Sí. Quien es?*"

"*Policia.*"

A sound of locks opening. The door cracked, admitting onto the front stoop a long dowel of light.

"*Identificacion, por favor,*" said Alvarez, the door held by a chain.

Gabriel stuck his ID and badge through the crack and Alvarez opened the door and they walked into a parlor with sea-green walls and secondhand furniture and a TV upon whose screen John Wayne spoke in dubbed Spanish to a grizzled cavalry sergeant.

"Gracias. Habla usted ingles?" asked the patrolman.

"Pocito. Mi espousa . . . " Alvarez, a short, scrawny man with a leathery face, looked over his shoulder and called out, *"Ylonda! Venga aqui. Es policia!"*

An immigrant couple, treading water to keep their heads above the poverty line, thought Gabriel. Willing to accept parolees as tenants.

"Policia?" a woman said from the bedroom in back. *"Que es problema?"*

"No say."

"Momentito."

Alvarez looked at Gabriel warily.

"Momentito. Mi espousa habla ingles muy bien. Siente se, por favor," he said, gesturing at a chair.

Gabriel declined, afraid that if he sat down he wouldn't be able to get up again. The eight-hour drive from Sacramento had brought spasms to his back, and an inflamed sciatic nerve had numbed his left leg. He'd gone to work as soon as he, Adrienne, and the kids were checked into the Ramada, first phoning Kincannon's parole agent in Santa Ana. Not much help there, Kincannon having been off parole for two years. He then called Dave Moran, the deputy chief in Westminster; then, to Adrienne's dismay, he left her at the motel and drove south to Westminster to pick up the only information Moran had on the case—the original arrest report, miraculously still on file, and a few newspaper clippings. That turned out to be more than enough, and he would have been excited if he hadn't been so tired. Kincannon was a Vietnam veteran, and he had gone on a rampage that night in 1974, randomly firing a pistol at the houses of Vietnamese refugees. The "V.C." were invading his neighborhood, his town. He'd been trained to kill those people and now they were living next door to him. Several of his bullets found their marks; one wounded an elderly man, two killed a woman and her twelve-year-old child. By the time he was paroled back to Westminster, the town had become "Little Saigon," and its Asian citizens protested his return. They picketed his apartment house, appealed to their state assemblymen, who persuaded the parole board to transfer him to Riverside.

Belting a blue robe to her ample waist, a heavyset woman, taller than her husband, emerged from the back bedroom.

"I can help you?" she asked the Mexican patrolman.

He pointed at Gabriel.

"So whachu need?"

"Sorry for bothering you so late, Mrs. Alvarez. I'd like to ask you a few questions about a former tenant of yours."

She lit a cigarette and stood in the hall between the parlor and the rest of the house, her hard, pockmarked face split by a sliver of smoke as she held the cigarette up in the air, her elbow resting in her left palm.

"Which tenan'?"

"Riley Kincannon."

"Mr. Riley doan live here no more. Gone."

"I know. Did he leave an address or a phone number? I'd like to talk to him."

She let out an explosive cough as she was inhaling, looked across to the sofa and her husband, and spoke to him in Spanish. He laughed sharply.

"Hey, mister," Ylonda said. "He doan leave no address, phone number. You wan' talk to him, you go there"—she motioned toward the ceiling—"he no there, you see him down there"—her finger pointed at the floor. "Me, I like Mr. Riley, pay his rent on time, no trouble, we're real friendly, so me, I hope he's upstairs."

This was not what Gabriel had expected or hoped to hear, and now he did sit down, holding his back straight against the chair, extending his leg, rubbing it.

"Do you know when he died?"

"Yeah. Febwary. He went to, how you call it, sojer's 'ospedal?"

"The V.A.—Veterans Administration hospital."

"Yeah, tha's it. So wha's this about?"

"Murder."

"Ooooo-hoo-hoo."

"Tell me what you can."

"Mr. Riley, he got sick real fast. Big man, *muy forte*, but in October, he got bad pains in his back. Bad, bad. No can go to work, not eating. He went to that 'ospedal, come back, tells me he got bad cancer in his back. We real friendly, y'know? Talk a lot together, he's so nice to me I can't believe he done what his parole officer says he done. This cancer, Mr. Riley tells me he got it in the Vehtnam War. Somsing he breathe there, some chemical . . . "

"Agent orange," Gabriel murmured.

"Oh, I doan know. But he was very brave. No cry, no looking sad, none of that. He jus' tell me this cancer so bad he gonna die from it real soon. Very sad. He got nobody, was in the prison long, long time, fi'teen, sisteen years I think, got nobody, so me and Emiliano, we have him with our kids for Christmas, then, Janwary, he goes back to 'ospedal, gives them people my phone number. They s'pose to call me when he dies. They call sometime Febwary, I forget when."

February. He would have to check V.A. records to make sure she had the month right. Gabriel looked off, toward a velvet bullfighter on the wall above the TV where John Wayne shouting "Adalante!" led a cavalry charge.

"Mrs. Alvarez, do you recall if Mr. Kincannon had visitors?"

"Oh, chur. Not too many."

"Remember anything about them?"

"Nah. Mr. Riley's door, its back the garage, up the stairs. I doan see who comes, goes. Hey, he doan commit another murder?"

"No. And you two got along? He was friendly?"

"Me, I was like older sister for him. Nicest tenan' I got. Y'know, before he goes to the 'ospedal second time, I help him pack his stuff. They givin' him those radiation treatments. Make him so thin! Thin, thin, thin! Hair fallin' out . . . "

"What kind of hair, Mrs. Alvarez, what color, I mean. Was it long or short?" asked Gabriel, feeling a stab of interest.

"Kinda short. Color? Light brown. Like sand. Got some gray. Now I think about it, more gray, less brown. And fallin' out! From those treatments? Almost gone. He's so weak, y' know, from those treatments, that I gotta help him pack. Very sad, what a sad thing." She picked up an ashtray, snuffed her cigarette. "Packin' up his underwears for the 'ospedal, shavin' stuff, then the stuff he's sendin' away to his boy . . . "

"His *boy*? I thought you said he didn't have anyone."

"Chur. Tha's what I'm thinkin' all the time he's here, two years. No *espousa,* no mama, papa, no kids. Then, this day, when he calls me to help him out, he's puttin' this stuff in a box, not much stuff . . . and he tells me it's for his boy, his son. I remember askin' him, 'Riley, you didn't tell me you gotta boy.' And he says, yeah, he does. He's not seen this kid since he's goin' to the prison, when the kid, he's a little *nino,* two, maybe tree years old . . . " She glanced down, cinched the belt of her robe tighter.

"This is really important. Everything you can remember."

When she raised her dark eyes again, he saw that they were damp.

"Hey, mister, this is real sad, no kiddin', makes my heart break. Mr. Riley's *espousa,* she's, y'know, *muy bonita, muy, muy bonita.* Seen her pitcher one time. Like a movie star. He's in prison not one year and this woman, she's a little bit . . . *puta* . . . and she finds another man. He's tellin' me all this stuff when I'm helpin' pack up. She divorce Mr. Riley, marries this other man, and then she's givin' the *nino* away."

"For adoption? A foster home?"

"Yeah. Like that. Mr. Riley, he's findin' out about this in a letter, not from her even, but from some friend. And he got so mad he's gone crazy and they put him, y'know when they put you all by yourself in the prison . . . ?"

"Solitary."

"Yeah, he's makin' so much trouble because he's so mad, first time he comes for parole, they doan give it to him. He got no idea what happened to this boy. Time goes. Time, time, time, and he doan care no more. Then, not one year ago, just before he gets sick, Setember I think, this boy shows up. Here! I doan see him. Mr. Riley tells me, when we're packin', that this kid shows up. Now he's big, like Mr. Riley, Mr. Riley's tellin' me. *Muy forte.* And in the college. But now Mr. Riley, he ain't this kid's father no more. The court give him another father, another mother. But some kinda agencia, they tell this kid who his real father is, where he's at, and he comes for a visit, but it doan go nice. No. *Malo.* Mr. Riley's tellin' me he treat the kid real bad because just seein' him makes him think about all the stuff he's forgot in prison and made him gone crazy. So they talk a little while, and Mr. Riley tells him to go away, doan come back, everything in the past. Like that."

"This was in September?" asked Gabriel. He had his notebook out now, and remembered where he'd heard about the Mender Foundation: a story on *60 Minutes* several months ago. It was an organization that broke the confidentiality of adoption records and reunited adopted children with their natural parents. The woman who ran the organization had been convicted of fraud.

"Yeah, Setember. Tha's what he tells me," Ylonda answered, firing up another cigarette. "Tha's what Mr. Riley tells me. So he feels real bad treatin' the kid bad. Not the kid's fault, he's got given away so his mama she can run away with this other man. He calls the kid, but now he's mad at Mr. Riley, and tha's that. So when he's found he's dyin' of this cancer, Mr. Riley says to me he wants to send his stuff to the kid, y'know, some photo books, some of those sojer medals, just a few things. And after he is died, one more package comes with his things he took to 'ospedal, and he gotta note, send these things to the kid, and tha's what I done."

"Do you recall his name?"

She paused, looking up at the ceiling with its swirled plaster, its dim light.

"Nah. Some kinda gringo name. I remember it was goin' to San Joaquin. The kid's in college there. And I seen the *espousa* in the photo book"—she raised her hand and shook her fingers in the air—"oooo-hoo-hoo. *Muy bonita.* But outside only. Inside, *puta.* Y'know, *puta*?"

"Whore," said Gabriel

"Yeah. In *ingles,* whore."

The two patrolmen, bored stiff, had joined Mr. Alvarez in watching John Wayne whisper endearments to Maureen O'Hara.

"One last question. Was there a blue carpet in Kincannon's apartment?"

She gazed at him as if he had supernatural powers.

"Yeah. Same one tha's still there."

"I need to take some samples from it."

"Hey, someone else livin' there now. I gotta wake him up at this time o' night."

"That's right, Mrs. Alvarez. You gotta. In a minute. I need to use your phone first." She motioned that it was in the hall.

He checked the field office's night number for messages first. There were two, the first from the agents surveilling Weathers. He'd been seen riding with another man in a dark blue Buick with Oregon tags . . . registered to a Benjamin Pickering, now residing at the Valley View residential motel, convicted of attempted robbery, felony possession of cocaine, aggravated assault . . . Pickering and Weathers followed to the San Joaquin Buddhist temple, then back to Pickering's motel . . . Weathers boarded a bus and returned to his apartment. . . . The second message was from Wilson Tipton: he'd received a second peculiar call, this one from a man purporting to be from a credit-checking agency. Sounded like the same voice as the credit card salesman.

Well, Gabriel thought, so far Weathers hadn't tried masquerading as a cop. Too smooth for that one. He hung up and gave himself a minute or two to absorb what he'd learned. Weathers adopted. In a way, he was a paper son, the natural son of a murderer. Kincannon's driver's license and other identification must have been among the effects Ylonda mailed. He would need to take a close look at that photo ID and currency exchange in San Joaquin, the one where Duane had had his final picture taken. Some of those places dealt in false green cards and border crossing cards for migrant farm workers, so it would have been no difficult feat of forgery for them to alter Kincannon's driver's license, replacing his photograph and birthdate with Weathers's. Then Weathers could rent a post office box under Kincannon's name, pick up Duane's checks, and cash them at the exchange.

Heartwood's voice was thick from sleep or lovemaking. Gabriel wasn't sure which and apologized if he'd interrupted anything. Heartwood said he wished that were true, and then Gabriel brought him up to date.

"So the seed's sprouted. He's found a new trainee."

"And a new target," Gabriel said.

There was a clicking on the line.

"What's that?"

"Me," Heartwood answered. "Clicking my tongue. That stuff you told me about his father. Interesting from a psychological bullshit point of view. I'll want to see whatever you've got on Kincannon. We're looking for Weathers's motives, okay? His dead father's going to give them to us."

"I'm learning. Kincannon's was racial bias. Mace was carrying on in dear old Dad's tradition, but carrying it about ten steps further."

"You've got part of it, but only the most obvious part."

There was a pause on Heartwood's end. From the parlor came the rousing chorus of the U.S Cavalry singing "She Wore a Yellow Ribbon." Standing, Gabriel's back ached, his left leg felt as if it were asleep.

"I'm worried," Heartwood said. "I'm worried this situation could get out of control."

"Got a handle on it. I've done shit like this before."

"Not with a Weathers you haven't."

He stretched the phone cord to peer around the hall archway into the parlor. Everyone was watching John Wayne. "It's my hunch Weathers would be up to this or something like it no matter what. I don't think we nudged him into it."

"Whatever's the case, don't you think we've got to warn people about what we think he's up to?"

"When we *know* what he's up to. We don't want too many people clued in yet. One press leak and he'll realize we're on to him." He stepped farther into the hall and said in a low voice, "Got a rough idea of what we need to do. First, we let Weathers run with Pickering until we get a clear idea how they're planning to hit the temple."

"Then what?"

"Tipton, next phase . . . "

"Yeah?"

"Hey, Mister Detective!" Ylonda called from the living room. "When you off the phone?"

"Can't go into it now," Gabriel said. "Need a little time to work out the details, but I think we can squeeze Weathers from two sides at once. We're gonna get him like a walnut in a nutcracker and break him open."

Wednesday, May 5th

WEATHERMAN WAS RIGHT. HIS OLD MAN HAD BEEN right, coming home from the bars after his shift at the mill, smelling of sawdust and sweat and booze, cracking him across the face for screwing up in school and sometimes for no reason at all, just for being alive, the hand with its scent of fresh-cut wood slapping him and then the shout borne on whiskey-soured breath striking him even harder than the slap, "You stupid little shit! You little fuckup!"

The Big Sad pinned Ben Pickering to his bed, an invisible force heavier than lead. He looked at the red plastic jerry cans racked against a wall and at the pipe bomb on the bedside table, and they seemed to mock him. Nothing he ever did turned out right. Everything he did turned out useless in the end. It had taken hours to make the bomb: drilling the hole for the firecracker fuse, installing it, cutting the casings from the shotgun shells shell by shell, emptying them of wad, powder, and shot, then tamping the powder dram by dram into the pipe until he had a good half-pound tamped down tight as the powder in the shells had been, and each end of the pipe capped off so that when the thing blew it would turn his car into a rolling napalm bomb. Righteous and there would be no more *yaaa-yaaa, uuumm-uuumm.*

Except now there would be. All the work he'd put into this, all the planning with Weatherman, and now it was all for nothing because he'd made that phone call last week. He'd just been messing with their heads a little! If only he'd known then what he knew now, if only he'd known then that he was—what was that word Weatherman used? Destined, yeah, destined to be somebody who'd put an end to all that *yaaa-yaaaing, uuumm-uuumming.* If only he'd realized that they'd take it so seriously, the dumb gooks. Boggs's tag or whoever's tag. Cat-eyes eat dog meat and W.A.R eats cats. So now there would be no final flaming moment, and he didn't know until the prospect of it had been removed by his own dumbness how much he'd been looking forward to it, how it had given shape and direction to his days.

Weatherman was probably mad at him. He hadn't talked to the Weatherman (we're only talking, Ben) since Monday, when he sold him the Charter Arms .32. But he knew the Weatherman was mad, disgusted with him. He could almost hear him. That voice that could make you feel like you were inside a meat locker. "If you hadn't made that call, Ben, then they wouldn't have gotten scared and called the whole thing off. You fucked up again."

He could go out there now, if only he could rise against the mighty gravity of his own sadness. Had everything—the bomb, the AK, jerry cans. Just fill 'em up and go on out there and take the place out. *But what would be the use?* the voice asked. *You'd only take out a few yaaa-yaaaing, uuumm-uuumming monks. It wouldn't be bigger than what Boggs did.*

Better than nothing, Pickering answered back. *You'd screw it up,* said the voice. *Because that's what you are, that's what you do. Screw up.*

And then the Big Sad raised its hands from his chest and put them under his armpits and sat him up in the bed. It clutched his own hand and moved it under the bed for his AK. He stuck the barrel in his mouth, he felt his lips touch the cool steel, tasted steel and gun oil on his tongue. Can't miss, can't fuck this up. He stretched one arm to touch the trigger, but then stopped himself, withdrawing the barrel from his mouth.

Not here. Not in this rathole Valley View Motel, not here, alone, like this. No!

■ ■ ■

He'd ridden in giant teacups at Alice's Mad Tea Party and survived a belly-wrenching tour through Space Mountain's invented galaxies. Eleanor saw Toontown while Leland overcame the humiliation of going to Disneyland with his parents and kid sister by braving the terrors of the Matterhorn bobsled and the runaway mine train in Thunder Mountain. Footsore and worn to the bone, Gabriel didn't complain as Adrienne, following the rigorous itinerary laid out in a Disneyland guidebook, marched everyone from attraction to attraction with strict precision.

He'd made her and his kids happy. His domestic life was back in place. His back wasn't, after the forced march. On Monday, he went to his chiropractor for an adjustment and ice-pack treatments, and then had to be fitted with a brace before he was in shape to go to work.

Then came two of the most intense days he'd known in a long time, which he was now relating in detail to Heartwood as they drove toward the DeLuca winery. Two interrogations of the Mexican guy who operated the currency exchange, the second producing results when the Mexican, told that he'd be investigated for forging border crossing cards if he didn't cooperate, finally remembered that, yeah, he had altered a driver's license for a big gringo, and yeah, the big gringo had been wearing mirrored sunglasses.

Later, an undercover agent entered the D.A.C.O. clinic to observe Mace's activities while Gabriel, with a postal inspector along, went to the Pacific Avenue post office to look at the deceased Kincannon's post office box. A lucky break: it contained a check from the Social Security Administration. He left the check there and drove to the S.S.A.'s San Joaquin office, where records showed that Benjamin Pickering had designated one Riley B. Kincannon as the recipient of his checks. The next day, a handwriting expert verified that the same man signed the Gold Hill registration card and the P.O. box application. Finally—the sweetest find of all—fingerprints taken off the box matched Weathers's.

"Slipped up. He figured things could never have gotten this far, and that even if they did, nobody'd ever find out that Kincannon was his natural father," Gabriel said, the fiberglass brace forcing him to sit like a West Point plebe in the mess hall. It was unseasonably warm today, and despite the air-conditioning, he was dripping under the brace.

Heartwood, who'd been busy himself drawing up profiles of Boggs and Weathers, looked out at the smoothly rounded hills, the vineyards ranked like battalions on parade.

"Sounds like you've got an airtight case of welfare fraud," he said dryly.

"Ha, ha, Professor. You bet I do and more. It's how he keeps these creeps under control. Controls the purse strings. And that's probably how he came up with three-sixty to give to Duane to buy the Taurus, if he didn't get it from his steroid sales. I'm gonna use that as a crowbar to open that son of a bitch up."

"More important matters. Your surveillance teams have Weathers and this Pickering guy together out behind the temple late Saturday afternoon, then again in Pickering's motel room early Monday morning and that's it."

"Yeah. But to me, yesterday's the key day. Pickering's shopping day. We've got him doing something definite, taking the first steps. Buys two jerry cans, pipe, shotgun shells. Sound familiar?"

"Boggs's truck."

"My pal Willow might think that everything's unpredictable, but criminals aren't. They establish patterns. This has the Mace touch."

"Ditto for his conversations with Pickering," said Heartwood, referring to the tapes from the listening devices Gabriel had had installed—legally—in Pickering's room. He'd heard them this morning, at the field office. Weathers's Southern California drawl, Pickering's voice harsh and nasal, both occasionally garbled or drowned by the TV. "Know what he's doing?"

"Conspiring to commit multiple murder is what."

"I meant from the pyschological bullshit point of view. Mace is no Manson howling 'Helter-skelter' to his little stoned family. Uh-uh. He's grooming."

"Grooming."

"It's almost identical to what some child molesters do to their victims. They take it slow, over a period of days, even weeks, making suggestions, planting ideas in the kids' heads so the kids begin to think that the sexual act is their idea. For a lot of reasons, but the main one is that it makes the kids much less likely to rat on them."

"Pickering's no kid."

"Not a child, but the emotional and mental level of, say, a fourteen-year-old. Easily influenced. And that's what Weathers is up to. Influencing. No direct orders, only suggesting, planting ideas. He's being deliberately oblique, talking as if he's just shooting the bull."

"You mean in case there's a disaster and Pickering's caught, that's Mace's fallback? I wasn't telling the guy anything? We were just bullshitting? He knows that Pickering would be impeachable on the stand? The dirtball loser's word against the squeaky-clean Mormon's?"

"Yes. It would muddy the waters anyway. But I think Mace's main reason for all this indirectness is that he's convincing *himself* that he isn't doing anything wrong."

"Yeah? Well, the law sees it differently and one thing he doesn't know is that it's all on tape."

"But it won't do much good if . . . "

"There's that goddamned word again, 'if,'" said Gabriel, turning off the highway onto a dirt road. A sign nailed to a white oak warned: SLOW! DUST HARMS VINES!

"If they don't make a move, then we don't have a lot to bust Pickering on. And right now they have no reason to make a move," Heartwood continued. "All we've got is two guys bullshitting."

"Well, as a last resort," Gabriel said, "we get a warrant, bust Pickering for possessing an incendiary device and an illegal assault weapon, then sweat him hard to see if he'll rat on Weathers. Also, we've got Tipton."

A large fieldstone house appeared atop a hill ahead, a steel-roofed winery below it. There was another sign, tacked to a fencepost. WINE-TASTING TODAY 10 A.M.–5 P.M.

"Tipton all by himself makes a one-armed nutcracker," Heartwood said.

"Let's see what this gal's willing to do."

She doesn't photograph well, thought Heartwood when he saw Joyce DeLuca, sitting on a stool behind the wine bottles and plastic tasting glasses arrayed on an oaken counter gone dark with age. The pictures of her in the papers hadn't captured the brightness of her hair, nor the way her small mouth, with its full lips, formed a natural pucker that did not suggest an imminent kiss but someone pondering a question, and because those pictures must have been drawn from old school files, the eyes in them lacked the peculiar look burned into the eyes of the living woman. He'd seen it long ago, embered in the eyes of men under tents: that passion—passion in its original meaning—of those who had been wounded. There was always an apartness about such people, and a reserve, as if they dwelled in some immense and impregnable solitude.

And so it was with her as she stood to greet them (they'd called, she was expecting them), her height contributing to her aura of unapproachable distance. He felt a little awkward, and after the introductions were done, pretended to an interest in the selection, picking up now a sauvignon blanc, now a cabernet, now a viognier.

"I didn't know this was made here," he said. "In the States. Viognier is rare even in France."

"And you're one of the rare people I've heard say it correctly. It's Tom's pride and joy. Tom Crenshaw, our oenologist." She pointed toward a slender, thirtyish man who, off beside some casks, was explaining a fine point to a visiting couple.

"You're from the Midwest, aren't you? The northern Midwest."

"Minnesota."

"Thought I recognized the accent. I'm from Wisconsin. Green Bay."

She stared in a way that said his origins were of absolutely no interest to her.

"May I?" he asked, pointing at the viognier.

She filled a tasting glass. He sniffed it, drank.

"Very nice. Bouquet like a dessert wine, but—"

With a brusqueness that was startling, she pushed an order blank across the counter and said impatiently, "I assume you didn't come here for the tasting, but if you did, here's our price list. You'll save by the case."

"That's not why we're here," Gabriel said with his own impatience. "Someplace more private, all right?"

She turned the tasting over to Crenshaw and, carrying a cane but not using it until the path went uphill, brought them to the big stone house and settled them in the living room, in front of a fireplace large enough for a child to stand in. An atmosphere of the baronial, augmented by a portrait of a white-whiskered man who seemed to cast a proprietary gaze upon the room and everything and everyone in it.

"My husband's great-grandfather," the woman said, drawing a blanket over her skirt as she propped her injured leg on a pillow. "He built this place."

Gabriel asked, "Mrs. DeLuca, you organized the memorial service they were going to hold out at the Buddhist temple, right?"

Heartwood inwardly shook his head. Good old Gabriel. He could ask for the time and make it sound as though he were interrogating you.

"The people at Concord House organized it," she replied.

"That's that church group?"

"First Methodist in San Joaquin. I teach English to refugees there now. Wednesday and Saturday evenings."

"Yes?"

"They did the organizing. All I did . . . They sent me around to sign people on. The Catholic priests, the Protestant ministers, the mayor and all. They knew that no one would say no to me." An enigmatic smile played across her lips. "The great heroine."

With a glance at Gabriel, Heartwood said, "We're here pretty much for the same reason. We'd like you to persuade those people not to cancel. To go ahead with the service."

Though she sat only five feet away, she seemed to be looking down from her remote and private citadel.

"Which people? The people at Concord? That wasn't their decision. That man, the old monk, it was his."

"Have you met him?"

She nodded.

"Could you talk to him? The argument would be that if it's cancelled, it would be a victory for the sort of people who don't want to see it come off."

Heartwood watched her smile again. It wasn't enigmatic this time. Ironic rather.

"So what's going on? You're crusaders or what?"

"Whatever we tell you would have to be confidential. Hundred percent confidential," Gabriel said, leaning toward her.

"I don't care for these theatrics."

"We're not being theatrical," said Heartwood. "We're going to ask for your help. We're sure we know who was responsible for what happened to the kids in your class, what happened to you. We're sure he is—was—planning an attack on the memorial service. We need an announcement that it hasn't been cancelled."

She pursed her eyebrows.

"You'll excuse me for being a little confused? I thought that story about an accomplice was denied. It was phony."

"Phony and not phony. We planted it," Gabriel explained. "Part of the plan we've worked out to catch this guy. Put him where he belongs. We need your help."

She didn't move, her leg outstretched beneath the blanket. She only looked. Did Heartwood see it in her cold northern eyes or was he imagining it? A spark of fury? Directed at whom?

"You'd better explain everything, and then I'll decide about keeping it secret. That doesn't suit you, then you can leave right now."

So they explained, leaving all names but Boggs's out of the narrative, referring to Weathers as "Mr. X" and Pickering as "Y" until she, exasperated with such obliqueness, extracted the identities of the two men by threatening to withdraw the hope much less the promise of her cooperation.

"This man *planned* it?" she asked when they were done. "He sat back and planned and plotted the whole thing? Way ahead of time? Like he was, was a . . . a . . . That's what you're saying? It was all his idea?"

"Yes."

"Oh, my . . . my . . . " She looked out a window, looked over them and beyond them and into the distance. "I could kill him. If I saw him right now I'd kill him."

"We can understand how you—" Heartwood started to say.

"You don't understand anything. I'd take my time about it. I'd want him to know who I was. I'd take a long time. Why don't you arrest him right now? Him and this other man. Pickering. What's the matter with you?"

"The law," said Gabriel.

"Oh, yes, the law."

"Far as Pickering goes, we need to pop him for *something.* Can't arrest a guy for thinking about doing something, or wanting to, or even talking about it. There's got to be an act that shows intent, and that act would be Pickering leaving his motel the day of the service with a firebomb and an assault weapon in his car. That's when we bust him. It's like a drug sting. The drugs and the money have to change hands before you can make the bust."

"Oh, that's wonderful," she said bitterly and with a short bitter laugh. "How far do you let it go? Do you let him blow the place up and then, as you say, 'pop' him?"

"He's arrested as soon as he drives out of the parking lot and in case he somehow slips away, we'll have roadblocks up. We wouldn't let him get inside two miles of that place. We pop, I mean, arrest him. We sweat him like you can't believe—put it in the bank, Mrs. DeLuca. We screw him to the wall. We get him to implicate Weathers."

She said nothing, seemed to wait expectantly.

"But we don't want Weathers for criminal conspiracy only," Gabriel said in answer to her unasked question. "We want him for what he did to the kids in your class. We don't have witnesses for that, and next to zip for evidence. We need a confession out of the son of a bitch. We've got something worked out for that and I'm not going to go into it because it wouldn't involve you. We need for both plans to work at the same time." He spread his hands and clapped them together, the clap in that vaulty room causing the woman to flinch. "Crack him open like a walnut in a nutcracker."

"I'd like to be there. I'd take a long time, I really think I would. I'd make him feel it someway and then I'd stand over him and I'd look into his face and I'd ask him, 'Do you know who I am?'"

"Mrs. DeLuca . . . ?"

"Are you aware that if the service is held that I'd be there?" she asked. "That you're asking me to risk my life and the lives of other people? And that you're asking me, on top of all that, to lie to those people? At least to withhold the truth? Are you even aware of that? Because you don't seem to be."

"Wrong. Damned aware of it. But like I said, he wouldn't get near that place. The risk would be minimal," Gabriel said.

"How comforting. Minimal."

"Listen, you want a chance to get back at him, then this is it. Forget about playing one-woman vigilante, it won't happen."

Heartwood let him go on. For Gabriel had been wounded, too, had climbed to that high and inaccessible place and knew how to reach her there.

"You've got more reason than me or Dr. Heartwood or anybody to see that bastard where he belongs. Want to talk risk? I'll tell you who'll be at *maximum* risk. Whoever Weathers decides to go after next. And he's gonna try, because he got away with it once. Nothing succeeds like success. So you want to see that, then you go ahead and do nothing. The one thing that guy isn't gonna do is nothing."

"Stop lecturing me. You don't have any damned right to lecture."

"That's no lecture, that's a prophecy."

She said nothing and in the silence, Heartwood half-hoped she would refuse, for if anything went wrong he knew he couldn't live with himself.

"I need to think it over," the woman said finally.

"We're not asking you to convince them, Mrs. DeLuca," said Gabriel in a gentler tone. "Try is all."

"I still need to think."

"Today's Wednesday . . . "

"I'm aware of what day it is, Mr. Chin."

Teacher, is it true that Spiderman can climb up buildings? Is there a man called Superman who can fly with a cape? No. *Teacher, we do not go McDonald's because we hear McDonald's hamburgers made of ground-up babies. Is this true?* No. *My husband has stones in his gallbladder, but he won't go to hospital for operation because he is told doctors will eat his organs. Can you tell me, Teacher, is this true?* No. No. No.

"We're supposed to be learning English! Where do you people hear this nonsense?"

Joyce looked at the eight men and women looking back at her in the tiny room and never had the chasm between her world and theirs yawned so wide.

The class was silent, expressions impenetrable. Strange faces out of a land that seemed so far and alien as to be a mythic kingdom. Mrs. Or's face was among them. She couldn't or wouldn't see the blackboard, couldn't or wouldn't read her lesson book, and yet she came to learn English.

"Well? Who's telling you these ridiculous stories?"

Silence still. She turned to Sokhim, who translated the question. A man answered, one of the two men who'd shown up.

"Their children. He says the children hear these stories on the playgrounds and come home with them," Sokhim told Joyce. "Everything here—so strange for these people. They cannot speak English, have no way to make . . . what is the word?"

"Judgments?"

"Yes. To make judgments. But you see they have . . . common sense? Yes?" asked Sokhim, raising her eyes as she refastened the peony whose petals looked against her hair like the feathers of a red-winged blackbird.

"Common sense, yes."

"They can tell there is something wrong with these stories, but they are not sure. And so they come to you, asking for the truth."

Joyce laughed to herself. That's me. The font of truth. She dismissed the class.

Outside, the men's matches flared in the darkness as they lit strong-smelling cigarettes.

"I see Pandra didn't make it tonight," she remarked to Sokhim. "Not feeling well?"

"Not sick, except for Cambodia. Two of his friends and him, last night they were listening to the radio and they said, 'In one year's time, we will all go back and meet at Vith's house and eat pork and rice and drink a lot of beer!'"

"Do you really think he'll go?"

"I don't know," said Sokhim, a little sharply. She sat stiffly, hands folded in her lap.

"Would you?"

"I don't know. My two younger ones, they are used to electricity, water from the sink, TV, cars. How they going to live on a farm in Cambodia? Planting rice in mud to their knees? Riding on a buffalo? I tell this so many times to Pandra, but he does not hear. This one, she does not see, Pandra does not hear."

She had pointed at Mrs. Or, standing with a young companion against one of the two clapboard cottages that, behind the redbrick Methodist church, constituted all of Concord House's real estate. The four women walked slowly toward Joyce's car, Joyce limping slightly, her cane crooked over her forearm, Mrs. Or shuffling in her endless night, guided by her companion. *I have seen into the truth of things. . . . Maybe she has, maybe not, but now I know the truth of things and what should I do?*

"Was Mrs. Or planning to come to the memorial service?" Joyce asked as she headed toward the Park Lane Apartments.

"Yes."

"Ask her if she thinks it was a good idea to cancel it."

"Joyce?"

"Just ask her and don't ask me why I want to know."

Sokhim put the question into Khmer and Mrs. Or gave a long answer.

"She says no."

"She said more than that."

"She says not a good idea. She says what happened happened because we are supposed to remember what happened in Cambodia. She says we are supposed to remember and the memorial for remembering, so they should have it."

They rode without talking through the menace of downtown—shadowy figures sleeping in the doorways, graffiti-splashed walls VERT . . . EROC . . . MERLIN.

Is this why I didn't die there? To do this one thing? Can I do it?

The answer wasn't going to come flying down from heaven on a stone tablet. She lived because she lived because she lived, and any reason or purpose beyond that was hers to create or not create, as she chose. She pulled up to the park in front of the apartments and walked the three women home, though Sokhim protested that she needn't.

Returning to her car alone, she felt vulnerable, limping as she did—the injured animal in the herd, the one the predators set their red eyes upon. She opened her purse and rested her hand on the revolver, but it did not make her feel any stronger or safer. The park was unlighted, and its crowded oaks, so tall and ancient-looking that hooded friars and conquistadors in their armor might have passed beneath them, cast all below into a blackness such as only Mrs. Or could know. And yet Joyce saw a movement beneath the trees, a shadow among the shadows. She walked faster, her cane's rubber tip squeaking on the pavement.

The bright gun at his side.

Now she sensed that someone had come out of the park behind her. In the next moment, she heard his footsteps and a sound as of someone panting. One hand on the cane, the other in her purse, fingers working past the revolver for her keys, she quickened her pace, her gait like a crippled bird's. She opened the door, slammed and locked it and fumbled in the darkness for the ignition switch. A stooped, elderly Cambodian man walking his dog crossed the street behind her. She let out a breath, drew in another, and lay her forehead on the steering wheel. Only an old man, taking his dog to the park to pee. The recognition failed to quiet the pounding in her chest, and she realized in the tenacity of that fear, occupying her heart without reason or sense, that she'd been afraid every waking moment of the past two weeks. Nearly three now.

I'm sick of it, she thought, pulling away into the night. *Sick of being scared.*

Interlude

Inside Duane Leonard Boggs

CORONER'S AUTOPSY (CONT'D)

INTERNAL EXAMINATION (CONT'D):

CRANIAL CAVITY: Reflection of the scalp reveals massive egg-shell fracturing of the calivarium in the biparietal region and fractures of both temporal bones. There is massive associated purple-black hemorrhage in the soft scalp tissues and extensive grotesque laceration of the left scalp due to the exit wound. The bullet has passed right to left, upward and slightly forward, and rendered a path of jagged explosive laceration of the parietal lobes of the brain, coursing approximately 2" deep to the convexity surface. There are extensive and extreme salt-and-pepper commotion hemorrhages involving the white matter, especially on the left hemisphere. There is extensive laceration destruction of the left posterior frontal lobe and parietal cortex. There is no antecedent abnormality of the brain, cerebellum, or upper cord. No brain tumor present. The circle of Willis is normal.

CERTIFICATION: PERFORATING GSW OF HEAD

Gordon Kendricks, M.D.

PSYCHOLOGICAL AUTOPSY: DUANE LEONARD BOGGS (CONT'D)

PREPARED BY LEANDER T. HEARTWOOD, M.D., M.P.H

Partial Transcript of Interview with Sara Jane Pittman, 25, Boggs's Sister, Conducted at Mrs. Pittman's Home in Elbow Creek, Idaho (cont'd)

. . . and they told me down there at the coroner's office that it looked like Duane might've turned his head when he . . . The way the wound was? And, oh, Dr. Heartwood, I want to believe that at the last second he decided not to kill himself but the gun went off. Kind of accidental. Because we believe that suicide is the worst sin. You don't give yourself a chance to repent of your sins. Him and his guns. Do you see that one up above the woodstove? My husband made that. It's called a Hawken, a muzzle-loader. Jim's in a club, where they dress up like those mountain men and shoot black-powder guns. Duane wanted to fire it. He just loved that Hawken, but that gun . . . that was the cause of Jim getting so mad at him that he made him leave here.

Things had been getting bad between them. Jim would tell me, "He's been here three months and he's making good money at the mill and he hasn't even tried to find a place." And we heard that Duane was smarting off a lot to his boss at the mill. I told Jim to be patient, that we were all Duane had. He was really getting to Jim, though. Jim's so much older, I guess Duane started to look at him like a dad. Followed him everywhere when Jim was home, like he was tied to Jim by a string or something. And I was starting to have problems with him too. One time, it was early in December, I told him he had to start behaving himself at the mill or his boss was going to forget that him and Jim were friends and fire Duane. Duane said, "That lard-ass! I do my job." I mentioned that there were a dozen grown men with families in town who'd be glad to have his job and wouldn't call the boss a name like that. Duane was making good money, him not even with a high school diploma. And then he said, "Like you, you mean? You figure that makes you some kind of well-educated person? Who can tell me that I gotta shuffle like a nigger for that lard-ass?" I said back, "There's something deep down wrong with you, Duane Leonard," and he laughed and said, "Must be that high school diploma give you such a sharp mind, Sara. I got a witchbitch for a mother who kicked me out when I was fourteen and give me so many stepfathers I can't remember what last name she's got. And a retard dad who crashes his car into a wall. And I'm supposed to be just fine?" So I told him to listen to himself: I got—gave me—I, me, mine. They were my parents too, and then he said, "Well you ain't in no great shape neither," and for some reason, the way he said that, so mean, it made me mad and cry and then—I was washing dishes at the time—I dropped a dish and broke it and he didn't help me pick it up, just walked away.

It was about a week after that that Duane violated Jim's two-beers rule. He got drunk at a bar in town and banged into somebody's car backing out of the parking space. Jim was all for kicking Duane out right then, but . . . you know, it was like I knew beforehand that Duane would do something real awful if we cut him loose, so I begged Jim to give him another chance and then I had another talk with my brother.

That wind was blowing inside Duane. I mean that wind that blew Grandpa Clovis and Grandma Addy out of west Arkansas in those Dust Bowl times. Grandpa told me what those dust storms looked like—like a brown-and-black ocean wave hundreds of feet high and the storms chased him and Grandma two thousand miles to California and I guess they did all right for themselves after a lot of hard work, but I've always had this feeling, this wondering, what would've happened to our family if Grandpa and Grandma had've stayed? Far as I know, there weren't any bad drunks or criminals or murderers in our family in Arkansas. There weren't any women with three, four husbands. It's like nothing was right in our family after they got pulled out of their roots. They put down new ones, but the tree that grew out of those new roots got all crooked someway, like Grandpa and Grandma left more than a cotton farm but the best part of themselves behind. Grandpa Clovis told you about our Uncle Gene, their firstborn? He didn't tell you the half of it. Uncle Gene was committed to a home for the criminally insane when he was thirteen. He started fires and one day burned down a farmhouse and it was a miracle nobody got killed. And our dad . . . well, you know about him. He was born almost two months premature, did you know that? He was just kicking at Grandma Addy's womb like something was driving him crazy. Grandpa beat his boys something terrible, like he did Duane. With that stick. He drank a lot when he was younger. And Grandma Addy was getting drunk on that holy-rolling religion of hers and just like a whiskey drunk, she started to see things that weren't there—devils in her own three boys. That thing Grandpa told you? About chastising the flesh to save the soul? That didn't come from him, that came from Grandma.

The thing was, that was a successful farm, still is, but when Duane and me lived there, I never once saw Grandpa and Grandma take joy in anything. Not when the corn came up tall, not when those walnut and pear trees would blossom. They didn't trust their good fortune. I think they were afraid to, afraid that one day the sky would stop raining and that dusty wind come back and blow them off the land again. That wind blew so hard and so long and did them so much harm it got inside them and made them a little crazy, and because they were, Dad and Uncle Gene got crazy too. And then Duane, the craziest of all. Only one who turned out all right was Uncle Dave. There's times I wonder if what was making Dad crazy inside Grandma's womb was that wind, like he could hear it in her blood, and he just had to get out and away from it.

I wonder that because there'd been times I heard it. When I was living with Grandma and Grandpa, I'd hear the windows rattling and the shutters banging, but when I'd look outside, I wouldn't see a branch moving. Except one time. I looked out across the orchards and I saw a dust storm just like Grandpa described—a big brown wave so high it blacked out the moon. It wasn't really there and I knew that, but I shut the window anyway, because I was afraid it would blow inside and get inside me and make me crazy. . . .

But up here, it's different. Up here with Jim, I feel like I've outrun it and it can't ever get to me, and that's what I told Duane. I told him that sometimes I'd look at him and see the worst of Mom and Dad in him. I said, "I'm talking about the way you *are*, Duane Leonard. It's like you're that wind that tears things apart, like it caught up to you and made you *it*. Jim and me are going to give you another chance, but if you can't get out ahead of that thing and stay ahead, I'm not going to let you tear Jim and me apart. You play by our rules, you watch how you behave in this town, you aren't going to ruin things for me, little brother, not in a million years, and I can't tell you how much I mean that."

He got the message for a little while. But then came New Year's. We had a party here—all of Jim's friends from his club. Close to midnight, we all got in our parkas and went out into the snow, and the men were going to fire their muzzle loaders at twelve o'clock. Duane wanted to shoot the Hawken, but earlier on Jim had told him he couldn't. He didn't trust Duane with it. Duane was sneaking drinks, pouring whisky into his beer, I saw him, I should've said something, but it was New Year's. . . . Somebody counted off till midnight, ten . . . nine . . . eight. And when we shouted "Happy New Year!" all these black-powder guns went off and we could hear the echo going through the mountains when we heard this noise like a machine gun. It was Duane, shooting off, well, it looked like a big pistol, the police later on told us it was something called a Tec-9. We didn't even know he had it! It fired and fired and fired, like a machine gun and one of our neighbors called the police. By the time they got here, Jim had already taken the gun away from Duane, but Duane started fighting with the police. He said it was his right to shoot the gun on his own property. *His.* He was so drunk that he kicked one of the cops in the knee and then tried to bite him. Like a wild animal! So they arrested him, and the last favor we did was to bail him out day after New Year's. I drove our car to the jail and Jim drove Duane's clunker of a truck, with his bags packed inside it. Jim gave him the keys and he got in the truck and he looked at me in this way and he said, "You're a bitch just like her," meaning our mother. And I said, "I told you, Duane Leonard, I told you I wasn't going to let you mess things up for me." Know what he said, Dr. Heartwood? "Fuck you, big sister." Know what I said back, me, a Christian woman? "Fuck you too, little brother. I don't ever want to see your face again." And I never did, not till I saw it that Friday on the six o'clock news.

Friday, May 7th

APRIL TURNED TO AUGUST THAT MORNING. IN THE freakish heat, Mace walked briskly toward the entrance to San Joaquin's police headquarters, but was stopped in mid-stride by a sudden terror when he saw a prisoner, flanked by plainclothesmen and bound in manacles and leg irons, escorted out of the city jail into a patrol wagon. For no good reason, he saw himself in the prisoner's place, chained like a dangerous animal, deprived of the freedom even to move his arms and legs normally. He tried to banish the terror, reasoning with himself that it was irrational, but precisely because of its irrationality, reason couldn't banish it.

Inside, he gave his name to some flunky clerk and said that he had an appointment with Detective—make that Agent—Gabriel Chin and Dr. Lee Heartwood. The clerk paged them. While Mace waited, a black man in handcuffs was led past him and up the stairs. The guy was jabbering and bobbing his head—a crack addict, probably—and had climbed two or three steps when he turned to look down at Mace with rheumy red eyes and an idiotic smile; then he gave a slow nod and said, "You!" before the cop jerked his wrists and pushed him up the rest of the stairs. Of course he'd meant nothing, but that nod had seemed knowing and the word *You* had sounded like an accusation.

Where did this paranoia come from? This wasn't how it had been three weeks ago—*three weeks to the day.* He'd been taking notes in a class on the history of the American West, while Duane wrought his vengeance some fifty miles away. He'd been aware of everything that could have gone wrong, and yet he'd known that nothing would. He'd been as serene as the Zen archer who knows his arrow will strike the bull's-eye before it leaves his bow. Why that serenity had deserted him now was a mystery. This unseasonable heat possibly. Or possibly the strain of last night, trying to raise Pickering out of the blue funk he'd sunk into. "I'm a fuckup, Weatherman, I'll just fuck it up." And Mace: "You idiot! It's going to come off. They're going to go through with it! Can't you see that that's a sign? What more do you want?" He roused Pickering eventually, but he still had doubts. Pickering didn't seem ready, at the peak of his training so to speak, balanced on that keen edge between rage and despair that makes a man destructive and self-destructive.

He sat down in a heavy wooden chair, feeling giddy and petrified at the same time, excessively alert to every sound and movement in the grimy little room. It was as if he were perched on some fragile platform above an abyss, and he had an almost irresistible urge to break out laughing.

This hysteria got worse when Heartwood and Chin came down the stairs, for each became the incarnation of the two emotions pulling him in opposite directions. Heartwood, with his protuberant nose, his kinky hair thick on the sides but almost gone on top, looked comical, like a clown without his greasepaint, while Chin's squashed boxer's nose and penetrating eyes were terrifying.

"Hello, Mace," Heartwood said amiably, holding out his hand. "Sorry for asking you to come downtown. Would've gone over your statement at your apartment, but we're damned busy here."

He felt too light-headed to stand when they shook hands.

"C'mon upstairs and look it over."

"Upstairs?" He dreaded going any further into this dingy, oppressive building, of possibly encountering again the black man with his knowing grin and nod. "I can read it here. I'm kind of in a hurry. Going home for the weekend. Bringing some of my stuff home before finals week. That's next week."

This was true as far as it went, though he had another reason for being far from San Joaquin this weekend. He was disturbed by the way the words were tumbling out of his mouth. Like Duane when he popped pills. *You don't need to go into all these explanations,* he cautioned himself.

"Back to Redlands?" Heartwood said. "Well, Gabriel and I might be in that neck of the woods soon. C'mon up. It won't take more than fifteen minutes."

There was nothing more for it. He got to his feet, steadying himself as blood rushed from his head, and followed the two men up to a long corridor. Signs stuck out from the doors on both sides: ROBBERY . . . RAPE/SEXUAL ASSAULT . . . TACTICAL UNIT . . . HOMICIDE. . . . *Homicide*—a hideous word. Detectives passed by, patrolmen girded like warriors with guns, flashlights, hand-held radios, and handcuffs hanging from their shiny belts.

He was taken into a small room with one dirty window, a marred wooden table, chairs like the one downstairs, and bare walls the color of clotted cream. *Interrogation room.* No. Interrogation rooms had soundproof tiles, one-way windows, built-in mikes. He'd seen them on TV cop shows.

As he sat down, the words Heartwood had spoken only minutes ago came back to him. *Gabriel and I might be in that neck of the woods soon.* If he hadn't been so agitated he would have realized right away what that meant. Fontana was close to Redlands and Tipton was from Fontana. Tipton had come out of hiding.

"Read this through, Mace, and tell me if there are any inaccuracies," said Heartwood, sitting beside him. Chin was across the table, unsmiling, silent, sitting stiffly and grimacing every now and then. That rigid posture—it was as if he were about to pronounce sentence. Why didn't he say something? What was he staring at?

Lowering his head, Mace pretended to read through the three-page summary, his mind elsewhere, actually in several different places at once, his thoughts a muddle of the trivial and the monstrous. *What should I bring home besides my winter clothes? Will Pickering go through with it? Is that really going to happen? No. It's a lurid fantasy. We were two guys talking, that's all, a lot of talk. Of course it's going to happen. It has to. I've got to study for the history final. Mr. Benedict didn't like my paper, only a C-minus. I've been so distracted this term. Well, at least I won't have to watch losers offer urine samples during summer vacation. They aren't going to forget Pickering as easily as they did Duane. This time they will see that in this chaotic time there can't be any safety or security for anyone anywhere. Should I bring my CD player back? No. Need it to relax while I'm studying for finals. Need to relax period.*

"Looks good to me," he said, handing the papers back to Heartwood.

"Thanks for taking the time." Heartwood raised his eyebrows and smiled broadly, heightening his clownish appearance. The ludicrousness of his expression was such a relief from Chin's stony glare that Mace couldn't help himself—he laughed.

"Have I missed a joke?" asked Heartwood.

"No . . . *no* . . . the way you looked just now . . . funny . . . "

"Nothing worse than being unintentionally comic."

The psychiatrist's expression had changed instantly to one of injury and resentment. Mace realized how inappropriate his laughter had been and commanded himself to get control of his emotions. Celestial. Terrestial. Telestial.

"Sorry. I've been under a lot of stress. Getting ready for finals. And that thesis, that's been a bear . . . "

"I understand. Been there, a long time ago. You've been up late, probably not much sleep, and the strain of it, the strain . . . "

"Of what?" Mace asked, alarmed by Heartwood's tone. Like the black man's nod, it seemed knowing.

"Studying for finals." Heartwood gave him a puzzled glance. "So we'll let you get going. By the way, could you give us a number where we can get in touch with you over the weekend? As I said, we might be down that way."

They've already arrested him. The thought blazed in his mind like lightning. *And he's told them that Duane told him . . . That's why they've called me down here. They want to question me . . . me! . . . Wait. Get a grip. If they wanted to question me they would've started already. And if Tipton was already in custody there would've been something on the news. They're going to arrest him this weekend. But why are they waiting . . .*

"Sure," he answered offhandedly, wrote out Lewis and Anne's phone number, then turned toward Chin, convinced that if he could stare without blinking into those black, gun-barrel eyes he would recapture his self-mastery.

"Mind my asking if you've caught your suspect yet?"

Chin shook his head. "We'd just mind telling you."

"And is it Duane's brother?" He offered Chin the smile that had charmed the most skeptical people he'd met in his days of mission work.

"That's another thing we'd mind telling you. We'll let you know."

"Why're you guys screwing around with me like this? Any idiot could figure out it's Tipton." A hatred for both of these men welled up in him. A mediocrity with lame notions about moral compasses, a chink cop. The Shrink and the Chink. "Do you think I'm a retard? If it's Tipton and I can go along when you question him, then tell me. Stop talking to me like I'm some halfwit."

Heartwood drew back, apparently startled by the outburst.

"We don't think you're an idiot. We're not screwing around. Are you all right, Mace? Is it too hot in here? I can open the window." He paused, screwing up his eyes. "I forgot. Finals. Late nights, stress . . . "

"I'm not stressed out, all right? I just don't like having my intelligence insulted."

He flinched when Chin slapped the table.

"Nobody's insulting you, Weathers. All right, you want to know. Our man's come out of his hidey hole, he thinks he's safe."

"Then why haven't you arrested him?"

"Maybe you'll get the picture of our situation if I turned things around. Suppose it was *you* we suspected and Tipton was sitting where you are now, and then we tell him you're the one we're after. He blabs it to the media or to someone else who blabs it to the media. If you're innocent, we get sued for slander. If you're guilty, you disappear."

Mace got some of his old self-assurance back. If they had the least suspicion of him, then Chin never would have used that illustration, out of the fear that it would alert him to their suspicions. No sooner did this happy thought occur than it was overcome by a doubtful one: *Unless that's exactly what they want me to think.* This was like a chess game. Trying to figure out why your opponent made a move, working out all the permutations, looking for traps.

"I promised I wasn't going to say anything," he said, feigning—and pretty well, he thought—an offended tone. "You threatened me with obstruction of justice if I did."

"Can't take any chances. Why are you so anxious to know who anyway?"

The question was barbed. He had to be more cautious, not press so hard. He'd probably gone too far already.

"It's only curiosity."

And to show that he wasn't anxious to know, he stood up languidly and said that he had to leave.

"One last thing before you do. In all your readings, did you ever come across this book?" Heartwood pulled a tattered paperback from his briefcase and handed it to Mace.

"*The Turner Diaries?* Never heard of it."

"It's a white supremacist novel. Interesting if you've got a strong stomach. I've been browsing through it because we think it might have a bearing on Duane's motives."

"Duane couldn't read a comic book cover to cover."

He was grateful for the chance to say that. Now that he knew they believed Duane too dumb to have committed the crime alone, the more he agreed with their judgment, the better. Obviously, a guilty man would want them to think the opposite.

"Though he could play a good game of chess, right? I misspoke," Heartwood said. "I meant Duane's accomplice's motives."

Mace saw then the reason why they hadn't pounced on Tipton. *He must be mixed up with some racist group and the cops think it had something to do with the massacre. They're still investigating that angle and don't want to show their hand by arresting Tipton. That's got to be it . . .*

"You know what I found fascinating? *The Turner Diaries* expresses some ideas very similar to the ones you expressed to me," Heartwood said.

He couldn't believe what he'd just heard. It was appalling. He wasn't going to put up with it. But he would not lose his temper, no, he was in control again.

"I think you owe me an apology for that, Dr. Heartwood," he said, pulling from his collection of masks one of affronted dignity. "You know that I've been dating a Korean girl for way over a year, you know that I lost this eye protecting her from those goons. I'm not going to stand here and let you say that I'm a racist."

Heartwood jumped up, pressed Mace's shoulder, grasped for his hand.

"I am sorry, okay? I didn't mean that at all. You're the last person I'd call . . . No, the accomplice . . . you see, we think he teamed up with Duane to prove himself to . . . Okay, I won't go into that. Please accept my apology."

And though he had some doubts about its sincerity, he said he accepted, then turned to the door. Heartwood tugged his sleeve.

"Wait. Please. A few minutes. I'm not going to feel right about this until I explain what I did mean. This novel has, oh, a vision, of an America wracked by anarchy, out of which arises a cry for order. And the only ones who can restore order are—this is the conceit of the book—the very ones who'd helped to sow disorder, the neo-Nazis. A kind of fascist New Jerusalem rises from the ashes, and it's lily white, believe me. Now about the similarity . . . well, you see it, don't you? How it echoes what you told me last week, about harmony and disharmony, about the necessity for certain *things* to happen. You suggested that perhaps the massacre was one of those tragic necessities. I'm a student of perceptions, Mace. And more, of how people act from their perceptions. And I imagine this perception you have . . . Now don't get your hackles up about this, okay?" He raised both palms as if to fend off an imminent attack. "I imagine they derive from your Mormon upbringing. Joseph Smith and Brigham Young believed that the New Jerusalem would arise in the American West, didn't they?"

"New Zion."

"Same thing." Heartwood turned on his heel and took two steps to the opposite side of the room.

"But I'm not trying to build any New Jerusalems, Zions, or anything," Mace said, and then criticized himself. *That wasn't necessary.*

"Damnit, there I go again. Not making myself clear. I know you're not. You've left the Mormon church. But—correct me if I'm wrong again—the Mormons do believe that we are in the latter days. Which is why they're called . . . "

"Of course," Mace said, dismissing this evident point with a wave. "What's any of this got to do with that damned novel?"

"Why, nothing . . . and yet, everything. Perceptions. Men are disturbed not by things but by the view which they take of them. Epictetus. But that view is determined in large part by one's experiences. Our experiences create for each of us, oh, a personal little prism"—he narrowed his eyes and formed a diamond with the thumbs and forefingers of both hands—"which bends and colors the light of our view of things in an idiosyncratic way, and that in turn affects how we act on those perceptions or react to them. Are you following me, Mace?"

He nodded, though it was difficult to tell where Heartwood was going, if he was going anywhere. The man was acting a little screwy, pacing about the room, twirling a finger in the air. Chin, still sitting as formally as a judge, wincing once in a while, appeared to have mentally left the room. He didn't seem quite so frightening now. He looked a little stupid. *That's why he's wincing. He doesn't understand a word of this. The dumb cop probably thinks Epictetus is a skin disease.*

"Now then, as a Catholic who left his church, I can understand someone like you, who's left the Mormon church. You can take the boy out of the church, but you can't take the church out of the boy."

"Dr. Heartwood, I've got to . . . "

He lifted his hand. "I know. Home for the weekend. Finals.

Patience. I'll come to the point. Let's take two people. You and Duane's accomplice, who *must* remain anonmymous. You first. Raised a Mormon in the affluent city of Redlands, California. A life of cleanliness and order and, above all, predictability. A life and a world that make sense."

"Where effect follows cause like night does day," Mace murmured.

Heartwood again turned sharply on his heel. "Nicely said! But what happens one awful day? Through a series of random occurrences—remember, you described them to the school newspaper—you and your girlfriend pull into a gas station at the precise moment that three skinhead bikers are about to pull out. What are the chances of that? A million to one? Why, if you'd been traveling only two or three miles an hour slower, you'd have missed them, but you weren't and . . . we know what happened. The external event, that is. But what about the internal event? What happened in here?" He tapped his temple. "Your perceptions changed radically. Suddenly you have encountered effects that seem to have no cause. The mere act of pulling into a gas station becomes the cause of a vicious assault. You've been horribly maimed for no sensible reason. Because you were driving at sixty miles an hour instead of fifty-five or -six or -seven. For the first time in your life, you encountered disorder, irrationality. The order of your world has been shattered. How do you react to this personal catastrophe? *Your* prism transforms it into a revelation. The order of the world itself is broken. Your . . . please excuse this, Mace, it's not meant as a pun . . . your eyes have been opened to the chaos that possibly lies at the heart of existence. You begin to see disorder everywhere. Riots. Violent crime. Epidemics. And your old Mormon ghosts rise, slightly transfigured. That millennial bent of mind. You interpret these events as signs of a coming apocalypse. And you struggle to make sense of it, above all to make sense of what happened to you. You need to create a coherent narrative, the same need that drove this writer"—he picked up the book, brandishing it like a weapon—"to create his narrative. But the narratives in the Book of Mormon won't do. You consult other texts, works of Eastern philosophy, the Tao . . . "

"What the hell's wrong with that?" Mace felt as if Heartwood were physically pinning him to the wall with this assault of words.

"Why, nothing."

"You sound like a D.A. on cross-examination."

At that, Chin laughed, shook his head, and stood.

"I don't think there's a police station on the planet ever heard a conversation like this. I gotta take a whizz."

And he brushed past Mace and walked out, straight as a soldier on parade.

"I didn't mean to sound accusatory," Heartwood went on, as if Chin had never been in the room. "I am merely . . . ah, let's get down to it. You have made sense of it. You said it to me several times. Nothing happens without a reason. It's just that sometimes the reasons aren't so apparent, but you are determined to wrest order out of disorder, to find the sense in the senseless. Nothing else will do. You cannot accept randomness, the capricious tornado that smashes one side of a block to smithereens and leaves the other side without a broken window. And what is the reason you lost your eye? To enhance your inner sight, to perceive the truth. That things are falling apart all around us. Like the blind prophets of ancient Greece, okay? We must suffer, suffer into truth . . . "

"Aeschylus," said Mace, more haughtily than he'd intended.

"A-plus. The blind prophets. And—here it is again—Mormonism is a religion of prophets. And what is the prophet's role? To make others see. You also said that to me several times. People are blind to what's going on. 'Blind to this mess,' is how I think you put it. You've donned the prophet's mantle and you're going to show them . . . "

"What the hell are you getting at? That I want to make other people suffer?"

"I don't believe I said that, and if I suggested it, I apologize again, though of course people don't need to be shown. They're not as blind as you suppose. They see all right."

"Personally, I don't think they do, but I guess that's my perception," said Mace with deliberate irony to hide his agitation. This was uncanny. It was as if Heartwood had walked through the whorled ravines of his brain. Had he underestimated him?

"Now what about the other guy? A loser. A lumpen prole with a chip on his shoulder, yet . . . yet he too needed a narrative to explain why his life's so miserable. Where someone of your intelligence turns to the Tao, he turns to this bloodthirsty garbage . . . " Heartwood again picked up *The Turner Diaries* and flung it across the table with a disgust that might or might not have been feigned. "My life is miserable because of blacks and Mexicans and Asians. The one interesting thing the accomplice did was to use Duane. Yes, that was interesting."

He stopped, leaned with both hands flat on the table, and looked down at its surface. Then, raising his eyes, he said, "As his weapon. Duane was a human weapon. A disposable one."

Mace regarded him in silence, but made sure not to take his eye off him, made sure not to look anywhere but squarely into his clownish face. What game was this man playing? Had he spoken to Tipton after all? He couldn't think straight in here. He had to get out of this room, which seemed to be shrinking, out of this building with its manacled prisoners, its cops and bodiless voices squawking in code over the speaker system.

"Class over?" he asked insolently. "Can I go now?"

"You could've gone anytime you wanted, Mace. You're a free man."

Gabriel returned to the room. He'd been on the phone in the Homicide division, alerting his surveillance teams in San Joaquin and Fontana.

Heartwood was standing under an air-conditioning duct, holding his shirt open.

"Where the hell did this heat come from?"

"Pay us a visit in August. One-oh-five at noon," Gabriel, sweating under his brace, said. The cool air was like a benediction. "How about telling me what all that was about? All we were supposed to do is find out what he's up to this weekend."

"I was clearing the decks. Mace has concocted a rationalization for what he's done. He's a very nineties sort of criminal. He not only doesn't believe that what he's done is wrong, he's convinced himself that he's doing us all good. He's bullshitted himself. Which is why I wanted to get it out of the way now. So we don't waste any time on it tomorrow. I also wanted to make him a little nervous."

"Didn't need to do that. That white boy came in here nervous."

"My guess is that he's anxious about his new kamikaze. I wanted to raise that anxiety level, but just enough to muddle his thinking, okay, okay?" Heartwood closed his eyes, and tilting his head backward, moved it back and forth under the shower of refreshing air. "I wanted to suggest that we know more than we do, and that we're about to find out more."

Gabriel buttoned his shirt. "Best catch that plane so we don't miss him. If he goes for it."

"He will."

"You're sounding damn sure of yourself."

"I *am* damned sure of myself. I know him now, better than he does himself. We handle it my way first, okay? If he knows what he's up against right off, the only thing he'll say is, 'I want a lawyer.'"

"Hey, nobody hates the L-word more than me. But you know, I don't think this guy will yell for a lawyer. Because he thinks he's smarter than any lawyer." Gabriel was concerned, wanted to do it by the book. "Anyhow, we've got to assume he's gonna have a gun, so we take precautions."

"You and Youngblood'll be there. Mace doesn't want prison, but he'll take his chances in court if he has to. One thing he doesn't want to do is die. He's fundamentally a coward. That's one of the reasons he gets other people do his dirty work."

"Okay. But remember that this is now a full-bore criminal investigation and I *am* in charge. He starts acting funny or I see your way is going nowhere, I step in. Handcuffs, brace, body search, read him his rights, the whole nine yards."

▬ ▬ ▬

By the time Mace got back to Mrs. Van Huesen's rooming house, his conflicting feelings, reaching their extremes, neutralized each other and created a stable state. They were still there—the hate, contempt, fear, and doubt—but were immobilized for the moment. So when he greeted Mrs. Van Huesen and Pickett, who was going out as he was coming in, he was to all outward appearances in complete possession of himself. He didn't care for the way Pickett dropped his glance and mumbled, "Hi, Mace." That wasn't like Pickett. *Probably p.o.'d because I haven't paid his share,* he thought, taking the stairs to his room two at a time. *Sorry. Had better uses for the money.*

He sat down under the sloped ceiling and absorbed the cleanliness and order of his surroundings. It helped him to manage his thoughts. He tried to recall, from a course he'd taken on criminal law, the definition of criminal conspiracy as it applied to murder. He resented being forced to consider the question; it was sleazy, it was degrading. As if he were a common . . . All right, forget that for now, you've got to deal with this, degrading or not. How did it go? Damnit! He wished he had the textbook. *Any person or persons who orders, instructs, or otherwise acts in concert with another person or persons to commit murder, even though they are not present at the time and scene of the murder, shall be tried as a principal or principals, that is, as though he, she, or they had commited the act of murder.* That wasn't it exactly, but it was close.

He put his memory on rewind, and for the next fifteen minutes, reviewed every conversation he'd had with Duane. He couldn't recall a moment when he'd ordered or instructed him, much less *acted* in concert with him. Ambushing the bus was Duane's idea, for Christ's sake! And all the rest was talk. Yes, there'd been that Thursday morning, when they'd driven the road together, and he, Mace, had clocked the distances . . . *Wait. Got to think harder than this. Can't be too easy on yourself.* No one could possibly know what we talked about except Tipton—if Duane told him. But under the law, Tipton doesn't know. He only knows what Duane told him, if Duane told him anything. Hearsay. Inadmissable. Hell, anybody who's watched *L.A. Law* knows that. Let's take a worst case—Tipton takes the stand, testifies, Duane said this and that about Mace Weathers, and the judge allows the testimony. Christ, look at Tipton. He'll be charged with fourteen counts of murder, he'll be seen as a guy trying to save himself from the gas chamber or a lethal injection, and he's got a record. No one will believe him.

Mace took another fifteen minutes to examine and cross-examine himself and Tipton. The verdict came in: the jury finds Mace Weathers innocent of all charges. He jumped up, excited and happy, and banged his head against the low ceiling. Laughing inwardly, he went into the closet and began packing his winter clothes. As he removed a stack of shirts from the upper shelf, he saw the square of wallboard that concealed an opening where an old fuse box used to be. Pickering's Saturday Night Special was behind it. Mace had bought it from him against the possibility that he would have to . . . well, how to put it? Deal with the Tipton problem. An ideal weapon, untraceable because Pickering (if Mace could trust his word) had got it in a trade from a Portland pothead. Wasn't this the opportunity he'd been waiting for? His destiny looking out for him? Yes, a window of opportunity and it wasn't open wide and wasn't going to stay open forever.

As still as a figure in freeze frame, he stood by the closet holding the stack of shirts in midair. Another thought occurred to him. *If Tipton does know about me, and I'm investigated, what if the cops find something that'll be an equalizer between my word and his? Maybe I made a mistake somewhere.* He could not think of how, but the techniques they had these days. Cops weren't too smart, but the techniques were. Like blood-spatter analysis. He'd never heard of that. Figuring out an assailant's position by studying the blood spatters of his victim. Not that Mace had to worry about blood spatters, but what about something else? DNA testing, for example. Could they find samples of his DNA in Duane's old room, on his clothes? Like that shirt of Riley's. Mace had never worn it, but he'd touched it. Wait. He'd had it cleaned. Did dry cleaning remove all traces of DNA? The stilled molecules of his emotions began to swirl again. Only one thought brought them back into arrest: *I will never be investigated, suspected, or questioned if Tipton disappears again and for good. The cops'll think he found out they were on to him and that he slipped away under their noses.*

One o'clock already. Even if he left immediately, he wouldn't be down there until eight or nine. He had to take things carefully. Step by step.

He ran downstairs, got in his car, and drove eight blocks to the nearest pay phone, rehearsing as he drove. He'd had the number committed to memory, but suddenly forgot it, and dialed directory assistance.

Tipton's phone rang ten times without an answer. Mace hung up, waited a moment, and tried again. Still no answer. Friday afternoon. Tipton's father had to be at work, wherever that was, and Tipton himself?

Fifteen minutes later, he was back in his room, hurriedly packing an overnight bag, making sure to include a tie and blazer, notebook and pens, and the little .32-caliber. He would spend the weekend with Lewis and Anne in pretty Redlands, everything would look normal.

It was a little past two when he got on Highway 99, following it southeast through the long, green trough of the San Joaquin Valley, the purpled Sierra Nevada on his left, mile after mile, radio stations fading in and out: in-your-face rock DJs, talk-radio hosts ranting about liberals and taxes and fielding phone calls from the disgruntled, the angry, and the downright crazy—a lot of pent-up negative energy out there–baseball announcers giving the scores, all-news programs giving the urban body count—so many dead in Oakland in one day that the mayor was considering imposing martial law—NPR correspondents reporting with orotund British accents from distant war zones, country guys and gals whining about dee-vorce and honkytonk bars, death-metal guitar riffs screeching into Mozart concertos, a jazz station smoothie paying tribute to some saxophonist who'd died that day, the eulogy cut off by an airwave evangelist peddling his cure for AIDS. *I've got it rightchear in Fust Co-rinthians,* and a chorus of Amens and Hallejulahs: the sounds of the great Bear Flag republic cracking along its numerous fault lines, the hymns and voices of Chaos.

The sun was poised on the rim of the land by the time he turned onto 58 at Bakersfield. Twilight enshadowed the ravines and draws of the Tehachapis as he climbed into those mountains, and the zodiac had begun its long swing across the ecliptic when he passed through the town of Tehachapi and saw the glare of the lights over the state prison there, walls and razor wire. Not going there and neither is Jacob. The highway twisted down into the vast, empty blackness of the Mojave, shot past Edwards Air Force, where space shuttles touched down when the weather was bad in Florida, and carried him across the salt flat and lava rock desolation into Barstow. The long drive had done his mind a lot of good. He always did his best thinking in a car, and he'd had plenty of time to work out a simple, effective plan.

He pulled into an all-night convenience store and got a pocketful of quarters. It was a little after nine. Someone would be home by now.

A dull voice answered the third ring.

"Jacob Tipton there?" he asked in a deep, abrupt voice.

"Yeah?"

"Jacob?"

"Yeah."

"This is Bart Healy from the *San Joaquin Dispatch.* Half the world's been looking for you and it looks like I found you. I did the stories on your brother . . . "

"Half-brother" came the sullen reply.

"Right, right. Half-brother." Mace's heart was thumping, and he smiled as if Jacob could see him. "Jacob, I'd like to interview you about him. It so happens I'm going to be in your area on another story, so I thought . . . "

"Just a second."

He heard the sound of the phone being put down, voices in the background. He shuddered in the desert's night wind.

"Hello, who'm I talking to?" asked another voice, one Mace recognized from his previous calls.

"Is this Mr. Tipton?"

"It is. Who're you?"

"Bart Healy. *San Joaquin Dispatch.* I wrote a profile of Duane's brother. I'd like to interview your son, if that's all right. We think his take on things could give a new perspective to the story, and we're hoping we're the first who'll get to speak to him. The first media representatives, that is."

Not bad, thought Mace. Authentic.

"Jacob's not giving interviews to anyone. You're wasting your time . . . "

Mace, his mind racing as fast as his heart, said, "Mr. Tipton, this interview's very important to us. My editor's authorized me to offer Jacob payment for it. That's not usually done, but in this case . . . "

There was a brief pause and then the question, "How much?"

"Five hundred dollars."

Another second or two of silence.

"That's a lot of money for a seventeen-year-old kid."

"That's how important the interview is."

"I'll put him back on. If it's okay with him, it's okay with me."

Was that him with Duane in the bar last summer? Mace wondered as he waited. *Will he recognize me? Probably not, not in a jacket and tie and with glasses on.*

"So you want to interview me now or what? I'm not saying anything until I see the five hundred."

"That's understandable, Jacob. No, I was thinking about tomorrow. I'm down here on another story . . . " He feigned a laugh. "They took me off the crime beat for a while, I'm covering an environmental story, but if I can get this interview, the boss promises he'll put me back on the beat. So it's an important story for me, too."

"What time? You want to come to the house or what?"

"I'll tell you what would be convenient for me. Tell me if it is for you. I'm going to be interviewing a water pollution expert who's doing some studies in Crestline. Know it?"

"Little town up in the San Bernardinos, yeah."

"If you could meet me up there. It's not too bad a drive from Fontana."

"I gotta work tomorrow. And I haven't got a car. Mine's broke down."

Mace thought for a few moments. He hadn't anticipated this possibility.

"Where do you work? Maybe I could rearrange my schedule. Pick you up there and then we could go up to Crestline. Do some interviewing in the car. My interview with the water pollution guy won't take too long, then we can continue. Hell, you'll get a trip to the mountains and I'll throw dinner into the bargain."

"Sounds good to me," Jacob said, with some life in his voice. "I work at Funland Reclamation in Fontana."

"Funland . . . ?"

"Reclamation. It's a scrapyard for old amusement park stuff. Even got some junk from Disneyland. I get off at five. That okay?"

Perfect, Mace said to himself. *It'll be dark when we get up there. It's all working out. But I'll have to be supercareful. Tire tracks. Footprints. Every little thing. He'll just disappear, if it turns out that he knows anything.*

"I'll check with my source. I'm sure it'll be okay with him if I interview him at the end of the day. Tell you what, Jacob. Give me your work number. I'll call to reconfirm."

Jacob gave him the number, then said, "Hey, this isn't any bullshit, is it? You're a reporter from . . . ?"

Mace hesitated. Had he failed to bring it off convincingly?

"San Joaquin Dispatch."

"I mean, you're not a cop, right? I'm not talking to any cops."

So that was it. Did Jacob have an inkling that the cops knew about him? No, couldn't. He wouldn't speak to anyone then.

"Have any cops tried to talk to you?"

"Nah."

"Take my word, I'm not one. Better yet, take five hundred dollars. See you tomorrow, Jacob."

"How'd I do?" asked Jacob, shyly bowing his head, hands in his back pockets, like a kid who's auditioned for the lead in the high school play.

"Pretty good. You didn't sound too eager and that's what we wanted," said Gabriel, walking with him back into the living room.

Drinking a beer, Wilson Tipton turned his mournful, weatherworn face toward them as they entered.

"You did good too," Gabriel said.

"Yeah. We missed the boat. Natural-born actors, should've gone to Hollywood."

"Was I right or what?" said Heartwood, lounging back in a chair beside the TV. "He masqueraded as a reporter. The perfect cover."

"He's gonna call me again at work, then he'll pick me up at five, and . . ."

"Let me guess." Heartwood raised a finger. "He's told you that he has to be somewhere else but you're to come with him. He'll quote-unquote interview you in the car. He's going to some remote place. The desert or the mountains."

Jacob made a flinching movement. "It's the mountains. You got a tap into the phone?"

"Into his head."

Jacob's father looked harshly at Heartwood. Gabriel wished he wouldn't sound so damned arrogant and sure of himself.

"Well, I do know about him now, because you guys told me. So . . ."

"So if we let this go all the way, Mace's next step would be to find out what you know about him, and if you do, to cause you to disappear."

"But it's not going all the way," Wilson Tipton said. "Not near it. This boy's all I've got."

"And I'm not much, right, Dad?" said Jacob, walking into the tiny kitchen.

"You're the one who said it, Jake."

Gabriel looked at the color photograph of the USS *Galveston* on the wall above Wilson's chair. He placed a hand on the old gunner's mate's shoulder.

"Weathers won't get near him."

Saturday, May 8th

BEN PICKERING WOKE UP LATE ON WHAT HE HOPED would be the last day of his life. He'd turned in early, but woke at midnight drenched in sweat from a recurrent nightmare. A hundred cops were chasing him down a street in a strange city. There was no one else around, like everybody'd been wiped out by an epidemic or radiation or some goddamned thing. The only survivors were him and the hundred cops, chasing him to put him back in prison. He was never, never going back to prison, and he ran hard. When he looked back, he saw that the cops were closing fast and their skin was melting off their faces and hands, like the wax on the dummies in a burning wax museum. Maybe it was the epidemic or the radiation causing their flesh to come off in sticky gobs, their eyes to drip out of their heads. Ben ran and ran, but the cops kept gaining on him. Losing their skin and muscle didn't seem to affect them at all, and pretty soon they were skeletons. Skulls under blue hats, skeletal hands reaching for him, closer and closer. He tried to scream, but couldn't, and then the first bony fingers dug into his shoulder blades. . . .

He had one red left and washed it down with beer. The cocktail dropped him into a dreamless, hypnotic sleep. He imagined death was like that—a big, black, peaceful nothing. The trouble with reds was, they made you so groggy the next day. Now, lying in his bed in the Valley View Motel, he could hardly move, like he was strapped down. He had to move. It was late. He knew it by the light that came through the crack in the window curtains: a big square of light that hung at the foot of the bed like a shimmering table standing on end. He managed to raise his arm against the invisible restraints and look at his watch: one o'clock. Shit. The damn thing had started already. That was what the papers said. It would start at one. A sign, Weatherman told him. It was a sign. The bitch behind the whole thing was the same bitch Boggs missed. The blond teacher. It had to be a sign and he had to get moving. The little slants were *yaaah-yaaah-uuumm-uuumming* right now, and it would take forty-five minutes to get there by the route he and Weatherman had worked out. There were going to be police checkpoints at the intersections east and west of the temple, but if he went around the back way and came up from the south, he would avoid the roadblocks and get on the levee road without anyone knowing he was there. That's what Weatherman said he would do, but he wasn't going to because he was chickenshit. Hey, no guts, no glory.

He'd better leave right away. It was just so hard to move against the unseen straps of the Seconal hangover and the Big Sad. Ben felt the Big Sad, now on this last day of his life, but not because it was the last day of his life. There never was a reason for the Big Sad, which always dropped on him out of nowhere and made him feel worthless and stupid. Meth and legal drugs like Elavil held it at bay, but he didn't have any meth or mollies and he'd crunched his last Elavil two days ago. He wished he was back into that dark and dreamless sleep right now, but he didn't have any more reds, either.

A picture began to paint itself in his mind: his car exploding, like the truck the sand niggers used against the Marines. Those Hezbollah dudes. His car exploding, spraying burning gasoline all over the temple and the monks and everybody. Weatherman said those gook monks used to set themselves on fire back in the Vietnam War days, so okay, he'd do them a big favor and toast them himself. And when everybody else started running from the flames, Ben Pickering would be there, waiting for them with his AK, double-taped magazines, sixty rounds, and a spare mag with another thirty in his pocket. The great thing was, TV cameras were going to be there, filming the remoralizing service. And wouldn't those cameras start to roll when his car went off like a little napalm bomb, right in the middle of all that *yaaah-yaaah-uuumm-uuumm* shit. Wouldn't they start to roll when he opened up with his AK, blasting away while the flames rose into the sky, higher and higher. *Righteous.*

The picture thrilled him and put new life into his drugged body and blew the sadness from his mind. It gave Ben Pickering something he hadn't had in a long time: a good reason to get out of bed. And that is what he did.

■ ■ ■

Photographs of the children taken for the yearbook were encircled by wreaths on wire pedestals planted beside the two small boxes, each in temple shape, that sheltered the temple's guardian spirits. Seven photographs and seven wreaths on the right, seven on the left. Joyce could not look at them. She sat between Mrs. Or and Sokhim on the lowest row of bleachers, which extended along each side of the temple grounds, creating between them a grassy rectangle like a playing field, and at the head of the field rose a wooden platform crowded with dignitaries, Catholic priests and Protestant ministers in black, Buddhist monks in yellow, and the parents of the dead, the Cambodians wearing white clothes or white headbands. That was their color of mourning, not black, for death was a release from the sea of sorrows.

The mayor, a square-faced man in horn-rimmed glasses, was speaking now. ". . . know you came to our country seeking a better life, escape from tyranny and war . . . " his voice boomed through the speakers, drowned momentarily by feedback whine, and then continued, "No words of mine can possibly . . . The shock we have all felt and still feel . . . "

Joyce could not keep her mind on the speech, and she felt uneasy. She and Sokhim had passed through a roadblock to get here, but it didn't reassure her. The sight of the patrol car that with pulsing lights barricaded the road only reminded her of the menace waiting out there somewhere. If something went wrong, if that detective's promise of minimal risk proved wrong, she hoped she would die with everyone else. She'd been true to her word: she hadn't told a soul. Only she, of all the people here, knew the truth of things. Sokhim didn't know. Mrs. Or didn't know. Paul Lim and his mother didn't know. The old monk didn't know, the old monk whom she'd appealed to two days ago, earnestly, passionately appealed to, lying to him the whole time, and persuading him with her lies to change his mind. No, he didn't know; nor did Alex. She'd told Alex to stay home. Why put him at risk too? Yet she wished he were here now.

"You have lost your children, but we have lost something too—a sense of security," the mayor went on, holding the pages of his speech tightly against the breeze that rustled them. "We're doubting things we once took for granted. Can any of us raise our children to be safe . . . ?"

Last night, after Alex had gone to sleep, she climbed to the attic, musty with the smell of forgotten things, and rummaged in a trunk filled with old photo albums and antique dresses and other memorabilia. She was looking for her great-grandmother's diary and something she'd read in it long ago.

The diary was leather-bound, but the leather had grown cracked, and its pages, filled with a script written in a sepia ink, were as fragile as dried leaves. Joyce's mother had covered them in plastic and had inserted on the blank sides typewritten translations of the Norwegian. After some searching, she found the passage she was looking for. It was about Great-grandmother's neighbor, who poisoned herself on the morning she'd found her songbirds frozen in their cages.

In those days, the greatest enemy of farm women on the plains was not Indian or locust or tornado, but the silence of an isolated, treeless world where no birds sang save for carrion crows. The kind of silence that could get inside a lonely farm woman's head and whirl and roar there like a tornado. The women fought that unearthly stillness with songbirds ordered from catalogues. Bluebirds, redbirds, finches, mockingbirds, whippoorwills were caged and put on Great Northern trains that bore them from Chicago to northern railheads, and then freight wagons trundled them across the plains to their destinations. The imprisoned birds were hung in the kitchens, where the women spent most of their time and the iron stoves kept the birds warm in winter. That was the worst time, when blizzards rode Canadian gales, unrestrained by hills or houses or woods, and interred all the land under drifts as high as the hubs of wagon wheels. In the winter, you could not even hear the crows.

One bitter February morning in 1889, a blizzard struck. Snow piled up to windowsills, piled three feet high on rooftops, and sifted down chimneys and stovepipes and snuffed the coals in the ovens. When the snow stopped falling, an arctic cold set in and the caged birds died. They died in Great-grandma's kitchen, and in the kitchens of half a dozen of her neighbors, who woke shuddering to songless houses and scraped the ice from their windows to look on to a landscape as white and still as a lunar sea. One of these women, an immigrant from Holland, that tidy little land of dikes and tulips, fired up her oven and put a dozen frozen birds on it, expecting them to thaw back into life. When they merely lay on the hot cast iron in puddles of melted ice, she boiled up a kettle of tea, poured a box of rat poison into it, and drank it down. *She was a nervous woman, poor soul,* Great-grandma had written. *As for the rest of us, we know spring comes and the wagons will bring us new birds. We must continue.*

We must continue. Those were the words Joyce was looking for. She read them and repeated them to herself. *We must continue.* Hadn't the world always been cruel and capricious, hadn't it always, in one form or another, given a wealth of reasons to give up on life? Not that Joyce had contemplated, even in her lowest moods, ending her own life, but she had decided not to allow life in her to begin, fearing its loss and the anguish that would bring. Yet that denial was a loss, and a death, of its own. *We must continue.*

Now, in the sun of an unusually warm afternoon, she came out of her reverie, aware that the mayor was finishing his speech: "While most of us cannot fully share in your personal loss, your grief is our grief, your sorrow our sorrow, your pain our pain, your loss our loss."

Yes, yes, yes, thought Joyce, joining in the subdued applause. Those are fine words, a nice balance, but our sharing in their grief is pointless, as all our lives will be rendered pointless in the end, and yet we are required to continue in the face of our pointlessness. *We must all continue.*

He pulled the blanket from the bed and wrapped the AK in the blanket and walked outside into a brightness that made him blink. He looked around, noticed no one watching, and lay the rifle in the front seat of his old Buick, then got behind the wheel and pulled out on the frontage road. In the backseat, under a canvas tarp, were the filled jerry cans and the pipe bomb. Ben drove along, watching his speed—Weatherman told him that if he was going to do something like this, which he wasn't, being chickenshit, he would be careful to obey the speed limit. It would be ridiculous to have put so much work into this and then get stopped for speeding. If the cops caught him with all this shit in the car, he'd be going back to prison and he wasn't going there again to get buttholed by niggers, no way.

As he drove, he rehearsed what he would do. Drive off the levee road and across the field behind the gook church, his approach masked by those whatchacall'em trees. Like pine trees. Cypress. When he got to the trees, he would park the car between two of them, the front aimed at the back of the temple . . . *Temple, shit.* A few doublewides nailed together, nicer than the trailers he'd grown up in, but trailers still, not like a real church. He would get out with the AK, leaving the engine running, and no one would hear because they'd all be speeching and *yaaah-yaaahing* and *uuumm-uuumming*, weight the gas pedal down with a brick, light the fuse, throw the car in drive, and let it rip. One thing he wasn't going to do, besides not go back to prison, was burn to death. No way. A really lousy way to die, burning to death, how those gook monks did that to themselves didn't make sense, but then, what could you expect from them? He would be firing into the crowd when the car blew up. He'd blast away with the AK until he was out of ammo or the cops brought him down. He saw himself falling, his rifle firing even as he fell, like Al Pacino in *Scarface*, and all of it on TV.

One of the Catholic priests and then the Methodist minister had spoken a few words, and now Sandra An's father rose from his chair and went to the microphone. The breeze ruffled his black hair, his white shirt and trousers were in the starkness of their purity almost blinding. He bowed to the monks, then turned toward the audience.

"For many years, our people have looked for refuge," he said without a translator, for he'd been an English teacher in Phnom Penh. "We have looked for a country to offer us shelter from dictators, safety from war, and so we came here, many of us beginning our journey in the jungles, where we walked for many nights, many miles, and those of us who survived then spent many months and even years in refugee camps, waiting for the chance to come here . . . "

Joyce looked to the side at Sokhim. She understood unconsciously what Great-grandmother had consciously. All things were required by their natures to go on.

". . . we came here, hoping this was our refuge, but now we have learned that there is no refuge here, no refuge anywhere. In this world of ours, safety is not possible and there can be no escape from suffering. Now our daughter is dead and the sons and daughters of these other people are also dead." He gestured stiffly to the families seated behind him. "Perhaps they were meant to die, I don't know, but I think they died for a purpose and did not give their lives for no reason. They have brought us all together. I look out now and see people with faces like mine, with brown faces, black faces, white faces, and we are all together because these children died. Perhaps they are telling us to stay together."

He paused, seemingly on the verge of losing his composure, and the wind could be heard, amplified by the microphone.

"So I do not cry now. I have no more tears. And I do not wish to go elsewhere because I am tired of running. I will stay here with my wife and our other children and be near to our daughter's grave.

There is nowhere to run to anyway. We know we cannot find safety, but we have found something here, today, that is greater than safety and that is love. We will remember this day always. That all of you people have come here to share in our sorrow is something we will treasure and not forget. . . ."

Comin' up on it now. Here I come, ready or not. *You come floatin' over here from your rotten countries in rotten boats, you walk over our borders like you owned this place, you stink of garlic and everybody kisses your feet, but not me, I'm goin' to give you a hot foot like you never seen.* Ben looked at the hand-drawn map as he turned right onto a narrow county road that ran through pear and walnut orchards, then past a vineyard and a highway sign that said, TOKAY GRAPES—FINEST IN THE WORLD. Three miles down this, then right at the next junction, two more miles up that, and he would see the levee road. He drove on, seeing it as it would look tonight on ten million TV screens. Maybe he shouldn't go down in a shoot-out with the cops. If he escaped, he could give interviews, tell the world what he thought. He drove on, one hand on the wheel, the other pulling the blanket from the AK, metal black and solid-looking, wooden buttstock and grooved foregrip shined up pretty. Glancing in the sideview mirror, he noticed a plain gray car about a city block behind. It looked like the same car that had been behind him before he'd made the turn. It *was.* No strobes on the roof, but these days state troopers drove almost anything. He checked his speedometer. Forty-five, five under the limit.

The road went up a little hill, and when he crested it, fear branched through him like summer lightning. The junction, less than a mile ahead, was blocked by two highway patrol cars parked grill to grill, their strobes flashing bluegreenwhiteredwhitegreenblue. There weren't supposed to be any here! Got to be some other way around, got to be, they couldn't do this, they'd never let him have a goddamned thing and now they weren't going to let him have this. . . . *Bullshit.* Got to be some other way. He touched the brakes, pulling over to the shoulder to let the gray car pass before he made a U-turn, but the gray car had gone onto the shoulder too and was rolling slowly toward him, dust spinning behind it, and then a blue light flashed on its dash. A voice called through a hailer: "You in the Buick. Get out of your car with both hands in the air! Get out with both hands in the air!"

* * *

The Mahtera, robed and sandaled, led a retinue of sandaled monks around the perimeter of the narrow green between the stands, the Mahtera chanting, the monks repeating, voices rising and falling like a multiplying echo. They rang small bells that glinted in the sun, the same sun destined to engulf and cauterize the earth but shining gently now on the monks and those they blessed; gently shining, thought Joyce, on her father's grave two thousand miles away.

"May all sufferings and sickness and fears of every kind disappear before they come near you," said Sandra An's father as he translated the benediction. "May all dangers, May all bad happenings, May all bad omens, May all that is not conducive to peace not come near you, May all despair and lamentations and such things disappear from you, May the enmity be destroyed before it approaches you . . . "

How did I know something like this would happen? Ben asked himself. Because it always does. Shit happens . . . and happens and happens. "Buick driver! We want to see some hands!" I'll show you hands. Ben stuck his arm out and flashed them the bird and floored the pedal, the rear tires flinging gravel. He aimed for the blockading patrol cars, the Buick's eight-banger turning some revs, the needle rising toward fifty, toward sixty. He figured the troopers would back the cars out of his way, but then, the speedometer coming on seventy, he saw that no one was in them. The troopers were on foot, four of them in wide-brimmed hats down in a culvert at the side of the road. In the first split instant, his leg muscles tensed to hit the brake; in the next, they relaxed and he kept going, the CHP insignia painted on the doors growing larger and larger and the strobes flashing bluegreenwhiteredwhitebluegreen growing brighter and brighter. *Righteous.*

▬ ▬ ▬

In a backroom of the small, cinder-block building that was the office for Funland Reclamation, last resting place for defunct Ferris wheels, bumper cars, whirl-a-bobs, and other rides and attractions that once thrilled, frightened, tickled, or nauseated thousands, Gabriel shouted into a cellular phone final instructions to the public affairs officer for the California Bureau of Investigation.

"I don't give a damn how many networks are calling you. You

don't give out his name, tell 'em the body can't be identified, and don't give out any details yet. Keep it out of the news for another hour. And put that word out to San Joaquin PD and the highway patrol. That's all I'm asking, one lousy hour, then you can tell 'em everything, right down to Pickering's shoe size."

He clicked off and sat down heavily in a creaking swivel chair and averted his gaze from Heartwood, Youngblood, and Jacob Tipton.

"That what it sounded like?" Youngblood asked.

Gabriel nodded and with his finger made a design in the dust on the desk.

"My old man used to say that if you want the job done right, do it yourself. They were supposed to pop him when he came out of the motel and got in his car. Instead, for some reason that I'm gonna find out, bank on it, they let him get to within three miles of the place, and squeezed him between the tail car and a roadblock. And that gave him the goddamned option of surrender or die."

Youngblood shook a cigarette from his pack.

"How?"

"He tried to ram the roadblock. The highway patrol cowboys opened up. Pickering must have been real dead, but his car hit one of theirs anyway, did about ten rollovers, and blew up."

Heartwood crossed his arms over his chest and gave Gabriel a look.

"Don't say it, Professor. I don't want to hear it from you or anybody."

"We have thus lost, through incompetent police work, one-half of our nutcracker. Is it all right if I say that, *Gabe*?"

Gabriel curled his lips around his teeth and looked idly at a waybill confirming the arrival of two damaged stone elephants from an L.A. zoo. "Listen, we know we lost it, Weathers doesn't, and he won't if that PAO does his job. It's four-thirty, time you got out of here," he said, turning to Jacob. "There's a couple of Fontana blue suits will give you a lift back, keep a watch on your house."

"Hope they're better at it than the guys you were just talking about," Jacob remarked, and went out.

Wearing his blazer and tie, a notebook in one pocket, the .32 in the other, Mace cruised past the remains of the Kaiser mill, blast furnaces and stacks rising like the plinths and obelisks of a ruined city over pyramids of bricks and twisted lengths of angle iron and steel slabs, the rubble reaching way across a flatness tented by a brown sky. A perfect home for Duane the Pain's brother: Fontana, desolate and mean, sunk in white-trash bitterness and blue-collar angst. The car radio scanned across the AM bands. Weird that there hadn't been any news yet. It should have been over two or three hours ago, Ben Pickering now a famous ghost. Unless . . . no . . . Maybe there would be something on at five, a bulletin at least.

He made a turn, drove through a block that consisted of an abandoned church, an abandoned Mexican restaurant, an abandoned pool hall, and, at the end of it, an abandoned corral, relic of the days when cowboys and land-grant vaqueros rode this range. Whoopeetiyo. In the distance, a new subdivision rose row upon row beneath the girded arms of electrical pylons. Another turn and he saw the wooden sign half a block ahead: Funland Reclamation, Inc. Behind its cyclone fence stood merry-go-round horses, ranked like a squadron of nineteenth-century cavalry, and behind them, a pair of concrete elephants aboard a flatbed truck. He drove around the block once, looking for suspicious, unmarked cars. If Tipton were under surveillance, a cop could spot him getting into the Camaro and take down its number. That's why Mace was now driving a rental car, which he'd taken out this morning on Riley's driver's license.

Spotting nothing suspicious, he parked across the street from the scrapyard's gate precisely at five. Still no news on the radio, and no Jacob, either. He switched to FM and searched for an NPR station, but all he heard was an A's game, now in its final inning, and some downhome country laments. Anxiety began to perk in him. Could Pickering have decided not to go through with it? Or had he tried, screwed up, and gotten caught? A possibility Mace found so appalling he willed it into impossibility. Ten past five. Other doubts stole into him. He knew where he was going to do it and how, but he didn't have full confidence that he could actually pull a trigger on someone at point-blank range. He wasn't a gangster. He was a college student! With a three-six-five average! The picture of himself shooting Jacob in the back of the head was too fantastic to dwell on. Maybe it would not have to happen. His deepest hope was that Duane, in his egotism, had not told Jacob anything, let him think that he, Duane, had worked out the entire plan.

Twenty past. No one had come to the gate. But a light was on in the little concrete building beyond it. Jacob had said it was only he and the manager in the scrapyard. Perhaps the manager had gone by now, and Jacob was waiting inside the office. Mace decided to give it another five minutes, but after three had passed, his anxiousness overcame him and he got out of the car and crossed the street.

Standing behind the door to the backroom, Heartwood heard the familiar voice ask, "Is Jacob here? Jacob Tipton?"

A pause and then the scrapyard manager's voice: "Who wants him?"

"Bart Healy. I'm a reporter? *San Joaquin Dispatch?* I was supposed to meet Jacob here for an interview at five."

"Popular kid, that kid. Not here. Let him go early today."

"Excuse me?"

"I said he's not here. Went home."

"What do you mean, 'popular'?"

"Everybody's wanting to talk to that kid today."

"Who? Another reporter? I was supposed to have an exclusive with him."

A nice job of theatrics, but let's see who wins the Emmy, thought Heartwood, and swung the door open and mimed a double-take when he saw Mace, dressed like every old-fashioned Mom's dream of a collegiate son in a dark blue jacket, pale blue shirt, and striped tie.

"Mace! What the hell . . . ?"

He took half a step backward, but other than that, showed no surprise.

"What did you do? Follow us here?"

Mace said nothing. Whatever emotions he was feeling at the moment were masked by the glasses, in which Heartwood could see his own face reflected.

"Mace?" said the scruffy manager. "Thought you said your name was Bart somethin'."

"Yeah, he did. I heard him. A reporter," Gabriel, standing alongside Heartwood, scoffed. "What did I tell you, Mace? What in the hell do you think you're doing?"

"Tell me?"

"Obstruction of justice. Posing as a reporter to talk to a suspect. I'd call that obstruction."

Heartwood could not help but admire Mace's self-containment. His mouth had stretched into a winning but embarrassed smile, his hands gestured his guilt of this petty charge.

"Think we'd better talk a little more about this." Gabriel turned to the manager. "Okay if we use your backroom again?" The manager shrugged his indifference to the matter, and Gabriel gestured to Mace to follow him.

"Am I under arrest or something?"

"Hell, no. If you were, you'd be cuffed and listening to me read your rights. We want to hear what you thought you were going to accomplish."

Mace hesitated.

"Listen, Weathers, you can talk to us informally in back or we can be more formal and go to the Fontana PD. They've got some nice, private rooms there built just for conversations."

Mace was amazed that he could control the trembling in his knees, much less walk. The room wasn't any more than ten by ten and was cluttered with boxes and tools. There were stacks of papers on the desk and clipboards hanging from pegs above it. Chin motioned to him to sit, but looking at the filthy chair, with stuffing coming out of the rips, he shook his head.

"I want you to sit down."

"Like I'm a dog? Sit, Mace!" he blurted out, then commanded himself to stay in control. Everything, *everything* depended on his being cooperative and self-possessed. He fell into the chair.

"Okay, now you weren't thinking of telling Jacob anything, were you?"

Mace made sure to keep eye contact.

"Absolutely not! I was only going to see what he had to say, and I figured he wouldn't talk to me if I told him why. So I made up that reporter story."

"And we're supposed to believe that? A college kid goes through this masquerade to interview a murder suspect for a goddamned term paper? Stand up a second."

"You just told me to sit."

"Now I'm telling you to stand," said Gabriel. For safety's sake, he'd persuaded Heartwood to allow one change in strategy. He patted Mace down and drew a revolver from the side pocket of his blazer. A Charter Arms .32.

"You must've been expecting a hostile interview." He went to his carrying case and slipped the gun into a plastic evidence bag.

"I always carry that when I leave campus. You know what happened to me. If something like that happened to you, wouldn't you carry a gun?" Mace's tongue was working independently of his mind, which told him not to give unnecessarily long explanations. It would have been sufficient to say, "You know what happened to me.

"I suppose now I'm guilty of carrying a concealed weapon without a permit."

"If you don't have a permit to carry, you bet."

And then the three men stood staring at him in a silence that seemed to last minutes. Instinctively, Mace began to straighten up the mounds of paper on the desk.

"Don't do that," Chin said, pushed his hand aside, then moved to the open doorway and stood leaning against the post.

Mace returned his hands to his lap, resisting the urge to sit on them to stop them from moving toward the clutter. Celestial terrestial telestial, he recited silently, cricking his neck with each word. Did nothing, saw nothing.

"So where do I stand here? No, I don't have a permit. I won't try to bullshit you."

The third man, tall, with a long jaw and mustache, and wearing a ranchman's sport jacket, leaned toward him, his hand extended.

"We haven't met, Mr. Weathers. Captain Phil Youngblood. El Dorado Sheriff's Department. We did the initial investigation of the massacre."

Was this going to be the bad-cop, good-cop routine?

"I think we can set your mind at ease as far as obstructing justice goes. We interrogated Jacob. Cleared him. Turns out that he wasn't there on the day of the crime. Wasn't at Duane's motel the night before. He was in L.A. that whole week, and spent that Thursday and Friday in the Hollywood jail. Solicitation for prostitution. I can tell you that we feel pretty damned foolish."

Mace felt so relieved that he could have levitated off the chair.

"So you guys were trying to throw a scare into me?"

"Yeah. Throw a little scare into you," Youngblood answered in a rumbling smoker's voice. "But we also need your help. Jacob did tell us a few things that have left a few loose ends. We think you could help us tie them up and point us in the right direction. Do you mind?"

"Helping you out?" He was alert for a possible trap—the eccentric move, the sacrifice of a major piece.

"Yeah. Because there was an accomplice, that's for sure."

"There is?"

"Yeah."

"The guy who fired the other shots, signaled Duane, assisted in his suicide?"

"Don't worry. He's not in this room."

"Well, I'd hope to Christ you don't think so."

"The guy who did those things isn't sitting in any room anywhere," Chin said in a flat, dead voice.

Mace hesitated, thinking back to the conversation in Heartwood's apartment. Ballistics evidence of a 9-millimeter, some other sort of evidence, blood-spatter analysis or something.

"Dr. Heartwood's drawn up a profile of this accomplice. We thought that if you listened to the guy's—call it his psychological description—you might help us identify him," said Youngblood.

"I really don't see how."

Youngblood pursed his lips and nodded. "We think you can, but if you don't want to . . . door's open. Okay if we get in touch with you later?"

"Later when?" Mace asked, half-rising to leave.

Youngblood answered, "We're not sure when. Later on sometime."

Something told him it would be greatly to his benefit to walk out, yet the suspense of waiting for a call would be unbearable. It might be better to deal with this now. At least he would have a chance to look over the board and plan his game, if there was a game. They're on white, I'm on black.

"I've got a little time."

Heartwood bestowed a reassuring smile, then, shoving his hands in his pocket, turned and began that annoying pacing of his.

"I'll start where we left off yesterday, okay, okay?"

"Okay, okay," Mace mimicked.

"I'm talking about rationalizing. You're familiar with the Bible, I'm sure."

"Can't quote chapter and verse."

"I *can,*" said Heartwood, with a ridiculous pirouette that brought them face-to-face. "Romans, chapter three, verse eight. 'Let us do evil that good may come.' It's actually phrased as a question in St. Paul's Epistle, but for our purposes, let's consider it a statement. I believe our accomplice, who was actually more than an accomplice but in fact the author of this massacre, has persuaded himself that he was doing something, oh, socially beneficial."

"That fascist New Jerusalem you were talking about."

Against his will, Mace again began to tidy up the desk. Chin took a step forward and tugged his sleeve.

"No, but that's not important. The only thing important is the fact of a rationalization, which tells me that the mastermind has an intelligence and a conscience—a Freudian superego, if you prefer a more value-free term. He has a moral sense that needs to be assuaged, but it is a deformed moral sense."

He turned his back again, paced to one wall, then another. Mace flushed with an anger whose flame heated all his emotions into movement, a Brownian swirl.

"So now what I'll do is describe the killer's true motives, and in so doing, I'll describe him, and then you tell me if I'm way off base."

"Look, I don't know . . . I mean, if you're . . . "

"Yes, Mace?"

"Nothing."

He didn't have to say a thing. He wasn't under arrest, and if he were, he still would not have to say anything. Let the clown talk, let's see his gambit.

"Very well, the mastermind had two major motives—revenge and hatred. He hated Duane, he hated his father and mother, but that hatred was combined with a paradoxical desire to avenge certain wrongs his father suffered, which led to the mastermind's other hatred—racial hatred of Asians. Hatred was the mother of his desire for revenge. He wanted revenge against Asians, revenge against society in general. Let's take the latter because it's the clearest. It's there that the mastermind's motives and Duane's mesh quite neatly. Yes, very." Heartwood wove his fingers together. "The mastermind suffered a serious injury, physically and psychologically. His assailants were never caught and society didn't seem to give a damn if they ever were. Society was, oh"—He looked toward the low ceiling, twirling his finger—"*blind* to what happened to our hero, who, being young, intelligent, good-looking, and arrogant, considered himself the center of the universe. He wanted society to feel the hurt he had, but he knew this society was inured to pain and so he exacted retribution by striking society where it is most vulnerable, where it was bound to hurt. Its children. He manipulated Duane into killing children. Which, to digress, is another feature of his profile. He's manipulative, especially with people with near subnormal intelligence, a manipulativeness honed earlier in his life in a more wholesome endeavor."

"Interesting," Mace said, almost through gritted teeth. This was disgusting, an insult . . .

"By the way, is there some reason you're wearing those sunglasses?"

"Driving glasses."

"It's dark and you're not in a car."

He took off his glasses, put on his patch, and glared at Heartwood with a hatred pure as refiner's fire.

"Happy now?"

"So to continue. On to Duane. The mastermind hated him, enough to want him dead, enough to manipulate his self-destructive impulses at the same time he manipulated his destructive impulses. Duane would kill himself, saving the protagonist of this narrative the trouble, and the obvious dangers, of doing it himself. Duane's death *was* an assisted suicide, but it was psychologically assisted. Why this hatred? It was bound up with their relationship. A master-slave relationship, and the master must by definition despise his slave. A relationship with some sadomasochistic, homoerotic undertones, I would add. But a homoeroticism of a very peculiar sort. The mastermind feared that he was himself a homosexual, an idea utterly reprehensible to him owing to his religious upbringing, owing to his own machismo. Now I happen to think he wasn't a latent homosexual, he was afraid he *might* be, and might give in to forbidden desires with someone like Duane, who didn't come from his world and wasn't likely to give him away. He's obsessive, you see, and most obsessives suffer from irrational terrors of things they might do. They are terrified of dark, repulsive *possibilities.* And so, Duane becomes a source of temptation and he must be punished first and then ultimately eliminated. And punished for another, deeper reason. Duane represented an aspect of the mastermind's personality, not as it is but as it might have been. Possibilities again. Had it not been for a particular turn of circumstances, our protagonist could very well have turned out like Duane—child of an atomized family, a rootless, drug-addicted, white-trash loser. Do you recall the story I told you about General Taylor? Committing suicide because he couldn't bear the thought of the *possibility* that he and other seemingly normal men were vulnerable to gross moral failures, that there was no foolproof immunization against certain promptings of the innermost self?"

Mace, blood beating in his head and ears, nodded.

"This person was like that. Couldn't bear the thought that there was anything of Duane in him. Not unlike certain fundamentalists who can't bear the thought that they are genetically only one point six percent different than chimpanzees. And so Duane was beaten and hated for that, beaten quite methodically, by the way. The profile indicates a methodical, organized personality. At any rate, by prompting Duane to commit suicide, the mastermind killed the reprehensible part of himself."

"I don't have to listen to this shit!" Mace leapt to his feet as though something had exploded beneath him. "What the hell game are you playing with me!" His fists were balled, his arm muscles trembling with tension. He could take this shrimp of a shrink and break his spine. "If you've got something to say, then fucking well say it. Don't give me this 'mastermind, protagonist' crap!"

Startled, Heartwood glanced sidelong at Gabriel and Youngblood, the glance telling them to move away from the door. It wasn't yet time to cause Mace to feel cornered, physically as well as mentally. He should believe that he had room to maneuver or escape, for if he were to overcome his fears of the unknown and play his best move—challenge them to arrest him—they would be the ones with little room for maneuver.

"Of course you don't have to listen to me. You don't have to do anything. You're not under arrest," he said with a show of indifference.

Mace stood for a moment, wishing he could reach inside himself and grab those whirling emotional atoms and restore them to their proper orbits. *Be frosty, past frosty, he hasn't said a thing that would stand up in court for two seconds. Don't give yourself away, don't condemn yourself.*

"I can go on?" Heartwood asked.

"Why not?" Mace replied with a caustic laugh and fell back into the chair. "Why the hell not?"

"Very well, thanks. And so to the source of it all. That is what I try to do. To follow all the little branches and tributaries back toward the main channel, and that to its source. And what is the source of our protagonist's hatreds and lusts for vengeance? Archaic rage. Remember that? The emotional artillery shell that buries itself in someone's subconscious without exploding, but waits there for years, decades, until something—a footfall, corrosion, a vibration sets it off. We've learned a couple of interesting facts. The mastermind was the victim of a traumatic event in his very early childhood, not quite three years old." Heartwood's voice dropped to a near-whisper, a tone conveying sadness. "His father, a Vietnam veteran, probably suffering from post-traumatic stress disorder, went on a rampage one night and killed two Vietnamese who'd moved into his neighborhood. He was convicted and sent to prison. While he was behind bars, his beautiful wife ran off with another man, abandoning her child to a foster home. Later on, the child was adopted. His mother turned her back on him forever. Now, I have tried to imagine how that would affect me. I've tried to imagine my way into our protagonist's mind. Have I told you that's what I do, Mace? Try to find the truth of someone's personality through imagination?"

Mace motioned indifferently.

"The ages between infancy and three or four are critical. That's when the template for the adult is being cut," Heartwood continued, still in that compassionate, elegiac tone. "I imagined that if it had been me, I would have been enraged and terrified by such a rejection, but I would have in time forgotten what caused this rage. Oh, I might retain some very vague, fossil memory of the event itself, of the woman herself. But the emotions? The fury and fear instilled in me at that moment would remain. And later on in life, after I found out I was adopted, I would think to myself, 'I wasn't given up at infancy, but at almost three years old. The mother who surrendered me would have nursed me, would have seen me take my first steps, heard me speak my first words, watched me develop a personality, and yet she had it in her to give me up. What kind of woman could she be? A monster.'" He came close, leaned his arms on the desk. "But I also would wonder, What kind of child was I? Was I a monster as well? Is that the reason she gave me up? Perhaps I would hold those contradictory ideas in my head at the same time. Perhaps I was the monstrous child of a monstrous woman, a whore. *Whore . . .* "

A wire's snap away from strangling the man whose clownish face filled his field of vision, Mace made a slight movement with his shoulders. Chin and Youngblood shifted their postures just as subtly, Youngblood's hand brushing aside the break of his jacket, revealing the revolver holstered on his hip. Yet it wasn't them with their guns who held him here. He was under some other kind of arrest, from what law he didn't know.

"Now all I know at this point in my life is what I've told you." Heartwood spun away, to the opposite side of the room and stood talking to the wall. "I know nothing about my father, and if it were me, I would begin to wonder about him. Where is he, who is he, did he desert me, too? I would begin to search for him, as in fact the mastermind did, but before he found him, he suffered a shock. The injury I mentioned earlier. And that, so to speak, armed the fuse of the buried, unexploded shell. And then came the final shock. He discovered his natural father's whereabouts, met him, and what did he find? A broken-down ex-convict living in a shabby apartment. A white-trash loser, in other words. He also learned all the sordid details and that the mother who deserted him deserted her husband as well, as he languished behind bars. Our protagonist identified with his father in that sense, but what did the father do after filling his son in on their family history? Turned his back! The rejection was repeated!"

Don't want to set eyes on you again.

"Were you about to say something, Mace?"

"No."

"It's interesting, it really is, because the mastermind knows that if he'd stayed within his natural family, he very probably would've become something like Duane, that he was much better off as a result of his adoption, that his mother did him a favor. And yet, and yet . . . the loss of love is the child's deepest terror, the deepest wound . . . but . . . never mind that. After the father's rejection, the fury goes off, and like all explosions, it's—again, pardon the expression—blind. It strikes at the rejecting mother, at the rejecting father, and at the Vietnamese whom the mastermind, in his innermost self, perversely holds responsible for his father's imprisonment. He's playing the old game of blaming the victim. Now if it were me feeling this old, old rage anew, I'd look into the mirror and see in my disfigured face the incarnation of the monster I secretly believe myself to be. Here, I would say, is my true self at last, and because I've grown up in a society that considers self-expression to be the highest human endeavor, I would allow this Other Self to express itself. Yes, this is where the external factors come into play. It is all right to express yourself, regardless of the moral consequences. But our protagonist doesn't want to suffer the legal consequences; that is, he doesn't want to get caught, and so what he does is to mold and manipulate and encourage someone else to commit the act. So in one bloody, abominable stroke, he can vent the rage begun by his mother's desertion, get his revenge on society, get rid of the despised Duane, avenge his father with the blood of Asians, while proving that he is superior to the father not only by shedding more blood than he but by so cleverly disguising his involvement in the crime that he doesn't get caught. Duane is nothing more than an instrument that conveniently self-destructs, leaving no evidence, or so the mastermind thinks." Heartwood came across the room and again leaned on the desk. Mace was repulsed by his benign, stupid smile. "How does it hold together for you, Mace? It needs a good deal of polishing, but is the logic there, that Greek sense of the inevitable?"

This is what they had on him? A shrink's theory? The coldness had descended on him. The blessed coldness that was not a stilling of emotion but an absence of emotion.

"Who told you all this?"

"You did."

His blood was freon, his veins chill copper tubes.

"Then stop insulting my intelligence and drop the game playing now and just say that you're talking about me."

"Of course."

"I don't recall telling you anything."

Heartwood backed way, aware of the change in Mace. The sharpness of his look touched him like the breath off a glacier. Had he failed? He was sure the revelations about Mace's parentage, the references to homosexuality, would have shaken him.

"I'll tell you how you told me in a second," he said, hoping not to betray the erosion of his confidence. "But first, your opinion about my narrative? True or bullshit?"

"Bullshit."

"Know what? You're right."

"What are you . . . "

"Later. Later, later. So how did you tell me all about yourself? In a lot of ways. Remember my story about that Marine? Darryl Adams? When I talked about his father and that his uncle had married his mother, you became visibly upset, which told me not all was right between you and your father. You told me how deeply you hated Duane in the way you'd said *'feral,'* and it struck me later that there had to be some reason for such hatred. You told me that there was something peculiar about your relationship to Duane in the way you looked at his grandfather when he talked about beating Duane. You told me about your mother in the way you reacted to Duane's—another point of identification between you two, by the way. You told me you had something to hide in the little lies you told me—that you never had a beer with Duane, that you were doing a thesis on psychological autopsies, when in fact, being the control freak you are, you needed to know exactly what we were up to so you could manage our inquiry if you had to. Finally, there was your lie that you'd never seen Duane again after that night, when was it? The night he showed up at D.A.C.O.—March eighth, I think. In fact you did see him. You had to have seen him. Duane continued to receive disability benefits even though he wasn't participating in the rehab program, because you sent in falsified attendance records to his Social Security office. But there was one thing Duane had to do in person and that was come in twice a week to make a urine drop. And we know, Mace, *know* that you happen to be in charge of that part of the operation. What you did was to substitute your urine for his, and it was after those visits that you got together with Duane to plot something one helluva lot worse than fraud."

That they knew this surprised Mace, but he did not let it show. So what? A little scam.

"And you're telling me right now by your demeanor. All of a sudden I can tell that you're feeling pretty sure of yourself. 'They haven't got any *evidence*,' is what you're thinking. 'No *evidence* linking me to the scene of the crime, no *evidence* that I conspired with Duane.' I confess to being disappointed. I was beginning to find you, oh, exceptional in your way. Aware of yourself as a child of a society that wants most things to be permitted or at least tolerated, and so you were experimenting at the far frontiers of behavior. But that *no evidence* routine is the last refuge of Washington lawyers and crooked politicans and other mediocrities."

"Well, I'm sorry to disappoint you, Dr. Heartwood. No lie. Your respect is important to me," Mace said with only an edge of sarcasm. Wonderful. In the zone again. "But the fact is, there are no facts."

"Really? One fact beyond dispute is that you came here looking for Jacob with a gun in your pocket and an inane story about being a reporter."

The guy who did those things isn't sitting in any room anywhere. As in a chess match, Mace saw the trap he'd fallen into and, seeing it, he felt the inchworms again. Sweat tickled his brow. *No . . . Wait. The match isn't lost,* he thought. *Stay frosty.*

"Gabriel and Phil weren't completely sure you'd fall for it, but I was," Heartwood said with a disgusting, self-satisfied smile. "We crafted it pretty well, right down to the phony news leak, but they thought you might be clever enough to see through the charade. I knew differently because I know you. You can't stand uncertainty. You can't stand not being in control of a situation. You were compelled to find out if Jacob knew anything about your involvement and, if he did, to do something about it. The really smart thing would have been to do nothing. But that's not you. You *had* to regain control and end the uncertainty. Now imagine that we're in court. Gabriel and I testify that we set you up for a sting and why we did. The prosecutor presents as *evidence* the calls you made to the Tipton house, posing as a credit card solicitor, as this and that, and finally in your current disguise, Bart Healy, star reporter. That, too, is *evidence.* And then we have this . . . " His confidence returning, Heartwood opened Gabriel's carrying case and pulled out the revolver in the plastic bag, which he turned around so the marking tape was toward Mace. "See what that says? *Evidence.* Circumstantial, we'll admit, but think of what the jury will be thinking. Why did this guy pose as a reporter and come to see Jacob with a gun in his pocket? Oh, your lawyer may say that his client was writing a thesis on psychiatric autopsies and wished to speak to Jacob before the cops got to him. As for the gun, his client had been assaulted and carried it for self-protection. But then, a *witness* will *testify,* that witness being your abnormal psych professor, that she hadn't assigned any such thesis, that you had never suggested it. And a *witness's testimony* also is *evidence.* It'll be difficult for the jury not to conclude that you intended to do serious bodily harm to Jacob. And then, the jury will ask itself why you had such intent. Bishop takes rook."

Mace laughed silently. He'll sacrifice the rook. He'll sacrifice more. He held out his wrists.

"Arrest me."

"Oh, come on, Mace. Don't be theatrical."

"Arrest me. Black sacrifices queen. What else do you want?"

"For you to concede. Confess."

He could no longer contain his laughter, though he was thinking, *If I'm guilty of murder it'll be for killing this son of a bitch.*

Then Youngblood stepped in and placed his hands on Mace's extended arms and gently pressed them down.

"I can't arrest you because I'm out of my jurisdiction, but I'll give you some advice. You don't have as much going as you think you do. A good lawyer could probably keep you off Death Row. He might even find a way to get you off on an accessory conviction. But you need to get something going for yourself, Mace."

"No, you need to get something going for yourselves."

"Ah, Mace, Mace," Heartwood said wearily. "This denial of guilt. What is it? Something inside yourself or is it the age? What makes you unable to admit, even to yourself, that you gave in to the worst in yourself? Because you did give in." He drew closer. "That's why my narrative is bullshit. It doesn't explain your brand of evil. It justifies it. Poor Mace, victim of subconscious impulses over which he has no control. But you did have control. You made a choice."

"They," Mace said, gesturing at Chin and Youngblood, "want a bust. But you want to know. I read that about you. You know all about me? Well, I know you too, Dr. Heartwood. I read about you in that *People* article. The great explorer of the interior, finding out what goes on in there, but you're never sure, are you? Never. Because half the time your subjects end up dead or they're so far gone in the head they're incoherent. So what you want from me is confirmation that your ridiculous theory is true. You won't get it."

Heartwood shrugged off the commentary.

"That being the case, let's forget why you did what you did."

"I have a right to remain silent."

"Please. Remain silent. You in fact have the right to walk out this minute. But do you mind if I don't remain silent?"

Let him talk. Let's hear all they've got. Then I'll know, they won't.

"So let's take a look at what you did and how," Heartwood said. "You did the planning. You calculated the times and distances. You found the best place for Duane to conceal the truck. You figured out how to make sure the bus driver opened the doors. And then, your most overt act of complicity, you staged a dress rehearsal . . . "

Mace flinched when Chin made a sudden lunge across the room, as if he were going to strike him.

"You're wearing dark green boxer shorts."

For no reason he could identify, the disclosure of this irrelevant fact frightened Mace more than anything else he'd heard so far.

"Lucky guess or you peeked."

"No peek, no guess. Tomorrow you'll wear red, Monday blue, Tuesday blue and white stripes. You want to talk about knowing people, Weathers, I know you, put it in the bank."

"You searched my room?"

"Yeah, oh, yeah."

"Underwear," he answered with a laughter he knew sounded false. "You broke into my room and peeked at my underwear."

"Peeked at a lot of things. Peeked at your mama. Tits, ass, and all. Peeked at what you wrote on her picture. That might be the only true thing you ever said in your life, Weathers. Peeked at other colors. I like colors. A close relation of yours lived in an apartment with a blue carpet."

Chin stood staring with a fierce concentration, like a lion on its prey; then he pulled two more plastic bags from the case and held one in each hand.

"And you want to talk evidence, you goddamned sea-lawyer, you're looking at it. In this bag is a thread taken from your jeans, and in this one a thread taken from a bedspread in the Gold Hill Motel. They match." He seemed to be quaking with a fury barely contained when he pulled out a much larger bag. "This is a shirt that belonged to your father in Vietnam. Riley B. Kincannon. It was on Duane's back because you gave it to him, but you made sure to take the name tag off because you knew Kincannon's name could incriminate you, if somebody was determined enough to find out he was your biological father. It worked this way. You and Duane had a good time, you whacking on his ass, him taking it, and you bought him for that kind of whoring by using Kincannon as the name his checks were sent to. That was all going on *before* you and he cooked up your plan, and you knew the Kincannon connection could be a weak link. Evidence? We have a witness who saw you take the shirt into the Gold Hill on Wednesday night, April fourteenth. That's evidence. You were there to rehearse Duane, weren't you."

"I have the right to remain silent."

I'm going to have to push him, Gabriel thought. Push him right to that edge where he starts to lose it. But not push him over.

"So what were you in the motel for? A little more of your kinky fun?"

"I'm remaining silent."

"But then why check in, the both of you, under aliases? What were you afraid of? That somebody in that sleazehole would report you for whatever S and M garbage you two were into? Uh-uh. You checked in as R. K. Cannon, and that handwriting matches the writing on your application for a post office box under the name of Riley Kincannon. That was cute, Weathers. Using your old man's name as an alias, his driver's license, and then making an alias out of that. Very fucking cute, and also more evidence. Here's more . . . " He took out still another bag . . . fingerprint cards. "We got a set of your prints from your room and matched 'em to a print on the post office box where Duane's checks were sent, made out to Riley Kincannon . . . "

"All right," Mace said."All right, all right. It's what you said."

Gabriel stepped back. He saw that Weathers's shoulders had slumped, but he wasn't sure if he had surrendered. A guy like him wouldn't quit so soon, so easily.

"What's what I said?"

"We were there, in the Gold Hill, to, you know . . . "

"Kinky fun."

Mace nodded and lowered his gaze to the floor.

"I just didn't want to use my real name, and . . . and . . . one thing more." He raised his head and drew in a couple of deep breaths. "Duane told me that night what he was planning to do. That stuff I told you, Dr. Heartwood? About Duane's fantasies? About fire bombing the Mexicans on the Interstate? He told me all that that night in the Gold Hill. And then he told me about this school bus ambush idea. He said that he'd gotten into an argument with a Vietnamese kid and the kid's brother tossed a wadded-up school bulletin into his face and the bulletin announced when the bus was going on the field trip. That happened a few weeks before, I guess, so Duane had plenty of time to plan it out. But, you see, I . . . "

"You dismissed it as another fantasy. You didn't think your lover, your whipping boy, would go through with it," Heartwood said.

"That's correct."

"And nobody was as shocked as you on Friday, when you discovered that he had gone through with it. And your foreknowledge of his plan was what caused you to stay away from the media, to lie to me."

"That's right. Yes."

Heartwood applauded, then Gabriel and Youngblood broke into grins and joined in the clapping. Then their smiles vanished and their hands fell to their sides.

"The fact is, you were there to work out the details with him," said Gabriel coldly. "Just like you did with somebody else. Somebody else who was having his checks signed over to the deceased Mr. Kincannon. Thursday before last, April twenty-ninth. Where were you?"

Mace battled against the rising panic in his chest.

"With my girlfriend. Celia. Celia Kim. Ask her."

"You switch-hit, do you, Weathers? Okay, you were with your girl. And then where did you go?"

Mace said nothing.

"Remaining silent again, are you, Weathers? All right, I'll tell you where you went. To the Buddhist temple outside San Joaquin. To do a little preliminary reconnaissance, make some calculations. We saw you there, me and Detective Youngblood. And what was the recon for? Well, here, let's have somebody else answer that."

Mace watched as Chin removed a tape recorder from the case and switched it on. His gelid blood began to flow again, thudding in his ears when he heard Pickering's adenoidal voice and then his own . . . *Ain't they goin' to see me, comin' across the field? . . . No, Ben, the trees . . . They're all going to be sitting toward the front and the trees in back will hide you . . .*

Chin turned to him. Mace nearly shuddered when he laid a hand on his wrist.

"That's evidence, too. Legal wiretap in Benjamin Pickering's room, room sixty-seven, Valley View Motel. Been listening to the news today?"

Mace said nothing. He wasn't a racist, he certainly never thought of himself as one, but he couldn't help the thoughts that passed through his mind as he looked into Chin's face. An ugly man. That extra fold of skin on the eyelids, that mashed nose, that spare rice-fed body.

"Well?"

"I have a right to remain silent."

"So stay silent," Chin said, breathing on him. "If you were listening, you might have noticed that nothing unusual happened today. The unusual thing that was supposed to happen didn't."

"Pickering panicked," Youngblood said, closing in beside Chin. Now it was the both of them, crowding him. "Tried to run a roadblock. We've got him and he's told an interesting story. We know all about it, so c'mon, Mace, get something going for yourself."

"Told you before, I don't give a shit about the potty-training stuff," said Chin. "That stuff Dr. Heartwood was talking about, all about your rage and blah blah, that's all crap to me." He grinned horribly and waved the tape recorder in his face. "What I know is that if a criminal is successful once, he'll try again. And you did, but you weren't successful this time."

"Jesus Christ, get something going for yourself. Let's see if we can't get something going for you."

"Check," Heartwood said from behind the two policemen.

Thoughts sped through Mace's mind, too fast for capture. They streaked like lasers. If he could stop one for a second he could see his next move, a way out of this.

"That's an old one," he said tightly. "Telling one guy that some other guy is ratting on him."

"Watch a lot of cop shows, Weathers?" Gabriel asked. A chilly one, all right, and I've got to push him a little harder. "Here's what I can do." He picked up the phone and slammed it down hard on the desk, making its bell ring. "Put a call through to the San Joaquin PD and put you on the speakerphone in the little room where Pickering's spinning his yarn. You can talk to him yourself. You guys seem to like talking to each other." He squatted down in front of Weathers's chair, his hands on its arms. "I'm wondering what else you liked to do together. Just curious, Weathers. I've never been into rough trade stuff myself. Did you get a big hard-on beating on his ass like you did Duane's? Or did you give it to him up the ass? Or maybe you took it from him." Gabriel saw it then—a tightening in the jaw muscles, a curling of Weathers's fingers. Getting to him now. "No, Mace? Okay, it's a personal question." He rose and laid his hand on the phone. "So should I call or save you the embarrassment and tell you what Pickering's told us so far? Let's take Thursday, April twenty-ninth, after your predawn recon. The two of you had a late lunch at the Burger King out near Hangtown Road and then took a short drive out to an old levee road that runs behind the temple. Stayed over an hour, getting the lay of the land. There's more . . . "

They had Pickering.

"So we've got Ben's version of events. Want to give us yours or what?"

Youngblood said, "Still got a chance to get something going."

Heartwood said, "He wants to sacrifice his queen. Pretty hard to get something going without the queen."

He couldn't think with these two cops breathing down on him like this. *They had Pickering.*

"Okay, last chance or we continue the conversation at the Fontana PD."

He saw the prisoner he'd watched yesterday. Like it was a premonition he'd failed to heed. Leg irons. Manacles. No way was he going to any police station—the mouth of the beast whose belly was prison.

"He hasn't . . . You don't . . . "

"No? Ask you something, Weathers. If he hasn't given us all this information, this evidence, I'd be pretty dumb to arrest you, wouldn't I? One little chat with a lawyer and I'd be cooked, wouldn't I?"

Mace said nothing.

"Wouldn't I?" Gabriel shouted, aware that he was pushing the case to its edge.

"I'm remaining silent."

"Have it your way." All right, take it to the edge, Gabriel thought. To and over. "You're under arrest, Weathers, for the crimes of first degree murder, conspiracy to murder, welfare fraud, and criminal possession of a firearm. Do you understand these charges?"

He nodded. A thought, a plan was forming in his mind, his blood was congealing again. He was not going to confess anything. He would make the move they didn't expect. They don't believe I'll try to get away. They think I'm some docile college kid.

"You have the right to remain silent. You have a right to have counsel present. Anything you say can and will be used against you in a court of law. Do you understand these rights?"

Chin and Youngblood had backed away a step or two, giving him some room. His gaze slanted toward the .32, lying in Chin's case on the desk. They'll want me alive, he thought. Heartwood especially. That's their weak point.

"Weathers? Do you understand the rights I just read you?"

He nodded again.

"Understanding these rights, is there anything you have to say to us?"

He shook his head.

A clarity of thought, a purity and sureness of motion. He pictured what he was going to do so that the doing of it would be like the repetition of something that had already happened.

"Stand up against that wall, brace your hands on the wall above your head, spread your legs," said Chin, and as he reached behind his back for his handcuffs, Mace lunged off the chair, threw a shoulder into the detective, putting all his two hundred and twenty pounds into it, snatched the revolver still in the bag, swung it into Youngblood's jaw, bolted into the front room, ripping the bag open at the same time, and threw himself through the front door.

Outside, in the floodlit yard, he ran to the gate, a big gate on rollers. The yard manager had shut it when he left. With his free hand, Mace reached for its handle and pulled. It didn't budge. He jerked at it again. It still didn't move.

"*Freeze!*" Chin shouted behind him.

He froze inside and out.

"Drop it, Weathers! Drop it and raise your hands!"

Instead, he snapped the muzzle to his temple, cocking the hammer as he did, then turned to face Chin and Youngblood, crouched with their guns aimed at his chest.

"You drop yours." Like freon in his veins.

He saw Chin lower his semiauto, pointing it toward his legs or feet.

"Don't think about it! I'll squeeze this off before you can! Drop them!"

Gabriel had never seen this before: a criminal holding himself hostage. Pushed him a little too hard. If he could kneecap Weathers . . . The range wasn't twenty feet, but the bashing from Weathers had left him shaken and made his spine feel as if it had cracked under the brace. He didn't trust his aim, and a Saturday Night Special, hair trigger at full cock . . . go off with a twitch . . . and then I've got two dead suspects, both suicides . . . Pushed him a little too hard.

"No way, Weathers. No way a police officer is going to disarm himself. Put that damn thing down."

Weathers hesitated. "I'm going to go out this gate. You're going to let me out this gate." He grasped the handle behind him, shook it.

Gabriel, with Youngblood alongside, advanced a step, Glock held low. Youngblood's cheek was bruised and bleeding. Pickering a kamikaze, now this.

"Don't take another step!" Weathers screamed. "I will do it!"

"No, you won't."

It was Heartwood.

"Lee, you'd best get back," Gabriel said. "This is no place . . . "

"Yeah, it's my place because it's all about me." Knees unsteady, Heartwood moved to the side and looked toward Mace. "Isn't it all about me? You think that *I* want you alive so I can know if it's all true, isn't that right?"

Heartwood stepped sideways to a small yellow box atop a concrete post. Beside it was a kind of car park for broken-down bumper cars.

"Stop!"

Heartwood did and casually rested his hand on the box. He knew he was taking a grave risk, but was sure he could pull this off. Without someone to kill for him, Mace wasn't a danger to others; nor was he a danger to himself. He thought too much of himself.

"The gate's electronically controlled and I'm standing by the button."

"Then push it," Mace snarled. "Push it or I'll . . ."

"Shoot yourself? Go ahead. I don't want to know if my theory about you is right. I really don't give a damn why you did it."

He could no longer control the trembling in his knees and sat down on the front of a bumper car. For some reason, he noticed that its color was the yellow of diner mustard and that it had red fenders and the words DODGE-'EM painted on the hood. "I am interested to see if you do kill yourself. That's something losers like Duane do. That'll tell me more about you than you could with your mouth."

"Shut up! Shut the fuck up!"

The way he was speaking, oh so mellow, oh so patronizing, like he knows everything. A little arrogant clown.

"Well, I'd say if you're going to do it, now's the moment. I really really really don't give a damn about the why of it. You taught me something, though, something I learned when I was seven but must've forgot. Evil's a choice. It's saying yes to the worst in ourselves, yes yes yes, and no to our angels, no no no. And that's what you did. A terrible idea came into your head and you acted on it. You're a mass murderer of children, you're a reptile that happens to stand upright. Fuck you, Mace. Kill yourself."

Heartwood paused, sensing the fear in him would soon be communicated by his voice. This was like talking someone down from a window ledge, but someone who had a live grenade in his hand.

"Well, if you're not, then you come along with us, or you wait until Gabriel and Phil shoot your knees off. It looks like check and mate to me, Mace."

"There's one more move, asshole!"

And as he squinted against the floodlight's glare, he saw that he'd judged Mace too well, for he swung the revolver down and fired, but Heartwood did not hear the shot. He was aware only of an impact in his left side, like a punch to the liver from a professional fighter, and then of staggering backward, his legs going out from under him, his hands fumbling for something to grab, and of Gabriel's and Youngblood's guns going off, and the warmth of blood soaking through his shirt and a drowsiness as he swung on the handlebar of the bumper car and fell into its seat.

"Take care of him, Phil!" Gabriel yelled and took off into the scrapyard.

He and Youngblood had both fired low as Weathers ran after his shot. They'd seen him grab his leg before he disappeared into the jumble of roller coaster cars, Ferris wheel girders, and Ferris wheel seats. Can't have gone far, not hit like that. Strong guy, though. Goddamnit! Should've dropped him or let the son of a bitch blow his brains out. Gabriel followed the blood trail, droplets glittering like melted rubies in the floodlights. He climbed over a wooden horse, smeared where Weathers had touched it, then over a merry-go-round . . . He heard something moving up ahead, beyond a barricade of rocket cars.

"I've called for backup and an ambulance. Here soon," Youngblood said, breathless after running back from the car.

Growing drowsier, Heartwood slumped in the seat, holding his hand tight to his side. Like getting punched hard. Exactly like that. All the breath gone out of you, legs turned into pipe cleaners.

"Phil . . . get me out of this thing . . . don't want . . . I don't want to die in a bumper car."

Youngblood took him under the arms and pulled him out and lay him on the ground. It was strangely cold. Cold, cold ground. The floodlights above blazed like electric moons.

"All right, now put my feet up on the seat. In case . . . shock . . . "

He held up his bloody hand, saw the color, and it told him everything. He could not help the sob that broke from his throat.

"David . . . got to see David. He's graduating . . . "

His grief was for that. If he died, and he was now almost positive he was going to, he would not watch his son graduate *cum laude,* there in the New England hills. Should stop blubbering. What would the old man say? Ronald Heartwood, M.D., he who'd picked, patched, and sewn up the pieces left in General Patton's wake? The hell with him. He gets to die in bed, full of years, not in the middle of his life in an amusement park graveyard because of a mistake in judgment.

Youngblood lifted his shirt and pressed a handkerchief against his wound. The pressure sent an arrow of pain through his abdomen. Can't cry in front of him, either. Still have to prove I'm as tough as the tough guys. Stupid stupid.

"Thanks . . . getting me out . . . " He attempted a smile. "Stupid to die in a bumper car . . . "

"You're not going to die, all right? Small caliber, through and through the side . . . "

"Liver, Phil. Through and through . . . liver . . . see . . . " He raised his hand again. "Color's almost black. Liver. Very complex organ."

Youngblood snatched a hand-held radio from off his belt, and spoke in a series of urgent codes. Voices responded in code through the static.

"The liver . . . many functions . . . controls level of blood sugar and lipids . . . detoxifies the blood . . . I am likely to go into toxic shock soon . . . dead in an hour . . . "

"Take it easy. Save your strength."

He wanted to talk, though, wanted to describe exactly what was happening to his wounded body at every stage so he could hold at bay the great terror of what those physiological changes would inevitably bring. He was a medical man, after all, fighting the unknown with knowledge. Funny, though. What good would his knowledge do now? He could describe what was happening, as if he were speaking at a physiology lecture, but he was powerless to change anything. The body would do what it would do, quite apart from his knowledge or will. Same was true of the mind, he supposed. The fallacy of analysis. That self-awareness will lead to mastery of the mind and the emotions. You can know why you act a certain way, but still, you act, prisoner of your own darknesses. Prisoners of biology and psychology, that's us. Ah, but what of the soul? Was there such an entity? Walt would say it's a neural network, like conscience. If there is a soul, as the Jesuits taught me, will it live on? Will I be taking a journey soon? Pascal's wager. Maybe I should say an act of contrition just to be on the safe side. *O my God I am heartily sorry for having offended thee* . . . The old prayer. New one now. Don't know it and can't recall the old one . . . Something about fearing the loss of heaven and the pains of hell . . . Well do I? Ha! Dealt with some big questions all my life, but here's the biggest staring me in the face. Is death annihilation or a passage? Pascal's wager. Can't prove it either way, so bet that it's a passage, considering the consequences . . . Interesting guy, Pascal. Science and philosophy. His math the basis for computers and he tried to prove man's relationship to God as if it were a geometry problem. He sought the equation for good. And what is the equation for evil? Would like to see David graduate. There's a reason to go on if I can.

He began to shiver.

"Shock, Phil. Not toxic yet. Ordinary shock. Going into . . . Blanket?"

Youngblood shook his head, took off his jacket, and laid it over Heartwood's torso, still holding the handkerchief on his wound.

"Can't believe this happened. Me, like this. Didn't . . . didn't think he'd do . . . "

"We didn't, either. Our fault."

"Well, Gabriel . . . right. Wasn't my place."

Youngblood looked away, at the sound of distant sirens.

"Here they come. You'll be okay in a minute."

"Liver. Tough to repair . . . tough to transplant . . . so many chemical and metabolic functions . . . Ah, there! Just now, Phil? A wave of dizziness. Blood sugar level dropping . . . "

He blacked out for a split second and yearned in that swift darkness to hear a Gregorian chant, a melody of order.

Crouched, still, Gabriel listened. A scraping, rustling sound. Weathers dragging himself. Down for good now. He peered into the maze of junk for movement, crept forward, and raised his gun when a shape suddenly loomed in front of him . . . huge, arms outspread . . . a spook house dummy . . . a vampire. They were all over the place, standing, sitting, prone. Werewolves. Witches with hooked, mole-covered noses. Bogeymen in black cloaks. Monsters with glow-in-the-dark faces that no longer glowed in the dark. Something did move, off to the left . . . He crept on, around the dummies, over them.

"Don't kill me, please. Can't go any farther. Don't, please."

Gabriel, his throat narrowed to a straw's diameter, didn't quite believe that. The voice had come from his left, perhaps ten yards away. He moved in that direction, staying low, and then saw him, lying on his back, both hands on his leg, his head resting against the first of a long line of green cars, this one shaped like a pair of toothy jaws and bearing the words, THE DRAGON COASTER. Gabriel stood up straight and held the gun on the handsome face, aiming just below the black eye patch. I could do it now, he thought. Got every reason in the world. Out of the corner of his eye, he saw the revolver lying about a foot from Weathers. He went over to it and picked it up and slipped it into his pocket. Weathers threw his head back, eye shut, grimacing and clutching his leg, his hands as red as a barn painter's.

"Jesus! It hurts like hell!"

"Good."

Gabriel stood over him and aimed the muzzle straight down into his face and watched the cold pale eye open and saw the terror flood into it.

"Aw, God, please . . . don't . . . Aw, don't please . . . "

All I have to say is he pointed the .32 at me. Gabriel's finger took up trigger slack, then relaxed. He lowered the Glock, remembering who and what he was. Got to keep the malignancy out and you start by keeping it out of yourself. He jerked Weathers's arms over his head, cuffed his wrists, and gripping the handcuffs by the chain, dragged him as a hunter drags a deer to a junked merry-go-round, unfastened one of the cuffs, then refastened it to a stanchion. One heavy son of a bitch. Winded, he sat on the platform and pressed the Glock under Weathers's good eye.

"Maybe I'll blow this one out. Match 'em up," Gabriel said.

"Don't!"

"What's my name?"

"Chin! Agent Chin!"

"First name."

"Gabriel."

"I've got to add one more charge," he said, almost placidly. "Attempted murder, which will be upgraded to murder one if Heartwood dies. You're going to confess to everything else, Weathers. If you don't, I'm going to pass some word to some people I know in whatever slam they send you to, and those guys'll make you wish for the gas chamber, a lethal injection, a fucking noose. And if you still keep your mouth shut, the very first face you see when you get out is going to be mine. Bank on it. If I'm seventy-five, if I'm eighty, if I'm a hundred, I'll be there. My name is Gabriel and I blow the horn on Judgment Day."

The gate rolled open, and Heartwood saw strobe lights bursting like stars. Electric stars to twinkle with the electric moons. In a few moments, paramedics were kneeling over him, wrapping his torso in a body compress, raising him onto a stretcher. Turning his head, he watched the ambulance back in, its doors swing open as if in welcome. Inside was another paramedic and plasma bags and antibiotic bags, respirators. He was lifted up and he grasped Youngblood's hand as he was carried in.

"David . . . I want to see . . ."

"David?"

"Son . . . I would like to see him . . . "

"You will," Youngblood said. "You will, Lee."

The paramedics laid him inside, the doors shut. Drowsy, so drowsy and cold. Toxic. There was movement now, the mad gulping of a siren. He closed his eyes and saw flowering dogwood and forsythia, a white steeple spiking the sky, and he and David walking together past the halls where ghostly Transcendentalists penned their reasonable essays.

Postlude

The People of the Neighborhood

SURFED.

Tonight was not a night for coherent narratives neatly packaged and boxed. Tonight was a night for surfin' USA . . .

For hanging ten on the electronic waves, seeking the perfect curl among a hundred channels. Cable channels. Broadcast channels. Satellite channels, beamed into their homes by steel dishes gathering signals from tiny steel balls spinning high above the planet.

A leopard crouches in a tree . . . *The leopard is a fearsome predator, strong enough to* . . . A game board . . . *Which category would you like to choose? Twentieth-century Authors or Geography* . . . *Geography* . . . *For five hundred dollars, this country was once* . . . Anchorman . . . *A dramatic arrest yesterday, in which a well-known forensic psychiatrist was shot, details in a moment.* A laughing black kid, a black father . . . Artificial laughter in the background . . .

A police car in hot pursuit, a high-speed chase . . . Gunfire . . . Madonna sings in her underwear . . . *It will be cloudy and cool over most of the northeast tomorrow, here in California, look for* . . . *You got it! Sunshine* . . . A handsome face, broad shoulders, suit . . . *A heartbreaker for the Dodgers today, Jerry, but the A's* . . . Anchorman again. *We now go to a press conference in Sacramento, where* . . . An Asian face, the tag at the bottom of the screen identifies him as Gabriel Chin . . . *We were questioning the suspect when* . . . *Boggs* . . . *school bus* . . .

Oh, yeah. Boggs. The school bus. The tragedy. A new development in the tragedy.

. . . *the suspect attempted to escape by threatening suicide* . . .

Dr. Heartwood was trying to talk him out of it when he turned the gun on him . . . Captain Youngblood and I returned fire, wounding the suspect . . .

Anchorman. *The suspect, believed to be the mastermind of the school bus massacre, was identified as Mace Weathers, twenty-two, a student at San Joaquin State College . . .*

The tragedy was three weeks ago.

Surfin' USA . . .

Bogey asks Sam to play it again on American Movie Classics . . . The leopard leaps from the tree, powerful predator strong enough to bring down prey many times its own size . . .

No, I'm sorry, the correct answer is Andorra . . . An all-star lineup! Murphy Brown *followed by* Love and War . . . A *Cosby Show* rerun . . . Madonna finishes her song, voicing-over quick cuts of herself emerging from the water in her underwear, pouting . . . *A big fight tonight on ESPN* . . . The leopard is chasing a wildebeest, leaps, rakes it with its claws, killer cat and wildebeest go down in dust, wildebeest's legs twitch as the powerful predator bites into its neck . . . *And it looks like we'll have a fine week ahead, with moderate temperatures . . .*

Surfin'. Clickers click. Images appear, vanish, reappear. Songs. Laughter. Surfin'.

Anchorman. *Authorities believed that Weathers had assisted another man, Ben Pickering, in a plot to . . . Later foiled by police . . . Pickering died when . . .* Anchorwoman. *Dr. Heartwood died two hours after being rushed to a hospital in San Bernardino . . . He was fifty years old . . .*

And that's the news for tonight. Good night, Jerry . . . Good night, Audrey . . . Good night, Dave. And good night to all of you . . .

DELAFIELD PUBLIC LIBRARY
Caputo, Philip.
Equation for evil : a novel

FIC CAP

RSN=00046676
MR 1 5 '96